A MIGHTY ENDEAVOR

Stuart Slade

LION BY LION
PUBLISHING

A Forecast International Company

1

Dedication

This book is respectfully dedicated to the memory of
Air Chief Marshal Sir Wilfrid Rhodes Freeman

Acknowledgements

A Mighty Endeavor could not have been written without the very generous help of a large number of people who contributed their time, input and efforts into confirming the technical details of the story. Some of these generous souls I know personally and we discussed the conduct and probable results of the actions described in this novel in depth. Others I know only via the internet as the collective membership of the History, Politics and Current Affairs Forum, yet their communal wisdom and vast store of knowledge, freely contributed, has been truly irreplaceable.

The assistance of Shane Rodgers was invaluable in preparing the sections that deal with the political and economic development of Australia in the 1940/1941 era. His expertise and encyclopedic knowledge of these aspects of the story were utterly indispensable in ensuring the impact of the British actions described in this novel on Australia and the rest of the Commonwealth were properly represented.

I must also express a particular debt of gratitude to my wife Josefa; for without her kind forbearance, patient support and unstintingly generous assistance, this novel would have remained nothing more than a vague idea floating in the back of my mind.

Caveat

A Mighty Endeavor is a work of fiction, set in an alternate universe. All the characters appearing in this book are fictional and any resemblance to any person, living or dead is purely coincidental. Although some names of historical characters appear, they do not necessarily represent the same people we know in our reality.

Copyright Notice

Contents

Previous Books In This Series

Available From

LION BY LION
PUBLISHING

A Mighty Endeavor	(1940)
Winter Warriors	(1945)
The Big One	(1947)
Anvil of Necessity	(1948)
The Great Game	(1959)
Crusade	(1965)
Ride of The Valkyries	(1972)
Lion Resurgent	(1982)

Coming Shortly

Conflict of Interest	(1941)

CHAPTER ONE
STATEMENT OF WORK

Government House, Calcutta, India, 7:30 AM, 19th June, 1940

    "Get out of my way, you stupid man!"

    Heads emerged from offices, civil servants were startled out of their usual calm demeanor by the sudden yell and the sight of the august personage of Sir Eric Haohoa running down the corridors of Government House. In fact, it was hard to decide which startled them most; the completely out-of-character rudeness or the fact that an Assistant Deputy Cabinet Secretary was running at all. It was unprecedented and, what was much worse, deeply alarming.

    Sir Eric knew it; he realized he was creating an incident that would ripple throughout the whole of the building within minutes. The sight of the departmental char-wallah's tea-trolley being unceremoniously kicked out of the way would ensure that. It couldn't be helped. The char wallah watched him pass, his mouth hanging open in disbelief. Sir Eric grabbed a door post, swung around the corner and vanished from sight. Behind him, the quiet rustle of gossip spread and increased in volume as additional spectators added their opinions to the debate on What It All Meant. There was one consensus; between them, the operative word was 'trouble'.

    "What the dev . . . . . " Sir Martyn Sharpe's face ran through a quick gamut of expressions as his door burst open. First was anger that somebody dared enter his office without knocking, let alone advising his secretary and waiting to be called in. That expression faded quickly to pleasure at seeing his old friend, then even more quickly to concern that his friend was red-faced and panting for breath.

"BBC World Service, quickly."

Sir Martyn turned the radio on. It crackled and whined slightly as it warmed up, then clicked as Sharpe pressed the pre-set button for the World Service. A familiar voice emerged from the static; the educated accent and precise pronunciation were quite unmistakable.

"And that was the news on this momentous day, and this is Alvar Lidell reading it. To repeat the main item of this bulletin, the war between Great Britain and Germany is over. An offer of an Armistice was received from Germany at noon Greenwich Mean Time and was presented to Cabinet by Lord Halifax. The terms contained therein were deemed to be satisfactory and the Foreign Office was therefore instructed to contact Herr Ribbentrop with British agreement to those proposed terms. With the signature of the Armistice by Herr Ribbentrop and His Majesty's representative in Geneva, hostilities between Great Britain and Germany ceased at 6pm Greenwich Mean Time today, pending the negotiation of a final peace agreement."

"I can't believe it. I never thought Winston would just surrender like this." Sir Martyn was aghast, his face white with shock.

"We don't know he did. There's been no mention of him." Sir Eric coughed and took a deep breath. "We don't know much at all about what's happening over there. If one of the Secretaries hadn't turned the radio on for the cricket scores, we'd have no idea about any of this going on. Everybody who heard has been sworn to secrecy of course, but the word will leak out soon anyway."

"You mean we didn't know?" If anything, Sir Martyn's face went even paler.

"Nobody knows anything. Certainly not in the Cabinet Office, that's for certain. The Viceroy's office? I don't…"

"We'll soon find out." Sir Martyn picked up the telephone on his desk. "Operator, connect me with Lord Linlithgow's office. Topmost priority."

He covered the mouthpiece with his hand while the connection was being made. "I doubt if the Marquess is in yet but I might catch Gerry, his Secretary . . . . Hello Gerry? The boss not in? ……… Have you heard the news? …….. Britain's out the war……. No I'm not joking. It was on the BBC news…… Alvar Lidell, of course. Certainly, I'll hold."

Sir Martyn covered the mouthpiece again. "Gerry's checking the telegrams from London. So far nothing… Hello, Gerry, nothing at all? That's very strange. You'd better get in touch with the Viceroy right away."

"Is that as bad as it sounds Martyn? Has Britain caved in?"

"Worse. There's been no communications at all from London. As far as we're concerned, Britain has just dropped out of the war and left us holding the bag."

Family Shrine, Bang Phitsan Palace, Bangkok, Thailand

Princess Suriyothai Bhirombhakdi na Sukothai lit the incense in front of the Buddha statue and bowed down, listening to the quiet chime fade away. She had struck the small gong as she had knelt before the statue to pray. The sound had taken her back, recalling the sounds of all the gongs she had heard over so many years. The last few years had been quiet. There had been the coup back in 1932 that had established an elected government in Siam and turned the Royal Family into a constitutional instead of an absolute monarchy. That much had been essential to guarantee both the survival of the country and the Monarchy she served. Some hotheads had wanted to go the whole way and turn the country into a Republic, but they had been easy to defeat. The couple of years spent maneuvering to frustrate them had been barely more than keeping in practice. *Still, it did give me some practical experience in commanding modern military units.*

Suriyothai rebuked herself for not realizing that the present calm had been too good to last. Before it, there had been so many emergencies, so many problems to be solved, but none like this. It seemed a minor thing, far away. As she ran its implications and consequences through her mind, though, they spread and interlocked. Consequences and outcomes fell against each other, one influencing the next; each held potential for good or ill. All too many of those chains of cause and effect, of policies and consequences, led to disaster.

As she stared at the statue, her mind worried away at the problem. This was big, serious; it affected the whole world. Her country was but a small part of that world, dwarfed by the powers that surrounded it. *When elephants fight, mice get trampled.* The old saying ran through her mind, its implications stark and clear. If something wasn't done and done fast, Thailand would be trampled into the dust. For a moment, her mind raged at the idiots in Europe who had set this ball rolling. She crushed the fleeting urge mercilessly, grinding it down until all that was left was ice-cold clarity of vision. That was her gift. She hadn't always had it; once she had been as prone to allowing emotion to cloud her judgment as anybody else, but the art of crushing her emotions had been taught to her, patiently and comprehensively. The gift truly was a gift, and now she treasured it more than even the other gift, the one she so painstakingly concealed. She knew she would need every scrap of insight she had to maneuver her way through this situation.

The first thought that crossed her mind was that the sudden collapse of Britain and France in Europe put some of their prime assets within her reach. The lands stolen by France in the last half of the 19th century were one set of cherries ready to be plucked. The problem was that other people also had their eyes on those lands; most notably the Japanese. Once again, the images of elephants fighting crossed her mind. When elephants fought, there

7

were only three ways for the mice to survive. One was to be somewhere else. That option did not exist. The second was to ally with one of the elephants. That option very definitely did exist. The third was to become an elephant. That option was also closed.

Or was it? Suddenly, her mind snapped at the idea and bit into it, holding it hard. *Was it so impossible? Did the way things had so suddenly changed make it possible?* Suriyothai settled back on her heels. To any outside spectator, she was just continuing her worship at the family shrine. In reality, her mind was filled with a waterfall display; a sheet of colored lights interlocked and merged only to split apart again as the events that drove them eddied and swirled. As they did so, she assessed them and measured possibilities. One particular thread started to grow in greater prominence than the others; its color pulsed brighter and stronger than the rest. She looked at it and isolated it, examining it and its demands in depth. As she did so, she realized that it could be done. Not only could it be done;it was the only viable way out of the mess that had so suddenly been created.

She stood erect, holding her back rigidly straight, and stepped outside the shrine. Outside was her desk, an antique that had served her well for many years. If wood had a memory, this piece of furniture could tell a terrifying number of secrets. But if Suriyothai had believed that wood had a memory and could hold secrets, this desk would have been burned a long time ago. She started to write, her Thai script elegantly and perfectly formed. Once the message had been completed, she coded it from a book that was only known to her and her inner circle. Finished, she stood again, thoughtful and reserved. One of the implications of the course that she had set herself upon was that her anonymity would vanish. Her very existence was unknown outside tightly limited circles high in the Thai government. That would have to change. For good or ill, she was about to become a public figure.

"Lani, take this message. Ensure that it is sent by telegram to our embassies in London, Paris, New Delhi and Washington. Oh, and Canberra as well. Also ensure that it goes to our contacts at Jardine Matheson, Swire, Hutchinson-Whampoa, Hendersons, Hong Kong and Shanghai Bank; all the Hongs in fact. I will need to see their Taipans urgently. Finally, send copies to Loki in Geneva and Philip Stuyvesant in Washington."

"You, your Highness?" Lani's voice was concerned.

"Yes, me. And I will also need to see Marshal Plaek Pibulsonggram. I have urgent business that must be discussed with him."

Room 208, Munitions Building, Washington, DC, USA

"Have we any idea of what is going on over there?" Henry L Stimson was bewildered. He'd got up this morning expecting the usual bad news about the war in Europe, but he knew neither just how much worse the situation would get nor just how quickly the slide downhill would gather speed.

"None. I hate to say it, but we've got virtually no insight into what has happened. We don't even know who the British Prime Minister is. Is it Halifax? Or Churchill? Or somebody else entirely? Kennedy at the Embassy is worse than useless. All we're getting from him is a barrage of nonsense about how it doesn't matter to us who is top dog in Europe and it might as well be Germany as anybody else. Dear God, what is that man doing over there? A chimpanzee would make a better ambassador."

"A trained chimp would be better. People like chimpanzees." Philip Stuyvesant looked at the ceiling in despair. "The version I got was that FDR saw Kennedy as a political threat and wanted him out of the way, so he sent him to London in the hope he'd find his way under a German bomb. As it happened, of course, it didn't take that."

"Democracy is finished in England. It may be here. The whole reason for aiding England is to give us time. As long as she is in there, we have time to prepare. It isn't that Britain is fighting for democracy. That's the bunk. She's fighting for self-preservation, just as we will if it comes to us. I know more about the European situation than anybody else, and it's up to me to see that the country gets it."

Cordell Hull repeated Kennedy's notorious message with what amounted to open disgust. "The only good thing about that barrage of nonsense was it destroyed any chance Joe has of getting to be President. That doesn't change the fact that he's told us nothing about what has just happened over there. Even the British Embassy doesn't know what is happening. *They* came to *us* this afternoon asking us what was going on. Philip, what do your industrial people say? Any word coming out through the trade circuits?"

"Not much. The people we deal with are as bewildered as everybody else. One thing that is agreed, Winston had nothing to do with this. He spent more than a decade warning against the rise of fascism and the need to confront that rise before it got too great to take down without a major war. He wouldn't just fold like this. Somehow, he's been taken out of the picture. My guess would be that he's either been taken into 'protective custody' or he's on the run somewhere."

"You're making this sound like some sort of coup. Great Britain isn't a banana republic; they don't have coups there." Cordell Hull was more bewildered than anything else; the frustration of being Secretary of State and not knowing what was going on in one of the most important countries in the world was telling.

"A coup is an illegal transfer of power executed by the direct or implied use of force." Stuyvesant had an annoying way of speaking when it came to strategic matters. His disinterested lack of inflection could set people's teeth on edge. To those who listened, and got past the dispassionate manner, found that it was worth their while; the understanding of grand strategy was unmatched. Then they realized the importance of that flat monotone. It described the world the way it was, not the way anybody wished

9

it was or thought it should be. Stimson and Hull had both learned that lesson, just as their predecessors, Edwin Danby and Charles Hughes had learned it about Peter Stuyvesant, Philip Stuyvesant's father. *Like father, like son,* Hull thought, *for good and for bad.*

"So, no, coups don't happen in Great Britain. What does happen instead amounts to a legal means of achieving the same result. It could be said that a coup is the mark of an immature society, one that had not learned how to bring about a change in power without stepping outside the law. Britain may not be a perfect society, but it is a mature one. So we can conclude whatever happened over there, happened legally. Of course, being legal doesn't mean it was right or proper. Also, never forget the maxim about possession being nine points of the law. The fact that Churchill has been eased from power is a done deal. Unless there is something really outrageous about how it was done, it's going to stay that way. Nobody will rock the boat. They'll just content themselves with the idea they are waiting on events and that's that. "

Hull frowned at that. Brought up and trained as a lawyer, his friends still called him "The Judge;" he looked on the law as the bastion of right and justice. Hull stopped himself and gave his attitudes a quiet mental rebuke. The law should be the bastion of right and justice; that didn't mean it always was. The law was created by humans and that meant it was as fallible as any other human creation. Hull guessed that the British had just found one of the failings of the system they had created. "So who do you think is in charge over there?"

Stuyvesant thought for a moment. "It has to be Lord Halifax. He's the one who presented the Armistice terms to Cabinet, so Winston couldn't have been there. If he had been, the Brits would be mopping Halifax's political blood off the Foreign Office steps by now. By the same logic, Winston has to be out of office and out of the running. If he was still in power, he would be having Halifax hung, drawn and quartered. I don't know how it was done, but based on what we know now, which isn't very much I hasten to add, Winston is out and Lord Halifax is in. As a result, Britain is out of the war."

"Is there still a war to be out of?" Hull was mulling the situation over. It didn't help matters that he despised Lord Halifax.

"The French are still in." Stimson spoke thoughtfully. "It looks bad for them but they are still in. If they hold…"

"They won't." Stuyvesant had the same flat intonation in his voice again. "They might have done so before Britain dropped out but now? They'll fold. They've taken a hell of a battering over the last few days and having their primary ally cut and run will finish them. Today's Wednesday. They might hold to the end of the week, they might even last the weekend but don't count on it. Next week, for certain, they'll pack it in. It's over."

"So it's all over." Stimson was appalled; his desperation showed through his voice very plainly. "Where do we go from here?"

10

"FDR won't accept it." Hull spoke with flat assurance. "You've no idea how much he despises the Nazis. He will not tolerate the idea of them dominating Europe no matter what Joe Kennedy says. I can't say I disagree with him on that. There are too many countries drifting towards fascism at this time. Not just in Europe but all over the world. He's going to put them down somehow, even if it means getting us into the war by pulling some trickery or other. "

"He can't get us into the war, not if it's already over. And it looks like this one is. Getting into an ongoing war is one thing, but the current war is over. Joining a war that's already running is one thing, but us entering now will be starting an entirely new war and that's something nobody will accept. Let's face it, if Germany sits still now and does nothing, the war is over. We're out and we can't get in." Hull's face was grim; the other two men got a strange feeling that he was near to tears.

"And if we do get in, we're on our own." Stimson was much subdued by the impact of the disastrous British decision.

"That's not as bad as it sounds." Stuyvesant was thoughtful. "Economically and industrially, we can dominate pretty much the whole world. If we mobilize our production capacity, we outgun Germany by a wide margin, even with the resources they've just seized. The problem won't be the equipment and military power side of this; it'll be getting at Germany. We're going to have to fight from bases in the continental United States. Hitting Germany from them will be interesting. We need something we've never had before: a war strategy that projects power into Europe from across the Atlantic, and one that presumes the absence of any form of forward basing. In fact, I don't think anybody has ever considered doing anything like it."

"The Army Air Corps has been working on war plans recently. Nothing formal yet, but they've been talking over two scenarios. One that presumes a war against Germany that uses forward bases and one that does not." Stimson looked skeptical. "Looks like that decision has been made for us. Cordell, I suggest you and I approach FDR and ask him to approve formal planning on a no-forward bases presumption. The Army Air Corps have already started working on the basics of how to fight a transatlantic war. I think the Air Corps call it AWPD-1. Before that even starts to be a serious plan, we have to find out what we need to destroy in order to drive Germany out of the war. Philip, I'd like you to get a small group of your fellow industrialists together, start trying to work out how the German war economy functions and determine the best way to can wreck it. Call yourselves the Economic Intelligence and Warfare Section. Assume that we're going to be on our own. For it sure as hell looks that way."

Bestwood Lodge, Arnold, Nottinghamshire, United Kingdom

"The bounder. Caving in to the Huns like this. My old friend Marshall Bond would recommend a necktie party, you can be sure of that." Osbourne de Vere Beauclerk, 12th Duke of St Albans, was furiously angry. As an aide to

11

Sir Douglas Haig in The Great War, he had been incensed by the idea that his age would prevent him serving in this one. Even by British aristocratic standards, the de Vere Beauclerk family might be more than slightly eccentric, but nobody had ever doubted their determination to stand by their King and Country. In fact, the family was even odder than their fellow peers of the realm realized, but that was something they kept very carefully to themselves.

"I will have his head for this." The rolling, sibilant tones, well lubricated by brandy and given timbre by cigars yet also diluted by exhaustion and heartbreak, echoed around the room. Winston Churchill, until six hours earlier Prime Minister of Great Britain, etc., etc., etc., glowered at the room around him. "I will have his head, taken from his shoulders in the traditional style, with axe and block. I will tell you this your Grace, as God is my witness, I will have That Man's head."

"I don't think that penalty exists under law any more." The Duke actually highly approved of the idea of beheading Lord Halifax, but he was more interested in seeing how Churchill would react. Much would depend on Churchill in the months ahead. If the Halifax coup was to stand opposed, there would need to be a British Government in Exile and it would need a strong man to lead it into credibility. The sheer hatred and venom that had been injected into the two simple words 'That Man' bore witness to the fact that Churchill had the strength of purpose needed.

"Your Grace, by the time these affairs have run their course, there will be no rule of law in our country. Does That Man not understand what he has done? There will be no peace for this realm of ours while the Nazi shadow stains Europe. All he has done is buy a few months, a few years at most, of peace before the final showdown comes. Whenever that is, our position will be worse than it is today. He has mortgaged the survival of our country for the position of Prime Minister. He calls this an armistice and says he had brought peace, but all he has done is fill our future with doubt. And he has paid for that peace with the honor that is the lifeblood of our kingdom. Did you hear what that French general De Gaulle called us? *Singes capitulards du lait à boire!* And the worst of it is that he is right. This day will go down in shame, Your Grace; an unbearable shame that will endure through the years until we earn redemption. And That Man's head will be the first part of the price paid."

Churchill ran out of breath and took another swallow of brandy. He would have preferred a whisky-soda, but he'd taken what was available. It had been a long, hard drive up here from Oxford. The first instinct had been to head south to the Channel ports and escape to France, but the German armies were closing in on the French coast and the final result there would be worse than in England. So, he had turned north, heading for the one refuge he knew would be open to him and secure beyond doubt. The family home of the Duke of St Albans was the eye of the hurricane, somewhere he could pause and take stock of a situation that had gone so badly awry.

"Can we put this matter right? Halifax holds his position by a thread. What he has done can be undone, surely?"

The clinical depression, what Churchill called his black dog, overwhelmed his mind with its full force of blanketing despair. It had plagued his life; this time he could see no way it could be relieved. "Your Grace . . . . "

"Osborne, please. We are in league against a powerful and ruthless enemy now; formality ill becomes such desperate straits."

"Osborne, I don't like standing near the edge of a platform when an express train is passing through. I like to stand right back and if possible get a pillar between me and the train. I don't like to stand by the side of a ship and look down into the water. A second's action would end everything. A few drops of desperation is all that it takes. Today, I have never felt closer to the edge of that platform or looked down into water more inviting. If it hadn't been for Cadogan's call, I would be in a police cell now. Oh, I have no doubt it would be called protective custody and I have equally little doubt that I would not live to see the morning.

"Yes, Osborne, there are things that we could do, but against the forces arrayed that have been set into motion, they will be little enough. The party committee will not remove Halifax from the Prime Ministry now. To do so would be to admit they are wrong and that they will not do. If they were to do that, then their whole claim to power and authority would be fatally undercut. We could stage a no-confidence motion in Parliament, but the House is disinclined to stage such votes except under the most trying of circumstances. We have already had one this year and most members will think that is enough. Even if we were to stage such a vote, I question whether we would win. That Man represents a strong body of opinion within the Conservative Party and the party will split in the face of the vote. The Labour Party will oppose him, but they are split also and many of their members decry this war. Never forget, Osborne, that Herr Hitler and Stalin have signed an alliance and the minions of the Comintern do Stalin's bidding. Even the Liberals are split. How those factions would combine is anybody's guess and the outcome yet more uncertain than that. No, a vote of no confidence will not get off the ground. This was a constitutional act, Osborne, one entirely legal and we have no practical means of reversing it."

The Duke saw its effect in Churchill's eyes and bearing; he made a private note to himself to have this man discretely but carefully watched tonight. "Winston, why not sleep on this problem? In the dawn, things may come to us that will not be clear tonight. Evans will show you to your room."

Churchill nodded, his eyes swimming with misery and despair. Then he followed the butler out of the room. As he did so, he glanced at the Duke. Beauclerk raised one finger and touched it lightly to his eye. In a relationship between families that had been handed down, father to son, for generations, that was all it took. There would be a suicide watch on their guest tonight. After they had gone, the Duke remained sitting, staring into the fireplace much

13

as Churchill had done. Quietly, he believed that Lord Halifax had done far more damage to the fabric of the realm with this day's work than even Churchill had realized. Beauclerk looked out of the great windows towards the lights of Nottingham. It seemed to him that the darkness was already closing in.

CHAPTER TWO
TASK DEFINITION

Dumbarton Avenue, Georgetown, Washington, DC, USA

"Nell, there's a telegram for you. From Switzerland." It was a convention in this most unconventional of all households that telegrams from Geneva should be passed to Eleanor Gwynne first. She would take a quick look at the contents and decide whether it would cause an explosion or not. Usually, the answer was that it would; then some hasty diplomacy would be needed to prevent another row breaking out between Phillip Stuyvesant and Loki.

"Thank you, ducks."

Dido Carthagina grinned conspiratorially and handed the envelope over. "Oh, it really is for me." There was a pause and then a resigned sigh. "It's relayed from Osborne in England. I'd better see Phillip about this right away."

"They're all in the living room. Whatever is going on has caused some serious angst in there."

"Europe, probably. Phillip spent hours sitting, staring out the window, when he got back from Washington. Heading in?"

"Of course, ducks." Eleanor flashed a smile at Dido and turned to the door of the living room. Quietly, she felt a little sorry for her friend. Once, a long time ago, Dido had made a bad decision, one that had catastrophic consequences for a lot of people. She'd never trusted her own judgment since and found making even simple decisions difficult. Like whether to disturb a meeting with an important message or what to order in a restaurant. Generally, she waited for other people to make the decisions for her. It was a passive way of living and one that the gregarious and social Eleanor found hard to understand. Mentally, she shrugged the reflection off and opened the door.

"Hi, Nell. Welcome to the plotter's cabal." Igrat was sprawled out on a couch, one leg hooked over the arm. The lighting in the room was dimmed

15

right down. With Igrat's pose and the number of empty glasses around, the place looked like a seedy night club after a very busy evening.

Across the room, Phillip Stuyvesant was looking through a stack of papers. He glanced up and saw the envelope in Eleanor's hand. "Message from Britain?"

"In a way, ducks. It's from Osborne via Geneva. In code. He says there's trouble over there and he has something we want. That's rare. Usually when I get a message from the family, it's because they've done something foolish and need me to bail them out. I assume it came through Geneva because the lines from Britain are down. What's going on?"

"Halifax took over from Churchill and he's signed an armistice with Germany."

Eleanor went white. "You are joking, ducks? How did that happen?"

"We don't know, I need a constitutional expert to explain it to me. But, the outcome is clear. The war's over, for a while at least. This so-called armistice won't last long. The whole situation will break out again and we'll be right in the middle of it. I've just been asked to work out how Germany plans to fight the whole world single-handed."

"Guess what? I'm going to be the bosses secretary in a new Washington Department, the Economic Intelligence and Warfare Section." Lillith also had a file and had reeled the name of her new appointment off without a hitch. "We're all going to be in it, I guess."

Stuyvesant nodded. "We'll be staffing the section from us. I need people there who know how I work. Igrat's going to be our courier again. Achillea and Henry, enforcement as usual. No sneaking off into the Navy this time, Achillea."

"You want Mike for anything?" Mike Collins was the closest thing Igrat ever had to a long-term partner.

Stuyvesant shook his head. "He's a lightweight, a butterfly. He's got nothing to offer except the ability to throw good parties. If we need one of those, we'll call him in. Nell, we'll need you to be a liaison with the British, especially when the Nazis turn this armistice into an occupation."

"You think they'll do that?" Naamah spoke from a corner.

"Of course. Their occupation of Europe can never be stable while Britain is unoccupied. The British Isles are the great fortress that guards Europe from an attack based in the west or south and a perfect springboard for just such an attack. Which role it plays depends on whether the people in Europe are on the British side or not. Or, in this case, whether Britain is on their side. An Armistice won't cut it. Somehow, the Germans will occupy and not too far into the future. I can't believe that Halifax doesn't understand that."

16

"And then the British will fight." Eleanor sounded saddened, more by the news that her birth country had folded than by the prospect of a war being fought on English soil for the first time in centuries.

"And then they will fight." Stuyvesant agreed. "All Halifax will have achieved in the end is to shift the battle from everywhere but England to England itself. The English are going to find out what it's like to be occupied and when they do, they'll start a resistance movement. Then they'll find out what happens when resistance movements start fighting occupying armies. The next few years are not going to be good ones, people. What we have to worry about is working out how to strike at Germany from bases in the USA."

"Bombing. At least that'll mean no more fighting in the trenches." Eleanor sounded pleased with that. Stuyvesant shook his head.

"Strategic bombing sounds good, but it doesn't end with bombing armies. It goes to bombing the depots where those armies store their supplies, then the railways that supply those depots and the factories that produce the goods that are transported by the railways. It ends with the people who work in those factories and then goes beyond that to killing those workers in their homes along with their families. We're not ending the war in the trenches, Nell; we're extending it backwards all the way to the worker's family in their house. This war is going to be bloody." Stuyvesant looked out of the window. "Anybody want to bet on how long it will be before we have to have a blackout in Washington?"

Supreme Command Headquarters, Bangkok, Thailand

"But the Americans are opposed to us and the Japanese are not. The Japanese offer us arms and equipment; the Americans do not. The Americans criticize every move we make and the Japanese support us. Why, then should we position ourselves against the Japanese?" Marshal Plaek Pibulsonggram made the points carefully and rationally. In truth, he was afraid of the woman who was sitting in front of him with an enigmatic smile on her face. *A true Thai smile,* he thought, *one that could mean anything and everything.*

"We're not quite positioning ourselves against the Japanese. Not yet, at any rate. What we are doing is strengthening our economic base so that we can stand on our own feet. If we have to remain within the Japanese sphere of influence, then the proposed plan will allow us to do so on something closer to equality. If we do not, and I believe that our interests are elsewhere, then our plans will enable us to stand against the pressure the Japanese will place upon us. At the moment, this is a plan that grants us more freedom of action. That is all. As for the Americans, they are opposed to us because they see our nationalist movement as being akin to fascism. President Roosevelt is opposed to fascism with every fiber of his being. A part of our plan is to teach him that nationalism in a country such as ours is not fascism but a simple desire to rule our own lives. Expressed that way, the Americans will sympathize with us and come around to our side. And soon, they will be seeking every ally they can find."

Marshal Plaek nodded in agreement at the last comment. "But, the Japanese offer us arms, equipment, aircraft. At prices we can afford. We need them and the Americans will not sell."

Princess Suriyothai Bhirombhakdi na Sukothai dipped her head slightly in acknowledgement. "The Japanese offer us aircraft and weapons at a cash price we can afford. It is the political price that we cannot countenance. We are not short of goods we can sell in times of war. We produce enough rice and fish to feed most of the region. We produce gold and silver for export. We make the finest silk in the world and produce some rubber. Money is not a problem Field Marshal, not really. We are a hardy people; we can go short inside our country if doing so will make us strong. It is political strength we lack. In most of the world, people would find it very hard to find us on a map. The movement towards Japan saves in areas where we have a sufficiency and costs us where we are gravely deficient."

Marshal Plaek considered the logic and found it did make sense. "So, what does your Highness recommend?"

"Field Marshal, your plans to modernize the Army must be accelerated. We are adopting German-designed equipment, mostly to be license-built at Lopburi. That equipment must enter service without delay. The German advisors we hired in the early 1930s have worked wonders with our forces and we must build on that. We must surpass our teachers, Field Marshal, and we have little time to do it in. We must adopt new ways, for the world has changed around us and the old ways are gone forever. There is an Air Force officer, Wing Commander Fuen, who has ideas on how to organize air support for the ground forces that are a remarkable advance on anything I have heard of. I believe they are worth considering.

"But it our political and economic strength we must attend to. That is why we will be suggesting that the great Hong Kong trading groups consider moving their headquarters to Bangkok. With Britain surrendering to the Germans, Hong Kong will not remain out of Japanese hands for long. The Hongs will be looking for a new home and we need to get them here. For that, we have to make many changes. We have telegraph connections in-country and a spur line down to Singapore. We must spend all the money we need to need to in order to make those telegraph connections as good as any in the world. With Britain out, India and Australia will be separated greatly in distance. We can become the bridge between them."

"When one village has fish but no rice, and the other has rice but no fish, great wealth will not come to either village but to the man who builds a bridge between them." Field Marshall Plaek quoted the Thai proverb thoughtfully. He could see where she was going with this. "But this depends on India and Australia staying in the war."

"It does, and that is the first obstacle that we must overcome. But, if they do, then the center of Indian mass in particular is here." Her finger tapped a map. "In Singapore. Indian must retain the great fortress of Singapore. But, it is an indefensible fortress against land attack. If the enemy holds the Malayan peninsula, Singapore will fall. The front line of defense for Singapore is not here at the Johore Strait, but here."

Her finger moved and tapped the Mekong River. "And that makes us a very valuable ally for the Indians. An ally who will link us to the Americans again."

"If India stays in the war."

"Exactly, Field Marshal. If India stays in the war."

Conference Room, Government House, Calcutta, India

"Does anybody have any idea what is going on?" Victor Alexander John Hope, 2nd Marquess of Linlithgow and Viceroy of India since 18 April 1936, was mightily offended. He had been the driving force behind the implementation of the plans for local self-government embodied in the Government of India Act of 1935. Those provisions had led to government led by the Congress Party in five of India's eleven provinces. He had been quietly proud of that achievement. Yet he had torn it down when his appeal for unity in the face of Britain's declaration of war on Germany resulted in the resignation of the Congress ministries. He got his Indian declaration of war on Germany at the cost of seeing his life's work and proudest moments destroyed. Now, Britain had surrendered and nobody had even bothered to tell him what was happening or why it had taken place. It was an insult of monumental proportions and the Marquess of Linlithgow was not a man who forgot gratuitous insults.

"Your Excellency, there is no word at all from London. It is as if London has completely forgotten about us. I have heard from Prime Minister Robert Menzies in Australia, for all the good that has done us. The Australians have heard nothing either and they are not best pleased by the fact. Their National Party has paid a political price for entering the war on Britain's side and to be left in the dark like this is unconscionable. It has insulted them, My Lord." Gerald Tarrant, Private secretary to the Viceroy, spoke sadly. "They found out the same way we did, by hearing it on the World Service news broadcast.

"Outrageous. Sir Martyn, has the word spread to the Congress Party yet?"

The remark was addressed to Sir Martyn Sharpe, Assistant Secretary for Domestic Affairs and a protégé of the Marquess. Sir Martyn's official duties were to look after the routine activities of his Department. In reality, his job was to maintain relations with the Indian politicians in the Congress Party. It was the kind of unofficial, back-door communications channel that the British seemed to thrive upon. One uniquely suited to India's environment. In the frantic hours that had passed since the news had been broadcast, Sir Martyn had spoken, on an entirely unofficial basis of course, with Pandit

Jawaharlal Nehru, leader of the Congress Party. That conversation had not been helpful in maintaining his tranquility.

"Your Excellency, I can quote the initial reaction of the Congress Party to this meeting. Their position is and I do quote exactly, 'You have lost the war you forced on us, now you can leave while we make peace. Next week will be soon enough.' They offer us help in packing our bags and making our way to the railway station."

"Damned cheek." Tarrant growled to nobody in particular.

"Gerry, they have to say that. Their own membership will tear them apart if they said anything else. Their real position is held within those two words: 'next week'. They want to find out what the hell is going on as well before they commit themselves."

Lord Linlithgow frowned at Sir Martyn's final choice of words, but let the matter pass. Everybody was frustrated and edgy from the knowledge that great things were afoot and they knew nothing of them. "I suppose it was inevitable they would demand peace. They never wanted a part of this war in the first place."

"They never wanted into this war, that is true, Your Excellency. To be honest, your decision to take us in was almost as offensive to them as we have found London's treatment of us has been. That point was made, quite gently I may say, by Nehru who described the situation as 'Karmic Justice'."

A smattering of laughter ran around the room. Lord Linlithgow shook his head, "I can see their point on that. In retrospect, I think the Indian declaration of war was not one of my better hours."

Privately, Sir Martyn agreed, but he was not going to say so. "Nevertheless, India is at war and I suspect that having found themselves in it, they do not want out of it at the abrupt and unsolicited command of a dubiously legitimate Prime Minister in London. They want to end the war by their own hand and leave it with their heads held high. To accept this diktat from London would leave them crawling way like whipped dogs. They, also, are offended, Your Excellency. Their offer to help us pack our bags and make our way to the railway station should be seen in that light. It isn't cheek, Gerry; it's their way of telling us they want to work with us on our departure, not against us."

There was a learned nodding of heads around the conference table. Subtle meanings attached to apparently inconsequential words were meat and drink for those present. There was a wealth of experience in doing just that around the table.

"Which takes us to the next question." Harold Hartley, known to all as HH, asked the obvious question. "Are we still at war with Germany?"

"That, at least, I can answer." Lord Linlithgow answered firmly. "India is a Dominion, not a colony. We declared war by our decision; we end that war by our decision. We may take our lead from London, if they deign to give us one, but the decision is made here, not there. And so, the answer is a clear yes. We are still at war with Germany and will remain so until we, or our successors, decide otherwise."

"That also is the Australian position, your Excellency. Prime Minister Menzies points out that Australia had its reasons for declaring war and that those are not necessarily changed by a British surrender." Tarrant relayed that input with a certain level of relish.

"That is absurd." Sir Richard Graham Cardew, the Cabinet Secretary, had gone bright red. "If the India Office commands, then it is our part to obey. The final authority lies there, not here." Cardew was one of the oldest men at this table; his experience over the last 30 years had formed his opinions and attitudes to the point where they were set in stone.

"That may have been the case once, Sir Richard; it is not now. India a Dominion heading towards independence."

"Never!" Cardew's interruption was explosive.

"Inevitably, Sir Richard, and I will thank you not to interrupt me again. India is inevitably heading towards independence and most of us will live to see that day. The question is not whether independence will happen, but when and under what terms. Do we simply walk out and leave or do we arrange a slow and gracious hand-over of power? Sir Martyn, in your experience, what is the Congress Party position on this? Their real position, not the one for public consumption."

Sir Martyn thought carefully. "Their various demands that we should simply leave now are indeed for public consumption. Or, perhaps I should say, to the rank and file membership of their party for whom they have to display a continued militancy. Their real position is that they are prepared to accept an interim regime provided there is a steady visible transfer of power. I except Gandhi from this of course; he demands we quit now and he means every word of it. The wretched man is quite impossible, I fear. But, your Excellency, an early casualty of that transfer process will have to be your own position. The place you occupy must be occupied by an Indian. Probably Nehru. And membership of the Commonwealth is a likely casualty also. Not in the immediate future, perhaps, but at some time, an independent India will sever relations there."

"That is outrageous. You betray us, Sir Martyn." Cardew was deep crimson and appeared on the verge of a stroke.

"Sir Richard, I have warned you before about interrupting others here. Once more and I will ask you to withdraw."

"There is no need for that, Your Excellency. I will not stay here and listen to treason." Cardew flung his chair back and stormed out of the cabinet room. The crash as the door closed behind him caused the papers on the great conference table to flutter. Lord Linlithgow raised an eyebrow at the disturbance.

21

"Pray continue, Sir Martyn. I find your insight most important."

"Well, your Excellency, the position of an Indian as a replacement for the Viceroy is essential for any agreement on a transition. It will be a sign of real power and authority that will cause the rank and file of the Congress Party to accept much else. Leaving the Commonwealth will be more of a symbolic gesture, especially in the light of today's events. It will be a dramatic breaking of ties that will also justify much else. It may even make acceptable India staying in the war. There is an interesting aside to that question; we speak of India's membership of the Commonwealth but what of the position of Britain? Is the government in London the legitimate government of Britain? If so, should it remain in the Commonwealth? If it is not, and there forms a Government in Exile, should not that entity be the legitimate representative of the British people within the Commonwealth?"

"It is lucky that Sir Richard stormed out after all. Had he heard you say that, he would now be dead on the floor from apoplexy and poor old HH here would have weeks of paperwork to do." Linlithgow looked around the room.

"In that event, I would feel it my duty to offer him every assistance within my power. But, your Excellency, my point remains; Congress can be persuaded to stay in the war."

"You believe that's essential, don't you?" Linlithgow's voice had a note of sympathy within it. He was well aware that Sir Martyn's wife was Jewish. Indeed, that was one factor that had influenced him in placing his trust with the man. Somebody who had the strength of character to do what he felt was right despite the possible effects on his career and the unspoken but very real social objections to the marriage also had the strength to do his work well.

"I do, Your Excellency. There are some things that are such incarnate evil that any decent man should stand against them regardless of the price the act must demand. I believe that Prime Minister Churchill understood that."

The Marquess of Linlithgow nodded. "And so does the Viceroy of India."

Cabinet Office, 10 Downing Street, London

"Is there no sign of Mister Churchill?"

Sir Edward Bridges needlessly consulted the reports he had received and shook his head. "We traced him as far as Oxford and then kept all the roads out of Oxford under surveillance, but I fear Winston was not detected by any of the patrols. I can only presume that he is still in Oxford."

"That would be uncharacteristic of the man. He was always one for action, no matter how ill-advised. He will be on the move. With his affection for the French, he will choose to go there. Are all the roads south from Oxford under surveillance?"

"They are, Prime Minister. But, how completely that surveillance has been maintained is another matter entirely. We British do not have an

22

overweening police force. We do not even see the need to arm our police. As an orderly people used to the rule of law, we do not have the need for either large numbers of police or to have them armed. In this case, to maintain surveillance of all the thoroughfares, ranging from the trunk roads to farm lanes, is beyond them. And then there are the trains, of course."

Halifax drummed his fingers impatiently. "It is apparent, I think, that a small, well-trained police force as we have now is an estimable thing indeed. But the times have changed and many pairs of eyes will be needed on our streets. We must be ready to reinforce our existing police force with an auxiliary police unit, one whose loyalty can be absolutely guaranteed."

"I do not think the British people will take kindly to the return of the black-and-tans, Prime Minister."

Halifax looked shocked. "Sir Edward, I mean no such thing. Placing a para-military force on the streets would be an outrage. I simply mean recruiting well-meaning citizens to assist our existing police force and provide a presence where otherwise limited numbers would preclude the police from doing so themselves. I wish the Home Office to see to the formation of such a unit immediately."

And to hell with the Cabinet or any form of consultation, thought Bridges. *If this isn't going to turn into a paramilitary force on the streets, then nothing will.* He had a decision to make, one that had kept him awake almost all the previous night. There were a considerable number of very senior civil servants abroad at the moment, including a large party in Canada and the United States. They had been discussing arms purchases and other war material acquisition programs with American businessmen, all with the aim of ensuring American industrial support for the faltering British war machine. There were already discrete warnings that none of those men would be returning to Britain. Indeed, the words 'Government in Exile' had also been whispered. All they needed was a figurehead and support from the Dominions and the threat could become real.

Was it a threat? Bridges had to ask himself that question. *If it is, should I be part of it? Should I drop my position here, the authority I have and the influence I have built in exchange for a life of exile?* He thought of his house, his gardens and his beloved fishpond. *Should I abandon those with a strong possibility of never seeing them again?* There was another problem, or, rather, another aspect to the choice. He was well aware of Lord Halifax's limitations. The man was an appeaser, a temporizer, a man who tended to agree with whoever he was speaking to. Bridges had a strong feeling that Butler, now Foreign Secretary in Halifax's place, had been a much stronger driving force behind the coup than he admitted.

Bridges stopped himself sharply. Coups didn't happen in Great Britain; they were the preserve of small, far-off countries that mattered little in the scheme of things. *But how else would one describe what had happened the day before?* Bridges guessed that if he threw in his lot with those who had decided to refuse the call home, Halifax would be surrounded by those whose beliefs had caused this situation. *Do I, Bridges, not owe it to the country to remain here, to keep the country running smoothly and to avoid the excesses that would otherwise surely take place?*

"Well, Sir Edward?" Halifax sounded annoyed.

Bridges shook himself free from his mental debate and postponed it for another time. "An excellent idea, Prime Minister. I will set the necessary wheels in motion. Now, Prime Minister, there is the problem of the Dominions. They still have had no official word of what has happened here. We need to brief them on what has happened and why and we need to ask them to follow our lead in accepting the terms of the Armistice. We need to give the impression at least that we are consulting with them on this matter."

"There is nothing to consult about and nothing to discuss. The terms of the Armistice are binding upon them as much as they are upon us here. They will obey them." Lord Halifax crossed his arms, right hand over his withered left arm. It was an intimidating pose from a Prime Minister. In common with any civil servant, Bridges was skilled at reading body language. Halifax was signalling that his mind was closed to any argument. Nevertheless, Bridges felt honor bound to give it one more try.

"Prime Minister, this may be true with regard to the colonies that are ruled directly from London. But with the Dominions, we are dealing with essentially independent states that are self-governed. They declared war on Germany on their own account and they will make peace on their own account. We must go through the motions of discussing the situation with them. We must explain ourselves and convince them that ours is the route to follow. A blunt order from us is by far the least effective means of gaining their compliance. Our relations with them have a certain level of choreography. We ask them and they oblige. We make a discrete suggestion and they, after some thought, agree. If, by chance we must step on their toes we beg pardon and they smile and dismiss it as being of no consequence. But sadly when we give direct orders they tell us to go boil our heads. If you wish to count upon Imperial support for the actions you have taken, then I strongly urge you allow the Colonial and Dominion Offices to reopen communications and that we consult with them."

"We shall indeed do that, Sir Edward. The Colonial and Dominion Offices will communicate the terms of the Armistice with Germany that we have signed and they will be informed that these terms are binding upon them also. The matter is settled; there is no need for additional consultation. We will hold them responsible for completing their part in the terms we have found acceptable. There is no need for weakness in this matter."

Sir Edward Bridges was aghast. "Prime Minister, I must protest. A preemptory message of the kind you propose will have the most disastrous of effects upon our relations with the Dominions. A conciliatory tone, a gesture of consideration need not imply any irresolution on our part, only a desire to resolve what amounts to a very inconvenient situation for everyone. It will even be seen as a sign of strength, that we consider our position to be so secure and well-founded that it will withstand any objection made to it. We cannot drive the Dominions, Sir. We must lead them."

"You presume much, Sir Edward. And so do the Dominions. They hide behind our skirts while profiting from Imperial Preference. This country carries the burden of their defense and little thanks we get for it. When I was Viceroy in India, I tried to discuss issues with them and they defied me. When I showed them the rod, they deferred to me. That is the way it has always been, Sir Edward; that is the way it will always be. Arrange for the message to be sent by the Colonial and Dominion Offices. Immediately."

Or I will replace you with somebody who will do what I order. That's what you have left unsaid, isn't it? Bridges felt depression swoop down upon him, but mixed with it was a sense of relief. His belief that he had a way out was proven false. He was trapped here by his own existing position and his own sense of duty. He had to remain in office in order to try and ensure that the country and the Empire ran smoothly.

Wardroom, Battleship HMS Valiant, Trincomalee, India

"Is it true?" Captain Edgar Porteous Woollcombe guessed what the answer would be before he got a response.

"It's true. Winston is gone; Halifax is Prime Minister. He's signed an Armistice with Germany." Admiral James F. Summerville looked stricken, as if repeating the news somehow gave it extra weight. "You got here just in time by the look of it."

"What do you mean, Sir?"

"I received a message from the Admiralty this morning. It advises us that an Armistice has been signed with Germany and we should govern ourselves in accordance with standing order number 03-9839. Well, I looked up that order and it says that our orders in the event of England being forced to capitulate are to continue to prosecute the war against Germany under the direction of the governments of the Commonwealth countries. In this event, we will govern our operations to sink, burn and destroy enemy forces and personnel without mercy until victory has been achieved. All signals, orders or communications from Britain directing a surrender or cessation of hostilities prior to the defeat of Germany being achieved are to be considered false and disregarded."

"Oh." The import of the message was clear; the fleet still in the United Kingdom was trapped but the ships abroad were being slipped off the leash. A little bit, anyway. Perhaps it would be better to say the leash was being placed in new hands.

"Exactly, Captain Woollcombe. I propose to contact the Viceroy of India to place this squadron at his disposal and await his orders. If he decides to fight on, then he has a fleet to do it with. If he decides to follow the lead from London, well, then we follow that course. But, *Valiant* has not yet formally joined this squadron. On paper at least, you are still part of Force H based in Gibraltar and will remain so until you report to me. That is why I wished to see you privately before you do so. If you wish, you may not report to me, quoting the current situation and your assignment as a unit of Force H. In that case, since Gibraltar is not a Dominion, you may take *Valiant* home. Your other alternative is to report to me, join the India Squadron and remain with us. In that case, Captain, it might be many years before you see home again."

Woollcombe didn't hesitate. "Admiral, Sir. If it means fighting on, I would wish to report to you and to join your squadron as per my existing orders."

Summerville relaxed slightly. "Good man. It will be most beneficial for us to have a battleship out here. I am having a Captain's conference in 30 minutes, please join us. It will be a chance for you to meet the other Captains in the fleet."

Woollcombe saluted and left. Summerville left the wardroom, quietly thanking the steward for the opportunity to have this quiet meeting. An "accidental" meeting in a wardroom where Summerville was a guest was one thing; summoning Woollcombe to his bridge would have been quite another. Once out on a bridge wing, he looked over the expanse of the naval base. Trincomalee was the one reason why the Royal Navy was here in Ceylon. It was the finest naval base this side of Singapore and dominated the Indian Ocean. Over to port was the aircraft carrier *Hermes. Not one of the largest or best-equipped carriers in the world,* Summerville thought, *but better than nothing. At least she means I'll have some form of air cover if we have to fight.* Then there were two heavy cruisers, the modern 8-inch *Cornwall* and the 7.5-inch gunned *Hawkins*. His third heavy cruiser, *Dorsetshire,* was out on patrol. His light cruisers were all in, *Capetown* and *Colombo* were six-inch gunned veterans of the Great War. They still looked lean, purposeful ships. Their older sisters, *Calypso* and *Caradoc* were more archaic looking and their design showed their age badly. Still, they could take on any of the Japanese light cruisers in a ship-to-ship pounding match. His destroyers weren't so fortunate. All twelve were old V/W class ships and compared badly with the Japanese destroyers they might have to engage.

Despite the age of the ships, this squadron gave India a navy, a tool it could use. That was more than it had at the moment. The Indian Navy fleet consisted of two sloops and four escort vessels that were barely more than coastal gunboats. If India was going to go it alone, she would need the British ships. The corollary to that was having the ships presented to them on a plate might well make the Indians more likely to stay in. A lot depended on what the Australians intended to do. As if the young officer had been reading his mind, a Sub-Lieutenant arrived on the bridge clasping a message.

"Sir, message from Admiral Crichton in Australia."

Summerville took the flimsy and read it carefully. It was a simple note, one that stated the Pacific Squadron would be conducting itself in accordance with 03-9839 and would comply with the directions of the Australian Government. That didn't mean too much by itself; a fast minelayer and four destroyers were hardly crucial elements in the balance of power. What it did show was that others in the Royal Navy were preparing to carry on the fight. Suddenly, Summerville felt a lot less lonely.

"You, what's your name?"

The Sub-Lieutenant drew himself up. "James Ladone, Sir. Signals."

Summerville smiled at him. "I bet everybody calls you Jim Lad. How long have you been on *Valiant*?

"Three months, Sir. First posting. Most people call me Jim Lad One. There's another subbie in Signals, Sir; James Ladde. They call him Jim Lad Two."

"Sensible. Tale a message for transmission to Admiral Crichton. Message reads. 'Indian Ocean Squadron submitting ourselves to Indian Government Authority in accordance with 03-9839. Our actions will be determined by their decisions.' Message ends. Got that?"

"Yes, Sir." Ladone scuttled off with an enthusiasm that reminded Summerville of a young puppy. If *Valiant* was to be his flagship, he would need a signals staff and Ladone would suit him well as a junior member.

Audience Room, Bang Phitsan Palace, Bangkok, Thailand

"Thank you all for coming here today. On behalf of the government of Thailand, I welcome you to our country and will endeavor not to waste your time. You are all familiar with the events in Great Britain, I assume?"

There was a quick exchange of glances which resulted in John Keswick of Jardine-Matheson taking the plunge. Jardine's was The Princely Hong after all, and taking the lead was its privilege, however much Butterfield-Swire might dislike it. "We are, ... ," he stumbled not quite knowing what form of address to use.

"My apologies. I am the Ambassador-Plenipotentiary of the Royal Family of Thailand." She smiled demurely. "That means I am the direct representative of the Thai political system. All of it, not just the official government. I answer to the King himself, but beyond that to the people of this country. I am Thailand's official trouble-shooter."

"By which you mean you shoot those who cause trouble, Madam Ambassador?" Keswick smiled, but his eyes watched The Ambassador closely. What he saw in her eyes scared him. This woman would have no compunction about killing those who threatened her country.

"Exactly. And because of the events in London, there is much we need to speak about. Are you aware of the terms of the Armistice between Britain and Germany?"

Keswick shook his head, "No, madam. Except that the Armistice has been signed, we have no knowledge of its terms." He was embarrassed by that. The Princely Hong had a widespread net of information sources, all of which had let the group down. The only redeeming feature was that the other Hongs had failed equally badly.

"I have the text of the Armistice agreement here. Please accept a copy for each of you with the compliments of my Government." Suriyothai had an impassive expression but inwardly she smiled. The Piccadilly Circus in London had come through in fine style, despite most of its leaders being out of the country. She waved slightly and one of her staff rose to her feet and handed out the documents. There was a rustling of paper as the taipans quickly read through the papers.

"This document was dictated by the Germans." Keswick was in no doubt of that. "It shows no understanding of the structure of the Empire or the political constraints it operates under. The suggestion that a document such as this, negotiated and agreed in London, will extend its terms as a matter of course to the Dominions is ludicrous."

"That is our thought also. We understand that Australia and India are mightily offended by the situation and also by the fact that they still have not received official word of what has happened. We believe, but do not know, that South Africa and Canada are equally displeased."

Keswick nodded, noting the careful distinction the Ambassador made between what she knew and what she believed or deduced. There was something else as well. His own position of absolute authority gave him the skill of recognizing that power in others; the Ambassador had it. He guessed it was probably derived power, drawing on the influence of the Royal family, but power was still power. He looked at the Ambassador and understood that this woman not only had power, she knew how to use it. Ruthlessly. The comment about shooting trouble-makers had not been a joke.

"May I draw your attention to the section that relates to the status of British colonies? It appears to our analysts that this gives carte blanche for any German ally to make claim to any British colony that said ally believes was unjustly taken from them. We believe that this inevitably means Japan will claim Hong Kong. Your activities in China are already being restricted by the war being fought there. Those restrictions will increase rapidly and will soon amount to total exclusion. When Hong Kong is taken over, the exclusion will extend to you there. That will be the end of the Hongs, Princely or otherwise."

Suriyothai let her eyes roam around the group of men assembled in the room. Her expression was polite, helpful and concerned at the threat facing them. Her mind was filled with a fierce joy at the opportunity that was now unfolding before her. She noted the apprehensive tones of the quiet conversations that went on around her. Her point had struck home.

"So, what do you suggest, Madam Ambassador?" Keswick took the lead again.

"You must get ready to move your operations out of Hong Kong. You have a number of options, I believe. Chongqing and Kunming have been mentioned and I believe that offices in Bombay are also to be established at this time."

Keswick was stunned. The plans to move Jardine Matheson out of Hong Kong in the event of a Japanese take-over were a closely-guarded secret. She'd just named the three leading contenders for a new headquarters.

"She's got you there, John." Richard Leeming of Butterfield-Swire had a jeering tone in his voice at the obvious breech of the Princely Hong's security.

"Do not be severe on Mister Keswick. Your own company has similar plans." Suriyothai reproved the Butterfield-Swire taipan and was secretly delighted to see him flush. "So do the rest of you. I think though, that your choice of alternatives leaves much to be desired. Chongqing and Kunming will both fall to the Japanese in due course and you will face the same problem again. Bombay is more secure and has excellent telegraph communications with the rest of the world, but moving there will present you with all the problems of dealing with an entirely new business and cultural environment. Recruiting staff will also be a problem for you."

Keswick nodded. All those factors had already been considered by his staff. "You have another suggestion, Madam Ambassador?"

"I have. Move here. Bangkok is a major city. We have telegraph services already and have allocated funds for a major upgrade of our system. If you elect to move here, we would invite you to sit down with the Telegraph and Telephone Authority and specify exactly what it is that you need in the way of communications. We will then build it for you. We have educated people here, graduates of British and American universities. We are business-friendly and, to put it bluntly, we will keep out of your way. We are close to being in the geographical center of this region, within relatively easy reach of east, west, north and south. Our business community is well-established, has excellent contacts across the world. It is also largely Chinese and provides a cultural environment with which you are already comfortable and into which your existing Chinese staff will fit well. This is a medium-large country with rich resources in food, gold, precious jewels, rubber and opium. The latter in particular will be needed across the world as the war continues. Wounded soldiers need morphine more than anything else and there will be many millions of those by the time this war ends. Finally, you will have the best army in South East Asia standing between you and any threat. Six divisions in regular service, four more as reserves. All German-trained and German-equipped. Gentlemen, the Germans taught us how to use our tanks and artillery well."

"That claim to military prowess sounds impressive but, with respect, it is based on your word alone. Do you have experience to support it?"

29

Leeming's voice stopped just short of being openly dismissive. "It is not as if your country has an impressive military reputation to date."

Suriyothai looked at him, a sincerely helpful smile on her face. Behind that smile, she imagined herself flaying him alive before disembowelling him with a hooked knife. Then she dismissed that train of thought; brutality would not solve this problem. "As it happens, I hold the military rank of Colonel and have commanded an infantry regiment. I agree that our military history is not taught in Western staff colleges. However, we do have a six hundred year tradition of fighting every invader of our country to a standstill. We are still here and, I would remind you, alone in this region we have never been colonized. Before the colonial era, we took on the might of Han China and defeated them. I would refer you to the battle at Bang Rachan. There, a small group of villagers held off an entire army for eighteen months. The women fought alongside their men and died alongside them. That is where the tradition of Thai women wearing their hair cut short comes from. But, your point is well taken. However, given the scope of international events, I think you can be assured that a demonstration of our ability will be forthcoming."

"And you want our agreement to move now, I suppose." Keswick sounded amused but actually his mind was running over the prospect that had been outlined. It was unexpected and completely outside any of the analyses his staff had made. Yet, it had a hypnotic fascination.

"Of course not. Pressuring you to make a decision would be foolish. We cannot persuade you to make a decision, either here and now or at any time. You must make that decision on your own and for your own reasons. And in your own time. We stand ready to provide any information you need and to invest in the facilities you will require. But, we cannot interfere with the decisions that you might make. To do so would undermine the relationship which we propose to you. What we do suggest is that each of you open an office here and transfer the critical records and other things you need to continue your business to that office. If you choose to move to Bangkok, then your new headquarters will stand ready. If you do not, a regional office with a full reserve copy of your records will be a valuable property in its own right. Either way, a fall-back plan is always a wise precaution."

Keswick nodded again. "That is certainly possible, but any final decision on the location of our headquarters would have to be attendant upon a demonstration of your country's ability to secure and protect our investment here. Other than that, I have two questions, Madam Ambassador. How soon can Jardine Matheson set up this regional office here, and will you be involved in running this move?"

"Yes, I will be personally responsible for seeing that any move you choose to make. There will be no problem in you transferring key members of your staff here. We will welcome them and make them part of our community. As to how soon you can make your move, some property developers here have started to build an office block that seems entirely suited to your needs. It is called Sukothai House and has its own generators and air conditioning. I have the details of it here." She handed over a leaflet that showed a typical European-style office building; one she had designed and built by European architects and paid for it out of her personal resources.

Keswick glanced at the sheet and then read it more carefully. That The Ambassador had it to hand was the factor that decided him. "Madam Ambassador, please advise the developers that this building is to be known as Jardine Matheson House and that we will take it in its entirety. Do you allow us to purchase buildings or should we lease?"

"You may purchase the building. The land it is on must be leased but we will offer lease terms that amount to your ownership. I assume Jardine Matheson (Thailand) is now an operable concern?"

"At the very least." Keswick covertly cast his eyes around the room. Now that the Princely Hong had jumped into the offer being made, the others would follow. That meant Jardine Matheson was in the lead and would be well-established by the time the others got here. Also, he guessed that his lead would place the Ambassador in his debt and he had a feeling she always honored her debts.

Once her guests had departed for the Oriental Hotel, Suriyothai relaxed and stared out of the window. In her mind, the strange display formed again, a waterfall of lights and threads that represented the various options for the future. Now the tenuous thread that she had identified earlier was glowing much more strongly than before. What had been a pious hope a couple of days before was now a solid possibility.

"I have brought tea, your Highness." Lani bowed deeply as she poured, taking great care that her head did not rise above that of Suriyothai. "The meeting went well?"

"Very well. We have made many promises and now we must keep them. Also, we made a few boasts that are no more than that. Boasts remain just words until there are actions to back them up. Now, we must look for the excuse to take such actions. We said we had the finest army in South East Asia. We shall prove it by destroying French power in Indo-China. Once our military ability is demonstrated, the Hongs will come here and they will bring economic strength with them."

Trent Building, Nottingham University, Nottingham, United Kingdom

"Excuse me, could you tell me how to find the library?"

The soft voice broke through David Newton's daydream and focused his attention on the speaker. A young woman with jet-black hair, strongly arched eyebrows and high cheekbones. There weren't that many women in the University and very few that attractive. "Umm, there's several, depending on which school you're in. What are you studying?"

"Commercial art. I'm just starting. And you?"

31

"Chemical engineering. Second year. My name's David Newton. The library belonging to the Fine Art School is along this way. I'm heading that way myself since the Engineering School is on the next floor. I'll show you where it is."

"I'm Rachael Cohen. Pleased to meet you David. To be honest, I was afraid when I got here. Everybody seemed very remote and distant. Nobody seems to want to talk."

"I think everybody is a bit scared right now, to be honest. With the Armistice coming the way it did and all. We'd all assumed our call-up papers were on the way and we'd be Army conscripts by the end of the year. Now, the war is over we don't know what is happening."

"The war isn't over, David. It's just started. It has a long, long time to run yet. And then there's the greater war as well." Rachael looked at him out of the corners of her eyes, measuring him to see how he reacted to the comment.

"I agree, That Man has made a horrible mistake and we'll all pay dearly for it." Newton was suddenly aware of how quickly the phrase "That Man" with reference to Lord Halifax had slipped into the language. He wasn't even sure how it had happened. "What do you mean by 'the greater war'?"

"Why, the war between capitalists and proletariat of course. Between the exploiters and the exploited. The class struggle will go on no matter what That Man says."

The venom behind her use of 'That Man' was startling. "Well, I see things a bit differently, Rachael. I think that the Nazis will kill us all, capitalist and worker alike, if we don't finish them off first. We've all got to stick together or we'll all be wiped out. Look, this is the Fine Arts library. Perhaps we can talk a bit more about this later. Over tea in the canteen, perhaps? My classes finish at five."

Rachael hesitated. "I have a bit of a problem with the food offered at the canteen. It's not kosher, you see. But I suppose tea will be all right. See you there at six?"

Michael Collin's Home, Long Island, New York

Sir Humphrey Appleday drained his glass, but it was no good. He had come over from London as part of a delegation with the British Purchasing Commission and had consulted with Phillip Stuyvesant on the matter of small craft for the Royal Navy. This evening was his first opportunity since the catastrophic news from London to talk over more pressing matters. There was the mystery of Winston Churchill, for example. The man appeared to have dropped off the face of the earth; no mean achievement for such a rabid publicity-hound. Unfortunately, Appleday had run into Michael Collins first and the two had exchanged ill-tempered words after a little finely-judged provocation from Nell.

Igrat had intercepted him with a full glass and her most seductive smile. She might have a morally flexible outlook on life, even by the standards of New York, but she was an excellent hostess. Appleday sighed gently, his anger leaving him. It was simply impossible for a man to remain angry when Igrat was plying him with drink; although in most cases, her victim would have been wiser to remain angry, alert and sober. They had usually paid for their mistake with their wallets and, on one recent occasion, all their clothes. In that case, her victim had been an aspiring New York politician with strongly pro-Nazi views. One call to a newspaper had followed another to his wife and the scandal had ruined him. Appleday returned her smile with a rueful grin, "I really walked into that little dispute, didn't I?"

"Like a newling kitten." Igrat's humor took any sting out of her words. "Don't blame Nell; we all react to danger in different ways. Phillip gets all careful and calculating, Mike gets rash, I get lecherous and Nell gets playful. And what she's doing tomorrow and thereafter isn't safe. The Pan Am clipper to Shannon will be secure enough, but after that? But, family calls and she's off to do her duty by them. She'll have Achillea and Gusoyn with her, so that's going to help."

Igrat leaned forward and Appleday found himself looking down the front of her dress. "Now, if you want to get back at Mike, take me away from the party. That'll set him off nicely."

Appleday was appalled. "And what will he do to you?"

"He's drunk, so he'll take a swing at me. He'll miss, of course. I'm really good at getting out of the way. Hearing about it will make Nell feel bad as well, so you'll get a double-barrelled revenge. Want to try it?" Igrat wriggled her shoulders slightly.

"And put you at risk of taking a blow, for the sake of cheap revenge? I'd rather swallow the insult."

Igrat's eyebrows rose in surprise. "Why, Humpty, you say the nicest things. You are a gentleman aren't you? I'm touched, I really am. But really, don't worry about Mike. He knows very well that if ever one of those swings connects, I'll be gone and never coming back."

Appleday looked at her, slightly suspicious that she might be poking fun at him, but her sincerity was obvious. In fact, Igrat was always slightly surprised when she found out that people cared about her. The mental scars from neglect, exploitation and abuse in her early childhood were still there, underneath the stylish, hard exterior. He decided it was time to change the subject. "So how does everybody else react to danger?"

"Oh, Lillith takes off in the opposite direction. Naamah fades into the background and will probable poison the person responsible. Achillea goes towards it carrying every weapon she can find. Achillea's going to England with Nell, you know. Help look after her."

"There shouldn't be any risk." Appleday thought carefully. "If anything, this is probably the best possible time to go to England. It might be the last chance anybody gets for a long time."

"It's going to be that bad over there?" Igrat was genuinely surprised by the comment. "I know your team has elected to stay over here rather than go back to England, but I thought Lord Halifax was going to try and keep Britain out of Germany's reach?"

Appleday sighed, then reminded himself that anything he said to Igrat would be repeated back to Stuyvesant in exactly the same pitch, tone and emphasis that he had used. "Halifax has bought some time, that's all. Britain must be either within the German political gestalt or an enemy of it. Its economy, war industries and geographic position all dictate that. The Germans know that invasion is impossible. After all, the German is not an aquatic beast and crossing the Channel is a far more intractable problem than any mere river. They've foregone the direct, brutal and rapid approach in favor of a slower absorption, but the policy end is the same. German control over Great Britain. They'll make small demands, each quite reasonable on its own and Halifax will accept them rather than fight. Then, one day, he'll wake up and find the whole country has slipped through his fingers. One may always keep the peace if one is prepared to pay the asking price, but I have to ask whether Halifax has even bothered to ask for the statement of account."

Appleday paused and tried to fight back the tears that were forming in his eyes. He could see what was going to happen so clearly; the fact that Halifax and his accomplices couldn't filled him with despair. "We have to set up a government in exile, but to do that we need a leader, somebody people can identify with. A group of civil servants won't be good enough. We need Winnie out and over here, or somebody very like him, and there isn't anybody quite like Winnie. But, returning to Nell's visit, everything should be all right now. I think we can be sure there will be a few Gestapo officers in Britain already 'to find escaped criminals' or some such excuse, but as for the rest, that will take time. A thousand years of tradition and the slow, painful growth of liberty thrown out in a day. Yes, Igrat, if Nell or anybody else goes to England, now will be the time. Because a long, difficult night is coming and I do not know if we will see the end of it. Or what bringing in a new dawn will cost."

Government House, Calcutta, India

"Well, Martyn, we've had an interesting communication from Bangkok."

Sir Martyn Sharpe raised his eyebrows in surprise. "From Bangkok? What do they want?"

Sir Eric Haohoa took a delicate sip from his glass of sherry. "As a matter of fact, they asked for nothing. They just supplied us with a complete copy of the Armistice agreement signed between London and Germany on the 19th. They said we ought to have a copy for our records."

"You mean, they have a complete copy of the agreement and we do not!" Sir Martyn was outraged, and his anger contrasted sharply with the quiet calm displayed by the Assistant Deputy Cabinet Secretary. "That is too bad of London, it is just too bad. They have told us nothing?"

"Still no word, Martyn. London is as quiet as the grave. Our most urgent telegrams have met with no response. As far as they are concerned, the Dominions simply do not exist."

"What else did the Siamese say?"

Sir Eric coughed gently. "They are Thais now, Martyn. The message came from 'The Ambassador-Plenipotentiary for the King'. Who this person is, we have no real idea. We have asked our local sources out there and they do not know, although some say it has been rumored for many years that the Royal Family has an emissary who expresses their wishes and desires to the government in an unofficial manner. A fixer and trouble-shooter, if you will forgive the Americanisms. If this person is the Ambassador from whom their message to us is sourced, then his contact with us must be approved at the highest levels in the government."

"'We ought to have a copy for our files.' Whoever he is, this Ambassador has a nice sense of humor." Sir Martyn chuckled at the offhand remark.

"Indeed so. He also says that, once the situation stabilizes, there ought to be a meeting between our two countries to discuss security and trade arrangements in the region."

Sir Martyn looked reflective at that additional part of the message. "They're assuming there will be a break between ourselves and London over this Armistice. Otherwise they would be seeking a meeting with London directly."

"That's the Cabinet Office interpretation, certainly. Sir Richard was all set to send them a blistering reply to the effect that they should contact London, but he was reminded that doing so would be a Foreign Department matter and that a response should be approved either by the head of the Foreign Department or by Cabinet. He did not take that well. There is something else as well that may relate to this."

Sir Eric hesitated. "You know the routing of submarine cable communications in this part of the world? The main line comes from the Middle East and comes ashore at Bombay. From there, the main trunk route runs to Singapore and then splits, one part going south to Australia and the other heading east to Manila, Hong Kong and Japan. Of those three, the main lines are to Hong Kong of course. The line to Manila then goes across the Pacific to the west coast of the United States."

Sir Martyn nodded. "And?"

"Our contacts within American Telephone & Telegraph Company say that the Thai Government has approached them for a quotation on expanding the capacity of their telegraph link to that system. At the moment, it's barely adequate for local traffic only. The expansion requested would make their link equivalent in capacity to the main trunk cable. When they were told of the cost of that operation and the time schedule, their response was that the cable was needed urgently and they would pay a substantial premium if the work was started immediately. They would pay an even larger premium if the work was completed within a year. That's a deal AT&T can hardly refuse, and it will give the Thais as good communications with Australia and ourselves as any in the world."

"What the devil are they playing at? That's a huge investment for a country of their financial standing. How are they paying?"

"Our sources say, they offer payment in gold." Sir Eric spoke that softly. "Apparently, the management of American Telephone & Telegraph Company have gold fever and see bars of gold bullion decorating the accounts at the next stockholder's meeting. They're searching for a cable-laying ship while we speak. That doesn't answer why, of course."

Sir Martyn thought the whole matter over. "It could be that they see the Armistice as being the fuse that sets this whole region ablaze. They could be right there, you know. The Dutch East Indies are restive; with the Netherlands occupied, authority there is unclear. The French will not last much longer. With Britain out, they'll fold in a day or two at most. That means Indo-China is also on its own resources. Then we have our own problems here and there's the Japanese in China. This whole area could come apart at the seams and they may well want to be in a position to know what is going on. Good, secure communications would be worth their weight in gold. And that is just what they are paying."

Sir Martyn was interrupted by his intercom bleeping. "There's a diplomatic messenger for Sir Eric waiting. He says its very urgent."

"Send him in." The two men exchanged 'uh-oh' glances.

Sri Eric signed for the package and opened it. Then he went white with shock. "Martyn, we have just received our word from London. It states that we are to comply with the terms of the Armistice without question and that the terms of the agreement as negotiated in London are binding upon us. We are reminded that the system of Imperial Preference upon which our economy depends is contingent upon us maintaining the agreements signed by the British Government on our behalf. Martyn, this is as close to an 'or else' ultimatum as I have ever seen from London."

"Do as you are told like good little boys or mummy will spank." Sir Martyn spoke bitterly. "Who do they think we are?"

CHAPTER THREE
ANALYSIS OF ALTERNATIVES

Bestwood Lodge, Arnold, Nottinghamshire, United Kingdom

"This will not do; this will not do at all." Churchill chomped down on his cigar and stared ferociously at his whisky-soda as he stomped backwards and forwards. "These are times when we, as a nation, must rise to meet the challenge and end the threat of dark tyranny that hangs over us all. We must stand up and fight this abomination that has taken place. Let us therefore brace ourselves to our duties, and so bear ourselves, that if the British Empire and its Commonwealth last for a thousand years, men will still say, 'this was their finest hour.'"

The Duke of St. Albans applauded the bravado with a strong dose of irony at its incongruousness. "Well done, Winston. That would have made a great speech in Parliament."

"It would have been one. I had it all written, but That Man forestalled me. He has silenced me, and when the time comes, I will silence him. There will be no last speech from the scaffold for him. He will lose his head in silence."

"Speaking of losing heads, Winston, we cannot afford you losing yours. And you will if you appear now. You said it yourself the first night you appeared here. Protective custody one day, found dead in your cell the next. The Commonwealth is looking for leadership and you, you alone, can provide it. We have to get you to Canada. If we do not, the Commonwealth will not last one year, let alone one thousand."

"That may be easier said than done." Churchill was thoughtful. The dreadful depression that had blanketed him earlier was lifting at last; his mind was already beginning to range through the possibilities. "You are right, of course. There is nothing to be done here. It would be better if That Man had actually broken the law anywhere but damn him, everything he did was legal. He brings shame upon the whole concept of the rule of law."

The Duke mentally raised his eyebrows. Every time the subject of Halifax came up, Churchill went off into these diatribes. He was obsessed with revenge and it seemed he could think of nothing else. The problem was, there was so much else to think about. "Winston, it's not just a matter of getting you out. That will be difficult enough. We have to deny the Germans as much of our technical and operational expertise as well. I've spoken, discreetly of course, with Sir Henry Tizard about this and he's putting together a group of his people from the Aeronautical Research Committee. They directed the development of radar, so I am told. The object is to get to the United States as soon as possible to brief them on a number of technical innovations. This has been planned for some time, so I understand, with the original aim of securing assistance in maintaining the war effort. In view of the way circumstances have changed, I believe that it will be necessary simply to give the Americans every piece of information we can."

"A last bequest from a dying man to his children." Churchill's depression was re-asserting itself. He scowled at the room in general and drained his glass. Quietly, the Duke feared for the future of his whisky supply if this visit continued much longer. "Is that what we have come to?"

"Needs must when the devil drives, Winston. That Man has taken us out of the war; now we must hand the torch on to others. This is the reality we must face. The information we will be giving up will have immense value after the war, of that I have no doubt. Yet it is a sacrifice we must make if we are to emerge victorious. We will be a poorer and much-diminished state post-war, Winston, but it is either that or existing only as a subdivision of a Nazi empire." The Duke suddenly exploded in anger, his pent-up frustrations bursting out through the reserve his rank and position demanded. "Damn Halifax! Damn him to hell! He's destroyed us and he doesn't even realize what he has done. You called the Commonwealth and America our children, Winston. Well, I hope they have learned from the sins of their father, that's all I can say. I pray that our children will strike back with all the rage and power that we should have had but have become too enfeebled to muster."

The Duke stood there shaking as he tried to bring his emotions under control. He strode to the drinks cabinet, poured himself a stiff measure of rum, noted that his brandy and whisky supplies were in as sad a shape as he had expected, and drained it in a single toss. "Tizard's party and you, Winston, should go out together. One of my relatives is coming over. An American cousin, by the name of Eleanor Gwynne. She is bringing some friends who are skilled in this kind of operation. They will arrange the departure and conduct you and the rest of the party out of this country. Exactly how they will do that, I have no idea."

"Eleanor Gwynne? Nell Gwynne?" Churchill smiled for the first time since the coup. "I hope she has the wits and wisdom of her ancestor and namesake."

"I think I can safely say that she does, Winston."

There was something in the way the Duke made the comment that made Churchill look at him sharply, but he shook his head and dismissed the thought. "Are you not coming with us, Osborne?"

The Duke shook his head. "No. I will remain here. I am a peer of the realm for better and for worse. My place is here. And somebody has to organize the resistance to the night that is about to fall or we will all be gone and forgotten."

The Country Garden Tearoom, Calcutta, India

"Shall I be mother?" Sir Martyn Sharpe picked up the teapot and carefully poured a cup for his guest. Working on the hallowed principle of milk in first, he'd already poured a little into his cup. His guest, on the other hand, preferred his tea without.

"Thank you, Sir Martyn. Have you heard from London yet?" Pandit Jawaharlal Nehru sipped his tea delicately. "Ahh, an excellent cup. I do not know what we would do without this establishment."

"We have indeed. We received a blunt order from the Colonial and Dominions Office to obey the terms of the Armistice without question. Or else. The else is economic destruction. It is outrageous. Lord Linlithgow is still furious about it. I brought you a copy of the telex."

"Most kind of you. Could I trouble you for another cup of tea?" Nehru read the telex while Sir Martyn poured out the last of the pot and unobtrusively signalled for another pot of loose Assam. The Anglo-Indian waitress moved in almost immediately to see her guests had all their needs fulfilled. It wasn't just the tea that was excellent here; the service was as well. Sir Martyn looked at the cake stand and carefully removed a fishpaste sandwich from the lowest tier. The bread was superbly fresh, the filling home made and exquisite.

"As you say, an outrageous imposition. I can only imagine how badly you feel at having received such shabby and cavalier treatment at the hands of the authorities." Nehru hesitated for a beautifully timed second. "Well, of course, I don't have to imagine it. We have felt much the same way many times in the past. Not least with the current declaration of war against Germany. Thank you, Sir Martyn. Have you tried the egg finger-sandwich?"

"Indeed; the touch of garlic is an inspired addition. May I recommend in return the fishpaste? Of course, the tenor of the reply from London puts you in an even more difficult position than it does us. We are merely cast adrift, you on the other hand, are adrift without a paddle. More tea?"

39

"Allow me, Sir Martyn." Nehru picked up the fresh pot and poured. "How does this place us in a difficult position? Britain is defeated and forced out of the war. We can now withdraw as well."

"Indeed you could. But there is a problem inherent with that. By doing so, you would be seen as following Britain's lead in a most distasteful matter. Any claim you might make to independence would be seen in that light. A declaration would be treated as a matter of words, not backed up by any form of reality. Especially since Australia, South Africa and New Zealand are also ignoring the orders from London, for the moment at least, and remain in the war. India being the odd one out of the Dominions would be an unfortunate position for us." Sir Martyn bit delicately at a cucumber sandwich, relishing the taste and texture of the chilled cucumber surrounded by the soft, crustless bread.

Nehru took a fishpaste sandwich and ate it thoughtfully. That was one of the great advantages of discussing issues over High Tea. Consuming sandwiches and small cakes while sipping tea gave each participant an opportunity to think carefully before answering. "Australia, New Zealand and South Africa? Does London know this yet? And what about Canada?"

"London has not been told, yet and Canada remains silent. But all three countries are treating this matter as a declaration of independence and a renunciation of dominion status. If we continue with the war, we will be placing ourselves in that camp. Independence, Pandit, now. In 1940; not in five or ten years."

"But we could declare independence now. That is what much of the Congress Party wants. We could declare independence and also bow out of the war. That would gain us the best of both worlds. Shall we order another plate of sandwiches?"

"We could do as you suggest, Pandit. But if we declare independence, how would we then bow out of the war? If we follow the instructions from London, our declaration would be nothing more than an indulgence, lost and disregarded. But, if we underline our declaration with a decision to remain within the war, then the break is sharp and clear. Also, if we declare independence, how do we drop out of the war? One country may start a war, Pandit, but two countries must agree to end it. The Germans will not negotiate a fresh Armistice with us. In their eyes, the deed is done by the London Agreement. They have nothing to gain by recognizing our independence and much to lose."

"But India also has much to loose by staying in the war. Not least of which are the lives of our young men."

Sir Martyn's mouth twitched slightly at that. He took an egg sandwich and carefully ate it. "Actually, Pandit, not as much as one might think. We can stay in the war, but what can we actually do? We cannot get to Europe to attack Germany and Germany cannot get here to attack us. There are some local issues that need our attention, but they will face us regardless of whether

40

we are at peace or war. There is another factor here. This war will not end with the Armistice signed in London. It will go on. Germany will attack Russia. Probably not this year, but almost certainly next; if not then, the year after. The war will split the world into two parts, those who are aligned with the Nazis and those who are against them. Which side of that divide does India wish to be?"

Nehru nodded carefully and sipped his tea. His whole upbringing rebelled at the idea of remaining in this war, but the possibility of registering an effective Indian declaration of independence almost immediately was entrancing. He also knew what was happening in Europe and what sort or regime was in power in Germany. His spirit rebelled against being in their company. "What about Japan?"

"That is another good question. If we drop out of the war, effectively admitting that we are still part of the British Empire whatever we might say to the contrary, then Japan becomes a serious potential threat. They could make a claim that as the regional ally of Germany, they, rather than Britain, has a right to rule over us. You have seen how they have behaved in China. Their likely behavior here is beyond imagining. However, that lies in the future."

Nehru looked at Sir Martyn curiously. "You keep saying 'us' and 'we', not India and Indian."

Sir Martyn looked very pensive for a few moments. "In the years I have worked here, Pandit, I have come to know and love India. I have seen it in all its moods and tempers. In one sense, I go beyond you in ambition. Yours is to see India independent again. Mine is much more than that. I do not wish just to see India independent; I wish to see it become a great regional power again. To see India participating in the great councils of the world, to hear its voice spoken on a world stage.

"This is a great country, Pandit. It should be given the chance to become that again. No, that is wrong; it should not be given the chance, India should take every opportunity to seize its destiny. The final comment I would make is this. Staying in the war is buying time; it is a reversible act that we can change in the future if needs must. Coming out now is irreversible. We must live with the decision come what may."

Nehru nodded. "Persuading the rest of the Congress Party will not be easy. But with us gaining immediate independence and leaving the Commonwealth in the due course of events, I can gain enough support, I think. I need time to persuade them. Can you win me time?"

"We will try and buy some more time but our ability to do so is limited."

"That is good news, in part at least. But, we never decided on what sandwiches to order. Egg or fishpaste?"

Nehru took a deep breath and made his decision. "Fishpaste."

41

Boeing 314, "Dixie Clipper", Foyne Flying Boat Station, Shannon, Ireland

"Welcome to the Irish Republic, Madam." The white-coated steward was as deferential as his position dictated. Each of the forty odd passengers on the Pan-American Clipper had paid 375 dollars for a single ticket on the twelve hour flight over the Atlantic. They'd been served a six-course evening meal before the long night flight. Eleanor Gwynne had been woken by the jolt of the flying boat landing in the Shannon Estuary. She'd spent the night in her curtained bunk-bed, soothed into sleep by the drone of the engines and the tranquil rust and beige color scheme around her. Now she smelled the heady aroma of fresh coffee.

"Breakfast will be served shortly. In the mean time, please accept a glass of Irish coffee, with the compliments of Pan-American Airlines."

Eleanor looked at the glass in front of her. A brandy glass, filled with black coffee, topped with a thick layer of fresh cream. The steward had already moved to the next passenger and was repeating the morning ritual. She sipped the coffee; her senses were kick-started into action by the strong dose of Irish whiskey. She finished it off with relish. Eleanor still had time to visit the lady's dressing room before sitting down to the first course of breakfast.

"A fruit and cream cheese salad, Madam? Or perhaps you would prefer our green bean salad? We also offer a fine Caesar salad mixed to your order from the serving trolley. And your choice of fresh fruit juice?"

"I'll have the fruit please, with orange juice." To Eleanor's amazement, the juice really was fresh-squeezed and the salad was made with fresh-sliced fruit. She looked over to Achillea who had just settled into her seat across the table. "We don't eat this well at home."

"Did you try that Irish coffee?" Achillea had settled for the green bean salad and pineapple juice. "We'll have to try that out on Phillip when we get back. I'd like to know how they get the cream to stay on top of the coffee though."

"Pour it over the back of a silver spoon, madam." The steward was back. "I would caution madam that it takes some practice to get just right though. May we offer you a Creole omelette, eggs Florentine or a south-western scramble with your choice of meats and hashed potatoes?"

By the time Eleanor had worked her way through her eggs Benedict, croissants and another Irish coffee, she was feeling slightly comatose. It was with a certain degree of relief that she heard the engines start up and felt the big flying boat taxying out to take off. That was when Gusoyn entered the cabin and joined them. He also looked well-fed. "I hope you unmarried ladies have been fed as well as us unmarried gents."

Eleanor snorted slightly, one thankfully masked by a judicious roar as the four engines increased power. The passenger deck of the flying boat was divided into cabins; the cabin for unmarried women was well separated from that for bachelors. The niceties had to be observed. "Superbly. Thank you, ducks. How long until we get to Southampton?"

"I asked our steward. It is a two and a half hour flight so we should be landing in Southampton at ten. Our train for Nottingham leaves two hours later. We have a Pullman coupe reserved for us. We should be at your family home by six. Loki has told them which train we are on. By the way, I hope you did eat well. It may be our last chance for quite a while. Food is still rationed in Britain, you know."

"You mean they've kept rationing in place, even though the war is over? Why?"

"Last year, Britain imported 20 million tons of foodstuffs per year, including more than half of its meat and three quarters of its cheese, sugar, fruits, cereals and fats." Gusoyn reeled the figures off with gloomy relish. "Bacon, meat, tea, jam, butter, sugar, biscuits, breakfast cereals, cheese, eggs, milk and canned fruit have all been rationed. Bread and potatoes have not; not yet, at any rate. If it is any consolation, fish and chips is not rationed either although I am told it is very expensive. We will be given ration books when we disembark. If we stay at a hotel, we have to surrender them to the hotel management while we stay there and retrieve them when we leave. Oh, restaurant meals are not rationed but they are really expensive."

"That shouldn't worry us, ducks. We've got a big budget for this trip. Lillith's done us proud on the money front. I'm not sure why." Eleanor paused while the engines went to full power and the flying boat took off. Underneath, Ireland was richly green, the rolling hills running down to the deep blue of the Shannon River. She suddenly felt severely homesick and questioned her decision to leave her homeland. Then she settled down and common sense reasserted itself. England had held very little for her and the prospect of a new country had been overwhelming. Then again, there was a lot she had needed to hide.

Achillea was looking down at the same sights. In her case, she was seriously grateful for the fact that they were flying direct to Southampton. The last time she had visited the area they were now flying over, her behavior hadn't been calculated to win friends and influence people. She was quite convinced there were people with memories long enough to put a bullet in her back if she ever returned to the small village of Béal na mBláth. "I guess Phillip wants to know what things are really like on the ground over here. We're a reconnaissance party to him."

"Keep that thought to yourself, ducks." Eleanor looked around but they were alone in their section of the Boeing 314. "What's a reconnaissance to him there could well be considered spying by the people here."

Conference Room, Government House, Calcutta, India

"We have been given our instructions. It is for us to obey them." Sir Richard Graham Cardew stuck his chin out pugnaciously. "There may have been some point in discussing whether we should follow London's lead when we had no specific instructions to do so, although I could not see any merit in such a discussion and still do not for that matter. But now we have clear instructions and we have no option other than to obey them. That is the way it has always been and that is the way it shall remain."

Lord Linlithgow frowned mightily, not quite so much at the content of the words but at the tone in which they had been uttered. The truth of the words might be argued; the tone of disrespect within them could not. He was already aware that Cardew was attempting to assemble a supporting clique from the traditionalists within the old guard of the Indian civil service. "Is there any word from the other Dominions?"

"There is indeed, Your Excellency," Gerald Tarrant was actually having a hard job stopping himself laughing. The Australians might be an uncouth lot but they had a talent for a pithy phrase. They have sent a message to London which reads 'if the Colonial and Dominion Offices had sent us a dispatch of the tone and content exemplified by this message, we would tell them to get stuffed.' Prime Minister Robert Menzies has resigned, saying his identification with the London regime has rendered him unfit to lead Australia at this time."

"Don't tell me that cad John Curtin is the new Prime Minister there." Harold Hartley was appalled at the prospect.

"I think you underestimate Mister Curtin." Tarrant spoke somberly. "I believe he has every prospect of being an excellent Prime Minister whose leadership promises to serve Australia well. In his inaugural address to the Australian Parliament, he tore up the message from London and threw the pieces on the floor, saying 'good riddance to bad rubbish.' That won him much applause from the House."

"That is a disgrace." Cardew wattled furiously. "Who do those people think they are?"

"People who face a dilemma that is exactly equivalent to ours in form and content," Lord Linlithgow said mildly. "They have reached their conclusion with regard to their own opinions and interests, just as we shall reach ours with regard to India's needs and interests."

"Maintaining the Imperial Connection is the only need or interest India should have."

"'Should have' is a matter of opinion, Sir Richard. 'Does have' is another matter entirely. Let us not forget there is a moral aspect to this conundrum. Obeying the demands of London mean knuckling under to an accommodation with Nazi Germany and that thought is abhorrent to any civilized person. I have thought this matter over in great depth and I believe that we cannot, in conscience, do what Lord Halifax would have us do. In isolation, I would tend to believe that we should join Australia in our defiance of this order. But, we do not act in isolation. Let us not forget this is India and we should bear the interests and opinions of the Indian people in mind."

"Why bother?" Cardew' spoke derisively, an obvious sneer in his voice.

"Because this is their country, Sir Richard. We rule it in trust for them. Sir Martyn, you have spoken with Pandit Jawaharlal Nehru? How does the Congress Party see things?"

"As usual, Your Excellency, they want independence now, if not sooner. Within that framework, however, there are many divisions. Nehru is now of the opinion that knuckling under to this order would make any rapid attainment of independence most unlikely and unproductive if attempted. On the other hand, continuing the war, for a short time at least, would underline India's independence and bring their dream within easy reach. That is an attractive prospect for them. After some discussions, Nehru has come to the opinion that, since India is now in the war, it should stay in. May I add that his own abhorrence of the Nazi regime was of some importance in him reaching that position."

"Communist rabble-rouser." Cardew's sneer cut across the room and more than one head nodded in agreement with him.

"Where do Nehru's political opinions finally reside, Sir Martyn?" Lord Linlithgow spoke quietly while he marked down those who had nodded. They would need to be maneuvered out of the way.

"There is no doubt he is a socialist your excellency, one who believes that the best model for developing this country resides within the framework of large, state-run enterprises. He would fit very well within the Labour Party in that respect. But a communist? I do not think so. His guiding light is the future of India and all else takes second place to that. To be a Communist would mean that he would place the interests of international Communism over those of India and that he will not do. There are Communists in the Congress Party, of that I have little doubt, but they do not dominate its leadership. There are fascists also. I would name Subhas Chandra Bose as prime in their number. He is closer to the leading figures than any communist. I would suggest it is in our interest to support the existing Congress Party leadership and ensure that neither of those factions gains any significant power."

Lord Linlithgow nodded. "So the Congress Party would support us in continuing the war?"

"Nehru asks for time, Your Excellency. Time to persuade those who hold different positions from his own of what lies at stake here. That would allow him to present his position as that of the Congress Party, rather than just a faction of it. I have an idea of how we can buy some time at least."

"Pray tell?"

45

"I understand that the undersea telegraph lines are experiencing erratic problems at the moment. Some messages are being corrupted in transmission and I believe that this was one of them. It may possess real content that is quite different from the corrupted version we have received. We owe it to the responsibility of our positions here to ensure that we have received a true and fair copy. I suggest we return a 'copy corrupt' signal and ask for a retransmission."

"Your Excellency, I object. This is a lie; a damnable lie."

"I think not, Sir Richard. Can you prove to us, here and now, that the message we received was not corrupted in transmission?' Lord Linlithgow paused before continuing, "I thought not. Sir Martyn is right. Whole sections of critical importance may have been omitted. It has happened before. I would remind you of the time when the text of the Holy Bible was corrupted in transmission and the word 'not' was omitted from the Seventh Commandment. Sir Martyn, do as you propose."

Bank de Commerce et Industrie, Geneva, Switzerland

"There's one person who will know how to get this information used." Branwen felt like ducking for cover as she made the suggestion. Mentioning Phillip Stuyvesant to Loki was akin to pouring gasoline on an already-raging inferno. *Why can't these two grow up?* Sometimes Branwen felt as if she wanted to take both of them quietly to one side and bang their heads together.

To her astonishment, Loki nodded in agreement. "I hate to admit it, but you are almost certainly right. If we send this material over now, it will get lost at best. Nobody in authority knows who we are."

"May the gods be praised for that." Branwen spoke fervently.

"Right. But now that very anonymity is turned against us. To the world at large, we're just bankers and traders."

Loki shook his head. He had just returned from Germany. What he had seen there turned his stomach. The reason behind his trip was a simple one. Five years earlier, a member of his family by the name of Morrigan had been framed as a communist by a man Loki had trusted and left to the tender mercies of the Gestapo. That had left Loki with only one practical option. He had made a trip to Germany, found her and put a bullet into her head before she could talk. She would have talked, eventually, and there was far too much she could tell her interrogators. Loki knew that. He also knew that his rifle shot had been the only mercy she was likely to receive. On that trip, his eyes had been fixed on what he had had to do and he had ignored what lay in clear sight around him.

That hadn't been the case on this trip. It had been purely a matter of revenge. He had found Odwin Noth, the man who had betrayed Morrigan. Loki had framed him as a communist agent and then killed him. Only, this time his eyes had been open and he had taken full measure of the German regime in a way that not even Kristallnacht had made clear. He had also achieved something else. He was a banker, a Swiss banker; Germany was a country where everybody in authority wanted a numbered Swiss bank account of their very own. That made him a sought-after guest; in so doing, he had been able to recruit people right across the entire spectrum of German industry. Loki never asked questions that seemed to have direct military or political significance; he was far too astute for that. Instead, he expressed interest in little things that seemed to have no direct relevance to anything much. What his contacts never realized was that each piece of data was a part of a jigsaw. When fitted together, they provided a picture of German industrial production and planning that was completely unmatched. Quietly, Loki was proud of what he had created. Not just because nobody had ever achieved so complete a picture of a nation's industry at war before, but because even those who had helped prepare it never knew the product existed.

"I took the liberty of contacting Phillip. He's sending Igrat over to collect the information. She'll have Henry with her as a bodyguard." Branwen waited for the explosion. Dealing with a situation that involved both Phillip Stuyvesant and Loki was rather like juggling bottles of nitroglycerine. One could never be sure quite what was happening or when one would explode.

"That's good. Is there any word from England yet?"

Branwen relaxed slightly. "On Churchill? No. He seems to have vanished completely. The general presumption is that he headed south as soon as news of the Coup broke and made it to Ireland. Our guess is that he's still there, in hiding and waiting for things to settle down before flying over to Canada."

"Interesting. Head of a government-in-exile I suppose. A lot of people who were over in the U.S. and Canada have refused to return. The entire British Purchasing Commission for a start." Loki grinned at the thought. "And that gives any government in exile a useful civil service. Something most of them lack. Igrat's coming over, you say?"

"That's right." *And you're pleased because it'll give you another chance to get her into your bed. Something you only want because you think that sleeping with Phillip's daughter will be a gesture of derision aimed at him. And Igrat won't sleep with you because she's smart enough to understand that.*

"Good, I've got some German strategic plans here as well. One's on an abortive plan Noth came up with. He thought of going East through Turkey and Persia to try and hit India. The other is the German decision to invade Russia. I hope the Americans will know how to use them." Loki looked at the plan for the German advance on India. It had its author's blood on the cover.

Lopburi Army Testing Ground, Thailand.

The Carden-Lloyd machine gun carrier came to an abrupt halt, its long antennas waving in the air. The tactical situation had been set up for this particular display. The presumption was that a Thai unit was advancing down a road and had run into a hostile roadblock, built around entrenched infantry and supported by artillery and machine guns. It was a well-built, well-sited position that would hold up the advance for several hours if not dealt with. The book answer was quite simple; some of the advancing infantry would pin the roadblock with a frontal probe while the rest of the unit outflanked the defenses and either wiped them out or forced them out of their position. Simple, but requiring too much time. A different answer was being evaluated here.

The key component of that answer was the machine-gun carrier. Or rather, the vehicle that had once been a machine gun carrier. It had been rebuilt; an enlarged and much taller rear structure had been added that housed two radios, their operator and an Air Force officer. One of the radios was tuned to Air Force frequencies and would be used to contact the Corsair dive bombers circling overhead. The other radio was a standard Army communications set. Inside the vehicle, the Air Force officer had seen the defenses and decided to do something about it.

"Cobra Section, attack target on road five hundred meters ahead of position. Green to red."

Suriyothai watched as the flare arched upwards from the Carden-Lloyd and started to burn green. Half way through, the flare turned red. Overhead, the drone of aircraft engines suddenly picked up in volume. Then it changed to the wailing scream of a dive bomber in its near-vertical plummet on the 'enemy position'. The Air Force has taken a lesson from the German book and attached sirens to the fixed undercarriages of its Vought Corsair biplanes. She looked up; the four aircraft that formed Cobra Section were peeling over into their dive. It was a chilling sight; one that the world had become all too familiar with after the German displays in Poland and France. Her binoculars tracked the dive bombers down as they slammed their weapons into the enemy position. *We need better dive bombers; ones that can dive steeper and deliver heavier bombs than those old Corsairs.* On the ground, the troops were running forward while the smoke from the bombs was still clearing. By the time the defenders could have recovered, the infantry were all over them. The position 'fell quickly' and the Thai flag was waving over it before the aircraft could return.

"Five minutes from spotting the defense to the dive bombers taking it out." Field Marshal Plaek sounded more than pleased. "It took the Germans between twenty and thirty minutes to organize an attack like that, and everybody thought they were marvels for achieving it. And we took five!"

"Because we had the aircraft circling overhead and the observer on the ground ready to bring them in. That's the real breakthrough. The dive bomber attack was reasonably good but it was nowhere near as skilled as the Germans. Our dive bomber pilots need to train more. They must fly more often and keep practicing. See to it please, Field Marshal."

It was a sight that would confuse any conventional military officer. A woman in a Colonel's uniform was casually giving orders a man in the uniform of a Field Marshal. Only the tiny handful of people who knew who the woman was would have found it, not just unsurprising, but routine.

"Do you miss military command, Your Highness?"

Suriyothai smiled in response. "Yes, I do. And I miss fighting with you by my side."

Beneath her smile, her mind ran back to 1932 and the end of the absolute monarchy in Thailand. Her function, the whole meaning of her life, was to serve the monarchy and defend its interests. Sometimes, that meant changing it. 1932 had been one of those times. She had seen that the days of absolute monarchies had ended. They had ended years before, but a series of unusually able kings in Thailand had concealed that. But time had caught up with the monarchy and it had to change, become a constitutional monarchy, if the institution was to survive.

It had been the Great Depression that had ended things. The existing absolute monarchy had been unable to cope with the escalating financial crisis; economic ruin threatened. Suriyothai had moved to avoid the impending disaster. She organized a group of military officers and civilians and planned a coup that had taken place in June 1932. Her allies then had been a group of young intellectuals educated overseas led by a young French educated lawyer, Pridi Banomyong, and a military faction led by military officers Phraya Phahon and Plaek Pibulsonggram. The coup had been launched at dawn and was over by noon the same day. It went so smoothly that most people were hardly aware it had taken place. The King had acceded to the demands to avoid bloodshed and agreed to serve as the constitutional monarch. Not everybody approved of that. In October 1933, a rebellion by provincial garrisons led by Prince Boworadet, a former Minister of War, brought the country to the brink of civil war. Suriyothai had assembled a force of government troops and appointed Lieutenant-Colonel Plaek Pibulsonggram their commander. In order to make sure she remained in command, she had appointed herself a Colonel and so she had remained.

The fighting had started on 12 October when the rebels had captured Don Muang on the outskirts of Bangkok. Heavy street fighting had lasted for two days before they began to retreat. Suriyothai had led her regiment in pursuit and overrun the main rebel stronghold. Even then, she hadn't stopped. Her troops had pursued and advanced to the rebel base in Nakhon Ratchasima. By 23 October, the rebels had been dispersed, and the revolt was over. Implicated in the rebellion, the King had abdicated, stunned by the fact Suriyothai had taken the field against him. She had pointed out that she served the country and the monarchy, not an individual monarch.

She shook herself slightly, shaking off the old memories. Beside her, Plaek smiled; he had seen her perform as a soldier and found taking orders from her appropriate. It was simply recognition of ability. "Your Highness, may I introduce Wing Commander Fuen who devised the tactics we have seen today?"

"Well done, Wing Commander; a most impressive display. What do you call the observer on the ground?"

"A forward air controller, Your Highness."

"Then train many forward air controllers. We should have one with radio equipment in every battalion at least. You have six months. And make sure our dive bomber pilots train hard. Far more than you can ever realize depends upon their skills."

Boeing 314, "Yankee Clipper", Marseilles Flying Boat Station, Vichy France

"Well, Phillip was right. France didn't hold out very long after Britain caved in." The passengers from the Boeing 314 had already disembarked but were stacked up waiting to get through French immigration. The chaos wasn't the French officials' fault; everything was still confused after the armistice signed in Paris had ended the fighting. The northern half of France was now under German occupation; the southern half was not. Igrat looked at the staff checking papers. Mostly they were the traditional French police, but there were some others lurking around, watching suspiciously. *Gestapo*. The flying boat anchored out in the bay was the first to arrive here since services had been suspended during the war. That apparently being over, Juan Trippe had moved quickly to re-establish his clipper service to Lisbon and Marseilles.

"Your name, mademoiselle?" The customs officer was looking at her passport, so the question was superfluous.

"Igrat Shafrid. Resident in Georgetown, Washington and Long Island, New York. I am here on a vacation trip." Igrat's French was fluent and won her immediate points with the immigration officials.

Not so much with one of the Gestapo officers. He pricked up his ears at the sound of Igrat's name. "Do you have Jewish ancestry?" The question was snapped out.

Igrat switched smoothly to equally fluent German. "Certainly not. I am an American of Persian ancestry. You know, the *original* Aryans. My family has been in America since 1760. As for religion, the only God I believe in is printed by the United States Treasury and has pictures of presidents on it."

"You can sure say that, sweetie." Henry McCarty was playing the part of Igrat's sugar daddy. That was the overt cover. As usual, there was a cover within a cover. The second-line cover was that he was actually a shady businessman who was looking for black market opportunities in a German-dominated Europe. Anybody who did a detailed investigation of the Broadway Baby and her sugar daddy would discover the corrupt businessman who had brought Igrat along as his cover. The best security was always to give people things to find.

The French official looked down and smiled. He'd recognized Igrat as an adventuress almost immediately and slightly envied McCarty for his companionship with her. Although, he had no doubt the stunning brunette would empty his wallet with great efficiency. "My apologies, mademoiselle. You will be staying in France long?"

"Only a few days. We are on our way to Geneva. My daddy has business with one of the banks there." The note of boredom at the mention of business permeated Igrat's voice.

"Now, sweetie, if Daddy doesn't do his business, sweetie won't get her presents." Henry sounded almost pleading and the French official was desperately trying to not laugh.

"You promised we could go to the Champs Elysee." Igrat pouted.

"I am sorry, mademoiselle. Paris is occupied by les Boches and nobody can go there from here. But the shops here in Marseilles are just as good." The Frenchman spoke with the fervor of a man whose family had long resided in Marseilles and regarded Paris as having a collective case of a severely over-inflated ego. "And our restaurants are much better."

"So I hear. Daddy promised me some real bouillabaisse."

"Then you are in for the experience of a lifetime. Welcome to France." Igrat's passport was stamped and she was past immigration. McCarty followed her a minute of so later.

"Well done, Iggie. By the time you'd finished with him, I got through without a problem. The guy who spoke to you was Gestapo?"

"I think so. When I switched to German, he didn't even blink. Are any of them following us?"

McCarty carefully looked behind. "I don't think so. We're clear. How do we get to the station?"

"It's right there." Igrat waved at a building in front of her. Bringing Henry along as a bodyguard had been Stuyvesant's idea, not hers. Given her own preference, she would have come alone. She was utterly confident in her ability to slip through the backwash of a war without attracting any attention and was convinced she could do this trip a day faster without having to worry about her partner. "The train for Geneva leaves in just under an hour. The train trip takes three and a half hours. We'll be there for dinner."

"Not bouillabaisse tonight then." McCarty sounded disappointed.

"Don't worry, we'll have time for that later. The next clipper flight back is in a week's time, so we'll have to kill time until then. By the way, you'd better buy me some expensive presents. Keeping up the cover and all that. If we are being checked out, we don't want the checkers to think I'm losing my touch. And we may need this cover in future."

"That depends on whether Loki is for real or not. I've got a nasty feeling this is one of his practical jokes. This whole trip could be his idea of something funny."

"It could be. Or an effort to get me over there. He's been trying to get into my pants for years. We'll only know when we get there. If this is one of his jokes, Phillip will get really nasty about it. I had to turn down a negotiable bonds delivery run for J.P Morgan to do this trip."

McCarty nodded. The truth was that he was feeling a bit superfluous. The ease with which Igrat talked her way past obstructions was only matched by the sheer organizational ability she showed in getting her trips set up. He'd always watched her courier runs around the world from the outside and thought her reputation in that line was overstated. Now, watching her at work close-up, he understood how much skill went into making her work look so easy. Fees for her services as an utterly trustworthy courier were her major contribution to the family income and had made her wealthy in her own right. Now, he knew why.

"You've done this before, haven't you?"

She glanced at him over her shoulder, one eyebrow lifted and a broad smile on her face. "Why, whatever makes you think that?"

Bestwood Lodge, Arnold, Nottinghamshire, United Kingdom

"Eleanor, how are you? How did your trip go?" The Duke of St Albans was delighted and relieved to see Eleanor Gwynne arrive. Especially with two such formidable-looking friends in tow.

"The clipper was a real treat, ducks. And so it should be for the money they charged. May I introduce my friends? This is Achillea Foyle and Gusoyn Rivers. We didn't know what was going on over here, so I brought some help."

"I think you'll realize what the problem is when you meet my other guest. Come into the reception room, all of you."

The Duke dropped his voice slightly. "One room or two for your friends?"

"Two if that's possible, although one for the lot of us would be enough."

"No problem. Your own room will be ready of course. You always have a home here. Now, let me introduce you to my guest, the Right Honorable Winston Churchill, M.P. and rightful Prime Minister. I need your help in getting him out to Canada. There's a government-in-exile forming out there you know."

"God's fish, Osborne. You do know how to drop a basket of live eels into a girl's lap, don't you ducks?" Eleanor shook her head and then remembered her manners. "My apologies, Mister Churchill. It is a privilege and an honor to meet you."

52

"And I you, Eleanor; although I entirely understand the alarm with which you received the news of my presence here." Churchill paused for a second; he was familiar with the portraits of Nell Gwynne he had seen. "May I say you share more than just a name with your charming and beautiful ancestor?"

"Thank you, Sir." Ever receptive to compliments, Eleanor dimpled at Churchill's gallantry. "Have you and Osborne thought about how to achieve our ends?"

"Would you not rather wait until you have rested from your journey? An arduous trip over the Atlantic and then a harrowing ride on the London and North Eastern Railway requires some recuperation at least."

"Osborne, a clipper flight to Southampton is hardly arduous. Although the railway ride could fairly be described as harrowing." Churchill's tones rolled around the room. "And my stay here puts you in danger, a risk that increases daily. I think our charming Nell is right. The least time we waste, the better it will be for our enterprise."

"Perhaps you are right. Frankly, Eleanor, I'm at my wits end on this one. The ports are being watched, with special attention on the ones feeding the Atlantic liners and the ferries to Ireland. The airports too, and the flying boat terminal at Southampton. France has been cut off by its surrender. Then there is getting around inside England. The train stations are being watched; that much is obvious. Oh, the small country stations are all right, but there are passenger checks at all the main ones. Petrol is rationed and the number of cars around is much reduced. There aren't many roadblocks, not yet at any rate, but getting between the road blocks will be just as hard as getting through them. And Winston is, well. . . ."

"Osborne means to say I am easily recognized and well known. Frankly, Nell, I do not see how we can pull this off. Even the day of the coup it was hard enough, and now the steps taken by That Man make it much harder. The hand of the government is heavy enough already and I fear it will continue to get worse."

"Who mans these checkpoints and carries out the inspections?" Achillea was absorbing all the information that was flowing. "Surely the police don't have the manpower to do it? Or the firepower, come to that."

"That Man has formed a police auxiliary. He doesn't trust the armed services, so he's recruiting his own police force. We don't see them much up here; they're mostly in the ports and cities. You'd see more of them in the Home Counties than in the North."

"Police auxiliaries." Gusoyn was intrigued. "What are their uniforms? Nothing complex, I hope."

"Black shirts and Army khaki trousers. And a Sam Browne pistol belt." The Duke was indignant.

53

"Black and Tans." Achillea was reflective. "And nobody sees them much up in this part of the world . . . "

"They do bear the shame of the Black and Tans, yes. Now people already call them the Blackshirts."

"There was nothing to be ashamed about with the Black and Tans." Achillea was still absent, rolling over information in her mind. "They had a rough job to do and didn't do that badly at it."

"They killed, burned and looted." The Duke spoke heatedly. "In the name of reprisal, of course. No way for Englishmen to behave."

"You know something?" Gusoyn was grinning. "I think Lord Halifax has just solved our mobility problem for us."

The Duke had just been about to follow up on his disapproval of Achillea's ready acceptance of the Black and Tan's history. Gusoyn's comment stopped him dead. Churchill beat him to the punch. "How could anything That Man does be of any help to us?"

"Well, when the police control all movement, only the police can move freely, is that not right? And up here, nobody knows who is in the Blackshirts or what they are supposed to be doing. In fact, I would surmise that they do a lot of the dirty work that needs doing and so nobody inquires too closely into their movements. So, I think it is about time we formed our own Blackshirt unit. Get ourselves established and nobody will dare ask who we are or what we are doing. We need some vehicles for transport though."

"Army trucks." Achillea was interested in the idea. "Units like that always have Army trucks. Can we get some?"

"Osborne's nephew Charles is in the Army. Where is he Osborne? And does he know?"

"He knows. He's in the Sherwood Foresters. Major in their headquarters. Come to think of it, they're not far from here."

"There is your answer then." Gusoyn was happy. "He takes us to their motor pool; we pick up a pair of good, reliable trucks."

"Lorries, Gusoyn. Be careful to use the right words or you'll give yourselves away."

"Thank you, your Lordship. We pick up a pair of good, reliable lorries and a Humber staff car and there is the transport we need. With those and our Blackshirt uniforms, we can go where we please."

"That still doesn't solve the problem of Winston. How do we hide him? He can't pretend to be a Blackshirt?" Osborne was entranced by the sheer audacity of the plan that was forming in front of him.

"We don't hide him." Achillea had the ball now and was running with it. "We put him in the back of the lorry, handcuffed of course, and show him off to everybody who shows any interest. We tell them, in great confidence, that we're taking him up north to be 'disposed of' and imply that anybody who knows about it will also be 'disposed of'. Of course, we'll be too dumb to realize that the list of people to be 'disposed of' will include us. The people on the checkpoints will guess that and keep their mouths shut. They'll do anything rather than admit they've seen that lorry and thus qualify themselves for a trip on the next one."

Churchill gave a great laugh that finally drove his black dog of depression away. "My word, Osborne. When you said you were calling for help from your cousin in America, I had my reservations. But now I tip my hat to her branch of the de Vere Beauclerk line. We've been worrying over this matter for days without getting anywhere, but she and her friends turn up and have a workable plan ready in less than thirty minutes. Nell, I salute you and your accomplices."

The Duke's mind was running overtime as well. "Eleanor, you and your friends have solved more problems than you realize. Sir Henry Tizard is putting together a group of key personnel and some scientific information that he believes should be given to the United States as it will aid in our eventual liberation. For the converse reason, it should also be kept out of German hands. Your convoy of lorries will give us what we need to move the men and material away."

"Please, your Lordship, do not get ahead of ourselves." Gusoyn was running his mind through the scheme. "We have solved how to move around but we have yet to work out how to get out of the country. Did you have any thoughts on that matter?"

The Duke sighed. "Our best idea was to go to one of the small fishing ports and hire a fishing boat to take us to the Irish Republic and then make our way to Shannon and out on a Clipper. But, it was a faint hope at best."

Achillea shook her head. "Too many places that can go wrong. Although, eventually, it might do as a cover story. All it needs is somebody to ask questions or to pick the wrong fisherman and it's all over."

"I do not like any seaborne side of this; it is all too easy to get caught." Gusoyn was thoughtful.

"We can't help it. This is an island nation. We have to go by sea sometime." Churchill was frowning.

"Not necessarily. We can fly out. We came in on a flying boat. Why can't one pick us up from somewhere?" Eleanor was very taken with flying boats.

"All the flying boat stations are watched."

"Then don't use one. Isn't there a loch or a bay somewhere up in Scotland we can use?"

The Duke drummed his fingers. "There might be, but how would we use one? We can't just go and buy a flying boat."

"Actually, we can." Eleanor grinned. "It would have to come in from the States but we could buy one. Or rent one and not tell the owner what we are going to do with it. We need to talk to Phillip about that, and that means we need Iggie here."

"She's in Switzerland, won't be back in the States until the end of the week." Achillea had that piece of information to hand.

"Then telegram Loki. Get her to come straight over here once she's finished with her delivery to Phillip. We need to give her a briefing on the situation here so she can brief Phillip. If all else fails, he'll organize a flying boat to get us out of here. Now, let's get some sleep."

As the party broke up, the Duke stopped Achillea. "I am sorry I was short with you earlier, but I saw the Black and Tans at work. Surely you couldn't approve of what they did?"

"So did I, your Lordship."

"Ahh, so you are like Nell then?"

"I am and so is Gusoyn. When we had rebellions, we killed everybody involved, burned down their homes and salted their fields. We left desolation and called it peace. By those standards, the Black and Tans were merciful. But, soon I think, England and Ireland will learn what occupation by those who still regard desolation as a solution is like. What these Blackshirts will be like, we have yet to see."

CHAPTER FOUR
INITIAL APPROACHES

Dumbarton Avenue, Georgetown, Washington, DC, USA

With one part of his mind, Phillip Stuyvesant was thinking about strangling Igrat while the other was concentrating on what she was saying. It wasn't her fault; she was simply doing her job by relating what Loki had said to her. The problem was, she was doing so in exactly the same intonations and rhythms that Loki used when speaking. So, if her normally husky tones were ignored, she sounded just like him. And when Phillip Stuyvesant heard Loki's voice, he always wanted to strangle the speaker.

"The report contains details of a strategic plan conceived by *Standartenführer* Odwin Noth as an alternative to the invasion of Russia. The full details are contained within the report, but essentially Noth's idea was to strike south of Russia. He envisaged an assault through Turkey into Iraq and then using that as a bridge into India. This would establish a front along the Caspian Sea. The Germans would then give arms and political support to the Indian Fascist Subhas Chandra Bose, thus establishing German influence over India. Then, the Germans would link up with Japanese forces in the East and then assist them in flushing out the French in Indochina. The Noth plan was to have this effort taking up to the end of 1943, at which point Japan will be poised to eliminate Australia. By then, Germany would have encircled the whole of the Soviet Union and made the Indian Ocean into a German one. At that point, they would invade Russia from all sides. Noth believed this would mean their victory was assured." Igrat dropped the pitch and tones associated with Loki and returned to her own voice. "Loki says that he killed Noth and discredited both him and this plan."

Stuyvesant picked up the report, noting the bloodstained cover as he did so, and started to flip through it. "This is insane. It's a typical amateur plan, conceived by somebody who looks at an atlas and assumes moving his finger on the pages constitutes a viable concept. This Noth person has no idea of logistics or how to move armies around. He doesn't seem to understand how terrain or transportation infrastructure affects the operations of armies. The German General Staff must have had kittens when they saw it. It's exactly the sort of grandiose nonsense that would appeal to Hitler, but appall any professional strategist. Even the attack on Turkey would push German capability to its utmost. Achieving the rest? It just can't be done. You say Loki put a stop to this?"

"He did; he killed Noth himself and ensured this plan was abandoned."

"What a pity. If the Germans had gone with this, they'd have lost the war in two years at the outside." Stuyvesant spun his chair around and stared out of the window for a few minutes. Igrat sat patiently watching him while he thought through the implications of what he had just read. "The whole strategic plan is a complete crock, but it does make a kind of crazy sense to the uninitiated. Suriyothai will be able to make good use of this; we'll have to get it out to her."

"You want me to go to Bangkok?" Igrat was hopeful since she enjoyed visiting the city. It gave her a chance to stock up on top-grade silk.

"No. I've got another trip for you; one that has to take place immediately. Delivering this plan to Suriyothai can wait until you get back, I'll read it in full while you're away. I haven't had a really good laugh for a long time. Is this all Loki gave you? If it is, I'll get Lillith to bill him for the trip. And for wasting your time."

"He also gave me this." Igrat handed over a massive file, one almost three inches of legal-sized paper thick. "He says it's economic intelligence on German industrial plans and intentions. He's assembled a ring of industry experts who put it together. He didn't say where the intelligence had actually come from. He said what I didn't know, I couldn't tell."

"Quite right." Stuyvesant was flipping through the pages. As he did so, his whole attitude changed. He leaned forward in his seat and started reading the information in detail.

"It's all right for you to say that. You won't be there when somebody tries to beat information I don't know out of me."

"Uhh, yes. Of course, that's fine." Stuyvesant's attention was rivetted on the information he was reading. "What did you say?"

"I said, can I have a new wardrobe for my next trip?" Igrat grinned and started thinking about the jewelry at Tiffanies. She had an affection for really large diamonds.

"Sure. See Lillith and get a cash float. This information is unbelievable. In every sense of the word. If it's accurate, it fits right in to what we'll be doing at the Economic Intelligence and Warfare Section. This will save us months of research and mean we're working with what is really out there, not what we think German industry is like. We'll have to check this against what we know, or rather what we think we know. And then we'll have to get back to Loki to reconcile the differences. Is he still trying to seduce you by the way?"

"He is." Igrat smiled a little sadly. "If he was interested in me for me, he might have a chance. But he isn't. He only wants me because he thinks having me will hurt you."

Stuyvesant and Igrat looked at each other and burst out laughing. Nothing could have underlined how little Loki understood about the internal dynamics of the Washington circle so well as the idea that Igrat's amorous exploits would do anything more than amuse her father.

"Iggie, I've got to ask you to go straight out again. To England. We've heard from Nell. The transatlantic telegram service is back in operation again, thank the Gods, and she needs help. I need you to go over there, find out at first hand what is going on and why. Then come back and tell me what they need."

Stuyvesant got up and walked over to the door of his office. "Dido, could you find Lillith please and ask her to bring Igrat's tickets in? Thanks, honey."

"Why don't you get an intercom box?" Igrat was curious. "They're neat."

"Don't like them. Too much of a risk that one will get left on and broadcast what is going on in here to the world. And, sooner or later, somebody will find a way of turning the speaker on when it's off, if you get my drift. Ahh, Lillith; another clipper ticket I see?"

"Phillip, in the last month we have spent over four thousand dollars on transatlantic air tickets alone. Allowing for our other expenses, we've got precious little change from ten thousand and the bills are still coming in. At this rate it would be cheaper to buy our own flying boat."

"I've looked at that." Stuyvesant sounded disappointed. "A Boeing 314 will cost us a million dollars. And that's assuming we can get on to the production list. Pan-American have just ordered another batch of six and the Army Air Corps want a round dozen. Then there's Boeing's commitment to B-17 production. Even if we put in the order now, we wouldn't see the aircraft for at least three or four years. There are also rumors that a bigger and better flying boat is being built for Pan American. So, no private Clipper for us."

"Well, Igrat will just have to swim across the Atlantic. I've looked at the map in my pocket diary and it doesn't seem very far."

"Spoken like a true disciple of *Standartenführer* Odwin Noth." Lillith looked confused; Igrat and Stuyvesant burst out laughing again. "Lillith, give Igrat her ticket for the *Dixie Clipper* and then shoo both of you. I've got some reading to do."

Bang Phitsan Palace, Bangkok, Thailand

"We have received some intelligence from our sources in Saigon, Your Highness." Lani entered the room and deposited the files on to Suriyothai's desk. "They relate to a major change in policy with regard to French relations with us. Especially on border issues."

Suriyothai looked at the documents that had arrived on her desk. The official Thai government position was that after the fall of France, the mandate of French authorities in Indo China had changed. The Foreign Office was hoping that the new government would have a friendlier attitude than their predecessors and that negotiations over border demarcation issues could be concluded.

Suriyothai's personal agenda was quite different; a friendly, co-operative French government in Indo-China was the last thing she wanted to see. It wasn't the first time she had found herself working against the official government of the country and she sadly reflected that it probably would not be the last.

She opened up the file and started to read the contents. It took all her self-control not to whoop with joy when she read the policy statement. It announced that effective immediately, the French authorities in Indo-China would be adopting a policy they called 'dissuasion'. It expressly stated that if Thailand attempted to negotiate over outstanding border issues or complain about French military actions on border, French aircraft would overfly Thai territory and French artillery start to shell Thai border posts. There would be no negotiations over any issue connected with relations between Thailand and French Indo-China.

The change in policy couldn't have suited Suriyothai more if she had written it herself. That made it all the more ironic that neither she nor anybody she knew had a hand in formulating it. What the French officials were thinking was quite beyond her. They had prepared a disaster for themselves.

And that was only one piece of the puzzle in place. The other was a second report on Indo-China. This one suggested that Japanese ambitions in the area were beginning to come to a boil. The problem was quite simple; with the capture of Longzhou, the highway joining French-controlled ports in Indo-China with the Chinese forces fighting the Japanese was closed. The problem, in Japanese eyes at least, was that the Yunnan–Vietnam Railway still permitted shipment of material from Haiphong to Kunming, despite repeated air strikes by the Japanese attempting to close it. More than 10,000 tons of military supplies a month were moving along that railway.

The Japanese wanted that supply line closed and they wanted bases and other facilities in French Indo-China. They were already putting heavy pressure on the French authorities to grant them use of airfields and ports in the colony. The official reason was the supplies reaching China, but Suriyothai knew there was more to it than that. French Indo-China would be a springboard for an assault on the rest of the region. The ultimate prize was the rubber resources of Malaya and the oil in the Dutch East Indies. She also knew that Thailand lay directly in the path of that assault.

"Lani, call the British Ambassador, Sir Josiah Crosby, and ask if I might have a meeting with him at his earliest convenience."

60

British Embassy, Bangkok, Thailand

"As you can see, Sir Josiah, this is a problem that must deeply concern my country. As a result of the French incursions into our territory in the latter part of the 19th century and their seizure of our territory as late as 1908, many Thai nationals live under French control. Given Japanese performance in China, we can only be deeply worried about their safety in the event of Japan taking control of French Indo-China."

"I can quite understand that position, Madam Ambassador. Unfortunately, I am also in an invidious position. I have orders from the government in London that essentially tell me to do nothing and ensure that no action is taken that may involve Britain in any regional disputes. However, I doubt the legality of the government in London and have received no explanation of what is happening there. All I receive are blunt directives which show little understanding of the complexities in the situation out here. Now, I do report, eventually, to London but my line of authority runs first to the government in India and from there to London. I can honestly say there is no doubt about the bona fides of the Indian authorities and their instructions are that I should act as I see fit in defense of Indian interests. Frankly, I find that a much more agreeable set of instructions."

"Also, I share your concern about Japanese expansionism. Personally, if I were in your government's position, I would hold that if Japan takes Indo-China under its control, Thailand should ask for the return of those parts of the area where the people are of Siamese ancestry."

"Sadly, that is the problem, Sir Josiah. The French are making it very clear that they will entertain no negotiations with us on any issue. Indeed, they are making it clear that they wish no contact with us in any area. I have received reports that people attempting to trade across the border have been arrested by the French colonial police and severely beaten."

Suriyothai shook her head sadly. The incidents she had mentioned were quite genuine and she had had nothing to do with planning or executing them. *It's very strange how the French Indo-China authorities are doing almost exactly what I want, unprompted by me. Do they have a death-wish or something?*

"You must understand, Sir Josiah, that in these areas, family connections go back many generations, often to before the foundation of my country. It is family that matters there. Countries come and go, but the family is always there. So one part of the family trades with another regardless of where the border is or the names of the countries on either side of it. This French policy of 'dissuasion' strikes at the heart of social organization in the entire region. It is cruel."

"I agree, Madam Ambassador. This policy seems hardly enlightened, but what can you do about it?" Sir Josiah sighed theatrically.

61

"Therein is the problem. The growing Japanese position in Indo-China is a threat to us all. Most of all, it is a threat to India. The Japanese need oil, rubber and all the other raw materials that this region can supply. They also have covetous eyes on India itself for its riches and its population. Most of all, they want the great naval base of Singapore. If they establish a secure base in Indo-China, they will strike westwards. Once over the Mekong, the next viable line of defense is the Irawaddy. If that is held, it will still mean the loss of Malaya and Singapore. It will also mean that we get overrun of course. If the line of the Irawaddy doesn't hold, the next viable defense line is the mountains on the India/Burma border. At that point, the Japanese will have almost everything they need except India itself and they will be in a vastly stronger position to take that."

"I think you underestimate the strength of Singapore, Madam Ambassador. Its great guns make it impregnable."

"From the landward side? How many of those guns can be trained upon an attacker from Malaya? And do the guns have explosive ammunition suitable for firing at an Army?"

"More than one might think. And I believe the munitions stores are comprehensive."

"And the water supply? Singapore has little or no water available on the island itself. If the water pipes from the mainland are cut, how long can the garrison hold out?"

Sir Josiah looked at his guest sharply. He had noted the skill with which she discussed strategic affairs. And she had made an obvious point now she had mentioned it. The water supply was the great Achilles heel of the fortress. She was right; Singapore was vulnerable from the landward side, even with its great guns. "And what do you think they would do from there?"

Suriyothai thought for a second. "Singapore would become their forward operating base. Are you aware that the Japanese have assembled their six aircraft carriers into a single striking force? They call it the *Dai Ichi Kido Butai*, the First Air Mobile Striking Force. I do not believe its equal exists anywhere in the world. With all six carriers operating together, they can throw almost four hundred aircraft into a battle over a limited area. That will gain them air superiority. I think they would strike at Ceylon first, seize that and thus establish another forward base at Trincomalee. India would then be faced with a two-pronged assault, from the south and the north. Such an assault would strain Japanese power to the outer limits of the plausible, but the potential rewards for them may make the commitment worthwhile.

The sweeping concept made Sir Josiah blink. "What are you suggesting, Madam Ambassador?"

"That the only viable line of defense for India is along the Mekong. By the time the Irawaddy is reached, Japan will have already won. Frankly, I doubt that the Irawaddy can be held. It is simply in the wrong place. Too far from India to be supported, too close to Japanese base areas to be secure and it will have already conceded everything the Japanese want. Sir Josiah, the options are the Mekong or a massive loss and a desperate fight in the Imphal-Kohima mountains. Possibly supported by an assault in Tamil Nadu. If we hold the Mekong, the situation of India having to protect itself doesn't arise. The Japanese will never get there."

"You sound very sure of that."

"Very sure. Their Army is of no great concern to us. We outnumber their Indochina Expeditionary Force on the ground and our Army has been rebuilt by German instructors who preferred to live here than under the regime presently ruling Germany. It is in the air we are weak. We would like to re-equip with modern American fighters and bombers but the Americans are refusing to deliver our latest order. There are six P64 fighters and ten A27 bombers held up in America now despite the fact that we have already paid for them. We wish to use purchase more American equipment but we may be forced to acquire Japanese aircraft instead. And that will force us to ally with them, not you. That is not our wish."

"You would not consider British aircraft?"

"We would, if we were offered them. We would regard Spitfires and Hurricanes as gifts from the Gods. But, all we are offered are Gladiators and old, surplus Gamecocks. They are no advance on what we have already. Sir Josiah, we must ask the aid of India in this matter. We would beg you to intercede with the Americans, convince them that we simply wish to control our own destiny free from outside bullying and domination. Rather like a group of thirteen colonies some years ago. If America extends the hand of friendship to us, we need seek no other."

"Except India, of course."

"Of course, Sir Josiah. The fortunes of my country and India are indissolubly linked. Geography, simple geography, tells us that."

Room 208, Munitions Building, Washington, DC, USA

"So, where are we with the industrial analysis of Germany, Phillip?"

Phillip Stuyvesant produced a very heavy series of files from a carry case. "We've made a pretty good start in getting a picture of German industrial power sorted out. This is our initial overview of the situation, although it does leave much to be desired in the way of fine detail."

"That's the overview?" General George Marshall was dumbfounded by the sheer volume of paperwork that was being generated. "What, in the name of God, does the fine detail look like?"

"I can ask one of my assistants to bring what we have in. She's waiting outside with it. I warn you though, she'll have to wheel it in on a trolley; it's a lot of data. Nobody has ever tried to do this before. What we are attempting to do is create a picture of the economy of an entire country and then work out how to dismantle it. This is not just a matter of finding the factories and bombing them. We have to work out how the various industrial structures interlock. From that, we can plan a campaign that will paralyze the German war economy.

"There's something else as well we're learning from this effort. We're not just generating a picture of the German war economy. We're getting a very fine handle on what German plans are. For example, we're getting a picture of supplies, especially fuel, being shifted towards depots in the East. All the indications are that Germany is going to invade Russia. It's too late for them to do it this year, and anyway, their army is down for maintenance after the fighting in France. But, the build-up of supplies in the east is accelerating too fast for an attack in the far future. It looks like we can expect the German invasion of Russia next year. We can even suggest how they are going to do it. It looks like three primary depot areas are being established, one in the north, one in the center and one in the south. Combining that with a railway map of the Soviet Union suggests that three thrusts are planned: one in the north aimed at Leningrad, one in the center aimed at Moscow and a third in the south aimed at Kiev. As the supply quantities build up, we could even make a guess as to the relative strengths of those thrusts. That will tell us what their overall invasion strategy is. An emphasis on the southern thrust will suggest priority being placed on resources; a northern bias will suggest industrial and political targets.

"That's all a bonus though. The real meat is the data we're getting on industrial capacity and that is intriguing. It seems as if Germany isn't actually taking this war very seriously. They've mobilized, but not that much. They're still producing large quantities of civilian goods. They're even still making hunting rifles for the civilian market. I'd say we're already mobilizing to a higher level than they are. I'd say that, if anything, we're going to have a lead in that department."

"How are you getting all this information?" General Arnold was curious. "I've seen nothing like this before."

"A combination of sources, Sir. Some is simply assembling existing records and existing data. The commercial attaches in the Berlin embassy and elsewhere have been assembling this stuff for years, but nobody did anything with it. I've got people going through those files now."

"Women, I suppose." Arnold was slightly sarcastic at that. The number of women filling key positions in the Economic Intelligence and Warfare Section had already been noticed in Washington circles.

"That's right. For this kind of work, women outperform men. They're more methodical and detail-orientated. Comes from looking after babies, I suppose." Stuyvesant listened appreciatively to the ripple of laughter that went around the room. "We've also started developing industrial intelligence sources in the financial and industrial communities. We're still authenticating what we get back from them. Our initial inquiries into the industrial-economic structure of Hitler's Germany focused attention on the following: electric power, including sources of fuel and distribution systems; steel, including sources of raw material; petroleum products, including synthetic processes; the aircraft industry, including aluminum production and engine plants; and transportation, the most prominent components being the railway, canal and highway networks. We also included in our evaluations the nonferrous metal supply, machine tool production, and food processing and distribution.

"One thing we found out has been immensely helpful. It turns out that the electric power generating and distribution system of Germany is relatively new, and that it has been built with capital borrowed largely from the United States. Now, American banks do not lend large sums of money for capital equipment without making careful investigations of the proposed structures. So, we approached the great international banks, particularly in New York, as to the availability of drawings and specifications of German electric plants and systems. In doing so we've tapped into a gold mine of data.

"The long and the short of it is that we've been able to put together a comprehensive target study on the German electric power system and the electric distribution system. It has even been possible to prepare target folders, including aiming points and bomb sizes. We've also been able to do the same on petroleum and synthetic oil plants; partially through the same sources, partially through the oil industries, and partially through individuals. We were fortunate in that we have experience of work carried out in Germany, in the Rumanian fields at Ploesti, and in the Middle East. This demonstrated the extreme importance and vulnerability of the German synthetic oil plants and the related importance of the Ploesti refineries. Thus, we have started to prepare target folders for those systems also. In addition, we made an analysis of the German steel industry and its sources of raw materials. We were less successful in our analysis of German transportation, partly because of the extent of the rail and canal system. But we have found enough to place the transportation system high on the priority list of desired targets."

"Good God man, is there anything you haven't looked at over the last month?" Stimson was impressed by the volume of work that was being presented here. "I have to say this. The political appreciation at this time is hardly favorable. I can say that the President views the possibility of a Nazi victory with deep concern. Three dictators, all hostile to the United States, are driving toward domination of important parts of the world. They threaten to completely upset the balance of power and with it world peace. Hitler and Mussolini have completed the conquest of Europe and appear to be contemplating the conquest of Western Russia and North Africa. England has been forced into a humiliating accommodation. On the other side of the world, the Japanese warlords are tearing China apart and look set to do the same to the rest of the Far East. Meanwhile, a fourth dictator, Stalin, though hardly a friend of America, is about the most valuable asset we have left in resisting Hitler. It seems likely that he too will be overwhelmed. If we cannot find allies, then we must fight this war alone and that appears a mighty and desperate endeavor.

"Stuyvesant, at first I doubted the wisdom of bringing a private sector industrialist into these meetings. I must say that the amount of work you and your team has put in to date justifies your presence here beyond any expectations we might have had. For that reason, I have authorized you to receive something so secret that even the President does not know the full scope of what we are achieving. We have cracked open a large number of diplomatic and military codes. Collectively, this work is called Ultra. It gives an insight into German and Japanese strategic planning. I want to expand your section's responsibilities to include using that decrypted information in an effort to determine future German strategy. Our decrypts tell us what the Nazi leadership would like to do; we will use your section to determine what their resources will allow them to do. One thing I must say, right now. This information will not leak out. It must not leak out; for if it does, we may well lose the war that is surely coming."

Government House, Calcutta, India

"We can't sit on the fence any longer, Pandit. We've stalled the Colonial and Dominion Offices for ten days and that's about as much as we can do. We are now facing the point where a decision has to be made. Do we defy Whitehall and stay in the war, or do we comply with their wishes and obey their orders?"

"Speaking as the leader of the Congress Party, I have to say that staying in the war is proving a very hard concept to explain to our membership." Nehru spoke slowly and carefully. His meetings with the rank and file of the Party had not gone well. "Those who do not wish to remain under the British yoke also do not see why leaving it should involve us staying in a war that is far away and affects us little. Speaking for myself, I am convinced by your argument and believe that both honor and our safety as a new, untried nation demand that we remain in the war. I even believe that a continued alliance with the other dominions that have remained in the war will serve us best in the short term. But how to explain this so that our membership is convinced? This is beyond my abilities."

Sir Martyn Sharpe twisted his mouth. He understood the problem and appreciated something else that, perhaps, Nehru himself hadn't yet realized. That was that Nehru was beginning to set aside the beliefs of a lifetime in pursuit of the greater good.

"Perhaps, Martyn, you underestimate the degree of flexibility we have here. Or the use to which we can put any extra time that we buy." Sir Eric Haohoa sipped gently at his tea.

"How so, Eric?"

"Well, people have argued with the Colonial and Dominion Offices before, they have tried to defy them and they have even tried to bribe them. Only in the latter case have they been successful and then but rarely. But, nobody has ever ignored them before. I don't think they know how to cope with that. The longer our silence lasts, the greater will be the confusion at their

66

end. A simple reply will be dealt with at a low level using precedent, but an unprecedented non-response? Nobody at a low level will be prepared to take the initiative in dealing with it. They'll boot it up to a higher level for consideration and that will continue all the way up until it reaches the top. Then, the elephant principle will kick in."

"What, pray, is the elephant principle?" Nehru was fascinated by this glimpse of the British bureaucracy at work.

"Pandit, if I may call you so?" Sir Eric waited and got a nod in response. "Pandit, making important decisions in the Civil Service is like the mating of elephants. There is lots of dust and noise, everything happens at a very high level, and there is no result for several years. Martyn is being much too pessimistic; we have weeks or even months before that situation becomes critical and we have to jump. In the meantime, we have time to deal with much more important issues."

"What can be more important than the future independence of India?" Nehru sounded offended.

"Giving India a sound economy so that it can stand on its own feet as an independent country." Sir Eric's reply was smooth and urbane. "Avoiding the impending economic crisis would be a good first step in that regard."

"Economic crisis?" Nehru and Sharpe replied in almost perfect chorus. "What economic crisis?"

"The one that presents us with the economic equivalent of being hanged tomorrow morning. And, like that notional event, it should concentrate our mind wonderfully. Do you know how our trade is managed under the Imperial Preference agreements signed at Ottawa?" Haohoa looked around and took the absence of response to be negative. "Well, we export raw materials to the motherland and import manufactured goods in their place. It's a neatly-conceived system that means Britain has access to a guaranteed supply of raw materials and a guaranteed market for manufactured goods. Like all closed systems, it works very well as long as it remains a closed system. But, like all such systems, it cannot allow any degree of openness. It is either a completely closed system or it is no system at all. And Halifax's 'armistice' has just blown a great hole in it.

"You see, we have virtually no industry here. We produce our own needs in cotton goods but that is all. Other than that, all our manufactured goods are imported from Britain. Now, if we remain at war with Germany and Britain does not, that supply of manufactured goods stops dead. Also, if Britain is at peace with Germany and we are at war, Britain cannot purchase our raw materials. I don't think Halifax has realized the implications of that yet. What his armistice does is force Britain away from the Empire and ties its economy closer to Europe. That's their problem, though. Ours is that we now have to sell our raw materials on the international market and buy our manufactured goods in the same place. And there is the problem. We have to buy manufactured goods with rupees. Now, what is a rupee worth?"

That was a question Sir Martyn could answer and he rattled off the rupee vs pound sterling exchange rate. "One shilling and fourpence."

"You see, Martyn, that's the problem. The rupee is valued against the pound sterling. Fifteen rupees equals one pound sterling. And that value is set by artificial fiat. Essentially, the pound sterling is a basket of Empire currencies and the value of each currency within that basket is what the British Government says it is. All those exchange rates are artificial; they are what the Government in London finds convenient. Since the rupee is only traded within a closed system, that doesn't matter. That closed system doesn't exist any more. So, I ask again, what is the Indian rupee actually worth?"

Sir Martyn and Pandit Nehru exchanged looks, both unwilling to say what they both knew to be the answer. Sir Eric waited for a moment before continuing. "I am afraid you are both right. The value of the rupee is what the international market says it is and that is less than the paper it is printed on. The only currency we have that is worth anything is the silver rupee and that is worth exactly the value of the silver it is made from. No more, no less. So we have to buy our manufactured goods. With what? Piles of dirty paper? For that is all our rupees are to the market. Most currency traders don't even know what a rupee is. We would literally be better off selling the unprinted paper on the market than spoiling it by turning it into banknotes.

"The only way we can get currency that people will accept is to sell things to countries that have traded currencies. Like the American dollar. Only, what is it that we can sell to the Americans? We are barely self-sufficient in food, but we can sell tea. Americans drink coffee. We can also export raw jute, raw cotton and wheat. All three the Americans have in abundance from their own producers. We actually do export raw materials to the United States and Japan and we import manufactured goods from them and that is the one saving grace in the situation. Even better, the proportion of goods exported to and imported from those countries has actually increased over the last ten years. We export gold to the United States and that is our one hope of survival. It is also the one way we can retaliate against the British, for our gold sales were the major dollar earner for the Empire. They will kick us out of the Imperial Preference system and we will cut off the supply of dollars from gold sales. Britain will hurt but we will be in acute financial agony. Our reserves are already bleeding out as we buy the things we must have to survive as a country and soon, within six weeks in fact, they will be gone. And then we will be able to buy nothing."

"I think there is a solution to this." Pandit Nehru was appalled by what he was hearing, but in some ways it fitted well with his long-term plans for the country. "Not to mince words, the answer is socialism. The Indian princes have untold wealth, accumulated from centuries of exploitation. We can seize those funds and they will pay for the imports we need. And in doing so, we will be rectifying a grave injustice in the society of this country. Those princes roll in obscene wealth while the common people here starve."

"India is marginally self-sufficient in food." Haohoa was being his pedantic civil servant self. "But the specter of famine does still hang over the country. It takes just a few things to go wrong at the same time and we will see another great famine here. Be that as it may, the idea of confiscating the wealth of the princes is an attractive idea from many points of view, but it will not solve the basic problem that we face. The princely wealth is capital, not income. If we seize it and use it to pay for our necessary imports, then it will buy us some time. Eighteen months and then it will be gone, never to return. We will not even utilize its full value, for that wealth is mostly in the form of precious stones and other valuables. Turning them into cash we can use by selling them will flood the market for such things and severely depress their value. There is another point we must bear in mind. We can only develop the economy of this country by bringing in foreign investment. If we establish a reputation for seizing funds, then investors will fear for the safety of their money and go elsewhere. That would cripple us from the start. The princely wealth is indeed a tool we can use, but we must be careful how we do so; for it can easily break in our hands and leave us with nothing."

There was a long, aching silence as the implications of Sir Eric's summary of the impending economic catastrophe sank in.

"Then splitting away from Britain is impossible?"

To Sir Martyn, those words represented the end of a dream. From the expression on Nehru's face, his dreams also had just been crushed.

"By no means." Sir Eric decided that it was time to spread the good news a little. "What the current situation does mean is that we can't split away from the Commonwealth. Our trade balance with Britain is tremendously disadvantageous, that is true. But that position has just ended. Our trade balance with the rest of the Commonwealth is very positive. In fact, the Commonwealth is the route by which our monies are transferred to Britain. As long as the Commonwealth remains in existence, we can continue to trade within it. Of course, Australia, and most especially New Zealand, will be much worse off. They have much the same position with regards to us as we do to Britain. Australia is headed for an even worse economic crisis than we are, And New Zealand? Well, I honestly believe that New Zealand cannot survive as an independent entity even within the Commonwealth.

"The fact is that we have raw materials that the other Commonwealth countries need and the same applies in reverse. What we lack is a medium by which that trade can be carried out. Since Halifax's armistice has effectively torpedoed the pound sterling in the world exchange markets, we desperately need a substitute. The Commonwealth countries need their basket of currencies if they are to survive; it's just that we now need one that does not include the pound sterling. We also need a source of manufactured goods. More precisely, we need a country that can take our raw materials and supply us with manufactured goods in exchange. I can think of only one country in this region that can fill that need."

"Japan." Sharpe made the statement with a degree of finality that was heavy with dislike for the idea.

"And we should create an alliance with one fascist power to avoid a relationship with another?" Nehru also disliked the idea, although he guessed that there was a wing of his party that would be more accepting of the concept. "Forgive me for not seeing how this is much of an improvement in our situation."

"Forgive me for saying so, but Subhas Chandra Bose might disagree with you on that point." One of the responsibilities of the Cabinet Office in any British-run government was supervision of the intelligence services. It just so happened that was one of Sir Eric Haohoa's primary duties. His reward for the observation was an involuntary grimace on the face of Nehru. "But, there is saying, when supping with the devil, use a long spoon. We are not creating an alliance here, just finding a market for our raw materials to bridge the gap until we can stand on our own feet. Remember, Pandit, we're running against the clock here. We have to do two things; one is to find markets for our produce and the other is to find a currency the Commonwealth can use as a world standard. For, on that point, if we do not hang together, we will all hang separately."

"And we cannot have a new currency standard while the present situation remains unresolved." Sharpe felt slightly foolish stating the obvious, but sometimes the obvious got overlooked because nobody bothered to state it.

"Agreed. Nobody is taking the lead in jumping ship because nobody wants to take the chance of carrying the blame if it all ends in tears. We will just have to hope that something forces our collective hands."

Dumbarton Avenue, Georgetown, Washington, DC, USA

"What else is going on over there, Iggie?" Phillip Stuyvesant leaned back in his chair, fascinated by the insight into the current English state of affairs that Igrat was providing. She'd been speaking about her experiences at the Southampton flying boat terminals; reading between the lines, she'd enjoyed twisting the tails of the officials there.

"The big one? Nell, Gusoyn and Achillea have Winston Churchill and a dozen or so leading scientists and engineers either tucked away in an English stately home, or ready to move at a moments notice. They've gone and formed their own auxiliary police unit that's throwing its weight around in the Nottingham area, so that they are cordially loathed by the local people and thus accepted as being legitimate by them. They picked me up at the station which got me some sympathetic looks from the locals. I'd have been scared, but I saw Gusoyn was the driver. So I went along with it."

"Winston Churchill? They have him squirrelled away? Where?" Stuyvesant was amazed. The 'where is Winnie' question was causing arguments around the world, and the impression was already growing that he had been quietly killed by Halifax. Discovering that he was already in safe hands, if not precisely in a safe location, was a new piece to the intricate political puzzle that was forming.

"He's in Nell's ancestral home. He's quite safe there. Nell and the others believe they can move him around if they want using their phony police unit. That's why they formed it. By the way, they gave me something to bring out as an example of the sort of technology that they can smuggle out when we rescue Churchill."

Igrat reached into her case and pulled out a metal box. Carrying it as if it didn't weigh anything had nearly given Igrat a strained shoulder, but she'd pulled it off. She opened it and pulled out a contraption with wires hanging from it.

"A revolver cylinder. One with eight chambers and obviously too big for a hand-held revolver. And its got lots of metalwork attached to it. So?" Stuyvesant was curious.

"It's called a cavity magnetron." Igrat spoke in a voice that had the lilt and inflexions of somebody else. Stuyvesant knew he was hearing an explanation that she'd been given by an expert and that she was relaying exactly as she had heard it. "It is a high-powered vacuum tube that generates microwaves using the interaction of a stream of electrons with a magnetic field. This piece of equipment has been generated by two scientists called Randall and Boot. The high power of pulses from the cavity magnetron makes centimeter-band radar practical and thus allows the detection of smaller objects. It also drastically reduces the size of radar sets so that they can be installed in aircraft and ships." The alien timbre to her voice dropped away as she finished the prepared part of her speech. "There's a lot more where this came form. Stuff on new engines for aircraft; all sorts of things. Some basic physics stuff as well. Don't ask me if that's any use."

"And what's this going to cost us?"

"Nothing. The British are giving it all to us, for the common good. All we have to do is come over and get it."

Stuyvesant nodded. "So, we get the goodies if we rescue them and this cavity magnet is a good faith gift to show us the goodies are real. This is a deal I can relate to. Has the gang any idea of how to get this group out?"

"They suggest buying a flying boat and landing it Scotland somewhere. Either at the coast or in one of the lochs."

"They're very free with our money. Have they no idea how much a Boeing will cost us? Leave this one with me, Iggie. I want you to go out to Bangkok with the Noth report and deliver it to Suriyothai. Lillith has your tickets. Spending more money on Pan American's clipper service has broken her heart, but we've got no choice at this time. I need you back here as soon as Snake has that report."

"No time for shopping?" Igrat sounded heartbroken as well.

71

"None. Not this time. Straight in and out. If you can fit a shopping expedition in between flights, do so, but don't delay getting back here. No 'missing the plane' and 'getting the next one out'." Stuyvesant picked up the cavity magnetron and twisted it around in his hands. "I wonder why Samuel Colt didn't think of this."

Headquarters, Middle East Command, Cairo, Egypt

With nine hours difference between Canberra and Cairo, there was a tendency for things to turn up at awkward hours. Annoying as that might have been, when dispatches from home did arrive during business hours it was usually a good indication of trouble. Trouble was all Lieutenant-General Thomas Blamey could see in this latest communication from his Government. After an hour's solid contemplation and a telephone call, he summoned his staff car and left word to inform GOC-in-C Middle East Command to expect him forthwith.

Archibald Percival Wavell, General Officer Commanding in Chief of His Majesty's forces in Egypt, Sudan, Trans-Jordan, Palestine, British Somaliland, Cyprus, Aden, and the Persian Gulf, who's concerns extended to Libya, Ethiopia, Eritrea, Greece, Rhodes and such trifles, was waiting on the front steps when Blamey's car rolled up. Admittedly, he was as surprised to see the Australian as Blamey was to be met in person. Blamey had just swept up the drive when another General, Major-General George Noble Molesworth, alighted from another staff car.

'Molely' Molesworth might not have been on par with the Lieutenant-Generals in rank, but as Deputy Chief of General Staff for the Indian Army he was more than due his share of official curtsey. In any event, his arrival had been telegraphed in advance. Quite unlike Bernard Freyberg, Major-General, VC, CMG, DSO** and General Officer Commanding the 2nd New Zealand Expeditionary Force, who hauled his large and much abused frame out of the Chevrolet behind Blamey.

If Wavell was in the least put out by receiving three visitors for the price of one, he gave little sign. Instead, he welcomed them all warmly and made polite conversation about the weather, the tribulations of air travel and Cairo traffic until the four men were safely seated in his office, drinks in hand and doors shut.

"Well gentlemen, it would be too much to ask if you were all here for Genie's birthday . . . ?"

It was almost inevitable Blamey opened the batting. Never much of a diplomat at the best of times, and hardly one of the boys in such company, he wasn't inclined to take the back seat to anyone. Yet, for as far as Wavell had come to know his man, he was surprised by quiet almost tentative tone from the bullish fellow

"Sir . . . I received instructions this morning that umm . . . My government would like my opinion on the future movements of the Australian

Imperial Force. They ask if the AIF should be withdrawn to Australia wholesale, or if it might be more advisable to move directly to Singapore. I'm also to inform them of the earliest we can leave Egypt and . . . " Blamey choked down a curse. "The lilly livered bastards also want to know how much kit I can screw out of you before we go. I'm not meant to be telling you that obviously, but . . . Christ. It's one thing to cut and run. I'm not playing snake in the grass for the buggers too. Sorry sir, I'm so bloody sorry . . ."

Wavell's look of polite interest hardly wavered as he listened to this toll of doom ring out. "That's alright, Tom; and thank you, I do appreciate your honesty." He had, after all, been half expecting something along these lines. His only real surprise was that it had taken so long, and that Blamey was so upset about it.

On the other end of the settee Freyberg coughed, "My government," he rumbled, "has only asked my advice on the desirability of redeploying my command. We . . . that is, Tom and I, rather think our Governments have been talking between themselves, as the options I am to consider are essentially the same as his: Singapore or Australia. However mine are not orders, and Wellington say they will be guided by my opinion."

Again Wavell nodded politely. "Thank you, Bernard" He turned to Molesworth, who was already blushing. "I take it you are here for my Indians, Moley?"

Molesworth nodded, "Yes, Archie. We seem to have a political accord developing with the Congress Party, but they don't much like the idea of Indian troops defending British interests."

Wavell raised a curious eyebrow "Any you may well need them for keeping order too, dare I say?"

"If Jinnah AML can't be kept under control then yes, I rather fear we will." Molesworth agreed sadly. "I knew it was going to leave you in the most dreadful bind, but I had not realized things would be this bad." He glanced across at the two Dominion generals.

"No, that is quite alright, old man," smiled Wavell gently "Perfectly understandable, given the circumstances."

"So that's it then," said Blamey into the air before turning to Wavell. "Where do you intend to take the British forces? I'm instructed to invite you to Australia, but I'd understand if you told me to go and roger myself."

Wavell looked blank. "I'm sorry - take whom where? I assure you, Tom, I've no intention of going anywhere at all, nor shall I without orders."

"Oh come on, man" snapped Blamey. "Making bricks without straw is one thing, but you're not holding Egypt with the rest of us bottling out."

Wavell nodded "I take your point, Tom, and I dare say you are right, but I intend to do my best."

"So you intend to stay?" asked Freyberg.

73

"Yes" replied Wavell simply.

"Good." said Freyberg soberly. "Then so shall we. And I will inform Wellington to that effect."

For the first time, Wavell showed some trace of passion "Really? Oh Ber . . . Thank you, Bernard. I thank you, and the Empire thanks you."

"What's left of it" muttered Blamey.

"That is rather the point, isn't it," said Freyberg, accepting Wavell's gratitude with a gentle nod. "This is the Empire now, or so far as I can see."

A sigh ran around the group. Someone had to say it, and it was typical of Freyberg to grasp the nettle.

"What are your instructions from London – if I may inquire?" Molesworth asked.

"As they have always been," smiled Wavell. "London has had no end of things to say, but there has been no change to my strategic guidance."

"What are they thinking?" muttered Freyberg.

"God only knows." Blamey's laugh was drier than dust. "God knows if they are thinking at all."

"Be that as it may," Wavell carefully avoided any trace of a smile, "My position is clear, and not a little easier thanks to Bernard's great generosity. But any further help . . . I should not like to beg, but I need troops and time, gentlemen, and any of either you might spare would not go unwelcome."

Freyberg scratched his chin. "London may have gone mad, but our immediate problem, Archie, is that Tom over here is cursed with politicians not given the strategic vision the good Lord gave an ant. And, if you'll pardon me for saying so, the Indian Government appears to be rather flustered. Not without reason, but history offers little sympathy for even the best excuses."

"Is this really the sort of conversation we ought to be having?" asked Molesworth cautiously.

"If not us, then who?" asked Freyberg with no caution at all. "As far as I can see, everyone is worried over their own little patch, and praying like hell someone else is looking to the whole."

"And no bugger is" agreed Blamey reluctantly.

Room 208, Munitions Building, Washington, DC, USA

"It can't be done." Jack Hunderford sounded really regretful. He'd been flattered by the invitation to attend the meeting and even more so that his opinions were heard so intently.

"But, we can get a Boeing 314 there, even if it does need some extra fuel tanks." Secretary Cordell Hull was determined to make this rescue happen. Overnight the electronics engineers at the Naval Aircraft Radio Laboratory had studied the mysterious piece of equipment; they were already stunned by its implications. They'd wanted to know where it had come from and how, but those questions had been carefully evaded. The message was very clear, though; the technology the Tizard escapees would be bringing with them was worth its weight in gold. That was a separate issue from the political importance of bringing Churchill out.

"That's not the problem." Hunderford was the head of flying boat operations for Pan American and was reputed to be the only man Juan Trippe ever listened to. There was nobody around who knew more about operating big flying boats. That was why he was in the room. "Landing flying boats on water is a very difficult operation. We make it look easy because we train the living daylights out of our crews and only fly in and out of carefully-maintained operating bases. Every one of our pilots has landed a dozen times or more at each base on the route before we let them take a Clipper in there. Landing at an unknown Scottish loch, or even worse, a lake, is impossible. Think of it this way. The flying boats that could do it can't get there and the ones that can get there can't do it. The Clippers look big and tough, but that's just their size. They're really very fragile. Rough water or a floating log will do for them. You'd be better off with one of the British boats. The Empires are much tougher than our Clippers. That's why ours are economically viable and theirs aren't."

"Any other problems?" Hull was disappointed by the blunt rejection of the initial plan.

"Navigation will be the big one. We have homing beacons at all our staging points and the pilots fly to them. You won't have that for this flight. That alone rules a flying boat out. After three thousand miles, you could be hundreds of miles off and one lake or bay looks much like another. No, if this is going to work you need a landplane and you need the best navigator in the world. He has to fly that aircraft right to the airfield and get down first time. He can't mess around flying search circles or he'll have fighters on his back."

"We haven't got a landplane that can make a direct flight from the East Coast to Scotland and back. Not yet anyway." General Arnold sounded depressed. He'd seen the hurried first report on the cavity magnetron as well and wanted more. "We could fly in from Iceland, though. We have a base there; the British occupied it under Churchill in May and the Marines took it over immediately after Halifax pulled the plug. The last thing we wanted was an enemy-controlled base that close to us. A Flying Fortress could get from Iceland to Scotland and back. If a suitable airfield in Scotland can be found, of course."

"That doesn't solve the navigational problem." Hunderford was slightly relieved at the course the discussion was taking. He had been terrified that one of his beloved Boeing 314 Clippers would be commandeered for this madcap mission.

"If we're going to use the Flying Fortress, it might well. Remember the interception of the liner *Rex* a couple of years back? Well, the intercept was plotted by a Lieutenant Curtis LeMay; he gave up flying pursuit ships in order to become a navigator and a bombardment man. Well, he's a Captain now and he's available for this mission. Jack wanted the best navigator in the world? He's it. I can even offer you some aircraft. The British wanted Flying Fortresses, so we have arranged for twenty of the new B-17Cs to be delivered off the production line for them. The first B-17C flew a few days ago, but there is no way in hell we're going to deliver the British ones. Not this year and not next year when they were due to get theirs. We can paint that prototype B-17C up in British colors and fly it over there. With LeMay doing the navigation, we've got a good chance of pulling this off. Worst comes to the worst, we can always claim we were delivering the aircraft according to contract."

The meeting cracked up laughing at the idea of an unannounced midnight landing at an unknown airport in potentially hostile territory being a delivery according to contract. Eventually, Secretary Stimson wiped his eyes and shook his head. "This might just be crazy enough to work. Find that Captain LeMay. Tell him what needs to be done and see that he gets the mission ready. This raises another question, in passing. Those twenty B-17Cs the British wanted aren't all the aircraft we have stockpiled here for them. My staff tells me we've got 230 Hawk 75s of assorted types, 250 P-40Bs and P-40Cs and a hundred Hudsons all sitting on airports waiting for an owner. Why hasn't the Air Force taken them over?"

"They're all export birds, Mister Secretary. The Hawk 75s have 7.5mm French machine guns or .303inch British ones. Their throttles are French-style, meaning the pilot has to pull them back to increase power, not push them forward. There's other differences as well; mostly metric instrumentation and minor differences in the engine. The P-40s aren't really P-40s; they're Hawk 81s. Wrong caliber machine guns again, French-style throttles and instruments, different engines. They'd need a major rebuild to make them suitable for our use and they still wouldn't be up to the standard of the current production models. All taking them over would achieve is slowing down production of the ones we really need. We'd be better off giving them away. I reckon the Chinese could use them." Arnold looked around to see the other members of the meeting nodding.

"Not just the Chinese." Cordell Hull was thoughtful. "If we get Churchill out, he'll set up a government in exile. All the British Dominions and a fair number of colonies are sitting on the fence right now, waiting for a lead. He'll give it to them and they'll tell Halifax to stuff his armistice."

"Why?" Arnold had assumed the rest of the British Empire would follow London's example.

"Because they're like us in 1776. A few polite requests and words of regret for offense unwittingly caused would work wonders, but Halifax won't give them. He's like every other weakling who has been bullied all his life. When he has a victim of his own, he takes all his own life experiences out on them. Given a lead, the Colonies will stay in the war. I feel sure of that. Even if they don't realize it themselves, they're looking for an excuse to cock a snook at London. And when they do, we can offer them a whole new air force, all of their own."

"One other thing." Stuyvesant looked at the files he had in front of him. "We touched on this earlier, but it's becoming a critical issue in our evaluations. We don't have a bomber that can get from the East Coast to Berlin and back again. Even if we use Iceland as a forward base, that's a long haul. If we are going to prosecute the coming war from here, we're going to need an aircraft that can do that."

"We surely will. You're an aircraft man, Stuyvesant. As an investor, at least. Would you care to go over to Boeing and Consolidated and get briefed on what their aircraft can do? Seeing what they have in mind might help you get the plan of attack more clearly defined."

"I'll do that, Sir."

Bang Phitsan Palace, Bangkok, Thailand

"Welcome to Bangkok, Igrat. How do you like our new airfield?"

"I prefer flying boats, Snake. So much more comfortable."

Suriyothai smiled at the use of her nickname, something that was known only to a tiny handful of people around the world. "We don't have suitable landing points for flying boats. I've looked. It has to be land planes, which is a problem for us. Long haul airlines are built around using flying boats. Anyway, what have you brought me?"

"We came across this in our business. You know we are working for the U.S. Government now?" She handed over the Noth report, complete with its bloodstained cover.

"I do. I was pleased to see Phillip has finally admitted the correctness of my opinions."

Igrat sighed. The relationship between Stuyvesant and Suriyothai was complex. On some levels, he was her mentor and teacher; on others the two were deeply divided. Their personal relationship added extra layers of complexity to the cocktail. While the two had some pretty spectacular rows over the years, their mutual respect had avoided the simmering dislike that existed between Stuyvesant and Loki. "He hasn't. We are simply acting as advisors and analysts, providing that leadership with accurate information it can rely upon."

"Being part of the political leadership here works. And this isn't being involved in politics?" Suriyothai tapped the bloodstains on the cover.

"That wasn't us. That was Loki."

"Ahh, this comes from him then." Suriyothai grinned broadly at Igrat who was distinctly uncomfortable at having been caught. "Sit down while I glance at this."

Igrat watched while Suriyothai started to read the Noth report. Quietly, one of the maids brought in a bowl of fresh fruit and a pot of tea. The minutes ticked by as Suriyothai thumbed through the pages. Eventually, she looked up at Igrat. "And what did Phillip think of this?"

"He said it was probably the dumbest strategic idea he had ever read. And given some of the strategic plans he has seen over the years, that is saying something. After he finished making choking noises, he said it was a typical product of an amateur strategist who had no idea of logistics, movement constraints or political realities."

Suriyothai laughed delightedly. "He is not losing his touch then. Did he go red?"

"Oh yes. The plan there has been abandoned though. Germany will be hitting Russia next year. We will be getting confirmation of that shortly, but everything we know points that way."

"And that will be a bloody war indeed. Igrat, please tell Phillip that nobody else needs to know that this plan had been abandoned. Who was this Odwin Noth by the way?"

"One of Loki's people, but a renegade, so I believe. One who had god-like delusions."

"I see. Well, no self-respecting strategist would take this seriously, but I am not dealing with such people out here. The ones who understand strategy know well the threat that faces us and what we must do to overcome it. Those who do not will be convinced by this and will be scared out of their wits by it. Phillip has done me a great service by sending this over. Odwin Noth may have been a fool and a renegade, but he has supplied me with a vital piece of the puzzle I am solving here." She paused for a moment, "Igrat, is Phillip in a position to get Secretary Hull to ease up on us? The American refusal to sell us arms hurts us badly and may yet force us into the arms of the Japanese."

"No, I'm sorry. I don't think so anyway. I'll ask when I get back. However, there are great quantities of arms ordered by France and Britain stored in the United States. If you can find a way of breaking them loose, they should solve your problems."

"That is a useful thought. Igrat, I will have a car drive you back to the airport. Next time you come here, tell Phillip I will accept no arguments. You and I will go shopping together."

CHAPTER FIVE
GAMESMANSHIP

Egilsstadir Airport, Iceland

The B-17C lined up with the runway and made a near-perfect three-point landing. It came to a halt about three quarters of the way down the runway, then taxied off on to a parking lane. Once the engines started to spool down, Stuyvesant watched a hatch in the lower part of the fuselage open up and the crew drop out; four men, led by a stocky officer whose command authority was immediately obvious.

"Stuyvesant?" Stuyvesant had expected the voice to be overbearing and a near-shout; in fact, it was soft and hard to hear over the residual engine noise and the wind. He had to strain to catch the words.

"I am. Captain LeMay?"

LeMay nodded. "My crew. Captain Archie Smith, Second Lieutenants Harris Hull and John Paul Bobo. They told me this mission was critical, so I brought the best we have."

"Pleased to meet you gentleman. Would you like to rest up from your flight?"

"I see no cause for rest. The aircraft will be repainted here. Your party has been told we'll be heading into Prestwick?"

"They have and they'll be there. I've got your passenger manifest and other documents. My courier brought them out yesterday. She's in the control tower if you need any additional data. Party is Winston Churchill, Henry Thomas Tizard, Brigadier F.C. Wallace of the British Army, Captain H.W. Faulkner from the Royal Navy, Group Captain F.L. Pearce of the Royal Air Force, Professor John Cockcroft, a nuclear physicist and Assistant Director of Scientific Research at the Ministry of Supply, Dr Edward George Bowen, a radar expert, Arthur Edgar Woodward-Nutt, an Air Ministry official and Frank

Whittle, a propulsion engineer. Also, there will be Achillea Foyle, Gusoyn Rivers and Eleanor Gwynne. They're the security detachment. Twelve people in all. Plus three thousand pounds of scientific documents and prototype equipment."

LeMay nodded. "We can manage this. The aircraft has a bomb bay fuel tank. The cargo will have to ride inside. The two women can sit in the radio cabin; everybody else will fit where they can."

"Captain, why did you choose Prestwick? There are other bases further north."

"No fog there. Ever."

"I didn't know that."

"Not your job to."

Stuyvesant was getting used to LeMay's manner. The terse manner wasn't rudeness; the man habitually used the fewest possible number of words to get his meaning over clearly. Despite the man's reticence, Stuyvesant found himself liking the Air Corps Captain. That made the next bit uncomfortable.

"Captain, you have been briefed on this mission. It's top secret. We've got a cover story worked out, but it's flimsy and will probably fall apart. If it does, the next cover is that you were on leave and took on delivering this aircraft as a private venture. Earning a little money on the side, as it were, to deliver an embargoed aircraft. If it comes to that, your reputation will be pretty much trashed. If you want out, just say so."

"I was briefed, so I brought a minimum crew."

"Something else." Stuyvesant hesitated, not quite certain how to phrase this and not wanting to give offense. "Three members of my family are in the party you'll be picking up. That puts me, and my whole family, in your debt. If this goes wrong, we will look after you. If this goes really, terribly wrong, we will look after your family. They'll want for nothing. We've done that for other people who've helped us in the past and we'll do it in the future. We take pride in paying our debts in full."

LeMay said nothing but nodded slightly. "You coming, Stuyvesant?"

Stuyvesant was about to say no, but he suddenly realized it had been a long time since he had done something arguably stupid just for the sheer joy of it. "If you can fit me in, yes."

"You can ride in the co-pilot's seat." The two men walked over to the control tower. A hastily-built structure, it offered only nominal protection from the biting wind. Tucked in one corner, Igrat was reading a fashion magazine. The collar of her fur coat was turned up and her nose was reddened by the wind.

"Igrat, this is our navigator and mission commander, Captain LeMay. Captain, our courier, Igrat Shafrid."

Igrat gave LeMay her most charming smile and got virtually no response. LeMay looked at her curiously. "You went to England and relayed the plan details?"

"Yes. The code is a Morse letter V. Dit-dit-dit-dah. Flash it on your landing lights as you come in. I also weighed all the equipment and papers they wanted to bring and made each member of the party weigh themselves. The list of weights is on that manifest. I thought it might help you load quickly."

"It will." LeMay looked through the sheets of paper. "I find no cause for complaint here. Commendable."

He left to supervise the repainting of the Flying Fortress. It was already beginning to sport the British "sand and spinach" color scheme with its belly painted black. Igrat looked at Stuyvesant and raised a carefully arched eyebrow. "Why do I think that he believes the proper reward for a perfect performance is the absence of punishment?"

"Iggie, I think you just got the highest praise you're ever likely to receive. I doubt if he's ever told more than one or two people that their performance was 'commendable' in his life." Stuyveasant thought for a second. "People like him are rare. Planners and administrators are commonplace, but our Captain LeMay is an operator. He doesn't talk or lecture. He just makes things happen."

Bestwood Lodge, Arnold, Nottinghamshire, United Kingdom

""Osbourne, please, one last chance. Come with us." Eleanor Gwynne pleaded with the man standing next to her. She was shabby; her clothes were torn and her face streaked with makeup that appeared to have run from continuous weeping. In fact, the appearance was deceptive and the result of patient preparation. It was essential that she looked like a maltreated prisoner and that their safety could depend on it.

The Duke of St. Albans shook his head. "My place is here. Somebody will have to organize a resistance to That Man. The regular army wouldn't take me and I won't sit around on a pension in a foreign land. This is where the de Vere Beauclerk family lives and where we will stay. Charles has his part in all this and must stay. By the same logic, I must stay and do my part. Now run along Nell, and get our people to safety.

The trucks and the Humber staff car were waiting outside. Gusoyn and Achillea wore the black shirts and khaki pants of the Police Auxiliary. Both had Thompson submachine guns hanging over their shoulders and Webley revolvers in holsters on their Sam Browne belts. Eleanor had another Webley carefully hidden beneath her clothes. Her shackles, ragged clothes and bruised face would cause her to be ignored as a potential threat if the back of the lorry was searched. A little judicious weeping would add to the effect. The combination would cost the man taken in by it his life. Eleanor Gwynne wasn't a fighter and did not hold the principle of a fair fight in any great regard. She had no compunction about shooting people in the back.

Four other members of the party, the youngest ones, were also dressed as Auxiliary Police carrying Thompsons. The rest were in the trucks, also appearing to be prisoners. They too sported bruises and ragged clothing. Of course the primary 'prisoner' was the stout figure of Winston Churchill. The instructions that had been passed via Igrat were quite clear. He was to escape even if it cost everybody else their lives.

Gusoyn took Eleanor by the elbow and helped her up into the back of the small lorry. She settled down on the wooden bench and checked that the shackles she was wearing would slide off without any delay. If she had to spring an ambush, split seconds would be vital. Her job was to shoot the man nearest to her and the most threatening man and then draw fire. If it went well, Achillea would cut the others down with her Thompson before they had the chance to kill anybody. Eleanor didn't want to know what would happen if it didn't go well.

"Everybody on board?" Gusoyn had taken over the leadership of this party. He and the other "Auxiliary Police" pulled down the canopy on the two lorries and tied off the rear panels, sealing the occupants in and also concealing them from view. Then, he got behind the wheel of the Humber staff car and put the vehicle in gear to lead his little convoy off. They had a two hundred and fifty mile drive in front of them. He'd allowed a whole day for the trip, plus a little spare. *Twenty four hours has to be enough,* he thought, *but we have to be there when that plane comes in.*

Standing on the gravel drive, Osbourne de Vere Beauclerk, Duke of St Albans, watched the convoy leave. Sadly, he shook his head. *What kind of country has this become when to travel safely needs such deception? How low have we sunk?* Another question pushed its way into his mind despite his efforts to prevent it from doing so. *And how much lower will we sink before this is all over?* As the tail-lights rounded a curve and vanished he asked himself another question. *Just how does one start a resistance movement anyway? There has to be a book on it in the library somewhere.*

Junction of the A611 and the A60, Mansfield, United Kingdom

'Damn, I wasn't expecting a checkpoint this early." Achillea was worried. They'd been driving for less than an hour and were only roughly 20 miles north of Nottingham.

"I was. Two main trunk roads coming together just short of a major town? It is a natural place for a checkpoint. There will be others. We will just have to bluff our way through each."

The checkpoint was manned by two uniformed police officers. *Bobbies*, Gusoyn noted, *not the already-hated Blackshirts.* He stopped the Humber beside the line of old tires that had been placed on the road and got out. He saw the expression of dislike on the face of the policemen as they saw his uniform, but they also noted the revolver in its holster.

"Auxiliary Police Chief Inspector Rivers. Let us through." Gusoyn flashed his badge. It had been made up by guesswork with some helpful advice on heraldry from the Duke. The gamble was that nobody else would know what an Auxiliary Police badge looked like either. The same applied to his orders. They had the same badge printed on the paper and the typing looked authentic. The Auxiliary Police were virtually unknown this far north.

"Not so fast, Sir." The sir was grudging. Gusoyn had assumed that the Auxiliary Police would be over-ranked to give them the authority they needed. Also, the more the local police disliked them, the better. "What are you doing up here? We don't see your kind around here."

"Read my orders." Gusoyn never liked being rude to people, but his assumed identity demanded it.

"Taking prisoners up north." The police officer was hesitant. "Why? What's going on?"

Gusoyn winked. "Take a look."

He led the two police officers around to the tailgate on the first lorry and lifted the rear flap of the canvas. "See who we've got on board."

"My God, it's Winnie." The policeman gasped. He shone his torch inside, showing the unmistakeable features of Winston Churchill. The other occupants, two men and a crying woman, hardly gained any notice.

"That is right. In protective custody." Gusoyn laughed nastily. "And will be all the way up north. Down for disposal, this lot are. Subversives and saboteurs of the Armistice. All to be disposed of, if you get my drift. Quiet like."

"Get out of here." The police officer nearly snarled the release.

Gusoyn climbed back into the car and rolled past the checkpoint. The two lorries followed.

"Can we expect a checkpoint every twenty miles?" Achillea was concerned at how often their bluff would hold up. It only needed one checkpoint to smell a rat and the whole escape would fall apart.

"I do not think so. We must follow the A618 to Rotherham and then the A633 until we hit the A61 at Wakefield." Gusoyn had spent most of the previous night studying maps. "I think the next checkpoint will be where the A61 and A64 meet north of Wakefield. That is another fifty miles or so."

Behind them, the two police officers watched the trucks disappearing. The younger of the two men was angry. "Poor Winnie, he deserves better than this. Bloody Blackshirt bastards. Think we ought to tell somebody?"

"Poor bastards." The older officer was less excited. "Too stupid to realize they're on the chopping block as well. You think they'll be allowed to live with what they know? And, Bert, we tell nobody. Everybody who's seen that little procession and who's in it are dead men. We say nothing. They never passed through here, we never saw them and we don't know anything about them. As you value your life Bert, keep your blooming trap shut."

Egilsstadir Airport, Iceland.

"I wish I knew how Nell and the others are doing." Igrat wore her mink coat, a pilot's silk scarf wrapped around her neck. She was still shivering with the biting cold. "For all we know, they've been caught already and this is all for nothing. And why do you have to go?"

"We need to have somebody who recognizes our people when we get there. Iggie, this can all go badly wrong. We'll just have to keep going and hope that it doesn't.'

"You made that up to justify going on this flight, didn't you? I know you. You're bored and this is a little adventure. You could stay here."

"I could, but there are good reasons for going. I've got a feeling we're going to be working pretty closely with our Captain LeMay for a long time and I want our relationship to start off on a sound footing. Going along with him will be a good way to do that. And yes, I am bored. So are we all; you know that."

"I also know that doing foolish things from boredom gets us killed." Igrat was near tears. "Isn't organizing this bombing campaign enough for you?"

"It will be, once we get things really moving. But this is different. It's actually doing something instead of sitting behind a desk." Stuyvesant caught the warning in Igrat's eyes and carried on smoothly. "Anyway, I've never ridden in a Flying Fortress before."

"Four hour flight." Captain LeMay spoke from behind Stuyvesant. "Seven-twenty nautical miles. We have a thirty percent fuel reserve. This is satisfactory."

Stuyvesant looked at the B-17C on the runway behind them. It had been fully repainted in British colors. The red-white-blue roundels stood out in the moonlight. "You know, those full-color markings show up pretty clearly. Can't we dim them down a bit?"

"Attract suspicion. The British are still using full-color markings. We look different and people start to ask questions."

Stuyvesant nodded. "When do we take off?"

"Sixteen hours time."

"I've arranged for some hot food to be ready and the barracks are heated. The Marines did a good job up here."

"I have no cause for complaint." LeMay nodded brusquely. "Eat and get some sleep. Miss Shafrid, you need it. You look like hell."

Igrat eyed his retreating back. "Quite the diplomat, isn't he?"

The numbers flowed past Achillea's eyes as the convoy headed north. A642, A63, A6120 and now the A58. The one blessing was that they'd only been through one more checkpoint, where the A6120 hand joined the A58; they'd just been waved through. "How are we doing?"

"Very well. We stay on this road until we hit the A1 at Boroughbridge, then we follow that road all the way north to a place called Melsonby. The A1 is dead straight most of the way, Achillea; it is a Roman road. A good augury, I think."

"I hope so."

"Then we have to follow a road called the A66 from Melsonby until we hit the A68. They're both Roman roads as well, and they take us all the way to a place called Culgaith where we change to the B6412 to Langwathby. From there, follow the A686 all the way north to Brampton, switch to the A6071 over the Scottish border and join the A7. That puts us barely seventy miles out. We just have to wiggle through some B class backroads to join the A74. Then, take the B743 and it drops us right into Prestwick airport. We are doing very well."

"I should hope so. My rear is getting stiff."

Gusoyn laughed. "If you think you have problems in this comfortable staff car, imagine what it must be like in those lorries. Sitting in the cab will be bad enough; the poor people in the back on those wooden benches will be feeling really bad by now."

"Can't we stop and give them a rest? Or change around a bit?"

"Not really. We will need to stop for gas . . . I am sorry, petrol . . . but we will be in public view then. I am a bit worried about the last leg. We will have to wriggle across country on B roads for a bit and that will be slow and we could get lost. At least they have put the road signs back. I was a bit worried last night that I could not find a way through on that last stretch."

"You'll manage it Gus; you always do." Achillea closed her eyes and let herself be lulled into sleep by the drumming of the road on the tire surfaces. She woke briefly at another checkpoint at Melsonby after being on the road for ten straight hours. She was also awake then the convoy commandeered a resupply of petrol at a station shortly afterwards. Idly, she wondered just how much chaos Gusoyn's casually-signed requisition would cause.

By the time she finally woke up again, the convoy was moving along a narrow country road. She shivered slightly and looked around at the surrounding countryside. "Where are we? And has the car got any heat?"

Gusoyn shook his head. "Get the car warm and I'll start going to sleep. We're at a place called Chanlockfoot, in Ayrshire, I think. We're doing the backroads wriggle now."

"Do you want me to take over?"

Gusoyn shook his head. "I've got the route fixed in my head and I know where I am. If I take a break, I'll get us hopelessly lost. The A74 is a few miles ahead and once we're on that, we're nearly there.

"Oh, hell, what is this?"

A tractor had got stuck pulling a cart across the road . Achillea felt Gusoyn stop the car. Every nerve in her body screamed warnings. She had her Thompson on her lap. Her hands moved quickly, checking her knives and her pistol. Sure enough, half a dozen men stood up from behind the stone walls. The ones who didn't have shotguns had hunting rifles.

"Well, sure enough, we have us a lorryload of blackshirts. Morag from the village said they were coming through. Now, all of you. Out of those vehicles and drop your guns."

Achillea reached down and dropped the Thompson. She didn't think much of it anyway. She was more worried about it going off than losing it. "Don't get hasty or you'll regret it."

"Aye, we'll regret shooting a full half dozen of you fascist bastards. Be payback for Spain, it will." The six men nodded and obviously agreed with their leader.

"You were with the International Brigade?" Achillea spoke quietly. If she could get within ten feet, she would have the rifle out of his hands before he knew what happened. He might have served with the International Brigade, probably had, but she knew he was no match for her.

"Aye, I was that. And saw you swine at work there too. Now all of you get on your knees."

Achillea thought for a second, then made a considered reply. "No. And you're wrong, we're not Blackshirts. We're fakes; imposters. We've got some people we're smuggling out of the country."

"You'll not fool me with that, lassie."

"Then take a look in the back of the first truck." Achillea was quite unaware she'd used the wrong word, but it made the leader of the group look sharply at her.

He walked to the back of the lorry. The sonorous, rolling tones of Winston Churchill echoed out. "She is telling you the truth and very glad I am to be able to confirm it." Achillea grinned to herself. Churchill didn't know it, but he had just saved six resistance fighters from getting killed.

"I'd heard you were killed." The heavy Scottish brogue was shaken.

"I am pleased to tell you that the reports of my death are greatly exaggerated. After sitting on a wooden bench in this lorry for eighteen hours, only my rear end is dead. The rest of me is very much alive."

The resistance leader walked back to Achillea. "How did you get through the checkpoints?"

"Mostly, they saw what they thought we were and waved us through. The others, we showed them these." She produced her fake badge and the forged orders.

The man pulled another badge from his pocket and compared the two. "These are nothing like the real ones." He was suspicious again.

"We know. We made them up, assuming that nobody would know what the real ones looked like." Achillea paused for a few seconds. "Is that a real one? How did you get it?"

"Took it off a Blackshirt who came this way. Don't know why he came, but we buried him in the woods anyway."

"How did you kill him?" Achillea was professionally interested.

"We didn't. We just buried him." Achillea looked at him and grinned. The man continued after returning the smile. "What's a lassie doing leading this?"

She looked at him stonily. "I'm not a lassie; I'm a Roman gladiator."

The man paused for a second then burst out laughing. "That's good. Roman gladiator indeed."

Achillea acknowledged the laugh. "The other thing is I'm not in charge; he is. Name's Gusoyn Rivers."

"I have got a deal for you." Gusoyn was back in the game now. "We have got eight Thompson guns and a dozen Webley revolvers, plus ammunition. All courtesy of the Sherwood Foresters.

"You come with us, show us to the A74 where we have to go and come with us to Prestwick. Then, you can have the guns and ammo. Start your resistance movement off nicely, I think. You can have the trucks and car as well, but I suggest you burn them."

"And we have a crate of hand grenades in the trunk of the staff car. You can have those as well." Achillea tossed them in as a sweetener. "Although for a resistance fighter, a pistol is the best weapon you can have."

"Tommy guns, grenades and revolvers. Billy Boy, this could put us in real business." The speaker, like any true Scotsman, found the idea of throwing hand grenades at invaders irresistible.

"Aye. You have a deal. We'll ride with you to Prestwick."

B-17C Flying Fortress "Swoose", North of Prestwick.

"How did the aircraft get its name?" Stuyvesant was curious.

"This one? It just popped into our minds. It seemed right somehow, almost as if she was telling us herself. Sometimes the crew will vote on a name or the aircraft commander will pick one by himself." Captain Archie Smith made some minute adjustments to the controls. "We'll be making our approach in ten minutes. What happens when we get there?"

87

"If everything has gone right, we'll be able to sell the idea that this is an aircraft being delivered to the RAF and has just flown in via the Greenland route. We have orders to pick up some cargo and passengers at Prestwick and fly them down to Abingdon where the aircraft will be accepted by the RAF. By the time we are missed, we'll be well on our way home."

"Those orders better be convincing. Any fighters at Prestwick?"

"The orders are. Written in best British bureaucratese by a leading British civil servant. Sir Humphrey Appleday no less. They are a masterpiece. As to fighters, as far as we can tell, just a detachment of Defiants."

"Just *Defiants*? Damn it, those things are a menace. They cut a squadron of Hun 109s to pieces over Dunkirk. With that power-operated turret, it can sit in one of our blind spots and riddle us. The Air Corps does a lot of talking, but these C-models aren't fit for combat. No armor, no self-sealing fuel tanks, blind spots all over. And we haven't got the crew to man the guns we do have anyway. Just Defiants, indeed." Smith shook his head at the inability of civilians to understand the realities of air combat.

"Archie, course one-eight-three and drop to six thousand feet." The voice came up from the navigation table.

"I'll bet you ten bucks we drop out of the clouds and the runway is dead ahead of us." Smith was grinning broadly.

Stuyvesant guessed this was a sucker bet and avoided it. "Captain LeMay is that good?"

"Best there is. You hear about the *Rex?* Six hundred plus mile flight to a moving target with him doing her final position by guesswork. Weather about as bad as it gets. He says, 'drop out of the clouds' and when we do, we're right on top of her. Drove the squids wild."

Prestwick Airfield Perimeter

"And who are you?" Sergeant Christopher McCulloch of the County of Fife Constabulary shone his torch into the Humber staff car. Only long practice stopped him from catching his breath when he recognized two of the inhabitants of the car.

Gusoyn recognized the Police Sergeant as well and wondered if McCulloch's presence here on the airport main gate was a coincidence. "Good evening, Chris. I have a letter for you."

He fished out the paper from Sir Humphrey Appleday that Igrat had brought over. McCulloch took it and read the brief note. It was a comprehensive request for safe conduct and contained a few allusions that left no doubt of its authenticity. He didn't know what was going on, but he did have a distinct idea he didn't want to.

"I see. Good luck."

Gusoyn put the Humber into gear and drove through the main gate as the candy-striped barrier lifted. Behind him, the two lorries followed suit.

B-17C Flying Fortress "Swoose", North of Prestwick

"Bring her around to one-two-six; drop to two thousand feet. Prepare for landing." LeMay's voice betrayed no stress at all. Stuyvesant was watching out of the cockpit, looking for the first glimpse of the runway. This was a straight-in landing, no messing around with approaches.

"Acknowledged. Flaps twenty degrees, undercarriage down. Prestwick Control, this is RAF Fortress. I on final approach after transatlantic delivery flight. We have cargo and passengers to pick up. Request permission to come straight in."

"Prestwick Control here. We do not have your arrival logged."

"Blasted bureaucrats. This Fortress was available so we were told to ferry it over while the Government was still sitting on its thumb. Now, do you want this bomber or don't you?"

There was a laugh on the other end of the radio. "We'll take anything right now. Bring her in."

"Landing lights on. Stuyvesant, flash the recognition code. Electrical panel, second row of switches, first from the left. That's the one."

Stuyvesant saw the runway suddenly appear as the Flying Fortress dropped out of the clouds. It was an occupied, operational base with Whitleys parked on the apron beside the runway. For all its apparent insanity, that was a key part in the deception. A bomber arriving at a deserted minor airfield somewhere was highly suspicious; one arriving at an operational bomber base was not. Stuyvesant took a quick look at the runway approaching under their nose and noted that the aircraft was perfectly lined up for landing. He started to flash the agreed signal as Smith looked at him and mouthed 'told you so.' On the perimeter of the airfield, a small line of three vehicles flashed its headlights in response. The knot in Stuyvesant's stomach started to dissolve slightly.

The aircraft bumped as the main wheels hit the ground; then it settled as the tail came down. By the time it had come to a halt, a staff car and two trucks were approaching from one direction and a single staff car from another. An officer got out of the latter and stalked over to the Flying Fortress. "May I see your orders please?" The question wasn't quite barked at Stuyvesant, who was still only half way out the entry hatch. But it was that of a man who wanted to be convinced, and wasn't quite sure what he should be seeing and what was better left unseen.

Stuyvesant handed him the folded orders. "The other Fortresses are still on the production line, but this one was ready, so we were told to bring it over. Our orders are to pick up some passengers and cargo here and fly them down to Abingdon near Oxford." He spoke with a British accent that sounded almost painfully strangled.

The RAF officer read the papers. The combination of Whitehall Bureaucratese and Stuyvesant's obviously aristocratic accent caused his attitude to thaw noticeably. "Well, these seem genuine enough. Only Whitehall could come up with something this jawbreaking. Odd they painted her in Fighter Command camouflage though."

"Tell you the truth, Sir, I think they just slapped the first paint job they could on her. Between us, I've heard the Government is going to embargo the supply of these aircraft and Boeing won't get paid for them until somebody takes them over. So they wanted this one over and out of their doors before that happens. And, of course, the RAF wants every Fortress it can get. This is the new model, by the way. Have you seen the improved belly gun position? Captain Smith, show the Flight Lieutenant the new gun mountings."

Smith took the RAF officer to the rear of the aircraft and started to show him the twin .50 caliber machine guns in the ventral bathtub. That way, he didn't see the portly figure being hustled out of the trucks and squeezed through the hatch into the aircraft.

Once Churchill was on board, everybody else could behave more openly. Underneath the aircraft, the bomb bay doors whined as they opened. A team of men from the trucks started to pass crates inside. Once the last crate was in, they got back into the trucks and the little convoy left the airfield.

"You want an escort?" The RAF officer was definitely impressed by the Fortress. "Forgive my bad manners, I never introduced myself. Name's Cheshire, Leonard Cheshire."

"Archie Smith. Leonard, this is a Flying Fortress. We've got twin .50s in the belly, another twin in the radio cabin and single guns in the waist and nose. We could escort your fighter though."

"Bloody Yanks." A bomber baron to his fingertips, Cheshire loved the jab at Fighter Command; the insult was affectionate. "You're blind astern, though. You really need a tail turret on these things. Have a good flight down south. Do you know where these birds are going to be based? The Bomber Command base at Tangmere?"

Smith nodded and Cheshire gave a curious smile. The crew boarded the Fortress and went through the pre-flight checks. Eventually, Stuyvesant breathed a sigh of relief as the now-heavily loaded bomber turned back onto the runway and started to accelerate down its length. As the wheels lifted off, the last knot of tension dissolved from his stomach. Nell and Achillea were in the radio cabin; Achillea was readying the twin .50s in case of any problems. Gusoyn was aft, by the waist gun positions. All the other passengers were spread out around the aircraft. Churchill was taking a swig of brandy out of a hip flask he'd produced once safely on board.

"Flight time four hours; we will maintain twelve thousand feet all the way." LeMay's voice from the navigation table showed no sign of relief or even pleasure. Stuyvesant guessed that to him this was just another job done to the meticulous standards he demanded of himself and others.

Royal Apartments, Windsor Castle

It was called protective custody, but it felt more like imprisonment. Likewise, the Police Auxiliaries at the door were technically there for security but were actually jailors. Albert Frederick Arthur George Windsor, better known as His Majesty, King George VI blamed nobody but himself for his situation. He had blundered; blundered so badly that the scale of his error left him near suicidal. In his eyes, the error was so egregious, so utterly damning, that it made the faults of his predecessor seem inconsequential in comparison. To the King, his backing of Halifax against Churchill in the May leadership contest had set the stage for what would happen barely six weeks later. That should cost him his throne; the King believed that it would if there was any justice in the world.

"Major Charles Frederick Aubrey de Vere Beauclerk of the Sherwood Foresters regiment, Your Majesty."

The King pulled himself out of his brown study and greeted the young Army officer who had been ushered into the room. "My Earl of Burford, how go these sad days with you?"

Charles Beauclerk glanced around the room and touched his ear. The King nodded slightly. He was not bereft of resources and some of them had been used to check for listening devices in this room. "Your Majesty, it gives me great pleasure to report that the rightful Prime Minister of your realm, the Right Honorable Winston Spencer Churchill, has escaped from the United Kingdom and is presently on his way to Canada where he will declare a government-in-exile loyal to Your Majesty."

The King felt a fierce joy run through him. Somehow, the catastrophic error that cursed the nation he led seemed to lessen slightly. Now was the time to build upon the moment. "You bring me most welcome news, Your Grace. Now, I must charge you with the most important mission you are ever likely to receive. I have a message that must go out on the midday broadcast tomorrow. Most importantly, this message must be delivered to Daventry unseen and unread by anybody who purports to be in authority in this country. I charge you to deliver this message in time for that broadcast, protecting its contents with your life and accepting no obstruction in fulfilling this charge. Do you understand this mission, Your Grace?"

"I do, Your Majesty."

Government House, Calcutta, India, 7:30 AM, 29th July, 1940

"It's come, Martyn. We have a message from the King."

"Eric, what does it say?" Sir Martyn Sharpe's voice was urgent and a strange mixture of hope and foreboding. The contents of this message could spell victory or defeat for his efforts to keep India in the war and all the consequences that were attached to that policy.

"It was broadcast from the main overseas BBC short wave overseas transmitter at Daventry in place of the usual midday news. The communique is

91

in two parts. The first a spoken message addressed to all, and the second transmitted in encoded Morse directed at the various Dominion and Colonial governments. They sent the latter twice, each time in a different cipher, both of which were specifically for the use by the Crown. There's no doubt about its authenticity; this is the real thing."

"Eric, will you tell me now what is in that message, or I will have it forced out of you?" Sharpe knew he was being teased by his old friend, but that didn't make it any easier.

"It's the living will of the Crown. The effective part of the communique reads . . . " Haohoa took a deep breath and read the message exactly as it was written on the message strip he was holding. "Be it known that it is our will that in the event of direct communication with the Crown being severed. The Powers of the Crown will pass through the direct Representative to the DomCol Cabinet in Committee in trust George VI Rex."

"Now just what the hell does that mean?" Sir Martyn stared at Sir Eric as both men tried to decipher the cryptic communication. Then, slowly, a smile spread over Sir Martyn's face. "He's covering for us; that's what it means. It's a safety clause, intended to cover the actions we have already taken, namely ignoring Halifax and Co, as long as the King remains under the control of the Halifax Government. I think we're being told to wait on events and break loose only if and when we absolutely have to."

"There's more." Sir Eric's expression changed to that of a cat that had just found itself the sole heir to a cream factory. "Last night, Winnie went on the air, from Canada."

"Winnie? You mean Churchill has turned up?"

"That he has. In Canada, and a mighty force has been unleashed upon the world. He went out on short wave radio there as well, announcing the formation of a government-in-exile in Canada and damning Halifax with bell, book and candle. You listen to this, Martyn."

Once again, Sir Eric paused before reading the contents of the message. When he started, it was in a copy of Churchill's rolling tones. "I stand at the head of a Government-in-Exile representing all Parties in the State: all creeds, all classes, every recognizable section of opinion. We are ranged beneath the Crown of our ancient monarchy. We are supported by the whole life-strength of the British race in every part of the world and of all our associated peoples and of all our well-wishers in every land, doing their utmost night and day, giving all, daring all, enduring all. To the utmost. To the end. This is no war of chieftains or of princes, of dynasties or national ambition; it is a war of peoples and of causes. There are vast numbers, in every land, who will render faithful service in this war, but whose names will never be known, whose deeds will never be recorded. This is a War of the Unknown Warriors; but let all strive without failing in faith or in duty, and the dark curse of Hitler will be lifted from our age."

"Eric, this changes everything. That went out twelve hours before the King made his speech, so His Majesty must have known its contents. The Canadian Government must have known what Churchill was going to say as well, so the fact this was transmitted means it has official support. Take this speech together with the Daventry message and it's as clear an indication as we are going to get that we should fight on. Halifax is being completely cut out of the picture." He paused for a second and caught his breath. "This is going to be an interesting Cabinet meeting."

Student's Canteen, Nottingham University, Nottingham, United Kingdom

"You'd better divide these up between you." Rachael Cohen put the sideplate with her two pork sausages on it on the table. "Four of you; I make that half each. David, will you do the honors please?"

David Newton exchanged glances with the three other students on the table. With food rationing in place, a half-sausage was a princely gift. The problem was, they all knew Rachael was going short on food because the canteen offered no dishes that met her dietary laws. It wasn't the canteen staff's fault, since they were trapped by the rationing system as well. They did what they could and had given her extra portions of veggies to make up for the food she couldn't eat. Newton reached out and carefully divided each of the sausages in half. It was an old tradition; the person who divided the food up would be the last to choose which portion he wanted. It made for a scrupulously careful division. "Thank you Rachael. Are you sure there's nothing we can get you to make up for it?"

She shook her head and smiled. "That's very kind, but keeping kosher is important to me. With everything the way it is, we can either stand up and be counted or run and hide. I hate hiding."

There was another exchange of glances between the four students. Somehow, they'd get hold of a kosher meal for Rachael. Freddie Williams broke the silence. "Any word from Germany, Rachael?"

She shook her head sadly; the joy of a second ago faded quickly. "None at all. We thought that when the war ended and communications with Germany improved, we'd hear from Aunty Becky and her family, but there's nothing. My mother is getting frightened. Daddy is just worried and says we should give thanks for being over here where we're safe."

"Did you hear Winnie's speech last night?" Colin Thomas sounded excited. "He tore into That Man like a berserker. Shook him like a terrier shakes a rat."

Thomas loved his similes and his overuse of them brought a collective smile back to the group. George Jones looked around carefully. There were rumors that the Black Shirts had undercover people hiding in the university. People were beginning to watch what they said, even in private. "I couldn't believe Winnie was dead. He just wasn't the kind to just go to the grave in silence. I wonder how he got out?"

"They say he drove from Windsor to Portsmouth and then walked to Southampton and caught the Clipper to Shannon and New York."

"That's not what I heard." Colin Thomas frowned. "I heard he went to Holyhead and took a fishing boat to Ireland before catching a Clipper at Shannon."

George Jones shook his head. "I heard from somebody in the know that a Yank submarine picked him up from Portsmouth and took him to Canada."

"Why would the Yanks send a submarine?" Newton sounded doubtful. To him, the story just wasn't plausible. In fact, none of them were. Something smelt a little off about the whole business. "Anyway, that really doesn't matter. The important thing is that somebody's challenging That Man at last."

Cabinet Room, Government House, Calcutta, India, 11:30 AM, 29th July, 1940

"So, Winston is back." Lord Linlithgow spoke thoughtfully. "Have we any idea how?"

"The official story is that he was warned of the protective custody warrant issued by the Halifax government and went to ground somewhere in North Wales. Once the heat had died down a little, he got a fishing boat to take him over to Northern Ireland. From there, he crossed the border to the South and laid low again. Then, he caught a Pan-American Clipper from Shannon to New York and got the train from there to Ottawa. I should add there are other stories in the wind, including him going south to Portsmouth and then to the Channel Islands, after which he was taken out by Royal Navy submarine. Yet another version has him going out via France and Spain to Portugal and then another Pan-American Clipper." Sir Eric Haohoa put the text of Churchill's message on the Cabinet Room table. "This went out by short-wave radio. The very fact that it was allowed to do so means that Canada at least has repudiated the Halifax government."

"They have no authority to do so." Sir Richard Cardew was emphatic. "What DomCol says is the final word. Their decisions must be obeyed."

"One of the primary lessons of every commander, be he military or political, is to know when not to obey orders." General Claude Auchinleck, Commander-in-Chief of the Indian Army and thus a member of the Executive Council of the Governor-General of India, spoke very carefully. "The actions of Lord Halifax do not sit well with me."

"Then resign, retire and leave the role of government to loyal officers." Cardew spoke nastily, anger and contempt dripping from every syllable.

"Sir Richard, General Auchinleck is a soldier of the utmost integrity. He voices, as is his duty, thoughts which most of us entertain. The purpose of a council meeting is to hear all opinions, weigh all the evidence available to us and make a decision that reflects our considered opinion on what is best for the people whose governance we hold in trust. We are not a rubber stamp for the officials in DomCol and while I sit here, we never will be. Is that clear?"

Cardew grunted noncommittally and Lord Linlithgow let it pass. He was tempted to fire the Cabinet Secretary, but it was politically unwise to do so. The man represented a significant following outside this room and removing him from the bounds of collective responsibility would be counter-productive. "And so we move to the key business of the day. The Daventry Message. Sir Martyn, will you read the key part of His Majesty's message out please?"

"The Powers of the Crown will pass through the direct Representative to the Col/Dom Cabinet in Committee in trust George VI Rex."

"What the devil does that mean?" HH was bemused.

Sir Martyn looked at Lord Linlithgow and got a brief nod. "Well, 'The Powers of the Crown' are constitutional and laid down the Constitution and the Common Law; there is no real argument here. The next bit, 'will pass through the direct Representative to the Col/Dom'. The direct representative in the case of the Dominions is the Governor General, and the Crown's powers pass through him anyway. Col/Dom is a simple contraction of Colonial and Dominion. We've used it that way ourselves this morning, so there is not much to argue about there either. It's the last few words, 'to the Col/Dom Cabinet in Committee in trust George VI Rex,' where all the trouble begins. The way this message was sent, there is no punctuation in it and inserting commas in the passage allows it to be manipulated in any number of ways.

"If we add a comma after 'Committee', the message now reads 'to the Col/Dom Cabinet in Committee, in trust George VI Rex.' By associating 'Col/Dom' with 'Cabinet' it transfers power to the local authorities. Furthermore, by reducing the words "in trust' to a parting salute, it also removes a possible condition imposed by the His Majesty on that power. Essentially, this echoes the Canadian repudiation of the Halifax government. We should bear in mind that this message went out twelve hours after Churchill's message from Canada. I believe it is adding His Majesty's stamp of approval on the Canadian actions and encouraging all the other Dominions to do the same."

"I disagree." Cardew had moderated his tone, but the simmering hatred was still there. "I read this message differently. I believe a comma should be placed after 'Col/Dom' to read 'to the Col/Dom, Cabinet in Committee in trust George Rex.' This makes it quite clear that the final authority still resides in Col/Dom as a representative of the Cabinet in London. It identifies the only Cabinet with a general purview as being the one in London."

Harold Hartley shook his head. "That would rather defeat the whole purpose of the statement in context. Either way we read this, though, it opens an even bigger can of worms. What does 'The Powers of the Crown will pass through the direct Representative to the Col/Dom Cabinet in Committee in trust George VI Rex,' mean? The way I see it, the only legally supportable interpretation is the literal one. The authority of the Crown is to pass through the Governor General to the Cabinet; there it is to be held in trust by the Cabinet, sitting as a Committee of Trustees. In short, Your Excellency, the red-hot potato has just landed in your lap and we, your cabinet, can advise you as trustees. And, as you pointed out, we rule here as trustees of the Indian people."

"Thank you, HH." Lord Linlithgow hesitated, "I think . . . in this situation, it is apparent that we have to wait upon developments. His Majesty does nothing without careful thought and I believe the ambiguity of the Daventry Message is deliberate. It authorizes us to either follow London's lead or strike out on our own as is dictated by local circumstances and the pressure of events. We must take that as our lead and not commit ourselves in any direction, until the way forward is more clearly defined. On that note, I will declare this meeting over.

Sir Martyn, will you remain behind for a few minutes please?"

Once the room was empty, Lord Linlithgow relaxed slightly. "You're right, Sir Martyn. It is clear to me that the Daventry Message gives us the authority to cut loose. What is the present position of the Congress Party?"

"Your Excellency, on independence, they still remain adamant that the working principle should be 'as soon as possible,' but this does represent a major shift in their position from the original 'now'. Nehru is prepared to accept a two year official transfer period. During this time, he will hold the position of your Deputy Viceroy while you teach him everything involved in the post. Might I add, in passing, he and many members of his executive were quite appalled at the amount and variety of work involved in the administration of this country. At the end of two years, the position of Viceroy will be abolished and that of President instituted. Nehru will, subject to elections to be held at a later date, be that President. You will hold the position of Chief of Staff to the President and will continue teaching him how to run the country. Once that transition has taken place, the Cabinet will consist of Indian officials with us acting as advisors and facilitators. This will continue until such time as the new government is running smoothly. Congress expects that to be at least a decade. At some point in that process, India will leave the Commonwealth."

"That is a remarkable plan." Lord Linlithgow was genuinely impressed at the acceptance of a drawn-out transfer of power. "I am astonished that Nehru has accepted it."

Sir Martyn hesitated. "Your Excellency, our discussions were in good faith, both sides wanting what was best for India. We have all put aside our personal beliefs and opinions in pursuit of a solution that would serve the greater good."

"Does that greater good extend to continuing the war?"

"No, Sir. It does not. Nehru is personally convinced that India should stay in the war as a means of clearly marking the break with London. Getting the Congress Party to go along with him on that will be another matter entirely. For that, we must hope for an act of God."

Public Bar, The White Hart, Nottingham

"Perhaps they weren't so stupid, Bert. Perhaps they were very clever people indeed."

The police officer who had been in charge of the road block a few nights earlier was putting things together very quickly. "They made sure we kept quiet, didn't they? Put the fear of God into us. And have you heard of their Blackshirt unit? Because I haven't. They just appeared, took Winnie away and vanished. Nothing we can do about it now."

"We can lift a glass to them, Alf."

"Aye, we can do that. And they deserve the toast."

Foreign Office, Government House, Calcutta, India, 4:30 PM, 29th July, 1940

"Sir Martyn, there are unannounced visitors for you. Sir Josiah Crosby, the British Ambassador to Thailand, and the Ambassador-Plenipotentiary from the Kingdom of Thailand." Sir Martyn Sharpe's private secretary had a strange grin on his face. "They seek an immediate interview on a matter of the utmost importance to the security of India."

Sharpe looked up. Sir Josiah was an old friend of many years standing and would be welcome at a moment's notice at any time. The mysterious Ambassador-Plenipotentiary was another matter. Sir Martyn was curious to see what he looked like and, more importantly, what he was up to. "I will see them both right away. Could you hold them for a couple of minutes, with extreme courtesy, and then usher them in? I wish Sir Eric Haohoa to attend this meeting."

He picked up the telephone and called Sir Eric. "Eric, Sir Josiah and the Ambassador from Thailand are here. Yes, that one. Could you drop in please? I have a feeling you might want to attend to this."

Once Sir Eric had arrived, the guests were shown in. To Sir Martyn's complete amazement, the Ambassador-Plenipotentiary was a young woman; short, with close-cropped hair. She was actually quite attractive, although her face exuded power and character rather than conventional beauty. She was wearing the traditional long skirt, tunic and sash of Thai women, but the fabric was deep green silk and the outfit was obviously very expensive.

Sir Martyn gave little sign of the surprise that had taken over most of his mind. "Sir Josiah, good to see you again. Madam Ambassador, it is an honor and a privilege to meet you at last. May I thank you for the copy of the Armistice Agreement? So far, it is still the only full copy we have received of that document."

"I am not surprised." The Ambassador's voice was a level contralto. "If I signed a document like that on behalf of my country, I would want it kept secret as well."

In the background, Sir Eric snorted with laughter at the quip. He also had been shaken by the identity of the Ambassador, but he was getting a strange feeling that her presence on the scene would liven the situation up no end. And he liked her sense of humor.

"What may we do for you?" Sir Martyn had arranged for tea and refreshments to be served.

"It's more what the Ambassador can do for you, Martyn." Sir Josiah sipped at a cup of tea. "Her Highness has acquired a document that is both intriguing and deeply alarming from the point of view of Indian security. How she acquired this document, I do not know but I have inspected it most closely, along with our experts from the Embassy. We have no hesitation in vouching for its authenticity."

"The document Sir Josiah refers to is a report by one SS *Standartenführer* Odwin Noth. Essentially, it proposes that Germany's next move should be a strike through Turkey and the Middle East to assault India. It envisages linking up with one Subhas Chandra Bose and turning India into a German colony. Noth believed that an attack on Russia would be a disaster for Germany and evolved this plan as an alternative. Our sources suggest that this plan was well-received by the highest political circles in Germany. I have both the original document that you may authenticate and an English translation. Personally, I prefer the latter; I find trying to read Fraktur gives me a headache."

She handed the Noth Plan over to Sir Martyn. He started to read the translation and his eyebrows lifted sharply. He looked at her and then started reading more closely. "If I read this correctly, then any acceptance by us of the Armistice signed in London would be meaningless. The Germans are going to invade us anyway, and all dropping out of the war would achieve would be to deprive us of any chance we might have of defending ourselves."

"Certainly, I would not place any great faith in German expressions of good intentions."

"On that, we may agree. Madam Ambassador, we need to see Lord Linlithgow immediately. May I impose upon you to wait here until I can arrange a meeting? It should only be a few minutes."

Cabinet Room, Government House, Calcutta, India, 6:30 PM, 29th July, 1940

"Well, it's a very courageous plan." General Auchinleck put the Noth Plan down with a certain degree of reluctance. "Our people have confirmed the authenticity of this report and the accuracy of the translations?"

"Our experts here have checked the translation and it is accurate. Authenticating the document will take longer, but Sir Josiah's people in

Bangkok have done so and are prepared to vouch for it. That is not the question though. What I must know is, does this represent a practical plan?"

"In the final analysis, this is what Alexander did. The invasion of India part anyway. I would say that our SS *Standartenführer* Odwin Noth is a keen student of history. To attempt this with a modern army would be an operation fraught with peril, but I would hesitate to say it could not be done. I would merely say that I would not like to be the officer commanded to undertake it."

"But it is practical?"

"It would require skills of the highest order and an unprecedented effort. I do not say that it could not be done, but I doubt any country's ability to undertake this kind of operation. Of course, a political leadership that believes will is a substitute for capability may well be tempted by it." Auchinleck thought carefully. "No, it is not a practical plan, but that does not mean that it does not represent German intentions or that they will not try it."

Lord Linlithgow thought carefully. "Madam Ambassador, you have done us a great service by bringing this plan to us. I would like to ask how you acquired it, along with one or two other documents you have sent us of late, but to do so might cause embarrassment. I will ask instead, what do you seek in exchange for this service?"

The Ambassador leaned forward in her seat. "Something very simple. At the moment, the administration in Washington views my country with great disfavor. Why, we cannot tell; but we believe they misunderstand our efforts to modernize our country and stand on our own feet as members of the international community. We believe that Secretary of State Cordell Hull has misinterpreted these as being a move towards a fascist style of government. Nothing could be further from the truth. We see America, not Germany, as the example to be emulated. But, American policy towards us may yet force us into associating with powers we view with distaste. We would ask you to use your good offices to intercede with the Americans, to speak with them and to invite Secretary Hull to our country so that he may meet with our leaders and see for himself that, far from tending to fascism, it is to his country's standards of freedom and free enterprise that we aspire."

Lord Linlithgow spoke with gravity. "In as much as we are able, we will do as you ask. Whether it has the results that you desire, we cannot guarantee. As to the Noth plan, we will watch German actions. If they show German intentions are directed to this region, then we must assume that the others projected by SS *Standartenführer* Odwin Noth will follow."

German Auxiliary Cruiser Atlantis, *Off Ceylon, Indian Ocean*

"Two stuffed animals! We intercept a ship loaded to the gunwales with whisky and all you manage to bring back are two stuffed animals? Is this proper hospitality to our undersea friend here?" *Kapitän zur See* Bernhard Rogge was only partly simulating anger at the news. A supply of good whisky would have been a valuable contributor to morale upon his ship. The rage was partly feigned though. He and his ship were in an awkward position. The British capitulation had left them stranded in a world where they weren't quite certain who was the enemy and who was not. By an ironic turn of fate, they were in much the same position as their intended prey.

"The Captain of the *Kemmendine* claimed to be a British ship carrying a British bonded cargo to Burma. He refused to breach the bond on that cargo."

"Good for him." Rogge felt nothing but respect for a man who would continue with his duty under such threatening circumstances. Lying under the six 5.9-inch guns carried by *Atlantis* was the epitome of threatening.

"I felt so too, Sir. And in view of our orders not to interfere with British ships or cargoes, I accepted his refusal. He did give us these two stuffed animals though. A personal gift, he said."

"How kind of him. We'll hang one of them in the wardroom where we will admire him while we drink glasses of water. Take them below, Lieutenant."

Otto, my apologies. I am afraid a stuffed animal and oil fuel is all we can offer you at this time. And some fresh food, of course."

Captain Otto Kretschmer nodded in appreciation of the efforts that had been made on his behalf. A raider depended upon stealth and unpredictability for its success. Compelling one to be at a specific point at a given time was a serious threat to its survival. The problem was that his *U-99* was low on fuel. Not getting resupplied meant not getting home. A few weeks earlier, when *U-99* had set out on her maiden voyage, the idea of operating in the Indian Ocean had a hypnotic fascination. It would force the British to spread their anti-submarine forces over a huge area, weakening their power in the vital North Atlantic. Then, the Armistice had been signed and British ships were off-limits.

Captain Rogge returned to studying his charts. The truth was that the presence of both *Atlantis* and *U-99* out here was fundamentally pointless. *Atlantis* was doing little more than mark time while the world situation tried to resolve itself. *U-99* just wanted to go home. Rogge decided that his highest priority now was keeping out of people's way while the naval command in Berlin decided what he should do next. "Otto, good luck on your voyage home and give our love to the Fatherland. Helm, as soon as *U-99* is clear, steer one-eight-zero. We'll head due south for a day or two."

Rogge returned to his bridge wing and looked out across the sea, allowing the movement of his ship and the sound of his engines to sooth him. He watched *U-99* pull away and then slip beneath the waves. He didn't envy her the long, dangerous voyage home. The truth was that he wasn't sure if he wanted to go back to Germany at all. He had an uneasy feeling that the new Germany was no place for an honorable man. Lulled into near-sleep by the timeless rhythm of the sea, he very nearly didn't notice the smudge of black smoke upon the horizon. To his relief, he was still able to sound the alert before the lookouts spotted the new arrival. At first, he expected the distant smoke to vanish as the other ship went on its way. Those hopes proved fruitless. The cloud grew in size and was soon unmistakable. The other ship was steering a course that would bring her very close to *Atlantis*.

Reluctantly, Rogge pressed the alarm button. There was no external sign of the result. Beneath the ship's protective disguise, her 5.9-inch guns and torpedo tubes were being manned. She had two tubes on each beam and they could well be the deciding weapon if ever *Atlantis* had to fight for her survival. Her two twin 37mm guns and four 20mm weapons would probably be less valuable, but their crews were ready and waiting anyway. Oddly, the only gun that wasn't being manned was the single 3-inch weapon sitting uncovered and exposed on the bow. That was there because an unarmed ship in the middle of a war would be suspicious in its own right, but the gun was really useless.

Rogge looked at the cloud of smoke again. Now, there was obviously a ship underneath it; a long, low, lean ship. Not a heavy-hulled ponderous merchantman. Rogge knew that he was looking at the one thing he wished to see least of all, a warship. And out here, very few warships indeed were friendly.

"Sir, medium sized ship. Two gun turrets forward; two aft. Two funnels; catapult and aircraft between them. A modified *Leander* class cruiser, I think."

"Australian." That was something Rogge really did not want to see. The situation was confused enough already. A British ship would be bound by the terms of the Armistice, or so Rogge believed. Hoped, anyway. He had heard that the Royal Navy station forces had put themselves under the command of the local Dominion governments, not the authorities in London. But, the Dominions had maintained a steady silence over the whole issue. Were they still at war with Germany? No peace had been agreed with them, but London had said its word held for the Dominions. Germany had agreed and was also of the opinion the war was over. Only, the Dominions had remained silent.

Rogge watched the cruiser close in. He wasn't surprised to see her sheer off when she was around 10,000 meters away. He knew what Admiralty standing orders were when intercepting suspect merchant ships: stand off and cover with guns. Shoot at the first sign of a suspicious act. The cruiser was shower a proper, professional caution and 10,000 meters put the advantage firmly on her side. He watched the guns in the twin turrets foreshorten as the mounts were trained on *Atlantis*; Rogge also could see sailors on the upper deck leaning against the rails, watching the action play out. Obviously, the cruiser was not at action stations . . . . . yet. That changed as he watched. The sudden flurry on her decks showed that she was going to battle stations.

"Signal, sir. The cruiser has hoisted signal IK. Beware of cyclone, hurricane or typhoon. That doesn't make much sense." The signals officer paused. "She's signalling again, sir. Signal reads NNJ. She's asking for our signal letters."

"Play for time. We might yet bluff our way out of this. Make sure all guns are loaded and the torpedoes ready to fire." Rogge drummed his fingers on the rail.

"Another signal, sir. By signal lamp this time. It reads VH. That's an order to display our signal letters."

"Very well. Hoist PKQI." Those were the signal letters for *Atlantis'* cover identity, the Dutch MV *Abbekerk.* By now the Australian cruiser was clearly expecting trouble. Her Captain had sensed something amiss, although Rogge had no idea what it was.

"She's the *Hobart,* sir. Signalling again. Signal reads IIKP. They're ordering us to reveal our secret sign and prepare to be boarded."

"That must have been that IK signal. We just got the middle of it."

"Another message by signal lamp. We are ordered to heave-to and prepare to be boarded immediately."

Rogge knew his standing orders at this point and they were clear. Under no circumstances was he to allow his ship to be boarded. That left only one other option.

"Hoist the German naval ensign, drop the screens and open fire, every gun that can bear. Fire torpedoes as soon as the crews have a good aim."

Australian Cruiser HMAS **Hobart,** *Off Ceylon, Indian Ocean*

"Just what the hell is that damned merchie playing at?" Captain Harry Howden was frustrated. "We've been signalling them for the better part of half an hour and all they do is hoist some unintelligible nonsense. PKQI? That's the *Abbekerk* and she's in Batavia with engine trouble. Has been for weeks."

The movement on the ship in front of *Hobart* grabbed his attention. The German naval ensign was breaking out from the stern while metal screens were falling down. They revealed guns that belched orange flashes Howden knew to be medium-caliber gunfire. The howl of approaching shells confirmed that impression. The first two shots were clean misses. One fell short; the other screamed between the two funnels and exploded in the sea beyond. Misses they might have been, but they were still close enough to send fragments pattering against *Hobart's* hull.

"It's the Hun raider *Kemmendine* warned us about! For God's sake, open fire."

Howden's words were interrupted by a second pair of shots; this time, from the centerline guns mounted fore and aft on the raider. These missed as well. Again by a hair's breadth, but enough to turn what could have been catastrophic damage into the pattering of fragments against armor. The raider

102

had got off the first shots, but the long range and her crude fire control had robbed her of the decisive early blow she had hoped for.

In reply, *Hobart* squeezed out a four-round half-salvo that was just a touch short. A second half-salvo was a fraction over, but the cruiser now had the range.

"Make revolutions for 28 knots; bring us around in front of her. All guns, fire for effect. Full salvos."

The orders made sense and *Hobart* leapt to obey them. Her stern dug in; the ship shaking as her engines powered up. Everybody knew that converted merchant ships like the raider had their guns on the beam. The British armed merchant cruisers were the same. That meant they were almost blind ahead. At most, one gun could be brought to bear to *Hobart*'s eight.

Through the vibration of the engines and the beginning of her bows swinging, Howden felt the shudder as all eight guns crashed out a salvo. Four of the shots hit square into the German raider's hull, starting fires that quickly stained the sky black. They crashed into the raider's waterline, penetrating her hull and knocking out her engines.

On the bridge, Howden cheered his gun crews on. The six-inch turrets settled into a steady routine that methodically blew the raider apart. This was what every cruiser captain dreamed of: a raider caught cold and under his guns. His only regret was that nobody paid out prize money any more.

"Get a radio message out. Signal we've been attacked by a German raider. We're returning fire and we've got her, by George."

Control Room, U-99, Off Ceylon, Indian Ocean

"Periscope depth. Right now."

Kretschmer almost snarled the order out. His submarine had much better hydrophones that they were normally given credit for and the thunder of gunfire had been clearly audible to *U-99* cruising nearby. The scope ran up. He did the submariner's swing, a rapid scan that gathered as much information as possible while minimizing exposure. That brief swing told him everything he needed to know.

"*Atlantis* is gone. She's burning like a torch up there." The vast pyre of black smoke had been unmistakable. "There's a cruiser close by. She has our auxiliary cruiser under fire."

Kretschmer paused for a second. His eyes focused on the stuffed animal that he had been given just a few minutes earlier. Making a rendezvous was deadly dangerous for an auxiliary cruiser. Somehow this one had leaked out. *How else had a cruiser been on scene?*

"We should even this match up a bit. Prepare Tubes One to Four, target is . . . . range two thousand meters, bearing one-three-five, speed twenty six knots. Course one hundred. Fire One . . . . ."

103

Australian Cruiser HMAS "Hobart", Off Ceylon, Indian Ocean

Howden watched *Hobart's* aft six-inch guns fire, inflicting yet more damage on the already-battered raider. That was when he saw the white streaks on the water, heading for his ship. The first two passed ahead of him. The second pair were running straight and true. Despite the frantic effort to turn into them, it was too late. The range was too short.

The two torpedoes slammed into *Hobart* with almost surgical precision. One hit just forward of "A" turret and near the ASDIC compartment. That was the weakest point on the ship's hull. It ripped a hole in the side that extended down below the ship's spine. Her bows started to break off and angled down.

The other torpedo hit the screws, mangling the shafts and jamming the rudder hard over. *Hobart* veered hard to port, completely out of control. For a moment it looked as if the Australian ship was trying to ram the raider. It was an illusion, since *Hobart* was already out of control. The torpedo hit aft jammed the two stern turrets in train. With her forward turrets already mangled wreckage, her main armament was theoretically useless. Yet, somehow, the crew in the forward turrets managed to keep firing. They thumped their last shells into the hull of the burning raider.

It was merely a gesture of defiance and Howden knew it. His ship was shattered by the torpedo hits. Her bows were on the verge of separating and his machinery was useless. His ship was going down. As soon as the bows went completely, she would slide under the water. There was only one thing left to do.

He took a look at the raider whose torpedoes he believed had created this havoc. She was dead in the water as well, burning furiously and had ceased fire. That, at least, was a small mercy. *Hobart* continued to limp away from the scene of the battle, out of control and unable to change speed or steer. Howden sighed and gave his final order as her commander.

"Abandon Ship."

German Auxiliary Cruiser Atlantis, Off Ceylon, Indian Ocean

"Sir, main machinery is out of action. The firefighting system has failed, and the fires are out of control. The temperature in the mine storage compartment is rising steadily and we can do nothing to stop it. The ship is going to blow up."

Rogge looked at his ship. *Atlantis* was belching black smoke all along her length and listing severely. She was also dead in the water. That settled the matter for him. She was finished.

"Very well, Lieutenant. Order the men to abandon ship. Get the wounded into the life rafts and launch as many lifeboats as we have left. Spread the men out between them and put officers within each."

He looked at his ship again, and then across the sea to where *Hobart* was limping away. She was sinking as well; there was no doubt of that. The two torpedo hits that had come from nowhere left her with bows that were moving separately from the rest of the ship and clearly working free. Her course was erratic as her wrecked screws and rudder interacted. Rogge could see the surviving crew beginning to abandon ship. One question kept running through his mind.

What have we done?

Almost three hundred of his crew survived the battle. They managed to pull clear of the burning wreck that had once been *Atlantis* and survived the great explosion that had sent her down. Dusk was beginning to settle when the first patrol plane from Trincomalee turned up. A Short Singapore flying boat, it circled the column of lifeboats on the sea for a few minutes, obviously radioing the position of the little convoy to surface rescue ships. Then, it flew away. Rogge saw it starting to circle another area of sea. *The survivors of the cruiser*, he guessed. He looked over the other men in his lifeboat and shook his head. It had not been a good day.

Parliament House, Canberra, Australia

As the MP's settled in after lunch, the Honorable John 'Sol' Rosevear surveyed the chamber with a good deal of satisfaction. There was no doubt this was their time. Labour was ascendent; the Tories in utter disarray. Even if the Government rested on a wafer thin majority, they were as safe as houses. No one was in the mood for another change of government so soon after the fall of Menzies.

If there was one fly in his soup, it was purely factional. The hard Left of the party was in control. If that didn't sit to well with Rosevear, it had put him in the speaker's chair as a sop to the Labor Right. Things could have been a good deal worse. *We can get some bloody good work done here; opportunities like this don't come along too often,* thought Rosevear to himself. *If Red Johnny doesn't make a mess of it.*

"The House recognizes the Honorable Prime Minister"

John Curtin grinned up at the Speaker as he stood confidently and strode the few paces to the Government dispatch box like a man walking on air. "Mister Speaker, in light of yet another royal abdication of responsibilities and recent events in Europe, and Canada well known to the House, the Government has prepared a draft bill that we believe will address the most pressing issues facing this Commonwealth . . ."

There was a bit of hubbub around the benches as the Prime Minister droned on, some pleased, some not, but mostly surprised. By any standards, this was quick work; to lay a bill before the house within hours of the BBC broadcast. To those so inclined, such decisiveness spoke well of a new Government itself hardly settled in to office. Amid the Opposition, initial skepticism at such haste grew to outright alarm as the PM concluded introducing the bill and immediately began to read the contents out in full, punctuated by increasingly frequent interruptions and objections.

He'd been expecting Curtin to come out swinging this afternoon, and no one could ever say Solly Rosevear was shy of a good fight. Even so, this was turning out to be even hotter than he'd anticipated. The struggle to maintain order, and even more to retain any illusion of impartiality, grew harder as the Points of Order mounted and were stuck down by his gavel. After the preamble and first few sections of the bill had been tortuously ground through, Rosevear was starting to regret the Labor Party's principled rejection of the Speaker wearing robes. Rumor had it some Speakers had sat in nothing but a singlet under their robes. It was warm day to start with. The chamber was getting hotter by the minute and Solly was sweating like an alcoholic sponge in his sauna of suit, vest and tie.

Down on the floor, Curtin bore the mounting temperature with the same tolerant smile he gave to all the raucous objection and procedural insult. Discretely studying the House over his spectacles as he read, or gazing about more frankly during the frequent interruptions, to Curtin it was all poetry set to life. Sweetest was the dismay across the room. The coalition shattered and leaderless in the wake of Menzies' departure now clucked about like headless chooks as the tidal wave of Labour victorious crashed over their privileged ranks. The faint mutterings of dissent from his own party only served to confirm his judgment of the situation. Every ship had its rats; and so long as he knew where they lay, Curtin was confident in his grip. A consummate party politician, he had his numbers locked down tightly. With the support of the Party Caucus and Trades Hall, he had nothing to fear from a few grumpy backbenchers and lukewarm supporters.

But those lukewarm supporters were turning the heat up on Rosevear. This might have been all part of Curtain's plan, having set the man up as Speaker partly with this sort of situation in mind. However, it had the Speaker in a lather; both physically and politically. He was having to strike down a growing number of interjections from his own side of the Labor Party in addition to the Opposition, many of which were points he agreed with and would have been making himself.

Like any Parliament worth its salt, information traveled around the chamber almost by osmosis. Early doubts hardened into ironclad conclusions long before Curtain reached the end of his document. The bill may have been a little rough about the edges, but it was no work of hours. Depending on one's point of view, this was either proof positive of the new leadership's depth and insight, or the depths of their conspiracy and treachery. All felt a growing sense of urgency as the details slotted into place.

The interpretation of Daventry lay at the heart of things, Labor took it as permission to wrest the nation free of its links to Home and Empire and were taking this opportunity with both hands to set some cherished planks of party policy into law. In sum, this bill was paving the way to a republic. That notion was as controversial on the Labor side of the house as it was unthinkable among the Opposition. Torn between the duties of his office, his own inclinations, and the hard lines of party allegiance, Rosevear grew increasingly angry and in dire need of a stiff drink. His rage might have been expressed in his language and temper towards towards objectors, but inwardly it focused exclusively on his party leader and Prime Minister.

As Curtin concluded his reading of the bill, he tabled the bill for immediate debate. His well oiled machine kicked into top gear. Having pushed proper procedure somewhat beyond its limits already that morning, gagging debate might have out of the question. But that didn't imply he had to play fair. If anything, the first hour of debate was even more disorderly than all that had passed before. A solid stream of well primed Labor MP's stood to ramble on, asking back-handed questions their own front bench could answer with long winded positive replies in favor of the Government's case. Occasionally, Rosevear let one of the Opposition get a few words in edgewise, but each was snowed under in a blizzard of interjections and objections. It was an old game, familiar to all on both sides of Parliament. But it was not one used lightly for matters of such weight that verged on constitutional reform. The fury this provoked exceeded anything seen before in the Australian Parliament, and Rosevare verged on losing control utterly.

Around that whole room of angry, shouting, screaming men, the Speaker could only see one island of support. Ironically it was the man he had replaced less than a week before. George Bell, DSO, MP and senior of the two Deputy Speakers, knew exactly what Rosevear was going through. He had spent the past six years in the chair himself. While not unmoved by the politics, he sat there smiling up at Rosevear and offering what encouraging nods he could.

Bell's was more than a professional sympathy; he actually thought the fellow was making a dreadful fist of it. The Speaker's face was flushing deep purple when it wasn't pasty white and Bell could see he was perspiring like a fountain from 20 feet away. The Tasmanian MP thought it best to do what he could, lest Rosevear collapse and leave him with the job of presiding over this shambles of a travesty.

Just after 3 PM, and with no end in sight, the Sargent-at-Arms crossed the floor to deliver a note to the PM. The Minister for Transport, who had been using two hundred and fifty words to say 'yes' in reply to a yet another prearranged question, paused as Curtin read the message. The Prime Minster looked up and waved the Minister back in action, stuffing the note into his pocket before leaning back with a casual smile. If Curtin had hoped to down play this new piece of information, the parliamentary grape vine had other ideas. The news raced around the chamber, leaving something approaching silence in its wake.

Rosevear, sitting in splendid isolation, was the only man excluded from the bush telegraph, although he certainly noticed something was happening. For the first time in what seemed like hours, and probably was, he was not beating down waves of protest, or even facing angry glares. It was almost uncanny how quiet the Chamber had become. Every MP in the House was whispering to each other instead of shouting at him. Given a chance to draw breath, he waited for the Minister to finish and resume his seat. As if wired to some trigger, the ministerial backside meeting leather saw almost half the house spring to its feet in a jabbing roar of "Mister Speaker, Mister Speaker!" They all clamored to gain Rosevear's 'eye' and be called up to speak.

Scanning the crowd judiciously, and with his own eye on trying to re-inject some calm and normality to the proceedings, he chose one of the steadier heads off the Opposition backbench and the fringe of the United Australia Party.

"The House recognizes the Member for Lara"

Under other circumstances, the Labour front bench would have nodded appreciatively at this. If not quite an Independent, the MP for Lara was well known for taking a casual view of party allegiance and speaking his rather liberal mind on occasion. If anyone on that side of the House might support the Government he was as likely a candidate as existed. Even if he didn't – well the seat of Lara was a marginal and Labor had high hopes for it. If the sitting member cared to put a foot or two in his own mouth, the Government would thank him for the ammunition.

Rosevear saw he had made a mistake immediately. It was hard not to with his whole front bench staring daggers at him. *Bugger 'erm,* he thought. *Let the lazy sods deal with their own bloody problems; I've done more than my share today.*

Gregory Locock remained standing as the other aspirants sunk back into their seats. "Mister Speaker, thank you. I was going to ask the Honorable Attorney General to expand on clause 12, but instead might I ask the Prime Minister, if in light of this recent naval action in the Indian Ocean, might not this whole bill be reexamined? Again I refer in particular to clause 12, but also several others . . ."

The rest was drowned out under a barrage of sound.

Curtin rose to his feet as the Speaker hammered the Chamber into silence. "Mister Speaker. I'd like to thank the honorable member for his question," he said with great confidence "And reassure him, and any others who may be concerned, that while events remain unclear, the Government has things well in hand. In any case, it is hard to see how such matters might have any bearing on business presently before the House. There's nothing that can't be smoothed over and we should not be distracted from more important things . . ."

As soon as the words passed from his lips, Curtin realized he had made a grave mistake. It wasn't just the deafening silence, but the low grumble that replaced it. The sound, not of anger, but of men quietly saying hard words in serious tones.

Locock remained standing for the next ten minutes as the Prime Minister tried to unsay what he had just said. A fine job Curtin did too. Slathering on the butter of reason and jam of promise with a lavish trowel to the hearty Hear Hear's of his increasingly vocal supporters, once the Whips and Ministers had recovered their poise and got to stirring up his defense. But it was a hollow noise, and few in the chamber bought the line he was selling, no matter how hard they stamped their feet after Curtin made each point.

If Australian ship had fought German ship, whatever the outcome, it was an act of war.

Curtin might say what he liked, but Berlin would have their own view and that was nothing to brush under the carpet. Nor was there any point to pushing this bill though until there was some idea of how Herr Hitler felt about it all.

Locock was still on his feet as the PM resumed his seat. Rosevear would have graveled him down, but the fellow had asked the question that had to be asked and done it with unusual civility. There was no reason to be abrupt and every reason to encourage a return to the usual courtesies on such a day as this, so Rosevar nodded at Locock.

"Mister Speaker," Locock nodded back, "I would like to thank the Prime Minister for his clear and informative expression of the Government's position. And further, Mister Speaker, I would beg leave to move this House has no Confidence in the present Government."

Chaos descended, bringing with it pandemonium, bedlam and turmoil. It did not quite reach anarchy, if only because Parliament sat on benches so there was a shortage of ready weapons. Rosevear pounded his desk like a carpenter and swore like a bargee, turning ever deeper shades of puce in the process. He might as well have spared his voice and blood pressure the strain. Eventually it was George Bell who stepped up to the Speaker's chair, stuck two fingers between his lips and let out an ear piercing whistle.

"SHUT UP YOU BASTARDS AND SIT DOWN! Your pardon, Mister Speaker."

It took a few moments for the Speaker to regain control of himself. Rosevear felt the humiliation of Bell's assistance as keenly as his own embarrassment and anger at losing control of the House. So it was with some ferocity he glared down at Billy Hughes, nominally Locock's party leader. Although, at 79, Hughes' position was mostly honorary; one he filled in lieu of some more energetic man.

"Has this Motion a second?"

In his day, Billy Hughes would have eaten Rosevear alive and picked his toes with the bones. Now, a little past his prime and still coming to terms with recent events, Hughes hesitated. It wasn't that the room lacked for men who would have backed the Motion of No Confidence in a heartbeat, but the

Speaker had just made it a party affair rather than a private matter and so no one stepped forward.

Until, from the Labor benches, the Parliament's one true independent stood up. "I'll second the motion," said Alexander Wilson in his Irish brogue, "and what's more, I think I may take a small little stroll." Putting actions to words, he crossed the floor.

The man who had bought the curtain down on Menzies' government proceeded to leave Curtin's in a heap on the floor of the House.

Cabinet Room, Government House, Calcutta, India

"Telegram from the Governor General in Australia, Your Excellency."

Sir Martyn bustled in to the Viceroy's brightly morning room and handed the message over directly. He knew the contents, of course, but theoretically it was a private letter.

Lord Linlithgow slipped the flimsy from its envelope and read eagerly. Of all the sources of intelligence available to the Government of India, the back channel between the Crown's direct representatives around the globe was by far the most reliable. It was actually the official route for a good deal of correspondence between parts of the Empire that lacked more direct representation, but as a source of reliable gossip, it was without peer.

"Which way have the Australians gone?" asked Nehru anxiously from settee. Yesterday, Brigadier General The Right Honorable Lord Gowrie, VC, GCMG, CB, DSO & Bar, known to his friends as Alexander Hore-Ruthven and presently Governor General of Australia, had sent warning the new Government was clarifying its position in response to Daventry and he should have more news shortly. "Are they still in the war?

The Viceroy just shook his head. "This verges on the incredible! Two governments in almost as many weeks. Good God, one would think they were turning into some comic-opera republic, yet Gowrie believes they remain stable and has some hopes for a new Government by morning."

"They are so divided all over this one issue?" puzzled Nehru.

"Oh, reading between the lines, I suspect there is a little more to it than just the war," Linlithgow sniffed. "And I can't say I cared for the sound of this Curtin fellow, so perhaps there's a silver lining to be found in that. But what sort of government they might cobble up now, I should hate to think."

"They have three parties," offered Sir Martyn helpfully, "but only one has the numbers to govern on its own. The other two have a long standing coalition."

Pandit Nehru smiled "Yes and the Australian Labour Party was the first Labour Party in the world to form a national government . . ."

"Ahh . . ."

". . . even if it only lasted for five days. My knowledge is mostly historical, Martyn. As Australian affairs have taken some prominence lately, I thought it best to do a little reading, but I find there is not a great deal to be had on the subject."

"Oh?" recovered Sir Martyn easily "Well recent events are a little complicated but, put simply, the previous Prime Minister, or should I say now, the fellow before the last chap . . ."

"Menzies," supplied Linthgow. "A good man by all accounts."

"Yes, sir; thank you. Robert Menzies took the loyalist view and was, reluctantly, prepared to follow London. His party, by and large, disagreed, as did his coalition partner and they all seem to have parted ways. That let Labor in as a minority government – I believe resting on the vote of a single independent . . ."

"Who must have jumped ship," concluded Nehru.

"Precisely," agreed Sir Martyn. "Or, if not, then there has been some movement across the floor. But other than Labor no one else has the numbers to form government unless another coalition can be arranged."

"Damn messy," nodded Linlithgow. "Whoever does come along will have no choice but to make a stand on the war, one way or another. So

"I know what will occupy the bulk of our day, we must find a sound line and length for us to take should the Australians publicly accept the Armistice and step out of the war."

"And should they stay in, of course . . ." add Nehru

"Oh, I should think that very much depends on you, Pandit," returned the Viceroy with a smile. "What say the Congress Party on the events of yesterday?"

"Your Excellency," Nehru began gravely, "the revelation of plans to invade India and the sinking of the *Hobart* have swung enough votes on the Party executive towards maintaining the state of war. It is held that the act confirms the intentions. Many disagree, of course. Gandhi and his followers call for peace at any price and non-violent resistance to the German invasion. Subhas Chandra Bose actually believes that an alliance with Germany is the proper course. But with those exceptions, and with heavy hearts, most others agree that maintaining the state of war is required. Both as a prudent precaution against German designs and to highlight our independence from London."

Linlithgow smiled with relief. "Very well. With your agreement, Pandit, we will announce your appointment as my deputy tomorrow. One change I would like to make to the agreement you negotiated with Sir Martyn. In two years, when you become President, instead of taking the position of your Chief of Staff, I would like you to appoint Sir Martyn in that role. It would be of great benefit to all concerned, I think. - Oh and if you are agreeable, Martyn?"

111

Nehru's stately nod and Sir Martyn's stunned head jerk seemed to signify acceptance. The Viceroy took pity on his secretary. "Then, with your concurrence Pandit, two telegrams please, Martyn. If you would, type them out personally, and secure them until required. The first to London; in cypher of course: 'Regret to advise you that in accordance with the Daventry Message, India takes responsibility for her own internal government and external relations. God Save the King.'

"Very good, sir," said Sir Martyn scribbling hastily in his note book. "And the second?"

"To Reichskanzlei in Berlin. Two copies, of course; one for the Japanese as their protecting power, but in plain language. It should read 'Genesis 1:22.'"

Nehru looked confused. Sir Martyn leaned over and whispered, "Go forth and multiply."

"Ahhh." Nehru smiled. "How appropriate."

CHAPTER SIX
POSITION STATEMENT

Parliament House, Canberra, Australia

Stepping up to the Government dispatch box for the first time as Prime Minister, Gregory Locock paused to survey the Chamber and marvel at how different it looked from this one particular spot. A night's frantic negotiation and a series of political compromises put him in this position. The sulking opposition glowering across the way; his own variegated coalition: Country Party, United Australia Party, independents and the little cluster of floor crossing Labor members buried safely deep in the Government backbenches. He was simply the candidate who offended fewest people. A bemused George Bell struggled to look stern as he nodded.

"The House recognizes the Honorable Prime Minister."

"Mister Speaker, as the first matter of Government business bought before this house, we should like to move a motion reaffirming the state of war that exists between this Commonwealth and Germany along with her allies, principally the Kingdom of Italy."

The Speaker looked down at the Labor Party frontbench and saw a mix of resignation and simmering resentment, but little opposition. "What say the House?" he demanded "Those in favor, say Aye." The roar of affirmation rang about the chamber and left little doubt as to the temper of the Parliament that day.

"The Ayes would seem to have it . . . " A grim faced John Curtin nodded. "The motion is carried by a majority of the House!" concluded Bell under a second roar of approval.

It took several minutes of gavel banging and demands for Order to get the assembly back in its seats. "The Prime Minister retains the floor."

113

Locock nodded. "Thank you, Mister Speaker. What the future holds, we do not know; but this we can say with all the confidence we can muster. We will be victorious, however long and hard the road may be. Mister Speaker, it is also my duty to inform the House that certain communications have been received by the Governor General from London in the last twelve hours purporting to be from the Government of Great Britain at the behest of His Majesty. These contradict the clear message from His Majesty in his Daventry broadcast.

"I put the following motion to the House. 'That in accordance with the Daventry Message, this House accepts the responsibilities delegated to it in that the authority of the Crown will pass through the Governor General to the Australian Parliament, there to be held in trust by them sitting as a Committee of Trustees."

The roar of "Aye!!!" was deafening.

Room 208, Munitions Building, Washington, DC, USA

"What used to be the Commonwealth is now falling into line with the Big Three. Canada, Australia and India have all repudiated Halifax's armistice. South Africa followed suit this morning and the smaller colonies are doing the same. We've still got a war to join, gentlemen." Cordell Hull had a bold smile on his face. For the first time in the two months since Halifax had signed the notorious armistice, things were running the way he wanted them to.

"I still can't believe that crazy scheme worked." Secretary Stinson shook his head. "You should be in a British prison, all of you."

"If it's crazy and it works, it isn't crazy." Hull stared at Stuyvesant who had an innocent expression on his face. Hull had heard that Stuyvesant had been on the aircraft that had pulled off the rescue and he didn't approve. Not completely, anyway. "The scientific material you brought back alone was worth the risks we took. You might be interested to know that a few other refugees are starting to appear in Canada. We're not sure how they are coming out, but it does look as if the larger British companies are getting their key designers and engineers out to Canada."

"My people say there's a lot of ill-feeling towards Halifax and his administration. It looks like Halifax nearly missed the bus. People were swinging away from an end-the-war way of thinking towards a grim determination to win at all costs. Another couple of weeks and he would have been too late." Stuyvesant thought carefully about how much to say. "There's a resistance movement springing up already. Mostly in Scotland and Northern England, but it's there. It wouldn't surprise me to find out that a lot of companies and research groups are quietly getting their key people and files to safety. Not to mention burying the records on any work that might be of aid to the Germans."

"So, there is still a war going on. Where do we go from here?" Stimson was slightly confused by the whole situation. He could see that the simple fact that the British Empire was still in the war, even if Britain itself was not, worked in favor of American interests, but he couldn't understand what the Dominions were going to do. *Just exactly how did the Australians plan to wage war on the Germans?*

The same question interested Cordell Hull and Phillip Stuyvesant, but Hull in particular had larger concerns. "Britain's status within the Commonwealth is now open to dispute. Canada recognized Churchill's government-in-exile as the legitimate government of Great Britain as soon as Australia and India came out. As far as we can make out, that means that the Halifax government in London has effectively been suspended from membership of the Commonwealth. So, we now have a British Commonwealth that doesn't include Britain. How that is going to spin out is something that we can't even begin to guess at, but the economic consequences are grave. We may have to do some propping up there to make sure they stay in business."

"Military support too. We can start by giving them the aircraft that are clogging up our airfields. We're finding more of the damned things every day." Stimson sounded indignant at the amount of American production capacity that had been absorbed by British and French orders while the American forces were crying out for modern equipment.

"Do we really want to do that?" Hull was thoughtful. "The President wants to put an end to the great colonial empires and this is our chance to finish off one of them, at least. It won't hurt our position to let the political situation mature for a few months. The longer we take to incorporate the orphaned Dominions into our trading sphere, the deeper the economic hole they will be in, and the harder the bargain we can eventually drive when we finally get around to buying them up. The longer we keep things simmering, the more likely it is that something will break our way."

"Like Germany hitting Russia. That's the way they're going." Stuyvesant looked thoughtful while he assessed the likely consequences of the invasion. "However we cut this, Russia is going to be an ally when the Germans do invade and we'll be supporting them as well. We could carry the burden of doing that by ourselves, but why? We can use help, even if it isn't essential. The invasion will change those Dominions from geese waiting to be plucked into useful economic resources."

"And the longer we wait, the smaller the chance of Britain re-establishing its position at the head of the Empire. No matter what way we look at this, America wins all around by waiting a little. We might even get a modest boost in US economic growth from the number of people who want to buy from us."

"There's another side to this whole situation." Stuyvesant had been thinking about the whole British Empire situation since Achillea, Gusoyn and Eleanor had got back. Coupled with his own and Igrat's observations, he found the situation interesting. "Pretty much all the Royal Navy that isn't in the U.K.

is placing itself at the disposal of the Dominion governments, and that makes them reasonably potent regional powers. It's not just the number of ships; it's the skilled manpower that's critical. The crews know how to fight their ships and their officers know how to run a naval campaign. What could have been a power vacuum in the region is beginning to fill in. The Indian Navy alone is quite a potent force now, and the Indian Army has never been anything other than potent. If the Indians get their act together and don't implode economically, we could be seeing the rise of a major regional power there."

"Which is critical, because Japan is on the move again. They're demanding that Britain cede Hong Kong to them as of now, quoting their alliance with Germany as making them the regional guardians of the Armistice agreement." Hull was openly contemptuous. "That's just the start, of course. They want the whole of the region as part of their 'Greater East Asian Co-Prosperity Sphere'. They'll get it too, if nobody stands in their way."

"Well, we'd better find somebody who can." Stuyvesant sounded uncertain at the prospect, but he had a strong candidate in mind for the job.

Training Area, 11th Infantry (Queen's Cobra) Division, Kanchanaburi, Thailand

"Keep moving. We have a long way to go before you can rest." The sergeants were encouraging the men on in their usual style. Private Mongkut Chandrapa na Ayuthya resented it. He had actually done his hitch in the Army a few years earlier, but he had been called up from the reserves; part of the process of fleshing out the 11th Infantry and turning it into a battle-worthy formation. He had left his wife, two sons and eleven-year-old daughter back on the farm. They would be able to cope; he felt confident of that. Of course, they would have the rest of his family to help out if they did run into trouble.

"How are you doing, grandpa?" One of the young recruits had put a slightly jeering note into the question. There was a certain level of tension in the unit between the young recruits who were mostly in their late teens or early twenties and the recalled reservists who were at least a decade older. The latter had a level of unofficial authority simply due to their age and their experience was useful; but they had also softened due to their post-military life. Now, they were going through the toughening-up process all over again. The current 40 kilometer, day-long march was part of that process.

"We'll march you youngsters into the ground any day, you'll see. Why, during my first time in, we had pleasant little walks like this every day just to get to the mess-hall. And it was uphill both ways!"

There was an appreciative patter of applause from the surrounding troops. Mongkut glanced around; everybody in his vicinity really did seem to be doing quite well. That wasn't surprising. This was the third long forced march the battalion had been assigned and the training tempo had been picking up steadily over the last month or so. He shifted the Type 45 rifle on his shoulder. That was one thing that hadn't changed since his first term with the Army; they were still carrying the long Type 45. There were rumors that the

116

Army was shifting to the new, shorter and more powerful German kar98k, but he hadn't seen any of the new rifles yet. The troops had been issued new helmets, replacing their old-style French 'Adrian' helmets with the German coal-scuttle design. They also had German-style webbing now that was much more practical than the old design. The Army's character had changed too, in subtle and hard to define yet very real ways.

There was something up. Mongkut could sense it. He'd caught surreptitious grins being exchanged between their company officer and the battalion commander. One of the foreign advisors had been around earlier as well. They were the ones responsible for the change in the Army's character. During Mongkut's first spell in the ranks, the emphasis had been on doing everything in exactly the way specified by the book and obeying orders without question. Now, everything was orientated on gaining the objectives set and how the troops achieved that was of lesser importance.

His thoughts were interrupted by a crackle of rifle fire. "Everybody, into the ditch!" Mongkut led the way himself, almost dragging the soldiers with him into cover. Most of the other men in the battalion were still milling around on the road, uncertain of what was going on or what they were supposed to be doing.

Mongkut had a strong idea what was happening. *This is a tactical exercise, to teach us how to react when ambushed.* He worked the bolt on his rifle, cursing the dust cover that was supposed to slide with the bolt but actually just got in the way, and sneaked a look up over the edge of the ditch. There were flashes from a treeline a hundred yards or so away. Mongkut aimed at them and squeezed off a shot. From the recoil of his rifle, they were carrying blank ammunition.

"Come on, shoot at them. Otherwise, they'll kill us all." The men around Mongkut followed his example, but the patter of rifle fire seemed paltry compared to the amount of fire coming their way. By the time he and his men had fired off a full clip, bugles were sounding along the road. The firing stopped and the officers started to reassemble the battalion.

"You men. You stand over there." The Lieutenant had pointed out the small group who had followed Mongkut. They joined another group who had been singled out. Shortly afterwards, a few more men joined them. The rest stayed on the road.

The battalion commander was standing in the back of a small truck and he addressed the bulk of the battalion. "You are all dead. You died because you didn't think. When you are ambushed, you do not just stand on the road and wave your hands around. You take cover and return fire while your officers get control of the situation and decide what to do. Before anybody complains that you didn't know there was an ambush planned, what do you expect? The enemy to put up a big sign on the road saying 'ambush ahead?' You must learn to think and react for yourselves, just as these men did."

The battalion commander waved at the small number of men who had been separated out. "They acted like soldiers; they took cover and returned fire. You, there." The commander pointed at Mongkut. "Your name is Mongkut Chandrapa na Ayuthya and your rank is private. Correct?"

"Yes Sir."

"No, it is not. Your name is Mongkut Chandrapa na Ayuthya and your rank is corporal. All of you men, you get to ride in trucks back to camp, so you have time to clean your rifles before evening parade. The rest of you will march back. At the double."

A groan went up from the remainder of the battalion at the thought of double-timing the rest of the way back to camp. Mongkut and his men climbed into the backs of three waiting trucks and felt the drivers start to roll forward. A sergeant swung up into the back of the truck with Mongkut. "You, corporal. You will have a section to command when you get back to camp. See you do it well." His voice dropped. "And, if you need advice, always ask the other NCOs. Being a corporal is just the start; we'll help you along."

Cabinet Office, 10 Downing Street, London, United Kingdom

"They are suspending us from membership of the Commonwealth?" Lord Halifax was a shade of deep red that featured significant areas of purple and others of dead white, especially around the eyes. Sir Edward Bridges couldn't help thinking the communiques from the departing Dominions had brought about a very patriotic reaction from the Prime Minister. He'd gone red, white and blue in that order. Bridges was seriously concerned that Halifax was about to have a heart attack and drop dead on the floor. His mind running along those lines took him to the point where he wondered whether that wouldn't actually be the best thing to happen, although he recoiled at the thought of the paperwork that would result.

"Not really, Prime Minister, although that is how it might appear to an outsider and how it will doubtless be interpreted outside the Empire. In fact, what they have done is recognized the Government-in-Exile based in Ottawa as being the legitimate government of Great Britain and rejected your own claim to legitimate authority as being based of a usurpation of power. Therefore, since your government is not recognized as being of legitimate authority, it is not a part of the Commonwealth. Great Britain is still in the Commonwealth, it is just that the government headed by you is not."

The shade of deep crimson that dominated Halifax's face darkened still further. Bridges could see the veins pulsing on his forehead. "This is an insult; a personal insult. They will be made to pay for this. And His Majesty, what of his part in this? How dare he interfere in the running of the Empire this way?"

"Well, technically, and without putting too fine a point on it, it is his Empire. What is more, the Daventry Message could easily be interpreted as advising the Dominions that they were still subject to the authority of the

Cabinet in London. If we assume that the reference to Col/Dom is intended only to identify the Governors of the Colonies and Dominions, then the only Cabinet with a general purview is London. The problem there is that rather defeats the whole purpose of the statement when in context. Obviously this is the interpretation that is preferred here and now, and the text of the message was modified in just that way when we repeated the transmission at midnight. Unfortunately, and against my advice, Central Office rather over egged their pudding by making several other changes to the original. As a result, that midnight retransmission is already known as the 'Halifax Revision' and nobody accepts it. It didn't help its credibility that the BBC sent it in plain language."

The incoherent anger of Lord Halifax's face was replaced by suspicion. *Ah, the second stage,* Bridges thought. *Power corrupts and absolute power corrupts absolutely. The first stage is rage at opposition and the second is intense suspicion of anything that may seem to be opposition. The third stage will be pre-emptive retaliation against those identified in the second phase.* "Might I suggest, Prime Minister, that much may be gained now by a show of magnanimity. The actions taken by the Dominions are as much the result of hurt feelings and offended pride as anything else. A generous gesture, a conciliatory address, all will go far to soothe the inflamed situation and quiet the sounds of anger. Think of the Dominions as children who consider themselves unfairly treated and have stormed off to sulk in private. A calm word and generous gesture are the more effective in resolving the situation, while harsh words and actions will but inflame passions still further. Our attitude should be one of addressing them 'in sorrow, not anger' ."

"You exceed your remit, Sir Edward. This is a matter for the Foreign and Dom/Col Offices and I might say Mister Butler and I are in complete agreement. If we tolerate any dissension from the Dominions, it will strike at the very basis of the Empire. They must be brought to heel, and quickly. They will be shown the rod, Sir Edward, and that will put an end to their pretensions."

Bridges sighed inaudibly and felt the weight upon his soul increase. Every day that passed with him here in this building made leaving to join the slowly-increasing band of exiles in Canada that much more difficult. For a man who had the depth of experience in Empire affairs that Halifax had, he showed remarkably little understanding of how the administration of the Empire worked. That fact alone made Bridges' leaving so much harder. It would be irresponsible, a betrayal almost equal to that made by Halifax himself, to depart and leave the conduct of affairs in the hands of a man so manifestly unready to manage them. Bridges knew he would have to stay, simply to try and ameliorate the worst of the disaster that was slowly and steadily opening in front of him.

"And which rod do you presume to show them, Prime Minister?"

119

"Trade, of course." Halifax's irritation was painfully obvious. "The whole Imperial system has been tailored around Britain's import demands. Without the market represented by our demand for raw materials, the Commonwealth will collapse economically. We have some recourse to external supplies, but the Dominions depend on favorable British trade concessions to underpin their economy. If we shift the direction of our trade patterns to favor other suppliers, they will find it is a cold and lonely world out there. When we cut their currencies off from the sterling pool, they will learn just how worthless they are on the international market."

"I think you mean to say how worthless their currencies are." Bridges was horrified at what he was hearing and a cold knot of fear was beginning to tighten in his stomach. "Prime Minister, I must implore you. Think carefully upon what you propose. A trade war with the Commonwealth countries will achieve nothing except the destruction of us all. We have an opportunity here to offer a carrot to the Dominions, one that they will find very difficult to resist. We make them the offer of continuing trade relations on the existing terms and we gain the raw materials we need to revert to a peace-time economy. That leaves them with the decision of whether they wish a return to normality also; the impending collapse of their economies will concentrate their minds wonderfully. They will have no realistic choice other than to recognize the existing state of affairs. The Commonwealth may not be happy with the state of affairs here but it needs the trade too badly to let that get in the way. Once the breach is healed and the present unpleasantness forgotten, the relations between London and the Dominions will be as they always were, to the great benefit of us all."

Bridges paused, getting the distinct feeling that if looks could kill, he would be stretched out dead on the carpet. Halifax was glaring at him. The problem was that Bridges was sure he had to keep going, not just for the wider good of the Empire, but in the narrower interests of Britain itself. His sleep had been haunted by a ghastly vision of the future; one in which famine had struck Great Britain. It had started when the vicar at his local church had given a sermon based around the parable of the seven years of fat and the seven of lean. From then on, Bridges had seen himself walking down empty streets of British cities, the last survivor of a British nation that had ended through starvation. He shook himself, trying to forget the images that sometimes seemed drawn from a Lovecraft story.

"There is another matter to consider, Prime Minister. That is of our forces abroad. Many of them have cast their lot in with the Dominion Governments and take their orders from them. In doing so, they quote the Daventry Message as authorization from the Crown for their actions."

"Then let the Crown pay them." Halifax strode angrily backwards and forwards, his whole body twitching with anger. "Cut them off. If they do not serve this country, then this country should no longer pay them."

"There is a problem with that, Prime Minister. Some of the serving personnel have deferred portions of their pay to be held as savings against their retirement. The Government also pays a portion, the allotment, of the pay due to personnel on foreign postings to their families here in Britain. To terminate the allotment would leave those families destitute."

Halifax stopped pacing and turned to face Bridges, his voice and manner suddenly changing. "I had not thought of that. In conscience, we cannot break the agreement we have with our servicemen with regard to their families. I will reconsider what to do about the pay for our troops abroad. No matter what decision we may come to on that issue, the allotments for their families here will continue to be paid. We will also honor their deferred pay and hold it in trust for them. Quite apart from anything else, this will give us a moral claim over UK forces overseas."

"There is a problem here." Bridges was relieved; Halifax was not as set on confrontation as his initial comments had made him seem. "We can continue allotments and deferred payment according to the records held here. However, we cannot hope to keep these allotments updated to reflect the men's own wishes, unless there is regular administrative communication between the forces abroad and ourselves. In the event of hostilities continuing, as they seem set to do so in the Middle East at least, there will be casualties that we would be unable to track."

Halifax waved his good hand dismissively. "Then we shall institute a standardized 'Dependant's Sustenance' payment to be given out in lieu. This is nothing new; it can work just like any other government pension. We set a base rate with modifiers for number of children, residence status, rent, et cetera. Doing so will keep the people happy and reconcile them to the events of the last few weeks."

His anger broken, Lord Halifax sighed and looked at Bridges again. "I understand your point about trade and the Commonwealth. I will think on this matter further. There is much to be considered before we make a final decision on these issues."

Cabinet Room, Government House, Calcutta, India

"And now we have the problem of the princes. Or, more precisely, the wealth that they control. Putting that to productive use is likely to be a challenge." Lord Linlithgow wrinkled his nose slightly. "And then we have the related problem of what to do with the Princes themselves."

"The latter should more properly be considered a matter for consideration at a later date." Sir Eric Haohoa was concerned by several aspects of the Princes Problem, but none of them compared with the economic problems that seemed about to engulf India. "The princely wealth, on the other hand, relates directly to financial difficulties that are reaching a crisis point. Fortunately, South Africa has come up with what may be at least a partial solution. The basic problem is that the rupturing of the Commonwealth has left us without an umbrella currency. Without it, we are unable to mobilize

121

what economic strength we have. This leaves us with two choices. One is to go back with our tail between our legs and beg pardon while pleading to be allowed to return to the pound sterling basket, with all that implies."

"Never!" Sir Martyn Sharpe, Lord Linlithgow and Pandit Nehru chorused the denial in perfect harmony. The three men looked at each other in amazement, then burst out laughing.

"You know, I think this political alliance is going to work." Lord Linlithgow's observation was dry, but still tinged with unexpected humor. "Sir Eric, perhaps you can cement our friendship still further by proposing the second option?"

"Well, Your Excellency, if we must have an umbrella currency and the pound sterling is unattainable, we are left with but one choice. To create our own. That is what the South Africans propose."

"And how do they propose we do that? Have they any idea of the complexity of what they suggest? New currencies cannot be waved into existence on a whim." Harold Hartley shook his head. "How do we back such a currency?"

"But what was the pound sterling? Since Britain moved off the gold standard, it was just another currency based on collective faith as much anything else." Sir Eric started to count off points on his fingers. "Firstly, we need to replace the sterling as a common standard, Secondly, we need to stop the massive devaluation of our currencies on the international market and thirdly we must get some stability back into the utter chaos that is our international trading position. The current short term flux is undermining our international bargaining position across the board.

"So, the South Africans suggest that we invent a new currency specifically for international trade. Initially at least, it's not going to have any confidence in the wider market. Unless we can back it properly, such a construct would lack the gravitas to be taken seriously. There is one thing we have in the Commonwealth that we have in bulk. Gold. We've got gold mines in South Africa, Australia and here in India. In fact, we control a good portion of the world's gold supply.

"We've even been playing with names for the new currency. The South Africans suggested the Krugerrand of course, but the sovereign has much more support. We can mint sovereigns in South Africa, here and Australia but mostly we print them on paper using the gold still in the ground as collateral. And diamonds, rubies, emeralds, anything we can get that has value. Then, we peg all the Commonwealth currencies to the sovereign as they were to the sterling."

"You're putting us back on the gold standard?" HH was shocked.

"At a much reduced value to bullion, yes. We have no choice. Being a hard, gold-backed currency, the sovereign has immediate respect, while wartime restrictions on currency speculation around the world will stop us getting raped in the process. The sterling pool will be replaced by a free market that is not subject to the dreadful standing of our individual currencies. Best of all, it will hold off the Americans who are sitting in Washington, waiting for us to go bankrupt so they can essentially buy us up on the cheap. Pandit, what could mark India's independence more clearly that abandoning the pound sterling?"

"My God. Creating a new currency, even a limited use one, is a massive undertaking even under benign conditions and these conditions are anything but benign. I simply don't think it can be done." HH shook his head in awed disbelief at the suggestion. "The whole problem here is the extent to which the collapse of the UK kicks the center out of the Commonwealth system. The problem with establishing any collective position is that a collective position needs to have a lead voice to present that position. Who is going to be that lead voice? This is a question we must think about with care, because whoever that lead voice is will become the de facto head of the non-British Commonwealth. I would suggest to you that such thoughts have already occurred to the Boers in Pretoria."

"They almost certainly have." Nehru spoke carefully, keeping his own deep feelings about the Boers well under control. "They would be foolish not to. But I do not see this as a great problem. India will leave the Commonwealth at some point, that much is certain. It is also certain that Britain will return to it once Halifax and his clique have been removed and they will resume their previous position as its head. Leadership of the Commonwealth will be a sought-after prize but I feel it will turn to dust in the hands of the winner."

"Be that as it may; but something dramatic and solid is needed quickly if we are to survive. The sovereign is one of, if not the most, widely distributed bullion currencies in the world. We've already got the dies to make it and it's something everyone understands. Politically, it's also a sign of solidarity with the Crown. Which further puts the skids under Halifax." Sir Martyn nodded as he spoke; the idea of a new currency was indeed seductive. "I will say this; going back to a gold standard, however diluted, is going to cause some severe problems all around."

"It will. But it is severe problems in the future or an economic disaster now." Sir Eric shook his head. "The Boers may have their own motivations, but that doesn't stop them being right. A new currency basket based around our gold-backed sovereign is the only way to go."

Lord Linlithgow sighed deeply. "I agree. Gentlemen of the Cabinet, I put it to the vote, shall we establish a committee to evaluate the issues arising from the South African proposal and determine the measures necessary to support the relaunch of the sovereign? Those in favor, please raise their hands."

There was a pause as Lord Linlithgow counted the votes. Nine in favor, seven against, one absent. "The motion is passed by a majority of two.

This brings us back to the issue of the princely wealth. How do we make best use of that resource for the benefit of the country as a whole?"

"There is a point we must bear in mind here." Sir Martyn spoke precisely and with great care. "We are talking about six hundred or so of the best educated and most influential families in India. They do have a useful amount of cash. In a wider context, many have positions of social and religious power and they certainly do have an interest in India's future. The princely wealth will only be a brief palliative factor if we confiscate it in full, and once gone, it will never return. I would venture to suggest that rather than be used to defray the expenses of the Government, we should consider it as seed money India is going to need at some point.

"In this regard, I see three broad options open to us. One is that we confiscate the money outright or take possession of it via extraordinary taxation. Secondly, we can strip away the income that it generates and leave the capital in the hands of the princes. The third option is to harness that money to a useful end by coercing them to invest their capital in suitable enterprises and thus generate long term income."

"Perhaps the sale of war bonds might be a good start." Personally, Nehru was all for the outright confiscation solution leaving penniless princes sitting in the ruins of their moldering palaces, but he recognized that was impossible, now at least. "There has been the usual measure of patriotic fund raising by the princes anyway, so we add to it by converting their savings pool into war bonds. Perhaps some gentle words from this administration about how the evil Congress Party wishes to confiscate everything and only an enthusiastic response to the war bond drive can hold them at bay?"

A ripple of laughter ran around the conference room. Nehru smiled at the approving nods he received. "Of course, we must keep leaning on them to extract all the rainy day funds they have hidden away. A small tactful reminder now and then about how the hidden account with their name on it seems to have been overlooked in the latest bond drive? And always the reminder about how those Congress Party fanatics want to tax any private wealth over one rupee?"

This time, the laughter was a full-blooded guffaw in appreciation of Nehru's excessively innocent expression. Sir Eric Haohoa took off his glasses and wiped his eyes. "I think this could work. The Princes will see that things could be a lot worse and at least the bonds will offer a reasonable rate of return. As the situation stabilizes, they will begin to look safer and safer. Who knows? They may even be grateful that we steered them to such a sound investment."

"I think we have a workable plan here, gentlemen. I do not think this needs a vote, since it is already within the remit of the Treasury. Pandit, I note that Sir Richard Cardew has once again declined to honor us with his presence. Since he obviously does not share the opinions of this Cabinet and does not intend to take part in our deliberations, might I propose to you that he be

124

invited to reconsider his position and Sir Eric Haohoa be appointed in his place?"

Pandit Nehru gave every appearance of thinking hard, although in reality the matter had already been discussed and decided before the meeting took place. "Sir Eric has spoken well concerning the complexities we face and the views of the Cabinet Office should be reflected here. Since Sir Richard has declined to do so, and if Sir Eric is prepared to take on this onerous responsibility, then the Cabinet would benefit from the change."

"Well, Sir Eric? Would you assume the responsibilities of Cabinet Secretary?"

"Your trust honors me, Your Excellency. I would be delighted to do so."

Calcutta United Service Club, Calcutta, India

"It is intolerable; quite intolerable." Every hair of Sir Richard Cardew's moustache bristled with indignation. "First, His Excellency defies perfectly clear-cut and unambiguous instructions from DomCol. Then he appoints that damned communist Nehru as his deputy. It is too much I say."

"And your removal as the Cabinet Secretary has nothing to do with your indignation, I suppose?" Lieutenant Colonel Pierce Harvey Garry took a sip of his whisky soda and was amused to note that his sarcasm went so far over Cardew's head that it didn't even ruffle his hair as it passed.

"Nothing at all. I made my position on this quite clear from the outset. DomCol is the ruling authority and our responsibility is to see that its commands are carried out. Why, your battalion was due to set sail for the Middle East, was it not?"

Garry glanced around. The orders that had assigned the Third Battalion (Duke of Cornwall's Own) of the 7th Rajput Rifles to East Africa were supposed to be secret, although everybody knew what they were.

"We were, but those orders and our movement have been suspended. Can't say I'm sorry. The sepoys are always a bit twitchy over crossing the sea. Loss of caste, you see."

"Well, there you are then. Orders issued by the War Department through DomCol are just suspended without a by-your-leave to London. All because of some native superstitions. What more need I say?"

Hmm, we have some contradictions here, Garry thought. *On one hand, complaining about India not dropping out of the war at London's command and on the other complaining about stopping the movement of a battalion to the area where fighting is still going on.* "Loss of caste is no superstition, Sir Richard, Its consequences are very real. My sepoys have every right to be concerned."

"Well, if Linlithgow and those jumped-up guttersnipes Sharpe and Haohoa knew their duty, your Sepoys wouldn't have to worry about losing their precious caste."

Hang on a minute, old fellow. You've just finished criticizing the Marquess for staying the transit order. At least get your story straight. "Caste is precious to them. When the news spread that we were sailing for East Africa, we started to get a desertion problem. Not many, but a few here and there. As soon as Nehru joined the Cabinet and the sailing orders were stayed, the problem went away. In fact, some of the men have already come back. Shame-faced at not having been true to their salt."

"I trust you made an example of them."

"Good Lord, no. I gave them a severe talking-to, more in sorrow than in anger, you know, then sent them back to their platoon. Their own shame at having betrayed their salt will punish them worse than anything I could award. Their fellows will treat them as outcasts until they've redeemed themselves."

"Well, you know best, I suppose. Still, we have to ask what do we do now?"

"What do you mean?" Garry was suddenly very suspicious and very careful.

"We owe it to the better people here in India to restore our relationship with London as quickly as possible. If that means installing a new Viceroy who knows and understands his duty, then so be it."

Are you totally insane? Garry stared at Cardew in shock. *Have you forgotten what happened the last time the Indian Army rose in mutiny? And you want to risk bringing that horror back?* When he replied, he did so very slowly and very carefully.

"I do not think there is a legal mechanism for removing a Viceroy other than to have London recall him. And, if I understand the situation correctly, any such order from London would be considered invalid. I believe the Cabinet here holds that the government in exile sitting in Ottawa is the legitimate government of Great Britain. Is this not so? Now if we can get an order from them, replacing Marquess Linlithgow as Viceroy, you may be on to something."

"Of course, of course." Cardew gulped down his brandy. "Pleasure to meet you, Colonel."

Garry nodded as Cardew rose to his feet and stomped off. He waved to a steward and had another whisky-soda delivered. That gave him a few minutes to think the disturbing meeting over. By the time his second glass was empty, he had decided it was time to seek a meeting with Sir Eric Haohoa.

Building One, Consolidated Aircraft Corporation, San Diego, California

"Are you planning to cancel all our contracts?" Reuben H. Fleet put on a good show of polite courtesy, while inside he was boiling with fury. "We have a lot of production capacity here, you know. It seems a pity to let it go unused."

"I don't think that will happen. I happen to know the Navy is ordering a lot more Catalina flying boats. The problem is range. With Britain out of the war, we can't rely on having foreign bases any more. So, the PB2Y is a dead duck; it doesn't have the range we need. Nor does the XB-24." Phillip Stuyvesant sounded eminently reasonable as well.

"The XB-24 has more range than the B-17. A lot more and it carries a heavier bombload as well. We've got six of them sitting on the ramp right now. The French ordered them. Now they're just sitting there. That's my company's money sitting in the sun, doing nothing."

"Had things panned out differently, the XB-24 might have been really something, that I grant you. But it doesn't have the range we need. Nor does the XB-32, so that will have to go as well. If it's any consolation, Boeing's XB-29 is being cut back. But, it's not the cancellations I'm here to talk about. It's the long-range bomber. You and Boeing are competing for that one as well. Why don't you show me what you've got?"

Fleet pulled a file out from a drawer and ran down the list of names cleared to see Consolidated Aircraft's long range bomber proposal. "Right, Mr. Stuyvesant, you are cleared to see the work we're doing. Come with me."

He led the way to another section of the building, one which had armed guards in the corridors and combination locks on the access doors. Eventually, he opened a door to a room that contained models and drawings. "Let's start with this."

'This' was a model of a huge flying boat, powered by six engines . Stuyvesant looked at it curiously. "Why are the engines in the back of the wings?"

"Pusher configuration. It reduces drag. Everything about this flying boat is designed to reduce drag to a minimum. We used the Davis Wing design on the XB-24 due to its low-drag characteristics and that's the primary reason why it outperforms the B-17. We've got a transport version of the XB-24 designed, by the way; one that might be very useful."

"So, your proposed long-range bomber is a flying boat." Stuyvesant was thoughtful. The idea made sense; all the long-range passenger aircraft in the world were flying boats.

"Good Lord, no. This is our proposal for the Pan American Super-Clipper; the aircraft they want to replace the Boeing 314. If they listen to us, we can give them an airliner that can carry at least a hundred people for six thousand nautical miles with a fuel burn comparable to that of the 314. It will revolutionize air transport, but Juan Trippe won't bite."

"Why not?" Stuyvesant frowned. "It seems like a major leap forward."

"Two reasons. One is that the original specification was over-ambitious and Trippe has doubts about whether it would be possible to fill an aircraft this big with passengers. The other is that he has this picture of air transport as being some sort of super-luxury way of travel. Now, there is a good reason for that. The Pan-Am Clippers are relatively slow, so people are stuck in cramped surroundings for many hours. It's not like traveling by sea, where people can walk around the ship and forget they are at sea. So, Trippe believes his passengers need the luxury to compensate for the discomfort of a small aircraft. We think he's wrong; people will accept cramped conditions and a level of discomfort for a cheap and fast means of traveling between countries. But, he's the customer.

"Anyway, we designed a really efficient wing for the Super-Clipper, one that makes even the XB-24 look primitive. We've designed a downsized version of the Super-Clipper, the XP4Y, for the Navy as a Catalina replacement. We're waiting to hear if the Navy will bite. We used the same aircraft as a test-bed for our bomber. We took the full-size Super-Clipper wings and tail and mated them to a new fuselage, one that is optimized as a land-based bomber. "

Fleet put down the model of the flying boat and picked up another one. "Here she is. And she's a monster; more than twice the size of Boeing's B-29. I don't want to bad-mouth another company, but I think Boeing is making a bad mistake with the B-29. They're using a lot of advanced building techniques and unproven design art to get the performance they claim in the airframe size they want. There's too much there that can go wrong. We're sticking to design art we know: structural technology proven with our flying boats and the Davis Wing from the XB-24. The only really new thing we have, other than sheer size, is the pusher engine installation. We call this the Model 35."

Stuyvesant took the model and inspected it carefully. He noted the smoothly contoured nose and the great twin fins and rudders at the back. Turning it upside down, his eyebrows rose at the sheer size of the bomb bay. "This aircraft will fulfill the long range bomber specifications we issued?"

"Fill and exceed." Fleet's pride was obvious. "The Model 35 will be able to hit targets five thousand nautical miles away with ten thousand pounds of bombs and return. It's a truly intercontinental bomber."

Stuyvesant looked carefully at the model again. "You know, Boeing is tied down with the B-29; they don't have any design resources to spare. Jack Northrop is pushing a flying wing but that's a step too far. Douglas, they have the same design staff problems that Boeing has. Frankly, this is the only convincing design that I've seen so far."

Fleet grinned proudly. "And the Material Division agrees with you. They've endorsed our design. The Army Air Force has even given us a number for her. She's going to be the B-36."

Wardroom, Battleship HMS Valiant, Trincomalee, India

"We have the foundations of a great navy here." Captain Edgar Porteous Woollcombe looked around the crowded wardroom and noted the mix of dark blue, light blue and khaki uniforms. "And a great Army and Air Force to go with it."

"Well said." General Auchinleck responded enthusiastically. "The Indian Army has always been the mainstay of the Empire and now we have the sea power to go with it."

Admiral James F. Summerville coughed slightly. "Gentlemen, before we get too carried away with what we have, and while I also second Captain Woollcombe's statements, we must pay due diligence to what we lack."

"And that is air power." Despite Captain Woollcombe's enthusiasm, Squadron Leader Baldwin was almost abashed at the slight force he brought to the meeting. The fact that he, a lowly squadron leader, was the senior RAF officer present said much.

"We have three squadrons of Indian Air Force aircraft here: two with Westland Wapitis and one with Audaxes. Mostly they have Royal Air Force personnel, but 16 officers and 144 other ranks are Indian. That's about a third of the total. We've got a small training establishment with Tiger Moths, but we were left out of the Empire Air Training Scheme. The RAF in India adds six more squadrons to the total. One has Wapitis, two Audaxes, one Lysanders and one Blenheim bombers. We also have a squadron of Valentia transports. No fighters at all."

"What about Singapore and Malaya?" Woollcombe looked at the appendages to India. "Do we have fighters there? And can we use them?"

"We have four squadrons of bombers in Singapore. 36 and 100 Squadrons have Vildebeest torpedo bombers; 34 and 60 Squadrons have Blenheims. There's another squadron, 62, in Malaya with Blenheims. Nothing in Burma worthy of note."

"We have no fighters in Singapore?" Woollcombe sounded incredulous.

"None." Baldwin was defensive. "With the war in Europe, our modern fighters were concentrated there. Frankly, we didn't take the Japanese very seriously. I do have some good news though. We've been searching around and we've managed to organize six Coastal Defense Flights with a mix of old aircraft we found in storage or used as hacks. Mostly Hawker Harts and Audaxes, but one CDF flight has six Blenheim Is. And we have the Short Singapore flying boats, of course. We actually have a round dozen of them."

Summerville nodded. The situation was as bad as he and Auchinleck had feared. "We can add a little to that. We have HMS *Hermes,* of course; she has nine Swordfish on board. We also have the float planes on the cruisers and here on *Valiant.* That adds two Walrus and six Seafox. But . . . . "

Auchinleck finished the phrase for him. "That still means there is not a single fighter in the whole of India. We have no air defenses; none at all."

"I would suggest that we can shift our forces around a little to make better use of them. We can reassign the Wapitis from Number 1 squadron to the Coastal Defense Flights and replace them with the Audaxes in those flights. The Wapiti will be as useful for patrolling the sea as the Audax, but the Audaxes will be much superior for army cooperation flights." Baldwin thought for a second. "Before That Man took Britain out of the war, we were converting some of the Blenheims back home into fighters. This meant fitting a four-Browning gun pack under the belly and taking out some of the equipment not needed for the fighter role. Perhaps we could do the same thing here? 27 Squadron has Blenheims suitable for the conversion. That would give us some fighters, at least. We can also see to training Number Six CDF, they're the ones with Blenheims, to support the fleet. Admiral, may I ask the aid of your Fleet Air Arm pilots in doing so?"

There was a profound silence in the room. The idea of the Royal Air Force offering aid to the other services and asking for their guidance seemed shocking. In the middle of the room, Summerville and Auchinleck were speaking quietly to each other. Eventually, Auchinleck spoke to the meeting as a whole. "Squadron Leader, your comments and proposals are well-said and well-taken. We need to expand the Indian Air Force to meet the demands placed upon it. Your energy and initiative commend you to the command of the enlarged force. I am therefore, on my authority alone, going to promote you to the rank of Wing Commander with immediate effect. You understand that this promotion has only my personal authority behind it and it may be rescinded by higher authorities should they emerge when the political situation changes. Your first responsibility is to organize the conversion of 27 Squadron's Blenheim bombers into fighters. This must take the highest priority."

There was a murmur of approval at the decision, but few eyes were not focussed on the map of India that dominated the wall.

The Peninsula Hotel, Manila, Philippines

The man wouldn't have been out of place on any street corner. In the dining room of the Peninsula Hotel, he stood out like a farmer in his dowdy go-to-town best, attending opening night at the opera. Igrat noticed him, of course. She always noticed everything going on around her, even if she gave no outward sign of doing so. She also noted that nobody else seemed to remark on the stocky middle aged man with a head full of slicked down sandy hair in a plain grey suit, so she concentrated on the superb breakfast instead. Her curiosity re-emerged when the same drab fellow appeared again the Pan-Am terminal. He was sitting quietly in a corner with a newspaper and pot of tea as they waited to board the Clipper.

It wasn't until the Pan-American Hotel on Wake Island that their paths crossed again. In the early pre-dawn the silence awakened Igrat more

130

than anything. If she strained every muscle, there was a faint throb that might be a distant generator; otherwise, there was only the rattling of palm fronds and slap of the sea on sand. On her journeys out to Asia, she had discovered an enchantment about the dawn here. The isolation, the peace, was something to be savored. Dressing hurriedly, she slipped out of the Pan-Am Hotel and down the path to the beach.

It was still dark between the stunted palm trees. Although Igrat had no difficulty staying on the path, she didn't see the still figure standing at the head of the strand until she was far too close to back away. The man turned at the sound of her slippers. She recognized him as the curious 'grey farmer' from Manila.

"Good morning, Miss"

Igrat saw a square pugnacious face that could have been quite threatening if it wasn't offset by an unusually high forehead. There was something else as well, a strange feeling as if a light was flickering softly in the back of her mind.

"Oh, good morning" returned Igrat "I am sorry if I disturbed you."

"No, you stay as you are, Missie. I'll move off if you're looking for some room." The voice had a gentle fatherly gruffness, although she couldn't place the accent. "Not that I'd object to a bit of company either"

With any illusion of solitude shattered, Igrat decided to satisfy her curiosity instead. The light in her mind was still there and she was sure what it meant. "Oh I couldn't ask you to do that. You were here first. Anyway, I like company."

"No trouble," returned the man. "There's enough island for the two of us."

"Barely," laughed Igrat

"Ay," he agreed. "And there's not much here, either."

"Except the sunsets and the dawn"

"I've seen worse." he nodded. "There's far worse to be had, that's for certain. You'll have to pardon me. Lewis, Essington Lewis; my friends call me Essie for obvious reasons."

The hand he extended was warm and dry; the handshake firm but not hard,. Igrat took it in the same fashion. She'd already decided not to vamp this man. There was something about him she found attractive and, anyway, there was always the light flickering in her mind.

"Irene Shapiro. I'm an actress."

"Well pleased to make your acquaintance, Miss Shapiro, and I'd take Irene over Essington any day of the week. Oh, look out, here she comes." He nodded at the horizon where the sky was turning a magnificent deep mauve. There was the tiniest spot of light forming where the sky met the sea. Before she could remark on it, a long streak of brilliant green leapt skywards. It formed a distinct pillar for a few seconds and then vanished as the leading edge of the sun's disk peeped over the horizon.

"A green flash!" Igrat's voice was awed. "It's been a long time since I've seen one of those. Do you think it will bring us good luck?"

"I think it already has, for me anyway." Lewis was looking at her oddly and a bit guardedly. Igrat knew why, but it was a subject that would have to wait for another time.

Student's Canteen, Nottingham University, Nottingham, United Kingdom

"Just what is this?" Rachael looked at the meal on offer from the student's canteen very doubtfully.

"Bubble and squeak." David Newton sounded as doubtful as Rachael. "It's a mixture of leftovers, mostly potatoes and cabbage, all mashed up together and deep fried with sausage. The fat from the sausages flavors the vegetables, you see."

"Oh dear." The truth was, Rachael was very hungry and had been looking forward to having something to eat.

"I'm sorry, love." The woman behind the serving counter was genuinely apologetic. "It's the rationing, see; we have to use every bit of everything we have. Can't afford to throw anything away. More than our job's worth to get caught wasting food. We put some potato and cabbage aside for you, though. Best we could do."

"That's very kind of you." Rachael gave the cooking ladies a great beaming smile. In her heart, she guessed that the food that they had put aside had been ladled out with the pork fat soaked spoons that had been used elsewhere. Still, she didn't *know* that was the case and ignorance was an acceptable excuse. But to mention such things would be to insult the ladies who had tried to help here. Rachael didn't believe in knowingly giving offense to anybody, especially those who were doing their best to cope. She took the plate with the vegetables. "Thank you so much for being so thoughtful."

When she joined her friends at their customary table, there was an air that she couldn't quite understand. Almost conspiratorial. Colin Thomas looked at her plate and shook his head. "That doesn't look very filling, Rachael. Why don't you try this?"

He pushed a large bag over. She opened it curiously. Her heart skipped a beat when she started to smell the contents. It was a full kosher meal: a bowl of beef tsimmes, a noodle kugel and an apple-date Bundt cake. She was barely able to stop herself drooling.

"How? How did you manage this?"

"One of us knows a Jewish family that lives close our folks. So, our mam asked them what we should get for you. They spoke to some friends of theirs and they spoke to friends and, well, things got arranged and this turned up for you an hour or so ago. It's cold I'm afraid, but at least you can eat it all. We'll hide the other stuff so our cooks won't be offended."

Newton grinned as Rachael gave way to hunger and started to wolf down the meal that some kind-hearted friends-of-friends-of-friends had sent over for her. Then, he wondered at the spirit of humanity shown by people who would give up a portion of their scarce rations so that a girl they didn't know could have a decent meal.

Cabinet Room, Government House, Calcutta, India

"The armed forces are taking inventory of our assets now, Your Excellency. Put bluntly, we have an excellent Army, a small but capable Navy but no air force worth speaking about. We have not one single fighter aircraft in the region. Nor do we have any prospect of building any."

The Marquess of Linlithgow took off his glasses and rubbed his eyes. With every day that passed, the manifest unpreparedness of India to exist as an independent country was becoming more obvious. What had seemed like an intoxicating project eight weeks earlier was now a desperate struggle for survival. Even Nehru and his cohort from the Indian Congress Party were beginning to be demoralized by the sheer number of problems piling up.

"There are some Indian forces in the Middle East; can't we withdraw them from there? That would solve at least some of the political problems we face as well as reinforcing us here."

Sir Eric Haohoa shook his head. "The troops there are involved in stabilizing the administration in Egypt and the Horn of Africa. If we pull them out now, we will be inviting chaos in that region. This brings us to another problem that has so far gone unmentioned. There are a lot of Dominion personnel in the U.K. whose position is very uncertain, to say the least. There are not a few senior officers in the British defense establishment who come from Dominion backgrounds. This doesn't affect us too much as far as the Air Force and the Navy are concerned, but there are many alumni of the Indian Army in the upper echelons of the British Army and their position is decidedly uncomfortable. I would say that whatever Halifax and his allies might wish government policy to be, I can't see any of the services looking at the Empire and kicking it over the side without a qualm, if they can avoid it.

"I think it is safe to say that there is a widespread feeling in the War Office and Admiralty that they want to see us right. Oh, I doubt they will actively oppose Halifax at this time and openly defy the government to help out the Empire, but I can see a back room consensus developing, within the Imperial General Staff, and elsewhere, to try and do their best to set us up in terms of self defense. With Halifax cutting us off and leaving us out in the cold, I think they'd have a lot of support in that too.

"As far as the Dominion personnel in the UK are concerned, I think there will be a move to form them up into independent units and train them like any other British formation until forced to repatriate them. When they do come home, they'll be arriving as useful units, if not equipped ones. That makes the aircraft purchased by London but currently held in the USA of critical value. The Australians, Canadians and New Zealanders will have trained fighter pilots to fly them. So will the South Africans. We're out on a limb here. The fact we didn't participate in the Empire Air Training Scheme means that we won't have those cadres to build on."

"We have had word from General Wavell on the matter of the security of Egypt and the Canal Zone. Our intelligence has projected an invasion of those areas by Italy at several times in the last two months. According to General Wavell's staff, the order to invade was actually given ten days ago, on August 8th. The physical invasion is expected at any time. The same sources tell us that Herr Hitler is not supporting Mussolini in this matter, since he values the Armistice with Britain more than the alliance with Italy. Sir Eric, the Italians have reached almost fifty miles inside Kenya and General Wavell regards the Fourth and Fifth Indian Divisions there as being critical to maintaining the situation in that theater. We can't withdraw them. Nor can we ignore the air component there. At the moment, Commonwealth forces in East Africa are fighting modern Italian warplanes with obsolete biplanes from the early 1930s. I believe the South Africans are even flying Hawker Furies there."

"I think, Your Excellency, that Wing Commander Baldwin would look upon Hawker Furies as manna from Heaven. His best offering in the air defense sector is to convert some of the Blenheim bombers to fighters. I can think of nothing that more highlights how much we need those American aircraft."

"So, it appears, do the rest of the Dominions. There will be a hard fight over them and that assumes they will indeed be made available to us. This may be an awkward question, Sir Eric, but who actually owns those aircraft?"

Sir Eric consulted the papers he had brought with him. They constituted an extensive file, one several inches thick. Fortunately, the lawyers who had prepared them had also made an executive summary. "That is an interesting question, Your Excellency. The aircraft were purchased by the French Government in the period 1937 – 1939 and the British Government from 1938 onwards. These aircraft were paid for in gold; the monies placed in an escrow account, from which funds were released by the escrow administration at agreed stages. In most cases, this represented 25 percent when construction of aircraft started, 25 percent when the aircraft was completed and the balance when they were accepted by the national authorities. Therefore, although the aircraft have actually been paid for, the manufacturing companies have only received half of the agreed sums. The rest is still sitting in escrow until somebody accepts those aircraft.

"Now, the question is, who owns those aircraft? The obvious answer is the British and French Governments. That then gives rise to a further question, who are the French and British governments? The United States officially recognizes the Vichy government of France as a successor to the Paris Government, but this is disputed by General De Gaulle, who has proclaimed himself the head of the Free French Government. He also has a claim to the French-ordered aircraft, although where he would put them is a very good question. The French overseas possessions have fallen in line with the orders from Vichy almost to a man. So, if delivery of those aircraft to the Vichy government is ruled out, there is no obvious successor to take possession of them. We stand as good a chance of getting them as anybody.

"With us, the situation is completely different. The Daventry Message clearly transfers authority and legitimate government away from London and places it in the hands of the Dominions and Colonies under the authority of their Governor-General. That is our interpretation of it, at least. Therefore, the ownership of the British aircraft goes with the legitimacy of the government and that means they are ours. How we divide them up between us is theoretically up to us, although I would suggest the Americans might have something to say about that.

"However, there is another complicating factor. The aircraft have not been delivered or paid for in full. Technically, both the British and French governments are in default on their payments for those aircraft and their actual owner is remains the companies that built them Primarily, that is Curtiss with the Model 75 and Model 81 fighters, Douglas with the DB-7 light bombers and Lockheed with the Hudson patrol aircraft. Not to mention Consolidated with the Catalina flying boats and the LB-30 long-range bombers. If any one of those companies went to war with us today, they'd win.

"Finally, there is the question of the interest on the funds held in escrow. Who does that belong to?"

"There needs to be a conference." Lord Linlithgow shook his head. "These things need to be resolved face-to-face. The question is where? Whoever hosts that conference will be in a good position to claim leadership of the Commonwealth, pro-tem at least."

"We'd better make sure it is either us or on neutral ground then. The Canadians and Australians will be locking horns over just that issue and the last thing we want is either of them lording it over us."

Pembroke Dock, Wales, United Kingdom

"With respect, Sir, these aren't our aircraft."

Squadron Leader Joseph Alleyne looked at the line of twelve Sunderland Mark I flying boats. They were brand new, pristine and shining. A year earlier, Number 10 Squadron's Sunderlands had looked just like that, but a year of hard service patrolling around Great Britain had taken the gloss off their paint and the smell of newness from their cabin.

"They are now. Ruling from the Air Ministry. The Australian Government paid for a squadron of brand new Sunderlands, not a squadron

135

that have already seen extensive service. So, you are to swap your used aircraft for an equivalent number of new-manufacture Sunderlands intended for 95 Squadron and then leave the country before anybody says otherwise. There'll be some passengers coming down for you to take with you."

Air Marshal Sir Frederick Bowhill frowned mightily at the young Australian officer. In his opinion, the Commonwealth forces left much to be desired where conventional standards of discipline were concerned. On the other hand, if it hadn't been for their streak of rebelliousness, the whole Empire might have caved in when Halifax pulled the blanket out.

"Where do we go? What do we do?" Alleyne was bewildered and felt frighteningly lost. Suddenly, he remembered an event long ago, when a lost dog had attached itself to him and followed him home. The look in the dog's eyes all those years ago had been an eerie foreshadowing of how Alleyne felt at this moment. Lonely, dazed, disorientated, abandoned and vulnerable. When they had reached home, he'd seen a hopeless, forlorn look in the animal's eyes; the expectation that he would, once again, be chased away. That was what Alleyne had expected his mother to do. But she took one look at the poor hound, took him in and fed him. Alleyne also remembered how the expression in the dog's eyes had changed to joy at the realization he was, at long last, somebody's dog again. *Will we be that lucky? Or will we end up wandering lost and homeless?*

"Away from here, as soon as possible. We have telegraphed the Australian Government, telling them that you and your aircraft have been ordered to leave Great Britain with immediate effect. If you receive no orders to the contrary, I would suggest you head for Gibraltar first, refuel there and then make your way to Alexandria. You can find a home there, for a while at least. General Wavell has repudiated the Armistice Agreement in view of Italian attacks on Egypt and the Sudan.

"As for what you do, you will have to consult your Government on that. As far as we are concerned, they have gone their own way."

"Refuel, sir?"

"These aircraft are still technically assigned to 95 Squadron. All their paperwork refers to 95 Squadron. When you arrive in Gibraltar, you will be, as far as anybody knows, 95 Squadron. Any fuel you requisition will be charged to 95 Squadron. By the time the real 95 Squadron gets here, which will be 48 hours after we get word from Gibraltar that they have apparently arrived there, you should be well clear."

Alleyne had a hard job stopping himself laughing. This was a deception worthy of anything he and his men had pulled off over the years. "Very good, Sir. Gibraltar and then Alexandria it is."

"Good man. One other thing. Three G-class Empire flying boats will be going along with you. As far as anybody is concerned, they are route testing for the resumption of Imperial Airways flying boat services. When do you plan to leave?"

"Tomorrow morning, Sir. At dawn."

"They'll be here. Look after them, Squadron Leader."

Cabinet Room, Government House, Calcutta, India

"The next item on the agenda is raising monies needed for the operation of the Government and investment in our national infrastructure." Lord Linlithgow looked around the room. "I need hardly add that this is a most pressing problem and one that is critical for our success as an independent nation."

"If I might make a proposal to the Cabinet, I believe that it might go some small way towards addressing this grave problem, while also righting an injustice that afflicts so many of our fellow countrymen." Nehru spoke gravely; his eyes flickered around the Cabinet. With the departure of Sir Richard Cardew, the most outspoken opposition to the presence of the Indian Congress Party in Cabinet had gone, but there were other, less overt opponents. "I refer, of course to the activities of money-lenders in every small village and town across India. Their depredations bring poverty and hunger wherever they go. They drain away the life-blood of our farmers and keep them in perpetual debt bondage. They are an evil that we must remove from our midst."

"Surely you overstate the harm these people do?" George Edward Parkes was responsible for agriculture in the Indian Central Legislative Assembly. In Nehru's eyes, the very fact that he could say that showed how out-of-touch he was with the sector of the economy he was supposed to oversee.

"I think not," Nehru was speaking slowly and carefully. This was, after all, his first substantive contribution to a Cabinet meeting. "In the farming villages, the money lenders advance the cost of the seed to the farmers. They take payment of that loan in the form of a share of the crops grown from that seed. That share is never less than half and is often two-thirds or three-quarters of the total crop.

"What is left is barely enough to keep the farmers and their families alive through the rest of the year until the next crop comes in. They are unable to save money or seed for their next crop. So, once again, they must return to the money lenders. And where do the money lenders get the seed they sell to the farmers with the funds they so expensively loan? Why, from the share of the crop that they took the year before! These men do nothing but live off the labors of others. It is time we ended their activities, once and for all."

"Up to three-quarters, you say?" Parkes was shaken by the revelation. "That does sound excessive. Damned excessive, if you ask me. But how will doing something about this raise money for the Government?"

"The key to the power of the money-lenders is that they have a grip on the seed for the next year's crop and can charge what they will for it. In a nutshell, they lend money and then take it straight back as payment for the seed. Now, few of those money-lenders pay the proper tax on their incomes. If we inspect their declared earnings, we will find that they only allow for interest rates of perhaps ten percent instead of several hundred.

"So, before the next planting, we audit those money-lenders and confiscate their supplies of seed in lieu of payment on back-taxes owed. We distribute that seed, free of charges, to the farmers explaining to them that this is a once-only compensation for prior over-payment. Come the harvest season, the share of the crop that would once have been taken by the money-lenders is now theirs. Some, they will store as seed for the next harvest. The rest they will sell and turn into money. Ahh, my friends, but what will they do with that money? They will wish to save it, but where?"

"A bank, of course." To Parkes, that was an obvious answer, but it was one that again showed he understood little of the living conditions of the Indian country dwellers.

"There are no banks outside the big cities." Nehru astonished himself by how patient he could be. "But there is one thing that is in every village. A post office. I propose we set up a system of post office savings accounts. They will be suited to the small investor and will pay a small but reliable rate of interest. After all, the money-lenders are, I am ashamed to say, Indians. But, when an Indian wishes to make a solemn oath, he will say 'I give you the word of an Englishman.' A savings account backed by the word of the English will be considered as safe as gold. The farmers will save their money in the post offices, where it will earn interest. While it is there, we can use it for our own purposes, paying off any withdrawals with monies deposited by others."

"That's called a Ponzi scheme. I rather think it is illegal." Sir Eric Haohoa was impressed by the idea. The money coming into those post office accounts would not be any great sum individually, but there would be millions of such accounts and cumulatively they would provide a healthy income.

"In the final analysis, is not every government a Ponzi scheme?" Nehru looked around the cabinet room with a broad smile on his face."

"Yes, but it's not considered good form to say so too loudly." Lord Linlithgow sounded amused. "This scheme does sound as if it would solve some of our problems. I move that the Treasury and Post Office form a joint committee to adopt and enact Pandit's suggestion. Any objections?

"Very well. So moved."

Dining Room, The City of London Club, Old Broad Street, London, United Kingdom

"The smoked trout please, followed by the breast of pigeon." Sir Edward Bridges put down the menu and looked over at his host. Reading the elaborate menu had been a formality for him; the trout and pigeon were his established favorites here.

Sir Desmond Glasebrooke was hard put to make his decision. Eventually, he ordered the potted shrimps and applewood smoked venison. The wine waiter had brought the first of their bottles and poured for them. Then, they were discretely left on their own.

"Edward, old chap, how are things going in Downing Street?" Sir Desmond gave a strong impression of a walrus that had just learned of the death of a much-loved relative.

Bridges shook his head sadly. "Very difficult, I fear, Desmond. The truth is, I don't think that the Prime Minister quite understands how everything fits together. He really isn't one of us, you know."

Glasebrooke shook his head sadly. "Between us, Edward, the chaps in the City aren't terribly happy with the current course of events. I might even go as far to say the chaps are perturbed."

Bridges put down his fork. "As bad as that? They're not concerned, are they?"

Seconds ticked by while Glasebrooke thought very carefully before answering. "No, not concerned. Not yet. If things don't settle down soon, though, they might reach that point. A major row like this within the Commonwealth, well, it makes the chaps unhappy. Some of them are beginning to think that the current administration may well be just a little bit unsound."

"My word." Bridges was shocked. "I had no idea things had reached that point. The dispute with the Dom/Col isn't that serious. It's more a matter of insensitivity at this end and trampled toes on theirs."

"I'm sorry, Edward, but I really must beg permission to differ on that point. This whole affair might have started that way, but it has gone beyond that point. The situation with Dom/Col is getting serious. Are you aware that they are beginning to move their financial reserves out of London? And that the Australian Division that was heading for Britain has been diverted to the Middle East?"

"That is serious." Bridges hesitated himself, concealing the uncertainty about what he could say by carefully anointing a piece of smoked trout with roasted lemon jelly. "We knew about the South African Division going to Kenya, of course. That was no great worry; the IGS might have diverted them there anyway. The Italians have advanced at least fifty miles into Kenya and the presence of the South Africans there will stabilize that situation. The P.M. is more worried about the Canadian Division. Technically, they are still at war with Germany and he thinks they could bring down the armistice. He is considering ordering them home. And that would be another breach with the Commonwealth. One that would be much harder for all the parties involved to accept. But, if Dom/Col are moving their funds out of the City, it would be very serious."

"What is happening with the armies really doesn't worry the chaps too much." Glasebrooke waved his fork around dismissively. "The financial thing is perturbing them much more. Ever since the turn of the century, the hard core of Britain's wealth has been in global finance and investment. We own, or have serious interests in, sewers, water, electrical, telegraph, telephone, rail, shipping, warehousing, banks and retail companies all across the world. The chaps really don't think that is too much affected by where a division goes or what happens to a squadron of flying boats. The split in the Commonwealth is quite different; quite different. If this goes on, the Prime Minister will be handing all our investments abroad to our competition on a plate."

There was a long pause while the waiters cleared the first set of plates away and brought the next course, along with the appropriate wine. Glasebrooke waited until they had withdrawn before continuing. "Take Malaya. Because the Japanese will. Does the Prime Minister really want to hand over all that rubber and palm oil to the Japanese? The economic loss to the chaps in the City would be stupendous and it won't stop there. I don't want to sound excitable, Edward, but the chaps really do think this is vital."

Bridges sighed. "I understand all this, Desmond; I really do. You're preaching to the choir. I think most of the Civil Service knows that. The problem is that HE doesn't see it that way. To him, the Commonwealth is a bunch of unruly children who need to be sent to bed without any supper. No matter what anybody says, he won't change his mind on that."

"But this is madness!" The bereaved walrus had just found he'd been cut out of the family will. If Glasebrooke could have looked any more depressed, Bridges was unable to work out how.

"I know Desmond, but HE won't listen to me. He won't listen to anybody outside his own small circle of trusted advisors. They all agree with everything he says; because if they didn't, they wouldn't be part of that circle." Bridges sighed and moodily ate some of his pigeon breast, reflecting that it was a good thing rationing did not apply to meals eaten in restaurants. How long that would continue was another matter. The whole issue of food rationing was beginning to raise its ugly head, with people asking why it was still being imposed when the war was over. For a brief second, Bridges had a flash of his nightmare where he walked down the streets of a Britain that had died from starvation.

"Desmond, may we put that to one side for a moment? There's another matter I wish to raise with you. Food imports. How do we substitute for supplies from the Commonwealth?"

"We can't." Glasebrooke was emphatic on that point. "We need Australian and New Zealand meat and dairy products, Indian tea and rice, Canadian wheat, West Indian sugar. All the rest. Fortunately, we won't have to. The chaps have already had discrete inquiries from the Dom/Col about us continuing to buy their products. They need to sell to us as much as we need to buy from them. In fact, I would venture to say that if they were allowed to do so, they would actually increase food exports to us."

"That is something of a relief. I am beginning to believe that we need to build up our food reserves here against any future trade disruptions."

"Future, Edward? The trade disruptions already exist and are costing the chaps a lot of money. As to increasing food imports, the problem is that the Dom/Col want to be paid in gold for their products. You know they are going to introduce their own currency?"

Bridges was aghast. "They can't do that. It would mean the end of the Commonwealth!" Then the implications of what he had just said sunk in. "Oh."

"That's what the chaps said when they heard. That's why they are perturbed. The Dom/Col are set on reintroducing the Sovereign, gold-backed no less, as an international trading currency. One that excludes the pound sterling. If that currency succeeds in establishing itself, then the City will be sidelined as a major financial center. I can think of at least one other country that would be very pleased to see that happen."

"The Americans." Bridges spoke with heavy certainty.

"Of course. They may well support the Sovereign, at least at first, simply to downgrade the importance of the City and increase that of New York. I needn't tell you what the chaps think about that idea. There is another whisper as well." Glasebrooke looked around, making sure that he could not be overheard. "There are whispers that the Hongs are on the move."

"Are they, indeed? I suppose, with the future of Hong Kong in doubt, they must be considering some preparations."

"The future of Hong Kong is in doubt?" Glasebrooke opened his eyes wide. "That is indeed serious. I believe that is enough to make the chaps quite concerned. It would explain the whispers we have been hearing, though. It has been suggested that the Hongs plan to move their headquarters to Chongqing, Kunming or Bombay. Two of those are outside the Commonwealth. That does have the chaps perturbed as well. If the Hongs move, they'll take their access to the Chinese business community, the internal communications system it thrives upon and the wealth it represents, with them."

"The Japanese are making noises to the effect that, as the regional allies of Germany, they will become the responsible power for our Dom/Col in the area. The Germans have officially expressed no comment on that claim, but we have every reason to believe they are quietly supporting it as part of their agreement with Japan. A move on Hong Kong is, we believe, only a matter of time. The Hongs have much better intelligence than we do. If they are preparing to move, then they must be aware of the probability as well."

"If the Japanese successfully move on Hong Kong, then they won't stop there." Glasebrooke shook his head. "This really is very serious indeed.

Malaya and Singapore will be next and India cannot be far behind. You must get the PM to make a stand on this."

"He won't." Bridges sighed and waited while the plates were again cleared away. He settled on a banana crème brulee for dessert.

When it arrived, the sommelier leaned forward confidentially. "Gentlemen, we have a rather fine Psersigberg Gewurstraminer Grand Cru 1932 desert wine if you wish to complete your enjoyment?"

Glasebrooke sighed again. "That sounds very good; we'll indulge ourselves. A half-bottle perhaps?"

Once the sommelier had departed, Glasebrooke leaned forward to Bridges. "After all, I rather think that we should get used to drinking German wine, don't you? We may not have a choice much longer."

Pembroke Dock, Wales, United Kingdom

"Squadron Leader Alleyne?"

The figure was in civilian clothes, but Alleyne had an almost-irresistible urge to jump to attention. The man gave a slightly twisted grin and shook his head. "No formalities, please. The less obvious our departure is, the better for all concerned."

Sir Wilfred Freeman smiled sadly at the young Australian who was helping him leave the country and service to which he had devoted his life. Somehow, it didn't help matters to know that he wasn't the only one who had made this particular decision or that he had been helped by the abrupt closure of his department. He had been responsible for selecting the aircraft that would form the basis of the Royal Air Force's re-equipment program. Now that program also had been abruptly terminated. Literally everything he had worked for was either abandoned or rated as being of little account. Looking at the waiting Sunderland flying boat, he asked himself whether his departure really was a call of duty to aid the Commonwealth countries that remained in the fight or merely a response to wounded pride.

"We're glad to have you on board, Sir." Alleyne refrained from saluting, but he felt a surge of respect for the grandfatherly man before him who had made what must have been an agonizing decision. Behind them, boxes of files and other documents were being loaded into the Sunderland. Then, Alleyne saw another one of his passengers and the bottom seemed to suddenly fall out of his world.

"General Smuts, Sir. . . ."

"Quiet boy. We said no formalities." The voice was gruff; its South African accent sounded harsh in the soft pre-dawn light, but the words had an amused timbre to them that took any sting out of his phrasing. Jan Smuts looked more than a little amused at the situation. "You are Captain of this particular ship and we all defer to you."

The third member of the party looked as if he might have disagreed with that, but any comment he might have had was pre-empted by Jan Smuts. He frowned mightily as he introduced himself. "Air Vice Marshal Arthur Harris, Officer Commanding 5 Group, Bomber Command."

Alleyne took an instant dislike to the man. There was something about him that contrasted sharply with the gentlemanly demeanor of the other two members of the party he would be carrying to Gibraltar and Alexandria. He gave no sign of the impression, though. "Will you all be going all the way to Alexandria with us?"

Smuts nodded. "Harris and I will be leaving you there, though, and going back to South Africa. Wilfred will be going to Alexandria and then on to Australia. I hope he will do for your aircraft industry what he managed to achieve for us here. And that his life's work will see a more satisfactory conclusion than it was fated to receive here."

"Perhaps we will have the honor of flying you there, Sir." Privately, Alleyne doubted that. He already had a strong suspicion that his flying boats would be a key part of the power equation now being written in the Middle East.

His suspicions were confirmed when Freeman shook his head. "I strongly suspect you will be remaining in the Middle East for some time to come, Squadron Leader. Whatever the future may hold, and I sadly suspect that future is grim indeed, the Middle East at this point is time is the single most crucial area in play. It is the actual point of action and will remain so until the Italian question there is resolved."

Smuts nodded magisterially. "Deterrence against further aggression has to be the bed rock of the Commonwealth position. We have to face the truth; we are a collection of weak powers looking to assume a mantle of strength, and that can only be achieved through success in war. The Middle East is a running litmus test of our real resolve, both internally and internationally. It is our collective shop window and we'll be judged to a large extent by our deeds there. If we limp-wrist the conflict with Italy, we not only look weak to the rest of the world, but we'll also feel weak as a collective and with the individual dominions, and so be weak.

"Squadron Leader, the Dominions rejecting Halifax was just words. The Middle East is the critical point for the Commonwealth where we must turn words into deeds." Suddenly Smuts smiled. "It is not often that a mere Squadron Leader hears such matters of great political strategy discussed. But then, it is not often that a mere Squadron Leader gets to be a critical part in such strategic considerations. Your twelve flying boats may well become the key to all our futures."

"What bomb load do you carry?" Harris sounded as if he hadn't bothered to listen to Smuts.

"On paper, two thousand pounds Sir, but Shorts are very conservative in their loaded weight figures. As long as we don't exceed maximum take off weight, we can carry up to five thousand pounds of warload. Usually depth charges but we have carried mines and torpedoes."

Harris grunted. "And the Italian ports in North Africa are within range of Alexandria." Without further word, he climbed into the barge that was ready to take the passengers out to the anchored Sunderland.

Room 208, Munitions Building, Washington, DC, USA

"What do we do with them? Somebody better come up with an idea fast before Congress finds out about them and makes us take them."

"We impounded all of them on the grounds that the United States believes delivery to the governments in London and Vichy would be destabilizing to European security."

"With all due respect, Cordell, that's just made matters that much worse." Henry Stinson and Cordell Hull glared at each other.

"There are really two problems here."

"Just two? You do realize that if the manufacturers don't get paid for those aircraft, they'll go bankrupt and that won't do our aircraft industry any good at all?" Phillip Stuyvesant smiled benignly at Robert Jackson, who glared back in response. Casting an eye around the meeting, Stuyvesant noted that everybody seemed to be glaring at everybody else. *This meeting* he thought *has promise.*

Attorney-General Jackson was actually grinding his teeth. "I said two problems. There are two categories of aircraft: one owned by the British and the other by the French. The French and British orders represent entirely different legal situations. Both countries have actually paid for the aircraft in question, although the final payment for them is still in escrow. The British case is easy. In the Daventry Message, King George VI, who is the legitimate head of state in Great Britain, transferred authority and legitimacy from London to the Governor-Generals in the Empire. So, the various bits of the Empire own the aircraft and they have to settle amongst themselves who owns what. Nothing to do with us. As soon as they've made their minds up, the aircraft get delivered, the remaining funds are released from escrow and your precious aircraft manufacturers, Stuyvesant, get their money. It's the French that are the problem."

"Aren't they always?" Stimson was staring at the ceiling. He looked around, caught Stuyvesant's eye, and gave him a surreptitious wink.

"Henry, please." Jackson was getting exasperated. "The Vichy government has no legitimate successors outside Metropolitan France. Therefore there is nobody to whom we can deliver the impounded French orders. Indeed, we cannot deliver them to anybody without legally purchasing them. We can refund the purchase money to the French and hold that in escrow until there's a government over there we approve of, or a legitimate alternative arises. But we're still stuck with the aircraft. And Congress might find them."

Henry Morgenthau pressed his fingertips together. "There is a way around this. We refund the monies paid by the French, thus transferring the aircraft to our control. We can then sell them to the British Empire countries, thus ensuring that they are used against Nazi Germany, the purpose for which they were produced."

"The Dominions can't afford them." Cordell Hull shook his head. He knew all too well that the now-severed parts of the British Empire were in desperate financial straits.

"Then loan them the money." Jackson was impassioned. "We loan them the money in dollars, but allow them to make repayment in these new Sovereigns they are announcing. In doing so, we support their new currency and wean them away from the pound sterling and thus put a pistol shot through the head of the British Empire. We also give them the tools they need to reinforce their independence and stabilize their economies."

"The latter is too much to ask." Morgenthau shook his head. "Their economies need a lot more than a few dollars to stabilize them. They need industry, investment and so on. There's a killing to be made there for the right people. For a far-sighted man who is prepared to wait for a return on his investment, the rewards will be rich indeed. But I agree with the basic proposal. We make a very soft loan to any of the Dominions that are prepared to buy the ex-French aircraft from us. Low rate of interest; we loan money in dollars, accept payment in Sovereigns.

"This way, those aircraft get put to good use." Morgenthau's voice hardened; a note of almost fanatical hatred came into it. "And anything that hurts the Nazis is a good use. They must suffer for what they have done. *Germania delenda est.* Phillip, I look to you for knowledge on how to reduce Germany to a desert."

"I'll do my best, Henry."

Dumbarton Avenue, Georgetown, Washington, DC, USA

"Australia? Everything is poisonous there." Igrat put a note of distress into her voice.

"The salt water crocodiles and great white sharks aren't." Stuyvesant sounded remarkably unimpressed by his daughter's feigned misery. "But what really upsets you is that there are no decent shops in that part of the world."

"Well, that too." Igrat looked at her father and lifted her eyebrows. "But, no shops for me to spend my travelling companion's money in means half my cover is gone before I even start. Who do you want me to see, anyway?"

"There is a man called Mister Essington Lewis, who runs Broken Hill Proprietary Company. He's an odd character, Iggie. You'll have to be careful in how you approach him. He's strictly formal and he hates using the telephone.

That's why I want you to go and see him personally. He makes an absolute fetish of punctuality, so bear that in mind when you make appointments."

"That's how, not why." Igrat made the observation completely deadpan.

"Lewis is a gifted operator. He knows the steel and mining industries inside out; and, more importantly, knows how to make companies in that sector work. I want to offer him a partnership. We'll provide backing for a joint investment in India. If that country is going to succeed in standing on its own feet, it will need its own heavy industry, something it painfully lacks at the moment. The country even lacks the people needed to work out what it needs. So, Lewis is the right person to get involved out there. If we get in on the ground floor, the investment we make will grow. I happen to know that he wants to see the Commonwealth as the largest steel producer outside North America."

"How do you know that?" Igrat's curiosity was piqued by the offhand comment.

"There was a major confrontation between BHP and a group called Hoskins. Basically Hoskins was a front for a consortium of the big British steel makers who didn't like the rise of BHP and wanted to kill it. Their attitude was that if they couldn't stop Australia making steel, then they wanted to control the way that steel was sold. Lewis believed in constantly re-equipping his factories so that they were at the leading edge of technology. As a result, Australian steel was the cheapest in the world. Even with shipping charges, it was cheap enough to be a major threat in the UK home market. Anyway, the British steelmakers put a lot of money into setting up their rival to BHP but lost out.

"The important thing from our point of view is that, once they had won the trade battle, BHP cut a deal with the British backers. BHP would take over their raw steel production and go into partnership with them in a new joint venture to make alloys steels in Australia. That was typical. BHP has a long track history of amicably swallowing its competition rather than killing it. I think they can look at the Indian steel industry the same way. It will be a long, long time before India's steel production will meet the country's full needs and BHP would be happy to fill the difference in a cooperative manner. From India's point of view, BHP doesn't just supply product and better quality raw materials than can be sourced in India, but technology. BHP has been in the game long enough to start its own R&D; making its own developments and building its own plant when it had something better than it could buy. As a result, BHP is scrapping more plant in a year than India can buy at this stage. I think Lewis and his BHP can provide India with a useful mentor, and see a profit in doing it. BHP like profit, they like it a very great deal, and they do think long term. So they're a good partner for us.

"So, give Lewis the proposal packet and the word on how we see things and why. Make sure Lewis knows that we're in this long-term. He

146

doesn't need to know what we mean by long term, of course. This is part of another investment I'm planning. I've got a guy called William Pawley of the Intercontinental Aircraft Corporation of New York looking into setting up an aviation company in India. Pawley has been a primary exporter of American aircraft to India and I've arranged for him to obtain a large number of machine-tools and equipment from here. If India is going to get a big pile of ex-British and ex-French military aircraft, they'll need to maintain them. That's an opportunity for us. Lillith's done the financial projections and she's rubbing her hands with glee."

"Doing well by doing good again?" Igrat firmly believed that virtue brought its own rewards, although her definition of virtue was rather different from the accepted norms.

"Politically, yes. The policy of the present United States government is that the old colonial empires should be dismantled and their constituent countries placed on a firm economic footing." Stuyvesant paused for a second, then continued. "The empires falling will happen anyway and its better they go quietly than fighting the process every step of the way. We're helping the inevitable along by investing in the economic development of the Commonwealth countries. If it does us some good in the process, so much the better."

Short Sunderland Mark 1 F-Freddie, Over The Eastern Mediterranean

The fifteen flying boats were spread out in a loose gaggle; the three G-class boats in the middle with the dozen Sunderlands surrounding them. The first leg of the flight from Great Britain to Gibraltar had gone very smoothly, as had the refuelling at the naval base. That had simply taken time, although they had been fortunate there were specially designed refuelling barges manned by trained marine crews at Gibraltar. The great naval base was equipped to refuel many flying boats during the course of the day, so a full squadron in transit had been only an inconvenience.

Privately, Alleyne believed that this would be the last time they might see such luxuries. In the future, operating from extemporized bases would mean refuelling from drums or unpowered barges. That would take hours. Lack of properly trained ground crews would put the work of handling of the fuel nozzles and opening/closing the aircraft fuel tanks in the hands of his own crews. The bellies of the Sunderlands were stuffed with oil supplies and minor spares, while their accommodation was occupied by the squadron's immediate ground crews. All that meant they would be able to operate, for a while at least, away from any fixed base.

"Gunners, keep your eyes open for hostile fighters. We're getting into range of Italian airbases by now."

"Do you really think that the Italians will attack us?" Sir Wilfred Freeman was sitting in the co-pilot's seat, looking out across the Mediterranean.

"If they know we're Australian, yes. We're still painted up in 95 Squadron markings, but how long the ruse will hold, I don't know. There's fighting going on in East Africa; if Italy hasn't invaded Egypt yet, she will soon. I was half-expecting to hear that the invasion had started before we left Gibraltar. Come to think of it." Alleyne keyed his radio. "All aircraft, drop down to one thousand feet. Say again, one thousand feet. Keep your eyes skinned for wop fighters."

Without knowing quite why, Freeman was suddenly positive they would be attacked. He scanned the sky, certain in his own mind that the appearance of Italian fighters was a question of when, not if. It was with almost a sense of relief that he spotted a group of six shadows against the clouds scattering the sky above them.

"Squadron Leader, two o'clock high."

"Got them." Alleyne was terse. "All aircraft, we have hostiles coming in. Drop down to two hundred feet and tighten the formation up. BOAC aircraft, try and stay out of the way. We'll put up a screen around you."

"Ever so grateful, old chap." The voice on the radio was impossibly British.

"I don't envy them." Freeman sounded sympathetic. "Unarmed aircraft, waiting for fighters to attack them."

"They'll have to get past us first and the Eye-ties will be in for a nasty surprise when they try. They can't get underneath us; that's why we came down so low. And they'll have a hell of a time from our turrets and beam guns." Alleyne was confident of that. His Sunderlands had twin .303-inch machine guns in nose, dorsal and beam positions, a quadruple .303-inch tail turret, and four fixed .303s in the nose. They'd already proved they could give a good account of themselves against the best the Luftwaffe could offer. Once again, his stomach clenched slightly at the thought of the work his squadron had volunteered for and then been forced to leave undone.

Above them, a flight of six Italian fighters were peeling off to dive. Alleyne looked hard at them; radial-engined monoplanes with a curious hump-backed design,. *Fiat G.50s. Agile as all hell, but lightly armed and no armor. They are in for a nasty surprise.*

The Italian pilots were inexperienced when it came to attacking heavily-armed, multi-seat aircraft. They'd done the traditional peel off maneuver; each aircraft taking its turn to do a wing-over and enter its dive. As a result, they were coming in from the stern quarter in single file. Each fighter in turn would be the target of the concentrated firepower of at least three flying boats.

The Australian gunners were experienced. They'd fought fighters before and knew how to go about driving them off. They held their fire until the lead fighter was in close. Then they filled the sky around it with bullets.

Looking over his shoulder, Alleyne guessed that at least 16 machine guns were firing on the leader. He was almost masked from sight by the hail of tracer fire. The Italian fighter burst into flames and continued its dive downwards to plunge into the sea.

Behind him, the Italian number two was also lost in the glare of the massed tracers. Its path was marked by a black stream of smoke. It first turned orange as it mixed with fire, then ended in an explosion of ruptured fuel tanks.

The third fighter saw what had happened to the two leaders. He skidded away as the machine guns tracked in on it. Alleyne guessed it had been hit. His gunners stopped firing when it veered away. Ammunition on the Sunderlands was too precious to waste on aircraft that had already broken off their attacks.

That left four fighters circling the formation of flying boats. The Italian fighter pilots didn't lack courage, but they had the sense to realize they were up against something much more capable than the aircraft they were accustomed to facing. Two split away and came at Alleyne's Sunderland from head-on. That was a bad mistake.

Alleyne swung his nose slightly and opened fire with the four fixed nose guns, reinforced by the twin guns in his upper and nose turrets. Tracer fire envelopd the attacking fighters. They sheered away. One developed a thin stream of whitish gray smoke from its engine. It was last seen heading away, losing altitude.

Three fighters left.

The fate of their flight-mates left the remaining fighter pilots wary. They tried a few more tentative probes. Fierce return fire drove them off each time. Eventually, they turned away and headed for home. *Italian fighters were very short-ranged,* Alleyne had read in the intelligence briefings, *and they lacked combat endurance.*

"Any damage to report?"

There were a few holes from long-range .50-caliber machine gun fire, but the flying boats were essentially undamaged. Critically, the fighters had never even got close to the big G-class boats in the center of the formation. Beside him, Freeman was nodding contentedly. "Nicely done, Squadron Leader. I wonder if they'll come back with their friends?"

"I think that's very probable, Sir."

Training Area, 11th Infantry (Queen's Cobra) Division, Kanchanaburi, Thailand

His rifle had its bolt carefully wrapped in cloth to stop it rattling. All his other equipment was either wedged in place or carefully padded to avoid giving warning to the troops waiting in the defensive position ahead of them. Before setting out, he and his men had jumped up and down to make sure than there wouldn't be the slightest sound to betray the assault. It had looked strange, but there was good sense behind it. Noise was the enemy as much as the 'troops' in the dugout.

Corporal Mongkut Chandrapa na Ayuthya felt the thin white tape laid out by the reconnaissance squads in no-man's land. He was leading his section forward to its bounce-off point some hundred meters short of the enemy defenses. He had the picture in his mind: the zig-zag trenches, machine guns carefully positioned to cover the wire with an impenetrable hail of fire. Their instructors had been quite clear about what would happen if there was a deliberate assault on the position in daylight. The machine guns would slowly swing backwards and forwards, spraying the barbed wire entanglements while the troops struggled to get through. If the machine gunners did their job, the men would die on the wire. Some of the instructors had told stories of a great battle in far-away France, at a place called the Somme. A place where 60,000 men had fallen in a single day because the wire had held and the machine gunners had been skilled at their work. Mongkut couldn't even begin to conceive of that many men dying in a single day. It was almost his entire Army being wiped out.

The instructors had explained that night attacks were one way the devastating effects of barbed wire and machine guns could be offset. They had also explained that coordinating and mounting a night attack was one of the most difficult and complicated operations an Army could undertake. Faced with the alternatives of heavy casualties in assaulting fixed positions or learning the skills needed to fight at night, the Army elected to take the latter route. That was why Mongkut was following the white tapes in the middle of the night.

His hand felt the knots in the tape. His section reached their assembly point. His men spread out beside him, crawling close to the ground in case observers from the enemy should see them. Any second now, the assault would start. The seconds stretched into minutes. Mongkut felt the coldness of the night bite into his bones. Even in a tropical climate, the night air could have a chill to it. Especially for men lying motionless on the ground.

After what seemed to be hours, the horizon behind him lit up. A roar marked the guns firing. Mongkut recognized the howl overhead as outbound artillery fire. Shells crashed into the positions in front of him. It was real artillery fire. Live shells filled the air with fragments. That was the signal for the assault. He pushed hard with his feet, jumping up as he shouted out his first order since the move to the front.

"Follow me!"

All along the line, Thai infantry rose to their feet. They sprinted towards positions hit by the sudden blast of artillery fire. They swept over the trench, bayoneting sandbags representing French soldiers manning the defensive line. They shot others that were "hiding" in the bottom of the trench. Mongkut saw a gaping black hole in front of him. He guessed it was the entry point to a dugout. Almost by instinct, he tossed a thunderflash inside. The interior light up.

His section was spreading out, ready to beat off a counter-attack from the defenders; Mongkut had the firm belief that, if sandbags actually came to life and attacked him, it would be time to retire. There was another shout of "follow me!" Mongkut saw his officer ordering them forward. It was time to attack the second line of defenses.

Two hours later, the battalion assembled while the instructors evaluated its performance in the night attack. After general comments and praise for an attack carried out well, the officers and NCOs were taken to one side for individual briefings. *Praise in public, punish in private,* thought Mongkut. His lieutenant and one of the foreign instructors sat down at a table with him.

"You and your men did well, Corporal. You were quick on your feet and you followed the shells in closely. You overwhelmed the trench in fine style and were quick to set up your defense. You grenaded the dugout without delay. But, you should have followed that up; you can't be sure that the grenade got everybody down there." The foreigner produced a picture of a dugout with a deep, narrow pit in the bottom. "This is called a grenade trap. If the men inside are quick, one of them might have kicked your grenade into this and saved everybody. Also, you didn't clear the trenches on either side of you. That could have cost your entire section their lives."

"There didn't seem time to do everything, Sir." Mongkut saw his Lieutenant look surprised. It wasn't expected for a junior to speak up like that. Respect for position and rank was deeply ingrained. Yet the foreigner actually seemed to approve.

"It's hard, isn't it? You have to secure your section of the trench, grenade the dugouts, clear the sections to either side of you and make sure you are linked up with the rest of your unit. Yet, you also have to be ready to receive a counter-attack and get ready to follow up your own advance with an assault on the enemy second line. Everything at once.

"I wish I could tell you how to do it all, but I can't." The foreigner smiled sadly, shaking his head at the memories of trench warfare that flooded back to him. "All I can say is, remember everything you have to do and do what you can as the circumstances demand. If you have to leave things undone, leave them; but *never* forget you have left them undone. It's deciding what to leave undone that's the hard part. You've heard of Generalship? Well, this is Corporalship. Generalship wins wars but Corporalship wins battles. Remember that. And, for last night's exercise, a qualified well-done."

Mongkut saluted and left, feeling ridiculously pleased with himself. Inside, the German instructor made a mark in a file he carried. "Good NCO material there. I like the way he spoke up. We have to encourage that, you know. It's the NCOs who will make or break any maneuver the Army tries to make. They have to be taught to think for themselves."

"But . . . ." The infantry lieutenant tried to get his mind around a concept that did not involve the blind obedience he had thought was ideal.

"Think on it this way. You guide the unit and decide what it must do. But it's the NCOs at the sharp end who have to decide *how* to do, it then and there. That corporal shapes up well. We'll have to watch him and help him grow. He might even make Sergeant one day."

"Or an officer?"

The Lieutenant meant it as a joke, but the German advisor nodded thoughtfully. "Possibly. Time will tell."

Government House, Canberra, Australia

"The sovereign?" Thomas White made his question sound like an answer. The other two heads in the room nodded.

Fadden shrugged "Now, obviously there's a lot of details to work through, both from our side and across the Empire, before we get a new currency up and running. But, as I say, the basics are pretty clear cut. The one thing we can't do is wind back the clock. Our new currency is not going to have the British economy backing it in addition to the Empire, nor will it have the Bank of England and Whitehall looking after it and moderating the whole show. The sterling stood on its own two feet, not something we can say for our sovereign. The wider market has had little exposure to it directly over the years other than via London, so they've got no measure of its value, and without that yardstick, pessimism just snowballs.

"So, we have to establish a value for our pound against the sovereign. Just pinning it to gold will calm fears and get business moving again. But it's the rate that is critical to the sort of business we get, and no matter what rate we set, its going to step on someone toes just as they'll be stepping on ours. If we undercut the Kiwis, or more likely they undercut us, the Indians, Malays, whomever we cross swords with, will have a diplomatic bone to pick with us, as we with them. As I say, we won't have London to balance the scales. The right way to do things would be to set up a bank specifically to run the sovereign; they'd buy the gold from the producers, mint the coin, set the rates, issue any notes and do the whole business.

"But?" Locock had some idea of where this was going.

"But," Fadden sighed. "That bank would have an enormous influence over our economy and the economies of everyone else, which would make it an intensely political animal, and quite frankly, unworkable. so far as I can see. Yet, without one, we've got to work out some means of doing all the same things as individuals acting in concert; that is going to be interesting. Broadly speaking, the only alternative to a bank is a market. I'm just an out-of-practice accountant, but on the present advise I've had from Treasury and Commonwealth Bank, we end up with two options: chaos, or some pretty severe restrictions. The South Africans came up with this, and odds on, they think their gold production will give them a major say in things. God knows

152

where they got *that* idea. Once this thing hits the open market, it's going to be the trading countries turning over the money, and that means it's the Canadians who'll end up running the show, with us or India in second place, I should think. The keys to banking in this part of the world are the Hongs. We know the Japanese have covetous eyes on Hong Kong, so the Hongs will rebase themselves soon. There are already rumors they will be heading for China or India; probably the latter. With them will move any feasible chance of establishing a central bank and with it the economic clout that will mean."

Fadden shook his head. There was a problem looming in his mind that he couldn't quite put his finger on now. He had an eerie feeling he was staring out across a darkened field and hearing a dire wolf howling in the distance.

Locock probed. "Arthur?"

"Oh. . . Oh!" Fadden snapped back into the present, but was left with the stomach-tightening sensation that he was being stalked by a nameless, unseen predator. "I'm not sure if the Canadians will be too interested, you know. It occurs to me they've been cozening up to the Yanks for years. So, if they've got something to gain out of all this, they've also go a hell of a lot to lose . . . We need to talk to Ottawa and we need to do it now!"

"Oh what a tangled web, thought Locock, not for the first time. It really was a mess. It had to be for a semi-obscure back bencher to end up Prime Minister in one tumultuous night. He was only supposed to keep the seat warm while the power brokers thrashed out an acceptable solution to this three-way race. The problem came down to numbers; that was democracy, after all. If Labour had held off a few days more, White would have the support to take over the Party, but that was as leader of the opposition. There were far too many members who were happy enough to put White up as a punching bag for the Government, but would back Casey to actually lead the country, Locock himself not the least among them. Hughes had stepped aside, leaving White as his deputy leading the party. Without the numbers in his pocket, White dare not take the Prime Ministership he was entitled to, and they had a government to form in the morning . . .

Locock was under no illusions he was convenient, expedient and ultimately expendable, compromise. Privately, he took the job doubting he'd even make Sir Earle Page's record of 20 days. With Casey now bound for Canada and Fadden seeming to warm to him . . . Well, hope might spring eternal, but in the mean time, there was work to do.

"We need someone good in Chile," insisted Fadden. "They buy our coal."

"Right you are, Arthur. Chile is on my list, but apparently that means we've got to do Argentina as well or they'll get upset." White pulled out a scrap of paper. "I was thinking we need the Philippines if only to liaise locally with the Yanks, and if we put a big High Commission in Singapore, it'll cover the rest...."

"What about Bangkok and Batavia? I don't know about the Thais as yet, but we do a bit of business with the Dutchies." Again, the picture of a bleak, snow-covered field glittering in the darkness as a dire wolf howled far away forced itself into his mind. "The Governor General has been our conduit with the British intelligence services for many, many years. How the hell are we going to keep an eye on our friends and their money if we haven't got the eyes to see?"

"It's more like the ears to hear," sighed Fadden reluctantly. For the third time, he seemed to hear the dire wolf howling in the darkness. The nameless apprehension it caused returned. There was a threat out there; one that nobody had seen or even recognized yet as real as any they had seen. "I suppose we had better clear this up. It's got to be done at some point, and now is as good a time as any."

"Alright – alright," agreed Fadden with sigh. "Well, by my count, we've got one more thing before we call in the Cabinet. What are we going to do with the AIF in Egypt?"

Government House, Calcutta, India, September 17, 1940

"I have just received word from General Wavell in Egypt. Four Italian divisions, under the command of General Rodolfo Graziani, have crossed the Libyan border into Egypt and are advancing on Sidi Barrani. The Italians have carried out artillery bombardments of General Wavell's forward positions and tried to bomb targets in Egypt." Sir Eric Haohoa peered around the Cabinet Office from behind the dispatches. Those present were nodding thoughtfully. The news from Egypt was hardly a surprise, but it wasn't welcome either.

"Four divisions; that could be 100,000 men. And Archie has 30,000 at most. 7th Armoured Division and 4th Indian Infantry, if I am not mistaken." General Auchinleck was very rarely mistaken.

"I believe that is correct." Sir Eric consulted his briefing. "Yes. 7th Armoured and 4th Infantry, with 205 aircraft. The Italians have 300. Graziani has nine divisions: six regular Italian infantry and three Blackshirt militia divisions. And a small armored group. But, the initial reports are that only four divisions have been committed and they are advancing slowly. A battle group from the 7th Armoured is harassing them while the bulk of the division assembles at Mersa Matruh."

"Gentlemen, I think we are beginning to see the first steps of the Noth Plan taking place." Lord Linlithgow sounded depressed. "Is there any sign of German involvement in this attack?"

"No, Your Excellency. This, and the fighting in East Africa, appear to be a uniquely Italian effort."

"That proves it then. The Germans are holding their forces ready for the thrust through Turkey and Iraq." General Auchinleck drummed his fingers angrily on the conference table. "Otherwise, they would be supporting the Italians in the assault on Egypt. What is happening in Iraq?"

"The situation there is deteriorating fast. With the outbreak of the war, the Iraqi Government broke off diplomatic relations with Nazi Germany. However, they have refused to take the next logical step and declare war upon Germany. Our man in Baghdad, Nuri as-Said, has been replaced by the nationalist and anti-British Rashid Ali."

"Nationalist does not mean hostile." Pandit Nehru had a warning tone in his voice.

"Indeed, it does not; a point that we are trying very hard to impress upon the Americans at this moment." Sir Eric shook his head. "However, Ali has made covert contacts with German representatives in the Middle East, though he is not yet an openly pro-Axis supporter. He appears to be a much closer equivalent to Subhas Chandra Bose than is comfortable for us. It is due to his influence that Iraq did not break off diplomatic relations with Italy when they joined the war on the side of Germany. The Italian Legation in Baghdad has become the chief center for Axis propaganda and for fomenting anti-British feeling in the region. It would appear that the next scene of German activity will be in Iraq and the key to what happens there will be our position in Egypt and the Sudan. If the Commonwealth position there holds firm, then we will indeed be in a much better position to counter German moves on Iraq."

"What worries me is, if we can see that, why can't the Germans?" Sir Martyn Sharpe didn't like interfering in military and intelligence matters, but there was something about the situation that felt askew. "If this offensive in Egypt is so critical to their plans for Iraq, shouldn't they be supporting it?"

"Logistics." Auchinleck spoke decisively. "The transport facilities are inadequate to carry the supply tonnage needed for a larger force forward to the battle areas. The ports along the North African coast don't have the capacity to land supplies for much more than the present order of battle. Graziani actually has more troops than he can use at the moment. So, there is no need for the Germans to get involved and they're better off getting ready for the seizure of Iraq."

"There's a political aspect to this as well." Sir Eric picked up where Auchinleck had left off. "Egypt is technically neutral and the British troops deployed there are supposed to be guarding the Suez Canal. The British Army in Egypt reports directly to London. There is no Governor-General to whom authority might be considered delegated. So, an attack on the British troops there is a direct attack on London. An Italian assault is one thing; it can be written off as an affair conducted by a third party. Any German involvement would be an entirely different matter; a direct breach of the ceasefire they signed back in June. If anything, this Italian adventure must be deeply embarrassing to the Germans and put at risk all they gained from Halifax's actions."

"So, no German involvement then." Harold Hartley summarized that conclusion with a degree of relief. "But it appears that the mess in the Middle East will be the center of attention until it gets tidied up. And that may take some time."

"It will also require resources." Auchinleck was despondent. The truth was that with Britain out of the war, the resources needed for the Commonwealth to carry on were simply not there. Britain had been the center of the Commonwealth in much more than just name. "The Seventh Armoured Division is just about the only full-sized armored division outside the German Army at this time. Lot of armored brigades of course, but it's the only armored division available. How it will keep its tanks running is anybody's guess."

"Canada is gearing up to produce Valentine tanks, but it'll be next year before we see any." Sir Martyn shared the general depression. After the heady excitement of fulfilling a dream and setting India on the path to independence, the practical realities involved were crushing down on him. In his eyes, they could be summarized as 'a complete lack of everything.' "We don't even have the spares to keep what we have running."

"There may be a solution to that, at least." HH opened a file he had brought with him. "We have had an offer from an American gentleman, a Mr. William Pawley of the Intercontinental Aircraft Corporation of New York. He is known to us already; he arranged the export of Waco YQC-6 and Douglas DC-2 aircraft to Tata Airlines. Now, he has come to us with an offer to obtain second-hand aircraft production machinery from the United States and install it in a factory here. He suggests that the machinery he can obtain will not allow us to produce our own aircraft, but will permit the support of American–built aeroplanes here. Tata Airlines speak well of him; they describe him as a man of his word who drives hard bargains but is scrupulously honest in carrying them out."

"There is something else you ought to know about our friend Mr. Pawley." Sir Eric also had a file on the man. "Despite being a very active Republican, he is closely involved with the Roosevelt administration, and, in particular, its policy of sending aid to China. He is already reported to be forming a volunteer group to fly fighters for the Chinese Air Force. If he has approached us with this offer, we can conclude it is because supporting us has become American government policy. Why that is, of course, we can but conjecture."

"Doubtless we shall find out in due course. I wonder if the other Commonwealth countries have received similar offers?" Lord Linlithgow drummed his fingers on the table. "We need that conference of Commonwealth leaders. Is there any progress on that front?"

"All are agreed that it is essential. The Australians propose holding it in Melbourne, the South Africans in Capetown, the Canadians in Vancouver. We have suggested Bermuda. It is a compromise everybody can live with and

I believe it will be accepted. Having suggested the appropriate location will be a benefit to us, politically speaking, of course."

Pandit Nehru burst out laughing; the rest of the meeting looked slightly shocked. He flushed slightly and put his hand to his mouth before speaking. "I do most sincerely apologize. It is something I find most amusing; to discover that the same petty consideration that concern us in running a party at ground level are also important when considering the great affairs of international politics."

"Please don't tell everybody that." Lord Linlithgow had to admit Nehru had a point. "We do try to keep such things a secret. Maintaining public confidence and all that."

Short Sunderland Mark I F-Freddie, *Over The Eastern Mediterranean*

"You holding up, sir?"

Alleyne looked over at his passenger. Sir Wilfred Freeman was white-faced with shock but holding on. A .50-cal bullet from a Fiat CR.42 had struck him in the shoulder during one of the brief battles that had taken place over the last four hours. Fortunately, the bullet had been at the end of its course. It had been fired from long range and, by the time it had penetrated the cockpit of the Sunderland, it had lost nearly all its energy. Sir Wilfred had a bandage wrapped around him and his arm was in a sling. That was the best that could be done for him under the circumstances.

His condition was symptomatic of the formation as a whole. The Italian attacks had been incessant. Although each individual wave had done little damage, the cumulative effects were mounting. One Sunderland was streaming white smoke from a crippled engine. Others were reporting wounded and a handful of dead amongst their passengers and crew. The Australian Sunderlands had fought the attacks off; the G-class boats in the middle of the formation had remained untouched. That was the good news. The bad news was that the formations of Italian fighters showed no signs of giving up the battle.

"Don't worry about me, my boy. I've had worse than this." Freeman's voice belied his words. It was unsteady, quavering slightly. "Italians don't seem to press their attacks, do they?"

"They don't quite know what to make of us." Alleyne was still scanning the sky, keeping a look-out for the next group of enemies. "They've never come across aircraft this heavily armed before. They're learning fast, though. They've stopped trying to close in and are trying to pick us off from long range. It's working, too; they're wearing us down, bit by bit. And we're beginning to run low on ammunition. Once the turrets run out, it'll get bad."

"I said 500 rounds per gun wasn't enough." Freeman sounded bitter. "I wanted at least a thousand; preferably twice that. The endurance of a bomber isn't measured by its range, but how long it can keep its defensive fire up. We would have had the extra ammunition too, if only we'd had just a few weeks more . . . "

That seems to be the unending anthem, thought Alleyne. *Just a few weeks more and we'd have had the new tanks, the new aircraft, the new ships. Just a little more time and we'd have turned the whole situation around. We'd have stalled the Nazis and settled in for the long term. But Halifax and Butler made sure than we never got that time.*

"There they are, Squadron Leader. High and two o'clock." It might have been twenty years since Freeman had flown with the Royal Flying Corps, but he still had pilot's eyes and had seen the dark shapes of another group of Italian fighters.

"Six of them." Alleyne grunted. "We can handle that. If they came at us in mass, we'd be in trouble."

"Now there's a sore point." Freeman laughed, then gasped as the effort hurt his shoulder. "Fighter Command were having a major battle over just that issue when everything went to hell. Dowding in the South favored small squadrons operating independently because they could react faster; Leigh-Mallory in the Midlands favored big wings of three or more squadrons operating together to give coordinated blows. I suppose we'll never find out who was right now."

Despite the rank of the man in the co-pilot's seat, Alleyne was barely listening to him. The next group of Italian fighters were firing from extreme range. Their tracers seemed to drift across the sky. Alleyne started a gentle weaving to throw the enemy pilot's aim off. It worked. Most of the tracers never came close to his aircraft. "Standing off at long range doesn't seem to work either."

"Fire control. What determines range isn't the performance of the guns, it's the capability of the gun sights, and they're just barely able to handle .303 machine guns. Expecting heavier guns to outrange lighter ones is futile until everybody gets better gunsights."

"If we can just hold out a bit longer, we'll be fine." Alleyne was worried about Freeman; the man was visibly weakening. "We're nearly out of fighter range now. Just a few more minutes, and it's a clear run to Alexandria."

CHAPTER SEVEN
EXCHANGES OF PREJUDICE

Oval Office, White House, Washington, DC, USA

"Monsieur, this is an outrage."

"I think not." Secretary of State Cordell Hull was at his most diplomatic. "The President has made it abundantly clear that the policy of this administration is to support in every way practicable those countries which are defending themselves against aggression. It is our firm conviction that only by defeat of the powers now controlling the destiny of Germany can the world live in liberty, peace and prosperity; that civilization cannot progress with a return to totalitarianism.

"We have been much perturbed by reports indicating that resources of France are being placed at the disposal of Germany in a measure beyond that positively required by the terms of the armistice agreement. I have reason to believe that, aside from the selfish interests of individuals, there is unrequired governmental cooperation with Germany motivated by a belief in the inevitableness of a German victory and ultimate benefit to France. For this reason, we cannot allow some of our most modern warplanes to be delivered to France. At the very least, doing so will allow the enemies of civilization to assess those aircraft and determine their strengths and weaknesses. At worst, we may find those very aircraft being used against us.

"We cannot, in conscience, deliver these aircraft. So, we are refunding, in full, the cost of those aircraft to you. France will not suffer from this; the money will be added to the reserves of gold maintained by France and we will invest it for you to achieve the best possible return on those investments. When this war is over, your funds will be available, supplemented by the profits made on your behalf by our most able financiers."

Monsieur Herve Alphand, Ambassador of the Republic of France, could find little to say in response. The truth of the matter was that he could see the American point of view on this, while his own sympathies were not in accord with the position adopted by Marshal Petain in Vichy. Yet he was obliged to represent their opinions. He settled on a course that turned the old principle of damning with faint praise on its head. Instead, he would praise with faint damnation. "May I know how your banks will invest those funds?"

Hull spread his hands in regret. "Monsieur, the banks in this country are independent entities. They do not tell us how they invest our money; why should they tell us how they invest yours? But, be assured, they will seek the highest returns commensurate with prudent investment practice."

Alphand recognized that there was no more to be said on the matter. "On another matter, Monsieur Hull, may we expect food exports from the United States to France to resume?"

Hull sighed. "The hearts of the American people go out to the people of France in their distress. As you are aware, we are continuing our efforts to arrange for the forwarding, through the Red Cross, of medical supplies and also tinned or powdered milk for children in the unoccupied regions of France. Nevertheless, the primary interest of the American people, and an interest which overshadows all else at the moment, is to see a resistance to Germany continued. The American people are therefore unwilling to take any measure which in the slightest degree will prejudice such resistance. Before the American people would be willing to permit the shipment of food to France, it would be necessary that the American people be convinced that such action would not in the slightest assist Germany. I must add that the same considerations are applied to exports to Great Britain."

"But not to the Commonwealth countries." Alphand sounded bitter.

"Of course. The Commonwealth is carrying on the fight against Germany. They have committed their whole national strength to the battle, regardless of the cost to themselves. Can the French colonies around the world say the same?"

It was not a fair question; Alphand knew it and Hull knew it. The British Commonwealth countries had a much greater freedom of action than their French equivalents. Privately, Hull wondered just what the French colonies would be doing if they had the same freedom to maneuver as the British.

"May I at least ask what will happen to the aircraft that were once ours?" There was a note of genuine sadness in Alphand's voice.

"Our minds are not yet made up. Perhaps we may use them as trainers for our own forces."

"Perhaps." Alphand did not sound convinced. He had a shrewd idea where those aircraft would be going.

Short Sunderland Mark 1 F-Freddie, *Alexandria, Egypt*

"Will he make it?" Squadron Leader Alleyne watched the stretcher bearing Sir Wilfred Freeman being loaded into an ambulance prior to being taken to a hospital. The harbor was full of flying boats. All twelve Sunderlands and the three G-class aircraft had made it across the Mediterranean. The Sunderlands had succeeded in preventing any damage to the civilian aircraft, but they'd all taken wounds themselves in the process. Crews were getting ready to bring three of them ashore so that hull damage could be patched while two more had mechanics working on damaged engines. Still, considering the aircraft had been under sustained fighter attack for more than four hours, they'd got off remarkably lightly.

"He lost a lot of blood. The medics are hopeful, though. How about your crews?"

"We made it." Alleyne dismissed the question rather abruptly, without realizing he was doing so. He was exhausted by the long flight from Britain to Egypt by way of Gibraltar and badly needed some sleep.

Wing Commander Hesketh looked at the Australian sympathetically. The man was pale and his eyes were shadowed from the strain of his flights. He guessed that the uncertainty of Alleyne's position was also preying on his mind. *Well, at least I can do something about that.*

"Your people can get some rest here, for a while at least. I do have orders for you directly from your Government. You now report directly to them, not London. On their instructions, you are assigned to Middle East Command and will be stationed at Aden as soon as you can get down there. We need your flying boats to help counter the Italian Red Sea squadron. We're going to have to move you out of Alex quickly, though. You're too vulnerable here."

"We can use these aircraft as bombers." It was Harris who spoke, cutting in on the briefing. "They can hit the Italian ports and supply lines."

Hesketh shook his head. "Not from here they can't. Sir, the Italians have four bomber groups based in Libya. Two of them have Breda close support aircraft and we don't have to worry about them. The other two have sixty Savoia-Marchetti SM.79 bombers between them. Those, we *do* have to worry about. There's about forty of them operational at any one time and they can go where they want and do what they wish. They're faster than the Gladiators we're relying on for air defense. As soon as we bomb one of the Italian ports, those SM.79s will return the compliment by bombing us here. And they'll take out those flying boats in the process. We need them too much in the Red Sea for that. We'll fix them, fuel them, and then get them out of here. We've got some Bristol Bombays for bombing missions when the time comes."

Harris thrust out his chin. "The Italians have already invaded. We have to strike back at them. The Sunderlands will stay here for use as bombers."

"No, sir. They will *not*. Do you know how many front-line fighters we have here? One. Not one squadron, one *aircraft*. A Hurricane. We have 75 Gladiators and 34 Gauntlets as second line fighters. We have Blenheim and

Bombay bombers and those we use to strike at the Italians. But the Sunderlands go to Aden. Those are the orders of the Australian Government."

"Do you know who I am, *Wing Commander*?" There was heavy emphasis on the rank.

"Yes, sir. I do. I also know what you are not. You are not in the chain of command here and you are not part of Middle East Command. We don't know who we report to at this time or what our status is, but we do know what we have to do and what we have to do it with. With respect, sir, you do not."

Harris stared at the Wing Commander, then retreated back into the belly of the flying boat. Hesketh breathed a sigh of relief.

"I hate to do this to you Squadron Leader, but you need to get these aircraft out of here soonest. I'm not sure who is your bigger enemy right now, the Italians or Arthur Harris but neither of them are to be ignored. Get some sleep while we fix your aircraft and then we'll get you on your way."

Cabinet Office, Downing Street, London, United Kingdom

"The Royal Navy will obey my orders."

"Nevertheless, the fleet has its duties and responsibilities to perform."

Prime Minister the Lord Halifax and Admiral of the Fleet Sir Dudley Pound glared at each other across the table. Neither was prepared to give an inch on this issue; both knew that their authority depended on them not doing so. Pound knew something else, a fact that had been kept very secret.

He was dying.

He had an inoperable brain tumor that would kill him in a year or two, according to the best doctors available. In addition he had hip degeneration that was making his work progressively more difficult. In a strange way, that made Pound's job as First Sea Lord easier. His career was over and his life was ticking away fast. The only he thing he had left to do was to protect the Navy that he loved.

"Our Armistice with Germany specifies that the Royal Navy should return to its peacetime establishment and stations." Halifax shouted the words across the room, hoping to see the First Sea Lord back down.

"It does, Prime Minister, and that in itself confirms that we have a legitimate need to continue with those peacetime responsibilities. It recognizes our deployment and activities and nowhere is the situation more critical than the Mediterranean. That fleet has always been the major peacetime station for the Royal Navy, outnumbering even the Home Fleet. Thus, the Armistice legitimizes its deployment and stations in that area. If that upsets the Italians, so be it."

Pound sounded reasonable and convincing, leaving Halifax an out from an awkward position. Those who knew Pound well had remarked upon his ability to defeat by guile proposals that had been forced on him by higher authority. 'Intellectual ju-jitsu' had been the description applied by some of his

162

contemporaries. He had used the technique to prevent Winston Churchill from sending a battle fleet into the Baltic and now he would use it to prevent Halifax from pulling one out of the Mediterranean. He might have gained his position for want of a healthier candidate, but that same quirk made him the right man in the right place now.

"The Mediterranean Fleet is *not* at its peacetime establishment." The shout was still aggressive, but Halifax was already beginning to back away from the conflict. He had brought the matter of Mussolini's movements in North and East Africa up with the Germans and they had denied all interest in them. As far as they were concerned, what Italy did was Italy's business and they could do it on their own. If Britain chose to resist the Italian moves, that was their business as well and it would not affect German-British relations in the slightest.

"And we shall reduce it to that establishment." Pound sounded agreeable, but his mind was running through the options. *There are two old battleships out there,* Ramillies *and* Royal Sovereign. *They can come home without too much loss to ABC and we can use their crews for the new battleships* King George V *and* Prince of Wales. *Likewise three old cruisers can come home and we can use their crews for three of the new* Dido-*class. If ABC loses his four oldest and slowest destroyers, we'll have a paper compliance with the Armistice while maintaining our position out there.* "Those ships will come home and the rest dispersed between the various bases we have available."

It sounded reasonable and Halifax took the chance to back off. Pound saw him do so and smiled gently to himself. With one modern, capable squadron at each end of the Mediterranean, his Navy could still do its duty out there.

Buna Field, Kenya

"Watch those Italians. Their CR.42s have a hell of an edge over us."

Which, considering we are flying Hawker Fury fighters, is hardly a great surprise. Pilot Officer Pim Bosede was beginning to understand just how bad the situation was in Kenya. It wasn't that the Italians had achieved great successes; it was that there was so little stopping them from doing so. The South African Air Force had sent two squadrons to help hold the line in Kenya. One had Ju-86 bombers; the other had the Fury. On the ground, two brigades of the King's African Rifles were holding off six brigades of Italian troops. Quite how they were doing it, Bosede couldn't see; but they were, and in doing so, they had bought time for the First South African Division to arrive and form up.

"What do we do about it, broere?"

"We fight commando style."

Flight Lieutenant Petrus van Bram wondered just how long this fresh-faced recruit would last. The Italian pilots were skilled and fought well. Their

163

aircraft outperformed the mix of old aircraft deployed in Kenya across the board. Technically, there was no reason why the allied forces in the country should have survived. van Bram was a deeply religious man, and he assumed that the survival of the small group of fighters on the front line at Buna was due to divine intervention. The more secular members of the squadron agreed with him. There wasn't a more plausible explanation.

"We hit and run, try to pick off a bomber here, a reconnaissance aircraft there. Problem is, the bombers and reconnaissance aircraft are faster than us as well. Every so often, the Italians try to visit one of our airbases. They got a few Hardys on the ground the first time they tried, but we have observers out now and we get a few minutes warning."

"What are their pilots like?" Bosede was frantically absorbing as much information as he could.

"Individually, very good. They are well trained and they know their work. Operational planning is not so much so. They have the same attack patterns and schedules, so we know when they will arrive and what they will do. The fighters stay very close to the bombers. So we can get in, pick off a straggler and get away before they respond. We cannot break up the formations, but we can do a little damage here and there. How many hours do you have?"

"On the Fury? Eight. But I have flown much prior to joining the Air Force. Mostly Curtiss Travel Air 6000s."

van Bram grimaced. "I hope you have not picked up too many bad habits. We will take an orientation flight and see. Take off in 30 minutes."

An hour later, Bosede was looking down at the landscape of northern Kenya as it slowly unfolded beneath him. Right in the middle of the parched brown and light green was the rich dark green stain of the Ajao River. His briefing on navigation had been simple. All one has to do was to find that dark green strip and follow it south; that would inevitably lead a pilot to the airstrip at Buna. The problem was that Italian bomber pilots could do the same thing. Somewhere below him, in the reddish brown and green, the King's African Rifles were fighting to hold off the Italians. There was no sign of that; it was as if the vastness of Africa had swallowed the war whole.

Ahead of him, van Bram was rocking his wings. Bosede saw him gesturing downwards. There was an aircraft down there. Bosede quickly took its details in. A radial-engined biplane; very distinct from the inline-engined Hardy and Fury used by the South Africans. *An Italian Ro.37, probably on a reconnaissance mission.* He saw van Bram peeling over into a long dive and followed suite.

About half way down, the rear gunner in the Italian aircraft must have spotted the two Furies. A stream of red tracer dots poured out of the rear position, searching out van Bram's aircraft. The lead Fury held its fire, though. van Bram ignored the tracer lights all around him, until he had closed the range to nearly point-blank. Then van Bram fired. A long burst from his twin Vickers guns abruptly ended the fire from the Ro.37's rear gun. Bosede dived below the Ro.37 and came up from underneath, firing a burst from his twin guns into the reconnaissance aircraft's belly.

The two fighters swerved away. The Ro.37 streamed black smoke from a damaged engine. Bosede was expecting to make a second pass; van Bram pointed upwards. A formation of four biplanes was already closing in. They were instantly recognizable: Fiat CR.32s. Bosede knew their reputation from Spain. Not as fast as the later CR.42, but extremely agile. Even one on one, they were far more than a match for the old Fury. He was quite relieved when van Bram broke off the attack and headed south. Unwilling to get involved in a long tail-chase, the Italian pilots formed up around the damaged Ro-37 to shepherd it back home.

Following the river worked. The rich foliage that surrounded it was visible from a long way away. It was simple to find it and then head south. After landing, Bosede climbed out of his Fury and stretched. It all seemed a waste of time somehow, and he said so to van Bram. His flight leader didn't agree.

"We saw off a reconnaissance aircraft and that helps our broere on the ground. As long as we do that, the Italians will keep their fighters escorting the other aircraft and not have them running free to hunt us down. So we did a little good work today. Not much, perhaps, but a little. We are doing what we can and we will continue to do so until help arrives."

Cabinet Room, Government House, Calcutta, India

"Railways. Now there is a problem to conjure with." Sir Martyn Sharpe had an almost dreamy look on his face. In his youth, he had wanted, more than anything else, to be a train driver. Even today, he had an abiding fascination with the operation of steam locomotives mixed with a genteel dislike for their diesel equivalents. The idea of rebuilding an entire continent-wide railway network was immensely appealing to him.

"We already have made a good start on building a railway network." Pandit Nehru objected and bristled slightly. Railways were a sore point in the Indian Congress Party; one on which everybody disagreed with everybody else over everything.

"A start, yes; but hardly a good one. We have railway lines built in four different gauges: narrow, meter, standard and broad gauge. They don't link up well and the track-beds are so light they can't take heavy freight. It's a frightful mess. We need to have a strategic plan for the development of our railway system. Communications are key to modern development."

"Once again, we see the need for a controlling interest by the state." Nehru was hard-wired to see state control as the answer to every problem, but in this case he had almost total agreement. The chaotic state of Indian railway development could not be allowed to continue. Each princely state had built its own railway system; its configuration had been decided by the whim of the Princes. So had the routes followed by the tracks. They also had more to do with the wishes of the Prince than economic necessity. The investors who had built the lines had been guaranteed a five percent return on their investment by the government, so the financial viability of the lines had been of no great interest to them.

"In this case, you have an excellent argument, but there is a problem here. Under the 1849 agreement with the railway promoters, the railways built by them are to remain their property for 99 years. At which point, they will pass, without compensation, into the possession of the Government, which will have to pay for the machinery, plant and rolling stock. We can purchase the railway in question earlier by paying the full value of the capital stock and shares. Alternatively, the railway companies can surrender their line to us by giving six months notice and claim repayment of all the capital invested. We simply cannot afford to do either. We are barely surviving at the moment as it is. This kind of additional burden will finish us."

"There is always nationalization without compensation." Nehru liked the sound of that and knew it would resonate with the membership of his party.

"There is indeed." Sir Martyn agreed. "But we have a problem there as well. The vast majority of the finding for Indian railway development came from England. For all practical purposes, Indian capital played a negligible role in building our railway system. The capital that came from England to India for railway construction formed the largest single unit of international investment in the 19th century. If we suddenly nationalize that without compensation, it will be a massive blow at the English financial system."

"Is that such a bad thing?" Nehru was growing heated. "The railways destroyed much of our native industry. Traditional Indian goods have been replaced by factory-made items imported from England and distributed cheaply by rail. The construction of the railways created employment for coal miners, steelmakers and machine forgers in England, not India, and converted our countryside into an agricultural colony of England. The railways were not a commercial success until the early part of this century, yet the losses were not borne by the investors who built them but by the government and thus the Indian people. It is time those monies extracted from us were recovered."

The silence in the cabinet room was profound. The subject of the railways themselves was almost immaterial compared with the yawning gap in perceptions that had been revealed by Nehru's speech. It had literally never occurred to any of the Europeans present that the construction of railways had been anything other than an undiluted blessing for India.

"Perhaps this is an area in which we should advance carefully? The first step should be to arrange for the consolidation of the existing railway system into a number of regional railway authorities. The existing railway owners can be given shares in the new railway authorities proportionate to

166

their investment in the original lines. Then, as we invest further in those authorities, bringing the lines up to a common standard, the government's shareholding will increase. Thus, when the existing agreements expire in 1948, the transfer will have been completed in a proper and orderly manner.

"We *must* be wary that we do not alienate any of the likely investors in this country. Our economic success depends on attracting them into our fold and we should not mortgage that prospect by hasty action when, in eight years, the assets will fall into our hands anyway." Sir Martyn looked around the room. The majority of the occupants seemed to accept that concept, although Nehru was still agitated by the mere mention of railways. It was probably a good time to move on.

"I do have some good news to relate. We have received word from Canberra, Johannesburg, Wellington and Ottawa that the proposed meeting of the heads of the Commonwealth countries is to go ahead and that our proposal that Jamaica be the locale for the meeting has been accepted."

"I thought that Bermuda was our first choice?" The Marquess of Linlithgow sounded surprised.

"It was, Your Excellency. It was pointed out that Bermuda posed certain security risks should the Germans get wind of the meeting, as they undoubtedly will. A well-timed commando raid and our enterprise would end with us all inside a German prison. Jamaica is a much more secure and inviting location and has better meeting facilities anyway. We amended our proposal to Jamaica and it was enthusiastically accepted. Britain will be represented by Mr. Churchill, of course. The United States will be attending as observers."

"Is that necessary?" Leon Arnold Fitzgerald sounded distasteful. Of the current members of the Cabinet, he was the one closest to Sir Richard Cardew in outlook. So much so that Sir Eric Haohoa was keeping him discretely watched.

"Indeed it is. It is, after all, the disposal of British equipment produced in America and currently held under embargo there that will be the subject of much discussion. We cannot ignore the fact that those discussions will be meaningless without American agreement. There are other issues that we must raise with them as well. The American government has intimated that it can make funds available to us on very reasonable terms, provided they receive certain assurances about our future position."

"That means staying in the war, I presume." Nehru was beginning to calm down.

"Of course it does. The Americans will fight Germany to the lives of the last Commonwealth soldier." Fitzgerald spoke with scorn dripping from every syllable. Sir Martyn was disturbed to note how much agreement there was with that sentiment.

"They may not get that chance. I hope nobody believes that this war will be ended quickly or will pass anybody by?" Lord Linlithgow had a note of reproof when he spoke and it made its mark. Several of those who had partially agreed with Fitzgerald looked shamefaced about it.

"Pandit, I would like you to lead our delegation to the Jamaica conference. I have far too many commitments here to be able to go there myself, and, I believe, your presence there would highlight the new road down which we hope to take India."

Nehru's agitation from the railway issue evaporated as the realization he would be representing India at a Commonwealth conference. What that meant in the broad perspective of things sank in. In a very real sense, it was a partial fulfillment of a life's work. Watching him, Sir Martyn decided that Pandit Nehru had a lot to learn about what went on at international conferences.

Short Sunderland Mark 1 F-Freddie, Over the Red Sea

"Have you seen nothin' down there?"

The Sunderland was cruising about a thousand feet up and maintaining barely a hundred knots. Experience over the Atlantic in the first phase of the war had taught crews that this was the optimum combination of speed and altitude when searching for U-boats. Low altitude to improve the chance of eye-balling a submerged submarine and reduce the chance of being seen by a surfaced one; low speed to stretch fuel reserves out to the maximum possible. Guy Alleyne knew his job very well indeed.

"Nothin' yet." An Italian submarine had attacked the New Zealand cruiser *Leander*. The torpedoes had missed their target. Radio intercepts picked up a message from the submarine *Galileo Ferraris* claiming to have torpedoed a battleship. That had caused some mirth back in Aden from those who hadn't tried to work out the chaos of a naval action. The crew of *F-Freddie* had; they knew the problems of identifying a target and determining how much, if any, damage they had done.

"Any more word from the Mad Bomber?" Andy Walker down in the radio compartment sounded genuinely curious. He had been the radio operator on duty when Arthur Harris had sent the squadron a preemptory order to return to Alexandria for service as night bombers.

"Nah, he gave up the ghost. I heard Wavell put him in charge of the Bristol Bombay fleet to keep him quiet. Damned drongo sent them off to bomb the harbor at Tobruk and they didn't get a bomb within fifteen miles of the place. He's been quiet ever since." Alleyne wasn't particularly worried. There had been a telegraphed set of orders for him in Aden. His government had told him what to do and where to go. More importantly, it told him who to obey and, implicitly, who not to. That trumped everything else. The most valuable part of it had been the simple fact of its existence. It had told him they were

168

still part of something, not forgotten wanderers trying to find a home somewhere.

"You reckon that sub will still be around here? The Huns would have cleared off by now."

"He'll still be around. He'll want a second crack at that cruiser. If he really reckons he hit her, he'll want to finish her off. If not, he'll want to try again. Either way, he's around here somewhere."

"Boss, I got somethin'." Chris White was the portside lookout, using the beam machine gun hatch as an observation point. "Three o'clock; right on the horizon."

"Good on you, Snowy." There was a long pause while Don Clerk, the starboard lookout, crossed over and checked on the sighting. "Snowy's right, Boss. Connin' tower on the horizon; enemy one by the look of it."

"Stand by for attack. All gun crews ready. Midships crew, open the side ports and wind out the depth bombs. Fuzes set for 25 feet."

The casual atmosphere had completely vanished from the Sunderland. The two side hatches under the wings were already opening up. In the bomb room, the 250-pound airborne depth charges were fuzed and attached to the racks. The racks were then wound out on rails under the wings. Alleyne already had the throttles forward, pushing the Pegasus engines as hard as was prudent. Aden was a long way from the easy availability of spare parts; stressing the engines would be short-sighted, to say the least.

White's original sighting had been accurate. It was a submarine. Alleyne quickly put together the recognition details. *Single gun forward of a small conning tower; she's German. Bad luck for her she's not the one we were lookin' for.*

"You reckon the poor dumb bastards are asleep down there?" The distance was closing quickly and White had an almost proprietorial interest in the submarine.

Suddenly, the submarine was surrounded by spray as she started to dive. In the North Atlantic, the Sunderland crew had become used to rapid dives from German submarines. Alleyne was astonished at how slowly this one was starting to submerge. The conning tower was almost certainly deserted. He opened fire with his nose guns anyway, lashing the submarine with the streams of tracer fire. The submarine was supposed to mount a 20mm cannon and a 37mm gun; there was no trace of return fire from them. *Most likely, the German elected to dive rather than fightin' it out on the surface and thought he had more time.*

Alleyne ceased fire as the flying boat slashed over the diving submarine. *F-Freddie* lurched as the four depth charges dropped clear.

"Way to bloody go! Perfect straddle, Boss! Score one for the *Hobart*!"

169

The cheer from the midships lookouts was all Alleyne needed to know. He was already curving around, bringing the submarine into his field of vision. Two depth charges had landed just short of the boat. The other pair had landed just over her. They exploded under the submarine, throwing her upwards and breaking her back. By the time Alleyne could see her properly, she was already sinking; her bows and stern raised in the air and her midships section under water.

"Strafe it?"

"Don't be bloody. Leave her. She's done for. Radio base and see if anybody can pick up the survivors. If there are anyway." Alleyne guessed the submarine had been closed up for diving. The chance of anybody getting out, given the catastrophic damage inflicted by the four depth charges, were slight. Still, if there was a chance, it was worth getting the word out. He completed the turn and cruised over the sinking wreckage beneath. The submarine had almost gone; only the point of her bows stuck out of the boiling white stains on the sea surface.

"I hope some of you took pickies of that?" Alleyne had forgotten to order the photography in the rush of the attack, but the evidence was needed if they were to be credited with a confirmed sinking instead of a probable. The sea surface was littered with scattered wreckage, but there were no swimmers that he could see.

"Yeah, I got it. No heads down there I can see."

"Me neither. Poor drongos. Any idea who they were?"

F-Freddie circled the scene of the sinking. Her crew searched the floating wreckage with high-powered binoculars for any sign of survivors. Eventually, it was Chris White who gave the doleful epitaph.

"Nobody got out. All I can see floatin' down there is a few bits of debris and a stuffed animal."

HMAS Australia, *Scapa Flow, Scotland*

"Will ye no' come back again?

Will ye no' come back again?

Better lo'ed ye canna be

Will ye no' come back again?"

The haunting echoes of the ballad echoed backwards and forwards from the ships anchored across Scapa Flow as the heavy cruiser started her slow progress out to sea. Captain Robert R Stewart surreptitiously wiped an eye at the words and the meaning behind them. This was the worst way to end an assignment he could think of. Betrayed.

There was no other word for it. He, his ship and his crew had been betrayed by the government they had come half way around the world to help. The rest of the fleet knew it. The sad dirge was their comment on the way the cruiser had been treated.

"It was originally written about Bonnie Prince Charlie, you know." Lieutenant Colonel Beaumont spoke softly. "The Andrew always had a talent for knowing the right music."

Stewart nodded sadly. "This is such a damned shame. We didn't want ta go home like this. Not with our tails between our legs."

"Not your fault. At least you were around to give us a lift home. The lads would have paid for the tickets on a liner home themselves rather than stay any longer. After volunteering to help the old country out, being described as 'useless mouths' was more than they could stomach."

"At least we didn't have ta swallow that." Stewart veered away from the subject, watching the pilot take HMAS *Australia* through the boom and down the Hoy Sound. "Just being booted out was bad enough. Ronald, you'd better get your men together for training soon. We're still at war with Germany and they might reckon of putting a couple of torpedoes into us. Your men better know what ta do if that happens."

"Aye, I'll do that. We were half expecting to be bombed in Aldershot but it never happened." Beaumont looked out across the sound. Two British destroyers were paralleling the Australian cruiser's course. They weren't escorting her; they just happened to be close by and going the same way. Under the circumstances, keeping a close ASW watch out was only a reasonable precaution, wasn't it?

The thought of *Australia* being torpedoed was a nightmare. The ship was packed tight with men; her own crew, the Princess Patricia's Canadian Light Infantry Battalion and some 'passengers' that nobody was talking about. She had men sleeping in every open space of the ship. Simply feeding everybody was straining the ship's facilities to the utmost. Beaumont had his own cooks in the galleys helping out where they could, but with almost 1,600 men on board even that was little more than a gesture. It was going to be a cold, hungry crossing. The mood of his men was such that they preferred that to staying in a country that was suddenly unwelcoming.

They were being unfair and Beaumont knew it. The evidence was literally all around them. The number of men on board wasn't the only reason why *Australia* was crowded. The ship was packed with cargo; every square foot appeared to sprout crates, covered and lashed down. Even the gun turrets had packages and parcels stowed in them. *Australia* was in no condition to fight even a minor warship. When the ship had been stored for her transit across the Atlantic, the Royal Navy had filled her to capacity and beyond.

"You might still be. One of the things I want your men ta do is get every machine gun they can lashed ta the railings in the superstructure. God knows, they've got enough of them." Beaumont snorted; the British Army had equipped his battalion for its return to Canada on the apparent assumption that every Canadian soldier carried both a Bren gun and a Vickers gun in addition to his rifle, pistols and a terrifying number of hand grenades. He'd been quite amazed to discover that his battalion headquarters now included a six-pounder anti-tank gun. Beaumont would have been prepared to swear that the weapon only existed as a prototype, but one such gun was lashed to the deck amidships and a case of blueprints was stowed in A Turret magazine.

Stewart grinned understandingly. "It's all right for you; your people just have ta clean them. I've got ta worry about carrying them. This poor old girl is loaded so deep, her plimsoll line is completely submerged. We've got every round of ammunition we can fit in on board. But we might need those machine guns though. We can outrun submarines, even loaded the way we are; a Condor is a different matter. If they show up, we'll need that flak."

"You going home after you drop us off?" Beaumont watched Graemsay Island passing behind them. He felt the shudder as the engines picked up power. He was no seaman, but he could feel the ship was sluggish with the load she was carrying.

"We are, by way of Jamaica. We're taking some top brass down there for a conference, then heading through the Panama Canal for home. What we do there is anybody's guess. The rumor mill says patrol duty in the Indian Ocean ta replace *Hobart*. Who knows? We might get another one of those damned raiders. The boys would like ta get some payback in."

Cabinet Room, Government House, Calcutta, India

"Is everything ready?" Lord Linlithgow looked around the room.

"It is." Sir Eric Haohoa confirmed the fact. "We have had some preliminary discussions with the other Commonwealth representatives and the ground rules have been agreed. The Middle East is our primary area of strategic importance and it is there that our defense investments will be concentrated, in the short term at least. The Hawk 81s will be sent there. The rest of us will have to make do with the Hawk 75s. The same applies to the bombers and the patrol aircraft. We will send whatever equipment is needed to the Middle East and then divide up the rest."

"And payment for all this equipment?" Nehru had an inbred dislike for spending money on military equipment, no matter how pressing the need appeared to be.

"The ex-British equipment needs not be paid for. The monies for it are held in the United States and we, the Commonwealth countries, inherit it. The ex-French equipment is more difficult. I understand the Americans have refunded the purchase price of that equipment to the French but then impounded the monies. They 'offered' to invest the money for the French against the time when the funds would be released, an offer the French couldn't refuse. The Americans are now 'investing' that money by loaning it to us so we can purchase the ex-French aircraft."

"That's generous of them." HH sounded more than slightly sarcastic.

"I suspect not." Sir Martyn Sharpe had a shrewd idea about what the Americans had in mind. "They intend to ensure that we are dependent on American equipment for our defense and industrial sectors. Already, there are moves by their robber barons to put money into our industrial development programs. A Mister Essington Lewis of Broken Hill Proprietory wants to establish joint ventures for steel production and there are rumors that American capitalists are behind him. It is a clear objective of American government policy to oppose colonialism and break up the great empires. I would say they have seen a major opportunity for them to do just that."

Sir Eric nodded in agreement. The position of Cabinet Secretary included supervision of the intelligence and security services. One of the things he was doing at the moment was reorganizing both to meet India's needs. "We believe that is exactly the case. The Americans are playing a deep game here and we're just pawns. Their primary target is Germany, but dismantling the colonial empires is still something they view with favor."

"And Halifax opened the door for them." The Marquess of Linlithgow sounded almost personally aggrieved. "He always disliked the Americans and was prejudiced against them. I cannot help but think that weighed in his calculations when he decided to set upon the course he has chosen. It would be ironic if it was his acts that gave them the opening they seek. It adds all the more emphasis to the importance of the Commonwealth meeting in Jamaica. We must stand together and we must resist American efforts to break us asunder. If we are to go our separate ways, it must be at a time of our own choosing and for our own reasons. How are we going to get to Jamaica?"

"The delegation will fly there, Your Excellency. We will be using the *Golden Hind*, one of the three Short flying boats that arrived recently. We will be going by way of Cape Town where we will pick up the delegation from South Africa. The Canadians will be arriving by cruiser; the Australians flying in."

"Very good." Lord Linlithgow nodded enthusiastically. "That will reflect well on our delegation. Modern image, and all that. Pandit, as a lifelong socialist, you will of course want to ride steerage class on the *Golden Hind*? As a gesture against privilege and class distinctions?"

Nehru's jaw dropped with a combination of shock and outrage. He had been smiling happily at the thought of sampling the fabled luxuries of one of the great flying boats that dominated long-range air transportation. Now, the thought of sitting in the cramped steerage compartment for days on end faced him. It was only when he looked around and saw the grins on the face of the other members of the meeting that he realized his leg was being pulled. "But, of course. In fact, I will insist on it. And I will expect you all to join me there."

There was a ripple of laughter and appreciative applause at the rejoinder. Sir Eric answered gravely, "I am sorry, Pandit, but we will have to refuse your request. There is no steerage class on an S-26. You'll have to travel first class like the rest of us."

Nehru shook his head in simulated grief. "Well, in that case, I suppose I will have to sacrifice my principles for the common good. Just this once, you understand. It is a dirty job, but somebody will have to do it."

Wollaton Park, Nottingham University, Nottingham, United Kingdom

"Look, Rachael; deer." David Newton pointed at the small group of deer that were in the trees off to the left of the gravel road. "I'm surprised they're still here."

Rachael watched as one of the deer heard the sound and spotted the movement. The herd of deer in the park were tame. Normally, they felt comfortable in the presence of humans, but that had started to change. Some of the herd had mysteriously vanished; that had left the rest nervous. Rachael saw the stag looking at the humans carefully and she could almost read his mind. *They didn't seem a threat, but who knows?* She guessed that another unexpected movement would send the stag and his hinds bounding into the shelter of the trees.

"Do you think they are being hunted, David?"

"Poached, rather than hunted." Newton thought carefully. "They're mostly eating the grass, so they aren't eating food that we could use. Not yet anyway. But I guess the local black marketers see a market for venison developing."

"Not yet." Rachael weighed the words carefully, not liking the sound of them. "You think rationing is going to get worse?"

Newton sighed. The truth was that he really didn't like the way things were going. He was a lot more widely read than most of the students and, as a group, they were more aware of the world than most people. But this was the first time that he and Rachael had gone walking out together and he didn't want to sound depressing. He desperately wanted this afternoon to go well and had been doing his best to make that happen.

"I think so, Rachael. This country imports so much of its food, and nearly all of it came from the Commonwealth. Now we're at daggers drawn with them; we can't expect that to continue. I suppose it all depends on how much more we can grow here and how much we can import from elsewhere. Have your folks got an allotment? Mine have."

"Yes, and Papa goes there every evening to make sure our vegetables are growing well. Or so he says; I think he really goes there so he can read the newspaper in peace without Mama telling him what to do around the house."

Newton laughed at the picture of Rachael's father hiding in a little hut on his allotment. "I think mine does too. Talking about houses, Rachael, behold Wollaton Hall. Built around 1600, I think."

"It's horrible." Rachael was appalled by the building. "It's so fussy and over-decorated. Who built it?"

"Sir Frances Willoughby. He tore down the whole village of Sutton Passeys to build the house and park. It was designed by the Elizabethan architect, Robert Smythson."

"You'd think he'd have built something attractive after he'd turned all those people out of their homes. Still the bosses never care who gets hurt once they set their hearts on doing something."

Newton wanted to argue that point, but he didn't want to fight with Rachael the first time they'd walked out together. Anyway, with Wollaton Hall in front of him, he didn't feel on very solid ground to dispute her point.

"Do you see the rings in the outer wall? The architect had been to Venice and brought back some ideas with him. Those are gondola mooring rings, of all things."

He reached out to point Rachael at one of the rings. As he did, she moved slightly to keep a distance between them. He stopped immediately. *Have I offended her?*.

Rachael smiled and shook her head. "No offense meant, David. A good Jewish girl has to behave modestly in public. That's all."

Corporate Headquarters, Broken Hill Proprietory, Limited, Melbourne, Victoria, Australia

"I'm not just *a* Broadway Baby, I'm *the* Broadway Baby. Al Dubin wrote the song about me. Or, as he claims, I inspired him to write it." Igrat paused slightly and looked at the man she was addressing. "He seemed to like being inspired."

Bruce Phillips couldn't help smiling. "I should hope so. So, 'Lullaby of Broadway' was written about you? Something I've always wanted to ask. What the Hell is a 'daffy dill' when he's at home?

"A rich idiot. Person who has more money than sense. Usually trying to find himself a Baby to look after. Once he's got one, he gets promoted to a Sugar Daddy. But, yes, 'Lullaby of Broadway' was written about me, although it's been some time since anybody tried to push me off a balcony."

"Some say the whole sequence is fascist." Phillips was more interested in the tone of her response than its substance. His instructions were to feel out these people and form a picture of their real aims and intentions. He was surprised when Igrat suddenly looked very sad.

"You know, Buzz was heartbroken at the way that sequence was received. Remember it was made in 1935. The number isn't promoting or glamorizing fascism; it's screaming a warning about the birth of the fascist disease. Buzz is a song and dance man, so he put his warning into song and dance, but the message is there. It starts off with people waking up and going to work while the Baby comes home after her night out. Note how well she gets on with the people going to work and how she looks after the cat. It's a picture of a happy, friendly society in which work and pleasure are equally important; both are valued and the helpless get looked after.

175

"Then the Baby goes to a nightclub with her Daddy for an evening out when the dancers come in. They stomp in, crashing their boots and giving the Nazi salute. They take over the pleasant evening completely, drowning everything else out, showing how they destroy the happy society. Then, they seduce the Baby, luring her away from her Daddy and fooling her into joining them. Finally, they kill her by pushing her off the balcony.

"By doing so, they destroy all the pleasure in the world, leaving only workers as slaves, while the poor and helpless, represented by the cat, are left to starve. In 'Gold Diggers of 1935,' Buzz was warning the world of what was to come, yet they just ignored him. It broke his heart and he swore never to try and use his art to send messages again." Igrat paused and caught her breath. "I'm sorry, I didn't mean to get carried away like that."

"Don't worry about it. I never thought of the sequence that way before. Look, I'll be honest with you. Mr. Essington Lewis doesn't like small but influential investors. He asked me to speak with you first, to see if your people are the sort he can live with. He quite likes small investors; it's the influential part he doesn't much care for. He has enough of those already, and more an enough 'influences' to juggle. I can say he sees BHP as his ship to run his way. He's a pretty fair 'Captain of Industry,' but you know what the captain of a ship is like."

Igrat suddenly looked deadly serious. "Mr Phillips, I told you about myself to emphasize that I have no responsibilities other than to be an absolutely trustworthy messenger. I have neither the ability nor the authority to enter into negotiations. My job is to convey to you the messages my principal wishes to send and to do so accurately and reliably. If Mr. Lewis likes the information I have brought, my principal will be happy to meet with him. Either here or in America; the choice is his. Also, if he wishes to send written or verbal messages back, I will carry them. If verbal, my principal gets his words, exactly as he speaks them, unchanged and unmodified. They will also be carried in absolute secrecy. If he wishes to check my credentials in such matters, he may speak with the Vice President of International Transactions at J.P. Morgan, or his equivalent at any one of several other international trading banks. They gave me permission to use them as references and will vouch for me. They know me by my real name, Igrat Shafrid. Mister Lewis already knows me as Irene Shapiro."

Phillips nodded, equally seriously. "Your candor is noted. Mr. Lewis appreciates both candor and honesty. So if one hand can wash the other, then I'm sure he will be rapt to do business. I must warn you, though; he has been fending off hostile takeovers for years and now political developments mean Mr. Lewis has the national interest to consider officially, as well as his patriotic instincts. I will report to him that we have the makings of a good deal here; we just need to sort out an end state for our respective principals to reach. Oh and he is also a regular visitor to the US, has been for years, along

176

with Europe; so we have some room to make arrangements there as well. Will you be staying in Melbourne long?"

"As long as Mr. Lewis needs me here to carry his messages back. I am at his disposal. If I could meet with him again, it would be a bonus."

Phillips smiled at Igrat, who returned the sentiment. After all, they were two emissaries carefully exchanging pleasantries on behalf of their employers so that the important meeting they were organizing would go smoothly. "I think that might be arranged. I will speak to Mr. Lewis."

Room 25, Royal Australian Navy Annex, Brisbane, Australia

The office was stuffy, stiflingly hot and cramped; very cramped. Chunky filing cabinets lined every possible inch of wall, leaving hardly enough room for a tiny desk and two stiff backed wooden chairs. Given its owner was no small man himself, the room seemed about to burst at its seams even before his guest squeezed in through the partly blocked door. For all that, Lt-Commander Rupert Long, RAN was in full jacket and tie to welcome his visitor. Fortunately Richard Casey, MP had come to see the man, not his abode. A week's hard travel had led him in a circle; he only grunted with annoyance as his sleeve caught a locking bar on one of the security cabinets and grimaced in pain as his knee connected with a stout padlock.

"I had not expected to see you again so soon, sir" smiled Long, settling down to business

"I . . . " Casey paused "I have a problem, Commander."

"Yes, sir?"

"Time," said Casey. "I simply do not have enough of it. If this were a company, I should say I have a reasonable grasp of the books, but not yet a picture of the actual business. I certainly do not know enough of the work involved to make any worthwhile findings in detail."

Long was pleased, but not all that surprised, by such frank good sense coming from a politician. Keeping one eye on politics and politicians was a professional necessity for a man in his position; doubly so now, given Casey's present task and the recent past few months.

"I understood you were to set up a committee, sir?"

Casey grunted. "I do not make a habit of running away from a job half done, Commander, and in any case this matter is too important to delegate to the usual sort of committee."

"Perhaps an unusual sort of committee, sir? Ask the experts, as it were," suggested Long. "You'll have no argument from me about the press of time and the risk of failure, sir, and speaking personally, I'm damn glad someone is finally taking us so seriously."

Casey only scowled. He had already formed his conclusions, at least as far as possible courses of action. His political instincts might have inclined him towards expediency; he had been an engineer and a businessman for too

177

long to ignore the guts of a real issue for some facile solution. "Oh I already have a committee in mind, Commander, and framework for your agencies to work under. I even have a fellow to run them both." *Not that there is a great deal of choice,* he added silently.

Long permitted his curiosity to extend as far as a raised eyebrow, but no further

"Oh yes," continued Casey. "I may not be a spy, but I have a tolerable grasp of administration and how establish a firm on a sound footing. I also know a little something of politics, sir; having met with all of your peers and seen their petty fiefdoms over the last few days. I don't believe there are any three of you who could be in the same room for half an hour without blood on the floor."

Long laughed. "I'll grant you four, sir, but I dare say I could find three."

Casey showed no sign of humour. "Maybe so, Commander; but no select committee drawn from the available experts we have to hand could possibly be trusted to reach any worthwhile conclusion. However, we must have a committee, if only to give sufficient weight to our recommendations . ."

Long noted with some interest the use of the inclusive tense.

" . . . furthermore, the committee must include an expert in intelligence, a man acceptable to all parties, and it must have a final structure in mind from the start, confining itself to the details," concluded Casey.

"I see," was Long's only comment.

"You'd disagree, Commander?"

"Pardon me sir, but it is Lieutenant Commander, and no, I can see that working; provided you find the right fellow and come up with the right idea for the committee to follow."

"I'm glad you agree, Lieutenant Commander," smiled Casey grimly. "Might I ask you a question?"

"Of course, sir."

"How far does your circle of agents extend?"

"As far as I could push it, sir, and not as far as I'd have liked too," replied Long casually.

"But how far?" pressed Casey.

Long hesitated, "Ahh, I should be reluctant to . . . "

"Oh damn it, man" snapped Casey "I am not asking you to name names, only give me an idea. I know you have contact with Singapore . . . China?"

Rupert Long was a man of deep thought, tempered by the decisiveness and drive of a lifetime in naval service. He had spent years immersed in problems Richard Casey had not known existed ten days before, and spent almost as long gradually laying his own irons in the fire to address them. Long still recognized this present flurry of activity as perhaps the one golden opportunity for reform; but he equally saw its pitfalls all too clearly. He had imperiled his career, probably ruined it, if truth be told, to build this little office into the finest intelligence service in the country and one of the best in the Empire. So it was only natural he devote some contemplation to Casey and his enquiry. What amounted to Long's life's work was on the table, along with the future of a critical function of government and, ultimately, the safety, security and prosperity of the nation he was sworn to defend.

Long took none of these things lightly; of no less weight was his personal commitment to those who spied for him. His operation had been built on trust and loyalty. There'd never been any money and patriotism could hardly be a motive for some of his 'correspondents.' So it was no small thing for him to say.

"The Cape up to Chungking, across to Japan, out as far as California, and down to Chile."

"Good grief," breathed Casey "I had thought perhaps Hong Kong, but . . . we are talking of your people?"

Long nodded solemnly

It was Casey's turn to repress rampant curiosity, but this information only confirmed his original idea. "So we need to work out what this committee is going to recommend when you hand in its report."

HMAS Australia, *North Atlantic*

Even if most of the gunfire was from .303-caliber machine guns, the sheer volume was impressive. The Bren and Vickers guns had been loaded with tracer; they turned the sky bright red. The effect was immediate. The approaching Kondor abandoned its attack run and turned away. Within a few minutes, it was a dot on the horizon, shadowing the cruiser.

"He didn't like the flak." Lieutenant Colonel Beaumont was satisfied at the performance his troops had put up. They'd done well for men who'd never thought they would end up fighting at sea.

"He didn't have to. Mostly, his job is to find us and then call in the U-boats. Only, with most merchant ships being barely capable of token resistance, the Focke-Wulf crews are getting over-confident. I doubt he was expecting the volume of fire we put up. Now he's going back to doing what he was supposed to."

"U-boats." Beaumont spoke the words as if they were a curse. "They're waiting for us."

"They're trying." Stewart was less worried about them than the bomber. "But we're holding 22 knots and that makes us a hard target. The bastards will be laying in wait, for sure. So, we'll make their job a bit harder. We'll swing north and that'll take us clear of anybody that Kondor had called in."

Stewart drummed his fingers on the bridge rail and thought for a second before giving out the new helm orders. He had to swing far enough north to take his ship clear of any U-boats in ambush positions, yet not so far north he would delay their transit to Canada any more than absolutely essential. He made another decision.

"Increase revolutions for 24 knots."

Cabinet Office, 10 Downing Street, London, United Kingdom

"How did things ever come to this?" Lord Halifax looked at R.A. Butler with distress compounded by confusion. "Any hope that Winston would take his removal with good grace was asking far too much, but as a distinguished parliamentarian who knew and understood the rules, I thought he would take it on the chin and retire quietly. I was expecting a bare minimum of public cooperation at least, no matter how bitter he felt privately. But, first he disappears, and then turns up in Canada breathing fire and brimstone upon us."

"What did you expect from a half-breed American whose main support is that of inefficient but talkative people of a similar type?" Butler nearly snarled the comment out. His antipathy, bordering on hatred, for Churchill was well-known. He had wanted Churchill arrested after the coup, but cooler and wiser heads had intervened. They had pointed out that Halifax and Butler had absolutely no grounds for arresting him other than that he had been on the wrong side of a party coup, and any attempt at an arrest would have alienated their support base. To arrest a man over a philosophical and policy disagreement was just not done. Churchill's continued presence in the House would have been awkward for all concerned certainly, but not anything that would justify detention or any breech of a very prominent person's civil liberties.

It had seemed such a good idea to distract Churchill by throwing out a rumor that his life was in danger should he return to London. Butler had always known that they had to keep Churchill away from a microphone for the critical hours after the coup. Support for the new government was just one cracking good Churchillian speech away from wavering and a couple of Beaverbrook editorials wouldn't have helped either. *How could we have known he would take that threat seriously?* Butler asked himself the question with a frustrated snarl. *Churchill had no reputation for cowardice, or reticence. By fleeing the way he did, he made our threat real. His absence from London and public view raised as many, if not more, questions and doubt about the new regime than any stink he might have kicked in the normal course of events if he'd returned. People would have seen a degree of sour grapes and thwarted ambition/revenge in any counter-coup effort, and tuned them out to some degree. But his silence was deafening, the genitive undercurrents playing much less softly, and get swamped by events in any case.*

Then he had turned up in Canada with rumors swirling of a daring escape, pursued by dark and mysterious agents of the coup. There had even been whispers that he had been taken on his way to a secret execution only to be rescued by a group of Scottish supporters and smuggled to safety. Instead of being delayed and entangled, he got away and formed a counter-government in Canada. We got what we wanted, an unopposed assumption of power, but arriving in Canada the way he did has only confused Imperial opinion and given them another reason to delay and again withhold legitimacy from our Government. Damn the man.

"Silencing Churchill is our first priority." Butler had one idea at least along those lines. It was an idea that his new National Security Service was well-placed to carry out, even though it seemed to take far longer to get things done than he had expected. "He must be made to cease his attacks upon us. We do have a tool for that purpose, one that might prove most effective."

Halifax looked up. "And that is?"

"When Winston cut and ran, he left his family behind. Lady Clementine and the children. I have instructed the Security Service to detain them. We can make it clear to Winston that the treatment of his wife and children will be determined by his conduct while in Canada. We can make the conditions of their detention sufficiently arduous to drive the point home."

There was a long silence while Halifax stared at Butler, his expression one of total disbelief. Eventually, when Halifax spoke, his voice was quiet and passionless.

"Are you completely out of your mind? Has your distaste for Winston driven every vestige of common sense from your wits? What you suggest is foolish beyond measure. I can think of nothing that would damage the standing or stability of our government more than the course of action you so lightly suggest. Even if that consideration did not apply, your proposal is reprehensible. You say you have issued orders for the detention of Lady Clementine and the children?"

"Yes, although . . . . "

"Then we must pray that the time is not already too late. Your Permanent Secretary is available?"

"Arnold Robins? He is outside." Butler was slightly bewildered at the sudden change in the atmosphere and the way Halifax had changed from a weak and pliant tool to a real authority figure.

"Send him in. Immediately."

Robins must have been waiting in the anteroom, for his appearance was delayed by only a few seconds. Halifax took the time to calm down and swallow his outrage at Butler's suggestion. When he arrived, Robins had a look of distinct concern on his face.

"Robins, I understand you were given instructions to order the detention of Lady Clementine Spencer-Churchill and her children. Have these instructions yet been issued?"

"Prime Minister, in view of the somewhat nebulous and inexplicit nature appertaining to the remit of the National Security Service and the arguably marginal and peripheral nature the subject of the instructions we have been given has to the political security of the realm, it was believed that the central deliberations and decisions that would result in the issue of the instructions in question would benefit from legal consultation as to their accommodation within the political process and that there could be a case for re-structuring the nature of the contemplated actions in such a way as to eliminate them from the immediate agenda pending a clarification of the responsibilities of the Service with regard to the population at large."

Halifax relaxed. "Thank God for that. Robins, you will take personal responsibility for ensuring that the safety of Lady Clementine Spencer-Churchill and her family and placing them on a suitable means of conveyance to Canada. You will confirm to me in person when these instructions have been fulfilled. Now, leave us."

Once the room was clear, Halifax returned his attention to Butler. "There is a time and a place for the adoption of dark methods, Richard: when the security of the realm is at stake and we are obliged to take that path in the cause of the greater good. Even then, we should regard that path as a last resort. Bear that in mind when you undertake actions on behalf of this Government."

Room 208, Munitions Building, Washington, DC, USA

"The Air Corps is crating up the 110 Hawk 81s built to French specifications now and we'll be shipping them to India and South Africa. They've named them the Tomahawk I, by the way. Meanwhile, Captain Chennault is organizing the expansion of the Chinese air forces in an effort to reduce Japanese expansionism in China. He will be purchasing newly-built P-40B aircraft and also recruiting pilots for the Chinese. If his plans hold true, those aircraft will be in service by the end of the year." Secretary Stimson looked around with satisfaction. He was clearing his airfields of the ex-British and French aircraft before he was forced to take them into USAAC service.

"We've heard from the Commonwealth governments on the 140 British Hawk 81s. They're calling them Tomahawk IIs. They've agreed amongst themselves that they are to be delivered to the Middle East. Forty aircraft, are to go to Kenya and will equip two South African fighter squadrons. The other one hundred will go to Egypt and equip two British, one Australian and one Indian squadron." Cordell Hull also looked very happy. The war was still on and the prospect of disaster that had seemed so imminent earlier had receded dramatically. The Italian invasion of Egypt had stalled at Sidi Barrani and the British forces in Egypt were gathering to expel them. Even more significantly, the rest of the Commonwealth was funnelling reinforcements to East Africa and the Middle East.

Stimson sounded enthusiastic. "It makes sense the way they've done it. Give them a few weeks and they'll have a major edge in both the Middle

East and East Africa while they use the ex-French aircraft to train new pilots and work up new squadrons. Any news on the rest?"

"There's a conference in Jamaica that'll sort all the other issues out. Main issue remains the Hawk 75s, the DB-7 bombers and the Hudson patrol planes. They're squabbling over those. How goes the industry side of this, Phillip?"

"Not bad." Stuyvesant consulted a file. "Bill Pawley is setting up an aircraft factory in India, using machine tooling the manufacturers here are replacing. The Canadians are already building Bolingbrokes, that's a version of the Blenheim, and the Australians Beaufort torpedo bombers."

"Our factories are re-equipping? We need those production lines running." Hull was confused.

"We'll get them going soon. We need them re-equipped now though so we won't have to do it later when we're straining for output. And, all those extra orders for machine tools get those lines running as well. By the way, the British also placed orders for P-38s and P-39s. Bell and Lockheed want to know whether to start work on them."

Stimson shook his head. "Not now. We need those aircraft. It's one thing to get rid of aircraft we've already built; quite another to divert future building capacity. We've got a problem with Japan and we'll have to address it. They'll come after us sooner or later."

Cordell Hull shook his head. "We're not interested in having a war in the Pacific. As far as the President is concerned, he regards Germany as being our primary enemy."

"The problem with that attitude is that it only takes one side to start a war. If Japan wants to have a war with us, we don't need to agree with them about it; they'll come straight at us." Stimson sounded grim. "The Philippines will be hit first, you mark my words."

"Then we had better make sure that our defenses there are up to par. Can we send additional aircraft to defend Luzon? And extra troops?"

"We'd better. We can shift some of the new production we're generating there within a few months."

Stuyvesant looked up at the ceiling. "You know, it's just possible Halifax has done us a big favor. If he hadn't folded back in June, we wouldn't be mobilizing the way we are now. And that means we're going to have a lot more forces available a lot sooner. It might just be enough to persuade the Japanese that moving against us won't be worth the effort. Of course, the more allies we have out in that part of the world, the better."

Kingston, Jamaica

"Hot run over the Atlantic, Bob?"

"Some aggro with Kondors early on, but apart from that, easy trip. The doggies were glad to get off though and we were glad to get rid of them.

They threw up in places we never knew existed. Parts of the ship still stink." Captain Stewart wrinkled his nose in disgust at the memory. Driving a heavy cruiser fast through the North Atlantic was a sure guarantee of a rough ride and the Canadian infantry on board had suffered from acute, universal sea-sickness. Then, his crew had barely had time to unload the equipment they'd carried over and clean ship before the Canadian delegates had arrived for the trip down to Jamaica.

The harbor was well-stocked with warships. In addition to *Australia*, there were three other British cruisers, *Frobisher, Emerald* and *Enterprise*. Then there were six old British destroyers, Admiralty S-class fitted out as minelayers. Finally, in the middle of the harbor was an American heavy cruiser, the *Houston*. Stewart reflected that she was probably the only ship in the harbor that knew exactly who she belonged to. Across in the flying boat basin, the group was completed by the two anchored aircraft that had brought the Australian, Indian and South African delegations. Stewart was proud of the fact that the Australians had flown in, even if they had arrived in a Short S-23 rather than the larger S-26 used by the Indians.

"We've found a home." Captain Roderick Glynn entered the bar and sounded pleased. As well he might; the status of West Indies Station and the ships that were based there had been indeterminate for all too long. "The Governor-General has announced that the West Indies will follow the example set by Australia, Canada, India and South Africa and continue the state of hostilities that exists with Germany. The warships of West India Station will govern themselves accordingly. Them's our orders."

"What *really* happened, Rod?" Glynn's father was a senior civil servant in the Jamaican government and it was presumed that the Captain of HMS *Frobisher* had his ear to the ground.

Glynn looked around to make sure nobody other than the Royal Navy Captains were present. "You might not know this, but there's a lot of discussion been going on about the future out here. Basically, London wants all the West Indies assembled into a federation that can then be given Dominion status. That's not popular because the rich trading islands believe that they'll end up subsidizing the poorer fishing ones. Since the existing administration is run by sugar planters and banana merchants, that argument carries a lot of weight. So, there was a Royal Commission appointed to examine the situation and come up with a workable solution.

"Well, they did. The problem is the disparity of development spread across the islands that makes up the West Indies. So, invest money in the development of the poorer islands, bring them up to the standard of the rest and the objections to Federation go away. So, the Royal Commission recommended that a grant of five million pounds a year be made from the Colonial Development Fund for that purpose. Just for good measure, they tossed in an extra half million a year for research into the development of viable industries.

"So far, so good. Only when the results of the Royal Commission were due to be released in the House, Butler announced that the whole report was being kept secret and we were told that the promised funds would only be made available if we stuck to the London line. If we didn't, we could go and whistle for the money. Of course, that went down like the proverbial lead balloon."

Glynn shook his head. "You know, if they'd done that quietly and privately, they'd probably have got away with it. But, announcing it in the House? There was no way the planters would allow it. Clem Attlee said just that in the House, of course, and much good it did anybody. Anyway, the West Indies are in, and there's the funny thing. Those Yanks who are 'observers' here? They were last seen heading in to the GGs office.

Governor's Office, Kingston, Jamaica

Henry Morgenthau looked across the polished wood of the great desk, taking in the surroundings that threatened to engulf him. The sheer volume of British historical associations tended to be overwhelming to those not accustomed to them. Sir Arthur Frederick Richards, Governor of Jamaica and now, for want of anybody better-qualified and drawing on the Daventry Message for authority, apparent leader of the West Indies, was fully aware of the impact this office had on visitors. That was why the meeting was being held here. Morgenthau cleared his throat and tried to concentrate on the issue at hand.

"I am empowered to state that the United States of America views with favor the decision by the West Indies, Australia, Canada, India and South Africa to join together in establishing the Sovereign as an international trading currency. I am also authorized, as Secretary of the Treasury, to advise you that that United States will accept the Sovereign in payment of international debts at the exchange rate specified. I am also empowered to state that the United States will no longer be accepting the pound sterling for payment of such debts, except in cases where the value of the pound sterling is expressed in Sovereigns."

The collective intake of breath that ran around the office was profound. The American decision had given the Dominions an economic weapon they could use against London. Morgenthau looked around at those present and nodded slowly. They got the message. *The pound is dead; all hail the Sovereign. And that is a blow right to the heart of the British Empire.*

"We are also prepared to loan your governments adequate funds to purchase necessary defense equipment and make the fundamental changes needed to your economic structures." Morgenthau looked around again. The response to this was less unified. It didn't matter much to South Africa and Canada. The former had its gold and precious stone sales to fall back on, while the Canadian economy was linked closely to the United States. India was staggering from day to day, trying to make ends meet and just about managing. It was Australia and New Zealand that were sliding downwards into

185

a severe economic depression the fastest. Morgenthau was already convinced that New Zealand couldn't survive on its own. Australia? That was less obvious.

"Secretary Stimson has asked if you have come to any agreement on the issue of the ex-British and ex-French aircraft currently in our custody?"

There was a general exchange of glances. Morgenthau got the feeling that a hard battle was going on behind the scenes. Eventually, John Fisher Boyd from Canada took the lead in replying. "Since Canada still faces a submarine threat from Germany, we have first call on the patrol aircraft. The six LB-30s and the Flying Fortresses will be the long-range element of that force. I assume we will be given a discount on one of the Fortresses since it has been – ahem – used?"

"They're already paid for." Not having been briefed on exactly how Churchill had been spirited out of Britain, Morgenthau couldn't understand why Boyd's comment had been considered so amusing. "And the Hudsons?"

"We believe there are one hundred of them outstanding? Thirty will go to India to replace the old biplanes they are using for coastal patrol and the balance will come to us in Canada. I trust that is agreeable to the United States?"

Morgenthau nodded.

"India will also have first call on the ex-French DB-7s, on the understanding that at least three squadrons of them will be deployed to the Middle East once the squadrons are up and running. Australia has surrendered any claim on them, since they will interfere with production of its own Hudsons and the Beaufort program. Canada has no use for short-range tactical bombers. The Marylands will go to the Middle East Air Force, where their greater range will be of use."

"And the Hawk 75s?"

"They will be divided between India and Australia, on the understanding that each country will send at least two squadrons to Singapore and Malaya. At the moment, there are insufficient trained pilots for all of them, so a school will be set up in South Africa with the earliest Hawk 75s being sent there."

"There is another issue which India wishes to raise with the United States." Pandit Nehru spoke softly, but there was a firm passion in his voice. "We agree that the Middle East must take absolute priority. The revelation of the Noth plan shows that. But India cannot forget it has a back door, and that back door is threatened by a powerful and militaristic Japan. Fortunately, we have an ally who guards that door for us, yet we are alarmed to discover that ally is not well-regarded in your capital. So much so that military equipment, bought and paid-for, remains undelivered. I refer, of course, to the Kingdom of Thailand. We ask you to reconsider your position with regard to our ally, lest

186

you drive it into the hands of Japan and thus leave the back door to my country unlocked and inviting."

Morgenthau frowned. This wasn't in the brief he had been given and he didn't have an answer to hand. "I cannot answer this question at this time. I will consult with Secretaries Hull and Stimson. They will explain to me what our position on this issue is and why it has been adopted. Perhaps we can revisit this issue once those consultations have been completed."

Buna Field, Kenya

"Just what good are we supposed to be doing out here, anyway?"

Pim Bosede snarled out the question, quite disregarding the superior rank of the officer he was addressing. Fortunately for him, Petrus van Bram overlooked the near-insubordination, not least because he was equally frustrated at the lack of success.

"We are maintaining an air presence. And we are gaining experience that will be put to good use once we get better aircraft." van Bram reflected that the latter at least was true. The squadron had gained experience and shed many of its old, bad habits. The tight V-formation had gone and the aircraft now flew in loose pairs. The old three flights of six aircraft had been replaced by four flights of four; although the loss of two aircraft had been as responsible for that as any sudden insight into tactical logic.

"And when will that be?" Bosede wasn't going to be mollified easily.

"Strange you should mention that."

van Bram had guessed this conversation would be coming up. It was hardly surprising, since the squadron's operations over the last two months had been one long exercise in futility. The Italian SM.79 and SM.81 bombers were actually faster than the South African Fury fighters, while the few aircraft that the Fury could catch were always heavily escorted by CR.42s.

The same problems affected any effort at offensive air operations. The handful of Blenheims and Ju-86s operated by the South Africans were too fast to be escorted by the Furies but not fast enough to escape interception by the CR.42s. In truth, the existing South African aircraft in Kenya were doing no good at all; it was only Italian inertia that was preventing them from further advances. The news he had now would change all that.

"You said you had experience flying Curtiss aircraft?"

"Travel Air 6000s. Flying mail."

"That's close enough. We've been told that we're getting the latest American fighters sent here. Something called a Tomahawk."

"Never heard of it."

"Well, you have now. They're being shipped to Mombasa and assembled there. You and three other pilots from this squadron who have experience with Curtiss aircraft will pick the first four up, get some orientation on them and bring them back here. The brass decided to convert the two Fury squadrons flight by flight, rather than squadron by squadron. Curtiss has sent some Americans over to help you convert. You'll have a week to get ready. Then we'll start taking the war to the Italians."

New Government Buildings, New Delhi, India

There were times when a man's duty was hard to perceive and times when he had to trust to his own judgment and the voice inside him that said he had to do thus and so, for the good of his soul. For Lieutenant Colonel Pierce Harvey Garry, this was one of those times.

Ever since Sir Richard Cardew had approached him in the Calcutta United Service Club, Colonel Garry had been torn by the belief that what he was doing was fundamentally dishonorable; yet he was also sure that not following the path he had chosen would have appalling consequences for the country he loved and the people he knew. That dichotomy, between what he knew to be right and what he knew to be necessary, had led him to the place and time he occupied now. Just as inexorably, it had led him to the actions that he was about to commit, for better or for worse.

"Pickets are in place. There's no movement yet." Captain Shashi Madhav was less uncertain of the rights and wrongs of this issue. To him, India was independent at last; broken away from the British who had ruled the country for so long and standing on its own feet. The regiment was in position to guard that independence and reverse the changes that had been made over the last four months. Had he had his way and followed his heart, the British would have been removed completely from power and sent packing, but he was a hard-headed, realistic man who understood the difference between wishes and practical reality. A transition period was needed to make the transfer of power as smooth as possible. The events that would be taking place here tonight confirmed that. They had shown Madhav something else; his Colonel's determination to defend the Indian government and, by definition, India's independence meant that some, at least, of the British were as Indian as he was.

"They'll be coming down the main road." Garry's voice was heavy at the impending tragedy. "In lorries. The plan was for us to open the way for them. Instead, we'll have to bar it."

The plan that had been explained to him was quite simple and yet profoundly, irretrievably, flawed. His Third Battalion, 7th Rajputs was assigned to guard the government complex in New Delhi. Instead, they were to secure that complex and await reinforcements from several more regiments that would converge on New Delhi and fortify the area. Sir Richard Cardew would then contact London, secure an appointment as the new Viceroy and take over the administration of India. His first responsibility once his authority was secured would be to arrest the previous Viceroy and his followers. A very simple plan indeed. Its primary flaw was also a very simple one. As any good civil servant would, Cardew had made the presumption that the center of administration, New Delhi, was also the center of power.

It was not. It would be, one day, but here and now, in October 1940, the center of political power still resided in Calcutta, not the nominal capital New Delhi. General Auchinleck had expressed it beautifully. "The idiot is trying to commandeer the train by taking over the dining car." That, of course, had highlighted the other minor flaw in the plan.

It presumed Garry would do his part by seizing the administrative complex for the mutineers; he was actually wholeheartedly on the side of the existing government and had been keeping their intelligence service under Sir Eric Haohoa fully advised on the situation. Once the mutineers had been committed by their attempt to join the troops they believed would be holding the Administrative Complex, other loyal Indian regiments would be moving to disarm them. Garry shook his head at that. The loyal troops would mostly be Ghurkas, the one force in India the existing government could depend upon without question. There was an age-old rivalry between the Rajputs and the Ghurkas and Garry would have been a lot happier if he could have had his Rajputs gain the honor of putting down the rebellion. Instead they would have to make do with firing the first shots.

A runner came up to the command post, his bearing filled with urgency. "Sir, they approach." Captain Madhav's voice was heavy. It was a hard thing to order troops to open fire on their own comrades, especially misguided ones that had been mislead by their commanders. Even with his devotion to his new India, Madhav had studiously avoided calling such men 'the enemy'.

Garry breathed heavily; to his great embarrassment, his eyes moistened. Suddenly, he bitterly regretted his thoughts of only a few seconds before about firing the first shots needed to put down this rebellion. He wished devoutly that the burden could have fallen to another battalion, even one of Ghurkas. He shook his head and breathed deeply for a second to steady his voice.

"Are our machine guns in position to stop them?"

"They are, sir." Garry was shaken to hear Madhav's voice trembling. A quick glance showed that he, too had tears in his eyes.

The machine guns were Vickers-Berthiers, a weapon the Indian Army had chosen when the British had selected the Bren Gun. The virtues of the two weapons were hotly disputed Both armies thought they had made the better decision. But, this was India, and the Vickers-Berthier was the weapon that would be used.

"We will give them a warning burst on my order. If that is ignored, instruct the gunners to fire at the engines of the lorries. They are to try and stop them without hitting the men in the cab or the back. If it is at all humanly possible, I would have this night go without bloodshed."

Madhav nodded in acknowledgement and passed the orders through. The end of the road suddenly seemed to brighten. The first of the approaching lorries turned the corner. Its headlights illuminated the buildings on either side. Silently, Colonel Garry damned Sir Richard Cardew for starting this whole sordid business. By the time he had finished the words in his mind, the lorries were rumbling towards the administration complex. He could temporize no longer.

"Captain Madhav, open fire on those lorries."

A stream of tracers from a single Vickers-Berthier light machine gun streaked through the night across the front of the lead lorry. From his vantage point by the side of the road, Lieutenant Colonel Pierce Harvey Garry saw it swerve to a halt and stand, swaying, in the middle of the road. The suddenness of the turn and braking came very close to causing the lorry to roll over.

Behind it, other lorries in the convoy were also coming to a halt, swerving to avoid each other. What had once been a neat, orderly convoy was now chaos. Troops started to jump down from the back of the stopped vehicles. Some formed a perimeter; others stood around in confusion. Which group did what said much about the junior officers and NCOs in the individual units.

There is still time. Garry knew it, but he also knew that time was the critical element in the situation that was developing. He desperately did not want this confrontation to end in a bloodbath. Once the firing started in earnest, that is exactly what it would do. He had to put a stop to it. His course was clear. For the first time in weeks, he felt happy with what his sense of duty demanded he do.

"Stop right there. Stand down immediately."

His voice rang across the road, cutting over the rumble of lorry engines. The lighting was dim but it still reflected off his rank insignia.

"Sir, we are under orders to enter the government building complex and aid in securing it."

The reply came from the cab of the first lorry, the one that had so nearly turned over. An officer dismounted. The same dim light revealed his rank as Captain. There was uncertainty and a hint of nervousness in his manner.

"And I am under orders to deny you access to this complex." Garry's voice continued to dominate the sounds of the street. In his mind, he could hear echoes of the burst of gunfire that had halted the trucks. *Would that they were the last shots fired.*

"I was told that you would be occupying the area and awaiting our assistance." The confusion was growing by the second.

"You were misinformed. The Third Battalion, 7th Rajputs remain true to their salt. Do the Garwhalis do the same?"

The comment stung every man who heard it. There was no worse accusation one could make to an Indian soldier than suggest he had not been true to his salt. Some historians had suggested that the horrors of the Indian Mutiny had come from the mutineers feeling so dishonored by their infidelity that nothing they could do would make matters worse. The Garwhali Regiment Captain looked as if he had been slapped across the face. British he might be, but he knew his men and knew the accusation would destroy his position if left unanswered.

"First Battalion, The Royal Garwhal Rifles also remains true to its salt. We move in obedience of orders from London."

Garry knew how to trump that. "And the 7th Rajputs move on the orders of the Viceroy acting on behalf of the King-Emperor himself."

The Garwhali captain showed nothing but confusion and near-panic. He had expected nothing like this. The whole situation was outside his experience. In that he was not alone. Nobody on the street that night had experience in this. In the end, he fell back on the one thing that he could rely on, the orders he had received from his Colonel.

"We have our orders. If you will not obey yours, stand aside."

Garry looked at him and then made his decision. He walked firmly, precisely, to the lead lorry and stood in front of it. Out of the corner of his eye, he saw the Garwhali Captain's hand move. Garry glimpsed the flash, but heard nothing. All he felt was the heavy impact that he knew was a bullet from a .455 Webley revolver.

Standing at the side of the road, Captain Shashi Madhav saw both the flash and heard the shot that had killed his Colonel. A brief hammer burst from a Vickers-Berthier cut down the Captain. The man hadn't even tried to take cover. He stood there with a dumbstruck expression on his face, a man pole-axed by the shock of what he had done. He died with that expression still on his face.

Madhav never thought about what he did next; nor did he have anything in mind other than to stop the killing. He ran out into the street, his arms held high.

"Stop! Cease fire! India is free. Shall we mark that freedom by spilling our own blood?"

His anguished words echoed around the street, reflecting off the buildings. As the sound faded away, there was a profound silence. It seemed strangely louder than his shout. It was broken by a rattle from the lorries on the road; the rattle of rifles being lowered, weapons made safe. Madhav's heart lifted as he realized the crisis was ending. His men wouldn't have to massacre the Garwhalis after all. Four Gharwalis came out and picked up the body of Colonel Garry, carrying it with respect and honor to the lorries. A few feet away, four Rajputs did the same for the body of the Garwhali who had killed their Colonel.

In his heart, Madhav knew he was watching the birth of a new, national Indian Army.

Cabinet Room, Government House, Calcutta, India

"What is happening out there, Sir Eric?" Pandit Nehru asked the question amid an office filled with foreboding.

Sir Eric Haohoa had entered the room with a sheath of signals. He shook his head sadly; the night was not one that he would remember with pride. "The attempt by elements of the Army to remove the existing government and return control of India to London is turning into a fiasco. The units that moved on New Delhi were intercepted by loyal regiments. There was some exchange of fire, but the hearts of the mutineers were not in their work. So far, the dead total eleven with another twenty wounded. Mostly they were British officers; their deaths left the men they commanded without a figure to whom their loyalty was attached. In the absence of such figures, they placed their loyalty to India above all else."

Those words were met with silence. The Indian Army had been the foundation stone of the Empire. It was disturbing for the British administration to see its final allegiance switching away from the Empire to the new state that was growing in India. On the other hand, Nehru was quietly delighted with the news; he had the tact and discretion not to make that fact public.

"The rest of the mutiny?"

Sir Eric continued after the silence had stretched for long enough. "Mostly a fizzle; units refusing orders until loyal troops turned up. The Royal Deccan Horse are holed up in their barracks area and putting up a fight, but they're the only ones who are making a real show. Everywhere else, it was the same story as in New Delhi. The officers led, but their men only followed out of loyalty to them. Once the chips went down and they saw they were being led down a blind alley, they gave it up in the name of a greater loyalty."

"What about the Deccan Horse?" Viscount Linlithgow was almost afraid of the answer.

"A Ghurka regiment is moving in to deal with them. We're sending Blenheim bombers in to hit their base at dawn, with an assault to follow. Once that's over, this sordid little affair will be done. One thing I should mention. One of the dead officers in New Delhi was Colonel Garry of the Rajputs."

"The man who alerted us to the danger." Sir Martyn Sharpe spoke sadly. "India is in his debt. And what of Sir Richard Cardew?"

"Under arrest." Sir Eric spoke grimly. This was, perhaps, the most difficult aspect of the whole situation. "A policy decision with regard to him and his fellow conspirators will have to be made."

That thought caused another long silence. Eventually, Nehru voiced the thought that had caused so much concern.

"And the decision we make will decide what kind of country we would like this to be."

192

"China." Cordell Hull's voice echoed around the room with tones that portended doom.

"China." Henry Stimson repeated the words with equally gloomy connotations.

"What's happening in China?" Henry Morgenthau was curious. His long visit to Jamaica left him out of touch with the developing world situation.

"Nothing good and that's the problem." Stimson shook his head. "Ever since the Marco Polo Bridge Incident, the Chinese have been trying to prolong the war for as long as possible, with the aim of exhausting Japanese resources while they build up their own military capacity. They showed they could fight at the Battle of Shanghai. Their German-trained divisions there held the Japanese back for three months and chewed them up, but they still ended up retreating towards Nanking. At least they proved their army could fight, which was a relief.

"Since then, they've adopted a strategy they call 'magnetic warfare:' attracting advancing Japanese troops to definite points where they are subjected to ambush, flanking attacks, and encirclements in major engagements. They did this during the successful defense of Changsha last year and the defeat of the Japanese at Guanxi soon afterwards. They followed that by launching a large-scale counter-offensive against the IJA a few months ago. That got beaten back.

"The truth is that China has a low military-industrial capacity, limited experience in modern warfare and their army is poorly-trained, under-equipped, and disorganized. They lost the only well-trained and equipped units they had in the Battle of Shanghai. The only things that are saving them is the influx of supplies from abroad and that the Japanese have encountered tremendous difficulties in administering and garrisoning the territory they have seized. They recruited a large collaborationist Chinese Army to maintain public security in those occupied areas, but it's largely ineffective. Japanese control is limited to just railroads and major cities and vast Chinese countryside is a hotbed of Chinese partisan activities.

"In short, Japan has occupied much of north and coastal China, but the central government and military have successfully retreated to the western interior and are continuing their resistance. However, the Chinese ability to continue fighting is dependent upon supplies from outside. They just don't have the resources to continue fighting on their own. The Japanese have realized that it's going to be impossible for them to achieve a decisive victory in the interior of China as long as those supplies flow in. So, they've started a major effort to cut them off. They're occupying the ports along China's coast for a start and they're pressuring the French to shut down the Yunnan railway from Indo-China. If they succeed in doing all that, the supply line to China will be shut. The stalemate in the Chinese interior won't last that long after that happens."

"It is U.S. Government policy to support China in its defense against Japanese aggression. We have some rather odd allies in doing that. The Soviets have their own hand in the game. They're supplying arms and equipment, mostly to the Chinese communist forces, but some is going to Chiang Kai Shek and his nationalists." Cordell Hull grimaced. As a classical liberal, in his eyes the Communists were little better than the Japanese when it came to totalitarianism. On the other hand, he was realist enough to know that 'a little better' was still 'better' and the memories of what had happened at Nanking still sickened him.

"What we need is a new supply line." Stuyvesant sounded thoughtful, but his mind was already ranging through the possibilities. "One way or another, the Indo-China ports and railways are going to be closed to us sooner or later. We have to build an alternative."

"Easier said than done, Phillip. Have you seen the ground out there?"

In greater detail than you can possibly imagine. Stuyvesant thought. "I have. It is bad, but there is a road already out there. It runs from Kunming to the Burmese border. It was built between 1937 and 1938; by hand, if you can believe that. It's amazing what 200,000 people working with their bare hands can achieve. If we can hook up to that, then we can shift supplies through there. Roads aren't as good as railways for shifting large quantities of good, but they're better than nothing. We can use the ports in Burma, especially Rangoo;, shift the goodies by train to Lashio on the China-Burma border and then along the Kunming Road into China proper. At the very least, we can replace the Yunnan Railway that way."

"You're not mentioning the obvious problem, Phillip," Hull was wary. "The Japanese won't just sit still for that. Burma is British territory. They'll pressure Halifax to close down the links you're just mentioned and we know how Halifax reacts to pressure. He goes to pieces so fast, everybody around him is in danger from the shrapnel." Hull sounded mightily disenchanted with the British Prime Minister.

"Well, he might well do so, but here's the interesting thing. Some industrial colleagues of mine have been negotiating with the Indian Government recently and they picked up some revealing insights. One of them is that it's open to question exactly who Burma reports to at this time. Until 1937, they were essentially a sub-office of India; and with the changes in London, there's a strong move to return to that arrangement. The Indians might well be a lot less inclined to succumb to Japanese pressure than Halifax. Asserting their independence and standing as a nation, all that good stuff. Some judicious aid might well reinforce that desire."

"We've given them several hundred aircraft; won't that keep them happy?"

"It's a start, but they need economic help as well as military. That's why they're moving to reincorporate Burma. They need the export goods. You see, Cordell, they can't ignore Burma. They need the export earnings too badly. If they're going to make a go of standing on their own feet, then they need to mark out a position in the world trade system as soon as possible. For that, they need Burma. Now, if we offer aid to them in exchange for no interference with us running supplies up to the Burma Road, they'll take it."

"Not if it means upsetting the Japanese. The whole reason why they jumped ship on the Empire was because they were afraid the terms of the Halifax Armistice gave the Japanese claim on India." Hull shook his head. "Given a choice between forgoing our money and a Japanese occupation army, they'll turn down our cash in a shot."

"Perhaps not." Stimson was thoughtful. "The Japanese had a lever against England. They could threaten Malaya, Singapore and Hong Kong. They don't have a lever against India; they can't get there from where they are now."

"They can invade Burma." Hull sounded very unconvinced.

Stimson laughed. "Not a chance. Not over the border between China and Burma. The only ways into Burma from China is either across some pretty impassable mountains or from Indochina, through Thailand into Malaya and Burma from the east."

"There's your answer then. The Thais are in Japan's pocket. All they will do is direct traffic." Hull set his jaw in determination.

"What makes you think that?" Stuyvesant sounded idle, but his mind was moving fast. *This could turn into the opportunity Suriyothai is praying for.*

"They've got a fascist government and they're buying aircraft from the Japanese."

"Come on now, Cordell." Stimson jumped in with both feet. "They're approaching the Japanese for aircraft because the State Department stopped delivery of NA-68 and NA-69 aircraft that the Thai Air Force had bought and paid for. Of course they're looking for another supplier, and there aren't too many options out there for them. As for a fascist government, they've just deposed an absolute monarch and replaced him with a constitutional monarchy and an elected parliament. That doesn't sound like fascism to me."

"They could have given those aircraft to the Japanese. Betrayed our secrets." Hull was both obdurate and petulant. Listening to him, Stuyvesant wondered what was driving his opinions.

"Oh come on, Cordell; those aircraft are hardly the best we produce. They're modified trainers, mostly. The Japanese may not have a first-line, world standard air force and navy, but they're better than that. Anyway, I hear the Indians smile upon the Thais. I believe Nehru speaks well of them. If he does that, they can hardly be fascists or Japanese allies."

"I second that." Henry Morgenthau reinserted himself into the debate. "When I was in Jamaica, Nehru himself said exactly that. He claimed the Thais had been of great service to India already and have showed themselves to be a trustworthy ally. He says that the Noth Plan makes it essential that India look west to its defense against the threatened German attack and that leaves them wide open to the East and Japan. They look to Thailand to guard their back door and specifically asked us to resume normal diplomatic and trade relations with Thailand in order to ensure that back door was properly guarded. And, very specifically, to resume arms sales to them."

"The Noth Plan?" Stimson looked confused.

"A German plan for an attack on India. Essentially it involves two thrusts: an Italian push from North Africa, through Egypt and the Sinai, into Transjordan and a German thrust from the Balkans, through Turkey and Iraq, into India. There's no doubt the plan is genuine, although how the Indians got hold of it is a mystery." Morgenthau blinked owlishly. "If Indian intelligence is that good, they might be a more valuable ally than we thought."

Stimson snorted. "Their intelligence might be good, but their strategic insight isn't. I find it hard to see them taking a plan like that seriously. The Indian Army have a staff college in Quetta that's the equal of any in the British Empire, and there's no shortage of trained professional soldiers out there who know the actual terrain and the true scale of the maps. If anybody can see all the flaws in this so-called Noth Plan it's them.

"To the Indian Army, that whole area isn't a backwater; it's been their strategic front yard for a hundred years. They have generals serving who fought across Palestine, in Salonika and the Balkans in World War One. I believe there were even officers who had bicycled from India to the UK using much the same sort of routes though Turkey as an invasion force would use. They can't believe this plan is practical. The force required to carve through Turkey is completely excessive, the supply lines to the base areas are totally inadequate and the transport facilities just don't exist in the quantities needed to support an invasion force of the required size."

Not bad, Stuyvesant thought. *I made up a list of ten reasons why Odwin Noth should have had his plan stuffed up his fundamental orifice and you just got three of them. I'll make a strategist of you yet, Henry.*

"I think that the reason why the Noth Plan is accepted is that it's simply so convenient to so many people. It gives the existing administration in India a reason to stay in the war; a reason for the Indian Army to stay in the Middle East. It gives the leaders of the Congress Party a tool to keep their wilder supporters in line and an excuse to maintain armed forces that a significant minority of the party would like to see abandoned altogether. The Noth Plan may be impractical, I'll take your word for that, but it suits everybody who matters to accept it as gospel.

"Anyway, we're dealing with Nazi Germany here. They have an established track record of accepting crazy plans and making them work. Look at the way they came through the Ardennes, for example. I'd say the Indians might have reservations about the Noth Plan but they can't afford to assume that it's not serious."

196

"Very good, Stuyvesant; we'll make a strategist of you yet." Stimson gave the industrialist a friendly grin. "Cordell, Phillip is right. The Indians can't afford not to take the Noth Plan seriously. That means they have to leave their back door open. If they believe the Thais will cover it for them, then we have to take their opinion seriously."

"I see no reason why we should accept Indian opinions on this matter." Hull was, if anything, more petulant than ever.

"We don't have to." For those who chose to listen carefully, there was a hint of real anger in Morgenthau's voice. Stuyvesant heard it, Hull did not. "We have been advised by Nehru that you are welcome to visit Thailand, discuss the situation with their leaders, see for ourselves the conditions within the country, judge the progress they are making to a representative democracy and gauge the temper of its leaders."

"I see no reason for that."

Hull spoke with a flat and final note that, more than anything else, pushed Morgenthau over the edge.

"You see no reason for that? And you served for many distinguished years as a judge? How many defendants did you convict, Cordell, because you couldn't be bothered to hear their defense? How many guilty verdicts had you decided on before you even entered the courtroom? We call you the "The Judge." We believe you look on the law as the bastion of right and justice, and now we find you condemn an entire nation without allowing them to say a word in their defense. How could we have been so wrong about you?"

"Now, wait a moment." Stimson was shocked at the outburst.

"A moment be damned!" Morgenthau was in full flow and was not to be interrupted. "If a government is fascist, if its people represent any part of that evil creed, I will be the first to call for their destruction. I will wish fire, plague, starvation and death upon each and every one of them. But I will not condemn them without giving them a hearing. I will judge by deeds, not by prejudiced opinions held absent the knowledge of hard facts. Cordell, when you refuse to give these people the chance to speak, you deny the very basis of the law you claim to have spent your life supporting."

There was a long silence. Henry Stimson was shocked at the outburst and the unheard-of abuse of the Secretary of State. Stuyvesant was outwardly solemn but inwardly delighted at the turn of events that had saved him the need to intervene himself. Morgenthau was trying to get his temper under control after his impassioned speech, while Cordell Hull was struggling to dampen down the fury that consumed him. Hull knew that the task of doing so would be much easier if Morgenthau hadn't been right. In the room, time and the atmosphere seemed to creak as the seconds turned into minutes.

"Very well." Cordell Hull spoke softly, although the strain he was experiencing in keeping his anger in check was painfully obvious. "Henry, I will do as you urge and accept the invitation to visit Bangkok. The law *should* be the bastion of right and justice, but it is the creation of humans, and that means it is as fallible as any other human creation. It is also as fallible as any of the people who administer it. I will hear what the Thai leaders and the Siamese people have to say and I will judge accordingly.

"Now, I believe this meeting has run its course and I declare it closed."

Technically that should have been proposed, seconded and put to a vote, but nobody cared to argue the point. In any case, Stuyvesant, for one, had other places to be. One of them was telling Lillith to get Igrat on the first Clipper for Manila and Bangkok.

Dumbarton Avenue, Georgetown, Washington, DC, USA

"What I don't understand is why I have to keep buying Iggie presents every time I go with her on a trip. It's breaking my personal bank." Henry McCarty sounded seriously aggrieved.

"It's because we're the only opposite sex men have got, ducks." Eleanor Gwynne sounded vaguely amused. "We cornered the market. Anyway, it's necessary for the cover you two are running."

"I don't really need Henry along with me." Igrat shook her head thoughtfully. She was clutching her return air tickets to Bangkok in her hand. The $1,400 round trip price-tag had almost caused Lillith to have an attack of the vapors. "I really don't; not now. It might get that way, but I'm fine. An American passport protects me much better than anything else. The Germans don't want to do anything to upset us right now."

"Not now, no." Stuyvesant agreed. "The German collective sets of eyes are focussed on Russia. When that turns into a real war, everything will go to hell very fast. I'll defer to your judgement on this, Iggie; make your runs alone until your gut instinct says otherwise."

"Thank the Gods for that." Henry McCarty was a deeply relieved man. "I can't afford to keep saving her life like this."

"You save my life?" Igrat put on a good pretence of being outraged. "If it wasn't for me, you'd have been arrested at Marseilles as an undesirable alien. If the French guard hadn't been looking down the front of my dress, you'd have been toasted for sure."

"That's another point." Stuyvesant was curious. "How do you get that dress to stay in place? I thought that one deep breath and everybody would see the cherries on the sundaes."

Igrat giggled and looked down at her dress. "It's taped to me, of course. Every Broadway Baby knows *that* trick."

"Ahh, right. OK, Iggie, go tell Lillith that you're risking your life to save her from spending money on Clipper tickets. Then get on the China Clipper out. You're running against the clock on this one."

The Lodge, Canberra, Australia

The Lodge was a quiet, modest residence, as 40 room mansions went; like so much of Canberra, it was a temporary structure that after sixteen years had taken on shades of permanence. Of the two studies provided for the Prime Minister, Locock liked the private chamber on the first floor, even if he found the formal room more practical for business. Although he was of two minds about the decor.

"Rum, single malt, Dimple, gin, brandy, and I mean brandy – not cognac, or.... well there's a bottle of Pims lurking back here, and is that Benedictine? The cupboard is pretty bare, Arthur; or I could get us up a bottle of Red Ned, a drop of Muscat?"

"Oh, whatever you're having" replied the Treasurer casually.

"Well, to tell the truth, I rather fancy a cup of tea," chuckled Locock. "But, if there's any gas in this soda bottle . . ." There was.

"Ta. So Curtin cleaned you out before he left, then?" asked Fadden, leaning back into a deep armchair with his whisky and soda.

"They had a bit of a shindig before they left." Locock eased back into his own armchair. "And, with all the comings and goings, the staff have been a bit busy. Have you read Dickey's report yet?"

"The Casey Enquiry into matters of Security and Intelligence? No; it's still on my desk, although I did see your minute about a committee."

"Well, the committee can wait a little," nodded Locock. "But I was hoping you'd read it, as I need to twist your arm on some funding."

"Oh, the spies need paying, do they?"

"It's more a matter of the estimates." Locock rubbed his ear. "I need to pry half of Naval Intelligence out from under the Naval Board and into my office, and I thought grabbing them by the budget might be the easiest way to do it."

"Half?" Fadden was puzzled. "Of Naval Intelligence . . . ? It looks like I *do* need to read that damned report."

"Under the circumstances, Casey felt he needed to pick a winner for us to build on, rather than try to start something new from scratch, and apparently the chap running Naval Intelligence is best we have." Locock shrugged. "Putting it directly under the department of Prime Minister and Cabinet seems about the only way to short circuit a lot of petty jealousy and obstructionism. I get the impression the old boy system we have worked well enough in peacetime, when everyone knew who they needed to talk to; but now, with people going everywhere and new faces all over the place . . . Do you remember Strahan mentioning the Governor General was our principal source for overseas intelligence?"

Fadden nodded. "Aye, and I didn't need Frank Strahan to tell me either."

"No? Well you might have mentioned it to me chum," smiled Locock. "In any case, it seems the good Sir Alex gets a great deal of his information from Long. It's the only way he's found to get around your precious civil servants and the all the bloody bureaucracy. We are just not used to taking that sort of thing into account on a day to day basis and we must," said Locock firmly.

"Well it's not generally all that useful," shrugged Fadden. "A few ominous whispers and vague hints without much a fellow can get his teeth into. About as much use as weather forecast for Wednesday a week."

"No? Then it would not have helped us any to know the Thais were wooing the Hong Kong trading houses?"

Fadden looked a little stunned. "You're joking?"

"No, but I wish I were. Dicky has seen the correspondence; dated correspondence. Apparently Long passed it up to the ACNB, but somewhere between the Navy Board and anywhere useful, it vanished. There's something big stirring there and we don't know what it is. And then there is that wretched coup attempt in India. Halifax loyalists trying to get back into power. We think that's over, but how do we know? The Halifax people could be regrouping and planning another attempt while we sit here speaking. . .

"We need this, Arthur; we need this. You keep telling us we need to trim expenditure and maximize tax revenue.

"Oh, it's only temporary." Locock said, lying through his teeth. "The Committee will sort out a permanent structure, and then you can punt Long back into the wilderness if it makes you happy."

200

CHAPTER EIGHT
GIVE AND TAKE

Over Buna Field, Kenya,, October 19th, 1940

It was a set-up. The Italians had got into the habit of sending Ro-37 reconnaissance aircraft over the area occupied by allied troops escorted by a flight of four CR.42 fighters twice a day. The aircraft would cruise over the allied lines with almost perfect impunity. If the South African Hawker Furies showed up, the CR.42s would move to intercept them and the obsolete old fighters would be forced to flee.

Today, things would be different.

The Hawker Furies would take off from Buna all right. They would move to intercept the Italian reconnaissance aircraft as normal. The CR.42s would move to attack them, also as normal. Only there was a new element to the situation. Flying high over the battlefield, four Tomahawk Is were waiting in ambush.

The first of the fast, heavily-armed fighters to appear in Kenya, their job was to drive the Italians out of Allied air space. The reason was quite simple. The 12th King's African Division had arrived and was moving into the line alongside the South African Division. Along with the 11th King's African Division, the three divisions would mount a counter-attack that would drive the Italian Army out of Kenya. So the planners hoped.

Every precaution had been taken to ensure that the Tomahawks would achieve complete surprise. They hadn't been based at Buna, in case their presence was detected. Instead, they'd used the aircraft's long range to fly in from Mombasa where they had been uncrated and assembled. They would land at Buna after the mission was over. Then another flight of four Furies would go to Mombasa to receive the new fighters instead.

Looking down, Pim Bosede saw the Furies closing in on the Ro-37. Above them, the CR.42s peeled off and started their dive on to the South African fighters; hoping, this time, to get close enough to engage before they made their escape. The four Furies curved away, once more running for the interior of Kenya. The Italian fighter pilots wouldn't chase them too far from the Ro-37. The CR.42s continued to give chase, their pilots fixed on the biplanes in front of them.

The Tomahawks closed the gap quickly. The Curtiss fighter was almost 100 mph faster than the CR.42. It had 200 horsepower more and its extra 2,000-pound weight meant it could dive that much faster. Bosede saw the CR.42s swelling quickly in front of him. The Italian pilots weren't fools; they kept a watch out for an ambush exactly like this. But they were used to the relatively slow pace of conflicts between biplanes. Now, they were up against modern monoplanes. The situation had changed much faster than they had ever experienced before. The Tomahawks grew from almost-invisible dots to full-sized aircraft, painted olive drab except for the snarling red-and-white shark's teeth marking their noses. The Italians started to swerve out of the way. It was too late.

Bosede saw his gunsight slide along his target's fuselage. The CR.42 could easily out-turn the Tomahawk. Delaying fire would simply give it a chance to escape the ambush. Bosede squeezed the trigger on his guns. He heard the heavy thud of his two nose-mounted .50-caliber machine guns joined by the faster rattle of the four .303-cals in his wings.

The enemy fighter lurched as the stream of bullets tore into it. Bosede could have sworn he heard the whumph noise as the fuel tanks exploded. The CR.42 became a streaming comet of flame. The Italian pilot threw up his arms in a hopeless gesture to protect his face from the fire that engulfed him.

First kill.

Bosede didn't try to maneuver. The American who had given him his painfully brief lessons in how to handle the Tomahawk had made that very clear. *Don't hang around to dogfight with biplanes. Dive on them, shoot them up and then climb away to repeat the process on somebody else. The Tomahawk climbs almost 700 feet-per-minute faster than the CR.42; you will be clear of the battle before the Italian pilots can do anything about it.*

Bosede did a wingover at the top of his climb and surveyed the chaos underneath. His victim had gone; nothing but a cloud of black smoke to mark its grave in the sky. Another CR.42 was spinning down; smoke and flames poured from its fuselage. A white flower erupted behind it. The Italian pilot had bailed out and was riding his parachute down. A third CR.42 was just a pyre of smoke from the ground. That left the fourth and last. It was heading north, trying to escape from the battlefield. A pair of Tomahawks were already closing in on it. Escape was a faint hope. A little to the west of the battle, the Ro-37 as already trying to escape from the disaster; the Furies had turned and were chasing it.

Bosede pushed his nose down again and went into a long dive that would bring him behind and below the Ro-37. Tracers flashed out from the single gun in the aft cockpit as the Italian pilot tried to evade.

It did him as little good. Bosede's six machine guns tore into the flimsy biplane. The two crewmen lurched around in their seats. Its crew dead, the Ro-37 peeled over into a long dive that quickly turned into a fatal spin.

Second kill.

The airfield at Buna was only a few minutes away. Bosede knew the way there well. He saw the runway before him and only just remembered to lower his undercarriage before carrying out a neat three-point landing on the long grass strip. Hoping nobody had noticed the near-goof, he taxied to the hangars before turning off his engine. That was when he saw how the Tomahawk was surrounded by ground crews who had run out to see the new fighters.

Petrus van Bram listened to his story of the fight with something close to amusement. "Do you realize, Pim, that your four fighters shot down 11 CR.42s and three Ro-37s in that dogfight? That's what we get if we add up all the claims you four are making. And that's not including the Ro-37 *my* Furies shot down. A great air victory, I believe?"

Bosede flushed. It was obvious that the air battle had been much more complex than he had realized. But, he was quite sure that it had been *his* guns that had killed a CR.42 and the Ro-37. His memory of the kills was so clear, so positive.

"Petrus, I . . . ."

van Bram held up his hand. "Pim, we have reports coming in from the Army who watched the battle from the ground. They will confirm your CR.42. They saw it explode in mid-air the way you describe and say only a single Tomahawk attacked it. But there were six aircraft firing on that Ro-37 and nobody can say who really killed it. At best, you have a small part of it. But, I will ask you to forgo that small part and allow me to credit one of the Furies with the kill. It will be very good for their morale after so many weeks of achieving nothing."

Bosede thought for a second. He knew in his heart that it had been his guns that had brought down the Ro-37, but he could see how a kill would encourage the remaining Fury pilots. He nodded.

van Bram slapped him on the back. "Good man. Get your aircraft ready for a fast take-off. After this day's work, the SM-79s will be paying us a visit and we would not wish to be caught on the ground like the Rhodesians."

Back by the hangars, Bosede saw the ground crew reloading his machine guns and fuelling up the Tomahawk. He saw something else; a single red-white-green roundel painted under the cockpit. The crew chief stepped back with a proud grin on his face. He had waited a long time to paint a kill mark on one of the fighters in his care.

"Sergeant, please do something for me. On the nose, paint the name *Marijke*, please."

"Your wife, sir?" The sergeant asked the question as he went to get a pot of white paint.

"No. I don't know where the name came from. It just popped into my mind somehow. As if she was telling me her name herself."

Jardine Matheson House, Thanon Witthayu, Bangkok, Thailand

"We're running out of time, Your Highness. All the intelligence we are receiving suggests that the Japanese will move on Hong Kong in the very near future. We have a couple of months, at most; perhaps much less than that."

Princess Suriyothai smiled politely at the businessman who sat before her. The builders of the new office block had done her proud; the facility was complete and as modern as any in the Far East. The new communications system was also being built; the choke point there was the underwater telegraph cable needed to improve the capacity of the link. There were only a limited number of suppliers of such cable and orders for it were placed months in advance.

"I think you have longer than you believe, Simon. The Japanese cannot move on Hong Kong at the moment since they are painfully short of troops. The war in China is already grinding them down as it absorbs more and more of their army. They will move on French Indochina first, since doing so will close off the most important remaining supply line for the Chinese forces.

"They call this force the Indochina Expeditionary Army and it is commanded by Major General Takuma Nishimura. It has as its main element, the Fifth Infantry Division, commanded by Lieutenant General Akihito Nakamura, supported by two independent infantry brigades and a cavalry regiment. The Fifth Infantry Division will need to be detached from that force before the Japanese can contemplate an assault upon Hong Kong. We intend to make sure it cannot be so detached."

"How do you plan that, Your Highness." Keswick had his own sources of information; they had reported the quiet mobilization of the Thai Army. Some of the German advisors training that army had also spoken to Keswick; their comments made him realize that The Ambassador's claims of her army were not exaggerations. His question was curiosity, not doubt.

Suriyothai understood that perfectly.

"We intend to take the southern half of Indochina, all the way to the Mekong. That gives us a strong defensive line and puts our army in a position to dominate the rest of French Indochina. The Japanese will be forced to keep their Indochina Expeditionary Army in place. They will have to bring additional forces down for the seizure of Hong Kong and that will take them time."

"An ambitious plan, Your Highness. When will you start?"

"In eight weeks. As soon as the Americans have had their feelings soothed."

HMS Warspite, *Alexandria Harbor, Egypt*

"Another ship lost to us."

Wavell's voice was heavy with disappointment. HMS *Ramillies* was in the shipping channel, heading out for Gibraltar and home. She was the latest in a long line of departures. Some ships were heading for their new home port of Gibraltar; others going all the way back to Britain and an uncertain future. The only really good news was that *Ramillies* would be the last. She had been drydocked in Alexandria for months; that was the only reason she had stayed so long.

"She's no real loss; her engines are done for. With her in a squadron, we're hard put to hold 15 knots. She and *Royal Sovereign* look good on the homeward bound list, though. With *Malaya* still in Gibraltar and *Warspite* here, we're still in business. We haven't done badly, Archie. I still have a fleet here and it's a damned good one. And the fleet at Gibraltar is nothing to be sneezed at: a battleship, two really modern cruisers and eight destroyers. We've got both ends of the Mediterranean covered; for the moment, anyway."

Wavell wasn't entirely convinced. He'd looked at the standard naval reference book before coming to *Warspite* for this meeting. The count had shown four old but rebuilt battleships in Italian naval service, with at least two more modern ships due to enter service at any time. Six to one was bad odds. Then there were the seven heavy cruisers, a dozen light ones and more destroyers than he could shake a stick at. He honestly couldn't see how the small squadron left here in Alexandria could secure his seaward flank.

"Andy, with Graziani stuck at Mersa Matruh, what happens at sea could be decisive. I've got a coordinated offensive planned. The South Africans in Kenya will push north while O'Connor tries to take down Graziani's supply base with a division-sized raid. If we can destroy those supplies, Graziani will stay stuck and we get a breathing space to sort out East Africa and the Horn. Even more critically, with any Italian advance in Africa stalled, the Germans might think twice about executing the Noth Plan."

Cunningham looked at him quizzically. "The Noth Plan. I keep hearing about that. Do you really believe it's serious?"

Wavell grimaced. "Every time I look at it, I try to logically persuade myself that it is a nonsense; a scheme dreamed up by some wild-eyed theorist who has never commanded troops in the field. Just as I am succeeding, I remember all the other wild-eyed schemes the Nazis have come up with and how they have then made work. We can't afford to assume it's not serious and, to be honest, there's quite a lot of evidence to suggest that the Nazis are really thinking along these lines. There's all the political trouble in Iraq, for example, and we know the Germans are trying to cozy up to the Turks. They're also making friendly noises to Subhas Chandra Bose. You heard he escaped from

205

detention at his home in Calcutta after the mutiny and has turned up in Germany?"

"So I heard. That mutiny was a bad do all around."

Wavell agreed. The attempt by a handful of units under the command of traditional-minded officers to re-establish links with London had already caused some regrettable ramifications. The escape of Bose was one of them. On the other hand, it had the perverse effect of solidifying the rest of the Indian Army behind the accelerating Indian independence process. The ideas of India continuing the war and Indian independence were becoming intertwined, despite all Gandhi's attempts to separate them. A major Commonwealth victory right now, with Indian troops at the head, would cement that. *But, one battleship against six? Four cruisers against almost twenty? Eight destroyers against sixty?*

"What I need is for Graziani to be cut off from supplies. When our raid takes out his main supply dumps, the Italians will try to run convoys through to replace the lost supplies. They're short on road and rail capacity to move them, but if they get replacement supplies ashore, that will make the difference between a serious inconvenience and a major reverse. Andy, you have to stop those supply convoys from getting through."

Cunningham nodded thoughtfully. "We can do it."

He saw the disbelief on Wavell's face and crushed down a moment's irritation. Halifax may have stabbed Churchill in the back but he, Cunningham, commanded a picked squadron of the Royal Navy and had virtually a free hand in how he used it. That was the one great thing about the present situation. With the de-facto decision to ignore messages and orders from London, he could use his fleet the way he knew it had to be used.

"Don't worry about it, Archie. I know the numbers look bad. But remember, the Italian fleet is spread all over the Mediterranean and Red Sea. They have to worry about keeping ships in service and they have all too many other responsibilities. We have just one and we can concentrate all our power on that single mission."

And we're the Andrew and the Italians are not. And there are just one or two other things we have running for us.

Tomahawk II **Marijke,** *Over the Buna Front, Kenya*

There were three roundels under *Marijke's* cockpit now. The Italians had responded to the destruction of the reconnaissance flight and its escorts by sending a formation of Savoia-Marchetti SM.79 Sparviero bombers to hit the Buna base. Ground observers had spotted the formation and passed the warning. Four Tomahawks were airborne and waiting for them. It had been a massacre; one that Bosede had felt slightly ashamed about.

The Sparviero had been 50mph faster than the Hawker Fury; its immunity to interception made the Italian crews careless. Never having been under serious attack before, they had little idea of how poorly-defended their aircraft were. The SM.79 was armed with a single fixed machine gun forward, another flexible gun in the dorsal position and one more gun in each of the two beam windows. They were completely blind from below and behind. The Tomahawks had swept in from that angle. Their six guns gutted the Italian bombers. Not one survived.

This flight was different. There were eight Tomahawks in 2 Squadron now and the South African Air Force was on the offensive at last. The second flight had arrived back from Mombasa with its new aircraft. Convoys of trucks loaded with spare parts and supplies had arrived at Buna, turning the airfield into a fully-equipped fighter base.

The eight remaining Furies had been relegated to ground attack work, equipped with racks for four 20-pound bombs under each wing. They were spread out underneath the Tomahawks; their target was the Italian troops north of Buna. It was the start of the campaign to drive the Italians out of Kenya and Somaliland and, eventually, liberate Ethiopia. Bosede knew the outlines of the plan. Its first objective was to ruin the morale of the Italian troops. Shooting down eleven aircraft in less than a week had been a good start.

Even better, a second Tomahawk squadron was also entering the game. They were a Rhodesian outfit whose four aircraft were further east, escorting some Ju-86 bombers hitting one of the Italian forward airbases. Soon, the Italian pilots would learn that if they wouldn't come up and fight the new South African fighters, they would be bombed out of their bases. The battle was changing. The desperate days when the Italians ruled the skies seemed a long time ago.

Bosede glanced down. The Italians were dug in around a road junction some 15 miles north of Buna. It was their foremost position; one that was isolated by distance and the almost non-existent road system in this part of Kenya. Unfortunately, it was also in the way of the planned offensive and removing it was a vital preliminary. Far below, the two remaining flights of Hawker Furies in 2 Squadron swept into the attack. Bosede imagined he could hear the flat crack of the vicious little 20-pound Cooper bombs, but his eyes were scanning the sky for Italian fighters. Sure enough, he saw them as they approached the beleagured outpost.

"B Flight. Bandits approaching from two o'clock; Angels Five." By agreement, B Flight would handle these fighters. A-Flight remained high up, guarding against the same kind of ambush that had caused an entire flight of CR.42s to die under the guns of the Tomahawks.

The aircraft below were CR.32s. That hardly surprised Bosede; it had become quickly apparent that the Italians were short of fighters. It hadn't seemed that way when he'd been flying a Hawker Fury and the CR.32s and -42s appeared to be everywhere. Now that they were as outclassed as he had once been, they were rare sights. According to intelligence, the Italians had a large number of Ro-37 and Caproni reconnaissance aircraft, but few fighters and only a handful of bombers.

The CR.32 pilots spotted the diving Tomahawks early and turned to flee. Bosede held his breath. If the Tomahawks set off in pursuit, the Furies would be left unguarded. B Flight knew their duty though. With the CR.32s in full retreat, there was no need to go chasing after them. The Tomahawks pulled out of their dive and climbed back to rejoin A Flight.

Infantry Detachment, Granatieri di Savoia Division, Buna Front, Kenya

Sergeant Gasparo Bonaventura dived for cover as aircraft swept overhead. It wasn't supposed to be this way at all. Other people were supposed to get bombed. All around him, the men of his detachment were finding nooks and crannies in the rocks to protect them against the fragments from the bombs. Intellectually, he knew the bombs had to be tiny; the old biplanes couldn't carry any really significant bomb load. When they went off, they were the loudest things he had ever heard. Fragments zinged, ricocheting off the boulders that made up the perimeter of the outpost. They gave good cover against fire from outside, but they trapped the fragments from the bombs and caused them to buzz around inside the laager.

"The perimeter. Quickly."

His call went out as the biplanes arched away to make another run. There was a reason why this outpost had been positioned here. There weren't many roads in northern Kenya and none of them were much good. Two of them joined just below the low rise the outpost was sited on. This was the most forward of all the Italian positions on the front. 'The point of the tip of the spearhead' his Captain had described the position, before taking off to somewhere safely to the rear. If the enemy were to move in this area, they would have to come through this point. Bonaventura's job was to see them making the attempt and warn the main defensive positions further north. What they did afterward was unspecified, but he had a feeling it would not end well for him.

Cautiously, he glanced around one of the boulders and looked at the road below. It was as he had feared; a small column of trucks had already pulled up and were unloading their infantry. What shocked him were the number of small, four-wheeled armored cars that were with them. He could count at least six. They were a problem. His men only had their Carcano rifles, without a single weapon capable of defeating armor. Bonaventura was forced to duck again. The biplanes had returned and their twin machine guns were strafing the little outpost.

When he could watch again, the situation had deteriorated badly. The infantry had spread out and were making their way up the slope. Even worse, the armored cars were following them. One stopped. There was a brilliant flash from its left-hand side. A heavy bullet struck a rock, barely a meter from his head. The rock split wide open. Fragments spalled across the gap and slashed at his face.

If that is a Morris down there, and it surely looks like one, then it has a Bren gun and a Boys anti-tank rifle. Just what are we supposed to do now?

"Open fire!"

The order was almost an automatic response. A feeble patter of fire resulted from it. The infantry attacking them to took cover, but that was hardly a good thing. There were Bren guns down there. They started to put short bursts into his position. His men only had a single light machine gun between them, a Model 30. Bonaventura was rather surprised to here it snap out a burst in return. He was not, though, surprised when it jammed. He heard the crew cursing as they tried to clear the weapon. *They will be lucky; once they jam, it takes hours to clear them. Oiled cartridges indeed! Which idiot thought that was a good idea?*

The Brens obviously had no such problems. Every time one of his men fired a rifle shot, a Bren would lay down a quick burst in reply. Then the infantry would dash forward while his own men took cover. Every so often, there would be another flash from the armored cars. Another heavy bullet would go whining off the rocks. Bonaventura squirmed around and looked behind his position. Sure enough, the South Africans had worked around his flanks and sealed off his position. *That's it; nobody is getting away from here.*

It was almost as if the South African commander had heard him. The shout from below was labored and the Italian pronunciation was terrible, as if the man was reading from a note he had been given. The awkward, mispronounced words echoed around the rocks.

"Soldati italiani, la posizione è senza speranza. Abbiamo carri armati e supporto aereo, e vi sono più numerosi. Non c'è disonore nel cedere a tale forza superiore. Nessuno deve morire oggi."

Italian soldiers, the position is hopeless. We have tanks and air support, and we are more numerous. There is no disgrace in yielding to the superior force. No one should die today. Bonaventura shook his head. The officer below spoke terrible Italian, but he was right. There was nothing more to be achieved here today. "Everybody; cease firing and put down your rifles."

He sighed, took off his scarf, fixed it to his bayonet and waved it in the air. The South Africans closed on his position. As they did so, he stood up, his hands raised. They jumped into the little redoubt and quickly took possession of the weapons his men had placed on the ground.

"Do not worry about the machine gun. I never had the damn thing fire more than three shots in succession."

The South African officer looked at the Breda, shuddered slightly, and nodded. "You have no casualties?"

Bonaventura looked at his men. Some had scratches and cuts from flying rock fragments, but that was all. For all the bombing and firing, nobody was seriously hurt. That was a miracle to be thankful for. "None. Thank God."

The South African smiled and nodded. "My men, also; not one with a hurt worth speaking of. Indeed, we should thank God tonight for his providence to us both." He paused for a second and looked around. "What were you supposed to be doing here?"

"Warning of your advance." Bonaventura suddenly realized he had no idea how he had been supposed to get the message back. "They never told me how. They just left it to me."

The two men exchanged long-suffering looks; both were all too familiar with being given orders but not the equipment needed to carry them out. "Come on, Sergeant; bring your men down. We'll give you a ride back in our lorries."

Cabinet Office, 10 Downing Street, London, United Kingdom

"Where is Mersa Matruh?" Lord Halifax was most confused by the geography of North Africa.

"It's here, of course." Butler strode arrogantly towards the map of Egypt on the wall and stabbed his finger towards the western section. Then he stopped and started to search the area for the town in question, Watching him, the Chief of the Imperial General Staff, General Sir John Dill, permitted himself a slight smile of amusement. It was obvious to him that Butler had no real idea of where Mersa Matruh really was. Dill timed his intervention to a nicety.

"Arabic is a very hard language to transliterate, you know. We all had terrible problems with it at the College. Here you are, RAB; it's called Marsa Matrouh on this map."

"My God; it's only 90 miles from Alexandria!" Halifax was appalled at how far the Italian Army had penetrated.

"Oh, no; it's closer to twice that. But don't be deceived by distances, Prime Minister." Dill had an earnest, helpful tone in his voice that appeased Halifax and set Butler's teeth on edge. "The really important detail here is the lay of the land. See how this ridge angles towards the coast? Well, south of that ridge is a pure undiluted hell called the Quattara Depression. An impassible wasteland; the only water comes from marshes so salty, they make seawater taste sweet and the ground is quicksand under a hard crust. A man can walk on it one moment, then break through and drown in sand the next. The area is riddled with scorpions and venomous snakes. The temperatures hit far over 100 degrees in the day and drop to freezing at night. There's no way anybody can run military operations there. An army might go in there, but it'd never come out.

"Anyway, the ridge that marks the northern edge of the Depression closes on the coast and it forms a funnel. As an army advances eastward, that funnel compresses it, making it harder and harder to deploy the troops available. It becomes very easy for a small force to defend itself against a much larger one. Also, there are no ports here. The supply line stretches all the way back to Tobruk, Benghazi and ultimately Tripoli. As an army advances eastward, it becomes harder and harder to support. Everything, even water, has to be brought forward from ports hundreds of miles to the rear. But, as the opposing army retreats eastward, it gets closer and closer to its port of supply, Alexandria and the Suez Canal. So, it gets stronger and stronger as the invading army gets ever weaker. Eventually, a point of balance is found where the invader simply cannot advance without a massive supply injection. That is the point Marshal Graziani has reached now. He needs a great injection of supplies before he can advance. He needs to bring those supplies up and stockpile them close behind his lines. That will take weeks or months. Only then will he be able to advance on Alexandria."

"So we have time to negotiate an agreement." Butler sounded satisfied.

"We have better options than that." Halifax was looking at the map intently. "Much better options. We have an opportunity here to re-establish our authority and stamp our mark on the situation. General Dill, you say Graziani is at the end of his tether and cannot attack our positions in Egypt without great risk, yet we are in a secure position ourselves, well-defended and well-supplied?"

"That is correct." Sir John Dill was fascinated by the change that was coming over Halifax while he watched. The man was swinging from servile appeaser to school bully within a moment. Quietly, Dill wondered what he would have done if the campaign in France had gone just a little bit more favorably.

"And General Wavell is determined to hold fast?"

"He is."

"Then it is up to us to support him. Herr Hitler has said that this is a matter between us and the Italians and that how we resolve it is of no interest to the German nation. So, if we are in such a secure position, it makes sense to use it to gain the best terms that we can from Senor Mussolini. Yes, that is the way to go. Sir John, telegraph General Wavell and advise him that we will be guided by his opinions on the situation and he can count on our support."

"Yes, Prime Minister."

Family Room, Bang Phitsan Palace, Bangkok, Thailand

"I don't understand why." Achillea took a drink out of her bottle of beer and sighed.

"Perhaps because, when you took your last boyfriend out for a country afternoon, you rode him into the ground, outshot him on a skeet shooting range, out-fenced him, arm-wrestled him for the restaurant bill and won, and finished off by drinking him under the table." Igrat surreptitiously winked at Suriyothai.

"But, I just . . . "

"On a first date?" Igrat's voice was incredulous.

Suriyothai burst out laughing. That segued into a fit of coughing as the beer went up her nose. She delicately wiped her eyes and put her own bottle down. Quietly, one of her attendants checked it, saw it was empty, and replaced it with a full one. It was very hard to stay sober in a Thai party. "So, Achillea will be helping you with courier runs from now on, Iggie?"

Igrat thought for a second. "Perhaps. I'm trying to find qualified couriers to help me out, but it's harder than it seems. I thought Nell would be perfect, but she isn't hard enough. I set up a little test and she allowed herself to be bullied into handing a package over to an assistant rather than the person it was destined for. I've found some outsiders who qualify for the routine stuff; a couple of them are pretty good, but I've struck out with couriers for family stuff."

"I got my package through and gave it to the right person." Achillea sounded aggrieved.

"You did." Igrat admitted that readily. "But the whole point of this job is to avoid confrontations, rather than to go looking for them. And you must remember spoken words exactly, not paraphrase them. That way, if they are misunderstood, nobody can blame you."

Achillea looked upset and took another drink out of her beer. Suriyothai looked at her sympathetically. "Igrat's work is harder than it seems, I think. So, Iggie, what are the developments in Washington?"

When Igrat spoke, her voice was flat and uninflected. To the initiated, it was the sound of Phillip Stuyvesant in briefing mode. "The U.S. cabinet, as a whole, is sympathetic to Thailand, but Cordell Hull is violently antagonistic to you. Why this is, I do not know, but his mind is set on the matter and he will not listen to argument on the matter or on any issues related to it. There was a major confrontation between the State, Treasury and War Departments on this issue. Treasury and War took note of the intervention of India on your behalf and suggested that a further investigation of the position adopted by your country was merited by their favorable counsel. Cordell Hull tried to shut them down and close off the avenue of approach but Treasury would not countenance this and forced him to re-open the issue. Cordell Hull will be visiting Thailand soon. You should prepare for him and show him where your true interests are placed, but do not forget you are dealing with a person who, if not an avowed enemy of yours, is something very close to it."

Suriyothai sighed. The adverse relationship with the United States was the greatest single roadblock to her plans, and she honestly could not understand why it was there. "One person has so much power in your government? To block the desires of the rest?"

"Where that man is Cordell Hull, yes." Once again, Igrat's voice dropped into a near-perfect facsimile of Stuyvesant's. "Cordell Hull is an intimate of FDR and greatly trusted by him. He is a man of firm beliefs and opinions and does not easily change his mind. You would do well to recall the *St. Louis* incident in 1939 where his advice caused almost 900 Jewish refugees to be sent back to Germany. He did try to persuade Cuba to accept them, but when that failed, he would not retreat from his decision that they should not land in the United States. He uses his close relations with FDR to by-pass any government decisions that he does not like. Snake, even getting him to come and visit you is a major achievement. Do not waste this opportunity; for you will not get another."

Igrat looked up and her voice snapped back to her own husky tones. "Snake, I'm going to break a rule here and give you my own impressions, alright? I've met Cordell Hull, and he struck me as being one of those people who is too proud and arrogant to change his mind once it is made up. He won't change his mind about you, but he might be persuaded that his opinion of you is of lesser weight than his opinion of the situation out here. Show him, however much he dislikes you, the alternatives are much worse."

"That makes much sense." Suriyothai noticed that Igrat had finished her bottle of beer. "There is more beer on the way."

"Don't give Igrat any more." Achillea still sounded resentful. "She'll get drunk and end up dancing naked on the table top."

"Not," Igrat said firmly, "on a first date."

GHQ, Middle East Command, Cairo, Egypt

"Just what the devil is happening in London?" General Archibald Percival Wavell was stunned by the telegram he had just received. He had been expecting one that instructed him to surrender his forces to General Graziani; he would have consigned that to the waste paper basket. Then he would have struck out on his own, for better or for worse. But the message that had arrived threw everything into doubt.

"A message of support, promising reinforcements? And they're sending *Illustrious* to Gibraltar?"

"Perhaps somebody has injected some backbone into Lord Halifax?" Major-General Noel Beresford-Peirse, commander of the 4th Indian Infantry Division, sounded doubtful of the possibility. Wavell couldn't blame him; whatever sentiment and tradition might say, political facts had placed the Indian Government in opposition to London. Beresford-Peirse looked to Calcutta for his orders now. The same disbelief was evidenced by Lieutenant-General Thomas Blamey; he had surrendered command of the Australian 6th Division to take command of the new ANZAC Corps that was forming in Egypt. His response to the idea was a disdainful snort.

"What exactly does the telegram say?" Freyberg was being cautious. The first echelon of the 2nd New Zealand Infantry Division was already in place and would join the Australian 6th and 7th divisions in the ANZAC Corps when that formation was activated. His caution stemmed from the briefing he had received from the New Zealand Government. Essentially, the country was bankrupt; only minimal support for his division could be provided. It had been discretely suggested that he ought to seek local sources for supply. The result of that suggestion had the nascent 2nd New Zealand Division nicknamed 'Freyberg's 40,000 thieves'.

"It states that London enthusiastically supports the idea of offensive action against the Italian forces under General Graziani and will support any such actions to the best of its ability." Wavell looked over the telegram, shaking his head in disbelief. "It goes on to say that London's position will be guided by my decisions here as the commander on the spot. It approves our dispositions of the Mediterranean fleet and informs me that the squadron in Gibraltar, currently consisting of battleship *Malaya*, cruisers *Gloucester* and *Liverpool* and the H-class destroyer flotilla, will be reinforced by the addition of the aircraft carrier *Illustrious* and four K-class destroyers. We are advised that the Gibraltar Squadron is now designated Force H."

"This is something of a relief." General Sir Richard Nugent O'Connor and his 7th Armoured Division had been orphaned by the Armistice and the subsequent break-up of the Empire. He had kept quiet, allowing the political and strategic situation to mature, and it now looked as if his prudence was paying off. "But it appears to me that the telegram is long on encouragement and short on actual deeds."

"There is an option that may clarify the situation a little further." General Henry 'Jumbo' Maitland Wilson had a strange grin on his face. "General Graziani is slowly and painfully building up his supplies in front of Mersa Matruh for the next stage of his advance. The dumps behind his positions are already large and grow a little every day."

"Mmmm, supplies." Freyburg's interjection caused a ripple of sympathetic laughter around the briefing room. More than one of the Generals present made an ostentatious gesture of protecting their wallets.

"Exactly." Wilson nodded. "Graziani has a lot of troops deployed forward, but they are almost all infantry with few heavy or support weapons. Such units matter little in desert warfare. The only Italian force that is of any account is a single motorized group with some 70 armored vehicles, mostly machine gun carriers. In contrast, we have the 7th Armoured Division, the 6th Australian Division and the 4th Indian Division all of which are fully motorized. It's a strange thing; for all the apparent disparity in forces, in the troops that actually matter, we seriously outnumber the Italians. I propose that we launch a raid on the Italian positions, destroy that motorized group and seize those supplies. At the very least, we will set all of Graziani's plans and operations back months while he rebuilds his supply base. At best, we could put all those infantry sitting in the desert into the bag.

"If it's a matter of pillaging, we ought to bring Bernie and his marauders along." Blamey grumbled in the background. He had been moved upwards just in time to miss the action.

"I think so." Wavell looked at the map for a second. "Jumbo, you are right; we can do this. You can't have 4th Indian, though. I need them to join 5th for an assault southwards out of the Sudan. We'll hit the Italian positions in

214

East Africa from the north at the same time as the South Africans move up northwards out of Kenya. Jumbo, you can have 7th Armoured and 6th Australian, plus Bernie's New Zealanders. Your primary objectives are those supply dumps; capture them pretty much at all costs. But don't neglect any opportunities to develop the situation further to our advantage. Nothing wins a battle more conclusively than a vigorous pursuit."

There was a stunned silence as the extent of the planned offensive sank home. Wavell was attempting to wrap the whole situation up with two simultaneous offensives. Maxims about not dividing one's forces in the face of the enemy weighed heavily on the Generals' minds.

"If I may make an addition to this plan?" Admiral Cunningham had been quiet during the strategy meeting but he could see a glowing opportunity developing. "If Jumbo and Dick are as successful as we hope, the Italians will have to run a massive supply convoy through to their ports in Africa to restore the situation. This offers us a good opportunity to being the Italian fleet to battle and give it a proper trousering."

"One battleship, against six?" Wavell couldn't help asking.

"There won't be six; not with this new Force H in the Western Mediterranean. They'll have to hold back a lot of their fleet to face that. We'll face three battleships at most; the rest of the Italian fleet will be split as well. We have naval aircraft; they don't. We can hurt them badly enough to swing the balance of power our way for months, if not years."

Wilson looked at the map. "This is certainly ambitious. If we pull it off, we'll have eliminated the threat in East Africa, driven the Italians out of Egypt, sent the Italian fleet back to harbor and probably chewed up their air force. We're biting off a major mouthful here, gentlemen. I hope we won't choke on it."

Wavell nodded in agreement. "We're risking everything on one roll of the dice. London is behind us now; why, and for how long, we can only guess. But we must assume that if we have a partial success, enough to save face, we'll get a cease and desist order from London while they sign another Armistice. We have to clear the board in one go."

Wavell looked around the room and noted the unanimous nodding. The game was on.

Odeon Cinema, Nottingham, United Kingdom

"Two student, please; front stalls." David Newton put two shillings down on the ticket booth counter.

"David, being so close to the screen hurts my eyes. Could we go in the rear stalls please?" Rachael glanced around and saw the cinema staff hiding their smiles. The front stalls were easily visible; the rear stalls, underneath the balcony, were in the dark, even by cinema standards. That was why they were the traditional place for couples to indulge in discrete courting.

"Of course, Rachael." Newton added another sixpence to the price of the tickets and picked them up as the cashier took them out of her drawer. "Would you like some snacks? I thought we'd have some fish and chips later. That should be OK for you, shouldn't it?"

Rachael nodded. Fish and chips were unrationed, but very expensive. "Cod and six-penn'oth of chips will be lovely. Until then, could I have some Mint Imperials?"

Newton bought a packet of Mint Imperials and a bag of Pontefract Cakes for himself, then escorted Rachael into the theater. By the time they had taken their seats, the lights were already dimming and the Pathescope News was starting.

Today, all eyes are fastened on North Africa where 200,000 Italian troops under Marshal Graziani sit barely 100 miles from Alexandria. The question asked across the world is, when will this mighty force complete the conquest of Egypt? When will it seize the Suez Canal? Barely 30,000 Commonwealth troops stand in the way of the approaching Italian juggernaught. Meanwhile, in Kenya, Italian troops there are being driven slowly back by South African troops supported by their new Tomahawk fighters.

Pathescope had obtained footage over the Tomahawks in action. The cinema screen was filled with pictures of the fighters with shark's teeth painted on their noses. There was one sequence that was obviously camera gun film. It showed an Italian SM.81 bomber staggering under the impact of gunfire from a Tomahawk. Smoke erupted from its left wing and nose engines; then it nosed over and spun downwards in a train of flame. The cinema audience erupted into cheers at the sight. As if in reply, the commentary restarted.

The South African and Rhodesian squadrons are competing to see who can down the most Italian aircraft. The leader is South African pilot Pim Bosede with his Tomahawk Marijke. *Just after this film was taken, he shot down another SM.79 bomber, making his total score ten victories. He is the first double-ace in East Africa!*

The newsreel showed a young, fair-haired South African jumping out of his Tomahawk and being applauded by the ground crew. Rachael looked at him and jabbed Newton in the arm. "Look, David. He's *so* handsome."

Newton looked sideways and saw the flash of Rachael's teeth. She grinned in the darkness. That made him realize he was being teased.

"You wait until I fly a Spitfire. I'll show *you* handsome."

The main feature was *The Sea Hawks,* starring Errol Flynne. Set in the reign of Queen Elizabeth, it showed a Britain with its back to the wall fighting the overwhelming power of Spain. Only the Sea Hawks, the captains of the British warships, stood between Spain and England. What neither they nor the queen knew was that the Prime Minister, Lord Wolfingham, was a traitor, in league with Spanish. He betrayed the leader of the Sea Hawks,

Captain Geoffrey Thorpe, and caused him to be captured by the Spanish. When the Spanish soldiers seized him, Rachael let out a cry of dismay and seized Newton's arm.

Newton noted that the scene hadn't really been that frightening, and that Rachael had kept a firm hold on his arm afterwards. A few minutes later, her head was resting on his shoulder and he had his arm around her. The film ended with a long speech by Errol Flynne about how no level of treachery, even that committed by a Prime Minister, would stop England from winning in the end. The cinema erupted into sustained cheering that drowned out the closing music. As they stood for the national anthem, they both thought it had been a very satisfactory visit to the cinema.

Conference Room, Government House, Calcutta, India

"We are organizing four additional divisions. Of them, the 7th and 11th Divisions will be assigned to secure Burma against foreign aggression. The 8th and 10th Divisions will be assigned to Iraq and will secure the Commonwealth position there." Lord Linlithgow looked up from the report that he had received. "It goes without saying, of course, that a considerable force of those regiments who proved their loyalty to India in the recent unpleasantness will be held here in case of additional disturbances."

"We are most fortunate that so few regiments were deceived into moving against us." Pandit Nehru had been pleasantly shocked by the loyalty most of the Army had shown to the newly-independent India. Even the few regiments that had rebelled had done so by following their officers. The rank and file had abandoned them when faced with the reality of firing on other Indian troops. Quietly, Nehru gave solemn thanks in memory of Colonel Garry, whose self-sacrifice had prevented a blood bath on the streets of New Delhi. His name would be honored, Nehru promised himself that. When things settled down and there was time to consider how best to memorialize the man, it would be done.

"And so, we become the policemen of an empire again." Despite his new-found respect for the Army, Nehru also remembered that traditionally the Indian Army had been the security force that had upheld British power across the world. It was less honored in Indian eyes than in British for that very reason.

"There is a big difference this time, Pandit." Lord Linlithgow guessed what his deputy was thinking. The months that had passed since the stunning news from London had revealed much to him. One abiding theme was how little the British had understood of the people they ruled here in India. Linlithgow had taken for granted that Imperial rule had always been for the benefit of India, and that he and his predecessors had been benign, enlightened rulers. He still believed that, but he also knew that many of their actions were not so well regarded by the Indians. He hoped and prayed that the Indians politicians, now working throughout the Indian administrative systems as part of the slow transition process, were beginning to understand why apparently unjust decisions had been inevitable.

"This time, the Indian Army goes abroad in the interests of India, not Britain."

Nehru nodded. "A big difference, indeed but our young men still leave. And Mohandas Gandhi still opposes their departure with every fiber of his being. Even the arrival of our new aircraft attracts his ire. You know he held a demonstration to block access to our new aircraft maintenance plant? It appears, though, that he was misinformed and held his demonstration outside the wrong building. A matter of an unfortunate clerical error in the transposition of two digits, so I am told."

The Marquess of Linlithgow raised questioning eyebrows at that. Nehru saw the gesture and shook his head. "No, this was not organized by Sir Eric's intelligence services or, indeed, the result of any official act. It was an Indian clerk, proud of the fact that Indian squadrons would receive the new aircraft while the ex-British squadrons had to make do with the old, who made sure information leaked to Gandhi's clique was false. In its way, that is more important that the fact the demonstration was planned at all."

"We still have no fighters in service, though." Linlithgow had never quite recovered from the shock of discovering there was not one single fighter aircraft in India. "But, at least, we have trainers. Our pilots have already started to learn to fly modern aircraft."

Quetta Airfield, India

"This is the Harvard I. A two seat advanced trainer. Compared with the Westland Wapitis you have been flying to date, it is an entirely different machine. A hundred miles-per-hour faster, it stalls at higher speeds than your old Wapitis cruised. It climbs faster, dives faster and will kill you faster if you do not take care. We will all work with these aircraft together. When you are familiar with handling a modern monoplane, we will transition to the Hawk 75, the Mohawk, fighter and you will become the first Indian fighter pilots." Gregory Boyington looked at the group of pilots surrounding him. They were young, earnest and painfully inexperienced. "Just remember, there are two kinds of people on this planet. Fighter pilots and lesser men."

Boyington had resigned his commission with the U.S. Marine Corps to join the Central Aircraft Manufacturing Company, run by Bill Pawley. He'd been under the impression that he would be going to China to fight the Japanese, but Pawley had taken a look at his degree in aviation engineering and his experience as a draftsman at Boeing and assigned him to the training program in India. Boyington's age had been part of that decision as well; he was a good half-decade older than most of the pilots in the CAMCO program. Boyington had two responsibilities with CAMCO. One was to train the pilots in the three Indian Air Force squadrons in the arts of flying high-speed monoplanes. The other was to get aircraft production at the CAMCO plant in

Bangalore off the ground. India also needed the ability to maintain its new Mohawks, Bostons and Hudsons. CAMCO was the answer to that need.

"How soon will we be able to fly the Mohawks, sir?"

"As soon as they, and you, are ready. The aircraft have to be delivered here, uncrated, assembled and test-flown. That will take some weeks. The delivery of Tomahawks to the Middle East takes priority. Then you must qualify on flying the Harvard before you can transfer to a Mohawk. After that, you will have to learn the operations demanded of fighter units. Intercepting raids, conducting sweeps for enemy fighters, escorting our own bombers. There is much to learn and little time. So we will start with familiarizing you with the Harvard."

Elsewhere in India, Boyington knew the coastal reconnaissance flights would start converting to the Hudson while the flying boat squadron was set to convert to Catalinas. In that case, at least, the transfer should be relatively trouble-free. The first Indian bomber squadron was presently flying Audaxes and would be converting to the Douglas DB-7. If anything, that was more challenging than even the fighter conversions. The Audax was notoriously docile and easy to fly, but the hot DB-7s were anything but. "Right. The first thing to remember about the Harvard is that it has a retractable undercarriage. Don't forget to pull it up after taking off and most especially don't forget to lower it before landing. Failing to do so makes the accountants very angry."

Boyington looked around at the trainees crowding around the Harvards. *God, I need a drink,* he thought. *Preferably several.*

Short Sunderland Mark 1 F for Freddy, *Approaching Massawa, Eritrea*

"So we ended up as droppin' bombs after all." Andy Walker sounded aggrieved. "Don't tell me the Mad Bomber was right."

"The top brass promised this was a once-only job. Lot of thin's goin' down tonight and we're just a small part of it all."

Alleyne was staring out of his cockpit, searching for the black shadows that would show another Sunderland making its bomb run. The original plan had been for the flying boats to make the trip to Massawa in formation and bomb the port in mass. He'd had to point out that his crews weren't trained to fly in tight formations in daylight, let alone at night; he would lose half his aircraft to mid-air collisions. The Sunderland carried its bombs in an internal bomb room and cranked them out on underwing racks when needed; a maximum of four bombs at a time. That meant at least two runs to deliver the eight 500-pounders they would be carrying. The one thing his crews could do better than most was navigate.

Eventually, the planners had listened to reason. The aircraft would fly out alone and make their runs individually. One virtue was that the Italian naval base would be kept under a steady rain of bombs for a long period.

"Massawa comin' up."

"I got it." Alleyne made a few minor course corrections and lined up on the port. Incredibly, there were lights still on down there. *Had the Italians never heard of a black-out?* "Midships crew, open the side ports and wind out the first set of bombs."

Noise increased as the side doors to the bomb room were opened; the controls felt slightly different as the bomb racks slid out under the wings. The Sunderland wasn't built for this kind of operation; it didn't even have a suitable bomb-aiming position. Alleyne was going to have to release his bombs by dead reckoning. He visualized the picture in his mind, trying to work out where the bombs would land in relation to the nose of his aircraft.

Far below, the lights of Massawa still twinkled. They went out just as Alleyne felt his bombs drop. For one weird moment, he wondered if their descent had caused the blackout. He saw flashes as the four bombs impacted somewhere in Eritrea. He was enough of a realist to accept that he couldn't expect much more than that.

"Midships crew, get the second set of bombs out."

He put his Sunderland in a long, gentle curve. The bomb room crew wound in the underwing racks, winched the remaining bombs into place and then got them back out under the wings. All hard, backbreaking work; all the more so when undertaken on a darkened aircraft over hostile territory. The people who had thought of this raid hadn't allowed for that.

The reloading took longer than he'd expected. Eventually, the aircraft was ready. Alleyne arched around, making another run. By this time, the target as completely blacked out. He made his drop using the shape of the coast as a guide. This left him slightly uncertain as to whether he'd hit Eritrea.

Straining his eyes to make out details on the ground had taken all his attention. When he looked up, his first reaction was that a nearby area of sky was a little more solid than it should have been. His second was that he had a split second to avoid a collision with a Sunderland coming in the opposite attention.

He broke right, heaving the controls over and standing the big flying boat on its wingtip. By a miracle, the other Sunderland broke right as well. The two aircraft missed by inches. Shaking with nervous tension, Alleyne pressed the switch on his intercom. "All you bastards all right back there?"

"All right? All right, yoos ask? I've just shaken flamin' hands with his starboard gunner, that's how all right I'm. And the bastard had me wristwatch in the process." Don Clerk's voice was shaking. Alleyne guessed he knew just how close the two aircraft had come to colliding. *Reassurance is in order.*

"That settles it boys. This night bombing stuff is for the birds. We're goin' home and that's the end of it for this game. Top brass wants us to do this again, they can fly the flamin' raids themselves."

Natal Mounted Rifles, El Yibo, Northern Kenya

"All right, broere; get ready to move." Sergeant Dirk Klaas passed the word quietly, although there was no real need to do so. What was about to hit the Italian positions opposite made any advance warning from a carelessly spoken word almost superfluous. The Transvaal Horse Artillery were about to wake the defenders up.

Flashes seemed to ripple along the horizon. There were two batteries back there. One had two troops of six 18-pounders; the other a troop of 18-pounders and another of 4.5-inch howitzers. The shells whined overhead, the pitch of the noise clearly defining them as being 'outbound'. Klass had been in the South African Army a long time; he knew from the noise that only the 18-pounders were firing. The eight 4.5-inch howitzers were holding their fire in order to support the infantry when they made their approach.

Ahead of him, a series of flashes erupted in the Italian positions. Another pattern arrived before the after-images of the first shell bursts had fully faded. The 18-pounder had been criticized by European armies for being 'too light.' That relatively light shell made it fast-firing and that was critical when it came to keeping people's heads down. Klaas had no doubt that the gunners were working like dervishes back on the lines, serving their pieces as fast as possible. He took a quick glance at his wristwatch and noted the time.

"Up, broere. Follow the shells in."

The South African infantry surged upwards from their trenches, running across the gap that separated them from the bursts of the 18-pounders. Overhead, the sound changed slightly. The pattern of bursts lifted by about a hundred yards, slamming in on the second line of trenches that backed up the first. In their place, the howitzers dropped their shells on the first line trenches, cutting any wire that was in place and keeping the defenders pinned down. The lead elements of the South African infantry went to ground, covering the Italian front with their rifles and Bren guns. The next wave passed between them and closed on the defenders. Then, they too went to ground. The troops they had passed rose up again and assaulted the trenches.

The Italians fought hard. Klaas gave them that. They surged out of their dugouts, those that had not been crushed by the artillery fire, and met the assault with fixed bayonets. Lee Enfield crossed with Carcano. The men carrying them fought desperately; all knew when two men fought with the bayonet, only one would survive. Other men fought with entrenching tools, spades with their blades sharpened to turn them into a vicious battle-axe that cleaved their opponent. Some, a few, turned to run. Their reward was a bayonet thrust in the back or a skull caved in by a swing from an entrenching tool. Klaas never remembered the details of that fight. Only that he had waded in with bayonet and entrenching tool, and that the Italians had died.

At some point, the sun had risen. It was daylight when the South Africans climbed out of the advanced trenches they had taken and moved on the second line. They left behind them a trench filled with bodies; some

221

Italian, some South African. Further behind them, another wave of infantry was crossing no-mans land and moving up to support the lead elements. Ahead of Klaas and his men, the 18-pounders and 4.5-inch howitzers were still pounding the main line of resistance.

That was beginning to crumble already. Klaas could sense it. There was a feel to a battle, a sense of its tempo, and he knew that this one was going to succeed. The Italians were already beginning to fall back; their positions abandoned or marked with small white flags. Klaas didn't blame them. They had probably seen and heard the horror in the advanced trenches and wanted no part of it.

What started as an advance became a pursuit. Klaas's sense of the battle was right. The Italians were giving up the ground and retreating. By the time the main line of defenses had fallen to the South Africans, the Italian infantry was already streaming to the rear, boarding lorries and heading north, away from the artillery fire and the men with bayonets that followed it. A few rearguards hung on; they bought just enough time for the rest of their units to escape. That didn't matter too much, for one very simple reason. It was the whole reason why the battle had been fought here, at a small village in northern Kenya whose very existence was of so little consequence that a detailed map was needed to find it.

There was no water between El Yibo and the Ethiopian border.

Tomahawk II **Marijke,** *Over the El Yibo Front, Kenya.*

The sixteen Tomahawks were spread out, four flights of four aircraft each; all were hunting for Italian fighters. They would be coming to remedy the situation that had erupted on this front. *Hunting for the Italian fighters* was a phrase that echoed happily in newly-promoted Flight Lieutenant Pim Bosede's mind. Gone were the days when the pathetic, obsolete Hawker Furies had run at the first shadow of an Italian fighter. Now, the Tomahawk ruled the skies and it was the Italians who fled at their approach.

"We see them."

The message was from the Blenheim bombers below. The Natal Mounted Rifles reported the Italian forces that had been holding the front east of Lake Rudolf were in full retreat, heading north. The Italians themselves were in trucks; their Askaris, local auxiliaries, were on foot. That difference would be very important in the next few minutes. There were no real roads up here to disrupt the yellow-gray ground; only tracks, and few enough of them. The Blenheim crews knew where the Italians would be. The cloud of dust thrown up by the trucks drove the message home.

Here we are, come and get us.

The Blenheims did.

They swept over the column of lorries, dropping their load of 250-pound and 40-pound bombs on the troops beneath. Compared with the blast of the bombs, the patter of fire from the single machine gun arming each aircraft were of little account. The effect of the attack on the convoy was disastrous. Many of the lorries were hit. They started belching black smoke and blocked the track. The others turned off in a desperate attempt to escape. Their tires broke through the thin crust of hardened mud that covered the ground and spun helplessly in the fine sand underneath. The infantry in them knew that their ride northwards had just ended. From now on, their retreat would be on foot.

Watching them, the Askaris noted the development. They dropped their rifles. Being an Italian Askari had been a way of earning a little extra money for doing very little work. The possibility of being shelled, bombed and strafed hadn't figured in that equation. It was time to leave. Word spreads fast in African villages. Soon, all across the front, the Askaris deserted and, very sensibly, went home.

High over the veldt, Bosede knew nothing of the word rippling through the African villages. What he did know was that the Blenheims had finished their attack and were on their way back to base. That released the Tomahawks to resume their free-chase. The squadron swung south, to where the Natal Mounted Rifles were advancing. Bosede had no doubt that the Italians would be trying to do to them what the Blenheims had just done to the Italian infantry.

"Bandits." Flight Lieutenant Petrus van Bram, now acting squadron leader, spotted the Italian aircraft. Twin engined aircraft, their yellow and gray paint made them hard to see against the ground below.

"Pim, take them with your flight. The rest of us will stay up here and cover you."

Bosede made a wingover and dove on the aircraft below. His eyes took in the details. The extensively glazed nose told him all he needed to know. Caproni Ca.311s. Almost an exact Italian equivalent of the Blenheim and as weakly defended: one 7.7mm machine gun in a top turret and one firing from a ventral hatch. Tracers licked out from the top turrets of the Italian aircraft. Light defensive fire that gave him little concern. His gun sight closed on the nose of the Caproni. His thumb squeezed the triggers, firing off a burst from both his nose .50s and the four .30s in his wings.

The effect on the Ca-311 was as disastrous, as it had to be. The aircraft staggered and flew apart under the concentrated blow. Its wings separated from its body as it disintegrated. The fuel tanks erupted into flame. What was left of the aircraft plowed into the dry, dusty veldt. Bosede swept upwards, climbing away from the scattering Italian formation. Three of the eight aircraft were already down;a fourth was trying to escape northwards, leaving a thick trail of black smoke behind it. Bosede watched a Tomahawk close in. A stream of tracers turned the aircraft into a flying torch. One more pass would finish the formation off.

One again, a wingover and a long dive down on to the poorly-protected Capronis. Instead of firing from above, Bosede came in from behind.

His fire raked the rear fuselage and engines. His target went down; three parachutes emerged as the Italian crew bailed out.

"Pim, you're trailing white vapor. Head back to Buna. The rest of your flight will escort you." Petrus van Bram's voice brooked no argument.

Bosede glanced at his instruments. There was no sign of trouble yet, but the Tomahawks were precious. They had made the offensive that was driving the Italians out of Kenya possible and their numbers were carefully conserved. Bosede set course for Buna.

On the way, he noted that his engine temperature was starting to rise. By the time the runway at Buna appeared under his nose, it had reached serious levels. He wondered if *Marijke* would make it. By then, what had started as a thin line of white vapor had turned into a thick stream behind the Tomahawk. She didn't let him down. By the time she came to a halt, he was surrounded by a white mist. It didn't take the ground crew long to spot why.

"There's your problem, sir." The flight sergeant pointed at a single small hole in the nose. "Looks like a bullet from a 7.7 caught your cooling system. Another few minutes and she'll have seized solid. Don't sweat it; we'll have her fixed by morning."

The telephone rang and a voice came warbled on the other end. The Flight Sergeant grinned broadly. "And that was a Lieutenant van der Haan from intelligence. Confirmed your two Capronis shot down."

Bosede staggered under the vigorous back-slapping and cheering. It was a long, long way from the days on the Hawker Fury. He threw his cap skywards to celebrate. Then he saw the single tiny hole that had nearly brought him down. A sudden sense of mortality weighed him down to earth.

GHQ, Middle East Command, Cairo, Egypt

"We have word from General Cunningham in Kenya, Archie." Maitland Wilson had a conceited expression on his face that reminded Wavell of the time one of his dogs had stolen an entire leg of roasted lamb. "Alan seems to be quite happy with the way things are going down there."

"I'll need more than that, Jumbo." Wavell wasn't in the mood for playful games.

"The South Africans have broken through in both the northern and southern sectors. In the south, they have captured Gorai and el Gumu. Their columns are advancing north towards Kismayu and the Jubu River. In the north, they captured the wells at el Yibu and el Sarbu and sent the Italians packing there. Our aircraft are bombing and strafing the Italians as they retreat, and it looks like that retreat is turning into a rout. Alan doesn't expect any serious resistance inside Italian Somaliland and thinks the Italians will try and concentrate on holding Ethiopia."

"Italian aircraft?" To Wavell, this was the crux of the matter.

"The Italians are throwing them in to try and slow down our advance. The Tomahawks are having a field day. They've shot down more than forty aircraft, mostly light bombers, but with a handful of CR.32s and .42s thrown in. We've had one Tomahawk shot down and three or four are damaged, but the odds are enormously our way. Even better, the Italians have brought the aircraft from northern Ethiopia down to try and regain air superiority. It won't do them any good; they've only a handful of fighters and they're CR.42s. Alan has ordered all our biplanes grounded; not that they were of much consequence anyway. That leaves the sky free for the Tomahawks down there; they can shoot at anything that isn't a monoplane."

Wavell nodded with a measure of relief. The first blow had been launched in Kenya because that was where the Italians were weakest and where the first squadrons of Tomahawks were based. He was gambling that the Italians would see this as a major thrust and would shift their air and ground forces south to match it. That would open the way into northern Ethiopia for the two Indian divisions in the Sudan. They would drive south, taking the Italian formations defending Ethiopia in the rear. Finally, with that battle under way, Maitland Wilson could launch his attack on Graziani and the supplies around Mersa Matruh with some hope of achieving tactical surprise.

The beauty of it was that each of the three operations was genuinely independent. Not one of them actually depended for its success on any of the others working. Each might work or fail on its own merits. In each case, the benefits they would bring by their success would be worth having. But, if all three worked together, then the success achieved would be, literally, world-changing.

4th Battalion, 11th Sikh Regiment, Kassala, Sudan

"Jai Hind!"

The call went up from the ranks moving up the hill. Subedar Shabeg Singh repeated the cry. He relished the sun gleaming off his bayonet and the sight of the waves of infantry that were moving against the railway junction at Kassala. The area had been seized by the Italians during the first days of the fighting in Sudan. A previous Indian attempt to recover it had been defeated due to heavy Italian air attacks.

Today, Italian aircraft were absent from the battlefield and the 7th Infantry Brigade was advancing in fine style. Having tanks in support was a help. Six Matilda IIs were moving in a manner that could best be described as stately. Their machine guns were rippling fire across the Italian positions. That was their job; to support the infantry. There were light tanks for the chase that would take place once the Italian positions were broken.

Overhead, the sound of artillery fire slackened slightly. The Indian gunners had been laying a barrage down on the Italian positions from their 4.5-inch howitzers. Those guns were more useful than the 18-pounders in very hilly terrain; one reason why the Indian divisions had a much higher proportion of them in their artillery regiments. The Italians were using reverse slopes to protect themselves from artillery fire, but the howitzers could lob shells over the crest to land on that reverse slope. It was an open question as to *what* they would hit that way.

The reduced artillery fire allowed Shabeg Singh to hear the sound of approaching aircraft. That had meant disaster a few weeks earlier. The Italian Breda ground attack aircraft had strafed and bombed the regiment, making the positions they had won untenable. They'd had to fall back; the shame of doing so still stung the Sikhs.

Today, though, was different. The aircraft were coming from the north. That meant they were supporting the 11th Sikh Regiment, not harassing it. *Assuming that the pilots do not make a mistake,* thought the ever-realistic Singh. The flight of Fairey Battles swept overhead. Bombs dropped on the defensive positions. The blasts and towering columns of smoke from over the ridgeline were the signal for the final push up the hill.

"Jo Bole So Nihal, Sat Sri Akal!"

The Sikhs sprinted across the remaining few yards of ground and jumped down into the Italian positions, preparing to take them with the bayonet. Instead, they found empty entrenchments and deserted defenses. The artillery fire had pounded some portions of the defenses, the bombing from the aircraft had done more, but the lack of Italian casualties was painfully obvious. The preparation had landed on mostly empty trenches.

The implications of that were still sinking into Singh's mind when he heard the renewed whistle of artillery fire. This time, the difference in sound was immediately obvious.

"INBOUND!"

The Sikh troops scattered and took cover in the deserted Italian positions. In some cases, the safety they offered was illusory. Foxholes and trenches had been booby-trapped. The resulting explosions beat the arrival of the Italian artillery fire by a few seconds. The light cracks of the inbound shells told Singh that they were only 65mm mountain guns firing a puny 9-pound projectile. The placement of the rounds made up for any lack of power. The Italian gunners droped their shots into the positions just seized by the Indians with almost uncanny accuracy.

They've pre-registered all the positions. The thought ran through Singh's mind as he scrambled out from the dugout he'd occupied and got as far away from it as he could. Behind him, a pattern of the light shells covered the position he'd just vacated. Fragments whined around his head.

The artillery bombardment was joined by a crackle of rifle fire, punctuated by brief bursts from machine guns. Singh sneaked a look from the dip he had found himself in. The Italians were advancing quickly across the open ground. His eyes took in the black feathers on their helmets. *Bersaglieri.* Their rifle fire was accurate and, combined with the precision support from the little 65mm howitzers, they were making the Indian positions too hot to hold.

The Sikh troops, very reluctantly, started to give ground, dropping back over the ridgeline to the dead ground beyond. There, they were relatively safe from the Italian guns. When the Bersaglieri crossed the crest in pursuit, they were greeted by a barrage of rifle and machine gun fire. Tthat drove them back in turn.

In the brief pause that followed, Singh collected his surviving men and got them back into reasonable shape. Then the whistles blew. He led them back over the crest into an assault on the Italian line. Once again, the positions just over the crest had been abandoned and lay temptingly open, but the Sikhs had learned from their previous mistakes.

They kept going.

This time, without pre-registration on carefully defined targets, the light Italian mountain guns were much less effective; they were an annoyance more than anything else. The Indian artillery observers had caught up with the infantry. They directed fire from the comparatively heavy 4.5-inch howitzers on to the Bersaglieri positions in the rear. The 35-pound shells had an authority that the 9-pound Italian projectiles lacked; the barrage suppressed the Italian infantry fire long enough for the Indians to close.

The fight was bitter. The Bersaglieri had no intention of giving ground without making their opponents pay dearly for it. By the time they were driven out of their defenses, Singh's unit had lost yet more of his men. He doubted the ability of the remainder to advance further without rest and reinforcement. He was slightly surprised to see one of the Bersaglieri officers advancing with a white flag. *Surely they are not surrendering now, after the brave and honorable fight they put up?*

It was with an anomalous sense of relief that he got the message from the company headquarters. "There will be a three-hour truce so that the wounded can be collected for care and the dead recovered for burial."

A few minutes later, whistles blew on the Indian side to announce the start of the truce. Singh was amused to hear the same message being given on the Italian side by a trumpet fanfare. His men started to lay the Italian bodies out where the Bersaglieri could collect them and get their own wounded ready for carriage back to the battalion lines. Half way through the process, a stretcher team from the Italians turned up and started to pick up the Italian wounded. An Italian officer with them noted the first-aid work carried out on the Italian wounded by the Indians and caught Singh's eye. Singh himself had seen the Italian medics and stretcher bearers treating the Indian wounded and returned the glance. Two professional soldiers who didn't even begin to speak each other's language reached an understanding without any problems. There was a time to fight and a time to give aid and comfort. This was the latter and that it was being respected as such gave honor to them both.

Vickers Wellesley G-George, *Over Asmara, Eritrea*

The eighteen Wellesleys were formed into three flights of six and lined up on the Italian Air Force base at Asmara. 47 Squadron had been assigned the base as its primary target, mostly to persuade the Italian Air Force not to come back north. As far as Squadron Leader Sean Mannix was concerned, the absence of Italian fighters was an entirely good thing. His Wellesley had been a remarkable aircraft once; long ranged and capable of carrying what was, for then, a heavy bombload. Now, it was painfully obsolete, slow and very poorly armed. His aircraft's only real defense was a single .303 Vickers machine gun aft and that had a very limited field of fire. The fact that he and his gunner sat in separate cockpits made coordinating defense very difficult. All in all, it was fortunate that the Italians had moved all their fighters south, where the South African Tomahawks had cut a swathe of destruction through them.

Mannix peered over the nose, trying to see the airfield that he was supposed to be approaching. It was hard to make out the runway against the prevailing yellow-gray color of the bare African soil. Even black-topped runways quickly adopted the universal khaki color as they absorbed the wind-blown dust. The airfield was supposed to be south of the town, but he couldn't see anything.

It didn't help that he was his own bomb-aimer. He had to fly the aircraft, search for his target, keep in formation with the other aircraft in his flight and watch out in case any enemy fighters were around. He swept his eyes quickly around the sky before transferring attention back to the ground. That was when he saw two large, square buildings with a long, straight patch of desert in front of them. *Hangars, runway, south of the town. This has to be it.*

It took a minor change of course to line up his aircraft on the target. Around him, the other five members of his flight saw the change and adjusted their own path accordingly. Their pilots watched his aircraft with their thumbs on the bomb release. As soon as he dropped, they would do the same. His was the only flight in 47 Squadron trained that way; the other two flights both relied on individual bomb-aiming. There had been long arguments over the technique Mannix had come up with. The other flight commanders pointed out that if he missed badly, everybody would. His counter-argument was that his flight would at least get a nice tight bomb pattern and damage something.

Underneath him, the hangars he had spotted entered his bombsight. He waited a second, allowing the cross-hairs to pass just over the target. Then he pressed his release. In the streamlined bomb panniers under his wings, the racks released the ten 100-pound bombs contained in each. They hit the bungee-loaded bomb pannier doors, knocking them open and then falling clear to rain down on the target below. The ground around the buildings erupted in a tight pattern of explosions, the buildings vanishing under the clouds of black and red smoke.

"Fighters; fighters." The voice from his gunner came over the speaking tube clearly. Mannix looked around and saw a flight of CR.32s descending on the British formation.

"Everybody, keep it tight."

Mannix tried to stay calm. *They promised us there wouldn't be any fighters here.* Behind him, he heard chatter; his gunner opened fire on a pair of CR.32s that had picked his flight. The other gunners in his formation did the same. Between them, the display of firepower looked impressive. Mannix was painfully aware of how ineffective it really was. In contrast, the other flights had dispersed as each aircraft made its own run. Now the fighters had a spread-out series of targets, instead of the compressed mass offered by Mannix's group. They went for the easiest targets: picking an isolated bomber, diving down and coming up from below, gutting them with their machine guns. Mannix saw one Wellesley break up. Its long wings folded around it as it started to spin down. Another developed a trail of black and orange flame; two parachutes separated from it.

There was more chattering from his formation. A CR.32 tried an up-and-under attack, but the aircraft were able to cover each other. The fighter pilot obviously decided easy kills were better and left them alone. Mannix's decision to keep a tight formation paid of in ways he had never expected. By the time the CR.32s pulled away, seven of the 18 Wellesleys had been shot down, not one of them from his flight.

Asmara, Italian Eritrea

"They all escaped?" Colonel Duilio Loris Contadino looked at the destruction and shook his head. The prison on the outskirts of the town had been the center of the attack and the bombers had done appalling damage. The walls had been knocked flat; the baked-mud bricks powdered by the bombs. The walls of the cell blocks had collapsed as well, leaving the cells inside exposed. The occupants of those cells took the opportunity the British bombers had so generously provided and fled. A handful had died from the bombs; the majority of prisoners, almost all leaders of the resistance to the Italian occupation of Eritrea and Ethiopia, had escaped.

"All of them, except the few we see in the ruins, sir." Captain Crescenzo Rico surveyed the destruction and whistled. "These must be the very best crews the British had. Just to hit a target like this from so high showed great skill and to get a close pattern like this, all around the prison but so few hits on it is truly remarkable. Our airmen could never do such a thing. And the way the other bombers drew our fighters away from the attack formation. I hope these were the elite British crews; because, if the rest of the British bombers are as skilled and ruthless as this, we will have much to fear."

"They were lucky, Captain. We were expecting them to bomb the airfield the other side of town and our fighters were stacked there, waiting for them. By the time the pilots realized the airfield wasn't their target, it was too late. The bombers had an undisturbed run." Contadino sighed; privately he was

229

shaken by the attack. *How had the British bombers known that the leaders of the bandit forces were held here? Asmara must be saturated with British spies.*

"What of the rest of the town?"

"The bombs are scattered all over the town. No great damage; a few buildings knocked down here, a road blocked by craters there. It's annoying more than anything else. If it hadn't been for those bombs disrupting our efforts to move through the town, we would have been here in time to chase the escapees. As it was, by the time we got here, they had got clean away. This was a very well-planned raid; an accurate main strike and well-executed diversions."

Contadino nodded. "We underestimated the British badly. I will seek a meeting with the Duke of Aosta and tell him that he will now have to face a resumption of bandit attacks in this area. I do not think he will be pleased with that information."

GHQ, Middle East Command, Cairo, Egypt

"Bill Slim shapes up well." Wavell sounded pleased.

Maitland Wilson agreed. "Fifth Indian Division is pushing forward into Eritrea and advancing on Asmara. If he can just forget that he isn't commanding a brigade any more and stop running around on the front line, he'll make a good divisional officer. Fourth Indian Division is hung up on the ridges south of Kassala. We expected that; they're pinning down the 40th Infantry Division there. Slim's Indians will be taking the *Cacciatori d'Africa* in the flank very soon."

"We're taking a hell of a chance moving 4th Indian Infantry down there, Jumbo." Wavell was flicking at the map with his fingers. "The 6th Australians are as green as grass and I doubt if any of their officers have commanded more than a battalion. Blamey makes a big show, but expecting those men to equal the performance of the Indians is pushing it. I hope we don't have a disaster in the making."

Maitland Wilson stared at the map. "We don't really have much choice. We know Halifax will call for an armistice as soon as he has enough gains to make securing one politically worthwhile, or plead for one as soon as it looks like we're losing. We've got to grab everything in one go. Once we have momentum on our side, we get freedom of action. If we let momentum slip, we're going to lose that freedom."

"Just how green are the Australians, Jumbo?"

There was a long pause as Maitland Wilson thought the situation over. "Very, but I'm not entirely sure that it matters. They want to fight. There's no doubt about that and the treatment of the Canadian division back home got their dander up. On the other hand, they lack experience in combined arms operations and large formation actions. The question is, will they need to do either? If 7th Armoured defeats the Italian armored battle group and spearheads the advance, the Australians following behind will be doing little more than clearing up and taking prisoners. Looked at that way, this may even be the training exercise they need to shake down. Anyway, I say again, Archie; do we have a choice?"

Wavell shook his head. "No, we do not. We cannot rely on any coherent policy out of London. Between us, Jumbo, I must admit that my position here is about as uncomfortable as it gets. I'm supposed to report to London, but I am an Indian Army officer who is now supposed to report to Calcutta. Well, that's always been something of a problem, we all know that; but we've never had a situation where India is at war and Britain isn't."

"Britain *is* at war with Italy; effectively, at any rate." Maitland Wilson was looking for some ray of sunlight to illuminate the situation.

"Yes, now. And that brings us back to our initial problem. For how long will Halifax keep up his present position? Anyway, Jumbo, I have another problem. Have you ever heard of an officer called Wingate? Major Orde Wingate?"

"Heard of him? I've had the misfortune of dealing with him. Insufferable, arrogant, conceited man, with excessive religious beliefs. Did well in Palestine, but got convinced he was the messiah come to Earth and ended up part and parcel of the Jewish forces there. Working as much for them as for us. Why? He's not in Egypt, is he?" Maitland Wilson's face was so distraught at the possibility, Wavell couldn't help but laugh.

"No, he's in Ethiopia. Bill Platt knew his success in raising and commanding irregular forces in Palestine and brought him out. Anyway, I've had a message from our Major Wingate claiming to have organized a jail break in which nearly all the leaders of the Ethiopian anti-Italian groups have escaped. He wants to set up an irregular group in Ethiopia to help drive the Italians out."

"That fits the man. He's obsessed with irregular warfare and deep penetration operations."

"They worked in Palestine."

"Yes, they did. Give him credit for that, but he was operating in a very friendly environment for what he was doing. He could trust his own people implicitly and they knew exactly who the enemy were. Neither will be true in Ethiopia. Anyway, I have my doubts about his deep penetration operations theories. I think he's going to try it one day against an enemy who know what they are doing and he'll get cut to pieces. The problem is that he'll take a lot of good men down with him.

Wavell nodded thoughtfully. "There's a lot to be said there. I've got a different question, though; one that strikes right at the heart of this proposed operation of Wingate's. Do we really want to go around starting up these irregular insurgency groups? It strikes me that the whole idea could backfire very badly."

"You mean start something that will return to haunt us?" Maitland Wilson looked thoughtful. "That's a very real danger. However, there is something else we have to take into consideration. We're desperately short of troops. We've got five front line divisions, one independent brigade and two divisions that are second line. We've got the whole lot committed to action right now and we've not got a man in reserve. Archie, if there's a crisis now, you'll have to give me a pistol and tell me to deal with it myself, because I'm the only reserve you've got."

"I might have to take you up on that, Jumbo. But, I take the point. The two Indian divisions are over-extended in Eritrea already and their attack has barely started. We need that irregular force in Ethiopia or we just won't have the men to boot the Italians out."

11th Infantry (Queen's Cobra) Division, Sisaket, Thailand

"Do you know where are we going, Corporal?" The private was deferential, as befitted one speaking to somebody of higher rank.

"Of course." Corporal Mongkut had already noticed the differences in the 11th Infantry since he had first been recalled to the colors. Where once men had made hard work of a few kilometers march, now they swung along easily; their steps accompanied by light-hearted banter. Yet, despite the rhythm of the march, they were keeping a wary eye out for a 'surprise' planned by their officers. Or, much more likely, the German advisors who had directed their training.

"Well, where are we going?" After a marked pause, the same private asked Mongkut with carefully faked patience.

"Why, wherever our officers tell us to go, of course." Mongkut replied with equally carefully faked innocence. He listened appreciatively to the wry groan of disappointment that went up.

Mongkut had a shrewd idea where he was. His family came from Rattanburi and he knew the country well. After the train had brought them from Kanchanaburi and unloaded them at the marshalling yard at Sisaket, they had marched east. Combining that with his knowledge of the land, he guessed that the whole regiment was moving towards the Indo-China border; probably close to where the borders of Thailand, Cambodia and Laos intersected. There was no logical reason why an entire infantry regiment would be needed up here; not unless something big was about to happen.

Without being able to explain why, Mongkut knew that war was coming. It wasn't the troop movements or his sudden resumption of military life. Nor was it the intense training he and his men had gone through over the last few weeks. It was much less definable than that. It was just that there was something in the air; an electricity or a tension. It was as if all the decisions had been taken, all the preparations made and the war was a reality that hadn't quite happened . . . . yet.

His thoughts were interrupted by a blast of whistles. A rest period. Ten minutes rest for every hour of marching. He couldn't detect urgency in the movement; it was as if the planners knew that there was plenty of time and they preferred the troops on the move to arrive in good condition rather than exhausted from a forced march.

"Water carriers; fall out and refill canteens."

The order had come from the Sergeants, but it was for the Corporals to carry out. Mongkut didn't need to say anything; he just pointed at two of his men and watched them join the rest. There was a lake through the trees, gleaming dark blue in the sunshine. He recognized it; knew the shoreline and the square fish farm that lay across the width of the lake. They were just a little bit north of Non Sung; only a few kilometers from his family home. That really did put them close to the border with Cambodia and Laos.

Troops moving up to the Indochina border and a war in the air. Mongkut put the two together and came up with a very satisfactory answer. In his opinion, there were a lot of debts owed. It was about time that his country collected on them.

Don Muang Airport, Bangkok, Thailand

"My apologies, Mister Secretary, for the landplane. Unfortunately, we have no areas suitable for flying boats, so we have to use DC3 aircraft for even the most prestigious of dignitaries. Please accept the warmest hospitality of our nation." The Ambassador placed both hands together in the traditional Thai 'wai' gesture and dipped her head.

"This is a more modern airport than I had expected." Cordell Hull did not return the gesture or make an equivalent response. "And a much more active one. I assume you have arranged this as a demonstration of your country's modern outlook?"

The Ambassador ignored the discourtesy shown to her. She'd been insulted many times in her life and had long ago learned to ignore the slights. There were much more important things at stake here than her personal feelings.

"This is a normal day's activity for this airport, especially now at the end of the rainy season. You see, the whole of the river delta is low-laying ground and it floods very easily once the rains start. By this time, the end of the monsoon, most of the area is underwater. This is wonderful for our farmers who will produce rice on the newly-enriched ground, but it makes the construction of roads and railways in the region difficult. To make matters worse, most of our population lives in the flooded areas. So we have developed air travel to maintain communications. The aircraft you just saw taking off is taking some passengers and, most importantly, the mail to Aranyaprathet. If you wish to look at the logs of the Civil Aviation Division, you will see this is a regularly scheduled flight."

"I am sure I will." Hull looked skeptical. "Who runs this airfield?"

"It is a joint civilian and military operation. The plan is to transfer the civilian part of the airfield to civilian employees as soon as they are properly trained and qualified. The actual airfield is run by our air force and they use the northern part. The fighters charged with the defense of the city are based there."

"What fighters and how many?"

"We have six Curtiss Hawk IIs based here; that's the export version of the U.S. Navy's F11C-2," The Ambassador sighed. "They are old, of course, and quite obsolete. Six more are at Chiang Mai in the north. We had hoped to replace them all with North American Model 68s, but the six aircraft we bought are being held in Hawaii."

"We cannot afford to allow the Japanese access to our latest technology." Hull slid into the waiting limousine. The Ambassador sat beside him in the back. "Not with the Japanese set on a course of territorial aggression across this whole region."

"And as one of the potential victims of that aggression, we could not afford to compromise the effectiveness of our air defenses by giving away their details. The secrets of your aircraft are safe with us. Secretary Hull, Bangkok is a densely crowded city built largely of wood. If anybody was to bomb it, the way the Japanese have bombed cities in China, the fires would be a catastrophe. Our fire fighting services would be overwhelmed and the only thing to stop the blaze spreading would be the canals that divide the city. Thousands, perhaps tens of thousands, would die. Without modern fighters, if our major cities are threatened with bombing, we would have no choice but to submit."

For the first time, Cordell Hull paused to question his basic assumptions. It was one thing to look at a map and make theoretical assumptions; quite another to deal with realities on the ground. The vulnerability of Thai cities to fire had never occurred to him. In passing, he wondered how many other cities in Asia would burn just as easily or as catastrophically.

"And why should the Japanese bomb you? It would appear to me that your government and political systems are very much akin to theirs."

The Ambassador smiled politely. Mentally, she imagined the American Secretary of State being burned at the stake; using a slow, carefully controlled, fire. "To the Japanese, other nations fall into two categories. Those who must be conquered and turned into slaves or those who acknowledge Japanese superiority and become willing servants. We would prefer to be neither; but, if forced to make the choice, we would become the second rather than the first.

"As to similarities, yes, there are many. We are both monarchies where the King is held in high esteem. There is an important difference. In Japan, the Emperor is held in high regard because that is the religious duty of the people. In ours, we hold our King in high regard because he has earned that respect by his service to our people. If the respect is not earned, it is not given and he is replaced. You may remember this happened, less than ten years ago." *And let us see if you remember who commanded the troops that did it.*

"Replaced by a military junta that wields authority in the name of the monarchy." Hull's voice injected a healthy dose of contempt into the phrase.

"Again, I will concede a superficial similarity." The Ambassador's voice remained polite and deferential. "But the reality is very different. In Japan, the military junta is an end in itself; it is the final product of a flawed system. Here, the military dominance of our government is a temporary thing; a step on the road to a functioning democratic government. In any case, our Prime Minister may be an Army officer, but he also functions within the rules and limitations of an elected assembly.

"By 1942 we will have full elections and we already have opposing political parties ready to contest them. The leaders of those parties already freely express their opposition to our current administration and its policies. They even have their own newspaper. What would happen to them in Japan?

"No, Mister Secretary, we have little in common with the Japanese. They believe they are already perfect and seek to impose their will on others. We recognize our imperfections and ask only to be given the chance to learn from others. And we ask you only to give us the chance to choose from whom we wish to learn. For without proper air defenses, we will have no such choice."

4 Battalion 11th Sikh Regiment, Bitama, Eritrea

It had only been a short advance. But it had a significance much more than just the ten miles they had moved. They had crossed the border from the Sudan and were now driving the enemy 40th Infantry Division backwards on their base at Bitama. The 40th Infantry, also known as the *Cacciatori d'Africa*, had held the ridgeline east of Kassala for two days before a flanking move by a brigade of the Fifth Indian Division had made the line untenable and forced them to evacuate.

Subedar Shabeg Singh felt gravely shamed that his Skihs hadn't managed to take the position and had to be helped out by the Jats of the 9th Brigade. Somehow, it made matters worse that the same flanking threat made the position at Bitama untenable and the Italians would not be trying to defend it. The critical high ground, the Bara Ghazi, to the west of Bitama had fallen without a fight.

Brigadier Harold Rawdon Briggs had called the meeting of his battalion officers to outline the next stage of the campaign. Scattered amongst the august ranks of the British were the much more junior Indian officers. Briggs was keenly aware that the political circumstances of his brigade had changed. It was now an Indian Army formation, in all its attributes; the process of handing it over to Indian command was, if not absolutely urgent, something all the better for being started as soon as possible.

The command structures of the battalions was being changed; each of the British officers now had an Indian 'shadow,' who would be learning to take over. Briggs had spent long hours looking at the men involved and their records, carefully picking out pairings that would work together. As far as he was concerned, the longer these men had together in the transition phase, the better for the Indian Army that was being born here. That was why an early start had been so essential.

"Major Hamby, sir." Singh recognized the man he was supposed to meet here. They'd worked together in the past and made a good team. The news that they would be working together again pleased him greatly.

Major Joel Hamby turned around; his own face was split by a friendly smile. "Shabeg, my old friend. It is good to see you again."

In the background sitting at his briefing desk, Briggs saw the two men greet each other as old friends and allowed himself a smile of satisfaction. To his knowledge, there was no parallel in modern warfare for what was happening now. An entire army was changing nationalities in the middle of a campaign. *The Indian will be the British officer's second-in-command and assistant while he is taught the new responsibilities. Then, when the Indian officer is ready, the two will switch positions. Finally, command will be handed over to the Indians and the British officer will . . . Well, that is the problem, isn't it? What will happen to us once command of the Indian Army is fully returned to the Indian Government?*

It was time to start the meeting. He tapped the glass of water on his desk and the room froze into silence. Briggs glanced around and saw how the Indian and British officers had completed pairing off. That part of the meeting, actually the most important part, was accomplished. He just hoped that other brigade and battalion meetings would be going as well. "Gentlemen, I have news for you that will change our plans for the immediate future. The armored cars of the Central India Horse have taken Bitama from the Italians without resistance."

There was a series of polite cheers from around the tent. Briggs paused for a second, acknowledging the moment before continuing on a cautionary note. "Let us not be misled. We all know that the Italians can fight and fight well. They are retreating because they do not believe that they can put up an effective resistance here. Our assessment is that the Italian garrison in Eritrea is falling back on Asmara and, eventually, Massawa. We believe that they will form a defense line at Keren to defend that position."

Briggs cleared his throat and drank some water before continuing. "The Fifth Indian Division will be pursuing the Italian force back to Keren and will be occupying Eritrea. The Italian moves appear to be similar to those adopted in Kenya and Somaliland. Put briefly, the Italian garrison in all the Somalilands are retreating without putting up much of a fight. They are regrouping in Ethiopia and it is there that they will make their final stand. The South African Division is already entering Ethiopia from the south, while the 11th and 12th King's African Divisions complete the occupation of all the Somalilands. Now, we can't let the Boers have all the glory can we?"

There was a patter of applause and a discrete Sikh war-cry. Briggs smiled to himself. *There is nothing like providing a common rival to weld people together.* "Just because the South Africans and their Tomahawks have shot down large numbers of Italian aircraft doesn't mean that nobody can win a battle or two without them, does it?"

Again a patter of applause rippled around the room. The way the two squadrons of Tomahawks had cleared the air of Italian air support had made a compelling story for the newspapers, but it had left the ground troops feeling unappreciated and resentful. Briggs waited again until it had settled down. "Well, we have our part to play in Ethiopia. Effective immediately, we will be heading south. And, I am reliably informed, we will soon be having our own Tomahawks to support us, along with other American aircraft, including a new light bomber called the Maryland. Our job will be to drive south and link up with the South Africans. I needn't say that honor demands we meet them as far south as possible, need I?"

There was another subdued roar of agreement.

"I am advised that we will be cooperating with other forces on our move into Ethiopia. One will be an Ethiopian irregular force that will be conducting a partisan campaign against the Italian forces in the country. There is also a British group doing much the same thing, under the command of a Colonel Wingate."

Briggs paused for a few seconds, running over that issue in his mind. When he spoke again, he did so very carefully. "I would caution you all that irregular forces and partisan groups invariably have their own agenda, and their long-term interests may not coincide with ours. I would counsel caution in your dealings with them. Be aware that they may be on our side today, but we do not know on whose behalf they may act tomorrow."

There was much nodding around the room at that. Briggs was interested to see that the Indian Army officers were as cautious as the rest. There was a much greater degree of agreement than he had dared hope. Eventually, one Indian officer asked the question Briggs hoped nobody would.

"Sir, does this most appropriate caution also apply to Colonel Wingate's force?"

"He calls his group Gideon Force, and I believe Colonel Wingate is aware that his control over the men nominally under his command may not be as absolute as he would wish; nor are their interests and ambitions necessarily in accordance with his own."

He could see the officers he was addressing translating his words in their minds and coming up with the answers he had intended. The Indian officer nodded with satisfaction and sat down again.

"Is there any word of the French?" A British officer spoke up.

Briggs hesitated for a moment. "I have been advised that the French have shown no interest in the conflict between us and the Italians at this time. In the absence of any further information, I believe we will have to continue planning our operations based on that perception. I would add that the Italians did attack the French back in June, although they did not achieve very much. The French may resent the fact that we left them in the lurch, as it were, but they actually fought the Italians."

There was a deep silence around the room. The British officers remembered how France had fought on after the Halifax had accepted the German Armistice offer. The French fight might have been hopeless, but it had been gallant. France had gone down with its colors still flying bravely. The contrast with Britain's actions had echoed around the world.

Looking at the meeting, Briggs began to realize how deep the wound in British pride and self-confidence had been.

Supreme Command Headquarters, Bangkok, Thailand

"The greatest curse of any nation is illiteracy. No matter how free somebody may be in theory, if that person is illiterate, then they are imprisoned by their minds. A prisoner held by steel bars and iron shackles may escape his bonds, but one imprisoned by an illiterate mind can never escape its curse. That is why we *must* educate our children; so that freedom will be their heritage." Field Marshal Plaek Pibulsonggram leaned forward in his chair, his eyes flashing. "The teacher is in the vanguard of progress and the school is where the future is born."

Cordell Hull blinked at the unexpected lecture. This wasn't going at all the way he had expected. "And where does military rule fit into all this?"

Marshal Plaek folded his fingers together as he thought the question over. "In the long term, it does not. In the short and medium term, I believe our task is to prepare the country for truly democratic rule under the leadership of a constitutional monarchy. Once again, we come back to the problem of literacy. People who are illiterate, who cannot investigate matters and form their own opinions, are easily led. To be frank with you, Mister Secretary, my greatest fear is of some smooth-tongued scoundrel who will use wealth and charisma to dominate large numbers of illiterate peasants and bring them to our capital in order to wreak havoc. While illiteracy remains rampant in our country, then that is a danger we must guard against. That is why our constitution stipulates that the transition to full democratic representation in the Assembly should only be achieved at the end of ten years *or* when more than half of the populace has gone through primary education, whichever is achieved *first*.

"I am proud to say that we have met this target and when the new elections take place in 1942, more than half the population will indeed have gone through primary education. Many of them are not youngsters; but older members of the community who have sacrificed what little leisure time they have to go back to school and become literate. When they make such sacrifices, we cannot let them down."

"The American concept of democratic government does not include the concept of qualifying people for the vote. We have had such measures in the past, and they were used to oppress and disenfranchise the voters."

"Our constitution was actually written by an American jurist, Raymond Bartlett Stevens. It does not qualify people for a vote individually, but merely states that the present arrangement of our parliament, wherein half the members are elected and half appointed, shall be replaced by a parliament wherein all the members are elected once the primary education target is met. Which it was, well before the 1942 deadline."

Marshal Plaek's quiet, very precise English had the desired impact. Very reluctantly, Cordell Hull had to concede the point made. Nevertheless, his primary concern remained unaddressed.

"And what, may I ask, are your future intentions with regard to your neighbors?"

"Once again, I will be frank with you, Mister Secretary. Personally, I like Japanese weapons. They are inexpensive for us to buy, simple, easy to maintain and effective. My colleagues in the government disagree and the government has discussed the issue with the loyal opposition, led by Luang Pridi Phanomyong. After listening to the case made by the opposition, I agreed with their position that the political costs represented by any links with Imperial Japan were too high to countenance. However, the need for armaments still remains paramount, given the world situation. The North American P-64s we bought and the license we had been granted to build more would have resolved our problems but . . . . " Plaek sighed softly and noted the guilty bob of the head from Cordell Hull.

"Weapons are tools, not intentions; Field Marshal. I asked after the latter."

"But the availability of appropriate tools determines the range of intentions, does it not? If one has only a hammer, one cannot build a house using screws. The intentions of Thailand, Mister Secretary, are simple. We intend to preserve our independence and our way of life, while also modernizing our country to become part of the modern, democratic world. For this, we require strong defenses and secure borders. The greatest threat to those is Imperial Japan. We must either be strong enough to oppose Imperial Japan or friendly enough with them for them not to be a threat to us. We prefer the former.

"Part of maintaining strong defenses is the ability to recognize threats before they become critical. Every day, the Japanese position in French Indo-China becomes stronger. The French authorities in Indo-China are staunch supporters of the Vichy government and are so indirect allies of Japan. Our border with French Indo-China was forced on us by the treaties of 1893 and 1908 and was deliberately designed to be indefensible. It concerns us here in the government that soon Japan will be on the other side of that border. If Japan attempts the same absorption process that is being conducted in Indochina, it will leave Malaya, Singapore and Burma gravely exposed. Ultimately, India itself will be at risk. As responsible members of the international community, this causes us much concern. We would make some minor changes to the border to improve our defensive positions and negotiate cross-border trade agreements to benefit the lives of the people living along that border, but the French authorities refuse to negotiate with us."

Cordell Hull shook his head. As a long-term diplomat, a refusal to negotiate was one of the worst cardinal sins he could imagine. It had been the way he, himself, had nearly committed the same sin that had shocked him into undertaking this mission. In his mind, the only worse sin that refusing to negotiate was to negotiate in bad faith. Determining whether the people he had met since his arrival were speaking in good faith was his next priority.

"If Thailand will accept my services as an intermediary, I will go to Hanoi and attempt to organize a meeting where trade and security issues may be discussed. In the meantime, I would like to visit some of the towns and villages here."

"We will be most grateful for your aid, Mister Secretary. Let us know where you wish to go and we will arrange transport for you."

The meeting ended much more cordially than it had started. Cordell Hull returned to the Oriental Hotel while Field Marshal Plaek Pibulsonggram read reports on the progress of the communications work that was finally in hand. Even so, he heard the quiet steps as the Ambassador entered his office. Unannounced, of course.

"I trust you did not tell him that the minor border adjustments we have in mind will take us all the way to the Mekong?" Her voice was droll.

"Of course not, Highness. It will be a nice surprise for him."

CHAPTER NINE
EARNEST MONEY

Ministry of Defence, Canberra, Australia

Sir Wilfrid Freeman sighed softly as he tried to settle comfortably into his seat. The damage done by the bullet that had struck his shoulder still troubled him gravely and he had the resigned feeling that the mobility of his arm would never be fully restored. Still, the report he was reading cheered him up greatly. If the Commonwealth Aircraft Corporation could pull this off, then the genius of the British for inspired improvisation still survived.

"So you've converted the Harvard trainer into a fighter?" Sir Wilfrid deliberately put an incredulous note into his voice. If the CAC could defend this project properly, they would also be capable of driving it to a proper conclusion and taking it even further.

"Not the Harvard; nah. The Wirraway. A cousin ta the Harvard. We took the basic NA-16 design, gave it a R-1340 engine, beefed it up for dive bombin' and gave it two forward-firin' machine guns, not one. More or less what North American did with the design ta get the AT-6, which then became your Harvard. Then, of course, North American beefed that aircraft up to be a dive bomber and light attack aircraft, then sold it to the Siamese."

Sir Wilfrid nodded, taking due care to make his expression as skeptical as possible. "Converting a trainer to a light bomber is one thing. Converting it into a fighter is quite another."

"It's a bit more than just a conversion, cobber. We gave it a license-built R-1830, reworked the whole airframe ta cope with the extra power, messed around with the undercart and gave it a pair of 20mm cannons in addition ta its .303s. Changed the wing profile as well. Truth be told, there ain't much of the ridgy didge Wirraway left there."

It took him a few seconds to translate the comment into English. When he had, he was impressed. The file on the aircraft had the estimated performance data and Sir Wilfrid had already made his assessment of that information. The new fighter would be slow at altitude and virtually useless over 15,000 feet; low down, it would be the equal of anything believed to be in

241

the area. Most importantly, it was made using Australian resources and was quite independent of anything that had to be imported. Except the 20mm cannons, of course. They were going to be a problem.

"How long? A year? 18 months?"

The CAC representative looked unbearably smug. "Nah. We've rolled the first one out already. We're doin' the ground tests now. We'll fly her in less than five weeks. January 29th is the date we have pencilled in. You're welcome to come down and see her fly. I know, she ain't important in the run of thin's . . . "

It was time to end the charade. Sir Wilfrid knew that CAC had done an incredible job in getting their little fighter ready in such a short time. It was time to make sure that achievement was recognized.

"Not important? My dear sir, this CA-12 fighter of yours could turn out to be the most important project Australia is currently involved in. The deliveries of American fighters have staunched a gaping hole in our air defenses, but they are a short-term expedient only and they leave us open to unwelcome pressure. One change you will have to make will be the 20mm cannon. We cannot be sure of their supply; make certain the CA-12 can carry four .303 machine guns in their place."

"The order is confirmed, then?" CAC had an order in hand for 105 CA-12 fighters but they knew Sir Wilfrid was tasked with choosing the aircraft to rearm the RAAF, and controlling of their production, by the Australian government. The CA-12 would be competing with the Department of Aircraft Production Beaufort for the R-1830 engines

"Of course. And I will be honored to attend the aircraft's first flight. What do you want to call it, by the way?"

"We thought ta' Boomerang. Always comes back, ya see. We'll be proud to see ya at CAC anytime ya like. To be honest, we thought DAP would be takin' us over."

Sir Wilfrid shook his head. "They're all set up to build the Beauforts and their design team will be fully-absorbed in bringing the Beaufighter into production. Anyway, it never hurts to have a little competition, does it? That brings us to the subject of your future. I assume that, with the first flight impending, your design team is reaching the end of their involvement in the CA-12? That being the case, you would be well-advised to come up with some concepts for its successor. You might like to look at some of the wing designs the Americans have come up with."

The representatives from CAC left with delighted expressions on their faces. Once they were gone, Sir Wilfred opened the next file on his desk. de Havilland Australia were already building Tiger Moth trainers and Dragon Rapide light transports but their capacity was under-utilized. Amongst the treasure trove of documents brought out of Britain were the blueprints for a medium transport aircraft, the Flamingo. Building that aircraft in Australia was the next project to get under way. The problem was getting anybody in Australia to trust a de Havilland-built transport after the DH.86 disaster. He sighed again and shook his head. He'd gone through this whole process once before as the Air Member for Research and Development. That hadn't ended well, but all he could hope was that his work would have a better outcome this time.

Cabinet Office, 10 Downing Street, London, United Kingdom

"Now is the time to call a halt."

R.A.B. Butler had the situation reports from the Middle East in his hands. They showed that Italian resistance in East Africa had crumpled completely, with Italian forces heading in full retreat back to Ethiopia. "The 12th King's African Division has taken Mogadiscio, while the South Africans have cleared Kenya and are moving northwards into Ethiopia. In the north, General Wavell's troops are advancing on Asmara while his forces are also entering Ethiopia. A diplomatic engagement with the Italians now will pay dividends and consolidate our gains. We have a victory that we can point to, as justification for our adjustments to Britain's political outlook."

"Did you see what the newspapers have said?" Lord Halifax gave no sign of having heard Butler's words. His own voice was querulous and petty. "They refer to the *South Africans* driving the Italians out of Kenya. It is *South African* Tomahawks that swept the skies of Italian aircraft. *Indian* troops are advancing on Massawa and invading Ethiopia. *African* troops are occupying Italian Somaliland. Where is mention of us in all this? According to the newspapers, these victories are being won by the Dominions without any contribution by ourselves. *I* approved the operations in North Africa and supported General Wavell. Where is mention of *that*?"

Lord Halifax was genuinely bewildered by the newspaper coverage of the war in North and East Africa. He had expected his friends in the Cliveden Set to ensure that he got all the credit for the apparently remarkable turn-around in the military fortunes of the country. Instead, his name was barely mentioned.

"I suspect that Geoffrey Dawson and Robert Barrington-Ward are doing you a great kindness in keeping your name out of this." Butler sounded sincere. "This whole business will end in tears. Wavell has his troops stretched to the absolute limit there, and he has still done nothing to remove the Italians from Egypt. I suspect that the Italians were not expecting him to attack, so he had the element of surprise working for him. When they counter-attack, we will see another disaster out there; you mark my words."

"What I see is the Dominions getting all the credit for winning a series of victories out there. They're taking the credit for a situation that is *my* creation. If *I* hadn't backed Wavell, he'd never have dared move like this."

"Prime Minister, the fewer people who know that, the better. Wavell is horribly outnumbered in North Africa and as soon as Mussolini moves against him, his entire position will crumble. With it, the credibility of the Dominions as independent powers will be crushed and they will be forced to come back to us, cap in hand, to rescue them from the wreckage. I would urge, though, that we do not let matters reach that pass. We can approach Signore Mussolini now and offer him a ceasefire; one that returns to the prewar boundaries. We have a window of opportunity here; one where the balance of power is in our favor. We should take advantage of it."

Halifax looked out of the window, at the miserable darkness of a British winter. There had been plenty of dry weather during December, and the rain that had fallen during the month was mainly light. The temperature was on the way down, though; there had already been several slight frosts. That wasn't the reason for the grayness that seemed to blanket the country.

Halifax could sense what was really the problem. The atmosphere of reluctance to accept defeat; a resentment at the way the war had been suddenly ended. Now, with the news of the Commonwealth victories in East Africa, there was a growing sensation that the Armistice had been a mistake.

To make matters worse, the demands from Germany were growing. Some of them had been quite reasonable, Halifax had thought at the time. Closer economic ties between Germany and Britain, for example. The Germans were placing large orders with British factories. The shipyards were building merchant ships for German companies; light engineering groups, a variety of supplies. Then, the Germans had asked for the use of a small number of British airfields so they could improve surveillance of the eastern Atlantic. Tangmere had been one such airfield; Manston another. There had been a few more. A handful of German reconnaissance aircraft on a handful of British airfields hadn't been too high a price to pay for peace.

"Very well, RAB. Instruct our Ambassador in Rome to seek an appointment with Mussolini so we can negotiate a cease-fire."

Bridge, HMAS Australia, off Berbera, Italian-occupied British Somaliland

"Perhaps it was for the best after all?"

Lieutenant Colonel Beaumont sounded almost amused by the situation. Standing beside him, Captain Robert Stewart couldn't help smiling. Any reply was forestalled by *Australia*'s eight-inch guns crashing out a salvo. A thousand yards a stern, HMAS *Canberra* fired at the same target: an orderly group of buildings that were the home of the Italian garrison. The buildings were empty and deserted. Early in the morning, a Sunderland flying boat out of Aden had dropped leaflets on the area, warning everybody that the base would be bombarded at noon and that anybody who did not want to see what eight-inch shell bursts looked like at close quarters ought to evacuate.

"The warning leaflets?" Stewart shook his head. "I can only think that we've got some very good intelligence on this garrison. Otherwise, those leaflets could cost us dear."

"I meant getting thrown out of the old country." Beaumont looked back on the last few weeks with almost fond exasperation. His battalion had disembarked from *Australia,* and been divested of all their extra equipment, before being put on trains and sent over to the Pacific Coast. There, they'd been put on a hastily-commandeered liner and sailed for the Middle East. They got there just in time to match up with *Australia* again. They'd been three-quarters of the way around the world to end up more or less where they had started. His thoughts were interrupted by the ship shaking as another pair of broadsides crashed out.

A group of boats was \assembling in the water between the two cruisers and the shoreline. They contained two battalions of Canadian infantry; an extemporized expeditionary brigade under Beaumont's command. It was a mark of just how stretched the Commonwealth was for troops that they were here at all. With the South Africans committed in East Africa, the Indians in Eritrea and Ethiopia and the Australians and New Zealanders in Egypt, these two battalions of Canadian troops were about the only available forces that could be found. It was the old story; wait six months, let the mobilization take effect, wait until the men being trained were ready and all would be well. Only, the war had its own momentum; it wouldn't wait.

"Sir, the landing force commander wishes to speak with you." The sparker had a radio set positioned on the bridge for just this eventuality.

"Mark, what's going on?"

"The Italians are waiting for us." There was the sound of teeth being sucked around the bridge. The troops having to fight their way ashore had been the worst-case scenario.

"Are they putting up much of a fight?"

"No, sir. They're drawn up in parade formation on the beach. About sixty of them, waving a white flag." There was a pause. "Sir, war can be very embarrassing sometimes."

Beach outside Berbera, British Somaliland

"Sir, I must ask you for your assistance." Colonel Nerio Amedeo Amerigo was almost completely white and was barely able to stand. "My men are accursed by malaria. Only a handful are in fit condition for duty; the rest need medical attention urgently. I implore you to send as much aid as you can spare. Our own doctor, Rosa Dainelli, is overwhelmed and without supplies."

Beumont took a horrified look at the desperately ill man before him. His condition was no worse, and no better, than that of the other Italian soldiers on the beach. "You paraded your men in this condition? In the sun?"

"It was necessary for us to surrender honorably."

Beaumont nodded and turned to his radioman. "Get word to the cruisers and the two transports. Tell them we need every medic and every ounce of quinine here right away. Colonel, we will transfer your men to the transports *Chakdina* and *Chantala* immediately. We will do everything in our power for you."

GHQ, Middle East Command, Cairo, Egypt

"We knew it was coming." Maitland Wilson sounded infinitely depressed. "That Man cannot maintain a purpose from one minute to the next."

"He's maintaining a purpose, Jumbo; and, from his point of view, it is a very logical one. He's trying to gain the maximum credit for his administration at minimum cost. Since our operations began, we've cleared the Italians out of Kenya, made a landing in Somaliland and pushed the Italians back in Eritrea. That's a pretty impressive set of achievements and he wants to take full advantage of them now before they fade away." Wavell sighed slightly and looked out of his window at Cairo bustling in the afternoon sun. "I think I understand him better for this. That Man does not believe he can win, ever. He assumes that no matter how well things appear to be running, they will always turn around and move against him. So his eyes are set short; to take what advantages he can seize in the short term, for he believes that the long term will always hold worse."

Maitland Wilson looked at the telegraph message from London and his mouth twisted. "He's certainly looking at the short term here. We are ordered to cease all offensive actions against Italy immediately, pending the outcome of cease-fire negotiations between London and the Government of Italy. The Ambassador to Rome is seeking an audience with Benito Mussolini today to negotiate the terms of said cease-fire. We all know that that means. Musso will shout and scream, waving his hands like a demented fishwife, then make some appalling threats. That Man will read them and back down, giving Musso everything he wants."

"I know." Wavell spoke mildly. "There is, of course, a small problem with that. I report to both London and Calcutta, and my orders from Calcutta are quite clear. They are to stabilize this area, eliminate any Italian threat to our position here in Egypt and ensure than the Italians will not be able to launch a supporting thrust when the main German attack through Turkey and Iraq starts. Tom and Bernard have received more or less similar orders from their governments, with the codicil that they are to subordinate themselves to me."

"A divided command and conflicting orders. The old recipe for disaster. I feel for you, Archie."

"No need to. In the final analysis, I am an Indian Army officer; with the split between London and Calcutta, it is to India that I must look for final authority. If I receive an order like this from Churchill in Ottawa, then I have a problem. At the moment, I do not." Wavell took the telegraph paper, tore it in half and then applied a match to the remains. "Operation Compass starts tonight on schedule. *Warspite* is on the move?"

246

"She is indeed, with a screen of course." Maitland Wilson looked at the charred paper in Wavell's ashtray. "Is it really so easy to break with London? And does Egypt realize it has more or less just joined the British Commonwealth?"

"The Commonwealth of Nations." Wavell corrected Maitland Wilson reprovingly. "There is more to that than just a change in the name, Jumbo."

Maitland Wilson nodded and left to issue the orders needed to start Operation Compass. Behind him, Wavell also stared at the burned paper in his ashtray. It hadn't been easy to break with London at all. Wavell knew his decision this day would haunt him for years to come.

HMS Warspite, *Off Maktila, North Africa*

"Prepare to open fire." Admiral Andrew Cunningham gave the order to Captain Douglas Fisher with a certain degree of relish. He was well aware that orders had been received from London ordering an end to the offensive, but they meant little to him. Wavell had ignored them and ordered Operation Compass to proceed. Cunningham was throwing his lot in with Wavell and the Commonwealth. His 15-inch guns were about to provide the most emphatic repudiation of the Halifax government in London that it was possible to imagine.

"Ready, sir." Fisher saw Cunningham nod and he took the gesture as it was intended. "Main battery open fire on designated targets."

Italian Encampment, Maktila, North Africa

For a brief moment, General Pietro Maletti believed he was back in his childhood, when he had heard the trains passing through his home town of Castiglione delle Stiviere. His earliest memory, one that came from so far back that he could recollect neither time nor context, was of his father lifting him up so he could see the flashing lights of a train passing in the darkness and hear the roar of its passage. The roar overhead was the same overwhelming pitch as those passing trains so many years before. To his shock, it was followed by a rapid series of brilliant flashes of light. He wondered, for one brief second while trapped between sleep and waking, whether he had somehow gone back to his childhood in Lombardy. Then, as the floor of his dugout heaved beneath him, he knew he had not.

The explosions of the shells across the cantonment occupied by Raggruppamento Maletti were drowned out by the thunderous roars of the big shells hitting the Libya Army Group's command positions. Maletti guessed, by the size of the explosions he was seeing, that they were naval gunfire; almost certainly the British battleship that had been reported in Alexandria. She must have left after dusk and proceeded up the coast to carry out this bombardment. It seemed an insane thing to think, but seeing the great balls of fire reaching into the sky from the 15-inch shells made Maletti grateful for the 18-pounders that were rippling across his positions.

This wasn't possible. Maletti was having a hard job forming a mental picture of what was going on. *The British were more than a hundred kilometers away, at Mersah Mutruh, where the infantry forming the Italian front line were gathered. They can't be here. But the guns firing on us are field guns. They have to be here.* A grim lesson was running through his mind, one that had been hammered home by his instructors at Modena but was all too often forgotten. *Amateurs thought surprise was a matter of a radical new weapon or a clever maneuver nobody else had thought of. It wasn't. Surprise is the overwhelming result of the situation changing faster than the victim that can adapt to it. The most commonplace maneuver will produce a devastating surprise if it causes the situation to develop before the victim can react.* Maletti knew he had been surprised.

He forced himself to sit down and think. *Artillery fire means an attack. Field artillery means the attack is coming now. We are far behind our front line, so the forces attacking us must be motorized at the very least. There are tanks coming and tanks mean infantry in support.* As if to confirm the analysis he had just made, the rippling crashes of the fire from the 18-pounders was supplement by a crackle of rifle fire. In an odd way, Maletti welcomed it; for it showed he was getting his mind ahead of the situation. That meant he had the opportunity to do something other than just react. To be trapped into reaction was a sure way of losing a battle.

Maletti got to his feet and headed out of his bunker. Over to his left, he could hear the sound of rifle and machine gun fire backed up by the roar of engines. That was where the attack was centered.

Once he had a view of the situation, he realized just how bad things were. There seemed to be British tanks everywhere. They were advancing slowly but steadily through his outer defenses, crushing down the wire with almost contemptuous disregard. Maletti watched their turrets swinging backwards and forwards. The coaxial machine guns cut down his men as they left their dugouts and tried to get to their tanks. A chill swept him as he realized just how easily he could have been one of them, killed in the early stages of the attack before he had ever brought the situation under control.

Not that he had very much chance of controlling this battle now. He recognized the tanks. *Matildas.* Infantry tanks intended to support an assault on a heavily defended position. Sure enough, there were indeed infantry behind the tanks, swarming over the positions behind the wire and tossing grenades into the foxholes. His eye told him that they were far less experienced than the tank crews; they were going through the drills well enough but they were doing them as drills. They hadn't developed the familiarity that turned drills into a well-executed battle maneuver. Maletti realized it would hardly make much difference now. It was the tanks that were deciding the battle. It was already lost.

How much so was quickly illustrated. Somehow, a crew had reached one of his M11/39 tanks and got it started. The twin machine guns in the turret opened fire. The troops behind the Matildas sprawled for cover. The M11/39 started to turn, to bring its hull-mounted 37mm gun to bear. The movement attracted the attention of the British tanks. Their turreted two-pounders could swing much faster. There was a ripple of flashes. The Italian tank was hit at least half a dozen times. There was a brief, split-second, interval that made Maletti hope that it had somehow survived the tattoo of hits. The eruption of smoke from the stricken vehicle showed such hopes were groundless. Despite being diesel-engined, the M11/39 was burning.

The position was nearly hopeless. Maletti could see that. His two tank battalions were already overrun; he was suffering the humiliation of seeing his tanks captured intact. The Matildas were grinding through his infantry; their inexorable progress marked by the streams of tracer fire cutting down his men as they tried to stop the juggernauts with rifle fire. There was only one hope left, his artillery. Firing over open sights, they might be able to stop the Matildas.

By the time he reached the artillery position, the Matildas and their infantry had already overwhelmed the rest of his camp. The survivors of his six infantry battalions had retreated to the guns as well. They were forming a perimeter around the 65mm howitzers. This was the last ditch. Maletti knew it; the only hope of holding it was the guns of his artillery battalion. The Matildas had seen the way the Italian infantry had fallen back to consolidate their position. They changed their majestic progress through the camp to assault it. Once again, the streams of tracers lashed through the darkness. They raked any defensive positions that revealed themselves. This time, though, the machine gun fire was answered by the flash of the 65mm artillery pieces. Manetti cheered. One of the first shots struck an advancing Matilda full on its frontal armor.

For a moment, he thought the tank was killed. It stopped. Its turret swung backwards and forwards, as if the tank were trying to clear its head. Then it started moving forward again. Its machine gun sought out the artillery piece that had struck it. Another shell hit square on the front of the turret. That had as little effect as the first hit. Manetti had heard of how the heavily-armored Matildas had plowed through the Germany infantry at Arras. Now he saw it for himself. His 65mm guns were useless. They scored hit after hit on the Matildas, but nothing seemed to stop them. A few were damaged, tracks broken or engines stalled, but he knew they would be repaired.

The lack of damage didn't stop his gunners. They fought their weapons to the muzzle; often firing their last shells at ranges of a few meters, before they and their guns were crushed under the tracks of the British tanks. With the guns methodically destroyed, the tanks swung around. They started to move along the infantry defense lines, crushing the hastily-dug foxholes with their treads. Maletti knew this was pointless slaughter; the ability to make any meaningful defense had died with his guns.

249

He took a white shirt, stabbed it on to a bayonet and waved it in the air.

A Sergeant saw the gesture and advanced carefully, his rifle trained on Maletti. Maletti waved his surrender flag more vigorously. He saw the Sergeant nod. Around them, the battle seemed to pause. "I am General Pietro Maletti, commander of this battlegroup. I ask you to accept the surrender of my command."

"Sergeant Joe Solomon. You'd better talk to my officer."

Around them, the fighting was already dying down. The Italian survivors were being collected together. The sun was rising with the speed typical of a desert dawn. Maletti could see the large number of his men who were being herded into an extemporized detention area.

"Sir, I have a General Maletti here. Says he wants to surrender his command."

"Ah, thank you, Sergeant. Return to your unit."

Maletti looked at the immaculately-dressed brigadier before him and was painfully aware of his dishevelled state. "Brigadier, our position is hopeless and I would like to surrender my command."

"Quite. I accept your surrender, General. I trust we will have no naughty tricks?"

Maletti knew what the British Brigadier meant. The Blackshirt militia divisions had a habit of fake surrenders that served little purpose but increased casualties, mostly their own.

"No tricks, Brigadier. This was a battle honestly won and we will abide by it." Maletti looked at the scene. British trucks were already pulling up and refuelling the Matildas. Crews were gathered around the handful of stalled tanks, repairing damage. "May I ask how many men you lost today?"

"So far, eight officers and 48 men. I'll let you know how many of your men are lost as soon as I find out. All I know is that, so far, we have taken around 2,000 prisoners here."

Maletti did the maths. His command had numbered 2,500 men; at least 500 were dead or wounded and the rest captured. This hadn't been a battle; this was a disaster.

Martin Maryland I G-George, *Over Sidi Barrani, North Africa*

"This beats the old bird."

The voice over the intercom caused Squadron Leader Mannix to lose concentration for a moment. He cursed to himself. The ex-French Martin Maryland had replaced his old Wellesley a few days before. He was still trying to get used to the American-built aircraft. Normally, he would have had a conversion course lasting months. These were not normal times. An American civilian pilot from the Glenn L. Martin Corporation had familiarized him with the cockpit and the aircraft's general layout; then Mannix had been left to his own devices. It didn't help that the aircraft was so cramped that his first flight in the Maryland had, by definition, been solo. He'd left his crew behind, in case it was also his last flight in a Maryland.

He'd been relieved to find out that, while the Maryland was a hot ship, it was also docile and relatively easy to fly. It cruised 20mph faster than the maximum speed of his old Wellesley and carried twice the bombload. It was also much better armed; four fixed forward-firing machine guns instead of one, and two machine guns aft in each of the upper and lower positions. Better still, he had a dedicated bombardier in the glazed nose. It was the new man, Warrant Officer Charles Cussans, who had interrupted his concentration.

"Have you sighted the target, Cussans?"

Mannix's voice was icy. In the rear turret, his gunner cringed. Many people claimed to run a taut ship; Mannix was one of the few who actually did. An icy question was usually the prelude to an impressive dressing-down.

"Dead ahead. Yanks make a good bombsight and the view from here is fantastic. Makes the old Bombay seem sick." Cussans sounded positively cheerful and quite oblivious to the trouble he was talking himself into.

Mannix was about to make a sharp reply about chattering on the air when Cussans spoke again. "We need to come to port, about one degree. I'll take the aircraft on five. One . . . two . . . three . . . four . . . five. Pilot, I have the aircraft." The idle chatter had gone from the voice and it was purely professional.

"All aircraft, we are under bombardier control. Form on me; drop when we drop. Gunners, keep a keen eye open. There are CR.42 fighters and reports of some G.50s here."

Mannix scanned the sky around him. One of the problems with the Maryland was that it only had a single gunner to man the two rear firing positions. A little early warning meant the gunner would man either the upper or the lower guns as the situation demanded. Still, there seemed to be no fighters around. *Probably the fighter pilots are still having breakfast, like normal civilized people.*

This time his concentration was broken by an unexpected whine. It was the bomb bay doors opening. RAF aircraft had their bomb bay doors on rubber bungee cords but the Maryland had doors that were opened mechanically. The aircraft lurched as four 500-pound bombs dropped from the bay. The whine was repeated as the bomb bay doors closed.

"Pilot, I will return the aircraft to you on five. One . . . two . . . three . . . . four . . . five. Pilot, you have the aircraft. My God, look at that!"

Far below them, the parking area at the Zauiet airfield erupted in a mass of explosions. Mannix assessed them coldly. It was a nice, tight pattern; well-placed on the parking apron. With a little luck, the bomb pattern had done a lot of damage. He wondered how well the other flights of 47 Squadron had done. These raids were supposed to keep the Italian Air Force's heads down, so the armored column attacking the Sidi Barrani area would be free of Italian air attack.

He was turning the Maryland as quickly as he could, given the tight formation of aircraft. The Italian gunners had woken up at last. There was a scattering of black puffs around them. *I wonder if they thought we were SM.79s?* The first series of bursts were way off target. The second were much closer; near enough to cause the Maryland to jolt.

"Any damage?"

The firing ceased. There was relief from the crews as they reported in. A couple of the aircraft had minor fragment damage, but none seemed seriously hurt and there were no casualties on board. It was quite a change from the earlier raid in Eritrea.

Mannix relaxed slightly for the haul back to Alexandria. That meant he could attend to other business.

"Bombardier. That was a good pattern. Well done."

"Thank you, sir." The chatty tone was back in his voice.

"And, in future, do not use the intercom for anything other than essential communications. I don't want a fighter to get us because the spotting report got lost in chatter. Natter away like that on the comms again, and you will walk home. Do we understand each other?"

"Yes, sir; perfectly, sir. No more chatter, sir." Cussans still managed to sound enthusiastic.

Mannix shut off the intercom and shook his head. *Times are changing; all too quickly.*

United States Embassy, Bangkok, Thailand

"Is there any reply from the French authorities?"

Cordell Hull was not accustomed to being ignored. Two days before, he had sent a diplomatic telegram to the French colonial authorities in Hanoi; one suggesting a conference to discuss issues in the region and offering his services as a mediator. So far, the only reply had been a deafening silence.

"No, sir."

Hugh Gladney Grant, American Envoy Extraordinary and Minister Plenipotentiary to the Kingdom of Thailand, sounded frustrated. Normally, this Embassy was considered something of a backwater, as indicated by his official title. According to the State Department, Thailand didn't rate an Ambassador Extraordinary, merely an Envoy. Grant had a bad feeling they were making a mistake.

"Not even an acknowledgement. I must admit that is one pleasant thing about doing business here, sir; the Siamese are meticulous about courtesy."

"So I noticed. That woman who organized their side of this visit has turned common courtesy into an uncommonly beautiful art form. I don't trust her further than I can throw the limousine she rides in. Who is she?"

"That's an odd thing." Grant thought carefully. "She appeared on the scene about six months ago, but our inquiries have shown her position goes back a lot further than that. She's the direct representative of the Royal Family and has a lot of power as a result. Her role seems to be to present the opinions of the Royal Family, without involving them directly in any dispute. We've tried to do some research on her, but all we can find out is that her position is hereditary, passed down from mother to daughter. How far it goes back, we have no idea. It seems as if her existence was unknown outside a small circle until very recently. Those who were in that circle don't say anything."

Grant hesitated. The story he was about to tell sounded foolish, yet he thought it was important. "A few weeks ago, we were walking in the Palace gardens; not far from here. Discussing the situation with the aircraft they ordered, in fact. Anyway, we turned a corner and there was a king cobra on the path in front of us, just resting in the sun. Huge brute; at least ten feet long and we had angered it. It reared up, spreading its hood. The king cobra is deadly, sir. It injects so much venom with each bite that survival is most unlikely. I was about to run away, but she just stood there, looking at it. The cobra dropped its hood and slithered away. Afterwards, she told me that the members of her family had a truce with the king cobras. Neither would attack the other, except in self-defense. She said it was probably superstitious rubbish and that cobras tended to back off from confrontations with humans. But, she added that in a thousand years, no member of her family had ever hurt a king cobra or been bitten by one. So, we know her family is that old."

"If she is telling the truth, of course." Hull sounded skeptical.

"There is always that. But, if it is true, it means that for generations her family has kept an agreement they believed in. That's worth bearing in mind."

Hull nodded. There was a knock on the door. Colonel Jude Roland Wilford entered the meeting room, carrying the latest newspapers. "Mister Secretary? Envoy Grant? I have the latest newspapers from home. They came across on the Clipper to Manila and were flown here from there."

"Anything interesting, Jude?" Grant had seen the diplomatic cables, of course, but the newspapers all too often had better information earlier.

"South Africans continuing to advance in Ethiopia, supported by widespread native uprisings. Indians doing the same in Eritrea, sans uprising. There's a huge battle going on close to the Egyptian border between the Australians and the Italians."

"Wait a moment," Hull was confused, "I thought the Italians were deep inside Egypt?"

"They are."

Wilford's voice was a mixture of awe and professional admiration. "The Australians are behind them. If the reports in the *Post* are correct, and their foreign staff is pretty good, they've broken through to the coast and encircled some 80,000 Italian troops. That means they're outnumbered four or five to one, yet are on the verge of taking the Italian Army apart. It's the most remarkable victory since . . . "

Wilford hesitated, "I can't think of a parallel. Cannae, perhaps. Anyway, there are also reports of air strikes all over the region. The Italians are taking a hammering in the air. The Aussies, Indians and South Africans are putting the aircraft we gave them to good use."

Hull snorted. "And what is Halifax's reaction to all this?"

"That's the confusing bit. The information we have is that the afternoon before the attack started, the London government approached Rome and offered an Armistice. Word from our embassy there is that the Italians are furious, regarding the offer as a ruse de guerre." Grant shook his head. If those accounts were true, the blow to the diplomatic credibility of the Halifax regime was profound.

There was another knock on the door. A young woman clerk came in, carrying a message flimsy. She looked around, confused by the presence of Cordell Hull. Grant waved to her and took the flimsy. As he read it, his eyebrows rose in surprise.

"Mister Secretary." Grant's voice was strained and formal. "This is the reply from the French Colonial authorities to your message of two days ago. They state that it is not their policy to discuss any issues with the Kingdom of Thailand and that their opinions and decisions are final. They add that there is no room for any form of mediation and that the normal reply will be given directly to the Thai authorities."

Hull pursed his lips. The flat rejection wasn't just uncompromising; it was also bereft of any diplomatic niceties. In fact, it was downright insulting.

2/1st Battalion (Australian), West of Sidi Barrani, Egypt

"What's the word, Sarge?"

Sergeant Joe Solomon looked at the speaker quizzically. "Well, 'hot' might be a good one. I'm partial to 'dingo' myself. You have any particular words you're especially fond of?"

A theatrical groan went around the temporary bivouac beside their lorry. Dobson flushed with embarrassment. The battalion was having a brief rest after the capture of the Italian camps at Nibeiwa and Tummar. Behind them, the rest of the 7th Armoured and 6th Australian divisions were pouring through the gap cut through the Italian positions. The 16th Infantry Brigade was establishing a perimeter to their east. The road underneath the 2/1st's lorries didn't look like much, but it was the main one that led from Sidi Barrani to Buq Buq. With the Australians sitting on top of it, the entire leading edge of the Italian North African Army was cut off in a pocket that ran from Sidi Barrani to Mersah Matruh.

Solomon had no idea how many men were trapped in that pocket. He did know that there were a lot, and that they had only the supplies they carried with them. Most particularly, that meant water. Every drop drunk by both armies had to be brought up from a rear base. For the Australians, that was Alexandria; but they had the Misheifa railway to bring it. The Italians had to use the ports at Bardia and Tobruk, and there was only the road now blocked for them to use. Thirsty might be a good word for the Italians to get to like.

The tea was ready. Solomon had his cuppa; thick with condensed milk and sweet with added sugar. The Commonwealth, as it was, had gone; who knew what would replace it. But, as long as there was plenty of tea, everything would be all right in the end.

"Of course, tea is a pretty good word too. Right, boys?"

There was a stir of appreciation at that while the men slurped down the precious nectar. Idly, Solomon wondered what their Italian opposite numbers were doing and whether the full extent of the disaster had dawned on them yet. *Surely it has,* he thought. *If a sergeant sitting in the arse-end of nowhere can see it, they must be able to. Three days, I reckon, four at most and the poor Eye-ties will have their tongues hanging out. If what's left of their army can't break through to relieve them, they're done for.*

"Where do you think we'll be going next, Sarge?"

Private Dobson had learned from his mistake and phrased the question much more carefully this time. *A lesson learned,* Solomon thought to himself. *Confusion and vagueness gets people killed.*

"West." Solomon had been in the militia for years before transferring to the expeditionary force; he could see how the situation had to develop. "We've got half the Eye-tie army bottled up behind us. The only hope they've got is for the rest to break through and relieve them. The brass will want the encirclement ring as thick as possible to make sure they don't pull it off. The last thing they'll want is a single battalion holding off an assault all by itself. So, we'll go west. In fact, I reckon the pommy tanks are already heading that way."

"The Tillies ain't." Another private had finished his tea and was sanding out his mug.

"Tilly ain't going anywhere fast." Dobson spoke with certainty. "We can walk faster than them."

"Yeah, but see them go at Nibbi? Waddled forward with wop shells just bouncing off them. All we had to do was follow them in. Reckon they deserves their rest."

Solomon nodded to himself as he finished his tea. The stunning victories at Nibeiwa and Tummar had him slightly worried. The boys were enthusiastic enough, but he knew how green they were. They could do a simple 'two-up, one-back and follow the tanks in,' but that was all. They didn't know how much they had to learn. Solomon knew he was slightly better off due to the service with the militia; he knew how much he had to learn. At least some of them also realized how green they were now. The rout of the Italians at Nibeiwa could easily have made them over-confident. It still could; when the memory of the Matildas grinding through the Italian defenses, shrugging off the shots from the Italian anti-tank guns, had faded.

"Sergeant, get the men mounted up. We've been ordered to follow the road west. Fourth Armored Brigade has reached the second 'B' in Buq Buq and we're needed to hold the ground they've taken. Solomon, a word please."

Solomon had the men breaking their bivouac and getting the gear stowed while he turned to his officer. "Sir?"

"Joe, load your wagon up with as much in the way of supplies as you can scrounge. Buq Buq is just the start. I think we'll be going on to Bardia and possibly all the way to Tobruk. God knows when we'll get a chance to resupply next."

"Will do, sir." Solomon watched his officer move across to the next bivvy and repeat the orders.

I just hope the brass don't get overconfident as well.

GHQ, Middle East Command, Cairo, Egypt

'I hope we're not biting off more than we can chew here."

Wavell looked at the situation map with something close to disbelief. The huge Italian Army that had been threatening Egypt was split in two, with the largest portion trapped inside Egypt. Its vast supply dumps were already in Allied hands. The spearhead of the attack was broadening by the hour as the cruiser tanks of the Fourth Armored Brigade chewed westwards, forcing the two parts of the Italian Army further and further apart. Looking at the two sausages that indicated the Italian positions, Wavell was reminded of a worm that had been chopped in half.

"Oh, we are." Maitland Wilson spoke with what Wavell could only describe as unholy relish. "The situation on the ground is ridiculous, bordering on the absurd. I'd guess our opposite numbers in Tripoli and Rome are in a state of denial right now. What they're seeing can't be happening; at least, not to a conventional way of thinking. On the other hand, if they realize that leg infantry just don't matter in this kind of war, then it all makes sense."

"What's the score so far?" Wavell was still fascinated by the situation on the map.

Maitland Wilson shuffled his reports. "So far, we have reports of 73 Italian tanks and 37 artillery pieces being destroyed or captured and approximately 8,300 Italian soldiers killed or captured. Our losses to date are 18 Matilda tanks disabled, but all have been recovered and are repairable. The Australians lost 21 officers and 194 men killed and wounded. The real problem is going to be when the Sidi Barrani pocket collapses, which it will do in a few days time. That will throw some 80,000 Italian prisoners into our lap. We're already capturing huge supply dumps and there are more to come. Bernie Freyberg's New Zealanders are in heaven. They've motorized themselves on Italian-made trucks and they've now got a tank battalion with thirty-odd Italian M11/39 tanks."

"I see a problem there."

"So do I, Archie; two, in fact. One is the one you're thinking of: they'll get shot up by mistake. So far, they're being kept well back from the front line as GHQ reserve to avoid just that happening. The other is that all that Italian kit is diesel-engined and we don't have much diesel fuel available. I suggest we send them to Palestine; guard our back door, as it were. The French in Syria don't look kindly on us at all. The Kiwis are as green as the proverbial grass, so the more time they get to shake down, the better."

Wavell nodded thoughtfully. With considerable effort, he tore his eyes away from the situation on the North African coast to take in what was happening elsewhere in his region. Italian resistance in Ethiopia was collapsing as the Indian and South African troops moved in to support the tribes that had risen in revolt. Another Indian division was hammering on the gates of Asmara in Eritrea. Palestine and Syria were the only unguarded sections of the region and they offered scope for his New Zealand troops to settle down. "Good idea, Jumbo; make it so. You know what will happen next, don't you?"

"The Italians will try to break through to relieve the troops we've cut off? Archie, they've got 50,000 or 60,000 men left in Cyrenaica, mostly around Bardia and Tobruk. They're just more leg infantry; they can't go anywhere. In fact, I'm getting a mobile group ready to put them in the bag. I'm using the 11th Hussars with their armored cars as the core, with a battalion of lorried infantry and some artillery. I'm planning to send the Australians along the coast road to keep pressure on the Italians in Bardia and Tobruk, while the mobile group goes across the neck of Cyrenaica, south of the Green Mountains. There's some desert tracks that can be used; they'll take the column by way of Bir el Gubi and Bir Hacheim to end up on the coast just north of El Agheila. Place called Beda Fomm. We'll block there and the whole Italian North African Army will be gone. There'll be nothing between us and Tripoli."

Wavell stared at the map, following the movements with his eyes. "Don't count on that, Jumbo. The Italian generals aren't stupid; they'll be learning fast from this debacle. You can bet they've seen the threat to Tripolitania and are moving their forces around to block any thrust we make. The geography of Cyrenaica is a gift to us but once we're past it, we won't be able to pull a similar operation again. And, with Cyrenaica behind us, it's just as much of a trap for us.

"Also, they'll be moving reinforcements in. Sending some to Tripoli, no doubt, but you can bet your life they'll be trying to move tanks into Tobruk.

257

When the Cyrenaica force tries its breakout, they'll have tanks to support them."

"Unless Andy Cunningham's fleet stops them." Maitland Wilson didn't sound that hopeful.

"Unless he does." Wavell agreed.

Martin Maryland I G-George, *Over the Mediterranean, Near Taranto*

"Anything down there?"

Mannix called down to Charlie Cussans, who was responsible for taking the photographs. It had finally dawned on somebody that the Maryland's combination of range and speed, along with a high cruising altitude, made it an excellent reconnaissance aircraft. Mannix missed having the other members of his flight around him, but drew comfort from the fact that his Maryland was 20 miles per hour faster than the Italian monoplane fighters. Up at 15,000 feet, the brass had assured him that he would be safe from interception.

He had, however, noticed that none of them were on the aircraft.

"Nothing." Cussans had learned his lesson from the first flight; he kept his reports clipped and to the point. From 15,000 feet, ships were but tiny stick-like outlines. It was still painfully obvious that the Italian fleet was not at home. They'd been told to expect at least four battleships, half a dozen heavy cruisers and two dozen or more destroyers and light cruisers. Nothing like that fleet was in the great kidney-shaped harbor of Taranto.

Mannix swung *G-George* away from the harbor. There would be heavy flak guns down there and he didn't want to try conclusions with them. As if to reinforce his caution, a few black puffs of smoke flowered ahead of him. *Right for altitude and directly on our course,* Mannix noted. *Whoever the gunners are down there, they know their business. If I hadn't changed course, we'd be in trouble.*

"Sean, hold that report. There's one battleship down there; looks like she's in drydock." Cussans was staring through the high magnification setting on his bombsight. It was more effective that the binoculars he'd been using, although the field of vision was far less. "And two cruisers; light ones. They're not where we were told, though; they're in the outer basin. Along with six, no, make that seven, destroyers."

"South side of the outer basin?"

Mannix had studied the map of Taranto before taking off from Malta on his way here. He'd memorized the layout of the port as best he could and was trying to visualize where the ships left in harbor were.

"All of them. That's the naval arsenal, I think."

"It is. Well done, Charlie. Now, lets get the hell out of here and back to Malta before those gunners have another crack at us. Wherever the Eye-tie fleet is, it isn't here. They're out."

Balcony, Government House, Calcutta, India

"Now that is an early Christmas present I can really welcome."

The Marquess of Linlithgow looked up at the formation of aircraft flying overhead. Although he didn't actually recognize the aircraft, he knew what they were from the briefing he had received. Mohawk IV fighters led the formation; four neat flights of four that formed a diamond in the sky. The lead fighter was flown by an American civilian advisor called Boyington; the rest by the Indian pilots of No.1 Squadron. They had just finished their conversion program and were making this flypast before being assigned to a new operational base in Northern India. At long last, India had fighter defenses. One of the gaping holes in its military infrastructure was being slowly filled in.

"An independent India; defended by Indian fighter pilots. A year ago, I could only dream of this."

Pandit Nehru looked at the squadron of DB-7 bombers that were following the fighters over Calcutta. Long a proponent of massive reductions in India's armed forces, he found himself thinking differently now that the aircraft flying overhead and the troops parading through the city served India, not Britain. It was symptomatic of the way his thinking had changed over the last six months.

Once he had seen the British as interlopers and foreign adventurers; ones whose motivations were, at best, equivocal and whose absence was urgently demanded. Now, he realized that they had been doing their best in an honest, if sometimes misguided, effort to rule India fairly. He also realized just how complex the modern world was and how out-of-place in it India would have been, had its old governing system continued. For all their faults, he realized, India could have done much worse than spend a few years under British rule.

"Our second fighter squadron will be going down to Ceylon to protect the Trincomalee naval base." Linlithgow repeated the news he had been given with relish. Many of the RAF pilots from the six squadrons based in India had volunteered for secondment to Indian units. In theory, they were simply providing the Dominion squadrons with a cadre of experienced pilots and would return to the RAF units as soon as the Indian Air Force squadrons had gained enough experience to stand on their own feet.

In reality, Linlithgow knew that their motives were more mixed than that. There was an element of envy in it. The Indian Air Force squadrons were getting the new American fighters and bombers; ones that made the Wapitis, Audaxes and Blenheims in the British squadrons seem antiquated. Pilots were pilots; they wanted to fly the better aircraft.

There was more to it than that though. Even a desire not to be stained by Halifax's collapse wasn't all there was to it. It was the idea of India itself. There was something about the country that, after a few years here, worked its way into a man's soul.

259

"And we must send more forces to the Middle East as well." Nehru spoke again as the roar of aircraft engines from the fly-past died away. He confused himself there as well; the fall of Keren to the Indian troops advancing on Asmara had caused jubilation. *The Times of India* had even called it a "re-affirmation of traditional Indian martial values." Privately, Nehru had thought that was going a bit far, but there was no doubt the achievements of the Indian Army in Eritrea and Ethiopia were establishing India as an independent country in the eyes of the world. Soon, more Indian troops and aircraft would be in Iraq and Iran; providing a forward line of defense against the German Army, when the Noth Plan finally got into high gear.

"We have had word from Churchill's government in Ottawa. They've issued a statement confirming that standing orders prior to June 1940 are still in force and that DomCol forces around the world and British forces along with them are to continue fighting, ignoring any ceasefire orders that come out of occupied London. That eases the situation on our guests, of course."

Nehru nodded at Linlithgow's words. The ambivalent status of the British forces in the Dominions was a source of running concern to everybody. Now, at least, they had some semblance of authority to link their chosen actions to. "Of course, the question is, can London be considered occupied at this time?"

"I don't know," Linlithgow suddenly sounded very old, very tired and utterly broken-hearted. Quietly, Nehru cursed himself for causing the man who had done so much for India such distress on what should have been a happy day. "I never thought, never dreamed, that I would see a day like this. Halifax's Armistice is against everything that I thought we stood for."

"Look overhead; Hudsons of the Indian Naval Air Force. India stands on its own feet today and we stand for the ideals Britain taught us. We may be going our own way, Victor, but we still stand for them. The Empire still stands for them all. Britain taught us well and we will hold to those lessons. In us, Britain lives on; in time, we will bring her back to life again." Nehru meant the words as meaningless comfort to a distressed friend; but, as he spoke them, he suddenly realized he believed every one of them.

CHAPTER TEN

HEATED WORDS

Pilot's Briefing Room, HMS **Eagle**, *At Sea, Off Gavdos*

"I see you're off to for your afternoon nap. Could I organize a nice cup of cocoa for you?"

The remark sounded impertinent; but, in truth, the Swordfish pilots heading for the briefing room were definitely on the old side compared with the young lieutenants from the ship's company. But, there was a reason for that. They were hard-core Fleet Air Arm veterans; ones who had started their careers flying the long-forgotten Blackburn Baffin and the almost equally obscure Blackburn Shark. They were low-ranked for their age and service careers; a residual effect of the limited career prospects in a Fleet Air Arm dominated by the Royal Air Force. Yet they had been quietly and diligently pursuing their craft throughout the lean years of the 1930s. The eighteen Swordfish crews on *Eagle* were probably the finest torpedo bomber pilots in the world. It was a pity their equipment still didn't match their skills.

"Cheeky little bastard." Lieutenant James MacFleet growled at the impudent snottie who had dared to remark upon his comparatively advanced age. The youngster stepped to one side as MacFleet bore down upon him. Inside the briefing room, all eighteen Swordfish crews were assembling.

"Gentlemen, settle down please." Captain Stuart Munroe tapped his podium with a pointer. "We have a critical mission to perform. We have been informed by Maryland reconnaissance aircraft that the Italian battle fleet is out. A Maryland from Malta confirmed that they had left Taranto yesterday evening and this morning we got confirmation that they are heading our way. They were reported south of Zakynthos at 0920; course one-three-five, speed 20 knots. The Maryland reported three battleships, four heavy cruisers and eight destroyers. If that formation holds course and speed, they will be eighty-three miles west of us at 1300. According to our current plans, that is when you gentlemen will sink them. All of them, for preference. I need not tell you that Britain needs a cheerful Christmas present right now."

MacFleet looked around. Eighteen crews and fifteen ships didn't augur well for the wholesale destruction Munroe appeared to be expecting. "Sir, am I to assume that the battleships will be the priority targets?"

Munroe shook his head. "No. The situation is this. The group we will be attacking are the covering force for a large convoy heading for North Africa. There are at least twenty of Italy's largest merchant ships in that convoy and their loss will be a massive blow to the Italian ability to support operations in North Africa. In addition, there are ships carrying an armored group of the Italian Army. Those ships will split away later on and head for Benghazi, while the supply ships head for Tobruk. It will be the job of *Warspite* and her cruiser-destroyer group to make sure they do not get there. To do that, we need to clear that covering force out of the way. It is not necessary to sink all the ships in that group, just hurt them badly enough to send them home. We want hits made on as many ships as possible; not a lot of hits on a few of them. Is that clear."

"Sir. Enemy fighter cover?"

"As far as we can determine, there will be none. Technically we will be just in range of land-based fighters, but coordination between Italian ships at sea and aircraft based on land does not appear to be good. The Marylands are reporting no fighter interference."

"Sir, do we have any information on which ships are in the group?" The leader of B-flight, Lieutenant Colwyn Caradoc, was Welsh through and through. His accent added something undefinably melodic to the briefing. It also made a number of the pilots feel homesick. They were all aware that the split between Britain and the rest of the Empire meant it could be a long time before they went home.

"Our information is that it includes the battleships *Andrea Doria, Caio Duilio* and *Conte di Cavour.* Heavy cruisers *Bolzano, Zara, Fiume* and *Gorizia.* That's what the Marylands say, anyway." Munroe added the comment quickly. The ability of RAF crews to recognize warships was not one of their most advanced capabilities. "We don't know who the destroyers are. One thing I must stress, if *Warspite* and the group with her can get into the Italian convoy, it will be a catastrophe for the Italians. Not just in terms of ships and supplies sunk, but in the position that their troops in Italy will be left holding. Headquarters now believes almost 100,000 of their men are cut off along the coast between Mektila and Mersah Matruh. They will have to surrender within three or four days at the most, unless a relief effort can be mounted. Every day that passes means that relief effort gets more difficult. We had news this morning that the Australians are moving into Bardia. If that city falls, then the nearest port to the Italians will be Tobruk. We believe that is why the merchant ships are heading for there; the Italians evidently believe that Bardia cannot hold out."

Munroe stopped speaking as a messenger from the Signals Division entered with a message flimsy. He took it and read the contents. A slow smile of satisfaction spread across his face.

"Gentlemen, I am pleased to inform you that the Italian battleships are continuing to head south at a somewhat higher speed of advance than originally thought. They are currently off Cape Methoni, some 120 miles north west of us. "

He turned to the map behind him and marked the latest position report on the chart. Then, he drew the connecting line joining their position to that of *Eagle* and her four escorting destroyers. The navigators in the crews quickly noted down the positions and the course needed for the intercept.

"We have 15 Swordfish ready to launch and will hold the remaining three, plus our three Sea Gladiators, in reserve. Man your aircraft, gentlemen; we launch immediately."

Outskirts of Bardia, Libya, North Africa

"There are how many Eye-ties in there?" Sergeant Joe Solomon couldn't quite believe what he was hearing.

"About 45,000, so the big brass says." Lieutenant Garry Oswin repeated the numbers he had been given. "With thirteen tanks and about a hundred machine gun carriers. And nearly 300 guns; ranging from our old friend the 65mm mountain howitzer to 150mm heavy guns. All defending an 18-mile perimeter."

"Strewth." Solomon was surprised at the sheer size of the force that was trapped in Bardia. "And we're attacking it with a single battalion?"

"Not us, Joe. Our part in this is a demonstration. The 16th Brigade will be doing the real work, hitting the defenses on the western end of the perimeter. They get the Tillies supporting them. Our job is to draw the attention of the Italian defenses here, in the east. We've got some porteed two-pounders to back us up if the Eye-tie tanks show up. We're not supposed to get into a real fight though. Just prevent the Eye-ties from moving any of their troops westwards."

Solomon snorted, guessing that limiting a fight was hoping for too much. He was about to say so when he was interrupted by an express train roar; one he recognized as inbound 15-inch gunfire. "You didn't say we had battlewagons in support, sir."

"We haven't. That's the monitor *Terror* and three gunboats. They were in the Red Sea, but they came through the Canal and have been moving up to support us. Should even things up a little, I reckon. Especially since we captured the plans of this place at Sidi Barrani. We know the exact positions of each one of those bunkers." Oswin grinned at his Sergeant. "And if the Navy don't get them all, we've got more of our own artillery in place. The new 25-pounders, no less. We may be a demonstration, but we're not lacking for support. Anyway, get your men ready to move out, Joe, on the whistle."

Solomon carefully looked at the ground he and his men would have to cross. There was a continuous anti-tank ditch, with a steep, 200-foot embankment on the opposite side. The slope was festooned with barbed wire and heavily mined. Once at the top, there were company- and platoon-sized strongpoints with anti-tank and machine guns. Each of them had its own anti-tank ditch and there was a second line of strongpoints behind them. All in all, it was a well-designed defensive system.

Solomon was glad he and his men wouldn't have to fight their way through it. All they had to do was to reach the ditch, then use the captured Italian picks and shovels they'd been issued to break down the banks. That would convince the Italians that the Matildas were coming. They would have to move their own forces to match them. Stories of the battles further east and the sight of invincible Matildas plowing through the defenses had spread worldwide; the Matilda was now an iconic image of the war being fought here in the desert.

The huge roar of the 15-inch shells seemed to slacken slightly. The three gunboats more than made up for that by hammering a rapid tattoo of six-inch shells into the Italian defenses. Overhead, Solomon heard the drone of a Lysander circling to spot for the artillery fire. As if the sound was the signal for the attack, a blast of whistles ran along the front. The Australian infantry rose to surge forward. Solomon yelled out "Come on you lazy bastards, we've got some digging to do." There was little need for it. His men were already up and out of their jump-off positions.

By the time they reached the anti-tank ditch, the Italians were beginning to return fire. There was dead ground from rifle and machine gun fire at the foot of the escarpment, but the 65mm howitzers in the strongpoints at the top dropped shells on to the infantry beneath. Solomon's men were hard at work. Their picks broke up the hardened sand of the trench sides. Others with shovels spread the dirt out to form ramps for the tanks that they hoped the Italians believed were coming.

The light cracks of the 65mm guns were supplemented by the roar of the Italian big guns. A bit down the line from Solomon's platoon, 150mm shells slammed into a group of Australians who were working on another section of the ditch. Those that weren't killed outright were buried in the sand as the shells caved the walls in on them.

"Screw this for a game of soldiers. Up and at 'em, lads."

Solomon didn't know who had yelled out the words, but its effects were immediate. His men dropped their picks and shovels. They started climbing the embankment. Some grabbed the posts of the wire entanglements to help them make the ascent.

"Stop, get back here!"

Lieutenant Oswin shouted the command. He was speaking to the backs of his platoon, already swarming up the slope. He shook his head and looked at Solomon helplessly. "We're in command here. I suppose we'd better follow them."

"Just as safe to go forward as back," Solomon agreed. He followed his officer up the slope. The platoons on either side of them had already seen his men starting the climb up; they dropped their tools to follow suit. Off to their left, there was a break in the embankment where the coast road led into Bardia. It was blocked by barbed wire entanglements and a concrete redoubt. The roadblock was already under assault from the Australians. Whatever the brass had thought about this being a simple demonstration, it was turning into a full-blooded assault on what was probably the most heavily defended part of the Italian perimeter.

It was a hard climb up the embankment. Solomon was gasping for breath by the time he reached the top. When he got there, he could see that the Italians had made a bad mistake. The two rows of strongpoints were individually well-sited, but there was too much space between them. They weren't mutually supporting. Each could be isolated from assistance and taken.

There was a well-established drill for that. Each position would be subjected to six-round concentrations from the artillery, while the infantry moved into place. Then, the Bren gunners would keep the defender's heads down. The grenadiers would move up and start lobbing grenades into the defenses. The concrete walls would keep the fragments in and turn the positions into death traps. With the defenses silenced by the grenades, the riflemen and Bren gunners would move in and take the position. It was a simple drill; well-tried and very effective.

The Australians were having none of it.

They were simply swarming forward, overwhelming the strongpoints with a mad rush. They jumped the concrete walls and killed the defenders with the bayonet. Solomon was appalled. All it would need to turn this situation into a blood-drenched catastrophe was a single Italian officer with the presence of mind to take a brief pause, compose himself and launch a coordinated counter-attack. The Australians would be caught out in the open, between the hammer of the counter-attack and the anvil of the remaining strongpoints. They'd be lucky to escape with just a massacre. About the only good thing at this point was that the gunfire from offshore had stopped. The Lysander crew overhead must have seen what was happening and radioed an emergency cease-fire order through to the ships.

Solomon was already up with his men, trying to bring them into some sort of order and start the process of reducing the strongpoints in a rational manner. By which, he meant according to the book. He was quick to realize that the book had already been thrown out of the window. Nothing he or Lieutenant Oswin could do would get it back. The only hope now was to keep up the momentum of the assault and not give the Italian officer he feared the moment he would need to get control of the battle.

A brief look around told him two things. One was the tiny number of figures in khaki lying on the ground. For all the insanity of the assault, so far, the casualties were remarkably few. The other was that the Australian breakthrough was spreading sideways, ripping an ever-larger hole in the Italian defenses. Already, the coastal road was being opened up as the defenses fell to simultaneous attacks from front and rear.

Then Solomon saw what he dreaded. Italian tanks. At least a half-dozen of them rumbled towards the milling mass of Australians. His men had no anti-tank guns; nothing that could stop them. *Now it's our turn*, he thought; remembering how the Matildas had crushed the Italian infantry under their treads. The tanks continued to advance. Solomon tried to get his men under control and into the overrun Italian fortifications. *There might be anti-tank guns or rifles there. Now that's a slim hope at best.*

Over on his left, a Bren gun carrier had seen the risk. It tried to engage one of the tanks with a peppering of machine gun fire. *Gallant but useless. He doesn't stand a chance.*

One of the Italian tanks fired its turret gun. The Bren gun carrier exploded into a ball of flame. That told Solomon something else. The tanks were M13/40s; better armed and armored than the M11/39s they'd faced earlier. *This time, there are no Matildas here to help.*

That made it all the more surprising when one of the M13/40s stopped, black smoke belching from its engine compartment. After briefly contemplating the possibility the sight represented divine intervention, Solomon realized that the portees with their two-pounders had arrived. *They must have made it up the road*, he thought Anti-tank shots snapped out across the battlefield, knocking out one tank after another. Solomon could only see a single portee, but its gun destroyed four of the M13/40s. Then it was hit, silencing the gun.

A second portee entered the battle. It knocked out a fifth tank, sending a cloud of black smoke high into the sky. That portee was destroyed by fire from the sixth tank; the third portee soon knocked the remaining M13/40 out.

The tanks being knocked out in quick succession broke the remaining Italian infantry. They started surrendering as the Australians swarmed through the remaining defenses. The Italian line caved in completely; the way to Bardia was open.

Solomon led his men forward towards the Italian rear area. An Italian soldier, on one of the strongpoints that had been overrun but not cleared, pulled himself out of the ruins. He took over a Breda light machine gun that had been left there. He fired just three rounds before the machine gun jammed. Two hit Joe Solomon in the back, killing him instantly.

GHQ, Middle East Command, Cairo, Egypt

"The strongest position on the western side of the perimeter, with the Italians dug in deep along the top of a wadi, tons of wire, MG's etc, above an 'unclimable' slope and the battalion went straight through them on nothing but pluck, pride and ignorance. God bless the buggers."

Wavell spoke with something very close to reverential awe. The initial reports from the assault on Bardia were in. They told a very different story from the carefully choreographed plan that had been evolved to counter a

266

resolute defense. The battle had descended into chaos, with multiple assaults breaking through the Italian defenses in a variety of directions. It was truly chaotic; a battle with no discernable shape or form.

Wavell had little doubt that in years to come, the historians would draw lines on a map and explain how the various attacks were supporting each other. They might even speculate as to what his basic plan had been. Wavell knew the truth, though; his basic plan had been thrown out of the window within minutes of the attack starting. The battle was being shaped by the troops on the ground. Privately, he had no objection to that. In the swirling madhouse that was the assault on Bardia, the Italian defenses were dissolving.

"We had some problems with 17th Brigade's assault."

Maitland Wilson was having a hard time making up his mind about the formless battle that had developed. On one hand, he gloried in the sheer audacity with which the offensive was shredding the Italian Army. What had been intended as a mere raid for supplies and a spoiling action against a later Italian attack was turning into a major offensive that was ripping apart the Italian position in North Africa. On the other hand, if the Italians got their act together, the situation could swing the other way with frightening speed. "They got pinned down by artillery for a while and took a lot of casualties. The battalion support company eventually got the attack moving and they broke through."

Maitland Wilson hesitated for a moment. The next part was difficult. "We're taking a lot of prisoners, Archie; thousands of them, in fact. We're getting the problems of false surrenders again, though. That led to a bad do all around at Strongpoint 24. A company of the 2/7th, backed up by a couple of Matildas, were attacking the position when the Italians hoisted the white flag. As the prisoners were rounded up, one shot the company commander dead, then threw down his rifle and climbed out of the position; smiling broadly, by all accounts.

"The troops didn't like that, Archie; not at all. They took the law into their own hands. They shot the bugger with a full magazine from a Bren gun, then threw grenades in with the rest of the Italians and bayoneted any survivors."

"Just because an Italian will knife you for suggesting he is not a gentleman, doesn't mean he is one." Wavell thought carefully. "The Italians put up a white flag and *then* our troops were fired on when they came forward to take the surrender?"

"That's one way of putting it, Archie." Maitland Wilson was wary.

"That's how the official report will put it. The Italians opened fire from under the cover of a white flag and the troops returned fire. Unofficially, make sure the troops involved get the riot act read to them. We can't have this sort of thing becoming commonplace. It would have been nice to have hanged that Italian for murder; it might put a stop to this false surrender nonsense." Wavell's voice hardened while he was speaking.

"There's another minor problem. Colonel Godfrey is claiming all the credit for 2/6th Infantry Battalion's assault. Says he saw the opportunity and took advantage of it. Disgraceful case of a CO seeking to make his mark at the expense of his men. Truth is, he lost control of them and they did the job on their own."

"Well. If we take him at his word, the assault he 'planned' was in defiance of the clear instructions he had received, and against all basic military logic and common sense." Wavell hesitated, aware of the operational and political implications of the situation. "That's the trouble with the Australians; they just don't have the experience to season them. Not yet, anyway. An Indian Army battalion wouldn't have gone out of control like that. But, they *did* breach the line; so, we'll leave Godfrey where he is for a while. Jumbo, I want you to have a word with him and haul him over the coals. Get Iven Mackay to speak with him as well. And his brigade commander. You organize the details, Jumbo; you know the drill."

Maitland Wilson smiled grimly. A series of reprimands from ever-more senior officers would ensure that Godfrey never lost control of his men again; or, if he did so, he wouldn't try and seize the credit for their success. Idly, Maitland Wilson wondered what would have happened had the attack been the disaster military logic suggested it should have been. Godfrey would have been quick to blame his junior officers he guessed. *Sly, devious and cunning; the man bears considerable watching.*

"I'll see to it, Archie. 16th and 17th Brigades are through the defenses by now and consolidating. One of the problems is that all the infantry units are severely under strength from detaching PoW guards. Stan Savige's 17th Brigade is spread out too far to do much more at the moment. 16th Brigade will be launching a night attack once they've consolidated, but they'll be exhausted by tomorrow evening. Iven says we need to move 19th Brigade up to reinforce them both."

"He's the man on the spot. Give him a free hand."

Maitland Smith nodded and noted down the order. "Dickie O'Connor says that his flying column is already south of Tobruk; a place called Bir al Ghabi. There's a maze of camel tracks, but the column is steering west by compass. There's a major wadi to the west that is causing some concern, but the column is still expected to make it to Beda Fomm within a week. Then the Italians will have nowhere left to go."

Swordfish Mark I V4373, off Cape Methoni

The flight of a Swordfish could best be described as stately; its evasive maneuvers could only be called majestic. As Lieutenant James MacFleet was all too aware, those characterizations were hardly complimentary when attacking an enemy battlefleet. Even the light patter of anti-aircraft fire coming from the Italian ships seemed to be threatening enough. The volume might be small by British standards, but the closing rate was so slow that the gunners seemed to have plenty of time to correct their aim.

The Swordfish torpedo bombers from *Eagle* were approaching in a wide arc as their scouting line closed in on the Italian ships. MacFleet had a good idea of what they were up against now; the news was only marginally reassuring. There were fewer ships in the formation that the Maryland crews had reported. Three battleships, two heavy cruisers and six destroyers. MacFleet's navigator had already identified the two cruisers as the *Trento* and *Trieste*. Older ships than the heavy cruisers reported by the RAF crews, with much less effective anti-aircraft batteries. The eleven Italian ships had only a handful of 90mm guns and 13.2 mm machine guns between them. The volume of fire that they generated was unimpressive to anybody who had seen the Royal Navy's eight-barrelled pompoms at work.

Another look at the three battleships showed that they had grown only marginally larger as his Swordfish had closed the range. MacFleet had a strange fear that if the Italians turned into the wind, they would actually outrun his Swordfish. Fortunately, with the British aircraft coming in from ahead of the formation, turning away from him would mean heading towards another group of torpedo bombers. The Swordfish crews had been practicing exactly this kind of attack for almost a decade. They were performing a well-known drill that had been methodically refined and perfected. The only slight differences were that the torpedo hanging under their aircraft were live. So was the ammunition being fired at them.

"We'll take the nearest cruiser." MacFleet yelled the remark into his speaking tube and got a thumbs-up from his navigator. The Italian heavy ships formed a V. The three battleships lead, and the two heavy cruisers brought up the rear. MacFleet felt sorry for the lead battleship. No matter what orders said, there was an irresistible tendency for crews to drop on the first enemy ship they came to. With the torpedo planes coming in from ahead, the battleship at the point of the V would attract most attention. He had a feeling she was the *Conte di Cavour,* but the four rebuilt Italian battleships were so similar, it was hard to tell the difference between them.

He kept weaving his Swordfish, trying to throw off the gunners who were hosing machine-gun fire at him. Every few seconds, there was a thud as one of the machine gun bullets hit his aircraft. That really didn't concern him too much. The wood and fabric-built Swordfish might seem flimsy, but it was resilient enough to take a lot of punishment.

"We got one!" The navigator yelled out the news with glee.

MacFleet sneaked a quick look over to the head of the formation. A great tower of water rose from the stern of the leading Italian battleship. "Right in the arse. That's got to hurt."

MacFleet was surprised how quickly he seemed to be moving as he finally closed in on his target. There was a destroyer between him and his chosen cruiser. Tracer fire streamed from its machine guns. He took a quick look; the midships 4.7-inch twin mount that defined her as a member of the Navigatore class. Another quick glance at the battleships that now seemed terribly close yet were also passing behind him showed that a second tower of water had erupted from the already-injured battleship. He would have held the sight longer, but there was another thud. Something hit his aircraft. This one sounded very different. *The deep thud of something important getting hit, not the lighter noise of a bullet passing through wood and fabric.*

The vibration told him his engine was hurt. Oil starting to spray on to his windscreen suggested the hit was bad. MacFleet abandoned the idea of going for the cruiser and decided to settle for a destroyer. *After all, the attack is supposed to hit as many ships as possible wasn't it? And my Swordfish might not stay airborne long enough to get into a drop position on the cruiser.*

A quick check showed he was barely 300 yards from the destroyer and in a near-perfect position just off the bow. Turning away from him would present the destroyer's broadside to his torpedo; turning into him would mean that closure speed was so high, the torpedo would hit before the destroyer could escape. He corrected the angle slightly and released the torpedo.

It ran straight and true, hitting the destroyer dead under the midships gun mounting. For a sickening moment, MacFleet thought it had malfunctioned and sunk without exploding. Then the column of water erupted around the destroyer. Only for a second, though. The torpedo hit was perfectly placed to detonate the magazine that fed the midships guns. The destroyer vanished in a black and orange fireball. The blast wave threw the damaged Swordfish out of control and nearly tossed her into the sea. MacFleet only just managed to get her back in hand. He felt sure a wingtip at least had dipped in the water. The aircraft was still flying despite the blast damage and the smoke streaming from its engine.

"Give us a course for home, Harry." The voice tube at least was still working.

"Try 180 for a few minutes. I'll give you a course as soon as I get a hit from the '79."

That was the Royal Navy's secret weapon, a homing beacon that would allow her carrier aircraft to make their way back. For a battered and damaged aircraft, it was a gift beyond price. MacFleet wondered if other navies had similar equipment, but dismissed the thought. He had a damaged aircraft to worry about.

Admiral's Bridge, Conte di Cavour, *off Cape Methoni*

Admiral Inigo Campioni hauled himself back on to his feet as the *Conte di Cavour* rocked from the third torpedo hit she had taken. Off to port, a

270

tower of water beside the *Guilio Cesare* showed that she too had suffered at the hands of the infernal torpedo-bombers that were breaking his fleet apart.

"Sir, the *Nicolo Zeno* has blown up!"

The lookout's report confused Admiral Campioni. They were under air attack. It was supposed to be impossible to torpedo a destroyer moving at full speed and taking evasive action. He looked across the fleet. A black pyre of smoke told him the report was correct. One of the Swordfish torpedo bombers was on fire as it crossed Campioni's field of vision. He watched the crew jumping from the open cockpit. They were far too low for their parachutes to open and far too high to stand a real chance of surviving the jump without a parachute. He guessed they'd decided it was better to jump than burn. The Swordfish wallowed for a split second and then it bellied into the water. The pyre it made drifted through the formation of ships and was left behind in their wake.

"Brave men." Campioni did not grudge the tribute to the pilots and crews of the old biplanes. He was under no illusions about the weakness of his anti-aircraft fire, but flying so slowly into the tracers still needed cold nerve. The British pilots had that; skill, too. His listing, crippled flagship was a clear tribute to that.

"Sir, *Guilio Cesare* has been hit again. She's signalling she is out of control."

Campioni looked aft towards where *Guilio Cesare* was starting to circle helplessly. *Another ship with a torpedo in the screws. The British pilots aren't just hitting my ships; they're putting the torpedoes where they will hurt the most. Damn them.* There was a light rattle as machine gun fire struck the bridge. One of the Swordfish had actually had the gall to strafe him as it passed. The single Lewis gun was unlikely to do any real damage. It would take the foulest of foul luck for it to hurt anybody, but it was the thought behind it that counted. He felt the ship shudder slightly under his feet. Campioni thought she had been hit again, but it was the echoes of a distant blow.

"It's over, sir." His flag Lieutenant sounded relieved. "We have taken three hits, *Guilio Cesare* two, *Trento* two, *Trieste* one and *Nicolo Zeno* one. The destroyer has gone and *Trento* is sinking fast. "

Nine hits out of 15 torpedoes. Just who were those pilots? "How many aircraft did we shoot down?"

"Three sir, with two more seen flying away badly damaged. *Andrea Doria* is trying to get *Guilio Cesare* under tow."

"What about us?" Campioni was shocked at how much damage the small formation of bombers had wrought on his fleet.

"Sir, the damage control crews report that the torpedo protection system has failed completely. All three torpedoes hit the same side and they cannot stop the flooding. We can limit the list if we counterflood but doing so

271

will mean our remaining machinery room will be lost. We're sinking, sir." The damage control officer sounded hopeless and defeated. "All we can do is to buy the time needed to get the crew off the ship. The destroyers can pick us up."

Campioni could feel his ship was going down. The rolling motion under his feet was getting consistently more sluggish. She was rolling reluctantly, but each successive recovery from the rolls was even more reluctant. The list at the end of each was just that little bit worse. Soon, she wouldn't stop the roll and she would capsize.

"Make it so. Get the men off. Make sure the crew in the engine and boiler rooms know what is to happen. What about *Trieste*?"

The Flag Officer took over the reports again. "She's dead in the water now, but Captain Avila reports she should be able to make five knots in a quarter of an hour and fifteen within the hour. He requests permission to head for port since it is proving hard to stop the flooding."

That should not surprise anybody. The *Trentos* were built so lightly that they get shaken up by their own guns, let alone torpedo hits. "Tell him to proceed at his own speed and at his own discretion. *Andrea Doria* is to take *Guilio Cesare* under tow and make for Taranto. I will transfer my flag to her. With five destroyers left in operational condition and those crowded with survivors, our part in this is over."

Campioni looked at his mauled fleet again and shook his head, thinking of the crew he had seen jump from their burning Swordfish. *God help me, I would be honored to shake the hands of those men.*

Goofers Gallery, HMS Eagle, At Sea, Off Gavdos

"Here comes another one!"

The chorus of cheers from the bridge of the carrier marked the appearance of another Swordfish returning from the strike. The first few aircraft back were already below, sitting in the hangar while they were repaired, rearmed and refuelled. The day was still early and there was the possibility of launching another mission. It all depended on what the pilots had to report.

The Swordfish making its approach was in serious trouble. It was streaming thick black smoke from its engine and its progress was unsteady. On *Eagle's* flight deck, emergency crews were getting ready to deal with the crash landing that seemed all too probable. The aircraft seemed to slip sideways and lurch down; then it recovered. It shook some more as it crossed the turbulence behind the carrier deck. Again, it seemed to falter, but the pilot caught it just in time. Then, his aircraft dropped on to the flight deck. Its arrester hook snagged a wire. The Swordfish came to a halt, quickly surrounded by emergency crews. They doused the smoking engine with foam. A cheer went up from the watchers lining Goofer's Gallery as the pilot jumped down. It turned to a roar of appreciative laughter; he knelt down and kissed the deck.

"*V4373*. That's Jim MacFleet Take him off the strike list, he won't be able to fly that kite again today."

The Pegasus engine on the aircraft was obviously wrecked. It was questionable if a replacement was available. It was rumored that *Illustrious* and her escorting destroyers had arrived in Gibraltar loaded down with all the spare parts and supplies that could be physically stuffed into them. Despite that, spares were in short supply. *Eagle's* aircraft were a quickly-declining asset. Nobody knew for sure what, if anything, would be coming out of Britain or when. The same problem was cropping up in all sorts of unexpected places. Without Britain as a source of supply, there was a slow, creeping paralysis of the equipment that was still in service.

Beneath the Goofer's Gallery, the damaged Swordfish was already being pushed towards a lift so it could be struck down for repair. On the horizon, another Swordfish was already starting to make its landing approach. Just how long *Eagle* could continue to operate her aircraft was a question that was starting to worry a lot of people.

Admiral's Bridge, HMS Warspite, North of Tobruk

"*Eagle* is claiming two battleships, two cruisers and a destroyer sunk, sir." The lieutenant had the message flimsy in his hands and was waving it around in what seemed to be near-triumph.

Admiral Cunningham looked at the young officer with a certain level of severity. The Lieutenant was brash, to the point of being insubordinate, and was never afraid to speak his mind. Neither trait seemed to be very favorable to the prospect of a successful naval career. Nevertheless, Cunningham believed that he would go far; it was just that he wasn't sure whether it would be to the top of His Majesty's Navy or to one of his prisons. Still, one had to make allowances for anybody cursed with a surname like Schleswig-Holstein-Sonderburg-Glucksberg. *How did a Greek end up with a name like that?* he wondered.

"And why is my searchlight officer bringing messages to the bridge?"

"Casting light on the situation, sir." The lieutenant seemed quite unabashed by the question from the commander of the Mediterranean Fleet. "Signals is swamped, sir, with all the traffic coming in, and are out of runners. I was passing, so I was just helped out."

"Hmph." Cunningham wasn't quite certain whether that was commendable or not, but there was much to be said for an officer who wasn't reluctant to help out another department in an emergency. *Especially with a message as important as this one.* "We had another message from the RAF a few minutes ago. They say that the Italian battle squadron is retiring on the naval base at Taranto with three large and five small ships. How do you reconcile the two messages?"

"I'd assume that either the debriefing on *Eagle* or the RAF made a pig's breakfast of things, sir. Probably, both of them. The important thing is what they both say; the Italian Battlefleet has been hit hard and is retiring."

Well, that was probably accurate, if tactless, Cunningham thought. *And he got the crux of the matter right. *Eagle* sent the battle squadron running for port with their tails between their legs. That means that the Italian convoy is wide open.*

"Quite. Captain Fisher, make to the rest of the squadron that they are to form on us and prepare for a night action." Cunningham looked at the four light cruisers and four destroyers that surrounded *Warspite* and couldn't help but reflect that the battleship looked rather like a nanny surrounded by her charges. "Make 23 knots and steer to intercept the Italian convoy. We want to hit them after dusk, so we can hunt them all down before dawn. I had expected to spend most of the day beating off air attacks, but we haven't seen a single aircraft. This is most encouraging. Lieutenant, get to your searchlights and make sure your crews are ready. Much may depend on you tonight."

Martin Maryland I G-George, *North of Tobruk*

"There they are." Charles Cussans sounded triumphant from his position in the glazed nose of the Maryland. In the gathering gloom, the merchant ships far below were hard to see, but he had managed to spot them. It was, perhaps, symbolic of the rapidly changing fortunes in the Middle East that the Marylands that had been brought in as bombers now spent most of their time as reconnaissance aircraft. The Commonwealth problem now wasn't beating the Italians; it was finding them, so they could be beaten.

"Get the position." Relaying it to the fleet was the top priority. In the cockpit, Sean Mannix knew that four cruisers and a round half-dozen destroyers were closing in on that convoy. There were even rumors that they had a battleship along, in case of heavy opposition, and that Andy Cunningham himself was in charge. Even as a long-term, RAF, career professional, he had to admit that the situation had promise.

"Got it." Cussans read off a string of numbers. They were sent out almost immediately. The message had to go to Cairo, then taken to the Naval section there and retransmitted to the fleet, but that wasn't going to be a problem. What the numbers essentially said was that the Italian convoy was where it was expected to be.

"They're firing down there."

The flash of fire from the anti-aircraft guns on the ships down below was almost invisible; the operative word was 'almost'. Cussans had seen them. The warning gave Mannix the opportunity for some sudden evasive action. The Maryland bounced from the shell bursts, but none of the explosions inflicted any damage. Below them, the rapidly-approaching night masked the formation of ships. *It was time to go home.*

"Good job, Cussans. As a special reward, you can natter on the intercom while we head for home." Mannix smiled to himself. He'd sat in the bombardier's position on his Maryland and realized just how lonely and isolated it was down there. That was a problem with the Martin aircraft; it was a hot-rod but its fuselage was extremely cramped. The three members of the crew were pretty much isolated from take-off to landing. Chattering on the intercom helped to relieve the isolation. Mannix had written a report for the high-ups drawing attention to the problem and discussing the good and bad points of the American design. He doubted if it would do any good, but one never knew.

Admiral's Bridge, HMS **Warspite,** *North of Tobruk*

He was seeing into the future as well as the nighttime darkness, Admiral Cunningham had no doubt about that. The equipment was crude and its performance needed to improve a lot before it would become an essential aid. More importantly, the Navy would have to learn how to use the tools properly. At the moment, they were still floundering around, trying to get the system perfected. Yet for all that, the radar equipment fitted to *Warspite* had spotted the enemy convoy and allowed the Commonwealth formation to make its approach unseen. In the country of the blind, the one-eyed man is king.

"Range to primary target?" The flagship of the convoy was the heavy cruiser *Bolzano*, presumably along to provide heavy gun cover against a raid. The covering force, now on its way back to Taranto, was supposed to deal with anything more than a small attack, so a single heavy cruiser was good insurance. Or, so it seemed; Cunningham actually had the gravest doubts about the whole concept of 'distant cover'. To his way of thinking, the battle would evolve so fast that a 'distant cover' squadron wouldn't be able to react in time.

"Five thousand yards, sir."

That sounded frighteningly close. The big thing about radar was that didn't just tell people what was there; it told the lookouts where to concentrate their attention. Technically, lookouts could easily spot a target at this range; on a dark night, with no moon and against blacked-out ships, reality was different from theory. Knowing where to look made all the difference.

"Very well. Open fire."

What happened next happened so fast and so perfectly that it could only have been the result of long practice and fingers waiting anxiously on firing switches. *Warspite's* searchlights snapped on, perfectly illuminating the unsuspecting Italian cruiser. Every detail of her superstructure stood out in the glaring white light. A split second later, *Warspite*'s four-inch anti-aircraft guns cracked out starshells that burst over the cruiser, further bathing her in light. Her eight fifteen-inch guns, already levelled at their target, crashed out, sending the great projectiles slamming into *Bolzano's* hull. All eight hit; a spectacular sight that silenced everybody on the bridge. *Bolzano* staggered under the blows, reeling as they penetrated deep into her. The explosions didn't just belch orange flame. They sent huge chunks of the ship's structure spiralling skywards as the blast ripped *Bolzano* apart at the seams. The cruiser was out of the battle; she would be hard-put to survive.

Down in *Warspite's* turrets, a well-ordered drill had started. Hoists lifted the shells themselves and the bags of propellent up to the guns. Rams then pushed them into the breach. As each gun was readied, a green light went on in the fire control room. Tiny realignments shifted the positions of the gun turrets slightly. Then a finger closed the switch; all eight guns fired again. The cycle time had been twenty seconds.

It was only a split second longer than that before the second devastating broadside tore into the dying Italian cruiser. Cunningham saw her gun turrets hurled high into the air by the blast, spinning and spiralling as they flew upwards. Perhaps mercifully, the sight was masked by the sudden shutdown of the searchlights. *Bolzano* now was only illuminated by the starshells and the red glow of the fires engulfing her.

Cunningham became fixated by the sight. The brilliant glare of the searchlights illuminating a destroyer was a shock. The destroyer seemed to be turning to engage the British battleship. She had been caught by the searchlights halfway through the turn. *Warspite's* six-inch secondary battery opened fire. The first salvo straddled the destroyer; the second gave the brilliant red flash of direct hits. The third salvo must have been fired. If it had been, it was lost in the roar of *Warspite's* main battery sending its third broadside into the blazing wreck of *Bolzano*.

Admiral's Bridge, Bartolomeo Colleoni

"Order the convoy to scatter, immediately."

Rear Admiral Ferdinando Casardi was horrified by the sudden discovery that there was a battleship attacking his convoy. More to the point, battleships never appeared alone. *There are cruisers and destroyers out there and they will tear us apart.*

"Order the *Bande Nere* and the destroyers to join us in attacking the enemy and holding them off while the merchant ships make a run for safety."

"Sir, *Grecale* has been hit by fire from the battleship's secondary batteries."

And so it begins. Casardi realized that a major disaster was already in the making. *Bolzano* was a pyre of smoke and flame. Even from this range, he could see her disintegrating as the British battleship pounded her with another salvo. *Does that make it four or five full broadsides she has taken? Does it matter? She's finished.*

"*Grecale* is returning fire." The lookout was trying to keep his voice under control, but the tinge of sheer, blind panic was already working his way into the reports. "She's lit up, sir."

The Italian destroyer was starkly visible in the black of the night, standing out in the white tracks across the water created by the British searchlights. *Whoever was operating them was a master of his craft.* The searchlights would flick on for a few seconds. Just long enough for the starshell crews to drop their rounds around her and then the searchlights would go off. Once they did so, the battleship seemed to vanish into the night again. It was *Grecale*'s turn again. She was already burning. That was her doom; the fires made an excellent point of aim for the British gunners. Grimly, Casardi realized that was the one hope the merchant ships, already turning away from the attack, would have. *The first ships to get hit will attract all the fire. That buys time for the rest. There is a sacrifice that has to be made.*

"Searchlights on. Bearing oh-nine-oh."

Casardi had made a quick guess at the position of the British cruisers and destroyers. He wanted his lights on to try and fix a target while he still had the guns to engage them. More importantly, he had to draw the British fire away from the merchantmen.

Bartolomeo Colleoni's searchlights snapped on, but the sea they illuminated was empty. To some extent, they achieved their purpose, though. For around him, he saw the orange flare of British guns. *Eight guns per ship. Does that mean they are eight-inch Counties or six-inch Leanders? And does it matter? My* Colleoni *was designed to fight French destroyers, not British cruisers. Our armor won't keep out either shell.*

That was when the world got very bright. Casardi realized what the British were up to. *The battleship is using her searchlights to illuminate targets and her armor to absorb any fire we can throw at her when she gives her position away by doing so. Meanwhile, the cruisers and destroyers stay in the darkness to fire on us.*

He felt *Colleoni* lurch under his feet. Her guns fired on the muzzle flashes of the British cruisers. She took a deeper and much more serious roll; a pattern of six-inch shells smacked into her amidships. He felt his cruiser dying. The vibration from the engines and the movement of the ship slackened as the hits took out her engine rooms.

"Keep firing under local control."

There was another brilliant flash from off to port. For a horrible moment, Casardi thought another British battleship had joined the fight. Then he realized that it was the *Bande Nere*. She'd been torpedoed. The explosion had torn the hull, one optimized for speed, not strength, in two. It was barely five minutes into the action. Already, all three Italian cruisers were crippled or dying.

Bridge, HMAS Sydney

This was what every cruiser captain lived for. Captain John Augustine Collins watched the eight six-inch guns on his cruiser hammer the Italian ship trapped in the glare of *Warspite*'s searchlights. He'd fired three half-broadsides, patterns of four shells in quick sequence, that laddered the target and got the guns ranged in. Now he was pouring full eight-gun broadsides into the cruiser's hull. She was already burning and slowing

277

notably. As she did, the ripples of hits along her hull seemed to grow in intensity, outlining her hull with orange fire. *The Italians always made much of the speed of their cruisers,* he thought. *The day they make one that's faster than a shell, I'll believe they have a good idea.*

"Is that Eye-tie trying to commit suicide?" Collin's executive officer seemed bemused by the spectacle.

"He's drawing our fire. Very well, too. Buying time for the convoy to scatter and escape. A brave man is dying over there, Billy."

His comment was interrupted by the splash of shell patterns all around him. *Sydney's* crew were well-rehearsed. The shooter was illuminated by her searchlights before she could get a second salvo out. *Sydney's* four-inch guns fired almost as quickly and with deadly accuracy. Two brilliant red flashes lit up the destroyer's stern, tearing into the two twin mounts there and starting the dull red glow of fire.

"Cease firing; that's *Mohawk!*" Collins had recognized the big destroyer with her eight guns almost as soon as she had been illuminated. "And get those lights off her."

It was too late. In the brief seconds *Mohawk* had been illuminated, an Italian destroyer seized the opportunity to fire her torpedoes. One hit *Mohawk* directly under the forward gun mounts; the second in the aft machinery spaces. Columns of water blew skywards, enveloping the ship. *Mohawk* was finished. Collins knew that; no destroyer built could take two well-placed torpedoes. She was already coming to a halt and settling fast; her crew going over the side in a hurried 'abandon ship'.

Collins swung his attention back to the light cruiser being hammered by his six-inch guns. She was already silenced and listing rapidly; a floating wreck being left behind as the Commonwealth ships pushed through the Italian screen to the merchant ships beyond. The flares of the six-inch shells hitting her were suddenly swamped by a series of massive explosions, as *Warspite* brought her 15-inch guns to bear. Then those blasts too were dwarfed; the Italian cruiser's magazines exploded.

Bridge, HMS Nubian

"We can worry about picking up survivors later."

Nubian and *Mohawk* had been flotilla mates for a long time, and the crews of the big Tribal class destroyers tended to stick closely together. Leaving the crew of *Mohawk* behind came hard. Commander Mason tore his eyes away from the sinking wreck of *Nubian's* sister-ship and stared into the darkness. The brilliant displays of starshell and searchlights, combined with the angry glare of shells and heavy gunfire, had effectively destroyed his night vision. Even so, the patch of darkness ahead of him seemed a bit more solid than the rest. When the darkness resolved itself into the shape of an Italian destroyer, Mason realized what had happened.

The destroyer saw Mohawk *illuminated and fired her torpedoes. Then, she sheered away in an effort to clear the launch point. A sound and sensible maneuver. She couldn't turn one way because that would bring her into* Sydney's *arc of fire so she went the other and that put her right across my bows.*

"Stand by for collision. Brace for impact!" Mason only just managed to get the order out. *Nubian* slammed into the center-section of the Italian destroyer, just aft of the single funnel. For a brief second, Mason saw the letters FG painted on the destroyer's bows, identifying her as the *Folgore.* Then the sight was masked out as *Nubian's* bows rose over the Italian ship. *Folgore* seemed to be writhing under the impact, reminding Mason of a snake being crushed under a boot. Then *Nubian* slammed down; the Italian destroyer's back snapped under the stress. *Nubian's* momentum carried her forward, completing the job of cutting *Folgore* in half. *Folgore's* own momentum carried her onwards, twisting *Nubian's* bows to one side. There was a scream of tortured steel as *Nubian's* bows detached. Then silence. Both destroyers were dead in the water. *Folgore* was already sinking fast. The crew aboard the larger and more toughly-built *Nubian* swarmed into the ruined bows, trying to reinforce shattered bulkheads and staunch the floods pouring in through the riven forward hull.

Bridge, HMAS Sydney

"We're through."

Collins looked at the situation plot with unalloyed pleasure. The chaos of the night battle was falling behind. *Warspite, Neptune* and *Orion,* plus the two remaining British destroyers, slugged it out with what was left of the Italian escort. *Sydney* and *Perth,* along with five Australian destroyers, were past that battle and racing towards the merchant ships, who were undoubtedly scattering. The task left was simple; hunting the merchant ships down, one by one, and sinking them.

This isn't a battle; this will be an execution, Collins thought. He wished, for a moment, he and his ships were back in the fight with the escort, facing a real enemy that could defend itself.

"Captain, *Waterhen* reports she has sighted one of the merchant ships and is firing torpedoes." There was no need to report a location; off to port, torpedoes exploded against a darkened hull. "And a message from *Warspite,* sir. The enemy transports are to the west and south of us and we are to form our movements accordingly."

And so it starts. Collins thought grimly. *Twenty-plus defenseless merchant ships loaded with men and supplies being hunted down by two cruisers and five destroyers. This will be bloody.* Then he glanced down just in time to see the chronometer click past midnight and in to the next day.

"Merry Christmas, everybody."

David Newton's Home, Mansfield Lane, Calverton, United Kingdom

"Rachael, could you come into the kitchen for a moment please?"

May Newton stuck her head around the kitchen door, smiling to herself when she saw her son's guest hastily move a little further away from him. The two women went into the kitchen where the smell of dinner cooking dominated everything else. "I just wanted to show you what we have for Christmas dinner in case there's anything that will cause you problems. We've got vegetable soup to start off with, followed by a chicken with vegetables from Ernie's allotment and the nearest we could get to a Christmas pudding. I made sure there's no pork in anything, but I didn't know what else to look out for. We've never had a Jew in the house before."

"That sounds delicious. You got a chicken? In spite of rationing?" Rachael was impressed.

"Ernie got a load of brussel sprouts and potatoes from his allotment, so we traded them for a chicken. There's a lot of trading like that going on in small villages like this. Black market, some people call it. We just say we're going down to the corner. Oh, there's stuffing for the chicken as well. Bread mixed with onions and chopped-up carrots." May Newton had left the sausage out of the stuffing in deference to her guest's religion.

"Could I help you out here?" Rachael was aware that her status as a guest was causing a burden on these people, but she'd been unable to go back down to her parents in London and didn't want to spend the holiday alone in Nottingham. David Newton's invitation to come for Christmas dinner had been a blessing in more ways than one.

"If you could help me carry out, that would be wonderful. Mind your dress, though; who knows when clothes will come off the ration."

The chicken worked out perfectly. David Newton and his father had a leg each, while Rachael and May Newton shared the wings and breast. The bird may have 'come off the ration,' but the attitudes generated by rationing and shortages still applied. The chicken was picked clean. Halfway through the meal, Ernie Newton asked a question his son had been quietly dreading.

"Decided who to vote for if there's another election, Rachael?"

David knew that Rachael was either a communist or a very radical socialist. His father was a local Conservative councillor. He could see the prospect for a major argument looming, but Rachael just shook her head sadly.

"I could never vote for That Man, after what he did."

"Aye, there's a lot around here who think that way. Farmers are conservative folk but they can't stomach what That Man did. There'll be many voting Liberal, or even Labour, next election.

Three hours later, the food had been eaten and presents exchanged. It was an austere Christmas; the exchange of gifts had tended towards the severely practical. May Newton gave her husband a spade for his allotment.

David Newton had managed to find a box of scented soaps for Rachael. The two women were in the kitchen clearing up, while Newton and his father had quiet drink together. It was the first time that David Newton had been invited to have a whisky with his father.

"That's a good girl you got there. I'll be honest, lad; your mother and I were a bit worried when you said you were walking out with a Jewess, but now that we've met her, we can see how nice she is." Ernie Newton was reflective and a little hesitant. "Look, son, man-to-man. Since your brother's away in North Africa, we'll put Rachael in his room tonight. There'll be no creeping around after dark, will there? That would upset your mother."

"Rachael's a good Jewish girl, Dad. Very old-fashioned in some ways. You and Mum have nothing to worry about."

"Glad to hear it. Like I said, you've got yourself a nice girl there. Now, call your mother and her in and we'll listen to the King's Speech. Or, rather, what That Man will let the King say."

Prince's Suite, Oriental Hotel, Bangkok, Thailand

"Merry Christmas, Mister Secretary."

The Ambassador entered Cordell Hull's suite at the Oriental Hotel with some brightly-wrapped packages in her arms. "We are all so sorry you are spending the festival away from your family, but we hope it is some consolation that your sacrifices will be of benefit to both our countries."

Hull watched as she unloaded the presents on the side table. "I didn't know Buddhist people celebrated Christmas?"

"We don't, not as a religious event. But, we are a hedonistic people. For us, a good excuse to have a party is not to be wasted." She hesitated for a moment before continuing. "And we like to give presents to people. By spreading some joy, we make merit for ourselves and thus improve our status in our next lives."

"May I open my gifts now?" Hull was actually nonplussed by the situation. He was well aware that he was regarded as a hostile party by the Thais and honest enough to admit they had good cause to adopt that position. "I am afraid I didn't think to get any gifts for people here."

"Please go ahead. And do not concern yourself; this is a day for merriment. All over the country, people will be going to visit their friends and gathering in the market places to exchange small gifts and greetings. If you wish, we can go and visit a local market where you can try out some of our local delicacies. Those who own stalls serving food will be making a special effort today."

The Ambassador looked pointedly at a seat and Hull reprimanded himself for undiplomatic discourtesy. *I don't trust this woman, but rudeness will achieve nothing.*

"Please take a seat, Madam Ambassador. You have been most kind; I really don't know what to say. May I offer you some refreshments? I can send down for some."

"I think you will find that room service is somewhat below its usual self today." The Ambassador's voice was droll. "The staff will also be celebrating. The working people of this country have little enough time off; perhaps we should let them enjoy it?"

Hull bobbed his head in acknowledgement. "A considerate thought, madam. How did you know my preferred brands of cigars and whisky?"

"I am expected to know such things. But, we did include one thing that is perhaps a little undiplomatic. We understand your father made his own whiskey, so we included a bottle of the whiskey we brew here. We thought you might like to compare the products of our moonshiners with yours."

Hull chuckled delightedly. "An excellent idea, madam. Perhaps, when I return home, I could send you some jars of . . . "

He was interrupted by the ringing of the telephone. He picked it up, listened for a few seconds and then handed the receiver over. "It is your office, Madam Ambassador. They apologize, but say it is very urgent."

The Ambassador took the receiver and listened carefully. Her face froze into an expressionless mask. Eventually, she put the receiver down and spoke, slowly and carefully, with a complete lack of intonation. "We have just received the promised reply to your diplomatic initiative from the French authorities in Indochina. Four French Farman bombers have just dropped ten tons of bombs on the border town of Aranyaprathet. The bombs hit the marketplace that was crowded with people celebrating Christmas. There are many killed and wounded; how many, I do not yet know. Please excuse me, Mister Secretary, I must go there immediately."

"May I come with you?" Hull was shocked by the news. *If what I have just been told is true, it puts an entirely new slant on the whole situation. This is what the Japanese are doing in China.*

The Ambassador hesitated, slightly confused by the sudden change in events. She had been expecting a French-inspired incident, ever since Hull had sent his diplomatic message to Hanoi a week earlier. She had not expected a bombing raid on Christmas Day. Once again, she marvelled at the way the French authorities appeared to be cooperating with their own destruction. "I think so. I'll have to arrange fighter escort for the transport aircraft, if you are on board."

She picked up the telephone again and dialled a number; speaking quickly once the receiver had been lifted at the other end. Listening, Hull caught the change in her voice. The polite, deferential tone was dropped and orders were snapped out. He had noticed this before with Thai women; once, in a very rare while, their mask of polite deference dropped and they gave orders that were to be obeyed. Things were not as they seemed on the surface; Hull was the happier for knowing that.

"There will be a Boeing 247 waiting for us at Don Muang. It is being loaded with emergency medical supplies for Aranyaprathet. The seats are being taken out so it can carry more. We will have to sit on the boxes. I hope that is all right? Also, our elite fighter squadron, FKP60, is getting three of its Hawk 75 fighters flown here to escort us, as soon as they can get the pilots in from their leave. We will depart as soon as they arrive."

"Sitting on the boxes will be fine, Madam." Hull hesitated. "May I use the telephone, please? I wish to call our Consulate and arrange for the United States to donate some additional aid to the victims at Aranyaprathet."

Suriyothai nodded. "That is a very kind gesture, Mister Secretary. On behalf of my people, I thank you." Inwardly, Suriyothai felt a fierce glee. One more piece had just fallen into place.

GHQ, Middle East Command, Cairo, Egypt

"Christmas presents, Archie." Maitland Wilson had a beaming smile on his face. "Lots of Christmas presents."

"Do tell, Jumbo. What have we got?"

"Well, from 6th Australian we have Bardia. The Italian garrison capitulated last night. According to Division, they've captured seven acres of officers and 22 acres of other ranks. We're pushing 200,000 prisoners now; how we're going to feed them all, I don't know. Then, we have a nice package from 7th Armoured Division. They have surrounded Tobruk, while their flying column has seized Beda Fomm. The whole of the Italian North African Army is now surrounded in Cyrenaica with their ports of supply either captured or under siege.

"Let's see, what else have we? Oh yes, Andy Cunningham has reported in. The Navy really did give the Italians a trousering in the Strait of Otranto. Sank a battleship, four cruisers and five destroyers, with another battleship and two more destroyers badly hurt. We lost a destroyer and three aircraft, with a cruiser and another destroyer in a bad way. The Italian convoy got scuppered; at least a dozen merchant ships sunk and more damaged. Bill Slim's Indians have broken through at Keren and are advancing quickly on Asmara. We'll have Eritrea wrapped up in a day or so. Ethiopia? Well, the South Africans are advancing on Addis Abeba from the south and the Indians from the north. We're expecting one or both to get there in a day or so. Kenya is cleared; all the Somalilands are occupied. It's a clean sweep, Archie. In two weeks, we've pretty much destroyed the Italian position in North and East Africa."

Wavell stood and stared at the map on the wall of his office, a great sense of relief pervading his soul. The tremendous gamble he had taken had paid off. Egypt was secure. That meant the Noth Plan had taken a serious blow, with its southern supporting thrust neutralized. After losses like the ones the Italian Army had taken, they wouldn't be going anywhere for a long time.

"I got a message from London, Jumbo. Very impolite one, as it happens. According to London, all our operations here are in defiance of their specific orders and contravene common sense."

"Well, Archie, we can't really disagree with the first part and Operation Compass in particular does look insane, unless one realizes that only armored and motorized units matter in desert warfare. So I would say That Man has a point, so far." Maitland Wilson beamed owlishly at Wavell.

"Perhaps, Jumbo; perhaps. But he demands we cease operations immediately before, and I quote, 'you are sent running like rats.' End of quote. It looks like the final break with London is very near."

"Rats, eh. That explains something; the contents of that telegram must have leaked out. Have you seen the new insignia for aircraft?" Wavell shook his head. Maitland Wilson produced a series of pictures.

"Basically, the Commonwealth nations have agreed on new markings for our aircraft. We're all keeping the traditional blue, white and red roundel, but replacing the red dot in the middle with a stylized red symbol for each nation. A maple leaf for Canada, a gazelle for South Africa, a kangaroo for Australia, a kiwi for New Zealand, a Chakra for India and so on. And, for us . . . ."

Maitland Wilson held up the picture. "A jerboa. We're now officially the Desert Rats."

Sululta, North of Addis Abeba, Ethiopia, Christmas Day, 1940

"There is a motorized column approaching." Subedar Shabeg Singh spoke thoughtfully. "I might suspect it was Italian, since Sululta is of critical importance, but I might also think that care is of the highest importance here. We are drawn to Sululta for the same reasons that the Italians would wish to defend it, but those same reasons again will draw the South Africans here."

4th Battalion of the 11th Sikh Regiment was on a small hill, just over a mile from the town. The position towered some 200 feet over the surrounding terrain; it gave a panoramic view of the countryside. That view showed why Sululta was so important. The town was built around a five-way crossroads and had two independent sources of water. It also occupied a pass through the low mountain ridges that ran across the terrain. A combined pass, water source and communications center; that made it a worthy prize.

"What do you think we should do now, Shabeg?" Major Joel Hamby was looking at the column with interest.

"I am thinking that this is a good time to let the situation mature. If the column is hostile, it may well stop in the town. That would give us only one target to attack. If it does not stop in the town, waiting will bring it in closer to us and make our initial attack more effective. If it is friendly, it will occupy the town with some fighting and save us the trouble. All the ways I think of this, I see only benefit from waiting and none from pressing the issue."

"I agree." Hamby nodded. "To let the situation mature is the best decision. It nearly always is. The column has lorries and armored cars. Four-wheeled armored cars."

"I think that makes it likely to be South African. The Italians would have those little tankettes. But it is still better to allow the situation to mature. Perhaps it might be in order to alert the men, so that we can move to the aid of the South Africans if they run into trouble down there." Singh looked again. "I am certain those are Morris armored cars."

"I think you're right. I'd say that column is going to attack the encampment, wouldn't you?"

No reply was necessary. The lorries and armored cars were already spreading out south of the tree-shrouded encampment that dominated the southern approach to Sululta. It was hard to make out the exact details of what was happening due to the dust and heat shimmer, but Singh could imagine the infantry leaving their lorries and spreading out to attack the position. The only thing that puzzled him was why they were taking so long about it. The answer to that question was quickly forthcoming; the drone of aircraft engines.

Six Blenheims skimmed over the ridge to the south of Sululta and made straight for the encampment. The attack had obviously been carefully planned. The pattern of bombs exploded all over the presumably Italian position. It vanished in a cloud of dirt and smoke. One or two of the bombs had overshot the position and exploded in the housing areas beyond. Measured against the vast expanse of Africa, the little hundred-pounders seemed to be insignificant. Singh doubted the recipients felt that way about them.

The South Africans started to move forward as soon as the bombs fell. Their armored cars snapped out bursts from their machine guns and rounds from their Boys Rifles. Singh was so busy watching the attack in progress, he forgot about the Blenheims. Hamby discretely drew his attention back to one of them; one that was circling the position of the 11th Sikhs on the hill.

"I suspect a recognition flare might be in order right now, old chap. Red then blue."

Singh got out the flare gun, checked the cartridge was of the correct type and then loaded it into the flare gun. The Blenheim overhead had reached the end of its run. It turned back to inspect the troops in more detail. The flare arched upwards, at first brilliant red, then turning to a dark blue. It was hard to see against the sky, so he loaded and fired a second flare. The Blenheim pilot was obviously confused. He circled the hilltop. Singh was about to fire a third flare when Hamby put his hand over the flaregun.

"I wouldn't do that. He can't see the blue flare against the sky and he's only got the red part to go by. I bet he's not sure whether it is a recognition flare or tracer fire from the ground. The more flares we put up, the more likely it is he'll decide they are tracers."

"I am thinking the man who decided on blue flares was a fatherless fool." Singh watched the Blenheim make another circuit of his position.

"I am thinking you are right."

Overhead the Blenheim straightened out. The pilot waggled his wings before heading south. Hamby and Singh breathed a sigh of relief. They took a look at the scene down by the encampment. While they had been dealing with the suspicious Blenheim, the Italians had surrendered. The South Africans were occupying the encampment and spreading into the town.

"We had better go down there and introduce ourselves."

A few minutes later, the leading section of the Sikh battalion was driving into Sululta. The South Africans had their vehicles parked in the shade. That left the Sikhs to park theirs on the sunny side of the street. Singh and Hamby got out and walked over to the South Africans, who were relaxing. As soon as they approached, the relaxed attitude vanished. One South African jumped to his feet and saluted smartly.

"Sir, Sergeant Dirk Klaas, Natal Mounted Rifles. Welcome to Sululta. The crabs warned us you were coming.

"Crabs?" Singh asked quietly.

"Royal Air Force." Hamby replied equally quietly. "Major Hamby and Subadar Singh, 4th Battalion, 11th Sikhs. My compliments on a well-executed attack, Sergeant; we were watching from the hill."

"The Italians aren't resisting too much, sir. They're afraid if they drive us back, the kaffir irregulars will get them." Klaas realized what he had said and flushed slightly. "Sorry, sir. But the Italians are deathly afraid of the irregulars. We've seen a couple of them who'd been taken prisoner by the . . . irregulars. What was left, it didn't look human. Poor bastards had been skinned alive and that was just the *start* of it. We shot them; only merciful thing to do."

"When you're wounded and layin' on the Afghan Plains." Singh quoted the line from Kipling. "We know what you mean, Sergeant. I am thinking, who really wants this place?"

Market Place, Aranyaprathet, Thailand

The stench of burned wood and charred flesh surrounded the party as they left the trucks that had brought them in from the airfield. The market place had been devastated. Smoke from the explosions mingled with the smell of explosives. What made the sight worse were the remains of the decorations; colored paper streamers still fluttered in the wreckage. Cordell Hull had seen the effects of bombing raids on cities before, first in Spain and then in China. but the Christmas decorations were a heartbreaking touch he had not expected.

Troops moved slowly through the wreckage, trying to find survivors in the shattered ruins of market stalls and food stands.

"We have had word from Nakhon Phanom."

The Ambassador was standing in the shade, watching the troops at work. "Four Potez bombers hit our market place there with three tons of bombs. There is no doubt in my mind that this was a deliberate attack on our civilians. This, here, might have been an accident. Two such attacks, no. They knew our families would be gathered here today."

"How many?" That was all Hull was able to say, but The Ambassador understood him.

"So far, six dead, forty wounded. Some of those have lost arms and legs. In Nakhon Phanom, only two dead, but about thirty wounded. We are lucky there was no fire here."

Hull nodded. He picked his way to the center of the market square. He could hear crying and whimpering from the wreckage and hurried to help shift some of the debris. A market stand had collapsed, but the wreckage had formed a triangle. The victims were in the safe zone. A soldier grabbed the other end of a wooden beam and helped Hull get it clear. There were two young children beside the stand; dirty, terrified but unhurt. They blinked in the afternoon sun, then saw the elderly European who had rescued them. Almost by instinct, they made deep wais to their saviors. The boy placed a hand on the back of his younger sister, helping her bow to the correct depth for their relative status. Hull carefully returned the gesture. His throat seized up and his eyes started to moisten as the soldier led them away.

He cleared his throat and turned to The Ambassador. "There were no anti-aircraft guns here, no fighters?"

"Anti-aircraft guns? No. Why should there be? This is a harmless market town. As for fighters, this is too close to the border. If they were based here, they would be caught on the ground by any attack. They are based further inland. Hawk IIIs. Our version of your BF2C. They were too slow to get here. The bombers had gone." She looked at Hull curiously, seeing the tears trickling down his cheeks. *It is time to tread very, very gently.*

"If you had faster fighters, they could have reached here?" Hull was having difficulty speaking.

"Probably not." The Ambassador spoke carefully. *If he feels too much guilt, he will become defensive and self-justifying.* "Aranyaprathet is too close to the border to be defended. That is why the French insisted the border be where it is; so that our towns could be held hostage. This is not your fault, Mister Secretary. It is the French authorities in Hanoi who ordered this raid and the one at Nakhon Phanom. We were lucky that the casualties were so few."

Hull looked again and the shattered market. A woman sat in one corner, rocking backwards and forwards while she wept. He didn't need to speak Thai to understand what she was moaning. Her husband was one of the six dead. Now she didn't know what to do next. For her, the casualties were not few; nor had the day been lucky.

"They weren't so few for her"

He was about to go to comfort her when he felt the Ambassador's hand on his arm. "No, Mister Secretary. Pay attention to her now, and she is too stricken with her grief to show you proper respect. Later, that memory will shame her. Leave her to her family; they will look after her. If you wish, you can see her in a day or so when the family will be ready to receive guests."

"I must return home. I have already been away too long." Hull looked around the devastated market place and whispered the next words. "This is like China. And Guernica."

The Ambassador stamped down her doubts over whether Guernica had actually been bombed the way the story said and put on her best sincerely-grave expression. "The Vichy authorities are allies of the Germans and the Hanoi administration is aligned with the Japanese. Is this so surprising? Or is it so surprising we consider all those people to be our enemies?"

Hull shook his head, convincing himself that the wetness on his cheeks was the result of the smoke and smell irritating his eyes. "Madam Ambassador. I will be candid. I do not like your military government and I do not like the way that government rules this country. But, I am convinced that this country has the ability and the desire to change and outgrow its present system. You have convinced me that your government shares that desire to grow and mature. Put together a list of the equipment your country needs to defend itself. It will be supplied. And do what you must to make sure this kind of atrocity does not happen again."

Comando Supremo, Regio Esercito, Rome, Italy

"The situation in North Africa is a catastrophe."

General Badoglio stared at the map that dominated the room, trying to absorb the speed and extent to which the situation had suddenly become dreadful. Almost 200,000 Italian soldiers had already either been taken prisoner or had been cut off in Cyrenaica. The only options for the latter were to break out or be added to the total number of Italians sitting in prisoner of war camps.

"The only reason why the situation in East Africa is less catastrophic is that we had fewer forces out there to lose. Ethiopia is gone. Somaliland is gone. Eritrea is gone. Italian East Africa no longer exists, except as a few scattered forces and isolated outposts. But for all that, North Africa is still the main disaster."

"We have received more approaches from the Halifax government in London, Duce. They are offering us a cease-fire and a return to pre-war borders in exchange for a non-aggression pact." Count Gian Galeazzo Ciano looked across at the room. "This would be a very satisfactory ending for us, were the offer to be of even the slightest importance."

"It is another *ruse de guerre*?" Badoglio was mildly amused by the idea of the Halifax government actually doing something effective.

Ciano thought carefully. He owed his position to having married Il Duce's daughter Edda, but that didn't change the fact he was an astute and skillful diplomat. "I do not believe Halifax's messages are a *ruse de guerre*. I believe they are sincerely meant and reflected the perceptions of the situation as seen from London. I now believe that those perceptions are wholly mistaken. There are, in effect, two British governments. There is the Halifax government in London and the Churchill government in Ottawa. The question, to which we must find an answer, is to *which* of these governments do the British forces in Egypt owe allegience? To answer that, we must look at their actions. We see they have ignored every message that comes out of London and gone their own way. So they obviously do not regard Halifax as being their head of state."

"So they have transferred their allegience to Churchill." Badoglio thought about that for a moment. "What is the position there?"

"I'm not so sure they have." Ciano seemed almost in despair. *I'm a diplomat and I have nobody to diplome with. I'm ready to lie, cheat and steal with the best of them but I can't find anybody to do it with. A lifetime of preparing for this job and nobody will play with me. It really is too bad.*

"As far as I can work out, General Wavell is taking his orders very literally. His job is to defend the Suez Canal and I think he believes he has to do that until the situation between Halifax and Churchill is resolved. He is defending the Canal so effectively that he'll be in Tripoli by the end of January, unless we are really careful."

Badoglio looked across the great table at where Benito Mussolini sat. In theory, at least, chairing the meeting. In reality, he was completely silent and motionless. "But it's not just Wavell is it? The whole Commonwealth is there. They've sent their best units, their best aircraft, their finest ships to the Middle East.

"Why? What do they hope to gain?"

"I don't know." Ciano's desperation was almost comical. "Nothing about this makes sense. The British Commonwealth has become the Commonwealth of Nations, but that's just a change of name. It doesn't mean anything, except that Britain isn't the head any more. But, they're pouring troops into the Middle East as if their very lives depended on it. One would expect them to look to defending their home countries first, but there's no sign of that. This doesn't make any kind of sense. General, I'm not a military man. You tell me what Australia and India and South Africa are doing in the Middle East? Because I don't know."

Badoglio started to speak and then stopped. He thought for a few seconds, started again and then stopped. Eventually he sighed with a level of despair that equalled Ciano's own. "I don't know. There's no great strategic need for them to be there. Persia and Iraq I can see, for the oil. But they have no need to be in the Middle East or East Africa at all. It's as if they perceive their major threat as coming through there and they are determined to pre-empt it. I think that isn't important, though. What is essential is that we take action to stop Wavell's rampage westwards. East Africa is gone; we must accept that. What is left is to try and save Libya. The naval expedition we sent to do that was a disastrous failure."

That is an understatement. One battleship sunk; one so badly damaged it will take months if not years to repair. A third with lesser damage. Half our heavy cruisers lost or damaged. Our best merchant ships sunk or bombed in harbor. Wherever we look, we see disaster. Ciano shuddered slightly.

"We cannot do this on our own resources. We have to get help from Germany. I have sent them a message, asking for mobile troops. Armored and motorized divisions are all that counts in the desert. The British have taught us that all too well. And aircraft. Those American Tomahawks have driven our colonial air force out of the battle, just as our CR.42s drove away the British colonial aircraft. German Messerschmitts will quickly put an end to them and restore air superiority."

"And what do the Germans say?"

"I have received no reply as yet. I was expecting one and hoped to have it for this meeting. My staff are on orders to bring the message over as soon as it arrives. I am very hopeful though; at this point a little assistance will go a long way. For all the achievements of the British in Africa, the forces they have available to them are very small. Given some aid, we can reverse this situation."

"I hope so." Badoglio sounded unconvinced. "I can see no way of recovering from this disaster without it. The aircraft are key. The Tomahawks are greatly superior to any fighters we have, but they are equally inferior to the Messerschmitt 109. Once we have recovered air superiority, we will be able to stop the bombing raids on our troops and consolidate our positions."

Badoglio had been intending to continue. He was stopped by the telephone ringing. Ciano picked it up, listened for a few seconds and then covered the mouthpiece with his hand. "The German Ambassador has arrived with the reply to our request for assistance."

"Well, get him up here." Badoglio sounded impatient; as, indeed, he was.

Hans Georg von Mackensen was an almost stereotypical picture of a German aristocrat and ambassador. Even so, he seemed exceptionally embarrassed at being asked to present the reply from Berlin personally. That alone gave Ciano a sinking feeling. von Mackensen's first words reinforced that sensation.

"Il Duce, gentlemen, I must stress that this is the reply I have received from Herr Ribbentrop himself. These are his words and are counter to the advice I provided. Herr Ribbentrop says 'Failure has had the healthy effect of once more compressing Italian claims to within the natural boundaries of Italian capabilities. You made your bed; now go whore in it.' I am sorry, both for the refusal of assistance and the unpardonable manner in which the refusal was made. I do not know what else to say."

There was a long pause during which complete silence dominated the room. Von Mackensen stood there, shifting from foot to foot in embarrassment; for all the world, looking as if he urgently needed to urinate. Eventually, Ciano sighed and shook his head.

"Thank you, Hans. There is no need to delay you further."

After von Mackensen had left, Badoglio spoke very quietly. "So that's it then. We have just been told that Germany considers Britain to be of greater value to its future plans than we are. The Commonwealth squadrons, with their Tomahawks and Marylands, control the air. The British Navy, and its aircraft carriers, controls the Mediterranean. Our forces in North Africa are doomed unless we can arrange an immediate ceasefire. We must contact London immediately."

"Not London." Ciano was emphatic. "Cairo. We have already discussed how General Wavell appears to have struck out on his own. We cannot be certain that any military orders Lord Halifax and his government issue will be obeyed by the armed forces they nominally control. There is only one person with whom we can negotiate and that is General Wavell himself. We must ask him for a cease-fire and save what we can."

The silence returned to the room, broken only by the scrape of a chair as Benito Mussolini got to his feet and quietly left the room. A split second later, there was a muffled thud from outside the door. A guard threw the door open in blind, undiluted panic.

"Summon assistance immediately. Il Duce had collapsed and is unconscious. I think he has had a stroke."

GHQ, Middle East Command, Cairo, Egypt

The radio crackled. The rolling tones of the speech were masked by the atmospherics, but there was no doubt that Winston Churchill was in full rhetorical voice.

"Rather more than half of a year has passed since the new Government came into power by nefarious and underhanded means. What a cataract of disaster has poured out upon us since then! The whole of Europe, from the North Cape to the Spanish frontier, is now in German hands; all the ports, all the airfields, all the resources of this immense block now stand against us. The perfidy of That Man and his betrayal of our gallant French

291

allies has led to a period of horror and disaster which could challenge our conviction of final victory, were it not burning unquenchable in our hearts. Few would have believed we could survive; none would have believed that we should today not only feel stronger, but should actually be stronger, than we have ever been before.

"The countries that once formed the core of the British Empire, finding themselves alone, stood undismayed against disaster. Not one of them flinched or wavered; nay, some who formerly thought of peace, now think only of war. The banner may have fallen from Britain's hands, but it has been taken up by the Commonwealth of Nations and waved defiantly in the face of our enemies. Our people are united and resolved, as they have never been before. Death and ruin have become small things compared with erasing the shame of our defeat and our failure in duty. We cannot tell what lies ahead. It may be that even greater ordeals lie before us. We shall face whatever is coming to us. We are sure of ourselves and of our cause, and that is the supreme fact which has emerged in these months of trial.

"Nowhere has our renewed spirit been more apparent than in Africa. The countries of the Commonwealth of Nations have stood together and ferried to the African theater an immense mass of munitions of all kinds: cannon, rifles, machine guns, cartridges and shell, all safely landed there without the loss of a gun or a round. The Commwealth Nations, led by Australia, India, New Zealand, South Africa and all the other members of our far-flung family, have poured forth troops into the theater. The great battle, which has been in progress in North Africa for the last few weeks, has recently attained a high intensity. It is too soon to attempt to assign limits, either to its scale or to its duration, but the victory won by the Commonwealth of Nations is already great beyond our poor imagination. Undaunted by odds, unwearied in their constant challenge and mortal danger, they are turning the tide of the World War by their prowess and their devotion. The lands liberated from cruel oppression, the sight of the columns of Italian prisoners and the mountains of captured war materials now in the hands of our gallant Commonwealth soldiers, is unparalleled. Never in the field of human conflict was so much surrendered by so many to so few.

"How much more might we have achieved if our cause had not been betrayed by Lord Halifax and his minions? The effect of their treason is an account that is already overdue and claiming payment is the task which lies before us. It is a task at once more practical, more simple and more stern that simply achieving victory. I hope - indeed, I pray - that we shall not be found unworthy of our victory if, after toil and tribulation, it is granted to us. With the aid of our Commonwealth brothers, we have to gain the victory and exact due and dispassionate penalties on those who betrayed us. That is our task and our privilege."

292

Maitland Wilson turned the radio off and took a deep breath. "Winnie certainly knows how to play on the heartstrings, doesn't he? The question is, where does that leave us?"

Wavell was having his work cut out stopping himself from laughing. "Beneath that bombast beats a political heart, Jumbo. When we get the transcript of that broadcast, read it carefully. He's recognized that the Commonwealth of Nations has replaced the British Commonwealth and paid tribute to all we have achieved over the last six months. Then, he deftly inserts himself as the leader of that Commonwealth and thus positions himself to take the credit. It's a classic 'I am their leader, I must follow them' gambit. I'd hate to play him at bridge."

"He's half-American. He probably prefers poker." Maitland Wilson opened the file he had brought with him. "The Italians have tried to break out through our blocking force at Beda Fomm. Our Flying Column arrived at the Benghazi – Tripoli road and set up roadblocks just 30 minutes before the leading elements of the Italian Tenth Army arrived. The Italians threw some 20,000 troops and a hundred tanks against what was little more than a reinforced battalion. The fighting was close and often hand-to-hand. At one point, a regimental sergeant major captured an Italian light tank by hitting the commander over the head with a rifle-butt."

Maitland Wilson paused for a second to think about that and shuddered. "The final Italian effort came this morning. The last twenty Italian M13/40 tanks broke through the thin cordon of riflemen and anti-tank guns. But even this breakthrough was ultimately stopped by the fire of our field guns, located just a few yards from regimental HQ. Our blocking force has been reinforced by additional elements of the 7th Armoured Division, but it doesn't really matter. The Italian Tenth Army is breaking up and surrendering. God knows how we're going to cope with all the prisoners on top of the ones we have already got."

Wavell wasn't really worried. "Jumbo, that's going to be a non-problem. We've had an approach from Rome. They are offering an Armistice leading to a peace treaty. They'll write off East Africa, in exchange for us pulling back to the Libyan-Egypt border and returning their prisoners of war. They'll return the few of ours they hold, of course."

"Can we rely on them? Or are we ourselves committing the same sin as That Man?"

That caused Wavell to stop dead. "It is a hell of a thing; isn't it, Jumbo? We hesitate to make peace and end a war on favorable terms, in case it is seen as following the example laid down by That Man. I can't think of anything more telling as an example of the damage he has caused. No, I don't think we are doing the same thing at all. If anything, we have reversed the positions. Now we are the ones who will be dictating terms and the Italians are the suppliants."

"Getting out of Cyrenaica is a good thing, Archie. The whole area is a deadly trap. It has to be occupied because that's where all the ports are, but anybody can push a mobile force across the desert and cut them off the way we did. I would advise we include an agreement on force levels in Libya and a demilitarized zone along the border to secure our position and then we'll be fine."

Wavell nodded. "I'll send the reply to Ciano in Rome."

Maitland Wilson grinned. "And a copy to London?"

"Why on earth would I want to do that? Send one to Ottawa though. Calcutta of course, and Canberra. In fact, Jumbo, everybody but That Man."

Government House, Calcutta, India

"We've won." Victor Alexander John Hope, 2nd Marquess of Linlithgow and Prime Minister *pro tem* of India sounded disbelieving. "India has won. With a little assistance, of course."

General Auchinleck made a polite choking noise. "I think, Your Excellency, that we had just a bit more than a little assistance from the Commonwealth of Nations."

"Not as far as our people are concerned." Pandit Nehru, Deputy Prime Minister *pro tem* of India, sounded more than thoughtful. "We have won a great victory over Italy and occupied Eritrea. It is with India that Italy is negotiating the surrender of that colony and its liberation under our tutelage. It is an absolute recognition of our status and independence. Our people recognize this and they rejoice in it."

"Not you, Pandit."

"Not Pandit Jawaharlal Nehru." Nehru sighed again. "I had dreams of an India that would stand for freedom, for peace and justice. An India that would use its power and authority to end wars and create a world of peace. Instead, India is becoming an imperial power, exerting its influence by force of arms. We have won a victory but it was one by our Jawans, not the force of our arguments. And my fellow Indians rejoice in this. Excuse my sadness, for this is indeed an auspicious day."

General Auchinleck forbore the temptation to quote the old adage about artillery being the final argument of kings. Instead he sought and found an argument that would reconcile Nehru to the fact that being an independent country had its penalties as well as virtues. One of the former was the need to resort to military force now and then.

"Pandit, what matters surely is the moral compass that guides us, regardless of the means we adopt. If our aim is justice and we moderate the means so that we do not compromise that end, is not that the objective that you seek? Our objective is freedom, peace and justice for all. Our arms have won that for the Eritreans. We have not become their colonial overlord; we have freed them just as we freed ourselves. We may not be happy with the means but our moral compass remains intact."

"Thank you, General. Your words comfort me a little, but they also highlight something that has been disturbing me for some time. The last six months have shown me how complex the problems facing our country are. They also show how ill-prepared I and my colleagues are to take over running the country in the face of these problems. General, you spoke of a moral compass. Mine must be the good of India and the proper rule of this country.

"Our original agreement was a two-year transition period from the colonial administration to an all-Indian government. I would like to modify that agreement to remove the time limit inherent within it. I believe we can achieve far more if we work together as the situation requires than if we try to comply with an artificial timetable. Also, I am not yet qualified to lead the government. I would like to suggest that Doctor Rajendra Prasad be considered as the first President of India, when the time comes. He is well-respected by every faction and a knowledgeable man of the world. We can present this change as a result of our victory in Eritrea; holding to the opinion that it shows how powerful India has become, provided all who live here work together."

The Marquess of Linlithgow was silenced by the enormity of the gesture he had just heard. In effect, Nehru was surrendering the goals and achievements of a lifetime in order to enhance India's chance of making it to a viable nationhood. *In some ways*, he thought, *that must be just about the most remarkable thing I have ever heard.*

"Pandit, India is indeed guided by a moral compass and I do not fear for its integrity, as long as it is in hands such as yours. Thank you for enlightening us and setting an example that the future will hold dear."

Once again, silence fell on the meeting room. For the first time, the Cabinet gathered was united; even the hold-outs who had supported Sir Richard Cardew were silenced by the magnaminity of Nehru's words.

Eventually, Sir Martyn Sharpe coughed quietly. "If I might move to the next item on the agenda. We have been in discussion with William Pawley, the head of the Central Aircraft Manufacturing Company (CAMCO). Their position in China has become untenable and they have agreed to move their operations to Bangalore. The move is being funded by an Australian businessman, a Mr. Essington Lewis, who recently gained access to substantial American investment funds. The new company will be known as Hindustan Aircraft Limited and will be 50 percent owned by the Indian Government." Sir Martyn gave a quick nod to Pandit Nehru at that.

"With them, they bring licenses to build two aircraft. One is the Hawk 75 that we already have in our inventory as the Mohawk. The other is the Vultee V-11 light attack aircraft. We are placing an order for 48 V-11s and for the same number of Hawk 75s. The first aircraft will, of course, be assembled from kits supplied by Curtiss and Vultee. However, as a result of a detailed memorandum from one of our American advisors, a Mr. Boyington, a new version of the Hawk 75 will be built. This will be powered by the R1820-86 engine rated at 1,450 hp and will be armed with six .303 machine guns. This aircraft will be called the Mohawk V; with its reduced weight and extra power, it will be the equal of any fighter in the region. The contract calls for the first Indian-built machines to fly on April 3, 1942. These are, of course, not just the first combat aircraft to be built in India; they are the first miltary aircraft to be ordered by *independent* India."

Sir Martyn's statement was capped by a thunderous burst of applause; the more enthusiastic pounded on the table. George Edward Parkes reached over and shook Nehru warmly by the hand. Watching the celebration, Sir Eric Haohoa realized that the crisis over India's continued existence had been weathered.

Whatever happened now, a newly independent India had been born.

Nagpur Central Jail, Maharashtra, India, December 31, 1940

"He has, of course, been properly treated?" Sir Eric Haohoa asked the question politely, but the prison governor took offense anyway.

"Of course he has, sir. We may be well removed from the center of administration down here, but we know what is right and what is not. I'll not say he is the most popular prisoner we have ever had, especially after our Jawans took down the Eye-ties in East Africa, but he has received every courtesy due to his previous rank and position."

Jawans, thought Sir Eric. Not so long ago, no British civil servant would have considered using the Indian word for an enlisted soldier. His thoughts were interrupted by the sound of a lock rattling and the creak of the cell door opening.

"Have you come to gloat, you wretched little guttersnipe?" Sir Richard Cardew spoke words loaded with venom. The hatred in his glare was so intense, Sir Eric actually felt himself taking a half-step backwards.

"No, sir; I have not. In fact, I have come to release you. The Cabinet has decided that it is no longer necessary to hold you in custody, nor would it be legal to do so without bringing you to trial. That option was seriously considered, since your actions caused the deaths of many good and honorable men. However, Deputy Prime Minister Nehru himself suggested that the disruption caused by bringing you to trial would far outweigh any benefits it might bring. So, on his initiative, it was decided that you should be released. You may remain in India if you so wish, or you may return to Britain. The choice is yours."

"I will not stay silent. I will fight you. I represent the true government of India and the true feelings of the better people here. I will not be silent."

Sir Eric smiled, just a little sadly. "You may do as you wish, Richard. It does not matter. You see, you have no constituency here. You have no power base, no support structure. While you have sat here, India has become a real country at last; one that stands on its own feet and whose voice is heard in the world. We have won great military victories and the Government of Italy is negotiating directly with us to end our war against them. With us, Richard; not London. The break with London is complete and final and even those who might once have had some sympathy for you are now swept up with the issues involved in ruling an independent country. Your voice, should you choose to raise it, will be an echo of the past."

"The Empire still stands . . . "

"No, Richard, it does not. You do not understand what I am telling you. Italy is negotiating directly with us; with Australia and South Africa. Canada has given its recognition to the Churchill government in Ottawa. The West Indies have struck out on their own as well. The Empire has gone; the British Commonwealth is now the Commonwealth of Nations and Britain's voice is not heard in its councils. Richard, we are a new nation that has already won respect. We have an Army with a record of victories won in its own name. We have a Navy that is enough to give even the strongest of enemies cause to pause for thought. We have an air force that grows in strength and power every day. Six months ago, there was not a single fighter aircraft east of Suez. Now, we have four squadrons; tomorrow, we will stand up a fifth. That squadron will be stationed in Singapore. We have bombers; we have transport aircraft, flying boats and our own training school. Compared with all that, your voice is a very poor and insignificant thing."

"You want to destroy the Empire. You treasonous, seditious, disloyal, subversive swine." Sir Richard was foaming at the mouth with almost uncontained fury.

For the first time, Sir Eric's voice lost its dispassionate tone. "Destroy the Empire? Never. My family have loyally served the Empire for three centuries; since a time when the Cardews were still stealing sheep from farms in Wales. It is Halifax and his cronies in London who have destroyed the Empire. It was always our policy that, in the event of Britain being occupied or forced to surrender, the rest of the Empire would fight on. The consequences of that policy, a policy that stemmed from and was promulgated by London, you will remember, were never realized until the situation actually arose and we had to deal with it.

"Even then, we were in denial until the abuse from London reached a point where we had no choices left. Complying with agreed Imperial policy and continuing the war meant we had to stand on our own and become truly independent countries. In requiring that, *they* destroyed the Empire. We have acted with sadness and reluctance; we have left the doors open, so that when we are victorious, we can rebuild what was torn down. That is a question for the future.

"Here, now and in this present, your opinions are just those of a relic from a bygone age and have no significance. How insignificant? You are not the only person being released today. I might mention Prithvi Singh Azad, for example; or Priyada Chakraborty. You might have heard of Achyut Ghatak or Adhir Kumar Nag. They also are being released today and many more of their

297

supporters. You are just one more prisoner; one released as an act of clemency by a government that views you as completely unimportant. "

"But, those men. They organized an insurrection against the legal government!" Sir Richard was appalled at the list of released prisoners.

"And you didn't, Richard?

"Now, come along. The warden wants to see you before you leave for home." *And I want you out of this prison before the idea of martyring yourself by suicide occurs to you.*

Cabinet Office, 10 Downing Street, London, United Kingdom

"They ignored us." Lord Halifax stared at the Foreign Office telegram with barely-contained fury. "They just ignored us."

And so our chickens come home to roost. Sir Edward Bridges looked at the Prime Minister with some shreds of sympathy. "Prime Minister, the Italians had to negotiate with those who held almost 200,000 of their men prisoner. Whatever their preferences, they had little choice in the matter."

"I speak not of the Italians, but of the traitors in Cairo. They ignored every message we sent them; they treated our instructions with contempt. They have betrayed everything that they are supposed to hold dear. Then, they signed an agreement with the Italians, without as much as a by-your-leave to us. I want them court-martialled and broken."

They did not treat your messages with contempt; they treated you in that manner. And, signing agreements with an enemy without as much as a by-your-leave is exactly what you did to them. Chickens returning to roost indeed. "That is a serious problem, Prime Minister. General Wavell is an officer in the Indian Army, not the British Army. At any court-martial, he would simply claim that as an Indian Army officer, orders from Calcutta overrode any orders he received from London. Indeed, he could well argue that a British court martial no longer has any jurisdiction over an Indian Army officer. I believe the court would look sympathetically on that claim, especially since the result of his decision was a remarkable feat of arms, leading to a stunning military victory. Such successes traditionally justify the means by which they were achieved. The traditional Army verdict on such circumstances is, I believe, 'Well done and don't ever do it again.' I would advise, Prime Minister, that you adopt the same approach."

"You can't do that, Prime Minister." Butler's voice was its suave self; Bridges was reminded of the times he had seen oil slicks spreading across water. "It will be showing weakness. The time has come, I think, to put a bit of stick about. Wavell and his cronies must be brought to heel and we must assert our authority over British forces outside these Islands."

Halifax looked desperate. For a moment, Bridges felt sorry for him. He was out of his depth and clutching for straws of support wherever he could find them. "Prime Minister, there is another Army principle it might be worth bearing in mind. 'Never issue an order unless one is sure it will be obeyed.'

That applies with great force here. At the moment, our authority over the forces abroad is tenuous and disputed. As long as we do nothing to bring the matter to a head, that is how it will remain. But, if we bring about a major confrontation with Middle East Command, a dispute which we cannot win, then all doubt will be removed and any authority we have left will be erased."

"Sir Edward, perhaps we have cause to doubt your loyalty?" Butler's voice was still oily-smooth, but there was a distinctly threatening element to it.

Bridges looked at Halifax and his lips formed a distinct phrase. "The Stone." That was all it took to cause Halifax to backtrack very quickly.

"Richard, there is no need to impugn Sir Edward's loyalty. It is his duty to raise issues that we might consider unpalatable." Butler nodded abruptly, but Bridges was in no doubt that he had just acquired a new and dangerous enemy. Halifax seemed distressed and uncertain as he continued speaking.

"Is there nothing good that can come of this situation?"

Butler took the opportunity with both hands. "We understand that the Italians asked for German help in resisting the forces commanded by General Wavell. They were refused in a message of unprecedented discourtesy. This makes it clear that Germany regards us as its most important ally in Europe and our position with regard to them is greatly strengthened."

"We are not an ally of Nazi Germany, Richard, and our interests only temporarily converge with theirs. Great Britain has decided to remain neutral; that is all."

"My apologies, Prime Minister." *Am I alone in hearing a note of derision in those words*? thought Bridges. "I mis-spoke. I did not mean to imply we should consider ourselves an ally of Germany; merely a country with whom Germany maintains friendly relations. However, we must take due note of the fact that the danger of Bolshevism means that our interests and those of Germany may be greater than you suppose."

Bridges was interested to note that Halifax did not look at all at ease with the line Butler was following. The Prime Minister quickly shifted back towards the subject of Wavell and the status of Middle East Command. "So what do we do about Wavell's insubordination?"

"Well, Prime Minister, the traditional options are that we recall him for court martial and cashier him, re-assign him to another post of such little importance that he will resign in disgust, ignore him completely or claim all the credit for his achievements and imply his contributions were of little import. He will ignore the first and second, take advantage of the third to further consolidate his position and it is already too late for the fourth. The fact that we, and the rest of the Commonwealth, are on divergent courses puts us in terra incognita here, Prime Minister. Anything we do will establish a precedent. May I suggest that a suitable one would be masterly inactivity?"

"Perhaps, Sir Edward. Please leave us now. The Foreign Secretary and I have party business to discuss."

That is a reasonable excuse to ask me to withdraw. But why do I not like the expression on Butler's face? Sir Edward Bridges backed out of the Cabinet Office and made a thoughtful progress down the stairs to the front door of Number Ten. Two of Butler's Auxiliaries were on guard, each armed with a Thompson sub-machine gun. *I wonder how long we will be able to get ammunition for them? It's been a long time since I had a drink with old Murray. I'll invite him over one evening, soon.*

There was an addition to that thought that Sir Edward Bridges resolutely kept even from himself. Sir Murray Prestcote was a long-retired veteran of the British Army in India. But, he had been very active in keeping in contact with the service and had many friends there. If somebody knew how to warn General Wavell to watch his back, it would be him.

Comando Supremo, Regio Esercito, Rome, Italy, January 14, 1941

"What are the terms of our agreement with the Commonwealth of Nations?"

Graziani, Badoglio, Ciano and the other occupants of the Army supreme command had expected Benito Mussolini to return either screaming with fury or venting bombastic nonsense. Instead, after almost two weeks sequestered in his private apartments, he sounded quiet and uncharacteristically unpretentious. The doctors said he had suffered from a severe stroke and complete nervous prostration.

Had the combination of the two made such a difference to the man's character? Ciano thought to himself. *Brought on by catastrophic military defeat and abandonment by our closest ally? That would be enough to dull the spirit of any man. Or restore humility to him.*

"Duce, we have secured Libya at its pre-war boundaries and the return of our prisoners of war. The Commonwealth will withdraw from Cyrenaica, but they will retain all the equipment and supplies they have captured. We have agreed to a 20-kilometer wide demilitarized zone on each side of the border; into which no military forces may enter, except by our joint agreement. The Commonwealth has agreed to joint patrols to ensure that these terms are observed. We have had to sacrifice Ethiopia, which has returned to its previous administration. Eritrea and Somaliland will be administered by the Commonwealth of Nations as if they were League of Nations trusts. In summary, we have managed to retain Libya, but at the cost of all our other African possessions." *Now order me shot. I have done my best for Italy and I will be content with that.*

"We kept Libya, but have lost the rest of our North African possessions." Mussolini paused and took a deep breath. The voice had changed as well; the ringing aggression and bouncing self-confidence were gone

300

completely. Now there was an almost thoughtful overtone; the tone of a philosopher, rather than a dictator.

"Well, I have decided I am not a collector of deserts. We can bid farewell to possessions that never benefitted us. Now is the time to look forward, not back. Our treatment at the hands of Herr Hitler has shown us that we can only become strong, I feel, when we have no friends upon whom to lean, or to look to for moral guidance. To continue this war would be national suicide. We must never consider the possibility of suicide; national or personal. We must despise and reject it. Rather, we must see these events as a part of life. As Italians, we must accept what life brings us and learn to love it. Our life should be high and full, lived for oneself, but not that above all; for we must also consider others. Those who are at hand and those who are far distant, contemporaries, and those who will come after us; their interests too we must consider.

"We have learned that Italy is not for export by force of arms. Instead, we must build the best and most beautiful Italy we can, and export Italy by those who choose to follow our example."

There was a long silence as Mussolini's words echoed around the room. He stood. The havoc the stroke had wrought becoming obvious as he wavered unsteadily on his feet. The left side of his body had been hit worst; his left hand was largely paralysed and he limped on his left leg. The left corner of his mouth was slack and every so often he dabbed at it with a handkerchief. "Galeazzo, you have done well. I commend you. Now, you must ensure that it is understood that Italy will maintain a policy of strict neutrality. We will expend our efforts on improving ourselves and our country. Our watchwords will be 'All within the state, nothing outside the state, nothing against the state.' Is this clearly understood? We will be neutral in any future conflict. There will be no more military commitments outside Italy."

Badoglio could hardly believe the change that was taking place in front of his eyes. If Mussolini was true to his words, this was the Italy he had always wanted. Perhaps the disaster in North and East Africa wasn't such a disaster after all. *Il Duce may be right, that we must accept what life brings us and learn to love it; for the benefits it bestows may not be immediately obvious and what seems unbearable today may well be the seed of a better tomorrow.* That left just one question in his mind.

"What will Herr Hitler have to say about this?"

"That horrible sexual degenerate? Egli può vaffanculo e morire come un uomo per una volta."

Room 208, Munitions Building, Washington, DC, USA

"Italy out of the war. The Commonwealth of Nations is off to a good start." Henry Stimson looked inordinately pleased with himself. The airfields in America were clearing rapidly as the aircraft originally ordered by the French and British were delivered instead to the Commonwealth countries.

"Not economically. India is staggering along from day to day, but Australia and New Zealand are sliding into an economic depression very quickly." Henry Morgenthau sounded deeply concerned. "They will need some additional help propping up their economies and need it quickly. I suspect New Zealand is beyond saving. I have already heard whispers that the Australians are considering absorbing them as an alternative to seeing them go bankrupt. There was provision for that in their constitution, you know."

"We must do what we must." Cordell Hull sounded detached and almost disinterested. "And no more."

"How did your trip to the Far East go?" Phillip Stuyvesant sounded mildly interested, concealing his real feelings carefully. He wasn't certain whether Hull's trip taking so much longer than originally planned was a good or a bad thing.

"I confirmed much that I already believed. The Siamese have a military government and is ruled by a regime supported by the force of arms. I deplore that regime and everything it represents. However, I do believe there is both room and desire for change and we should enable that change to whatever extent we are able. If we aid them, they may well evolve into a country we can support. But, if we do not, they will surely side with our enemies. At the moment, their enemies are our enemies. We must recognize that. I will withdraw my objections to the delivery of armaments to them, conditional upon them making the democratic development we expect."

Stimson interrupted him. "Cordell, we owe the Thais some aircraft. P-64 fighters and A-27 light bombers. How can we make good on the order?"

"Have we no equivalent aircraft we can give them in lieu?"

Stimson thought. "The A-27s are no problem. Northrop is building the A-24 for the Army. It's a version of the Navy SBD. The Army doesn't like it though; they think it's too slow, underarmed and its range is too short. They won't miss a couple of dozen for the Thais. For all its problems, it's actually a better aircraft than the A-27."

"Fighters; they need fighters. If you'd seen that market place, you wouldn't be worrying about the bombers."

Stuyvesant lifted a pencil. "The Indians have more Hawk 75s than they can absorb at this time and they have a more advanced version coming down the pike. Why don't we suggest they transfer a couple of dozen of their existing aircraft to Thailand and we give them a credit for the value they can use to buy other equipment they need?"

Stimson nodded. "That works for us. Means we keep the hard cash, the Thais get the aircraft and India gets more equipment it needs. You agree, Cordell?"

Hull nodded. "It sounds fair. And it gives us a chance to see if current Siamese words will match their future intentions."

CHAPTER ELEVEN
SERIOUS NEGOTIATIONS

11th Infantry (Queen's Cobra) Division, Border with French Indochina, Thailand, January 5, 1941

The border post was supposed to control the passage along the road from Kantharalak in Thailand to Angkrong in French Indochina. In fact, it blocked it completely. The French had brought in local labor to dig up the road surface. Their efforts left a deep ditch across the road lined with parapets made of the rubble from the road surface. There was barbed wire tangled along the mounds of earth and solid wooden stakes to hold it on place. There was even a guard box behind the earth banks that had a telephone. Corporal Mongkut Chandrapa na Ayuthya could see the telephone line heading southeast towards Angkrong. He carefully did not think that it connected the border post to Angkrong, since one of his men had cut the wire a couple of minutes before.

There were just three men at the border post. One was in the guard box and looked as if he was asleep. The other two were sitting on the embankment, smoking and surveying the neighborhood with monumental disinterest. They would have been much more interested if they had realized all twelve infantry battalions of the Queen's Cobra Division had moved up to the frontier and were currently in their jump-off positions for the invasion. *An invasion that had already started with a cut telephone wire.* Corporal Mongkut took a deep breath as the approaching dawn revealed more details of the target. In the back of his mind, he noted the birds were starting to sing. Then the hammering noise of a Lewis gun drowned them out.

The burst fountained soil around the two men outside the post. One died instantly, riddled with bullets. The other jumped to his feet, dropped his cigarette and frantically looked around to see what was happening. A second burst cut him down as well, long before he had learned anything. Mongkut saw him down on the ground, his body shaking as he died.

He focused on his primary target, the guard box. The man in it had grabbed the telephone. He was banging the handpiece on the desk, apparently in the belief that doing so would repair the cut wire. There was a short crackle of rifle fire from Mongkut's group. The glass in the guard box shattered, and he, too, went down. With the border guards neutralized, Mongkut got to his feet and jog-trotted towards the ruins of the border post.

His men worked fast. They took the bodies of the two men outside the post and their corporal from inside it and dragged them to the side of the road. Mongkut quickly checked the bodies, identifying them as members of the 4th *Tirailleurs Tonkinois*. The sun was already rising over the mountains on either side of their road. Behind him, other units of the 11th Division were crossing the border and beginning to push down the road towards Angkrong.

Mongkut's lieutenant waved. He and his men fell in with the rest of their unit and joined the march south. He had the map he had been shown clearly in his mind. Angkrong was a small rectangular village, but it controlled a vital crossroads; one that opened the way eastwards. Once Angkrong was in their hands, the real advance could start.

Behind Mongkut's unit, engineers brought up a quartet of elephants. They started the task of destroying the border post and repairing the road that led through it. Their orders were quite simple; they were to erase the border so thoroughly that nobody would ever know it had once existed here.

Hawk 75N Over Thakhek Airfield, French Indochina

Thakhek Airfield was the primary staging post for the attacks on Thai cities over the last six months. The Farman bombers that had carried out the most devastating of the raids were based far back in central Vietnam. That put them out of range of the Thai aircraft; for the moment, at least. But Thakhek was within range and it was a priority target for the Air Force. Other airfields were being attacked as well, but Thakhek was getting the main effort.

The primary strike was the half-dozen Martin 139 bombers; they formed two neat V-formations at 3,000 meters. Their stately progress through the air was marred by a very light scattering of black spots. The anti-aircraft defenses of the base were limited. There were few anti-aircraft guns in French Indochina, and it seemed as if the French believed that they could continue attacking Thailand without any form of reprisal.

Unaccountably, the anti-aircraft fire stopped as the Martins swung into their final bomb run. The export equivalent of the USAAC B-10B, each Martin 139 carried ten 250-pound bombs. Their bombing showed the inexperience of the crews. Most of the sixty bombs the formation dropped were within the airfield boundary, but the explosions were scattered all over the base. From what Flying Officer Suchart Chalermkiat could see, the vital hangars and runways were undamaged. That left taking the airfield out to him and his fellow Hawk 75N pilots.

As the Martins turned away for the flight home, Suchart pushed the nose of his fighter over and started to dive on the base below. Dive bombing was something every Thai pilot practiced. For the last six months, they had done little else but train for dive bombing missions. Even the Hawk III and 75N fighters had not been exempted. They had had to carry out their dive bombing training in addition to their other duties. Foong Kap Lai 60 was supposed to be the elite fighter squadron of the Thai Air Force, but their Hawk 75Ns had flown on this mission with a 250 pound bomb slung under their bellies. If French fighters showed up, they would jettison their bombs and fight. Otherwise, they were dive bombers. So was every other aircraft the Thais had. Even their Avro 504 trainers were carrying bombs today.

Suchart released his bomb. He saw it curve down into the center of one of the hangars. A smooth pull on the control column brought his Hawk out of its dive. He skimmed over the parking area, a few tens of feet over the grass. To his disappointment, there was only one aircraft in easy sight, a Potez 25. *Still, it is a ground attack aircraft and that's worth taking.* Suchart's four .30-caliber machine guns raked the old biplane. It burst into flames in front of him.

His flight formed up around him and he turned his nose west for home. Once the bombers that had struck the airfields were safely back at base, the fighters could do what they were supposed to do.

Hunt down and kill the enemy.

Forward Headquarters, Burapha Payak Corps, Thailand

The maps on the walls showed the developing situation quite clearly. The 11th Infantry Division was north of the Tonle Sap, crossing the border into Cambodia and advancing towards the banks of the Mekong River. So far, they hadn't experienced any serious opposition; just a few scattered patrols and the unfortunate border guards. Further south, two regiments of the 9th Infantry Division pushed along the road to Battambang. They were having a tougher time. Battambang was the headquarters of the French Indochina Army this far south; it was well-placed to organize a proper defense.

That was exactly what Suriyothai hoped they were doing.

"Your Highness, two farang ladies to see you." General Arthit Kongsampong seemed slightly surprised at the number of women who were descending on the command center of an army corps. Having the corps commanded by a woman was shocking enough, although the whispers about this woman officer were startling indeed. Two farang women turning up as guests was something quite else.

"Send them in." Suriyothai looked at the map again. The tiny piece of Laos that lay west of the Mekong was already well on its way to being secured by a battalion of infantry. A regiment of the 11th Infantry was moving west to cover its flank. It was a good start.

"Igrat, Achillea; It has been a long time since we met under these circumstances."

305

Igrat smiled broadly and made a creditable attempt at a respectful wai. Suriyothai solemnly returned it. Achillea followed Igrat in. She had grease on her blouse and smudges of oil on her nose and cheeks.

"What happened Achillea?"

"A couple of your men were having trouble with a Hotchkiss thirteen-point-two. Headspace adjustment screw had jammed. I fixed it for them. Just poured boiling water over it and that expanded the metal enough to get the screw loose."

"Ahh, I see." Suriyothai had no doubt that Achillea was now politely worshipped by the men she had helped. There was something about the combination of Achillea, oil, grease and guns that men found irresistible. "How did you two get up here and what do you want?"

"Hitched a lift on a supply truck headed this way." Igrat spoke as if cadging lifts on army supply trucks was the most natural thing in the world. To her, it was. "My father has some information for you. He says that Cordell Hull has softened his position and he is prepared to allow the transfer of American-produced arms to Thailand. They will be supplied from India. But, my father cautions, to consolidate this position, you need to do two things. One is to make visible progress towards a democratic form of government. The other is to kick a Japanese unit around very soon. You need to be seen as an enemy of an enemy."

Suriyothai nodded. Relief flooded through her. The single greatest obstacle to all her plans was crumbling. "I can promise the kicking around as soon as the Japanese move. That will be when they realize how far we will be advancing into Indochina. They will try and intervene with diplomacy; we will turn them down and they will be more forceful. Then we will demonstrate how foolish that approach will be. What will we get from the Indians?"

"Hawk 75 fighters, the latest model, and DB-7 light bombers. And, direct from America, thirty A-24 dive bombers. They are in compensation for the other aircraft you purchased and did not receive. Now, my father asks, can he have details of your plans for this campaign?"

"No." Suriyothai was absolutely firm on that. "I haven't even told me what our plans are yet. Now, what else have you got? Phillip wouldn't send you all this way just for this."

"Mostly reports on business involvement in this area. Phillip is investing in India especially and he wants you to be aware of what is going on. He has also picked up word that the Hongs are moving to Bangkok and he is curious as to whether you have a hand in this." Igrat's voice took on her own pitch and cadence. "He is, of course, being sarcastic when asking that. But he regards stabilizing the economies of the area as being a very high priority. That also reflects U.S. Government policy, although the decisions were not linked. Both he and Secretary Morgenthau came to the same conclusions for the same reasons."

"How did he hear about the Hongs?" Suriyothai was genuinely curious. She had thought that information was strictly controlled. Igrat didn't answer and Suriyothai realized she knew, but wasn't going to say anything. "Alright. Forget I asked. Tell Phillip this. We're going to destroy the French Army in Indochina. That is already in hand. Think Sedan. We're moving one division along the northern part of the Mekong now to deal with any Japanese incursion. The Japanese are desperately short of maneuver units and the most they can throw at us is a single division. We can handle that. Everything else is details and subject to change at short notice.

11th Infantry (Queen's Cobra) Division, Angkrong, Cambodia

Mongkut was quietly proud of both himself and his squad. In fact, of the whole platoon. Ever since they had eliminated the border post, they had been advancing at the double-quick-time: 180 paces to the minute. Six months of training had shown its value. His men chewed up the five kilometers that separated them from Angkrong in less than forty minutes. They'd been helped by geography. The road had snaked around, but after the crest of the ridge had been passed, it had all been downhill.

Looking behind him, Mongkut could see the mountains that delineated the border. In front of him was the flat plain that had so recently been part of Thailand, but had been seized by the French and made part of their Indochina empire. Now, it would be returned to its rightful owners. That thought cheered Mongkut. It offset the rawness in his chest from the prolonged quick-time march.

Angkrong was a basic rectangle of four unsurfaced roads, divided horizontally into upper and lower halves by a fifth. On a map, it looked like a figure-of-eight that had been squashed so it was wider than it was high. The road that Mongkut and his men were following led into the northeast corner of the town, the top right hand corner of the 8. The road that formed the bottom of the eight was the critical one. Once that was seized, Thai infantry could advance east or west, according to their desires. Their seizure of the road would also prevent the French Indochina Army from moving eastwards. It was a key part of the plan to split the French Army apart and dismember each section separately.

Mongkut waved his arm. His men scattered to the right hand side of the road. Behind him, the next squad was going left. The effect was simple. What had been a column of troops advancing down a road was now a line that would assault the village. The orders had been very strict. 'Remember, not so long ago, these people were our countrymen. Treat them with respect, for they are to be our countrymen again.'

The company had finished deploying for the assault. Mongkut heard the whistles blow. That was the signal for the charge. He broke into a jog-trot. Then, he was in a full run towards the town. It was quiet. No dogs barked or chickens crowed; just the pounding sound of army boots running on hard ground. Mongkut was panting as he reached the first line of huts. They were poor things by the standard of his home village; rotting wooden walls topped by a thatched roof. A piece of tattered cloth substituted for a front door. The obvious poverty made him hate what he had to do next, but the safety of his men depended on it.

He grabbed the cloth and flung it to one side, pushing his way into the hut. There were two women inside; one young and feeding her baby, the other much older. *Probably the young woman's mother*, Momgkut thought. The young woman screamed and swung away, shielding both herself and her baby from the stranger. Mongkut reacted quickly.

"I am sorry to frighten you. Are there any French soldiers here?"

The young woman showed no sign of understanding. Her mother broke out into a beam of delight at the Thai words. She replied quickly in the same language, the words coarsened from long disuse. "At the other end of the village. There are a few. You have come back?"

Mongkut knew what she meant. "We are back and this time to stay. We will not allow our land to be stolen today. Now, excuse me, Mother; we have much work to be done today." As he left, a thought occurred to him. "Where are your ducks and chickens?"

"The French did not allow us to keep them. They said we must buy all our meat and eggs from them. All we were allowed to grow was rice."

Mongkut was shocked. *A village of farmers not allowed to own ducks?* It was unnatural. In the short time he had been checking the hut, a crackle of rifle fire broke out in the far corner of Angkrong. He led his men to the sound of the firing. It was over by the time he had got there. Five men, a corporal and four privates of the 4th *Tirailleurs Tonkinois*, were standing with their hands raised; their Berthier rifles on the ground beside them. None were injured. A quick glance showed Mongkut that none of the Thai troops were hurt either.

"It wasn't serious." Mongkut's sergeant was watching the scene. "They fired a few rounds for honor's sake, we fired a few to show we were serious and they surrendered."

"Sergeant, may I speak with an officer? I have information they might need."

The sergeant nodded and pointed at a Lieutenant, who was reading a map. Mongkut went over to him and saluted. "Permission to speak, sir?"

"Corporal?"

"Sir, the importance of winning over these villagers was much emphasized. I have learned the French would not let them keep their own ducks. Perhaps, if we gave them some to keep, they might look on us as friends?"

Lieutenant Somchai Preecha nodded. In fact, Mongkut was the third man to approach him with that idea. "A good idea, Corporal. I will mention it to our Captain. Now, assemble your squad and head east. We have far to go today."

There was a steady crackle of rifle fire from the hills as the attack spread along the border. It was punctuated by blasts Mongkut recognized as mortar rounds. The French defenders were realizing this was a serious invasion and beginning to try and organize resistance. It was too late for them to defend the border. They would have to concentrate on a defense further inland. Mongkut wondered where that would be, then dismissed the question. He and his men would find out soon enough.

There was a sudden redoubling of the rifle fire from the area of a ruined temple just to their east, followed by a series of loud explosions. The lieutenant looked at the area and grimaced. "The old temple up there; the one surrounded by cliffs. If there are any enemy troops in it, they have nowhere to go. We have much work to do today as well as far to go, Corporal. And your men will lead the regiment."

That's phrased as an honor, Mongkut thought, *but it's a really dangerous job we could do without.* He went back to his men who were resting on the dried-out grass. "Time to move out, men. It is our honor to lead the regiment."

There were groans of displeasure at the news, but his men hauled themselves to their feet, picked up their rifles and got ready to head west. They returned to the double-quick time they had used to get here and left the village of Angkrong in fine style. As they did so, the men saw the villagers making respectful wais to them as they passed. *Perhaps there is something in this liberating business after all,* Mongkut thought to himself. They were supposed to advance to another small village, Choeteal Kong, some 16 kilometers due east of Angkrong. Mongkut hoped that it wouldn't be so poor and run-down as Angkrong had been.

French Sloop Dumont d'Urville, *At Sea, South of Muang Trat*

"Is there any news?"

Lieutenant Laurent Babineau stuck his head through the hatch leading to the radio room. Inside, the radio duty crew were scanning the airwaves, trying to find out what was happening.

"Sir, all we know is that the Siamese have crossed the border in large numbers and are advancing on Battambang. Their aircraft have attacked airfields all over Indochina. This is not a border clash, sir. This is a real war."

Babineau nodded. *Dumont d'Urville* was patrolling the Cambodian coast of Indochina, with emergency orders to bombard Thai coastal towns in the event of any border disputes. With three 5.5-inch guns, she was well-suited to that task. However, the authorities in Hanoi had not anticipated the situation breaking into a full-blooded war. With her feeble anti-aircraft armament of four old 37mm guns, she was hardly suited for an independent deployment within range of enemy air forces.

"Sir, message coming in." The morse code hammered for a few seconds, paused, and then hammered again. "Sir, it's official. We are at war with the Kingdom of Thailand. We are to execute Plan Green."

The operator tore off the message flimsy and handed it to Babineau. Up on the bridge, Captain Toussaint de Quieverecourt was scanning the horizon with his binoculars.

"Captain, message has come in. It's war. We are to execute Plan Green."

The Captain sighed. "The politicos in Hanoi have been asking for this. Now they've got it. I hope they're happy. Plan Green, you say? That's the bombardment of Muang Trat. Make revolutions for 15 knots. We want to get in and out before we are spotted."

Babineau rang the orders down to the engine room. He felt the sloop vibrate as her Sulzer diesels picked up power. Muang Trat lay at the end of a long inlet; one that had a finger of Thai territory on one side and a group of Thai-owned islands, including a major naval anchorage at Koh Chang, on the other. Toussaint de Quieverecourt tapped the islands with his forefinger.

"If the Siamese have a squadron deployed here, we will be completely out of luck."

That is the sort of understatement the milk-drinking surrender monkeys would come out with, Babineau thought, bitterness swelling at the memory of the way France had been abandoned to fight the Germans on her own. "Their Navy isn't up to much."

"No." Toussaint de Quieverecourt was thoughtful in his agreement. "Certainly their weakest point. But this sloop is hardly a front line warship. Order the crew to action stations. We're so close to the enemy coast that this situation can drop in the pot very fast. I think we would be well-advised to avoid the splash."

"Sir, aircraft approaching from due north." The starboard lookout's cry was urgent.

Babineau used his binoculars to scan the indicated direction. "I see them Captain. Biplanes; nine of them."

"Full speed; hold nothing back." Toussaint de Quieverecourt did some quick mental calculations. *If those are Thai dive bombers, we are in deep trouble.*

The aircraft approached steadily. *Dumont d'Urville's* pathetic anti-aircraft guns were unable to put up any form of defense before the attack was well underway. Babineau watched the first flight of three aircraft, now clearly recognizable as Curtiss Hawk IIIs, peeling over into their dives. Toussaint de Quieverecourt was watching them as well. He waited until the aircraft were committed to their dives before giving the next order.

"Hard to port, now."

310

Dumont d'Urville swerved; her side rails nearly submerged as the ship tilted over. She had been built to police far-off colonies and show the flag, not get involved in major battles. It all went to show that no plan survived contact with the enemy. Babineau watched a pair of bombs detach from under the wings of the lead aircraft. He saw them arc down towards his ship. He was convinced they were going to hit. But the last-second swerve threw off the Thai pilot's aim. They exploded in the sea, well to starboard. Another pair of bombs hit the water the other side of the ship, splashing her with water and causing fragments to bounce off the steel plating.

Only four bombs? Babineau looked around; he saw the second dive bomber had held its fire. It pulled up to repeat its dive. To his amazement, the pilot made three more passes before dropping finally his bombs.

The results justified his dedication. His two bombs straddled the hull neatly, neither more than a few meters from the hull plating. The sloop rocked with the blast. The men on the 37mm guns fell as fragments scythed through their positions. Babineau felt the ship slowing abruptly as the engines failed. Sure enough, the engineering officer was on the line.

"We've lost power. Those bombs stalled the diesels." There was a tinge of panic in the message from the engine rooms.

"Well, you had better restart them, hadn't you?" Toussaint de Quieverecourt spoke in a steady, imperturbable voice that seemed completely unaware of the fact his ship was dead in the water while under air attack.

"Lieutenant, do we have any anti-aircraft guns left?"

Babineau looked aft to where the 37mm mounts were located. The dead and wounded were being pulled off the mounts and replaced by other seamen. "Our 37s will be back in a moment, sir. And we still have our machine guns, if the Siamese try to strafe us."

"We'll just have to hope that will be enough, won't we?" The Captain's voice was still calm and collected. Hearing it steadied the bridge crew. So did the belch of black smoke from the forefunnel as the diesels in the forward engine room came back on line. *Dumont d'Urville* started to move forward again as the second flight of Hawk IIIs started their dives.

This time, there was no evasive action to throw off their aim. The three aircraft dropped a single bomb each. A 500-kilogram, not the 100-kilogram bombs the first flight dropped. Babineau watched the bombs drop down towards the sloop. This time, he knew they would hit. *This is going to hurt.*

One exploded in the water just beside the forward 5.5-inch guns. It shook the ship with the same ferocity that a terrier shook a cornered rat. Fragments from the explosion sliced into the hull, tearing up the great black letters A72 painted on the bows. The second was equally close, but on the other side. Again, the ship was sprayed with water and fragments; ones that rocked the ship and cut down exposed members of the crew. The third crashed home aft; a direct hit on the catapult and the Loire seaplane. The whole area erupted into flame. A black plume of smoke stained the crystal-clear, blue morning sky.

The burst of power from the engines had been stopped again. *Dumont d'Urville* was dead in the water and burning. Overhead, the Thai Hawk IIIs circled, surveying the scene. Babineau guessed that the three aircraft that hadn't dived were the fighter escort. They were probably debating what to do next. The sloop was badly hurt; there was no doubt about that in his mind. The question was whether more aircraft would be sent to finish her off.

"Sir, aft engine room reports the temperature there is rising quickly from the fire, but they have the aft pair of diesels back on line. We can make five knots now, perhaps ten in an hour, *if* we can get that fire out. We have flooding forward and amidships. The damage control crews are having trouble establishing a flooding perimeter because of all the fragment holes."

"Change course; head due east. Plan Green is abandoned. All available hands, fight the fire aft. Once that's out, they are to join the damage control teams trying to stop the flooding." Toussaint de Quieverecourt looked up at the Hawk IIIs circling overhead. "I think they are leaving us alone. I believe the Siamese are stretching their aircraft to the utmost and knocking us out of action will be good enough for them. We'll go home and lick our wounds. And report what happened here. That was a very well executed attack.

"I think the gentlemen in Hanoi have seriously underestimated our enemy."

11th Infantry (Queen's Cobra) Division, Choeteal Kong, Cambodia

"We've pushed the *Tirailleurs Tonkinois* back here. Now, we're going to engage them. Their officers have managed to organize a line of defense along this clearing east of Choeteal Kong. We're going to push them out of it and destroy the unit in the process."

Lieutenant Somchai Prachakorn looked up from the packet that had been dropped by an Avro 504 trainer a few minutes earlier. "Corporal Mongkut. Platoon Sergeant Kamon was wounded outside Angkrong. You are promoted to Sergeant and will take his place. Our platoon will form the lead element of this attack. We have a forward air controller with us. When we make contact with the *Tirailleurs Tonkinois*, he will call in dive bombers to support us."

Overhead, the puttering of a low-powered aircraft engine intruded on the briefing. The Avro 504 was back, circling overhead. After a few seconds, a small package with a white streamer attached was thrown from the back seat. It landed in the middle of the camp. Mongkut ran out and brought it back to his Lieutenant, who read the contents with satisfaction.

"The Avro says, the enemy positions are where we thought; a few hundred meters down the path. They gave away their position by firing on the aircraft. Foolish of them."

"Fortunate for us." Mongkut had just realized he had been made a platoon sergeant.

"Very fortunate. Sergeant, Kam asked me to give you these. They are his sergeant's stripes. He also sends a message; that if you ruin his platoon, he will beat you. Now, sew them to your uniform and move our platoon up. Oh, and recommend one of the men from your old squad for promotion to Corporal."

The hours they had spent at the double-quick time along dirt roads were now a fond memory. The platoon was moving through scrubland; country covered with bushes and the occasional outcrop of trees. This was also snake country, infested with kraits and cobras. Fortunately they preferred not to confront humans and were doubtless moving out of the way. It was just one more problem Mongkut had to think about.

He had his sergeant's stripes sewn to his uniform, quickly and clumsily, but still in place. Returning to his old squad, he'd felt a wrench at being parted from the men he'd served with ever since being called back to the colors. *Who do I recommend as squad corporal? Din, who everybody likes? Or Pon, who is the best soldier but unpopular?* Then he remembered the advice he had been given on his promotion to Corporal. *We will help you along.* He would consult with the other Sergeants.

He looked quickly right and left, checking that his men were spread out properly as they advanced. Over to his far left, the great ridge of hills that marked the old border still glowered down on the advancing infantry. The 11th was advancing parallel with that old border and would continue to do so until they reached the Mekong River. Then, they would fan out along it to establish the new border. *No, re-establish the true border.* Another glance behind showed the small truck that followed at a respectful distance.

The *Tirailleurs Tonkinois* battalion defending the treeline gave its position away by firing far too early. The patter of rifle fire was largely ineffective, although it did cause the advancing Thai infantry to go to ground. Mongkut heard a hammering noise; the platoon Lewis gun opened fire to cover the first step in a leapfrog advance.

"Hold positions." Lieutenant Somchai snapped an order out. "The dive bombers are coming in. We'll attack as soon as they've finished."

The word was obviously spreading along the line. The sounds of firing died down to a few isolated shots. Mongkut got a feeling than the enemy battalion was probably congratulating itself for having stopped the attack. If so, they were in for an ugly disappointment. He could already hear the sound of aircraft engines overhead. A quick look upwards showed two flights, each of three Vought Corsair biplanes, overhead.

They peeled over into their dives. The sound that erupted was an earsplitting cacophony of sheer terror. In addition to the scream of their engines, the Corsairs had sirens mounted on their fixed undercarriages. The trick was one they had learned from their German instructors; they placed considerable emphasis on just how demoralizing it was to those on the receiving end. The wailing noise reminded Mongkut of the ghosts that inhabited an old ruined temple near where he had grown up. The volume of the shrieking howls was so great it made him want to flee. He hugged the ground and forced himself to wait for the bombing to end.

The ground shuddered as the first explosions tore into the French positions. Mongkut felt a smack on his back and looked up. Lieutenant Somchai already on his feet and running towards the ripple of explosions that marked the *Tonkinois* defenses. Mongkut couldn't allow him to go alone; he rose to his feet and followed. Behind him, the rest of his platoon did the same. The unit sprinted across the ground towards where the 50-kilogram bombs were still landing. Clods of earth, sticks and fragments of metal were still flying as they closed in on their enemy.

The *Tonkinois* riflemen were stunned, incapable of resistance. Only a few seconds, a minute or so at most, marked the gap between the dive bombers finishing their work and the Thai infantry leaping the barriers and engaging the defenders. Miongkut saw the blue-clad *Tonkinois* throw down their rifles and hold up their hands in surrender. Some tried to run away. They were shot or bayoneted as they left their rifle pits. Others were on the ground, crying out for mercy as they writhed with the wounds from the bombing. Then there were those who were on the ground and would never move again. Between the dead, the wounded and the prisoners, the 4th Battalion of the *Tirailleurs Tonkinois* had completely collapsed as a fighting force.

Forward Headquarters, Burapha Payak Corps, Thailand

"First reports in, Highness. A battalion of the First Regiment, 11th Infantry Division has engaged a battalion force of the Tirailleurs Tonkinois. The air support techniques Wing Commander Fuen devised have worked very well. The enemy battalion collapsed with only nominal resistance. They have taken over 250 prisoners and four guns. Our casualties were three dead and eleven wounded. Very little resistance in Laos. We have already captured Pakse and the battalion assigned there is spreading out along the Mekong. Ninth Infantry Division is advancing with tank support along RC157 towards Battambang. They took Poipet without any opposition but they report French skirmishing is increasing."

"Keep those troops under control. We need the French to come forward to meet them, not retreat away from them." Suriyothai's voice was sharp and decisive. One regiment of the 9th Infantry was advancing along the Battambang road but it was little more that bait to draw the French Indochina Army into a catastrophic encirclement. Their job was entirely different from that of 11th Infantry. The Queen's Cobra Division had to sweep forward as fast as possible to secure the northern flank of the advance. The Black Panther Division had to advance slowly to lure the French forward.

"The commanders know that, Highness, and are gauging their actions accordingly." Suriyothai's aide swallowed slightly at the near-rebuke he had delivered. On being appointed to the position, he had been warned that the one unforgivable sin was to tell the Princess what he thought she wanted to hear. What she actually wanted was the truth and nothing else.

"In the air, our pilots report destroying 17 aircraft on the ground and three in the air. The latter were all MS.406s shot down by our Hawk 75s. We lost three aircraft; all Hawk IIIs. Every aircraft we have is hard at work, either supporting the Army or hunting the French fighters. Except the dive bombers of Foong Kap Lai 72. They found a French sloop moving towards Trat. They bombed it, leaving it burning and dead in the water. We believe the French are planning bombardments of our coastal towns."

"We cannot allow that." Suriyothai looked at the map pinned up on one wall of the headquarters. "What does the Navy say about this?"

"They have promised to move a squadron down to the anchorage at Koh Chang. A coastal defense ship and four torpedo boats. They believe that will deter any further French naval enterprises."

"I hope so. It doesn't matter too much, though. This war will be decided on the ground and in the air. French bombardments will kill civilians; that is all. Has the Foreign Office had any official word from anybody yet?"

"No, Highness. Although it is still very early for an official response. The French authorities in Hanoi have formally declared war on us though."

Suriyothai frowned slightly. "I'm not sure they can do that. The central government in Vichy can certainly can, but we have heard nothing from them?"

"Nothing, Highness. But Field Marshal Wavell agreed a cease-fire and peace treaty with the Italians just a few days ago. He has even less standing than Hanoi."

"No." Suriyothai was decisive on that point. "Wavell was acting as an Indian Army officer, not a British Army officer, and his orders from Calcutta were very clear. India had declared itself fully independent and was acting as a separate country. Hanoi has not made that declaration and it is still a French colony. They do not have the authority to declare war on anybody. I think they may have just played into our hands again."

Suriyothai waved and the officer left her alone. Once again her mind shifted into gear. The waterfall display of swirling colored lights formed. The strands interlocked and merged, only to split apart again as the events that drove them eddied and swirled. The thread that she had first recognized only six months ago was now pulsing brighter and more strongly than it had ever done before. She looked at it, evaluated it and carefully weighed its progress. Now, it dominated all the others; to the point where it had mass and momentum all of its own. As long as this war went well, it was the primary thread of the future at last.

"As long as this war goes well."

Suriyothai spoke the words aloud. Everything that she had to achieve, economic, political, military, social, came down to that one requirement. This war had to go well.

Room 208, Munitions Building, Washington, DC, USA

"Phillip, what do your business contacts make of this war?"

Henry Stimson was reading the initial reports on the fighting with some interest. True to form, the only really accurate reports so far were in the Singapore-based *Straits Times*.

"There's very little reliable information in the public domain, of course." Stuyvesant was speaking carefully. "But the consensus is that the recent bombing attacks on Thai border cities finally pushed the Thais too far, and they want to secure their population against further attacks. Of course, there's the matter of exactly where the border really runs. The French established the current border in 1907, literally at gunpoint. The Thais, many of them anyway, regard that as an unresolved question. However, in a strange way, that is probably only a side issue. The real conundrum here is where the French authorities in Hanoi stand."

"Hanoi has declared war on Thailand." Cordell Hull sounded uncharacteristically uncertain of himself. "After their bombing attacks while I was there, that would seem hardly necessary. It seems to me that Hanoi has been spoiling for a fight."

"Most of the business people I have spoken to agree with that." Stuyvesant thought for a second before continuing. "Ever since the Japanese seized key positions across northern Indochina last year, the actions of the authorities in Hanoi have confused everybody. They seem to be determined to provoke a major conflict in the region, despite the fact that they are at a serious disadvantage without support from metropolitan France. Their policies do not appear to be aligned with their interests. In fact, the only people who can benefit from their actions are the Japanese. We know the Japanese see Indochina as a secure basing area for a possible assault on the rest of South East Asia."

"The French start a war in Indochina; the Japanese move in as peacemakers and reinforce their position across the whole area." Stimson nodded, his mind running across the permutations. "That makes sense. Are the Hanoi authorities that much of Japanese puppets, though?"

"With a whole Japanese infantry division sitting around Hanoi, do they have a choice? I think it is very significant that this declaration of war came from Hanoi, not Vichy. After all, the only difference between Hanoi and Vichy is . . ."

"One Japanese infantry division sitting around the former." Stuyvesant finished off the thought, causing Hull to smile for the first time since he had returned from Thailand. "I agree. The actions of the French authorities in Hanoi are obviously quite distinct from those of the Vichy government in France and we must presume that they are being dictated by the Japanese. That would make Hanoi a Japanese ally, albeit probably an unwilling one." *And that, Suriyothai, honey, is as far as I am going to go. You're on your own from now on.*

General Marshall reached out and tapped a map of the area. "This is where the battle will take place. The French will have to assemble their forces and that puts the fighting near Battambang. This village is where the north-south road, RC-160, crosses the east-west road RC-157. It's on the banks of a river that gives the French a good defensive position. That's where the French will hold. The village of Yang Dham Khung."

Infantry Platoon, Second Battalion, *16e* Regiment d'Infanterie Coloniale, *Phoum Kham Reng, French Indochina*

The low ridge gave the roadblock at least some warning of the enemy approach. Lieutenant Jourdain Roul had positioned the block just behind the ridgeline so that it would be protected from direct fire. Pickets on the ridge line itself had a good line of vision that stretched all the way back to the hills on the Thai border. Given how little warning he had received of the attack now obviously in progress, it was the best he could do. Very soon, his work would be put to the test. He had been hearing sporadic rifle and machine gun fire all morning, getting steadily closer to his position. *The Third Battalion,* Tirailleurs Tonkinois *aren't holding the border the way they were supposed to. If that's true all over, then we have some serious problems.*

Roul's briefing had been brief but to-the-point. The Thais had invaded Indochina and were advancing down Route Colonial 157 to Battambang. They had to be stopped. That meant the forces in the area had to be assembled into a proper military formation. Doing that required time. Roul's platoon was to block the road and delay the Thais to buy that time. The briefing had been short; as far as Roul was concerned, the only important word in it was the one that hadn't been said. Sacrifice. He and his men were being sacrificed to buy time.

He scanned the ground in front of him with his binoculars. He had expected to see the Thai infantry swarming forward, but the swathe of relatively low-laying ground seemed deserted. They had to be there, though. The sounds of gunfire were proof of that. RC-157 was lined with small huts, the homes of local farmers. Every so often, a flare would go up from one. There was no discernable reason why; although Roul assumed they marked the position of the Thai lead elements. With the quiet drone of the aircraft overhead, it was actually a remarkably peaceful scene. It couldn't stay that way long. The Thais were advancing; it was their aircraft flying over the battlefield.

317

Nobody had seen any French aircraft. Rumors were spreading that they had all been destroyed on the ground.

Roul wormed his way back from the observation point and checked the defenses his men were digging. There was a slit trench on either side of the road, exploiting the reverse slope to gain protection from artillery fire. Roul had selected the ground himself, taking full advantage of a small area of bushes to provide a little cover. It was a scarce resource along RC-157. The ground seemed bare and almost desolate, other than the odd patches of crab bush and the occasional stand of trees. Almost a kilometer south of his position was a small stream that ran through a depression. Roul had marked that out as his retreat route. He'd noticed that RC-157 was commanded by higher ground on both sides. He had come to the conclusion that any attempt to retreat along the road would be a disaster. Once his position here was untenable, he would fall back on the stream and use its bed for cover as he retreated to the next holding position. The road actually made a loop and the streambed lay across the neck of the loop. He had his third squad dug in to protect the dirt track leading to the stream, thus protecting his line of retreat. It was the best he could come up with.

Having checked his men were digging in properly, he returned to the observation point. The situation didn't appear to have changed much during his absence, although one of the flares going up showed that the enemy infantry were a lot closer. Now, at last, he could see them. They moved carefully through the huts that lined RC-157. Their dark green uniforms and German-style helmets clearly distinguished them from the *Tirailleurs Tonkinois,* who wore the standard French horizon blue and the Adrian helmet. *Whatever had happened to the* Tonkinois *riflemen, they aren't retreating along the road.*

That was when Roul saw something that filled him with dismay. A pair of tanks supported the Thai infantry. He recognized them immediately; Vickers 6-ton Type B. Armed with a machine gun and a 47mm gun in a two-man turret, they were more than capable of destroying his roadblock. Once he revealed his position, the battle was going to get ugly very quickly. Roul began to suspect he knew what had happened to the *Tirailleurs Tonkinois.*

Beside him, private first class Léo Corneille had shouldered his Berthier rifle and taken a sight on the Thai infantry below. He was the platoon sniper; a skill that had gained him the distinction of being a first class private rather than a humdrum ordinary one. His Berthier had a three-power magnification telescopic sight. Roul watched his rifle moving as Corneille scanned for a suitable target.

"Corneille, on the road, beside the third building on the left. He looks like an officer."

Roul looked again. The man was definitely giving some sort of orders to the other infantrymen. That made him either an officer or a senior NCO. Beside him, Corneille nodded. He settled down into the authorized firing position. There was a flat crack as the Berthier fired. Roul saw the man spotted

318

crumple to the ground. He was hoping somebody would come out and pull the victim to cover; that would provide Corneille with another target. Instead, one of the tanks pulled in front of the victim, screening him from view. By the time the tank moved again, the ground was empty. Reluctantly, Roul was impressed. *Somebody thought that out.*

Overhead, the gentle buzz of aircraft engines changed. It seemed no more threatening than it had before, but it grew closer and seemed to pause above the platoon. Roul looked up. A biplane was circling overhead, obviously attracted by the shot that had brought the Thai soldier down. Roul couldn't recognize the aircraft. It looked a little bit like the French Potez 25, but seemed flimsier somehow. From behind him, tracers arched through the air. His three squad light machine guns fired on the aircraft. It turned and left the scene. Mentally, Roul cheered on his gunners who had driven the enemy aircraft away.

The whine of inbound shells changed the situation completely. Roul recognized them immediately; they were French 75s. For a moment he believed he was getting some timely artillery support, but the hope was quickly dashed. The shells exploded on the front slope of his position. That didn't worry him too much; he had used the reverse slope to protect his road block for exactly that reason.

"Time to drop back behind the ridge, sir?"

Sergeant Arsène Ambroise had put exactly the right note of respectful urgency into his comment. That was hardly surprising; he was a veteran who had served in the trenches during the Great War. The rounds from the 75s weren't actually that close to the observation point, but there was little reason to wait around until they were. The four men in the post scrambled back over the ridge and down towards the defensive positions.

Roul cound see that the Sergeants had done their work well. All the men were in position and alerted for the fighting that seemed imminent. A quick glance around him suggested that his unit was as well-positioned and readied as anybody could expect. All that was left was to wait for the Thai infantry and the two tanks to come over the hilltop. He was confident his men could handle the infantry; the tanks had him worried.

The wait seemed to stretch on. Roul knew that the Thai infantry had some six hundred meters to advance before they could assault the hill he occupied. It seemed like they were taking their own sweet time about it. He glanced down at his watch, surprised by how little time had actually passed since the first shots from the 75s. The artillery fire had ceased after those first few rounds. Roul was sorely tempted to go back to the ridgeline and find out what was happening.

A patter of rifle fire erupted from the low ridge off to his right. It was only some ten meters higher than his positions and was about six hundred meters away. That meant the fire was largely ineffective against dug-in infantry but it was more than annoying. The axis of attack against his platoon had changed. Now, he faced an attack from due north as well as from the west. He knew why the attack had been so long in arriving now. The Thais hadn't charged his position head on; they had outflanked him.

"A nice move." Sergeant Ambroise seemed quite impressed. "Should we order our squad on the right to return fire, sir?"

Roul thought for a second. The rifle fire seemed ill-directed and largely ineffective. As far as he could tell, not one of the bullets had bitten yet. "No, keep them quiet. No point in giving the enemy targets to aim at. We'll let the situation mature."

His orders were to block the road and delay the Thai advance for as long as possible. He was doing just that. That he had only expended one rifle round and a couple of bursts of machine gun fire to do so seemed to him to be a good thing. Nothing, even rifle ammunition, here in Indochina was in copious supply. There was no telling when any ammunition he expended would be replaced. His thoughts on the neglect of the Indochina Army were interrupted by a renewed crash of artillery fire. This time the shots had arrived from his right. For the first time, the fight had become serious.

"Damn, that will be difficult. They've brought up infantry guns." Ambroise recognized the distinctive noise of the short-barrelled Japanese 75mm infantry howitzers; quite different from the flat crack of the earlier guns. "And they're spreading along the ridge."

Roul swung his binoculars to the east. Behind his position, almost a kilometer away, were two hills. One was 218 meters high, the other 200. Hills 218 and 200 dominated the area, simply because they were the only really high ground in the area. Given his choice, Roul would have occupied them, but doing so would not have blocked the road. He could see what the Thai commander had in mind now. *He's spreading along the ridge and will occupy those hills. He won't be blocking the road, but he doesn't want to. What he wants is me out of the way. With those hills in his hands, he can sweep the entire platoon into the can.*

The infantry guns had got the range. Two of the shells slammed into Roul's squad on the right hand side of RC-157. What had been a good position to defend against an attack along the road was a bad one to defend against an attack from the north. It was obvious that the Thais knew where his positions were. With a flash of insight, Roul knew why. *The aircraft my men 'scared' off had seen where the machine gun fire had come from and reported back. Firing on that aircraft had been a really bad idea.*

"Sergeant, order our first squad to drop back. Their position is already compromised and the artillery is ranged in on them. They can achieve nothing where they are. We'll drop back to the ridge to the south here. We'll still be blocking the road but we'll be in dead ground for the guns to the north and west. And we'll still be covering our line of withdrawal."

Ambroise gave the orders. Horizon blue figures left their trench and headed backwards towards the huts that lined RC-157. Not all of them; two of the twelve remained behind, their figures still. The enemy artillery got two more before they reached cover. Shells from the infantry guns threw them in the air and left them twisted heaps on the ground. *A third of the squad gone*, Roul thought, *and nothing to show for it.*

"It's the guns that kill, sir." Ambroise sounded thoughtful. "They've got just two of them up on that ridge, but that section is all they need. Ahh, there they go. Clever little buggers, aren't they?"

The two infantry guns fired a pattern of smoke rounds. White clouds billowed in front of Roul's new positions. For a hideous moment, Roul had thought they were gas rounds. He almost gave a gas attack alert, but he realized what was happening when the Thai infantry broke from cover. He watched the small groups move forward, leapfrogging from point to point, with each group covering the rest.

Ambroise was watching them carefully. "*Stosstruppen* tactics. I think all the stories we heard about German instructors must be true. Or British veterans."

"Milk-drinking surrender monkeys?" Roul was openly derisive. "The Siamese are attacking us, not running away."

A stutter of rifle fire rose from the French positions along RC-157, but the smokescreen made the defensive fire ineffective. It was significant the squad machine gun hadn't opened fire yet. Machine guns were always a priority target. Gunners never fired unless they had worthwhile targets or fixed lines set up. No machine-gun fire meant the defenders were firing blind.

"The Tommies in the trenches were good, Lieutenant." Ambroise was patient, as befitted a veteran sergeant with a young officer to train. "In 1914, they knew all the tricks that the Germans claim to have invented for their stosstruppen and a few more besides. And they knew how to put them into practice. Their army lost that edge in the middle of the war, but they had it back by the end. But, those Siamese are German-trained. You can tell by the way they're moving forward."

Below them, the French squad machine gun finally opened fire. The two Thai infantry guns shifted fire to the huts occupied by the survivors of the squad. The pressure of the fire from the guns and the rifle fire from the advancing infantry started to push the French force back. With the smoke clearing, Roul could see further east along RC-157. The sight was not encouraging. The attack on his position was just one part of a company-level assault along the road. To make matters worse, He could see they were already in process of seizing Hill 218. That left his little command in a very precarious position.

"And its time for us to leave, Sergeant. We can't stay here." Roul knew the truth. In a few minutes, his position would be hopeless; its lines of withdrawal cut off. Then, his men would only have the choices of dying in a brave but futile fight or surrendering. "Order the men to fall back along the pre-planned route."

Ambroise nodded and passed the orders out. The survivors of the first squad retreated again, leaving their position on RC-157 and falling back to the dirt track. Second squad peeled off and followed them; the third squad acted as a rearguard. Roul sighed and led his command section south as well.

As they trudged along the dirt track, Roul couldn't understand what had happened. He had expected an infantry attack with bare steel and a desperate fight in the ruins of the huts. Instead, it seemed as if there had been hardly any fighting at all; just a few artillery rounds and a scattered series of rifle shots. Yet, he was retreating away from the position he had been ordered to hold, leaving five of his men behind. Somehow, he felt sick and disappointed in both himself and the morning's work.

"Why, Sergeant? What did I do wrong."

Ambroise looked around quickly. Fortunately, there had been nobody in earshot. "Quiet, sir. Don't want the men to hear you've got doubts. Cut right into them that will. Nothing went wrong back there, sir; you did well."

"But we're retreating."

"We got maneuvered out of position. That's the way professionals do things. It's amateurs who make gallant charges on heavily-defended positions. We had a good defense there; would have been a tough one to break. So the Siamese didn't try. They just made it impossible for us to hold on there. And they took their time about it; did it right and didn't worry about doing it fast. They've been taught well."

Roul felt better. If the veteran sergeant thought he had done well, that took the sting out of a defeat. Yet, for all of that, it remained a defeat.

Bestwood Lodge, Arnold, Nottinghamshire, United Kingdom

"I don't believe the current situation is supportable. I would give it two years at most. That Man does not seem to realize that Britain and Germany are on divergent courses and a confrontation between the two is inevitable. A confrontation that will mean the destruction of one or the other. He is trying to deny the widening gap between the two nations and in doing so he is merely stoking the fires of the future conflict." Captain Peter Fleming of the Grenadier Guards looked owlishly at Duke of St Albans. "You should hear my young brother on the subject."

Osbourne de Vere Beauclerk nodded thoughtfully at his two guests. The contents of his wine cellar had only just started to recover after the depredations of Winston Churchill; now they were taking another nasty blow. Peter Fleming himself was abstemious enough, but his companion, Captain Mike Calvert of the Royal Engineers, was sinking whisky as a phenomenal rate. *If he carries on like that,* the Duke thought, *his liver won't last two years.*

"What do you suggest we do about it? Stage a coup ourselves?"

Fleming shook his head. "That won't work, not now. For good or ill, Halifax is established in power. We must not forget that he gained that power quite legally, even if his use of legality was underhanded. Events now have their own momentum and we must run with that. The situation will come to a head in two years; three at the very outside. We have that long to prepare."

The Duke decided that being obtuse was probably the best approach at this point. "Prepare for what? Resuming the war?"

"That would be the best possible outcome, if fortune was to favor us. I do not think the Germans will make that mistake twice. To invade this country as an act of war against organized opposition is futile. Germany has neither the resources nor the expertise to do it. If they had tried last year, we would have slaughtered them. Damn it, we still might now. Look at what Wavell and his Desert Rats have achieved over the last few weeks. They knocked Italy out of the war and wrapped up the Italian Empire. We were safe here in our island, but Halifax and his cronies never saw that. No; next time, the Germans will come by stealth and we will not see the invasion for what it is until it is all but complete. We must prepare a resistance movement for after that invasion."

Great minds think alike. I've been trying to do that ever since Nell and her friends spirited Winston out of the country. I just don't know how to start. Nobody seems to write instruction books on how to do it. "What is that to do with an old man like me? Hiding in the woods and shooting up patrols is a young man's game." *And a sober man's game.* The Duke cast an anguished glance at Calvert who had killed a bottle of pinch-bottle Haig in five straight pulls.

"One might think of a fake auxiliary police unit smuggling a certain figure out of the country and a Flying Fortress that arrived at Prestwick, took off and was never seen again. Little Brother was enormously impressed by that, Your Grace; he swears he will write it up as a novel one day. He believes there is a market for novels about spies. You've got a rare talent for this game; and, with respect, your age makes you all the less likely as a leader."

"But what do you want me to do?" The Duke put an air of despairing confusion into his voice.

"We're going to set up the resistance forces." It was Calvert speaking, his voice steady and level. *Dear God; he's sober. How?* Listening to him, the Duke had sudden doubts about the authenticity and strength of his whisky supply. Calvert carried on in the same, steady voice. "Colonel Colin Gubbins has been appointed by Winston to organize the force. It will consist of two components. The first being a military arm that will be raised out of, and technically be part of, the Home Guard. We're calling it the Auxiliary Units, in the hope that anybody coming across the name will confuse it with Butler's Auxiliary Police. They'll be supported by a civilian arm, the Special Duty Sections, recruited from the local civilian population. This group will act as the spotters for the Auxiliary Units. In addition, a signals structure will link the isolated bands into a national network that can act in concert. That network will work on behalf of a British government-in-exile and its representatives still in the United Kingdom. We want you to keep an eye open for likely civilian candidates and we want to place the root of the communications system here."

"So my job will be to recruit members of the civilian resistance?"

"No." Fleming was sharp and very emphatic. "You will coordinate recruiting but, Your Grace, you must *never* be directly involved in any operations again. Mike and I will be your aides and do the leg work. We are the cut-out between the German occupiers and the head of the resistance movement. That's you. Your job will be to coordinate recruitment and oversee the organization. At most, to spot likely candidates. We will do the rest."

Abbey Street, Nottingham, United Kingdom

"Halifax OUT! Halifax OUT! Halifax OUT OUT OUT!"

It is the eternal prerogative of university students to demonstrate. It worked off excess energy. University College Nottingham might not have been a fully-fledged university yet, and it might have to rely on the University of London to award its degrees, but that merely added to the fervor of its students. If they weren't quite university students, they'd show everybody that they had the spirit and energy to become ones. And so it was that the demonstration poured down Abbey Street; their banners held high and their chant echoing off the buildings. For all its energy, it was a good-mannered demonstration. No windows were broken and the students made sure that passers-by had the room they needed to go about their business. The police recognized that. The handful of constables on duty watched with tolerant smiles. More than a few of them agreed with the students.

It was the crossroads by the White Hart public house that did it. The threat of a major demonstration had caused the National Security Service to bring in large numbers of Auxiliary Police. Their lorries blocked the way down Abbey Street. That forced the demonstrators to turn down Lenton Lane. Unfortunately, the road narrowed sharply as it approached a bridge over a canal. That compressed the crowd and made it more difficult to control. There were factories the other side of the bridge. The Auxiliary Police had been ordered to protect them. They'd blocked the bridge. The demonstrators had nowhere to go. Those at the front tried to stop. Those behind them couldn't see what the problem was. Their pressure pushed the front ranks forward. Even then, the situation might have been controlled, given skilled handling. The Auxiliary Police had little training in crowd control and too many of them had been sampling the beer served at the White Hart.

In the front ranks of the demonstration, David Newton saw the cordon of Blackshirts. He felt the crowd eddying around him. The pressure from behind was carrying him forward, leaving him helpless to do anything other than watch the disaster unfold. As the crowd surged towards them, the Blackshirts panicked. They started lashing out with their batons in order to stave off the pressure. Newton heard the thud as the batons, longer and heavier than the traditional policeman's truncheons, struck home. The victims fell. Others tripped over them; some falling into the Blackshirts in the cordon. What had been a neat division between demonstration and Blackshirt ranks collapsed into a swirling mass. That was when he heard the sharp crack of a pistol shot. There was a stunned pause; a moment of silence. Then two or three more shots. The students forming the demonstration broke and ran. Unable to go backwards or forwards, they went sideways, into the maze of old houses that lined the canal.

Newton ran, heading away from the Blackshirts. They were following the crowd, lashing out at anybody who was within their reach. He knew they were out of control; any semblance of discipline they might have had was collapsing under the pressure of events. Instinctively, he knew how dangerous they were. The screams and scattered shots from behind him merely reinforced that knowledge. Heaving for breath, he turned into a sidestreet to try and get clear. That was when fear really gripped him. He had turned into a dead end. A group of Blackshirts were already approaching. There was a small group of students between him and the Auxiliaries. That gave him a chance to hide. He grabbed a doorhandle. To his blessed relief, the door was unlocked. He dived in, slammed it shut and turned the lock. Then he put his full weight against it.

He was shaking as he heard the screams get closer. Then he heard a figure pounding on the door and a frantic plea. "For God's sake, let me in. Help me, for mercy's sake, let me in."

He recognized the voice. It was Rachael. He tried to move, tried to open the door for her, but his body wouldn't obey the orders from his mind. He kept trying to move, trying to get his arms to slip the catch and his legs to move him away so the door could open. It was as if his limbs were encased in mud. While he fought himself, he heard her pleading change to wails of fear and then screams. Behind him, the door lurched and banged. Its lock, reinforced by his back, held firm. It seemed like an eternity, but it was only a few seconds. He heard more screams and pleas from outside. Then silence. The sounds receded.

Only then did he realize he was weeping with shame and humiliation.

Hours later, he was cold and stiff from being braced against the door. The sounds of the riot had long since faded away, leaving him alone and sickened. It was safe to leave; safe to pick his way back through the streets towards the College and its halls of residence. It was strange; for all the fear, terror and violence there was little actual evidence of what had happened. The buildings seemed undamaged in the twilight. There were no shattered windows or broken doors. A broken streetlight was unusual enough to draw his attention. There were small dark puddles that he kept well away from. That was all he saw of the aftermath from the afternoon that had changed his life.

Back in his room, he was sitting, staring at the wall when there was a polite knock on the door. That was unusual. This was a hall of residence and people tended to barge in without knocking and apologize later. But, the whole area was like that, stunned by what had happened. It was as if common courtesy was a refuge people retreated to in order to deal with what happened.

"David. Thank God you're all right." Colin Thomas was an old friend of his. "We knew you were up near the front and thought you might have had it. It's a nightmare out there; those bastard Blackshirts . . . "

"How many?" Newton could barely speak.

"Dozens got beaten up and arrested. We know of three dead so far. George got shot at the bridge, right at the start. Freddie too. Shot in the back as he ran." Thomas hesitated, his voice shaking and his eyes wet. "David, you were walking out with Rachael weren't you? I'm sorry; a group of six Blackshirts cornered her. One of them recognized her, knew she was Jewish. The bastards knocked her down and started kicking her, right there in the street. A couple of the lads saw it, but they were too far away to help. By the time they got there, she was dead and the Blackshirts had legged it. I'm so sorry. Anyway, you're all right. Look, I've got to go. We're still trying to find out where everybody is and get an idea of who has been arrested."

The door closed. Newton stared at the mirror, guilt at what he inevitably saw as his craven cowardice ripping at his soul. Very, very quietly he made himself a promise. *Never, never, never again will I turn my back on somebody who needs protection.*

He didn't see his own reflection in the mirror. Instead he saw his memories. The girl who, when the student's canteen had served bangers and mash, had given away her pork sausages to her friends. Her great beaming smile when the students had got together to buy her a proper kosher meal in return. Her lying helpless on the ground, her ribs kicked in by men wearing hobnailed boots while he had cowered behind a door.

He realized he had something very important to do. Something that mixed atonement and vengeance, and was more than a little of both.

Queen's Road, Nottingham, United Kingdom

The woman walked with the practiced swing of an experienced prostitute. This was Sally's beat, her corner of Queen's Road and Arkwright Street. It was a good corner; lots of traffic and the entrance to the station was close enough for her to pick up travelling trade. There was even a pub with rooms opposite and she had a working agreement with the landlord. She didn't embarrass him by plying for trade in his bar, but she could rent one of his rooms by the hour and use the side door to get in. The fact she had such a good spot wasn't by chance. She paid the local 'Firm' their protection money without argument, didn't try to hold out on them and never stole from her clients. The Firm was a loose organization of local criminals who controlled the underworld in Nottingham. Every city had its firm, under one name or another. Some were relatively benign, others vicious. Nottingham had one of the better firms. She played straight with them; they played straight with her. They'd given her a good pitch and trusted her enough to send some of their better clients to her.

Things were changing in Nottingham. They had been ever since the Auxiliaries had arrived. What had been a pleasant, friendly city had turned into one with the brooding air of menace typical of a city under occupation. The Auxiliaries weren't police any more; not after the way they had smashed the demonstration. They were an occupation force and were regarded with sullen hatred.

Sally saw two of them approaching down Queen's Road. They were thick on the streets, had been ever since the riot the other side of town. The official line was that some students had started a brawl and the Auxiliaries had broken it up; but there were uglier rumors than that. Like students who had been arrested but had then vanished without explanation.

"Hey, Johnsie, you want some of this?"

One of the Auxiliaries grabbed her arm and spun her around. He grabbed her hair and pulled her head back so his partner could see her face in the yellow glow of the streetlight.

"You joking? Never know what you'll catch from a tom." The Blackshirt called Johnsie looked disgusted. "I'll bet it's rotting away down there."

"Nah, this one's clean. And she's going to give me a free ride to prove it. Aren't you love?"

"Look, I . . ."

"Because, if you don't . . . Remember what we did to that Jew-girl? You'll get the same."

Sally sighed and led the Auxiliary over to the side door of the pub. The other Auxiliary shook his head and leaned up against the wall, waiting for his partner to finish. The streets were empty, almost. It was too early to be crowded from people going home after a night out, too late for the back-from-work crowd. He turned around, wondering how long he was going to have to stay around out here when a youngster bumped into him. He smelled of beer and was obviously very drunk. He put his arm around Johnsie's shoulders and breathed heavily into the Auxiliary Policeman's face.

"You gave them students a seeing-to didn't ya mate. Stuck up gits, they all are. Deserve what they got. Let me buy you a drink." The youngster tried to push a ten shilling note into the Blackshirt's pocket. For a moment, the Blackshirt tried to push the young man away. He hesitated; ten shillings was ten shillings.

The hand with the banknote clamped over his mouth. He felt an agonizing pain in his back. Newton thrust the carving knife into Johnsie's liver. He twisted it around. It left the Blackshirt bleeding to death so fast he could feel his life draining from him. Newton let the body fall to the ground, then reached down and took the .38 Webley from the man's belt.

327

That was when he heard the side door of the pub slam.

The second Blackshirt was looking down at him from the step. He fumbled with the revolver holstered at his waist. A woman was standing beside him; one hand raised to cover her mouth, her eyes wide with shock. Newton didn't hesitate. He brought the Webley up and fired a single shot that took the Auxiliary in the forehead.

"Get out of here lad. That shot will bring the law. The real law." Newton backed away and then looked at the woman. One cheek was reddened and her lips were slightly swollen. There was a long pause. She nodded very slightly.

"Yeah, I did what he wanted and he smacked me around anyway. Why d'ya do it, lad?"

"The girl they killed? She was my girl. I didn't realize it was them though."

"Yeah, word is they were a couple of Mosley's boys before they joined the Auxiliary, so I heard. Those two have been beating on a lot of the toms here. They've really got the Firm mad at them. The cops will think that the Firm did it as a lesson to the others. The Firm won't care who did. Saved them the job, you see. You're in the clear, this time. Now, scat."

Sally was only two years older then Newton, but her years working the street gave her voice an timbre of experience that brought an immediate result. Newton dropped the revolver and left. As he ran around the corner, he heard the first blast of police whistles.

Bestwood Lodge, Arnold, Nottinghamshire, United Kingdom

"Nasty case." Fleming read the newspaper account and shook his head. "Still, if the Blackshirts go around beating up the local toms, they can expect the Firm to get upset about it. The word is that the police have already concluded this was a gangland killing and are just going through the motions. If it had been one of their own, it would have been different, of course. They'd be tearing the town apart and there would be help coming in from every police force in England. But, Blackshirts? Police don't really care one way or the other about what happens to them. The only witness they've got is a tom who says the first one was dead when she came out and the one with her was shot from the shadows. She didn't seem to care much either."

"And the Firm aren't denying it was them. Suits everybody for that to be the official verdict." Calvert was relaxed in an armchair. Where the local Firm was one of the more reasonable sort, they and the local police would have a tacit agreement over boundaries and conduct. Burglaries in unoccupied houses received little police attention as long as the local people were safe when inside their homes and could walk the streets at night safely. Toms could ply their trade as long as they did so in an agreed area away from decent people. Unwritten agreements that accepted some things so that worse ones could be avoided. Calvert was already establishing discrete contacts with Nottingham's local Firm.

"That wasn't what happened and you know it."

The Duke stared at the wall, trying to work out how he felt about what had happened. Two dead men, even if they were Blackshirts, was a lot to swallow.

"The whisper is, those were two of the Blackshirts responsible for killing that girl in the riot a couple of days ago. Seems like one of the lads decided to take the law into his own hands. Done both of them in." Calvert grinned. "One unarmed, untrained lad against two armed men and he gets them both. That lad has promise."

"We can't justify . . . " The Duke was still appalled by the reality that was opening in front of him.

"Oh yes we can."

Fleming spoke coldly; there was no mercy in his manner. "Did you see what they did to that poor girl? You often hear people say it, but this time it was true. They beat her so badly, even her own mother couldn't recognize her. And even that doesn't matter.

"What does matter is that the Auxiliaries are going to be running scared and angry now. They'll be even more aggressive, even more unreasonable. They watch the official police doing next to nothing about the killings. That makes them livid. They'll throw their weight around even more and, all the time, be watching out for the next likely lad with a knife or a gun. They'll treat everybody as a potential killer and, that'll make people hate them even more and build up support for the Resistance. And that'll set the Auxiliaries off even more. You see how the spiral goes from there?"

"I do." The Duke hated what he was hearing, but it rang terribly true. "But this was still murder. What sort of world are we creating?"

"Nothing that hasn't been created for hundreds of years. Your Grace, there's going to be a Resistance; that is as sure as anything can be. This is just the start. It's going to get worse. A time is coming when this kind of thing is normal. That Man thinks he stopped a war with his armistice, but he hasn't. He's *started* one; only it's being fought here, not on a battlefield a long way away. Once the Germans arrive, it will be a real war. What's just happened here has done so over and over again, all over Europe. We've been so far removed from it, we've forgotten the reality. Now we're learning it again. We're lucky in a way; we've got time to prepare and get things ready. A year ago, that lad wouldn't have dreamed of killing two men. Not in his wildest nightmares. A year ago, what he did would have been to commit two foul murders. A twelve-month later, it is now a courageous act of resistance. Now he's made that leap, we can recruit him, train him and use him. Make sure he kills the right people in future; not that he didn't, this time.

"That Man has changed the rules and he doesn't realize how much yet. We're in the middle of the change right now. It's happening all over the country. Up in Scotland, there are already areas the Auxiliaries dare not go, for fear of a pistol shot in the darkness. And as for Northern Ireland, when an IRA man shoots down an Auxiliary, the Protestants cheer him on. You wanted to start a resistance movement? Well, it's started. Now, we find that lad and bring him into the fold. Through a couple of cut-outs, of course."

Fleming sighed and helped himself to a brandy, to recover from his outburst. The frustration at having to explain such things was genuine, but it was mixed up with despair at the dark, dismal future he could see coming. *People think a resistance movement is glamorous and exciting. When they learn the truth about just how dirty a business it is, the realization always sickens them and they still don't know the worst of it. They have no idea what is to come and it's probably better that way. God help us all. England won't be a green and pleasant land again, not in my lifetime.*

Calvert took another drink. "Oh yes, that lad has promise. Just what we're looking for, in fact. Motivated."

CHAPTER TWELVE
THE HEART OF THE MATTER

Infantry Company, Second Battalion, 16e **Regiment d'Infanterie Coloniale, RC-157, French Indochina**

"Cowardice! Unforgiveable cowardice!"

Captain Grégoire Dieudonné crashed his fist on the table to give emphasis to his words. In front of him, Jourdain Roul stood to attention, trying to keep his temper under control. He was uneasily aware that a good part of him agreed with his Captain's assessment. The company was formed up around a small hamlet; one so small, it didn't even have an official name. Its importance was limited to the fact that it was here that RC-157 made a 90-degree switch in direction from south to due east and crossed a small stream. The curve of the stream and the arc of the road offered what appeared to be a good defensive position; on the surface, anyway. His experiences earlier in the day gave Roul good reason to doubt that.

"Do you have any explanation for your actions? Or must I assume that you are English?" Dieudonné was bright red with rage. Still, his words gave Roul a chance to explain himself.

"Sir, our position was untenable. The Siamese had occupied the high ground to the north and were making undisturbed artillery practice on my right. Their infantry demonstrated against my center, pinning it in place, while they advanced to cut the road in my rear. They had tanks in support. There was nothing I could do. If we had remained in place, we would have been cut off and forced to surrender."

Roul took a deep breath. "Sir, our position here is in equal danger. The Siamese are not advancing along the road, to the exclusion of everything else. They are methodically occupying the ridge to the north, parallel to RC-157. They are doing that while we speak. If they haven't occupied Hill 168, they will soon. From there, they can bring their guns up again. Captain, I must urgently recommend we detach a unit to secure Hill 168."

Dieudonné stared at the map, running permutations through his mind. Despite his behavior towards Roul, he was actually quite sympathetic to the young Lieutenant's dilemma. The French defensive plan had been based on the border battalions forming a series of roadblocks along the key east-west highways that would pin down the Thai forces. Then, the core of the Indochina army would counter-attack, envelop their left flank and drive them back. The problem was that the whole plan was built around the assumption that the Thais would keep to the roads. Obviously, they weren't doing that at all.

Dieudonné knew more about what was going on around him than Roul, although he was unpleasantly aware that his picture was very incomplete. He suspected that the disappearance of the Third Battalion, *Tirailleurs Tonkinois* had been caused by the same sequence of events that had taken place at Phoum Kham Reng. Only, the *Tirailleurs* hadn't disengaged and had been swallowed up in place. If Roul hadn't disengaged, his platoon wouldn't be here now. On the other hand, if he had remained in place, his sacrifice would have bought Dieudonné more time to prepare his defenses. Sometimes there were no good options.

"If you had held your position as ordered, I might have had time to do just that. The option is no longer open to us. We will have to extend our position on our right to defend against an envelopment. Take your platoon and prepare defensive positions on our extreme right. And Lieutenant, do not believe that your position on the right of the line means your actions today are considered creditable."

Lieutenant Roul snapped out a salute and stomped out of the tent, obviously angered by the reprimand. Dieudonné shook his head and studied the map again, trying to put some form of sense to the Thai advance. It was slow and methodical; a harsh critic might even describe it as lethargic. The image that came to his mind was that of a slow flood of water, perhaps from a dripping tap. It was quietly seeping past the French defenses, not forcing its way through them. *Obviously their commanders are determined to keep their casualties to a minimum but there is more to the situation than just that. They're just not trying to move quickly. Are they really prepared to cede the initiative to us?*

His thoughts were interrupted by a tattoo of rifle fire from his left flank. A breathless runner arrived a few second later. "Sir, Lieutenant Lucrèce sends his compliments and says he is under rifle fire from a low ridge some three hundred meters to his front. He seeks permission to return fire."

Dieudonné looked at his map and marked a red circle on the ridge in question. It really wasn't much of a ridge. At best it was only some ten meters higher than the position held by Lieutenant Benjamin Lucrèce. "Tell the Lieutenant to hold his fire. We will engage the ridge with our mortar." The company had a mortar squad with a single 60mm barrel. This was the kind of situation the weapon was ideal for. The captain left his tent and went over to where the Sergeant in charge of the mortar squad had set up. A quick inspection of the map and the mortar crew knew exactly where they had to drop their rounds. A few seconds after that and the ridge was marked by the series of small explosions that showed an infantry mortar at work. The Thai rifle fire quickly petered away and the ridge, such as it was, fell quiet.

Second Battalion, First Regiment, 9th Infantry (Black Panther) Division

"Any casualties?" Colonel Romklao had his maps out in front of him.

"None, sir. The men pulled back quickly. They're certain, though, it was mortar fire. A 60mm mortar."

Romklao knew the implication of that. A single 60mm mortar firing meant they had an infantry company ahead of them. His reconnaissance squad had goaded the French into opening fire with it. That had told him all he needed to know. It was probably a full strength company as well. Romklao regretted bitterly that the infantry platoon he had run into earlier in the day had managed to slip away. *They've had plenty of time to rejoin their company. It would have been better to have put them in the bag earlier.*

His battalion was flowing forward, mostly silently. That was part of the doctrine they had carefully absorbed from their German instructors. *Don't get hung up on every enemy force that tries to block you. Go around them; filter past them and leave them cut off in your rear. Follow-up forces will deal with the troops you have by-passed. Keep the initiative by continually moving forward. Don't get involved in fights you don't have to; but, if you have to fight, bring every scrap of force you can summon against your enemy.* The Germans had used the analogy of a man digging a hole in dry sand. As fast as he shovelled it out, it would flow back around him. The only problem was that, in this particular case, he was the follow-up element. The other two battalions in the regiment were already moving to occupy Hill 280 some 12 kilometers further east.

"Are the guns ready?" The Regiment had a battery of six 77mm infantry guns ,but it had been split down to three two-gun sections; one section was attached to each infantry battalion. That was another thing their instructors had stressed; most of the damage done by artillery took place with the first few rounds. After that, the effectiveness of the guns declined steeply. A few shells right at the start of an action were worth hundreds later on. Not for the first time, Romklao reflected grimly on how much hard-won expertise their advisors had passed on. Before their arrival, he'd never understood just how much his Army had to learn. Now, he knew enough to wonder whether his army was capable of translating lessons into practical experience.

"Yes, sir."

Lieutenant Kulap Kamon had brought his guns up and positioned them behind the ridgeline exploited by the recon section. This was their second time in action. A few hours earlier, they'd dispersed a French outpost at Phoum Kham Reng. It had been a minor action, starting with a sergeant wounded by a sniper and ending when a few rounds from his guns had sent the rest of the French unit running. But it had been enough to give his men some of the swagger of veterans.

"Have smoke ready. The machine guns will open the battle."

Romklao had positioned his four heavy machine guns carefully. They were screened from direct fire, but their bursts would graze the top of the ridge before plunging on the French positions. Each machine gun had its limits set. They would fire along those lines to rake the French positions with gunfire. Indirect fire from machine guns; Romklao knew he would never have believed it was practical.

"Colonel, we have the dive bombers waiting. Nine Hawk IIIs, with four 50-kilo bombs each. Their pilots await our word."

The comment from the Air Force officer in the truck sounded a little pompous, but rumors were already spreading on how the dive bombers demoralized the French infantry. The rumor mill was always more efficient than any regular communications system could be. There had been doubts within the Army about whether assigning Air Force pilots to Army units this way had been wise, or even sensible, but the idea was working.

"Ask them to hold please. We will mark the target with smoke when we want them to make their attack."

Romklao took a flare gun and fired a red flare into the sky. There was a pregnant pause. Then rifle fire broke out along the ridgeline to the north. Romklao had two of his four infantry companies spread out along the ridge with orders to pin down the French right and prevent them reinforcing their left.

"Machine gunners, open fire on the French positions."

Infantry Company, Second Battalion, *16e* Regiment d'Infanterie Coloniale, *RC-157, French Indochina*

Captain Dieudonné had been expecting the attack to develop on his right but the force that was taking part astonished him. The volume of rifle fire was much more than that of a company. He could count at least six light machine guns snapping short bursts into the positions held by his two platoons on the right flank. The firing spread quickly along the line. Now he heard the sustained jackhammer noise of heavy machine guns. For a moment, he thought that it had started to rain. The sight of some of his men, caught in the open, falling to the ground quickly dispelled any such notion. He was under indirect machine gun fire. *It's probably just suppressive fire. The enemy's main strength is on my right.*

In truth, after the initial surprise, the machine gun fire achieved very little. At most, it disrupted movement in the French position. Once the French infantry had gone to ground, their casualties were very few. So, it was no surprise to him that the whistle of inbound artillery fire dominated the noise of the battle. The shells seemed aimed directly at him. Their noise swelled to a crescendo before the shells exploded with soft, dull thuds in front of his positions. The white smoke billowed upwards. Just like Lieutenant Roul a few hours earlier, Dieudonné thought that he was coming under gas attack. His mind recalled ugly pictures of the time when he had been a young Lieutenant in the trenches of 1918 and had seen gas at work for the first time. *Thankfully, it isn't gas; just smoke. Roul mentioned that the Siamese like smoke screens.*

"They're coming."

The cry went up from along the trenches that marked the position of the platoon on his left. Dieudonné looked at the advancing infantry with a degree of shock. The main attack was coming on his left and was in much greater strength than he had believed possible. There were more than two hundred Thai infantry attacking; perhaps closer to three. They swarmed forward, beginning their descent of the long ridge that had shielded them. Beyond his left, Dieudonné saw another force of infantry, at least equal to the one on the ridge, moving to envelop his flank. There is no way that this force could be anything less than a whole regiment. Any further thoughts along those lines were disrupted by the scream from overhead.

Each Thai Hawk III had peeled over. The aircraft dove on the French positions beneath. The noise of their near-vertical, full-power descent hammered into the brains of the men below. It prevented rational thought and dispelled any attempt to organize a defense. Looking up at the aircraft, each and every man was convinced that the attack was aimed personally at him. The defenses started to break apart. One of the sections of Dieudonné's heavy machine gun platoon was trained for anti-aircraft work. The crews held firm. They sent two streams of tracers skywards. The effort only brought about their destruction. The dive bombers saw where the fire was coming from. The later aircraft to dive used that area as their target. The Hotchkiss machine guns were silenced by a combination of bombing and strafing before they could do any harm.

The biplanes grew as they neared the ground. The snarl of the engines and the howl of the wind through their wings combined to make a deafening roar. The Hawks didn't carry the additional sirens that were used by the Vought ground attack aircraft, but their effect on the morale of those below them was still devastating. The French infantry couldn't stand. They were already out of their defenses and running for the rear when the 50-kilogram bombs exploded around them. By the time the air attack was over, Dieudonné's left flank had collapsed as thoroughly as if it had never been. Now the Thai infantry were into his defenses.

The French fought as they fell back, firing their Berthier rifles from the hip. Officers tried to rally their men and used their pistols on the enemy who was enveloping them. It was fruitless. Some of the French troops rallied and tried to form a defensive line. They were too outnumbered, their tactical coherence already been shattered by the bombing. A few of their shots struck home. A handful of the advancing enemy fell. But the men of the platoon had no chance. They were either shot down while they fought or threw down their weapons and raised their arms.

Dieudonné drew his pistol and fired it until it ran dry, but his position was hopeless. As the green-clad infantrymen surrounded him, he threw his pistol to the ground and raised his hands. Behind him, he saw the positions on his right being rolled up as they were taken in the rear.

"Captain, please ask your men to surrender. You have done all that you can. There is no point in more bloodshed."

Dieudonné looked at the Thai infantry officer standing in front of him. Again, memories of the First War came back, triggered by the German-style helmet. French intelligence material all said that the Thais used the Fremch Adrian helmet, but it was obviously wrong. He found himself wondering what else he had been told was mistaken.

Infantry Platoon, Second Battalion, 16e Regiment d'Infanterie Coloniale, French Indochina

"Sergeant, we need to get out of here."

Lieutenant Roul gave private thanks that he had been positioned on the extreme end of the line. The dive bombing and artillery fire had been far enough away that his platoon wasn't too badly affected. It also gave him time to see the platoon on the left dissolve under the ferocious assault and the first of the two platoons on the right of the road break up. His unit was next and he didn't intend to sit still and let it happen.

"Down the road, quickly."

The NCOs passed the word and the platoon started to fall back along the road. It was a race. The prize getting clear of the trap they were in before the jaws closed on them. The Thai infantry on the ridgeline to the north extended beyond Roul's position. Their rifle fire was galling. Roul saw some of his men falling as bullets bit home. Other members of their squads tried to help the wounded back, but the delay meant they too fell from the increasing volume of rifle fire.

"Leave them! Everybody save yourselves. The Siamese will look after the wounded."

Roul hated himself for giving the order but he realized he had little choice. More Thai infantry were already closing in from the South. It was going to be a very finely cut thing for any of his men would get clear. His order gave no indication about running, but it might as well have. The entire platoon, Roul included, broke into a trot and then into a full run. Roul's humiliation filled his throat and made him feel sick. He was leading a rout, running away from a battle. *What would my father think of me?* The thought made tears stream from his eyes.

What was left of the platoon made it to an area of thick scrub and bushes about a kilometer east down RC-157. It wasn't just that the scrub and bushes provided cover; there was a slight, horse-shoe shaped rise around it that screened him from view. Roul knew he had learned something today. Even a meter rise in the ground could be tactically vital. That one-meter rise saved his platoon from total destruction.

Even so, he looked back on the road and saw the lines of figures in horizon blue that marked the path of his rout. He had started the day with four sergeants, four corporals and 32 privates. Counting the men he had left, he could see private first class Léo Corneille, Sergeant Arsène Ambroise and one or two more.

How many men survived?

"Corporal Frenais; eleven men, sir. Three of them are wounded but can walk."

It was as if the sergeant can read my mind. So answer me this. What do we do next? "Very good, Sergeant. The Siamese will be clearing the battlefield and that will give us a chance to break away. We must head for Yang Dham Khung. That's where the main body will be assembling." *Dear God, I started this day with 41 men and now there 14 of us left. And we have achieved nothing.*

Roul used his binoculars to watch the Thai infantry back at the position they had just seized. Three Vickers tanks and some trucks joined them. Some of the trucks had red crosses pained on them; stretchers were being placed in them. As one was lifted on, Roul caught a glimpse of horizon blue from the man on it.

Thank God. They are looking after my wounded.

Supreme Command Headquarters, Bangkok, Thailand

"We badly need those Ki-30s. If we had ordered them as I wished . . ." Marshal Plaek Pibulsonggram sounded reproachful.

"Politically, the order would have been disastrous. It would have linked us to the Japanese and ruled out any other options. There is more at stake here than just the fighting now in progress." The Ambassador snapped the reply out. She was tired, despite managing a quick nap while flying down to Bangkok on her private Boeing 247.

"Our pilots are flying five or six missions a day. Because of that, we have already lost a Hawk 75N from a crash. The pilots are very tired. We cannot go on like this."

"We can and we will." The Ambassador's voice was pitiless. "Every hope we have for the future now hangs on us defeating the French in Indochina. And we are defeating them. We have driven them back almost 30 kilometers and are only 20 kilometers from Sisophon. We have wiped out their border forces already. All that is left of them are groups of stragglers heading east.

"We know the French are assembling their main force at Yang Dham Khung. They have massed nine battalions of infantry, two battalions of artillery and a company of tanks there. When the French launch their counter-attack from Yang Dham Khung, we will have 15 battalions of infantry, three of artillery and two complete battalions of tanks waiting for them.

"In the north, we have already reached the Mekong in Laos and are digging in there. North of the Tonle Sap, we are swinging across country, peeling off units to guard the Mekong as we move east. Above all, the fourth regiment of the Queen's Cobra Division is swinging south to by-pass Battambang to the east. The first regiment of the White Horse Division is swinging north from Trat to the same destination. The other two cavalry regiments are heading for Phnom Penh. When they link up, the whole French Army in Indochina will be encircled around Battambang while we advance on Phnom Penh from north and south of the Tonle Sap. Soon, there will be nothing left between us and Saigon. The French have no idea what they are up against."

Marshal Plaek raised his hand placatingly. "I know what we are achieving. And I understand how important those achievements are. I just fear for how long our Air Force can keep up its efforts."

The Ambassador relaxed slightly. "Perhaps this may calm your fears. We captured these documents at a minor skirmish on RC-157. An affair of no great importance, except for the capture of these French intelligence assessments of our forces. Take a look at them."

She handed the role of documents over and Palek read them. As he did, his eyebrows lifted in surprise. "These are completely wrong. The French seem to think we have copied their triangular division and regiment structure. They don't realize our infantry divisions use the German square structure with four regiments per division and four companies per battalion. That basic mistake means they're underestimating our strength by over a third. They put our army at 44 infantry battalions? Now that we are mobilized, we have *seventy-seven* and that increases as more reservists join the colors."

"And those battalions are a third larger than theirs." The Ambassador sounded very satisfied. "The Air Force need only struggle for a few more days, my old friend. Then, our pilots can rest before we deal with the Japanese."

Anti-Tank Company, 3rd Battalion, 5th Regiment Etranger d'Infanterie, Yang Dham Khung, French Indochina

At least, this time, we have the high ground.

Here, the French forces were arrayed along a ridge that lay behind a twisting river. *It is,* Roul thought, *a good defensive position.* On the long march back along RC-157, he'd realized just how hard this part of Indochina was to defend. The ground sloped steeply downwards from the mountains along the Thai border, so anybody advancing from the west always had the high ground. This was the first point at which the geography changed. Here, the French positions were at an elevation of 30 meters while the low ground in front of them was, at most, 16 meters. What worried him was that the

338

Indochina Army would be launching its counter-attack from these positions and would have to pass through the heavily-forested areas that lay between their ridge and the river. Roul's two previous actions had taught him that the Thai Army knew how to maneuver and he suspected they would make good use of that jungle.

The problem was that Colonel Jacomy, whose "Groupement J" was assigned to conduct the attack, wouldn't listen to anybody. Especially a Lieutenant whose sole contributions to the engagements over the last few days had apparently been to retreat as fast as his legs would carry him. Roul's attempts to report on the actions he had fought and the lessons he had learned had been brushed aside with overt contempt. The survivors of his platoon had been assigned to reinforce an anti-tank battery belonging to the Fifth Regiment of the Foreign Legion. To an officer of the regular French Army, that was very close to being an insult.

The anti-tank unit had two Model 1934 25mm guns. Roul wasn't quite sure what the third gun was. It had originally been a standard *Soixante-Quinze*, but the Legionnaires had modified its carriage drastically so that it sat much lower on the ground and was easier to move around. He'd arranged the three guns in a triangle, with the 75 at the back. The 25mm gun was light and underpowered, but it could deal with any tank in this part of the world. Roul was more worried about the Thai infantry. Against them, the 25mm was just a very big rifle. The Soixante-Quinze had explosive shells as well as solid shot and could put up an adequate fight.

"Interesting defensive position."

Roul jumped at the unexpected comment. He looked around and saw Major Belloc, commander of the Foreign Legion battalion standing behind him. He jumped to attention and snapped out a salute.

"Sir?"

"Putting the *Soixante-Quinze* at the rear. How did you come to that conclusion?"

Roul took a deep breath. "Sir, I've fought the Siamese twice now. Each time, when they ran into opposition, they maneuvered us out of our defenses. They would never attack us frontally. They always pinned us down and then maneuvered against our flanks. If there was a position that was too tough for them to take with a quick attack, they would bypass it and continue on."

"*Stosstruppen* tactics."

"Exactly, sir. I've also seen the Siamese bringing up tanks. If we engage their tanks with our guns, they won't fight it out. The tanks will pull back, they'll bring up their infantry and try and outflank our position. So, I've got the two twenty-fives positioned forward to take on the tanks. Then, when the infantry move up, the *Soixante-Quinze* will be perfectly positioned to support the anti-tank guns and we can hold out here."

Belloc nodded. "You've fought the Thais before. You're Roul, aren't you?"

"Sir."

"Hmm. Colonel Jacomy suggested I put you somewhere you can't run away. Have you anything to say to that?"

Roul was outraged. "Sir, my platoon has lost more than two thirds of its strength fighting the Siamese. We held our ground until it was impossible to do so any longer, *then* we disengaged in as good an order as the circumstances permitted."

"I thought as much. Anyway, Colonel Jacomy forgets that we in the Legion have no personal history, save that we make for ourselves here. But, I need to know everything you have to tell me about the actions you have fought. Soon, we will start our counter-offensive and try to drive them back. I think this will be a much harder fight than our commanders realize. By the way, you may be interested to know that two border guard battalions of the *Tirailleurs Tonkinois* have been dispersed. To all intents and purposes, they have been destroyed as fighting formations. They were so unwise as not to disengage when the circumstances dictated that course of action."

1st Infantry Battalion, "Royal Guard," 9th Infantry Division, Yang Dham Khung, French Indochina

"We have a chance to redeem ourselves."

Major Wuthi Wirrabut spoke quietly in the pre-dawn darkness. A few years earlier, the Royal Guard battalion had made the worst mistake any military unit could make in a civil war. They had picked the wrong side. Following the coup that had ended the absolute monarchy, Prince Boworadet had led pro-royalist forces, including several infantry regiments, a cavalry unit and several artillery batteries, in a march on Bangkok to restore the traditional order. They reached the capital to find that most military units in Bangkok supported the government. The Royal Guard battalion had been the exception; they had sided with the traditionalists and shared in the defeat that had engulfed them.

The effect on the battalion had been disastrous. They had been reduced to company strength and lost most of their privileges. Only recently had they been restored to battalion status and received the heavy weapons their table of equipment dictated. That the battalion was still commanded by a major was a mark of how recently it had been restored to its original status. Major Wuthi was painfully aware that, even now, there was a question mark against the trustworthiness of his unit. After a moment's thought, he resumed his comments.

"The French are moving up their forces while we speak. And not making a very good job of it, I might add. Our scouts say that their units are stumbling around in the trees and getting lost. They've identified two separate

340

formations; a three-battalion group in the north and a two-battalion group in the south. It looks like they plan to start their attack about dawn."

"Fifteen companies to our four." Major Anansong Chirawatra, the battalion second-in-command, was thoughtful. "We will have to earn our redemption."

"It's not that bad. Most of the French units are understrength and have only two companies each. Third Infantry will handle the southern thrust. They have four companies and tank support, against five without tanks. They're already moving out into ambush positions. We're four companies against seven and we have artillery and armor. And once the sun comes up, we will have air support. I think this will be a fair test for us."

"We must always try to be our best." Major Anansong repeated the mantra cheerfully.

"There is no trying about it. We must perform better than our peers expect,;much better. When we were assigned to this division, Her Highness, the Ambassador, made it clear that she expected great things from us." Major Wuthi paused for a second. "It's not being reprimanded by Her Highness that frightens me so much; it's when she forgives me afterwards that I get really scared."

HTMS Thonburi, *Koh Chang Anchorage, Thailand*

"Have *Ayuthya, Maeklong* and *Tachin* left?"

Commander Luang Phrom Viraphan had completed the hand-over and taken responsibility for the squadron at Koh Chang. It was hardly a powerful force; the coast defense ship *Thonburi* as flagship, four torpedo boats and a minelayer. It was intended simply to deter any French attack on coastal cities to the west. That was where the minelayer came in. She would mine the waters between Koh Chang and the mainland. That would effectively bar the French from intruding.

Luang Phrom was keenly aware that his role, and that of the Navy in general, was purely defensive in this war. The major part of the burden was being carried by the Army and Air Force. The reports from Laos suggested that the war up there was already won and that all Thai territory west of the Mekong had been recovered. It wasn't surprising that had happened so quickly; the pockets of ground were small and Luang Phrom doubted if the French troops up there had amounted to much more than a corporal's guard.

"They pulled out a few minutes ago." The communications officer had come up to the bridge with the signal lamp message. "They delayed their departure by a few minutes due to a French seaplane that was buzzing around. Now they are on their way back to Satahip."

Luang Phrom looked sharply at the officer. "A French seaplane, you say? Not one of ours?"

"Definitely French, sir. A Loire 130. Quite unlike anything we have."

"Scouting us out." Luang Phrom paused, then came to a decision. "Send a signal to *Trad, Songkhla, Chonburi* and *Rayong* to maintain an increased watch. If the French are scouting us, they mean to attack. We can expect them at dawn. Order *Songkhla* and *Chonburi* to raise steam and take up positions off Koh Lao Ya, at the anchorage entrance. They'll give the French a surprise as they come in."

"And the mainland?" The communications officer phrased the question delicately.

"Send a warning to Bangkok that we expect a French attack here at dawn tomorrow. And contact the commander of Foong Kap Lai 72. He should have his dive bombers ready to engage any French forces that appear.

Hawk 75N Over Don Muang Airfield, Bangkok, Thailand

The chance of finding one of the French Farman 222 bombers at night was remote. Flying Officer Suchart Chalermkiat had absolutely no faith that his patrol would be productive, but it was necessary to at least make the effort. His Hawk 75N was heavier and more difficult to handle than he was used to. The wing .30-cal machine guns had been removed; each had been replaced by an underwing pod containing a 23mm Madsen cannon. The judgement was, if he did get lucky and find one of the big Farmans, he would have a major performance advantage so the weight and drag of the cannon wouldn't be disastrous. On the other hand, their extra firepower might be decisive in a fleeting engagement.

If he found one of the French bombers, of course.

Suchart had no doubt they were coming. The border lookout posts had reported hearing them pass overhead. An extrapolation of their course led here. Were they were heading for the city itself or Don Muang airfield on the outskirts? Most of the pilots in FKL-60 believed the French would bomb the city, arguing that the French had a long history of bombarding or bombing civilian targets. Suchart had disagreed. In his opinion, the French would realize it was too late for that and would try for the airfield instead. Thai air superiority over the battlefield was crippling the French Army's ability to fight. A few airfield raids might destroy enough aircraft to swing the balance away from the advancing Thai infantry formations.

The result was that, of the ten Hawk 75s airborne over Bangkok, nine were over the north of the city where the loop of the Chaophrya river made a target easy to find in the moonlight. Only Suchart's aircraft was to the east of the city. He flew in a racetrack pattern, looping around with his fuel mix thinned out as much as possible. Saving fuel meant extending the time he could wait for the Farmans.

Even though he was expecting the airfield to be attacked, the explosion of the bombs in the darkness was a shock. One minute, the night was dark; only the silver stream of the moonlit river told him where he was. The next, patterns of orange explosions rippled across the ground below him.

By the time the first group had flared and faded, another group had replaced them. The second batch was further away and behind him. Suchart's first thought was that, even if one load of bombs had hit Don Muang, the second couldn't have. His second thought was the realization that he was between the Farman and its home at Saigon. Suddenly, the chance of staging an intercept wasn't so remote.

He peered into the darkness, so intent on trying to pick out the shadow of the bomber that he missed the explosions of the third and fourth patterns of bombs. The Farman had to be out there, somewhere. Almost without thinking, he advanced his throttles and touched the mixture control on his engine. The extra power made his fighter a little more lively, but it was still sluggish compared with its normal configuration.

That was when he realized one of the stars had flicked out and then returned. Something had passed between it and his Hawk 75N. Suchart curved around and closed on the tell-tale star. Sure enough, in the darkness ahead of him, was a shadow; slightly darker than the blue-black of the tropical night. More throttle, another fuel adjustment and the shadow grew quickly. A big, high-wing aircraft with its engines slung underneath the wings. Now Suchart knew where to look. He could see the flames of the exhausts rippling in the darkness. There were two sets per side; that confirmed it. The Farman had four engines, two in each underwing gondola; one at the front and one at the back. The aircraft ahead of him was indeed a Farman 222. The near-impossible chance had taken place.

Suchart continued to close. Now that he had seen his target, he wondered how he could ever have overlooked it. He had a quick moment to think about his angle of attack. The Farman had a single machine gun in the nose, one in a dorsal turret and one in the belly. He settled on coming up from underneath, so that the aircraft's engines would be exposed.

He sighed slightly, steadying himself. Then he squeezed the upper of the two gun-switches on the control column. That fired his nose .30-cal machine guns. Tracer arched out. The first few passed low. Suchart corrected his aim and walked the burst into the fuselage, then along the wing. As soon as he was hitting in the region of the engines, he pressed the lower firing trigger. He felt the 23mm cannon firing. The heavy recoil caused his Hawk to lurch in ways that the .30s had never done. The effects were immediate and appalling. The whole engine gondola erupted into flame. Brilliant red fire lit up the fuselage. Suchart paused, then fired again.

The fire spread with stunning speed, turning the Farman into a great burning cross in the sky. There was a short burst of fire from one of the gunners, but it was wild. Anyway, Suchart had broken off his attack. There was no need to push it any further. The burning bomber was already heading down, slowly losing altitude and speed. For a moment, he wondered if the pilot was still alive at the controls. Pity for a fellow pilot made him hope that he was not. To be trapped in that inferno was a terrible way to die. The Farman

222 sank, its airframe now outlined as dark lines against the burning fabric of its skin. Then, suddenly, it was all over. The wings crumpled. The wreckage fell from the sky to become a flaming pyre on the ground.

Supreme Command Headquarters, Bangkok, Thailand

The great flaming cross in the sky made a fitting introduction to his visit. Sir Josiah Crosby looked up at it and imagined what it must be like for the crew of the burning bomber. *Those poor, poor men.* The thought came out with genuine sympathy. Sir Josiah might have cast his lot in with the Indian government, but the thought of Europeans dying so far from their homes still affected him. The sight was shut off as he went into the headquarters of the Thai Army.

The building seemed very different from his previous visits. The leisurely, almost lazy, atmosphere had gone completely. Now, men in dark green uniforms rushed from place to place with an air of determined urgency. His escort led him through the corridors, towards an office buried in the depths of the building. He knocked on a featureless, unpainted wooden door, paused for a second, then opened it and ushered Sir Josiah in. The Ambassador-Plenipotentiary was inside.

"Ah, Sir Josiah. Thank you for coming at this unspeakable hour. I must leave Bangkok at dawn and return to our forward Army headquarters and this is the only time I have. May I offer you some tea? We have a fine spiced mandarin orange tea, if you prefer?"

"Thank you, Madam Ambassador. Or, should I say Colonel? The orange tea sounds delightful."

"Whichever form of address makes you most comfortable. You saw we have just shot down one of the French Farman bombers? And our anti-aircraft guns hit a Potez 542 over Nakhorn Phanom? So far, the night is going well."

A maid appeared with a cup and a pot of tea on a tray. She poured for Sir Josiah and then quietly left. He took a sip and delight spread across his face. "This is indeed delicious. I have always reported to London by way of Calcutta; but, with the change in authority, this is no longer the case. I now represent only the interests of India and my actions are determined by the Indian Foreign Office. They have instructed me to tell you that we have received authorization from the United States to transfer some of the aircraft we will be receiving from them to your country, in lieu of the aircraft your Air Force ordered but never received. We have been assured we will be fully compensated by a finance credit for any such aircraft we transfer."

Suriyothai nodded. She had noted the tiny stress that Sir Josiah had placed on the 'you' in his comments. "That is very good news."

"The Americans took it for granted that we would transfer Hawk 75A-4s; Mohawk IVs, we call them. However, on the advice of our Air Force and its advisors, we have elected to standardize on the Hawk 75 ourselves. The

Brewster Buffalos we have received will be needed by the Navy, for our aircraft carrier. But, our share of the Hawk 81s, Tomahawk Is, amounts to 48 aircraft and we will offer all of these to you.

"At our first meeting, you expressed concern about Japanese intentions. We believe that the performance of these aircraft in the Middle East and Africa will give the Japanese pause for thought. In addition, we will also offer you 24 Hawk 75s and the same number of DB-7B aircraft. Our advisors say the latter will make superior intruders and are significantly faster than most Japanese fighters."

It took all Suriyothai's self-control to stop her jaw from dropping. An influx of aircraft on this scale would provide all the air defenses her country needed to refuse compliance with any Japanese demands. "Sir Josiah, on behalf of my government, there is little I can do other than express my very great gratitude for this generosity. Obviously, your offer is accepted gladly, with the hope this will mark the start of an enduring friendship between our nations."

Sir Josiah laughed gently. "It is not so generous as you think. We are giving you the older aircraft ordered by France and Britain more than a year ago. The Americans will be providing us with the latest models in exchange. A year is a long time in war, but I think this exchange benefits everybody involved."

Suriyothai looked out of the window at where a fire burned across the city. The French counter-attack was beginning; all the reports from the front stressed that. The night bombing of the airbases showed that the French were, this time, in real earnest.

A year was indeed a long time in war, but so could be a few hours.

French Sloop Dumont d'Urville, *At Sea, Approaching Koh Chang*

"The report from the reconnaissance aircraft is in. " Lieutenant Laurent Babineau passed the word through to Captain Toussaint de Quieverecourt. "We are in luck. Both the Thai coast defense ships are in the anchorage."

To Babineau's surprise, his Captain seemed decidedly unhappy. One reason was obvious; the blackened area of twisted metal where the ship's catapult and seaplane had once resided. The other was less tangible. "Commodore Berenger has sent his orders for the attack. He is forming the fleet into three divisions. *La Motte-Picquet* will go in east of Koh Wai, while we will take the channel between Koh Wai and Koh Klum with *Amiral Charner*. *Tahure* and *Marne* will take the passage between Koh Klum and the main Koh Chang Island."

"He's splitting our force into three groups?" Babineau realized why his Captain was perturbed. "If the Siamese move quickly, they could defeat us in detail. " *Tahure* and *Marne* are weak; they've only got a pair of 140mm guns and some 100mms between them. If the Thais are expecting this, they could cut those two ships off and sink them before we could come to their aid."

"I know what Commodore Berenger is thinking. Our squadron has three different speeds. *La Motte-Picquet* can do more than 30 knots, *Tahure* and *Marne* twenty; we are limited to 16. Splitting us up into three groups means that each group can maneuver at maximum speed." de Quieverecourt sounded as if he was trying to convince himself. "And we all have different guns. 155mm on the *La Motte-Picquet*; we have 140mms and the others mostly 100mms. Operating separately will ease our fire control problems."

And I know what Commodore Berenger is thinking as well, Babineau thought. *He can take his cruiser in fast, open fire first and claim the credit for any victories. But, if it goes wrong, he will have us coming up behind to bail him out. But to voice such ideas would be insubordinate, at best.*

Babineau saw his captain looking at him and realized that de Quieverecourt knew exactly what he had been thinking. "Should we come to action stations, sir? We are approaching the anchorage and dawn is not far off."

de Quieverecourt shook himself. "Yes, do so."

Tahure and *Marne* had already sheered away, heading for the channel that led into the anchorage from the north. Then, *La Motte-Picquet* started to surge forward and peel away to starboard. That left *Dumont d'Urville* and *Amiral Charner* heading directly into the anchorage. Babineau looked over to the east. He saw the first faint hint of purple that spoke of a dawn yet to come. In the minor degree of extra light it provided, he saw two shapes close to the island of Koh Krabung. He managed to make out the distinguishing feature of their design, the large single funnel amidships.

"Captain, two torpedo boats. Close by Nagam Island."

"I see them, Laurent. Bring the ship around to oh-nine-oh. Prepare to open fire on them as soon as we are clear of the Laoya islands in the middle of the anchorage. And order *Amiral Charner* to take its lead from us."

Dumont d'Urville was now parallelling the course of *La Motte-Picquet* but falling steadily behind the cruiser. Looking at the charts, Babineau realized that Berenger, on board *La Motte-Picquet,* couldn't see the torpedo boats, since they were screened by Koh Wai Island. "Captain, we have a clear line of fire now. I believe the Thais are trying to raise steam over there."

Babineau took another look. In the dim pre-dawn light, the threads of smoke from the two torpedo boats were only just dimly visible. Certainly, the two ships weren't moving. The three 140mm guns on *Dumont d'Urville* crashed out, sending the first shells of the battle towards the two Thai ships. It was a ranging salvo; three shots spaced out to straddle the targets. Actually, all three fell short. The next salvo was over. It was only the third that actually achieved the desired straddle.

The forward 3-inch gun on one torpedo boat opened fire. Babineau guessed that it was aiming at the gun flashe,s but the shots weren't even close. The next salvo from *Dumont d'Urville* fell all around the torpedo boat. *They must be taking splinter damage at the very least.* The 140mm guns fired again. This time the target reeled from the impact of a direct hit. The orange glow of a major fire started to spread from her midship section.

"Why the devil isn't *Amiral Charner* firing?" Captain de Quieverecourt was furious. The French force had achieved complete surprise, yet his was the only ship firing on what appeared to be a defenseless enemy. "Laurent, contact her and order her to open fire on those torpedo boats."

Babineau grabbed a signal lamp and sent out the message as ordered. While he did so, the Thai torpedo boat had been hit twice more. She was clearly sinking. Her companion was starting to move very slowly, but she was firing her trio of three-inch guns. Where the shots were going was another matter. Certainly it was nowhere close to *Dumont d'Urville*. The signal lamp on *Amiral Charner* started to wink. Babineau took down the message. Its content actually made his jaw drop with shock.

"Sir, with respect, the message from *Amiral Charner* says that Commodore Berenger did not place you in command of this division so, therefore, *Amiral Charner* will dictate her own movements in compliance with the Commodore's orders."

Babineau shook his head. It seemed incredible, but the Captain of *Amiral Charner* was actually correct. Commodore Berenger had divided his squadron into three divisions but not appointed anybody to command those divisions. Correct that may be, but it would take a mind of incredible pettiness to make an issue of such things in the middle of a battle. Babineau's thoughts were interrupted by more cheering from the bridge. The gun crews on *Dumont d'Urville* were into their stride; the guns fired with a rapidity they had rarely achieved before. The second Thai torpedo boat was already hit and her return fire was faltering. That was when a broadside of 155mm shells from *La Motte-Picquet* blanketed the position of the first torpedo boat to be taken under fire.

If she wasn't sinking already, she certainly is now. Babineau actually felt sorry for the poor ship. She was hopelessly outmatched by the cruiser and sloops that were pounding her and didn't even have the steam raised to make a run for it. She was rolling over already and was finished. *A sad way for a ship to die. At least she got a shot off to save her honor.* The other torpedo boat was in no better condition; her death was made certain when the *La Motte-Picquet* switched fire on to her.

"Bring us around to oh-oh-five." de Quieverecourt snapped the order out. He hoped that *Amiral Charner* would follow the maneuver, since there was a limb of the anchorage ahead and there might be game there.

"Captain, *Amiral Charner* reports we are under attack by a third torpedo boat approaching from the north. It has a merchant ship following it."

347

"What?" de Quieverecourt frowned. "A merchant ship?"

Any additional questions he might have had were broken by the firing of *Amiral Charner's* guns as she engaged the new targets. Babineau looked across to where the shells were directed. The ships were hard to see in the gloom and shadows of the nearby land, but he caught a glimpse of the targets in the light of the shells exploding. Two funnels amidships. Suddenly, he realized what was happening. He snapped out a signal to the other sloop. "Cease firing, those ships are the *Marne* and *Tahure!*"

To Babineau's sickened dismay, *Amiral Charner* continued firing. *Marne*'s silhouette was disfigured by the red flare of a hit and the orange glow of fire. That made the identity of the ship painfully obvious. Mercifully, *Amiral Charner* ceased fire.

HTMS Thonburi, *off Koh Krabung, Koh Chang Anchorage, Thailand*

"Get under way now."

Commander Luang Phrom Viraphan snarled the order out. *Thonburi* was the only diesel-engined ship in the fleet. That meant she was the only one that could move right away. The attack had come a vital few minutes earlier than he had expected. *Another quarter of an hour, 30 minutes at most, the four torpedo boats would have raised steam.* Faced with them, the French squadron would have been in an invidious position. But he'd never had those few minutes.

The fleet was still raising steam. The fate of the two torpedo boats slaughtered off Koh Ngam showed what would happen to the other ships if the French squadron got to them. There were two more torpedo boats, two fleet oilers, several transports and a minelayer back in the anchorage. *Thonburi* had to protect them until they got under way. Luang Phrom cursed the fact that *Thonburi*'s sister ship *Ayuthya* was not there to help him.

Luang Phrom felt the vibration under his feet as the diesels started to move the gunboat forward. "Navigation, keep us in shallow water. That's to make the French stay at longer range."

"Torpedoes!"

The scream of warning from the lookout was nearly panic-stricken. The eastern sky was much brighter now. Deep purple changed to light blue as the sun steadily neared the point where it would peek over the horizon. In the extra light, the white streaks on the water were clearly visible. *Thonburi* was moving, but just barely. The torpedoes were perfectly aimed. For a moment, Luang Phrom was dismally certain that his mission to protect the rest of the fleet would be ended before it started. Then, the tracks were replaced by white-capped blasts. The torpedoes exploded in the shoal water.

"And that's another reason to stay in shallow water."

A combination of relief at the sudden end to a near-mortal threat and the fact that the Captain's jokes are always funny caused a wave of laughter to sweep the bridge. The problem was that *Thonburi* was silhouetted against the pre-dawn sky to the east. The French ships were lost on the darkness to the west. Still, the flash of their guns had been visible and there was just enough light to see a vague shadow.

"And, open fire."

The gunboat lurched as her four 200mm guns roared out. Luang Phrom hoped against hope that he would see the brilliant flash of hits on the leading French ship but there were none. It had indeed been a faint chance under the conditions prevailing. He was still disappointed.

"Prepare to fire again. Wait on my command." *This is going to be a long fight. We will have to save ammunition.* Over to the east, there was a tiny white spot that marked the first tip of the sun coming over the horizon. In a few minutes, the sun would be up and the French ships would be staring right into it. That would swing the advantage back to *Thonburi.*

French Sloop Dumont d'Urville, *Koh Chang Anchorage, Thailand*

" *La Motte-Picquet* has fired torpedoes."

Babineau made the report with a slight degree of reluctance. He could see the Siamese gunboat by Krabung Island and the white streaks of water that marked the torpedoes on their way to destroy her. He lost track of them in the semi-darkness but say the white towers of water and then the brilliant flash of explosions. "We got her."

A few seconds later, there was the train-like roar of 200mm shells. Four towers of water rose between the *La Motte-Picquet* and the *Dumont d'Urville.*

"That must be the other gunboat." de Quieverecourt was surprised at the speed with which the Thai gunboats had opened fire. "Those gunboats are only 2,200 tons. The one we just hit won't be firing at anything with three torpedoes in her."

Babineau glanced aft. *Marne* and *Tahure* had fallen in aft of the two larger sloops. The fire on *Marne* had been put out very quickly. Mercifully, she had only a few wounded from the 'friendly' shell that *Amiral Charner* had put into her. Nevertheless, her captain was maintaining a hurt silence. Viewed objectively, Babineau couldn't blame him.

"Open fire, Laurent."

de Quieverecourt noted that the movement of the ships had brought a Thai gunboat into his firing arcs, while *La Motte-Picquet's* rush eastwards had meant that any shots she might have had were at Mai Si Yai Island. *Dumont d'Urville* was a well-drilled ship and her gun crews were filled with confidence after the destruction of the two torpedo boats a few minutes earlier. The only question that de Quieverecourt couldn't answer was where the gunboat *La Motte-Picquet* had torpedoed was. *Could she have sunk so quickly? Perhaps, after three hits on a small ship like that.* That thought was interrupted by the crash of 140mm guns as the French sloop opened fire.

349

"I can't see what's happening, Captain." Babineau sounded frustrated. "We're staring right into the rising sun and I can't see a damned thing. That's why *La Motte-Picquet* is heading so far ahead of us. She's trying to get clear of the sun."

There was another train-roar overhead. This time, there was no doubt as to which ship was the target. The four shells exploded in the water around *Dumont d'Urville*. Her side plating rang as a patter of fragments hit the steel. Her own guns returned the salvo. The glare from the rising sun stopped Babineau from seeing where they landed. The minutes ticked past, with the slow exchange of ineffective salvoes growing more hesitant. In Babineau's opinion, he was shooting blind. The futility of the exercise annoyed him.

"Captain, we can't engage under these conditions and our flashes are just giving the Siamese something to aim at. I suggest we cease fire until we can spot the fall of shot."

de Quieverecourt nodded. *Dumont d'Urville's* gun fell silent. A few second later, another salvo arrived from the Thai gunboat. This one was far aft of *Dumont d'Urville;* a close straddle on the *Amiral Charner*. For a moment, Babineau thought she had been hit, but there was no tell-tale burst of black smoke or red glow of fire from her.

"Close but not close enough, Captain."

"If she had more than four guns, we would be in serious trouble by now. She just hasn't the number of guns needed to give a dense shell pattern."

"Nor do we, sir."

"True, but we're not supposed to get involved in this kind of fight."

Behind them, *Amiral Charner* had been straddled again. The next rounds seemed to be a long time coming. That made Babineau look; first at the gunboat that was maneuvering away from the line of four sloops, then at *La Motte-Picquet*. The cruiser was firing her guns in full broadsides; eight 155mm weapons blasting out rounds at her target. The first broadsides were badly off; Babineau guessed that *La Motte-Picquet* had mistaken the shots from the *Amiral Charner* as her own. Four broadsides in, she obviously realized her mistake and corrected her aim.

HTMS Thonburi, *off Koh Krabung, Koh Chang Anchorage, Thailand*

"Move to intercept that cruiser."

Luang Phrom was buying time and he knew it. The sun was up and that was both a good and a bad thing. His position in the eye of the rising sun had allowed him to engage the four sloops and hold them at bay while expending relatively little ammunition and suffering no damage from the wildly inaccurate return fire. Now the sun had risen properly, he no longer had that advantage. The accuracy of the French gunnery was improving.

On the other hand, the fact it was now daylight meant that the dive bombers would soon be on their way, if they weren't already. And always, there was the question of steam. Every minute that passed meant the other warships would be that much closer to joining *Thonburi's* lonely fight against five French warships.

The tactical situation was changing as well. Up to now, the French cruiser had been out of the fight, masked behind Koh Mai Si Yai and Koh Mai Si Lek. Now she was emerging from their shadow and was threatening to make an end-run past the *Thonburi*. Capable of more than 30 knots, the cruiser could do that and there would be little *Thonburi* could do to stop her, unless she was physically in the way. Luang Phrom saw the ripple of flashes along the cruiser and heard the howl of the inbound shells. Fortunately, they were well off-target.

"Shift target to that cruiser."

"She's *La Motte-Picquet*. I saw her on a trip to Saigon not so long ago." Lieutenant Sunan Shinawatra looked at his Captain and smiled. "I was on a Dutch liner, travelling for my family's silk business. Met an American called Jim Thompson. Oddly, I just happened to have a very good camera with me when we passed the French warships." His reminiscence was interrupted by another broadside from the cruiser. This one was closer but it was still far enough away. In reply, *Thonburi's* 200mm guns sent a full broadside at the cruiser. The four splashes were all around her but there was no sign of a hit.

"We need more guns. Our salvoes aren't dense enough to give a good number of hits."

"The new cruisers will have six guns."

Luang Phrom knew that was irrelevant. What mattered were the forces here and now. *Where are those dive bombers? We need the support here.*

"Lieutenant, go aft to the secondary control position. If anything happens to the bridge, you will take over the ship from there. Your orders in that event are simple. Keep fighting until the French retreat or the ship sinks under you."

A third salvo from the French cruiser was also wild. In reply, *Thonburi* once again straddled her without scoring any hits. He next French salvo was different. It was on target. The eight shells were close enough to the gunboat to rattle her sides with splinters. *La Motte-Picquet* paid a price for her accuracy though.

Thonburi straddled her once again. This time, there was a brilliant red flash between the funnels. Luang Phrom heard the cheer go up from his ship at the long-delayed success. He saw *La Motte-Picquet* reverse course and return behind the shelter of Koh Mai Si Lek. The threat of an end-run was past, for the moment.

"Reverse course; head back for Koh Krabung. Let us see what our guests in their sloops are up to."

French Sloop Dumont d'Urville, *Koh Chang Anchorage, Thailand*

"What the devil is Berenger up to?" Babineau let the words slip out with much more force than he intended or was prudent.

"He is concentrating his force, I think. Perhaps he realizes that dispersing us all over the anchorage may not have been the best of policies. His orders are for us to circle Baidang Island until he joins us. Then his intentions are for us to assault as a group and force our way past that gunboat." *This is what we should have been doing an hour ago,* de Quieverecourt thought, *instead of wasting time messing around. We should have been in the anchorage by now, shooting up everything that floats. One look at the charts shows there is only one way in for ships that draw as much water as we do and that damned gunboat is blocking it.*

"She's hit!" Babineau's report was a gasp of dismay. "She's taken a hit amidships."

Every pair of binoculars on the bridge swung to look at *La Motte-Picquet.* The cloud of smoke amidships was apparent, but there was no red glare of fire and she didn't seem to be slowing. "Captain, a report from the flagship. She took a hit amidships that has penetrated the armor but damage is not serious. Commodore Berenger's compliments and the four sloops are to join him at Baidang Island for an assault on the main anchorage."

"Assuming the dive bombers don't get here first." de Quieverecourt muttered the words to himself, but he saw Babineau nodding. The threat of the Thai dive bombers was on both officer's minds.

The minutes ticked by as *La Motte-Picquet* closed on the four sloops that had rounded Baidang Island and were now heading west. Eventually she drew level with them and rounded the island again; the sloops fell in behind her. At that point, the Thai gunboat reappeared from behind Mai Si Yai Island. Her guns flashed again. The salvo of four shells landed all around the *La Motte-Picquet.* The cruiser picked up speed, heading east and leaving the slow sloops behind.

"Message from the flagship, sir. It says the Siamese are trying to escape via this channel and we are to remain here to block them. The flagship will go into the main anchorage by the eastern channel."

"Damn him, why can't he make his mind up? We're running against the clock here and he is going backwards and forwards." Babineau didn't care who heard him. He swung his binoculars up and watched *La Motte-Picquet* round Chan Island and head northeast. Then, he swung his gaze to the Thai gunboat. She had reversed course and was heading east as well.

"There he goes; determined little bugger isn't he?"

Despite the situation, de Quieverecourt was almost laughing at the comment. "You know, I think I like the captain of that gunboat. He's decided what he wants to do and has set his mind on doing it. There are others who could learn from that example."

HTMS Thonburi, *off Koh Mai Si Lek, Koh Chang Anchorage, Thailand*

Lieutenant Sunan expected *La Motte-Picquet* to emerge from the shadow of Koh Mai Si Lek any moment. *Based on her previous behavior, she should be at least 15,000 meters out, in the deeper waters beyond the Koh Sang anchorage itself.* That was the best range for *Thonburi,* one where her 200mm guns were still effective but the older 155mm weapons on the *La Motte-Picquet* were loosing effectiveness. He had the guns already loaded, trained and elevated so that he could open fire with the minimum of delay.

It didn't work out that way. This time, *La Motte-Picquet* came in on a much more northerly course and was into the shoal water. Sunan guessed that there was probably only a few meters of water between her keel and the jagged coral. More importantly, she was at least 8,000 meters closer to the *Thonburi* than he had expected. In the race to get the first salvo off, the lighter, handier 155mm guns on the cruiser won. At what was virtually point-blank range, the effects were devastating.

Sunan picked himself off from the deck. His ears rang from the explosions and blood ran from his nose. *Thonburi* had been hit at least four times. The forward section of the ship was devastated. The bridge was a shambles, the foremast down and the conning tower had been penetrated. He knew that Captain Luang Phrom could not have survived the blows. Nobody could, not in that shambles. He staggered to his feet, pummelling life back into himself and the rest of the reserve command crew. Before he could get them to do anything in the way of fighting back, a second broadside slammed into the gunboat. The forward gun turret was knocked out; its barrels drooped dispiritedly as the power failed. Another shot bounced off the roof of the aft gun turret, jamming it in train. Two more smashed into the already-wrecked superstructure, causing fires to erupt from the anti-aircraft guns.

"Bring her round, use the engines to bring her round."

"Yes, Captain."

Lord Buddha have mercy, I am the captain now.

Thonburi started to swing. The French were over-confident; so convinced that the gunboat was crippled that they hadn't bothered to correct their aim. The shots fell short. Only two of the 155mm shells hit the ship; they hit low on the hull where the armor stopped them. Despite that respite, Sunan felt the tilt of the deck as *Thonburi* listed. There was a blast and he wondered which of the ship's magazines had exploded. As it turned out, none of them. As *Thonburi* had turned, the guns in the jammed aft turret aligned with *La Motte-Picquet.* The gunners took the opportunity to unload them via the muzzle. The shots went wild, missing *La Motte-Picquet* by a wide margin but Sunan took comfort in the fact his ship was still fighting. He tried to turn *Thonburi* around so that her gunners in the aft turret could have another crack. He was rewarded by two more 200mm shells heading off towards *La Motte-Picquet.* They missed. Sunan felt the ship shift under his feet again and the list increased. The battle was nearly over and he knew it.

"Head for Koh Ngam. We'll beach her there."

"Sir, overhead."

One of the men was pointing skywards. Overhead, Sunan saw the glint of the morning sun on the wings of the Hawk biplanes. The leader made the traditional wing-over into a near-vertical descent. The dive bombers had arrived.

French Sloop Dumont d'Urville, *Koh Chang Anchorage, Thailand*

"Air attack! Air attack!"

The lookouts screamed the warning; the crew of *Dumont d'Urville* cringed, remembering the attack they had experienced a few days earlier. This time, though, they watched the dive bombers drop from the sky towards *La Motte-Picquet*. The first pair of bombs straddled the hull, so close that the towers of water seemed to touch the hull. There was no trace of the third bomb. Babineau wondered what had happened to it. The answer was not long in coming.

"Message from the flagship. She is under dive bombing attack, has taken two near-misses and one direct hit from 100-kilogram bombs. The bomb that hit did not explode but the near misses have caused severe splinter damage and the machinery compartments are suffering from shock."

Babineau looked at the cruiser accelerating to maximum speed and starting to weave. Perhaps it was the unexpected change in speed and direction that threw the next flight of dive bombers off, for their weapons well off target. Nevertheless, more were coming in. High overhead, Babineau saw a formation of four twin-engined bombers heading towards the formation of sloops. They didn't have the speed to evade bombing the way *La Motte-Picquet* did.

"Sir, Commodore Berenger orders us to withdraw to the west at best speed." The communications officer had brought the message up himself.

The starboard lookout added to the mass of information flowing in. "Sir, two more Thai torpedo boats are moving. They are heading up the anchorage now. And more aircraft are coming in."

"That's it. We're out here without cover and the whole Thai Air Force will be descending on us. The Commodore is right. Our time here is over." Captain de Quieverecourt sounded disgusted. He looked over to where a pyre of black smoke marked the position of the Thai gunboat and shook his head sadly. "One ship against five and she held us off for over an hour. I would say she deserves to make it home."

1st Infantry Battalion, "Royal Guard," 9th Infantry Division, Yang Dham Khung, French Indochina

"They're coming."

Company Guards-Sergeant Preecha Budisalamat passed the word quietly. He had seen the shadows slipping into place amongst the trees to his front and knew that the attack was coming. He had been expecting it for over an hour, but the observation outposts had reported the French were having severe trouble moving into their assault positions. Apparently, some of their units had become lost in the maze of paths through the trees and disrupted other units that had stuck to their assigned route. Preecha didn't condemn that; as a city man, he thoroughly understood just how easy it was to miss one's path in forest this dense. A few street signs nailed to the trees would make life so much easier.

His Guardsmen prepared the defense line as well as they could in the short time they had available. They'd dug rifle pits and dragged trees over to help provide protection against rifle fire. Major Wuthi Wirrabut had put three of his infantry companies up on the line, with the fourth held back in reserve. The line itself was buried deep in the trees. That had already proved its value; the French artillery bombardment had been concentrated on the treeline. It missed his unit completely. *Defend a treeline from in front of it or behind it, but never in it.*

Preecha checked the machine guns; both the two Vickers guns that were normally part of the company and the three additional guns assigned from the battalion machine gun company. There was a minor problem there. When the battalion had been reconstituted, their infantry weapons had been donated by a patriotic group, the Wild Tiger Corps. So, the Guardsmen carried Lee Enfield rifles and had Lewis and Vickers machine guns. The downside was that they all fired British .303-inch ammunition, not the 8x52mm rounds used by the rest of the Army. That was a supply problem and Preecha just knew that one day they were going to get sent the wrong ammunition.

Explosions raked across the positions held by his company. They concentrated Preecha's mind wonderfully. They were hand grenades, tossed across the clearing and into the Guardsmen's positions. The grenades were accompanied by a sheet of rifle fire. Brilliant white streaks of bullets flashed all around Preecha. He heard thuds as they hit the logs and whines as they ricocheted off them. The noise stunned him; compared with the silence of the forest a few seconds earlier, it was ear-splitting enough to drown out his own thoughts. Half-seen figures in the darkness were swarming towards his positions, climbing over the fallen trees or gathering in groups where the going was easier. Those groups attracted the fire of the Vickers guns as they joined the battle.

Preecha knew how to handle the water-cooled machine guns. They needed to be swept, slowly and methodically, across the line of the enemy advance in a pattern of interlocking streams. If they did, nobody could survive the web of bullets. But that wasn't possible. The range was far too short and the enemy were not advancing in regular lines. Instead, they tumbled into view; either alone, or in groups. The machine gunners were concentrating on those groups; hammering them with long bursts that cut infantry down in heaps. The Guardsmen left those groups to the experts; instead, they fired single shots at the men who were on their own. Preecha remembered the words of the advisors who had retrained the battalion. *It is the machine guns that do the killing. The job of the riflemen is to protect the machine gunners. As long as the machine guns fire, your position will hold.*

"Reloading!"

One of the Vickers guns had reached the end of its belt and a new box wasn't quite ready. Almost as if by magic, the French concentrated on the gap in the wall of defensive fire that was cutting them down. They funneled towards the silent machine gun, trying to get at it before it could start firing again. Behind the logs that protected the gun and its crew, the loader frantically tried to get the ammunition box open.

"With me." Preecha called the three men nearest to him. They ran to support the gun. The three guardsmen fired their rifles from the hip. The bullets probably went anywhere but into the enemy, but that didn't matter. The shots themselves started to stall the French. Some of them into a dove for cover. Some tried to return fire, but the three-round magazines on their Berthiers put them at a grave disadvantage. Preecha drew his revolver, an old British Webley, and fired two shots. One of them took an enemy in the chest, spun him around and dropped him into a heap on the ground. *That old .455 can knock an elephant off its feet.*

Preecha barely had time to compliment his revolver when another Frenchmen jumped up on top of the logs that provided top cover for the machine gun crew. He was preparing to drop a grenade inside the field bunker. Preecha put another pair of shots into him. Once again, the heavy bullets did their work. The man was thrown off the roof before he could arm his grenade. That was when the Vickers gun started firing again. The stream of brilliant white fireflies caught the attackers in the open and scythed them down.

"Well done Guards-Sergeant." Guards-Lieutenant Patma had seen the incident and made sure his Sergeant got the public commendation his actions had merited. The impromptu little counter attack had saved one of their machine guns. "That gun's crew owes you and your men some beer."

The cheer that met his words was cut by another scream of warning. "Here they come again."

This time, the French knew where the machine guns were. Their attack was concentrated on the gun nests. Hand grenades exploded around the impromptu bunkers, sending fragments ricocheting off the logs. The extemporized defenses didn't stop them all. Preecha heard the screams from inside one of the gun pits as a grenade bounced inside. He ran over to the scene, firing more pistol shots as he want. The gun was knocked out. One man from its crew was dead; another blinded and his face torn open by fragments. The third man had been lucky; he must have been shielded from the fragments by the bulk of the gun. His arm was pouring blood, but he would live.

The same fragments had knocked the gun off its tripod and lacerated the water cooling jacket. A quick glance showed Preecha that the French were closing in fast. He grabbed the heavy gun; the hot barrel burned his arm as he did so. He remounted it just in time to pour a long burst into the French. The charge on the position broke and the men were driven back into the cover of the treeline.

Preecha looked along the line. Mostly, it was holding. One section had started to fall back from the fire of light machine guns that had been concentrated on them. He picked up his machine gun and lifted it up on to the logs that surrounded its pit. That way, he could fire along the line of the defense and enfilade the attackers. The white flashes of bullets around him seemed to intensify. He ignored them and squeezed the trigger on the Vickers gun. It was so hot the barrel was beginning to glow. His long burst plowed into the source of the light machine gun fire and silenced the enemy guns. Protected from the galling fire, the corporal in charge of the section led his men back up to their original positions.

"Guards-Sergeant, get ready to move our men out." Guards-Lieutenant Patma had appeared, apparently from nowhere. "Fourth Company has set up a defense line to our rear. Major Anansong is assembling a force from First and Second Companies to extend our left. The enemy are moving armored cars up."

The lieutenant moved away, passing the word to the rest of his platoon. Preecha took the opportunity to look around the scene of the fighting. To his surprise, the sun was already rising. He could see the carnage in front of the battalion positions. There were dozens of dead and wounded scattered in front of the Thai defense line. Their horizon blue uniforms were mixed in with a much smaller number of figures in the dark green of the Thai infantry. Preecha shook his head, then gathered his men together. As he did so, there was a howl overhead and a series of explosions in the French positions in front of them. The regimental artillery was covering the withdrawal of the two companies that had held this section of the line.

Preecha's men abandoned their positions under cover of the artillery fire and dropped back. As they passed through the new defense line, he saw that the company here had properly-built field fortifications. Slit trenches and proper dugouts. Preecha's men had bought them the time they had needed to set their defense up properly and it showed.

By the time he and his men had reached their new positions, the sun had risen. Preecha could see what was going on. The Guardsmen had won the race and were spreading out into defensive positions. The scene was a small hamlet, just a few wooden houses and a road junction. Guards-Lieutenant Patma had his map out and called Preecha over.

"We're here; junction of RC-157 and RC-160. We've had word that the French are moving their armor up along RC-157. At least six AM-50 armored cars and six FT-17 tanks. All from the French DMC. Plus two

357

understrength infantry companies. My orders are to stop them here and drive them back. Major Anansong is in charge of us, while Major Wuthi has the remainder of the battalion in our old positions. Get the men into position, Guard-Sergeant; this looks like a hard fight."

Once again, it was a matter of building field entrenchments with whatever happened to be at hand. Mostly, that meant wood torn from the huts constituting the hamlets. The four remaining Vickers guns were the main priority. Preecha already knew they would be the backbone of the defense here. Around them, men who had entrenching tools were digging rifle pits, while the less fortunate were using their helmets in a determined effort to create at least some cover. Whatever they managed to dig by the time the French arrived was all they would have.

The first to arrive were a trio of motorcylists. Their machines were fitted with sidecars that carried a single light machine gun. Preecha actually felt sorry for the one in the lead. He was cut down by rifle fire before he realized that he was under attack. The other two crews abandoned their machines. They took cover in the ditch by the side of the road and tried to return fire. The platoon Lewis gunners started to exchange bursts with the French crews. *Give a child a new game and they'll be happy for hours,* Preecha thought indulgently.

The armored cars that turned the battle serious. There were indeed six of them. They had spread out into a line, taking advantage of the open ground before it closed in. They had the old, very short-barreled, 37mm gun, firing a one-kilogram shell at no velocity to speak of. Yet they were deadly enough as a fire support weapon.

The armored car crews spotted where the Lewis guns were firing from and started to fire on those positions. The AM50 armored cars leapfrogged forward in pairs; one pair moving, one pairing firing, the third pair spotting for targets. The equipment might be old and obsolete, but the crews knew what they were doing and were closing in on the Thai positions. Preecha looked at the Vickers gun crew closest to him. They were holding fire, ostensibly not to give their positions away needlessly, but really to ensure than the AM50s closed in as much as possible. The machine guns had a short belt of 100 rounds loaded. The bullets on each belt had solid black tips; armor-piercing ammunition. At 500 meters, those bullets would penetrate 12mm of steel. The armor on the AM50 was only 7mm thick.

He heard the nearest machine gun chatter and saw the brilliant flashes as the steel-cored rounds hit the front of the AM50. Some ricocheted off the sloping steel plates that protected the radiator. Others must have penetrated, for a cloud of white steam enveloped the front of the armored car. It swerved to a stop beside the road and stayed there, immobile in its cloud of white fog. Another AM50 wasn't so lucky. The Vickers gun caught it at an angle. The armor-piercing bullets penetrated its fuel tank. The armored car caught fire, sending a column of black smoke into the sky.

What happened next was something Preecha had never seen before. The stricken vehicle exploded as fuel and ammunition were ignited by the fire. It went up in a single blast that sent debris and white trails of smoke in all directions. What had been a recognizable vehicle was reduced to a blazing hulk.

The sight seemed to cause the other armored cars to hesitate before they opened fire on the machine gun positions with their 37mm guns. Preecha heard a whistle overhead. One of the remaining AM50s was suddenly surrounded by shell bursts. The battalion might only have the old 50mm infantry guns as its artillery, but firing over open sights they were enough to completely outgun the old armored cars.

One of the AM50s took a direct hit on the front. The shell crushed the driving cab completely. The armored car ceased fire and the survivors of its crew bailed out. They tried to take cover from the rifle and machine gun fire that seemed to be surrounding them. Another AM50 had already fallen victim to the black-nosed bullets from the Vickers guns. With all the assurance of a veteran who had seen a whole two hours in combat, Preecha knew that the battle for the Thai left flank was going well for the Guardsmen.

Anti-Tank Company, 3rd Battalion, 5th Regiment Etranger d'Infanterie, Yang Dham Khung, French Indochina

The day was not going well. Lieutenant Roul had known that ever since the armored car company that had attacked the Thai left flank had been pushed back with heavy losses. The sites of four lost armored cars were still marked by the smoke stains in the sky, but they'd been joined by more marks of battle. The FT-17 tanks had tried to support the Legion infantry. The Thai medium tanks had arrived and driven the FT-17s off the field. *This whole attack is turning into a disaster. The DMC has been decimated and our infantry are getting nowhere. And I wonder where the Thai infantry are now? Last time we were in this kind of position, they were already working their way around behind us.* The Legion infantry were fighting hard, repelling Thai attacks and pushing back where they could, but the French offensive had never really got off the ground. It was quickly turning into a quagmire.

"We have news from Phoum Preav." Major Belloc arrived with as little warning as he had on his previous visits. This time, though, his formerly immaculate Foreign Legion khaki was stained and blackened. The infantry of the 3rd battalion had been hammering the position held by the Thais for over four hours, with no success. "Groupement C under Colonel Cadoudal has been severely handled. 19th RMIC has been cut to pieces and Colonel Quelenc has been killed. Jourdain, what do you think the Thais are up to right now?"

"We've got the only high ground here." Roul was thoughtful. "They can't use the ridgelines for cover the way they did before. Not if they come through to the north of us. If they're going to try that, they'll have to come south; long way south, around Phoum Kdol."

"Turning our left flank, the way we tried to turn theirs." Belloc chewed the advice over. Roul was the only man in his command who had fought the Thais before and the Lieutenant's insights were precious to him. "The way they are pushing Groupement C back is consistent with that. And for us?"

Roul thought back over the engagements he had already fought. "They'll try and pin us down here while they cut us off. Expect to see an attack that is much sound and much fury but signifying nothing. A lot of fire, a lot of artillery and their dive bombers will hit us, but they won't push the attack home on the ground. When that starts, we'll know they are behind us. There will be a brief moment when we can get out; we can disengage and pull back to another defensive position. Leave it too late and we will either be encircled or we will have to break out."

He was interrupted by a drone of aircraft engines overhead. Roul watched Major Belloc look up at the biplanes in the clear morning sky. "Corsairs. There is only one problem with your analysis, Jourdain. Colonel Jacomy has sternly forbidden us to retreat."

Overhead, the drone of engines turned to the wailing scream familiar to anybody who had seen cinema films of the fighting in France the previous year. The Corsairs dropped almost vertically out of the sky. The scream of their engines was amplified by the sirens on their fixed undercarriages and the wind howling over the struts between their wings. To Roul's relief, the target was the French infantry position to his front. As yet, his anti-tank guns had not fired; the battery remained masked. He had a hunch that the situation was quickly reaching the point where he would be earning his pay for the day.

In front of him, the infantry broke under the dive bombing. They streamed backwards, abandoning their positions and fleeing the coming battle. Roul heard the shouts as they went.

"The tanks are coming! We are betrayed!"

He took a deep breath to steady himself. Overhead, the Corsairs finished their dive bombing runs and started strafing the retreating infantry. That brought them much closer to Roul's position.

"Steady, men. Sergeant Ambroise, the crews should be ready to open fire. The 25mm guns will engage the tanks. The Soixante-Quinze will hold its fire until we have a clear shot at the supporting infantry. Private Corneille, you know your duty. I leave you to carry it out. Without the infantry supporting us, the whole weight of repelling this attack falls on us. Let us show them what regulars can achieve."

The attack was following very closely behind the dive bombers. *Just how do the Siamese manage to bring their aircraft in so quickly?* Roul could see four Vickers 6-ton Type B tanks surrounded by the green-clad infantry. They already had an air of implacability about them. If the French infantry had remained at their posts, there would be a firefight going on now. But they had not; the positions were deserted. The effect on the advancing Thais was discernable even at this distance. Their advance picked up speed.

"Target the two tanks in the center."

Roul passed the word to his gun crews. They carefully aimed their pieces. The anti-tank guns had the advantage, for the first few shots at least. They didn't intend to waste them. Roul waited until the tanks had closed in and then gave the order to fire.

The first two shots didn't seem to achieve much. The tank targeted by one had turned at the last second. The shot sprayed dirt and stones all over it, but did no apparent damage. Roul saw a brilliant flash as the shot hit the frontal armor, but it seemed to ricochet off. The tanks stopped; it was obvious that the crews were searching for the gun that had fired on them. Roul understood their problem. Unlike the larger, and theoretically more capable, 37mm guns, the Hotchkiss 25mm had a negligible firing signature. Unless one knew where to look and caught it while firing, there was little to see. The tanks started to move again. Now they edged forward, while the infantry moved ahead of them. Then, there were two more cracks. The 25mm crews took their next shots.

This time, the two guns had concentrated on a single target. Their shots had effect. A tank spun to one side. Its tracks flailed; a drive wheel was destroyed by the hit. The other three tanks had seen something; they started firing their 47mm guns at the site of the anti-tank guns. Their supporting infantry moved forward fast, attempting to find and clear the anti-tank guns that threatened their advance.

The survivors of Roul's infantry platoon opened fire. Their light machine guns cut down the Thai infantry. Roul jumped down beside the crew of his 75mm gun and pointed to a group of the green-clad men.

"There, take them down!"

The Soixante-Quinze fired. The burst of the high-explosive shell scattered the attacking infantry. The anti-tank guns fired again; their shots hit the Thai tanks but ricocheted off their armor. The 25mm was a good gun for its size; but, at this range and against real targets, its penetration was marginal. The 75 did better. The crew loaded an armor-piercing shot. The effect on the Type B was devastating. The turret spiralled high into the air. What was left of the hull erupted into flames. With two of its tanks gone and the infantry driven to ground by the fire from Roul's platoon, the Thai attack faltered and fell back.

"That was well done." Major Belloc had reappeared. "A creditable defense indeed. However, I have to tell you that the Thais have taken Phoum Kien Kes and cut RC-157 some eight kilometers to our rear. And in the north, Sisophon has fallen to them. We are cut off; all six battalions of us. Colonel Jacomy has ordered us to hold our positions. The remainder of the forces at Battambang will break through and relieve us."

361

Belloc and Roul exchanged glances. It was Belloc whose quotation expressed what they both knew was going to happen.

"Nous sommes dans un pot de chambre, et nous y serons emmerdés."

5th Cavalry Battalion, 2nd Cavalry "White Horse" Division, Mung Roessei, French Indochina

The road was hard-topped. The black asphalt seemed to shimmer in the afternoon sun. A few tens of meters away, the waters of the Tonle Sap shone in the same sun. The great lake stretched from Battambang most of the way back to Phnom Penh; here, it cut Cambodia nearly in half.

The scene on the road was something that its builders had never anticipated. The Carden-Lloyd machine gun carrier rocked slightly on its suspension as it halted across the left-hand lane. Behind it, the trucks of the infantry battalions stopped as well and discharged their men to form the defense perimeter. It hadn't been a hard fight on the drive up from Chantaburi; the few French roadblocks had been shelled, dive bombed and bypassed. The only real problem had been the driving urgency to get to this point with minimum delay. That, the battalion had done. They had made it on time and done their duty. Now they, and their vehicles, could rest.

The same could not be said for the other two regiments of the division. They would be heading east, along the road that had just been captured. For the road in question was Route Coloniale Five leading from Battambang to Phnom Penh and it was the main supply line for the entire French Indochina Army now concentrated around Battambang.

FKL-60 Operating Base, Nakhorn Phanom, Thailand

"There is not much difference between the P-36G and the Hawk 75N you have flown up to now." The American civilian speaking to Flight Lieutenant Suchart Chalermkiat had landed the aircraft behind him just an hour before, after flying it in from India. "That's why we're getting them through to you first. The P-40Bs can follow later when you have more time to convert."

Suchart understood what the American was getting at, even while the interpreter was translating his words. FKL-60 had started with 11 Hawk 75Ns; now they had five. Two had been shot down by French Morane fighters; two by ground fire. Two had been lost in accidents. The eight aircraft that had just arrived from India were desperately needed. "P-36Gs?"

"Army Air Corps designation for the Mohawk IV. You've got the retractable undercarriage, of course. Don't forget to pull it up when you take off and lower it before landing. We've lost aircraft because of that. There's an extra machine gun in each wing, giving you six. We've replaced the French 7.5mm guns with British .303 Brownings. That's cost you some ammunition capacity. Otherwise, you'll find the aircraft is 40 mph faster then the 75N, and that's about all. Lands the same way and is a touch more agile. Take her up and try her out."

"Thank you, . . ." Suchart hesitated.

"Boyington; everybody calls me Pappy. How many kills you got?" It was the standard fighter pilot question; Suchart was slightly flattered by being asked. It meant this American recognized him as being one of the club.

"Does that include aircraft on the ground?" Suchart got a sideways look by way of response; he kicked himself for the obvious mistake. "Of course not. So far, three. Two Moranes and a Farman bomber. The last one was at night."

Boyington nodded. "Four here. All Japanese. When you fight them, the major one you'll run across is the Nakajima. You can recognize it by its fixed undercarriage. It's as agile as the devil, but only got two .30s. Your Hawk can handle it as long as you don't try and do a low-speed dogfight. There's a bigger version of it that's a bit faster and got a retractable undercarriage. The one to watch for is the new Mitsubishi. I've never run into one, but the rumor is that it's very fast, very agile and got wing-mounted cannon."

There was a pause while the interpreter caught up and got his breath back. Suchart grabbed the opportunity to ask another question. "You think we will fight the Japanese?"

Boyington looked around. He had strict orders not to discuss politics on this delivery flight, but he told himself that this was tactical advice to a fellow fighter pilot, not political at all. "You will. The two biggest guys on the block always end up fighting it out and the Japs will want to take you down before you get big enough to give them a hard time. Only, I'm getting a feeling they may have left it too late. Anyway, you watch their fighters. They love dogfighting. Just dive on them and get away before they can trap you into a turning match."

"That's what the German pilot who came here said. Aerobatics are for amateurs. Dive and zoom."

"Glad to hear it. That's good advice. Now, the most important thing. Anywhere I can get a drink around here?"

Forward Headquarters, Burapha Payak Corps, Thailand

The maps on the walls showed the developing situation quite clearly. To the Ambassador, it looked like a European fried breakfast. There was a big red circle around Battambang, with the town itself a red blob in the middle. That was the fried egg. North of it was an ellipse stretched out along Route Colonial 157 with a series of designations scrawled in it. That was the sausage. Then, north of that was a series of small red circles that marked the remnants of the French troops north of the Tonle Sap. They would be the hash browns. To the Ambassador, it looked like breakfast; but she knew to the French it was a military disaster in the making.

Six battalions of French infantry and an artillery battalion were cut off and surrounded north of Phoum Preav. Ten more French battalions of

363

infantry, three battalions of artillery and the survivors of an armored battalion were surrounded at Battambang. Only two battalions of infantry were left unbesieged. One was the first battalion of the 5th REI at Siamreap and the other was a *Tirailleur Tonkinois* battalion at Kompong Thum. Almost half the French forces in Indochina had been either destroyed or had been left with no choice but to surrender. On the other hand, the Ninth Infantry division was wholly tied down at Battambang, along with a regiment of the 11th Infantry and another of the 2nd Cavalry. The rest of the 11th was either spreading out along the Mekong to await the anticipated Japanese thrust or advancing along Route Coloniale 6 to Phnom Penh. South of the Tonle Sap, the rest of 2nd Cavalry was also heading towards Phnom Penh along Route Coloniale 5. She was confident they would get there. After all, there was nothing left to stop them.

"What excuses have the Navy offered us?" Her tone was icy cold; the naval officer waiting to report blanched at hearing it.

"We have lost two torpedo boats and the coastal defense ship *Thonburi* is grounded off Koh Chang. She'll be towed back to Bangkok for repair later this afternoon. The French were driven off and they were prevented from bombarding our coastal towns." Captain Chuan Jitbhatkorn sounded defensive and knew it.

"That's what happened. I asked why it has happened. Or is there no reason why the Navy has let us down?" The Ambassador's tones hadn't warmed in the slightest. In her own mind, she had a reasonable idea of what lay behind the naval losses at Koh Chang. The Army had been rebuilt with young, vigorous officers in command, men who had been selected on merit. The Air Force was recently-formed and had always been that way. The Navy, though, had been aloof from the political disruptions of the previous decade and had not been forced to change as a result. It was still wedded to the old ways. One of them was officers selected by connection and family, not ability. There was a place for soldier-politicians in the armed forces; the Ambassador was well aware of that, since she was one. But a military politician who was also an able military commander was rare. More normally, the two were mutually exclusive.

"We were outgunned and outnumbered. Our ships could not raise steam fast enough. The idea of a coastal defense ship with a few heavy guns is fundamentally flawed; such ships cannot fire effectively on moving targets. For all that, one ship held off five enemy warships for over an hour and saved the rest of the squadron. We lost a battle, tactically; but strategically, we may have won. That will depend on whether the French return or not." Captain Chuan was angered by the insinuations about the Navy's conduct and it showed.

"Very well. I have a task for you." The Ambassador eyed the Captain thoughtfully. He'd fought back when attacked; that meant he could be the sort of young, intelligent officer she sought out. Let's give him a job to find out.

364

"You are charged with interviewing all the survivors of the action and making out a list of lessons learned and actions recommended. If our naval policies are wrong, say so. If our present ships are useless, say that too."

Her voice softened. "There is no shame in losing a battle, Captain. That can happen to anybody. There is much shame in not finding out why the battle was lost and failing to correct those errors. Report back to me with the reasons why Koh Chang did not go as we desired and solutions for the problems so revealed. And remember. If anybody tries to prevent you from giving me your honest opinions, place them firmly out of your way. I have no wish to be told what I want to hear. Nobody has ever suffered at my hands for telling me the truth." Chuan glanced around and noted that several of the Army officers were nodding absent-mindedly.

A communications officer rushed in waving a message. "Highness, a message from the Foreign Ministry in Bangkok. The Japanese Ambassador has delivered a note to ourselves, and apparently to the French, offering to mediate an end to this war. The terms they dictate are attached."

"And what is the reaction in the Government so far?" The Ambassador spoke reflectively while she read the terms of the Japanese ultimatum. They were better-suited to her purpose than she could dream possible.

"Marshal Plaek wants to throw the Japanese Ambassador down a well and asks your permission to do it."

The Ambassador snorted. "This is not Sparta. I will compose a suitable reply for the Japanese Ambassador to send back to Tokyo. However, advise my old friend to pick out a suitable well; just in case."

Room 208, Munitions Building, Washington, DC, USA

"So, the conclusion so far is that the industrial infrastructure of Germany is such that there are no singularities that we can take out. We define a singularity as a point of failure, the destruction of which will bring war-making capability to a halt and which cannot easily be repaired or replaced. This means that any strategic bombing campaign is going to have to hit a large number of targets to induce the kind of failure we are seeking. The ball-bearing industry is a good example, as you will see from Chapter Twenty-Seven of our preliminary report. There are only four ball bearing plants in Germany and their destruction would bring ball bearing production to a halt. In theory, that will destroy German war production. In reality, they can replace ball bearings by roller bearings for many applications and roller bearings can be made anywhere. They can also replace internal production with ball bearings imported from, say, Sweden or Switzerland. Then, of course, there is the question of repairing the factories and there we move into unknown territory.

"The truth is that neither we nor anybody else have any idea what it actually takes to destroy a factory. The British believed that it would take four

250-pound bomb hits to destroy an average factory. Already, the experience available to date shows that this estimate was ludicrously wrong. Probably wrong by several orders of magnitude. We've already determined one problem; that is that all the bombs we were planning to use have impact fuzes. They explode immediately on impact and the factories have roofs."

"Oh?" Secretary Stimson sounded confused; suddenly, realization dawned on him. "Ohhh. The bombs hit the roof and wreck it, but the inside remains undamaged?"

"Exactly. We need to fit our bombs with delayed action fuzes. It sounds simple, but it appears nobody thought of that. A dead space between the roof and the ceiling of the factory floor is excellent protection. The roof sets the fuze off and the ceiling catches the debris. Reinforcing building roofs is also a simple defense. Anyway, we're going to have to do a lot of research on what it takes to blow a factory up before we can take a target list and estimate the force we need to destroy it. We'll probably need to take a real factory and bomb it just to see what happens. One thing I will say now, the 250-pounder won't hack it. We're looking at 500- or 1000-pounders, at least, to get real effects. Possibly much larger. We could be dropping 4000-pounders by the time this war is over. We'll have to bear that in mind when designing the bomb bays for our aircraft."

"Thank you, Phillip. I suggest you find a disused factory we can employ for that purpose. Now, I assume everybody has heard that the Japanese have offered to 'mediate' a negotiated peace between French Indochina and Thailand?" Cordell Hull looked around the table. More heads shook than nodded. "Mediated is a very polite way of putting it. Dictated terms that suit themselves would be closer. I have those terms here. Essentially they are that Thailand gets a small strip of land along the border. Quite a bit less than they have occupied over the last few days. Japan gets full basing rights and essentially complete political control over the rest of French Indochina, along with free access rights to Indochinese and Thai territory 'to monitor the ceasefire'. Oh, and the French authorities plus the Thai government will be expected to pay significant amounts to Japan to compensate them for their efforts."

"That's not a mediated ceasefire; that's a power grab." Stimson frowned. "Are the Thais complicit in this? In league with the Japanese?"

"Given the nature of their reply, I hardly think so." Hull looked around, his opinions conflicted. On one hand, he was delighted at what he had read; on the other, perturbed that his original judgment had been so mistaken. Driven by his instinctive prejudices against military governments, he had nearly made a catastrophic mistake by alienating a valuable ally. "To quote the Thai Foreign Ministry, 'Since the Empire of Japan has no legitimate presence, position or interest in the Indochina region, the Kingdom of Thailand firmly and unequivocally rejects the ultimatum masquerading as a mediated settlement to the current hostilities between the Kingdom and the French

Indochina authorities. These hostilities are a matter between the participants and will be resolved on a bilateral basis between them. Furthermore, the Kingdom of Thailand advises the Empire of Japan that it will not be allowed access rights to Thai territory and any attempt to secure such rights will be resisted by all the force at the Kingdom's disposal.' In non-diplomatic language that reads 'mind your own business and drop dead in the process.' It's about the most emphatic rejection of a diplomatic approach I have seen in forty years of public service. The French Indochina authorities have accepted the Japanese proposals. I would say that the two reactions have drawn the lines of political alignments quite definitively."

Suriyothai, honey, when you nail your colors to the mast, you sure use the largest nails you can find. Stuyvesant restrained himself from grinning at the thought. He was forestalled from saying anything by Henry Morgenthau's worried comment.

"Aren't the French doing quite well? The Thai advance seems limited and the French are claiming a major naval victory. They're saying they've sunk a third of the Thai Navy including both their largest battleships and three destroyers."

Stimson shook his head. "Not according to our military attache there. One of the ships the French claim to have sunk is in Sattahip. She's not just undamaged; she wasn't even in the battle. The other one was towed into Bangkok the day after the battle. She's badly shot up but afloat. They're coast defense ships, by the way, not battleships. The Thais say they've lost two torpedo boats; that's all. We do know they drove off the French squadron. It's in Saigon right now, with their cruiser and at least one sloop damaged. On land, the French are facing an imminent disaster. Their counter-attack was a complete failure and it seems like their army has been surrounded at Battambang. That's probably why they accepted the Japanese proposal. It's the only chance they have of stopping the situation unravelling completely."

"I think it is fairly obvious that reversing our position on arms supplies was a major factor in Thailand adopting its anti-Japanese alignment." Cordell Hull sounded almost sanctimoniously pleased with himself.

Given a week, you'll have convinced yourself that this was what you had planned all along. Stuyvesant contented himself with nodding thoughtfully at Hull's statement. Hull's next words caught him by surprise.

"Since they are obviously aligned with our interests, perhaps we should make our support clearer? Unfortunately, we appear to have run out of British and French aircraft to give away."

A ripple of laughter ran around the room. The truth was that the vast stockpile of undelivered French and British aircraft had been put to a far better use than its original owners could ever have thought possible. The political and strategic gains from their distribution far exceeded their actual military value.

Stimson raised a hand in a munificent gesture. "Actually, I might be able to help there. I was speaking with General Marshall this morning. Apparently, the British bought 100 M2A4 light tanks, which remain undelivered. They were scheduled for our own use, but we have a new model, the M3, being introduced. Their loss will not be significant. Perhaps, if we were to offer them to the Thais, the reinforcement would make their rejection of the Japanese all the more emphatic?"

"They belong to the Commonwealth of Nations as the legitimate successor to the British government." Cordell Hull was firm on that. The proprieties had to be observed. "Of course, if the Indians, Australians, Canadians and South Africans don't mind, the transfer would be possible."

"The South Africans want armored cars. The Canadians are building Valentines. It's just the Indians and Australians who matter and I think we know where the Indians stand on this. They won't object."

Cordell Hull acknowledged Stimson's assessment with a nod. "Phillip, you look like you have a thought on this?"

"It seems to me that a longer-term commitment is necessary. Speaking as a businessman, I'd want to know that the current relationship is stable before investing. After all, we have reversed course on Thailand twice now."

"Perhaps a long-term financial commitment?" Henry Morgenthau spoke diffidently. He'd seen the intricate detail of the studies on German industry and didn't like what he was seeing. The sheer complexity and number of variables in the picture that had been presented made him question the plausibility of theories based around central economic planning. That ran against the beliefs of a lifetime and made him pleased to get back to simpler and less disturbing ground. "Extend a substantial credit line, repayable over a long period at a low rate of interest? That would be a sign that the relationship now being established is an enduring one."

"And what they do with the money would also be useful information on their real policies and intents." Hull nodded approvingly. "An excellent suggestion, Henry. Has anybody anything else to add?"

There was a generalized murmur of denial and Hull looked around happily. "Very well then; I will present these opinions to the next meeting of the cabinet. Phillip, I will let you know when that will be. I understand that your team has finished the first draft of Air War Plan Directive One. Please hold yourself ready to attend the appropriate part of that meeting. I fear nobody else can present the information you have gathered in a way that will do it justice. On that note, I move this meeting be closed."

CHAPTER THIRTEEN
REACHING AN UNDERSTANDING

Town Hall, Phoum Dak Pay, French Indochina

This was a humiliation that Admiral Jean Decoux had never anticipated. In 1940, he had been appointed to the position of governor of Indochina with specific instructions to reverse the policy of appeasement towards the Japanese led by his predecessor, General Georges Catroux. When he had arrived in Hanoi, he had found that Catroux was far from being the appeaser Decoux had been told. Political realities forced them both to follow that road. Neither had received any support from the new government in Vichy and both had faced intense pressure from the Japanese. The Japanese wanted French Indochina as a base from which to strike at the rich resource areas further south. There was a further truth, one that Decoux had a harder job accepting. The government in Vichy may have condemned Catroux as an appeaser, but appeasement was the policy that demanded. In effect, his predecessor had been disgraced for obeying the instructions he had been given. Decoux had taken that lesson on board and concentrated all his efforts on trying to resist the Japanese advance while not giving them the excuse to seize complete control by force. He had never expected this devastating blow from the west. His civil servants had assured him that displays of force would be entirely adequate to eliminate any threat from that quarter.

"Is it really as bad as they say?" Admiral Decoux needed the advice on the situation at the front. General Catroux was the only reliable source he could consult.

"It is a disaster. Another Sedan." Catroux was a deeply worried and unhappy man. He was utterly disillusioned with the authorities in Vichy who had thrown him to the wolves and were now trying to do the same to Decoux. "The forces in the Battambang pocket tried to link up with the smaller pocket to the north yesterday. but the attack was repulsed with losses on our side. It is like the fighting at home last year; it is the air forces that are determining the course of the war. We have lost twenty-two aircraft so far, and another dozen or more on the ground. Our fighters have been shot down and our bombers driven from the sky. The Siamese dive bombers can go where they want and do what they wish. And they are very good at their work."

"How long do we have?" It was the most important piece of information Decoux wanted. It would determine everything else that he could achieve.

Catroux thought carefully. It was so easy to give in to despair and give up while there was still hope. Yet, it was also so easy to convince oneself there was hope when all chances of victory had faded. "A week; perhaps ten days. By then, the encircled troops will have had to surrender and we will have lost the one good card still in our hand. While they resist, we can negotiate a peace settlement on terms. Once they are gone, the Siamese will simply dictate what terms they will. At least we have one consolation. We have heard from the Swiss that the Siamese are treating the prisoners they have taken with great kindness. We should respond in kind, of course. We have fourteen of their aircrew as our prisoners and treating them as guests rather than prisoners would be wise."

"Of course; that goes without saying." Decoux was slightly annoyed at any suggestion the prisoners of war would be anything other than well-treated. The fact that the Thais had almost a thousand French prisoners of war in their hands took any decision on that point out of his hands.

The conversation was interrupted by the entry of the Thai delegation. The fact that the French had arrived first and had to wait for the Thais to appear was itself an admission of who was winning this war. Decoux was startled to see the leader of the group was a woman. There had been rumors for some time that a previously-unknown woman had been commanding this offensive, but it was the first time he had actually seen her. She was short, stocky and her hair was cut short in the style favored by Thai women. One look at her and the deference given to her was enough to tell him she truly was in charge here. And not just of the Thai forces. It was her will that was driving the whole situation. Decoux could feel the force of that will from across the room.

"Admiral Decoux, General Catroux, I am the Ambassador-Plenipotentiary of the Kingdom of Thailand. That title means that I have full authority to negotiate a settlement of the dispute between our countries. Let us do so now, and not waste more lives."

The Ambassador's French was smooth and fluent. To Decoux, who had heard his language butchered by faulty grammar and pronunciation so often, her perfect rendition was a pleasure to hear. He was sincerely distressed at having to disappoint her. "Madam Ambassador, your government has received the settlement terms dictated by the Japanese mediators of this dispute. These offer an acceptable resolution of the conflict and we base our position upon them."

The Ambassador shook her head. The Japanese had tried to insist that these negotiations be held on board the cruiser *Natori*, currently in Kompong Som, but her government had flatly refused to consider that demand. "I regret to inform you that the position of the Government has not changed. The Japanese terms are not acceptable and will not be considered as a basis for a settlement of this dispute. Our terms are quite simple; we require the restoration of our borders as they were prior to your encroachment upon them from 1860 onwards. We also require our borders to be defensible. For that reason, we require the return of all our territories south of the Mekong River and the establishment of the border between Thailand and French Indochina as the riparian center of the Mekong."

"What the devil is the riparian center?" Admiral Decoux whispered the question to General Catroux.

"The line representing the deepest part of the river in question. It's the normal way of defining a boundary represented by a river."

"We are sorry, Madam Ambassador. We have no choice other than to accept the Japanese proposal and reject any other. I mean that literally; we have no choice in the matter other than to accept the Japanese proposal. Or any Japanese proposal, for that matter."

"As will you." The words from the door cut across the Ambassador before she could start to speak. "The mediated settlement we have dictated will be accepted without change. That is our final word on the matter."

The Ambassador stared at the man who had stormed into the meeting room. He was almost a caricature of a Japanese Army officer. Short and bald, but with a bristling moustache; his eyes behind circular rimless glasses, which exaggerated the folds. He was wearing a British-style Sam Browne belt over his Japanese Army uniform and a katana sword hung from it. She shook her head slightly. "And just who are you?"

"I am Colonel Masanobu Tsuji, direct representative of the Imperial Japanese Army."

"Very well, Colonel Tsuji. If you have an intelligent remark to make, please do so. Otherwise, leave. I am not impressed by foolish men who pound on their hairy chests with closed fists."

Decoux looked at the two facing each other with something close to awe. The space between them seemed to crackle with energy from their clash. He also realized something else; a blood feud was being born in front of his eyes. Tsuji's fanatical hatred of the Ambassador was being met by her withering contempt for him. He also realized that Tsuji was confused. Decoux seriously doubted whether he had been openly defied in such a public and blatant manner before.

371

"I do not have a hairy chest." Tsuji nearly screamed the words in response. To Decoux it seemed a very strange thing to say. He guessed he was missing a cultural reference that the Ambassador had used to flick a very raw nerve.

The Ambassador seemed slightly surprised. "How strange. I thought you would have taken after your mother."

This time, Tsuji did scream with rage. He started to draw the sword at his waist. There was a rattle of bolts. The Ambassador's bodyguards cocked the heavy Thompson sub-machine guns they were carrying. The Ambassador herself had reached underneath her jacket and drawn two semi-automatic pistols. Decoux recognized them as German P'08 Lugers, but they were obviously chambered for a much larger round than the usual 9mm. He guessed they were .45s. As far as he knew, only three Lugers in that caliber had been made. *And this woman had two of them?* She now stood there with one in each hand, looking at the sword with unconcealed and blistering contempt.

"How like the Japanese to bring a tooth-pick to a gunfight."

Tsuji paused for a second, shuddering with the effort to control himself. Eventually, he slammed the sword back into its sheath and stared at the Ambassador with searing hatred. "You will die screaming for this."

"My enemies have often said that." The Ambassador's voice was reflective and, to Decoux's amazement, amused. "Instead, they all died; screaming soprano."

Tsuji glared at her, turned around and stormed out. The Ambassador holstered her pistols and sat down at the negotiation table again. "My apologies, General, Admiral, for the interruption. Sadly, I believe that the unwarranted Japanese interference in our relations means that we are at an impasse now. Might I suggest we meet again in a week? At which time, I believe you may have a window of opportunity to reach an agreement that represents our mutual interests, not those of Japan. Our troops will, of course, be continuing their operations during that period."

Decoux exhaled, suddenly realizing he had been holding his breath as long as Tsuji had been in the room. "Madam Ambassador, I don't understand what you said to him, but I have never seen that man so angry or filled with hate."

She smiled. "In Japan, there is a class of people called the burakumin, or eta. They are literally the lowest of the low, ranking even beneath whores, beggars, night-soil collectors and so on. They are regarded as being so disgusting that any other Japanese touching them, even those of the lowest and most degraded kind, has to be ritually cleansed of pollution. The burakumin are supposed to be distinguished by having hairy chests. There are rumors that the mother of Masanobu Tsuji was burakumin, but his father's family covered it up to save them from unspeakable disgrace."

General Catroux shuddered. "That man will come after you with every ounce of power at his disposal. He will throw the whole might of the Japanese forces in Indochina at your country."

The Ambassador's smile broadened into one of pure delight. "Oh, I do so hope so."

Forward Pickets, 11th Infantry (Queen's Cobra) Division, Ban Dan Ky, Mekong River, French Indochina

Sergeant Mongkut Chandrapa na Ayuthya sighed gently and shook his head. He'd just received a rare treat, a letter from home, and he treasured its contents. *Well, most of them*, he thought. His daughter Sirisoon was in trouble again, for fighting at school. Again. Apparently, one of the boys had kept pulling her hair while she was repeating her lessons to the teacher. She turned on him and scratched him so badly he'd had to be sent home. He was actually quite proud of her for doing that. Most girls of her age would have just run away or cried. My daughter had turned and fought her tormentor. *Come to think of it, I am actually doing much the same thing right now.*

"Sergeant, I can hear something."

Corporal Pon spoke very, very quietly. The observation point was right on the banks of the Mekong River, shielded from the water only by some tree-trunks and bushes. At this point on the river, the water flowed smoothly and steadily. Sound would reflect over it. *That is probably what the Japanese were forgetting.* The sounds of hammering and movement their side of the river was faint, but clearly audible.

"I hear it too. Stay alert and watch for any movement." One good thing was that the moon was up. The Japanese would be visible in the reflections of the moonlight off the water. Mongkut was pleased with the way Pon was working out. He'd selected him for promotion on the advice of the other Sergeants, who had reminded him that a popular Corporal might be so because he was too slack on the men. They'd been right; the very qualities that had made Pon unpopular as a private had worked well for him as a corporal.

Mongkut slid backwards and made his way to the platoon command post, set well back from the river. The plan was to drop back when the Japanese attacked so that their blow would meet nothing but empty air. Then, when the Japanese were over the river and trapped on the Thai-held side, the 11th would counter-attack and drive them back. There was no doubt that the Japanese would attack. Word of how the commander of the Burapha Payak Corps had insulted and publicly humiliated a very important Japanese officer had spread through the whole Army. Even better, the commander of the corps was a Princess; that had added extra spice to the story. By the time the story had finished spreading, it had been elaborated with extra details of how the Japanese officer had burst into tears at the humiliation and had been so demoralized that his men had to restrain him from committing suicide.

"Sir, we heard movement across the river. Hammering and voices speaking. I think the Japanese are assembling boats."

Lieutenant Somchai was looking at the map spread out on his table. North of his position, the Mekong had split into a vast maze of tiny rivers, each deep and fast flowing. The combination of thousands of small islands and an ever-changing maze of waterways made launching any kind of cross-river offensive impossible. South of his position, the river split in two around a large central island. Any Japanese attack there would have to occupy the island first. They hadn't. Further south still, the river entered another stretch dominated by rapids; a profusion of fast flowing streams and thousands of tiny, snake-infested islands. By the time the river became crossable again, it was not far north from Phnom Penh. The Thai Army hadn't got there yet, although the fourth regiment of the 11th Infantry was advancing fast in that direction. First Regiment was on the outskirts of Siem Reap. Second and Third Regiments were here, waiting for the Japanese assault that had to hit this single, 14 kilometer stretch of the river. There was, quite simply, nowhere else the Japanese could make the crossing. Somchai knew he was only a lowly lieutenant, but he could see that this particular stretch of the Mekong was going to be strategically very important one day.

"Very well. The observation points are on full alert?"

"Yes, sir." Mongkut noted a touch of reproof in his voice. He felt his lieutenant should have realized that would be the case; but he reminded himself that it was a lieutenant's job to check on such things.

"Make sure they remember the orders. As soon as the Japanese start to cross they are to drop back, keeping the enemy under observation but not impeding his move forward."

"I will remind them, sir." Mongkut guessed what the plan was. The Japanese had shown in China that they were attack-crazy; their first reaction was always to attack an enemy in front of them. There was a long ridge a kilometer or so behind the riverbank; one that the Japanese would have to take before they could go anywhere else. Mongkut was quite sure that ridge was defended by every unit that could be brought up. The Japanese would be trapped between the defenses and the river.

The only thing that worried Mongkut was that if he, a sergeant, could see it, the Japanese officers surely could.

Headquarters, 11th Infantry (Queen's Cobra) Division, Phoum Sam Ang, Mekong River

"We're getting reports in from all the forward pickets. The Japanese are active all along this stretch of the Mekong. You were right, Highness."

Suriyothai restrained herself from replying 'of course.' It hadn't actually taken much effort to see that the Japanese assault had to come here. It wasn't just that the river was crossable at this point. There was a good road network centered on this area; that would ease Japanese supply problems.

There were three airfields within a few minutes flying time. *The Japanese only had one division available for the assault, so they didn't have the manpower to do anything elaborate. Then, again, they don't think they will need to do anything more than a simple charge. They've learned a lot of very bad lessons from the fighting in China. Coupled with their overweening self-confidence, they'll destroy themselves on these defenses.*

"The reinforcements are ready?" There were two regiments of the 11th Infantry spread along the ridge, dug in to bunkers and entrenchments. A regiment of the First Cavalry had arrived as well; they were the reserve in case anything went wrong. Finally, she had moved the assault engineer battalions from the Ninth, Eleventh and First Cavalry Divisions up. They had unloaded their equipment and were waiting in the dead ground just below Ridge 77. When the time came to counter-attack, those assault engineers would lead the way. *And may the Good Lord Buddha have mercy on the Japanese when they do.*

"They are, Highness, and the artillery is in position, waiting. We have the 150mm guns on call." General Pridi hesitated before continuing. "Highness, the combat engineers. Do we have to use them this way?"

"The Japanese are foolhardy in attack but tenacious in defense. They have shown that in China. We will break them on our defenses here but throwing them back across the river will involve hard fighting. We will have to crush their defense thoroughly. I do not intend to sacrifice one more of our soldiers than absolutely necessary. Those engineers are the key to everything."

Suriyothai looked down on the ground that lay between the main line of the Thai defense and the river. It was invisible in the darkness but it was there. The Mekong, probably the strongest defense line in Asia. Once before, her country had held these positions; but they had been a medieval, primitive army where spears were still regarded as viable weapons. Against Europeans with breech-loading rifles, they had stood no chance. They'd had to compromise, prevaricate and appease their enemies. Now, they had tanks, artillery, machine guns, aircraft and, most important of all, the knowledge of how to use them. This, here, was the decisive battle and everything depended on it.

For a brief moment, the waterfall of colored lights filled her mind. She saw the thread of events she had first detected the previous year. It glowed strong and firm; all the threads converged here. Once this battle was won, the French would concede. Her country would have the Mekong back as its primary line of defense. Her Army would have crushed the French and the Japanese. That would provide the security and stability guarantee that would cause the Hongs to make Bangkok their base. With them would come prosperity for her people and tax income for her government. Defeating the Japanese would put her country firmly in the American camp and ensure their support. Her country's position secured, they would become the guardian of the back door to India and thus a trusted Indian ally. And that was the opening door to a real position on the world stage. The mouse would have become an elephant.

This battle was indeed the key to everything.

Mohawk IV, Over The Mekong River, French Indochina

They had taken off for this sweep along the Mekong just before dawn and had been patrolling the river by the time the sun came up. Flight Lieutenant Suchart Chalermkiat had taken that time to fall in love with his Mohawk IV. It was much faster than his old Hawk 75N and much more responsive on the controls. He was leading a flight of four aircraft; two more flights accompanied his. The older Hawk 75Ns had been consolidated into a single squadron and they also were patrolling the area. The briefing before take-off had been very clear. A major Japanese assault on this part of the front was expected. Their aircraft had to be cleared from the sky.

"I see them. Below, ten o'clock."

The washed-out light gray of Ki-27 fighters stood out clearly against the dark green of the jungle that bordered the Mekong. A closer look showed the dozen Ki-32 light bombers skimming the jungle below the fighters. They'd had green mottling painted over their light gray; obviously, they'd been in Indochina longer than the fighter pilots and realized how ineffective the light gray was. It amused Suchart that he probably knew more about Japanese Army aircraft designations than most people. A few months ago, the Japanese had been trying to sell aircraft to Thailand. Several types had arrived at Thai airfields for evaluation. Suchart had taken the opportunity to look at them closely. *I wonder of any of the aircraft I saw are down there.*

"Take them. Suchart, lead the way." The order from the squadron commander was terse. Suchart pushed the nose of his fighter over and started to dive. *Break up and disperse the escort first, then tear the bombers apart.*

The Japanese pilots were neither stupid nor ill-trained. They spotted the Mohawks early in their dive. The neat formation of three Vs scattered. When the Japanese had been trying to sell the Ki-27 to the Air Force, they'd made great play of the aircraft's agility and its unequalled ability to turn tightly. Later, the German pilots who had been hired to train the Thai Air Force after the political climate in Germany had turned sour gave their opinions on that theory. Now, Suchart could see why they had been unimpressed.

The tight turns looked impressive, but the Ki-27s bled off energy in the process. It did not get them out of the lethal cone of fire from the Mohawks. Suchart had picked his target carefully. His six machine guns lashed out with a converging cone of tracer. The first few rounds went past the Japanese fighter's nose. The rest walked along the fuselage. To his astonishment, the Japanese fighter blew up; disintegrating into an orange ellipse of flame as its fuel tanks erupted. *The Moranes I killed never exploded like that. They took a battering before they went down.*

He was through the Japanese fighter group but still in a dive, heading for the Ki-32s below. He banked right, hoping that one of the Ki-27s would see him do so and close in for the kill. *Their job is, after all, to stop us getting at the bombers.* To his delight, a Ki-27 took the bait and curved after him. That was why Suchart had broken right, not left. He was leading the Japanese fighter right across the nose of Suchart's wingman. In his mirror, he saw the Japanese fighter start to fire its two nose guns. Then the stream of tracers from his wingman enveloped the little fighter. It erupted into another orange fireball. *Teamwork, teamwork, teamwork.* Their instructors had hammered it home with ruthless persistence. *Wingman, cover your leader; leader, cover your wingman. That way you'll both get home. Most of the time. Don't make pretty maneuvers. Dive, gun, run.*

The formation of Ki-32s was right in front of him. Suchart approached them from the front quarter, but that was hardly a problem. He'd been taught the art of deflection shooting against fighters; the Ki-32 was a much larger, slower target. His first few shots went past the nose again; the remainder of the fire walked along the fuselage. The effect wasn't as dramatic as with the Ki-27s. The Ki-32 started to burn; a mix of black and gray smoke pouring from its engine. The stricken aircraft nosed over. The steepening dive only ended when it plowed into the treetops beneath. Another Ki-32 was already following it down. Suchart's wingman had seen the opportunity and raked it with his machine guns.

A quick glance at his instrument panel showed him that the needle on his speedometer was jammed against the stop. *Am I really going that fast?* The Japanese formation was already well behind him, so he pulled the nose of his fighter up and started to climb. There would be time for another pass or two soon enough. The other three aircraft in his flight had already formed up around him. Suchart started the long curve that would get them back into position over the battlefield. The Japanese formation that had approached so confidently was gone, scattered to the winds. There were a dozen or more pyres of smoke from the ground. The only question was, how many of them represented a precious Mohawk lost?

Far below him, over the muddy, gray waters of the Mekong, a formation of Hawk 75Ns were strafing the Japanese boats that were pouring across the river. Suchart wondered if his old Hawk 75N was one of the aircraft attacking the boats. He dismissed the question. He had enough to worry about.

Forward Pickets, 11th Infantry (Queen's Cobra) Division, Phoum Sam Ang, Mekong River, French Indochina

"Look at that!"

Corporal Pon was awed by the sight. The river was covered by a huge fleet of small boats, all of which were heading for the Thai-held bank. A group of Thai aircraft had swept over them, their guns firing into the swarm. It had all the effect of trying to wipe out an ant's nest by stabbing them individually with a needle. Overhead, the rumbling roar of artillery shells dominated the scene. The vast flock of boats was pock-marked with great white towers as shells plowed into the water. Every so often, a shell would bite home. A boat would be thrown into the air; men spiralled from it as the wooden craft broke up. Yet, despite the shelling, the approach of the assault boats seemed unstoppable.

"The great fish will eat well tonight."

The grim words were all too true, as anybody who lived near the Mekong was aware. The river was populated by giant catfish; scavengers who would eat anything. Literally anything. That was why the bodies of those who drowned in the Mekong were seldom found. Sergeant Mongkut saw something unusual in the midst of the swarm of small craft, larger vessels carrying a tank each. One of them exploded in a ball of orange flame; a 150mm shell made a direct hit on it. The rest continued their apparently inexorable advance.

"They're bringing tanks over. We'd better get out of here."

It was as if the Japanese heard him and decided to encourage him on his way. The sound of inbound artillery fire was quite distinct from outbound. Japanese shells hit all along the banks of the river. The shells burst in the trees and sprayed wooden fragments across the patches of clear ground.

That was all the pickets needed. Their job had been to warn the troops holding the high ground off to their left and the lower ridge that marked their center and right of any Japanese assault. That work was done. Now they needed to get back to join the main line of resistance, two kilometers to their rear. *An early start,* Mongkut thought, *would be a good idea at this point.*

He led his troops away from the river, slipping through the trees before the Japanese could arrive. To his relief, the Japanese bombardment was limited to the riverbank and treeline. He guessed that the Japanese guns were mostly 75mm weapons, firing on a flat trajectory across the river. That kind of fire was of limited value; the thick groups of trees along the bank stopped the guns firing further inland.

Once his men were away from the bank, they picked up speed as the trees thinned out. Two hundred meters away from the bank, there was a wide belt of open ground; an old farm that had been abandoned too recently for the jungle to reclaim. Mongkut saw another sergeant leading a batch of pickets back from the bank. The sight gave him a distinct feeling of relief. *At least I didn't abandon our positions too early* The scattered infantry picked up speed as they jog-trotted back to the main line of resistance along Ridge 70. The last thing any of them wanted was to be caught in the open by the Japanese.

Headquarters, 5th Motorized Infantry Division, Ban Dan Ky, French Indochina

The problem was that everything had to go right.

There were no reserves for this operation. Japanese forces in Indochina were thin on the ground to start with, and this operation had already changed into a full-scale assault. Lieutenant General Akihito Nakamura knew his 5th Motorized Infantry Division was one of the most powerful in the Japanese Army. He had more than 500 trucks to move his supplies and artillery and every man in his unit had a bicycle. That gave them unprecedented mobility, especially where the density of forest precluded the use of trucks to carry his men. He also had a tank battalion, in place of the horse cavalry battalion used by less-favored divisions. That gave him twelve Type 95 Ha-Go light tanks and twenty-four Type 97 Chi-Ha medium tanks. He had enough artillery as well: 12 105mm howitzers and 24 75mm guns. With four infantry regiments organized in two brigades, the 5th Motorized was a powerful formation indeed.

There was nothing else. Apart from the 5th Motorized Division, there were two Independent Mixed Brigades in Indochina. The 21st Independent Mixed Brigade was stationed around Hanoi, while the 14th was tasked with consolidating Japanese interests in the South. The latter was technically his reserve formation for this assault, yet it was more than 150 kilometers away. Given the poor road network and virtual absence of railways to the area his division was operating in, he couldn't expect any support from them. To make matters worse, his promised air support hadn't shown up either. He had been told that a formation of twelve Ki-32 light bombers escorted by nine Ki-27 fighters had been sent to assist in the assault on the Thai positions, but they hadn't arrived. It wasn't good when things like that happened before battle was even properly joined.

He also knew what he was up against. His information was that he was attacking the Thai 11th Infantry Division. That was, according to his intelligence data, a division remarkably similar to his own. It was a square division, with four regiments; the difference was that the Thais didn't use the intermediate brigade command level. It had trucks to tow its guns and a divisional tank battalion; although that battalion had fewer, weaker tanks than Nakamura could call upon. If both units were Japanese, this would be an even fight. Such fights rarely went well for the attacker. However, Nakamura knew he had the Japanese fighting spirit of his men to rely on. That is worth more than abstract mathematical arguments of numbers and force levels.

"Situation?" he snapped the word out to the divisional intelligence officer. "And where are those aircraft?"

"Sir, 9th Brigade is landing on the other side of the river now. They report little resistance on the riverbank, but both 11th and 41st regiments are taking casualties from enemy artillery fire and air attacks. They report no friendly aircraft over the crossing and say the Siamese are bombing and strafing them without interference."

"Where are those aircraft?" Nakamura repeated the question with growing impatience.

The reluctance with which the liaison officer with the air units spoke filled Nakamura with apprehension. "Sir, the attack formation we launched was intercepted by at least thirty Hawk 75 fighters. They shot down six Ki-27s and seven Ki-32s and then scattered the rest. Our fighters claim twenty enemy fighters shot down."

Well, that will be a miracle from the gods themselves, since it's twice as many Hawk 75s as the Thais have. "Get aircraft up to support our units now."

"Sir, we have no fighters left operational at this time. The 77th Sentai is bringing its remaining 24 Ki-27s up from Haiphong. They'll have to land at Pakse to refuel so they won't be operational for three or four hours at the earliest. Until then, we have only Ki-51 light bombers and a handful of Ki-48 mediums. Without fighter escort, they will be shot down."

There are no reserves. Once again, the thought passed through Nakamura's mind. It had the echoes of a temple bell tolling for the souls of the dead. *The Thais have air superiority over the battlefield, for a few critical hours at least. But until then, we will have to do without. The Thais have already made one bad mistake. They have refused to fight us at the water's edge. Instead they have allowed us ashore and let our units establish themselves. They will pay for that.*

Main Line of Resistance, 11th Infantry (Queen's Cobra) Division, Ridge 70, Phoum Sam Ang

"Who are you?"

Lieutenant Somchai was expecting many things at this time. One of them was for Japanese tanks to appear out of the woods and advance upon him. Another was to have Japanese infantry to do the same while Japanese artillery rained shells down on his head. What he had not expected was for a farang loaded with cameras to appear in his rear.

"Robert Capa. Photographer for Life magazine. I've been told to stay with you and cover the action."

The man handed over an order from the regimental commander. Somchai smiled politely, while mentally cursing the gods for lumbering him with a civilian just before a major battle. "You are most welcome, Khun Robert. You will be leaving before the fighting starts?"

Capa had a local interpreter with him, a member of Life's local bureau, who translated the question and relayed the photographer's response. "I could hardly cover the action if I did that, could I? Do not worry, Lieutenant. I covered the Spanish Civil War and the fighting in the Desert. I'll stay out of your way."

Somchai looked at him doubtfully, but orders were orders. "Then please take cover. Japanese tanks are coming."

It was an odd fact. Perhaps the direction of the wind or the way sound reflected from the ground, but the squeal of metal as the tanks edged through the woods below was clearly audible, even through the howl of shells overhead and the rumble of explosions from the artillery bombardment of the

380

Japanese landing force. The fluke sound effect lasted for only a minute or two. It was drowned out by another formation of dive bombers appearing.

Somchai watched them peel over and dive on the Japanese positions. Even at this distance, the sound of their dives and the wailing of the sirens fitted to their undercarriages drowned out everything else. They were concentrating on the artillery batteries, trying to eliminate them before the fighting really got started. For that, Somchai was profoundly grateful. This was going to be bad enough without the Japanese having their artillery operational as well.

He was so intent on seeing the dive bombers at work that he missed his forward pickets breaking out of the treeline, running for the ridge. They were half way towards the defenses dug along Ridge 70 when spurts of dirt started to erupt around them. The leading edge of the Japanese infantry had to be close. *How did they close up so fast?*

It was a hard thing holding fire while his pickets were brought under fire, but the cost of revealing his positions this early would be worse. In any case, the range was a little too long for the Japanese rifle fire to be really effective. A few men were hit, but the others picked them up and helped them to cover. Somchai breathed a little more easily; then suddenly realized that he was impatient for the Japanese assault to start. Waiting for the blow to fall was sapping at his nerves.

"Sir, the Japanese are right behind us. They're riding bicycles through the forest." Somchai turned slightly to face Sergeant Mongkut. The man was out of breath from the run back to the main formation and he was trying to compose himself."

"Did you see the tanks?"

"No, sir. We heard them though."

"Very good, Sergeant. Rejoin your men and make ready. It is time the Japanese were taught that they are not the only men in Asia who know how to fight." Somchai thought for a second. *That sounded suitably inspiring.*

That was when something very strange happened. The whole world seemed to go completely silent. The artillery fire directed at the Japanese positions on the far bank, the buzz of aircraft overhead, everything seemed to pause for a second. In one of the slit trenches, Capa took a look and dived for cover. Somchai guessed that, after covering all the wars he had, Capa probably knew what was happening. Somchai followed his example. His men saw him taking cover, assumed he knew what he was doing and followed his example. The silence only lasted a few seconds.

There was an intense howl of inbound artillery as the concentrated artillery of the 5th Motorized Infantry Division opened up on the positions along Ridge 70. It was followed a split second later by the crash and howl of the Thai artillery opening on the unmasked Japanese batteries.

Somchai curled up in the bottom of his slit trench. He had dug it in absolute conformity with the instructions he had been given. It was as narrow as possible, so that fragments from shells exploding around him would have as small a window for entry as possible. He'd hollowed out the bottom so there was an overhang to protect him from shells that exploded overhead. For all that, he knew that if one of the 105mm howitzer shells scored a direct hit, all the careful digging in the world wouldn't save him from the blast. He knew that his trench still gave him an excellent chance of survival against any reasonable kind of bombardment. It just didn't seem that way, now that the shells were actually arriving.

He knew something else. As an officer, he had to be aware of what was going on and make ready to receive the impending assault. He sneaked a look out at the ground in front of him. The shells threw up clouds of muddy fragments that looked like leaves falling in a windstorm. Combined with the smoke from the explosions, he could hardly see anything. The noise was so deafening, it was impossible to make sense of anything else. Then, the hail of shells seemed to slacken. Visibility cleared. Across the couple of hundred meters that separated him from the treeline, formations of Japanese infantry were running towards him. Between the infantry groups were Japanese tanks.

Somchai knew his voice would still not carry well enough to alert his men. There was an answer to that. The shrill blast of his whistle penetrated the bedlam around him. He heard the sound taken up by his NCOs as they led the men out of their foxholes and took up positions to beat back the assault.

The heavy artillery fire had lifted. Now the shells were landing in the gap between Ridge 70 and Ridge 77 a kilometer to the rear. That didn't mean that the forward positions weren't getting hit; merely that they were now under direct fire from the Japanese 70mm infantry guns, not indirect fire from the 105mm howitzers on the other side of the river. Sergeant Mongkut wasn't actually sure than was an improvement. The shells were still arriving. Now they were being deliberately aimed at points of resistance. He sighted down his rifle, looking through the showers of mud and debris and the clouds of smoke. Japanese troops were pouring out of the treeline. They were already starting to cross the open space that separated the trees from the Thai positions. His squad had a pair of Lewis guns, one for each of the two nine-man sections. The gunners were waiting for the whistle blast that would tell them to begin their work.

The Maxim guns fired first. Mongkut could hear their long tattoo of fire. The guns swept backwards and forwards across the Japanese troops. There were two Maxim guns per platoon, a total of 24 for the battalion. Mongkut knew the officers had spent most of their time making sure they had been properly placed and well protected. They were they key. As long as they remained firing, the Japanese could not survive an attempt to cross the open ground. The Japanese knew that as well.

Watching the groups of Japanese advance, Mongkut saw them being tumbled down by the machine guns. He also saw something else; small groups of Japanese taking cover. He knew from the information that had been passed down the line that each Japanese platoon had three 50mm mortars. They were more grenade throwers than mortars; sacrificing shell weight and range to lighten the weapon so that it could be carried around by the infantrymen and taken into battle. Their specific job was to take down the heavy machine guns. That was just what they were starting to do. That made them a priority target.

The explosions were small, but the Japanese crews had spotted the Maxim guns. The mortarmen were very good. Their shells were on target. The steady rhythm that was cutting down the assault infantry wavered. Now the Lewis guns would come into their own. Mongkut smacked Corporal Pon's helmet and shouted into his ear. The battlefield noise was so intense Pon could barely understand what was being said. But he saw where Mongkut was pointing. He was where he belonged, right alongside his Lewis gun. The light machine gun started stabbing out short bursts. That took fine judgement. The bursts had to be long enough to be effective, short enough to conceal the fact another machine gun had joined the battle. The bursts silenced the mortar. Fire from the nearest Maxim steadied as the harassment of the mortar fire ended.

Now it was the turn of Mongkut's platoon to be on the receiving end of the galling mortar fire. The small shells weren't really big enough to be a serious threat, but they were a nuisance. There was a big difference between a threat not being serious and not existing. He was being splattered with mud from the little shells. It was only a question of time before one of the splats was from a fragment of shell casing. To make matters worse, the burst of fire from his Lewis gun attracted the attention of the infantry guns. Their larger, much more lethal, shells had started to impact around his positions. The shriek of their shells was almost as terrifying as the bursts, but Mongkut knew that the sounds of shells arriving had never killed anybody. Blast and steel fragments were different. They were all around him. *Where is our artillery? Where are our infantry guns? Why aren't they silencing the enemy guns? Have they run away?*

In front of him, barely 50 meters out, the Japanese emerged from the clouds of debris-laden smoke. Not the ordered waves that had left the tree-line, but groups of men who ducked and weaved as they ran towards the Thai positions. Another whistle blast pierced the roar of the artillery fire and the hammering of the machine guns. Mongkut sighted on a Japanese infantryman. He squeezed off a round, cursing the useless dustcover that encumbered the action of his rifle as he worked the bolt. The man went down, but Mongkut believed he had simply gone to ground.

The deafening roar of the fighting was supplemented by high-pitched metal squeals and the growl of an engine. A Japanese Chi-ha tank approached. Its green and orange-red paint seemed to blend in with the smoke and explosions around it. The tank fired its short-barrelled 57mm gun at the positions in front of it; the hull machine gun sprayed the area in general.

This was what tanks are supposed to do. Mongkut knew that. They brought their gun up to close range so that they could combine a heavy shell with pinpoint accuracy. That helped the infantry cover the open ground and chew a hole through the defenses. He didn't see where the first two or three shells went. He did see the one that exploded in the pit used by one of his Lewis guns. He saw something circling up through the air. For a moment, he thought it was part of the stricken Lewis gun. It landed not far from him. He saw it was a foot, still inside its regulation Thai Army boot.

The Chi-ha lurched and started to move towards the entrenchments. Mongkut saw brilliant flashes as rifle and machine gun rounds bounced off its armor. The tank seemed to ignore them. An explosion on the front of the tank seemed to push it backwards. One of the battalion's 75mm infantry guns had waited for just the right moment to hit the tank from just the right angle. The Chi-ha stopped dead; burning furiously from the devastating shell hit that had torn its front open. Mongkut felt bitterly ashamed of what he had thought about the artillerymen just a few seconds earlier.

The Japanese infantry were still coming; still moving towards Mongkut and his men. He aimed again. This time, his bullet struck his target squarely in the chest. He could even see the little puff of dust from the front of the man's jacket and the spray of blood behind him as it left his body. Incredibly, the man was still coming. Mongkut worked the bolt on his rifle and fired again. This time his target went down.

There was hardly any time or space left. A Japanese officer came straight at him, swinging his sword back in preparation for a deadly blow. Mongkut fired his rifle. He hit the Japanese officer in the shoulder for all the good that seemed to do. Then, he blocked the swing of the sword. The katana sheered deep into the wooden furniture of his rifle; he felt the shock as the blade bit home. Having blocked the swing, he thrust with his bayonet. Mongkut saw his victim run right onto the point. His arm was flung back. The katana flew through the air, and his hat was hurled high above his head. Mongkut saw a flash out of the corner of his eye. He had much more important things to worry about. The officer had doubled up around the point, fouling the bayonet and dragging it down. By then, Mongkut had another round in the chamber. The recoil as he fired it pulled the bayonet clear of the officer's body.

The trench line was a primeval bloodbath. Japanese leaped into rifle pits and trenches. The fight was a brutal match of men in blood-splattered green or khaki gouging, clubbing and tearing at each other. One Japanese soldier had Corporal Pon down and was pounding at his face with his fist. Mongkut grabbed the Japanese by the neck and pulled him backwards, dragging him off the corporal. Another figure in jungle green swung at the Japanese with a meat cleaver and ripped open the man's chest. Even through the dirt and blood, Mongkut recognized the battalion cook. There was no time to ask questions. The Japanese were everywhere. Every man was needed. The meat cleaver was designed for this kind of butchery.

Mongkut moved along the trench line, stabbing and battering anything not dark green. In this confined area, his rifle was useless. He had drawn his entrenching tool. Its weight and carefully sharpened edges provided a much better weapon. It crushed heads or sunk deep into chests. He swung blow after blow. It was now literally dripping with blood and things that Mongkut dared not name. By then, he had lost track of time and space. He didn't know where he was or how long the fight in the trenches had been going on. All he knew was whether there was a khaki-clad target in front of him or whether it was time to go and find another one. He wasn't even aware that his men had formed up behind him and were methodically sweeping their sector of the trenches clear.

Headquarters, 5th Motorized Infantry Division, Ban Dan Ky, French Indochina

General Nakamura took another long look at the map in his command tent. *It wasn't supposed to be happening like this. Japanese willpower and fighting spirit always carried all before it.* The map was starting to show otherwise.

It wasn't that the casualties had been much heavier than he had expected. The ground in front of the Thai positions was carpeted with Japanese dead, but the soldiers were expendable. They could be replaced by conscripts for the cost of a postage stamp. It was that the Thais hadn't fled when the assault had reached their positions. This hadn't happened before. A few bombs from some aircraft, a few rounds of artillery and a determined charge supported by a light tank or two would send the Chinese Army reeling backwards.

This time, his men were locked in battle in the defense lines against an enemy that would not give up. Several times, in several places, his infantry had broken through the defenses, only to find a Thai officer had grabbed a few men and assembled a blocking force. Cooks, clerks, truck drivers, messengers, anybody who could hold a weapon, had been thrown into the battle. That small group of men would hold back the breakthrough until a reserve force could arrive on the scene and drive his men back into the bloody swirling chaos of the trench-fighting.

"Sir, we need to commit the 21st Brigade right away."

Major General Masao Watanabe, commander of the 21st Brigade, could envisage what was happening in the maelstrom that was engulfing Ridge 70 without being told the details. The whole of 9th Brigade was committed to the battle there. He doubted very much if anything was left of the 11th Regiment. That unit had spearheaded the assault and it had probably been cut to pieces. The survivors had probably made it to the Thai lines and died there, but they would have disabled the defenses long enough for 41st Regiment to get across no-man's land with far less loss. It was probably 41st Regiment that was engaged in the bloody battle of attrition taking place up there now. Watanabe believed that if he could bring both the regiments of his 21st Brigade in a coordinated blow at the same sector of the line, they could smash right through.

"One more good, hard push will do it."

Nakamura looked at the maps. He could see the same thing that Watanabe could. The Thai defenses on the ridge were bending under the ferocity of the Japanese assault, yet not yielding enough to allow the breakthrough he needed. On those grounds alone, hurling 21st Brigade into the battle on the ridge was a road to victory.

Yet, there were things worrying him about this battle. They didn't end with the lack of any reserves. Most of the Thai artillery had stopped pounding the crossing areas and moved to supporting the infantry defenses. They still had heavy artillery that was concentrating on the Japanese batteries. Nakamura had heard the shells and seen the blast; they were 150mm guns at least. The Thais also had control of the air over the battlefield. Their aircraft were arriving in relays. As soon as one group had finished bombing and strafing, they would withdraw and another group take over. Their fighters had driven off the Japanese defenses and it would still be hours before reinforcements arrived.

There was another reason Nakamura hesitated to release 21st Brigade. The Thai position along Ridge 70 was anchored on the Mekong at one end and on a mass of high ground at the other. Much of the galling artillery fire slowly destroying the Japanese batteries was coming from that high ground. That implied more Thai troops up there. Nakamura had elected to ignore those hills when he launched his assault. The hills didn't go anywhere; if he'd taken them, they'd simply expose a further stretch of the Mekong. He would have sacrificed much of his division simply to widen his hold on the river bank, leaving no reserves to exploit the crossing. To get anywhere, he had to take Ridge 70. But the Thais could use those hills to launch an attack on his right flank. If he committed 21st Brigade to the assault on Ridge 70 and that happened, they would roll up his entire division.

That was a prospect he could not accept.

Nakamura was in an agony of indecision. His only chance of breaking through was to throw 21st Brigade at the ridgeline; doing so left him wide open to the flanking attack he feared. Holding 21st Brigade against that flanking attack would mean that the chance of a breakthrough on the ridge was seriously in doubt. His thought train was stopped in its tracks by a dreadful screaming wail. Nakamura knew what it was from the films he had seen of the fighting in Poland and France. There were dive bombers overhead. They were already in their near-vertical dives on his headquarters. Their engines and sirens howled as they dropped on their target. One thing the films had never made clear was just how devastating the sound of the dive bombers was to those about to be on the receiving end of their attack.

Vought V93SA Corsair, Over The Mekong River

"They're down there."

Wing Commander Fuen's gunner/radio operator shouted the words through the speaking tube to his pilot. The snarl of the engine and the whistle of the wind through the struts and wires separating the wings of the biplane made communication between the crewmembers difficult. Fuen hadn't thought of that when he had evolved the air-ground coordination now winning this war.

Fuen wasn't quite sure what was down there; only that it was important in the eyes of the forward observer sitting on Hill 223. That was the key to the whole system. The ground observer was the final word on what targets should be attacked. The pilots did as they were told. That was why a Wing Commander was taking orders from a Flying Officer. That had been one of the hardest battles Fuen had fought, making pilots understand that for ground support to be effective, it had to be controlled from the ground.

Fuen speculated quickly on why the forward air controller had selected this particular target. The man was perfectly placed; if Fuen had designed this battlefield, he would have put Hill 223 exactly where it was. It commanded the stretch of the Mekong that was suitable for crossing and a wide swathe of the country to the north. Probably he had seen people going to and fro to mark a headquarters, or an artillery battery making practice on the Thai positions. Whatever the target was, it wouldn't be that much longer.

It was time. He flipped his sirens on, then pulled the stick back and rolled in the classic wing-over into a vertical dive that was already becoming the trademark of the dive bomber. Behind him, each of the aircraft in his flight followed suit. They formed a long chain aimed at the target below. As it grew larger, Fuen saw that it wasn't an artillery battery, even though nearly all the missions flown this day had been aimed at taking out the Japanese artillery. This one was just a collection of tents and vehicles.

A headquarters? Perhaps even THE headquarters? Fuen had high hopes. The Japanese had been spoiled by China. Only now were they learning what it was like to fight under a sky dominated by hostile aircraft. They concealed their headquarters and other vital targets well against observation from ground but were careless about being seen from above. *Every army should fight at least one battle under hostile air attack.*

The target was swelling fast. Fuen selected the largest group of tents. His bombsight was centered perfectly on them. A gentle press on the bomb release sent his six 50-kilogram bombs into the complex. By the time they hit, he was already hauling back on the control column, pulling out of the wild dive. He was skimming the jungle when he did so, moving fast from the pyre of smoke that marked the target.

There had been a loud bang during the dive; he thought his aircraft had been hit by gunfire. One of the wing struts had broken. The fabric around

387

it was torn and flapping. *Not so good. Still, we have to overfly the target on our way back to Nakhorn Phanom.* His flight around him, Fuen led the way back to the target. The four V93s swept over the base; their four forward-mounted machine guns raked the area. Fuen saw the great rising sun flag and another he couldn't recognize still standing. *That has to change.* His machine guns riddled the flags and chopped down the pole they flew from. As they roared over the toppling pole, his rear gunner added another long burst to the mayhem below.

An hour later he was standing with a maintenance sergeant, looking at the damaged wing. The wing strut had broken up further and the fabric was a mess. "Must have caught a bullet."

"Possibly. There might be another explanation." The Sergeant spoke carefully, but damage like this was becoming more common each day. He believed his Wing Commander had to know that. "I think the structure of the wing failed first and that broke the wing strut. Not the other way around. The strain of all these dive bombing attacks is more than they were designed for."

Fuen nodded. The V93 had never actually been designed as a dive bomber. They would have to serve that way though, until the promised American dive bombers arrived. "You may well be right. Fix it, Sergeant. The Army still needs us."

Headquarters, 5th Motorized Infantry Division, Ban Dan Ky, French Indochina

General Nakamura hauled himself out of the slit trench he had occupied and watched the biplanes vanishing on their way back to base. The warrior within him had to admire the attack and the way it had been carried out. The man within him had to wish they'd carried it out on somebody else. His headquarters had been devastated by the bombing and strafing. The tents were all down. Some were just shredded; others burning. The vehicles had been hit hard. The last two dive bombers released their loads directly into the park. The whole area was burning from the contents of ruptured fuel tanks.

"General Nakamura, sir." General Watanabe was nearly in tears. "Our flags sir; our flags."

Nakamura suddenly realized that the two flags that had dominated his headquarters area were gone. Then he saw the shattered wreckage of the flagpole and the tattered rags that surrounded it. *The flags, our colors; given to the division by the Emperor himself. Lying in the mud like discarded rags. What would the Emperor say should he hear of such disrespect?*

The sight of his division's colors lying in the mud settled Nakamura's mind. Japanese officers were indoctrinated with a maxim that dominated every other. 'When in doubt, attack. Even an extemporized attack will seize the initiative and then the fighting spirit of the Japanese soldier will bring victory.' That made the way clear and he wondered how he could ever have forgotten it.

"Watanabe, lead 21st Brigade in an attack on the enemy positions along Ridge 70."

Main Line of Resistance, 11th Infantry (Queen's Cobra) Division, Ridge 70, Phoum Sam Ang

"Here they come again."

The shout along the trenches filled Sergeant Mongkut with despair. The trenchline was a mass of bodies. Thai jungle green mixed with Japanese khaki in a chaotic tangle. Most of the bodies were hideously mutilated as a testament to the ferocity of the fighting. The use of clubs, spades, knives and swords at body-contact range was never likely to produce a pretty or attractive scene. Mongkut thought that his trench looked like a slaughterhouse after a bomb had gone off in it. That was, after all, a fair description of what it was.

One of the Japanese figures in front of the trench was moving, wounded but still alive. The platoon medic, still miraculously alive despite the carnage in the trench, started to climb up to go out to him. Robert Capa grabbed his foot.

"Don't do it. I saw the Japs try that in China."

The medic was confused, unable to understand English or why he was being stopped from aiding the wounded. Capa realized the problem. He picked up a rifle from one of the dead. He worked the bolt, took careful aim and fired a single shot that hit the wounded man in the head. As he died, his hand relaxed. The hidden hand grenade rolled clear and exploded.

"The Jap just wanted to take you with him. Don't ever go near a wounded Jap. Just shoot them in the head from a safe distance."

Mongkut didn't quite understand the words. He spoke a little German from their instructors and a little French; English was unknown to him. But, the message was quite clear and it appalled him. Up to then, the French and Thai troops had tended to each others' wounded as if they were their own and gone out of their way to respect the sanctity of the Red Cross. *We'd treated prisoners and the wounded with respect. Why were the Japanese so different?*

His train of thought was interrupted by sounds from a road behind him. He glanced sideways and saw an armored vehicle moving into position. A small one, but it had a water-cooled machine gun mounted on its front; one that could be fired from behind armor. Mongkut recognized it, a Carden-Lloyd machine gun carrier. Men were riding on it; men clad in Thai jungle green but distinguished by the bright yellow scarves of cavalrymen. They quickly spread out along the trench, reinforcing the savagely depleted ranks of the 11th. Behind them, in the area shielded by the ridge, more trucks were pulling up. Men debussed and formed up. They had the brown scarves of combat engineers. At least a battalion of them.

The sound of bugles from in front of his position focussed his attention on the Japanese again. More were pouring out of the treeline below, their flags flying and bugles sounding. Mongkut couldn't help feel that the

389

cavalry had arrived in the nick of time. *Perhaps the Hollywood westerns were right after all?*

The numbers pouring out of the forested slope below were impressive. Mongkut believed there was at least a full regiment already moving up the slopes and more were continuing to pour out. It was obvious to him that, without the cavalry reinforcements, the new attack would have overwhelmed the remains of his own regiment.

The Second Regiment of the 11th Infantry had lost most of its heavy machine guns in the first Japanese assaults. First of First Cavalry more than made up for the loss. Their Browning guns, mounted behind armor, methodically swept across the Japanese lines, cutting down the men as they crossed the open ground. Once again, the Japanese mortar squads started to fire their bombs at the machine gun positions. Tthis time, they had little success. As they started to get the range, the machine gun carrier would back clear and move to another position. The little 50mm mortars used by the Japanese were effective against normal machine gun nests, but lacked the power to take down an armored vehicle.

Faced with unrelenting machine gun fire and the concentrated artillery of two infantry and a cavalry regiment, the attack bogged down. The Japanese troops were half way across no man's land, the area between their bounce off positions in the treeline and their objective. They could get no further. The fire from the cavalry regiment, supported by what was left of the infantry, was too intense. The divisional artillery that should have supported them had been decimated by counter-battery fire and air attacks. They were securing positions in dips and hollows and trying to move forward in short bursts, covered by fire from the rest of the attacking force. That took time. There was no doubt, the momentum of the Japanese charge had been broken.

"Sergeant, get your men together and follow us." A cavalry officer snapped out the order. The machine gun carriers started to move forward. They drew fire as they did so. The Japanese soldiers made targets of themselves in the process. The machine gun carriers brought under fire started to squeeze out long bursts at the Japanese positions, suppressing the incoming fire.

Mongkut watched the cavalrymen working with their machine gun carriers with envy. In the battles he had fought with the French, support from even lightly-armored vehicles would have made things so much easier. Each machine gun carrier would pin down the Japanese while the cavalrymen worked close enough to throw hand grenades into their positions. Slowly and methodically, the Japanese were crowded back from their advanced positions into their original lines.

Headquarters, 11th Infantry (Queen's Cobra) Division, Phoum Sam Ang

"The Japanese have committed their second brigade to the assault on Ridge 70. Sending in our reserves there has meant that their attack has bogged down. The latest report is that the Cavalry are pushing them back. Now is the time, Your Highness."

The Ambassador nodded. She looked at the map spread out before her. The Japanese were too skilled, too experienced to leave their flank hanging completely open. There had to be some troops covering the approaches from the high ground currently occupied by 3rd Regiment, 11th Infantry. She guessed it would be no more than a company; probably one from the divisional headquarters troops. All the regular infantry were either dead or committed to the battle on Ridge 70.

"Order the third regiment to advance on the flank of the Japanese positions along Ridge 73. One infantry battalion to detach and capture Hill 151, supported by a battalion of the engineers."

She looked again at the map. Ridge 73 met Ridge 70 at a right angle. Hill 151 formed the pivot between the two. It was an odd position. Hill 151 was a critical piece of terrain, but only if both Ridge 70 and Ridge 73 were also held in strength. If those conditions were met, the Japanese would be trapped in a bowl; their rear blocked by the Mekong, their left flank anchored against another, smaller river that fed into the main waterway.

A further advance from Ridge 73 on their right flank would roll them up.

Second Regiment, 11th Infantry (Queen's Cobra) Division, East of Ridge 70, Phoum Sam Ang

Japanese resistance was stiffening as the Thai troops approached the woodline north of Ridge 70. It wasn't that the individual troops were fighting with greater determination. As far as Sergeant Mongkut could see, that wasn't possible. To the best of his knowledge, not one Japanese soldier had surrendered. They'd stayed in their defensive positions and held their ground until they were killed.

He honestly couldn't understand it. The instructors had taught their Thai students that positions should only be held until they were untenable. It was much more effective to abandon such positions and retake them later than to lose men in a hopeless defense. The Japanese obviously did not believe in that doctrine. Even their most hopeless positions had been held until every man in it was dead. *There was no such thing as bypassing positions or maneuvering them out. The Japanese had to be dug out and killed, one by one.*

"Sergeant, the engineers are moving in. We must cover them." The cavalry lieutenant obviously knew what he was doing. Mongkut recognized that, but he wasn't his lieutenant and he glanced around looking for some guidance.

"Lieutenant Somchai is gone, Sergeant. He never made it out of the trenches." Corporal Pon was wounded, his face swollen and battered with one eye closed and his front teeth missing. Blood stained his jaws and the front of his uniform and his voice was hard to understand.

Mongkut nodded, acknowledging both the news of Somchai's death and the orders he had been given from the cavalry officer. The sacrifice of the troops that had been trapped in the open had bought the Japanese time to build defenses in the woods. Tracer fire streamed out from a defense position, ricocheting off the Carden Lloyd carrier. The vehicle responded with a long burst from its Browning. A pair of engineers started to move forward. They kept perilously close to the tracer fire and used its suppression to get close enough to the source of the Japanese gunfire.

What happened next horrified Mongkut in a day already been filled with nightmares worse than he could ever have imagined. A long stream of orange fire erupted from the engineer team and arched into the Japanese defenses. The flamethrower operator was well-trained. He started squeezing bursts out in quick succession. Balls of red-orange rolled into the woods. The roar of the flamethrower was bad enough. Worse were the hideous screams from the Japanese positions. The occupants of their position ran out of the woods, living torches soaked in fire from their heads to their feet. They could hardly be seen in the inferno that consumed them. All Mongkut could see was the black outlines of the men as they writhed and burned. All he could smell was the ghastly stench of burning flesh and the petroleum fuel of the flamethrower.

"Forward, quickly."

The cavalry officer gave the order. His men moved quickly against the position they had just incinerated. Mongkut quickly glanced to one side and the other. He could see terrible, feather-like bursts of flame as the engineers got to work. Then, the forest closed in around him and the men were pushing into the shadowed ground. It was blackened, seared and stained with a filthy, black glue that stuck to everything. There was a charred trunk on the ground, one where the bark was broken open and roasted by the flamethrower. Then, Mongkut saw the dark red inside. It wasn't a tree but the remains of a man, burned until he was unrecognizable as anything human. All around him were bicycles; dozens of them were blackened by fire and their tires burned or melted. The Japanese infantry had ridden them into action, not knowing that they were cycling into an inferno.

More bursts of machine gun fire erupted from the trees up ahead. Some cavalrymen went down. Others had taken up their positions and returned fire while a machine gun carrier edged through the trees until it could bring its Browning to bear. It would suppress the position until a flamethrower crew could get to work. Mongkut lost track of time and space. Lost in the green world under the trees, all he was aware of was moving forward until they met Japanese resistance. There the ghastly sights and sounds of the flamethrower attacks would be repeated.

Sometime during the battle of the forest, Corporal Pon was killed. Mongkut was aware than the number of survivors from his unit was steadily shrinking. A section had a corporal and eight men; the battle had started with eight such sections in each platoon. Looking around, he guessed that the cavalry platoon and the engineers, plus his own unit, was barely equal to his own platoon's original strength. The engineers were suffering too. When the horror of the flamethrowers had sunk in, the Japanese made the engineers their primary targets. Every so often, their rifle and machine gun fire would explode the pressurized cylinders of fuel on the back of a flamethrower man. Then he would be the one turned into a screaming, living torch.

At some point in the battle, their axis of advance had swung from east to south. Mongkut realized they were driving the Japanese parallel to the river instead of back towards it. He had no idea where he was in the forest or why the unit was maneuvering the way it was. All he knew was that there was another Japanese position in front of him that had to be suppressed before its world would be turned into fire. He knew something else,; he hated the Japanese beyond anything he could imagine. *They have lost this battle, it's all over. Why must they make us fight like this when they must know they have lost the battle? Why are they forcing us to do these things?* As the hatred seethed in his mind, he started to welcome the sight of the flamethrower crews burning the Japanese in their dugouts and foxholes and relish the sounds of screaming from their victims.

Forward Headquarters, 5th Motorized Infantry Division, West Bank of the Mekong

Lieutenant General Akihito Nakamura knew defeat looming when he saw it. He had left his headquarters the other side of the river so he could lead his division when they broke through the Thai defenses and headed into the heart of Indochina. That hadn't happened. His division was being methodically destroyed, driven back on to a narrow spit of land where the Mekong and one of its tributaries joined. There was no way out of that position. That left only one option open to him and his division command staff. They were preparing for it now, loading themselves with hand grenades and picking up rifles so that they could make a last charge on the enemy. *Perhaps, even now, one last charge will turn the tide of the battle. It has before.*

The Thais were closing in. Nakamura knew that from the closeness of the sound. Machinegun fire, artillery, the crash of grenades and the evil roar of the flamethrowers. The last sound infuriated him. *How could his soldiers be expected to fight like warriors when they were burned alive in their defenses?* The Thais hadn't even charged like proper soldiers. Instead, they moved forwards slowly and patiently. Nakamura looked up at the setting sun. *A few minutes and it would be night. A pity I don't have that long. A night charge would have a better chance of breaking through.* He led his men out to their last-hope attack.

It was easy to find the front line. The noise and stench of petroleum identified it even without the orange streaks of rifle and machine-gun fire in the gathering gloom. Nakamura drew his sword and started to run towards the inbound fire. He sensed his men keeping up with them as they carried out their attack. The orange streaks were all around him, raking across his force, sending the soldiers tumbling down. One man was carrying a Japanese flag when he was struck by the bullets and sent sprawling into the ground. *Two flags in the mud is enough for one day.* Nakamura grabbed the staff and waved it defiantly.

He felt heavy thuds in his chest. His legs seemed to turn to jelly. He used the staff of the flag to support himself. A ball of orange fire engulfed him.

Headquarters, 11th Infantry (Queen's Cobra) Division, Phoum Sam Ang

"Second Regiment of the 11th Infantry has been effectively destroyed. Its casualties exceed seventy percent of its strength. Third Regiment is better off; they have taken about thirty percent casualties but they are suffering additional losses as they mop up isolated resistance. There's no sign of that ending yet. The Cavalry have suffered about forty percent losses. On the other hand, the Japanese Fifth Motorized Division has been obliterated. All that's left from the infantry regiments are the survivors scattered throughout the woods. We've chewed up the divisional base the other side of the river with dive bombers and artillery."

"Prisoners?"

"Five, Your Highness; all wounded so badly they were unable to resist. The Japanese fought until they were killed and those that could not fight any longer, killed themselves. When their position was hopeless, they would charge our lines to certain death rather than give up." The operations officer paused for a second before continuing. "We found the bodies of about a dozen of our men taken prisoner in the initial stages of the fighting. All murdered and their bodies mutilated."

The Ambassador nodded, carefully keeping her feelings to herself. She would add one extra term to the agreement with the French because of that piece of information. "The 11th Division will be withdrawn and reformed as soon as the French sign. They will be the first to receive the new equipment we are making under license."

She breathed out, unaware that the sound of her doing so had been shaky. "We have done well today. I want full reports from everybody. Every lesson we have learned this day about fighting the Japanese must be written down and saved. And send a copy of those reports to Chulachomklao for translation into English. I know somebody who will want to read them.

Town Hall, Phoum Dak Pay, French Indochina

It was a week after their first meeting, to the very minute. Admiral Jean Decoux was waiting by the table, mulling the news that had spread throughout the French High Command in Hanoi. The troops surrounded at Battambang, the cream of the Indochina Army, would have to surrender in a day or two at the most. They were out of food, out of ammunition, out of water. Further east, Thai units were already on the outskirts of Phnom Penh and moving further eastwards.

Above all, any hope that the Japanese might impose a settlement that was something short of a disaster had gone. A whole Japanese division totally destroyed. Very heavy losses on the Thai side as well. Decoux was an Admiral, not a General, but he knew the implications of that. The battle had been hard-fought, but the Thais had kept going until they had won. They were capable of achieving more than just easy victories. That had implications for the war that was now ending. Implications epitomized by the pen in his pocket. The destruction of the Japanese division left him with no real choices in the matter.

The Thai party entered the room, led by the woman who had been in charge before. She offered her hand to Decoux. He shook it firmly, with the respect due to somebody who wore their country's uniform. Then the two delegations sat down.

"Admiral, the terms of the agreement that will end this war remain largely unchanged since our last meeting. The new frontier will be defined as the riparian center of the Mekong River, from the Chinese border to the sea. The possession of islands in the river will be determined by which side of the riparian center they are located. All hostilities will cease. All prisoners who wish to be repatriated will be returned. No reparations will be paid by either side."

She paused for a few seconds.

"There is one additional term. You may expect that Japan will occupy the remainder of Indochina at some point in the near future. We have wiped out the greater portion of their strength and that will delay their plans, but you may regard that occupation as being inevitable. At this time, they have two independent mixed brigades; one around Hanoi, the other at Hue. That is not a sufficient force for their ambitions. Their need to bring in additional forces gives you a window of opportunity that may last for some weeks or months. As part of this peace agreement, my country will offer all the French population of Indochina, yourselves and your families, sanctuary from the Japanese. Those who take advantage of this provision will be our guests until they make permanent plans for their future."

Decoux nodded; he had heard of the atrocities committed by the Japanese in China and knew that the Ambassador's words were true. Fear of what a Japanese occupation would mean had been a specter haunting the French administration in Hanoi and a major factor in determining their policies. "A magnanimous gesture and one for which I am deeply grateful. The terms you propose are acceptable."

Decoux sighed, and took the pen from his pocket. It was an elegant tortoiseshell Penol Ambassador, one given to him by his father on his acceptance by the French Naval Academy. It had been his most treasured possession since he had been a young naval cadet. He consoled himself with the thought that his orders from Vichy had been to negotiate, not to continue fighting. Those orders had assumed he was dealing with the Japanese, but they applied to this situation as well. He sighed again, then carefully signed the agreement in front of him.

As he did so, he wondered what his actions would have been had the situation been reversed. *Would I have offered sanctuary to my enemies? Or handed them over to appease a greater and more dangerous foe?* That left a personal gesture that he felt forced to make. Perhaps he might have made it anyway but the offer of sanctuary for the French women and children in Indochina decided him.

"Madam Ambassador, please accept this pen as a gift. To mark this day in the hope that all the historical circumstances that led to this bloodshed will not be repeated."

The Ambassador gravely accepted the gift. She used it to sign the peace agreement. Her face was impassive; inside, her mind was filled with fierce joy. For with that simple signature, the mouse had become an elephant. It was a young elephant certainly, still little more than a calf, but it was a fine, healthy young elephant and it already had the ivory stubs to mark where its tusks would be.

But, for all its youth and the maturing it still had to do, her country was definitively an elephant.

The Ambassador's Private Suite, Bang Phitsan Palace, Bangkok, Thailand

Lani quietly entered the room where the Ambassador slept, carefully not noticing the man beside her. She touched Suriyothai lightly on the arm; she awoke almost instantly.

"Highness, Igrat is here, as you requested."

"See she is made welcome and tell her I will be down in a few minutes." Lani carefully withdrew.

The Ambassador turned to her partner and woke him with equal care. "Plaek, you should go and continue your re-election campaign. The voting will be in three days time."

"Will I win?" Marshal Plaek Pibulsonggram was joking when he asked. Under other circumstances, the election might be open to doubt; but, after the stunning military victory in Indochina, he could not imagine himself doing anything other than winning in a landslide.

To his surprise, the Ambassador was shaking her head.

"It will be desperately close; but, in the end, your National Party will lose by a handful of votes to Pridi Banomyong's Democratic Party. You will not contest the result, even though many will suggest that you should, and there will be a peaceful transfer of power. Pridi will respond by appointing you to his government."

"As Defense Minister?" Plaek sounded hopeful. Again, the Ambassador shook her head.

"As Education Minister. As Defense Minister, you would be seen as the power behind the scenes and that is politically undesirable. Anyway, you've always had a fondness for education. Don't worry; you'll win the election after this one."

"Pridi is a socialist." Plaek sounded doubtful.

"He is, but I have already taken the necessary measures to keep him under control. He will speak the words, but the policies will not happen. And he will learn that his ideas do not work in the real world. He is an intelligent, honorable man and he will see what is before him. Experience will be a better teacher than any books could be."

Plaek Pibulsonggram nodded. The last words had been a painfully truthful reminder. The army that had been created since the 1932 coup had been blooded and learned that lessons from instructors were one thing, putting them into practice was quite another. Anyway, being the Education Minister appealed to him.

Once he'd been in a village where the schoolteacher had been obviously incompetent. He hadn't just been teaching the wrong things; he'd been doing them in a way that bored the children and made them unwilling to learn anything. He'd seized the teacher by the scruff of his neck and literally thrown him out of the classroom. That afternoon, the affairs of state had been put to one side while the children were taught their arithmetic by the Prime Minister himself. Suddenly his mind snapped at his own thoughts. The words 'taught the right things' echoed strongly.

Suriyothai watched her lover's face light up and was content. *He's got the message.*

An hour later, she entered the room where Igrat was reading a fashion magazine. She'd done so as quietly as she could, but Igrat had still heard her and risen to her feet.

"Snake, words from my father. Congratulations are in order. A well-executed war."

"Thank you. Iggie, please, sit down. You and I have never stood on formality. Yes, the war went well, although taking down the Japanese unit was much more costly than we thought. Phillip should know that we lost 214 killed and 374 wounded fighting the French but twenty times that number fighting a much smaller number of Japanese. We killed 499 Frenchmen and wounded over two thousand, but took twelve thousand prisoner. By the time the fighting was over, we had killed over eleven thousand Japanese and took five prisoners. We were still running into resistance on the battlefield three days after the main bulk of the fighting was over. There is much to think upon there."

Igrat nodded while the courier part of her brain memorized the numbers. An unspoken part of her work was to keep her eyes and ears open. A street girl saw things and heard words that the diplomats and professional agents overlooked. Igrat had sensed wide acclaim among the Thai people; they looked on the victory of their Army over the French as something of a national rebirth. For the first time, Thailand had been able to extract concessions from a European power by force of arms.

She had also sensed shock and fear as realization of the terrible casualties suffered fighting the Japanese had sunk in. She had seen the huddles of men and women gathered around the news stands looking at the lists of dead and missing. When fighting the French, the lists had been barely a column long; usually less than that. The same lists for the battles against the Japanese had gone on for pages. The Hong Kong and Shanghai Bank had just moved its headquarters to Bangkok. To introduce themselves, the bank had paid the Thai Rath newspaper to produce a special supplement with the names of the dead and wounded, then to distribute it free of charge. Igrat had noted that she hadn't seen a single copy of that supplement dropped on the street or thrown away.

Suriyothai looked at her and knew what she was thinking. "I have some documents for you to take back to Phillip. Reports on the operations here. The originals are going via the American consulate here to the War Office but I want him to have his own copy. It is essential that your military authorities know what fighting the Japanese will be like. I've had them microfilmed so the weight won't break your arm."

Igrat relaxed slightly. "Thanks, Snake. I've got some paperwork for you as well. My father wants to set up a business here, a cement company. We're in partnership with an Australian, Essington Lewis. He's one of us, by the way, although he doesn't know it yet. We're putting up the money; he's supplying the expertise. He wants to set up a steel company as well. Between the two, we'll be well placed to support rebuilding the city. We supply the cement; his company, the rebars."

"We already have a Siam Cement Company. Phillip can buy that. We'll sell him 70 percent of the shares, with the Crown retaining the rest. I'll have the documents prepared for you to take back. You are going straight back to the USA?"

"Sure. Then out to Britain to see some of our friends there." Despite the friendly conversation, Igrat was careful not to say whom. "Going to Britain needs caution these days. Every time I go there, the number of Auxiliary Police increases and they get more aggressive. Always good to take care when visiting countries where the number of people's police exceeds the number of people's people."

Suriyothai snorted slightly. "It's not taking long, is it? Phillip always said that the first steps to tyranny are the hardest and going downhill from there is easy. By the way, that reminds me. Did you get the stuff I asked for?"

"I did." Igrat pushed a box over. "A dozen bottles. Excuse my asking, but what do you want it for? It's not a problem you have."

The Ambassador produced a very conspiratorial smile. "It's just a gift for somebody."

Natal Mounted Rifles, Nyang'oma Kogelo, Kenya

"God, this chicken is good. Makes the wait worthwhile."

Sergeant Dirk Klaas looked at the African woman running the roadside food stand. "Look, we really are sorry about that kid. We'd have stopped if we could, but a big truck like that, towing a gun. . . . "

It had been a simple road accident, almost mundane. The column of South African trucks had been heading south, on their way to an embarkation port, when a young child had run right out in front of the convoy. The lead vehicle had absolutely no chance to stop. It had run him over. The vehicle behind had done the same and so had the one behind that. By the time the convoy had stopped, the child was very obviously very, very dead. The local police had arrived and started to take statements, but Klaas had noted nobody seemed to care very much. One woman was weeping quietly, but that was all. From her age, she was probably the child's mother.

"Don't you distress yourself, Sergeant."

Klaas noted she had his rank right and spoke good English. *Mission-taught, no doubt.* "Nobody liked that little monster. Uppity child, always telling everybody what to do. More chicken? I can do you a special price if all your men buy from me."

The South Africans were milling around the market place while the accident report was finished. The chicken stand was, in Klaas's opinion, by far the best food there. "I'll tell you what, Mother. You give us a right price, and we'll buy enough to eat now and also for our meal this evening."

The woman beamed at the polite address and named a price. Klaas called his men over. She had a plate of samples waiting. They were enough to convince the platoon that this was indeed a deal that should not be missed. A few minutes later, the stand was the scene of frenzied activity as her family got to work making up the biggest order for cooked chicken her business had ever seen.

"Sergeant?" A painfully young South African officer was calling him. "The police have finished interviewing the truck drivers. They are reporting this as a sad accident caused by a child not being taught to respect traffic properly. Between you and me, most of the village does not seem too sympathetic to the family and the child was very unpopular with the others here. Anyway, the division has made a compensation payment to the mother and that has closed the affair. You organized all this chicken for your men? Good move; spending money like this will soothe any hurt feelings in the village."

"It's really good chicken, sir. Try a piece."

The officer did so. a look of sheer delight spread across his face. "My God, man; you're not joking. Mother, when this order is done, can you make up another for me? The divisional headquarters will have a feast tonight."

"It will be done, sir." The woman watched her children redouble their efforts to increase grilled chicken production while making sure they didn't take short cuts that would affect the quality of her product.

Around the back of the hut, the execution of chickens was reaching holocaust proportions. The family head was ecstatic at the sheer volume of business. He was already working out how to build his family a new home on the profits. He suddenly realized this could be the start of something big. He called out to his wife, "Nyarai, look after our guests well and they will bring many more back. And give the sergeant and his officer some free bottles of beer. You see, that horrible little boy was of some use to the village after all."

Lieutenant Piet van der Haan was careful to hide his smile. As divisional intelligence officer, he spoke Kikuyu perfectly.

Jardine Matheson House, Thanon Witthayu, Bangkok, Thailand

"And so, Madam Ambassador, I would like to formally welcome you to the new headquarters of Jardine Matheson. We're up and running as the formal headquarters of the Princely Hong as of today. All our key staff and all our records are here. Our agents and clients know that this is where the decisions are made. All the other Hongs are either already here or following. By the end of the year, there'll be nothing left in Hong Kong except empty buildings." Simon Keswick hesitated; leaving anything behind for the Japanese upset him. "I wish we could bring them over too."

"Have you somewhere comfortable to live?" Suriyothai well understood how valuable this alliance would be and it had to work. As much depended on this as it had on the war in Indochina.

"A very fine household, rented on a 99-year lease. And the accommodations you have found for our Chinese staff are more than acceptable. You have worked hard for us, Madam, and your efforts are appreciated. As are those of your army." Keswick spoke the latter with a dry sense of humor.

The Japanese Fifth Division wouldn't be capable of doing anything other than rebuild itself. Another division would have to be moved to Indochina to replace it. That meant the planned operation against Hong Kong would be delayed for months. The time so bought had been invaluable in making an orderly move. "I am sure Swire, Hutchinson-Whampoa, HSBC and all the other Hongs will be equally appreciative. It is a pity Lloyds of London have chosen to center their international operations on Bombay, but they were already established there . . ."

The Ambassador looked out the window at Thanom Witthayu and the construction work going on. The canal down the center had been filled in and the road turned into a modern, hard-surfaced, divided highway to join the city's administrative center with the explosively growing international business area here. Across the street, the Hong Kong and Shanghai Bank had its 'headquarters' in a dilapidated wooden house. They had gone to great lengths to be the second Hong to make Bangkok its home. Next to that existing building, foundations for their new office block were already being poured.

Less than a year into the great revolution she had planned and already her city was being fundamentally changed. The buildings going up were a symbol of that. Once, at six stories, this office building had been the largest in the city. It would be dwarfed by the new ones going up along Thanom Witthayu and Thanom Sukhumvit. Already, Jardine Matheson were planning a new and much larger headquarters. *Phillip is right; we are going to need a lot of cement.*

There was a copy of the latest issue of *Life* magazine on the conference room table. The cover picture had been taken by Robert Capa. It showed a Thai infantry sergeant bayoneting a Japanese officer. Capa had caught the moment perfectly. The sergeant was in a classically perfect bayonet thrust. The long blade transfixed the officer; its end clearly visible beyond the man's back. The officer was arching backwards from the force of the thrust; his cap hurled from his head and his sword flying through the air. The caption 'Japan Meets Its Match' was, in the Ambassador's opinion, premature. But, *Life* hadn't had access to the long casualty lists from the 11th Infantry to temper its judgement when the front page had been set.

"You kept your promise, Highness." Keswick looked at the picture also. "All your promises. Your Army fought better than anybody expected. But, I do not think that sergeant will sleep well for many nights to come."

"You are not concerned about our new Prime Minister?" The change in government had been politically essential, but she was worried about the effects it might have on the business community.

"Khun Pridi? Not at all. He is a good and honest man, an excellent Prime Minister. And one who knows his duty."

The Ambassador and the Taipan smiled at each other. As always, they understood each other perfectly.

Room 208, Munitions Building, Washington, DC, USA

"I know Pridi. A good man, he studied law at the Sorbonne."

Cordell Hull was ready to acknowledge the merits of a fellow-lawyer. The result of the elections and the ensuing peaceful transfer of power from the National to the Democratic Party had surprised him. He had honestly expected the National Party to win a massive majority, even without rigging the results. That it had not done so forced him to admit that he had seen everything he could have wished, a democratic government, the Japanese defeated and their allies driven back. The situation in the region had been stabilized; temporarily, at least. Even more importantly, with its back door protected, the Indians had felt secure enough to turn a blind eye to the supplies being shipped into Rangoon and then sent to China via the Ledo Road.

"Very progressive in economic matters." Henry Morgenthau echoed Hull's feelings. "I have their initial list of proposed purchases from the line of credit we are extending to them. Almost all civilian-sector industrial development. New power stations figure prominently. They want an asphalt plant for road construction and a new University. The University of Chicago has been approached to partner with them and set up their courses. They are also asking us for funding to set up an institute to research and develop snakebite antitoxins."

"No military equipment?" Stimson was curious.

"Some. Biggest item is 24 DB-7C torpedo bombers for a new naval air arm. They're the same as the ones the Dutch ordered for the East Indies. Otherwise, they are ordering some more tanks in addition to the M2 lights."

"Which ones?" Stimson was worried about that. The U.S. Army was desperately short of tanks itself. Even losing a hundred of the obsolete M2s had been a painful blow to an army that was frantically trying to mechanize.

"They want enough M3 medium tanks to equip a battalion."

Stimson sucked his teeth. He didn't think much of the M3 design; it was an interim product until a better vehicle was designed, but it was the only medium in prospect for a while. "We'll have to take that under advisement. The DB-7Cs won't be a problem. Anything else?"

"Artillery. They want our 105s."

"So do we. We can ship them surplus French 75s instead. That it?"

"They want more fighters in the longer term; they're asking about Republic P-44s or Bell P-39s. But they say that can wait, since they have problems absorbing the new aircraft they have. There's another thing coming up. We're picking up rumors that the Dutch East Indies, Australia and India are all being approached by Japan for supplies. Oil, rice, food, iron ore and so on. And those countries are responding. Viewed objectively, they don't have much choice of course. They can't sell to anybody else and Japan can't buy from anybody else. Good question whether it's a buyer's or seller's market. But, Cordell, we're going to have to admit that any trade embargo we mount against Japan is going to be very leaky."

"Have you read the reports we got from that battle on the Mekong?" Stimson shook his head in disbelief at what he had read. He had a copy of *Life* magazine in his briefcase. The article on the battle, illustrated by Capa's stark pictures, had shocked him. "We've had a lot of reports back from China, but nothing like this. This is the first time we've seen the Japanese defending against a counter-attack from a modern army. The Japanese simply didn't retreat and they didn't give up. They had to be killed in their foxholes, one by one. We haven't seen that in China, probably because the Japanese haven't faced a defeat of this scale there, but the reports are chilling. They took no prisoners; they just killed anybody who tried to surrender, including their own people. Not that they had much occasion to do the latter. Their infantry just didn't surrender. No quarter given or taken, even when they faced flamethrowers. Towards the end, they'd been driven back on to a spit of land with no way out. The survivors just kept charging the Thai positions until they were gunned down. We're going to have to accept that if we go to war with them, it will be bloody."

There was a moment of silence in the room that was broken by a thoughtful Cordell Hull. "Well, that brings us to you, Phillip. How's the study of the German synthetic fuel business going?"

Short Sunderland Mark 1 F-Freddie, *Approaching Sydney Harbor, Australia*

"It looks like we've made it home."

Squadron Leader Alleyne was making his final approach to the flying boat landing area. He realized just how homesick he was. The twelve Sunderlands of his squadron were strung out in a long line and he could sense the urgency of the crews. The flight from Aden had been a long one, punctuated only by refuelling stops.

"Any idea what we'll be doin' next?" Andy Walker sounded as if he badly needed some sleep. He did; so did everybody else in 10 Squadron.

"Word is, we'll be based in Queensland. We've got quite a maritime empire formin' and we'll need ta patrol it somehow. I dunno if we'll keep these old sheilas, but I doubt if that'll be possible. Where we goin' to get the spares from? We may end up flyin' Catalinas instead." Alleyne swung the Sunderland on to its landing run and felt the bottom of the hull kiss the water. The aircraft lurched and bounded a couple of times with the chop on the water, then settled down into a smooth glide through the landing area.

"You really think we'll be flyin' Catalinas?" Walker didn't sound impressed by the idea.

"11 Squadron already has them. They were supposed to be gettin' Sunderlands. We'd better make the most of these while we have them."

GHQ, Middle East Command, Cairo, Egypt

"The Italians are keeping their side of the agreement." General Henry 'Jumbo' Maitland Wilson sounded relieved. The great fear across Middle East Command had been that the peace agreement with the Italians would break the momentum of Operation Compass and allow the Italians to regroup. If that happened, they still outnumbered and outgunned the Desert Rats. Maitland Wilson was quite sure that, had the war resumed, it would not have been so easy a second time. But, the news from Libya was quite unequivocal. The Italians were withdrawing all the troops not needed for the security of their colony.

"And we ours." General Archibald Percival Wavell was very firm on that point. It was essential that either this peace agreement held or that

403

breaking it was seen to be the work of the Italians. With the second possibility eliminated, the first was guaranteed. "With the Canal and Egypt secure, we can address the problem of Iraq. There are rumblings from that country and I fear the situation there is coming to a head."

"The latest intelligence is that a group of four Iraqi nationalist army generals, known as "the Golden Square," are planning a revolt. The Golden Square intend to overthrow the regime of Regent 'Abd al-Ilah and install Rashid Ali as Prime Minister. Their objective is to press for full Iraqi independence following the limited independence granted in 1932. To that end, they are working with German intelligence and are accepting military assistance from Germany."

"The Noth Plan." Major-General Noel Beresford-Peirse sounded almost incredulous. "They actually mean to go through with it."

"It defies logic, but I must agree with you." Wavell thought for a few seconds. "Have your Fourth Indians ready to move to Iraq. They can join 20th Indian Brigade there."

"I'll need to get my Government's approval for that, Archie."

Wavell nodded. "Of course. My apologies; it's so easy to forget how much things have changed in a year. Please, consult Calcutta, Noel, and ask their approval to move your division. Perhaps we can shift some air power to Iraq. Moving aircraft doesn't have the political implications of ground forces."

"My New Zealanders are well-placed, Archie," Major-General Bernard Freyberg spoke. "We could move a column into Iraq damn fast, if you give the word. I'm not sure how long we'll be a viable force, though, the way things are going back home. The Government's bankrupt and the boy's pay is months in arrears. As far as you're concerned, if you don't use us, you could lose us."

"Thank you, Bernie. I'll bear that in mind. So far though, we'll just have to let the situation mature." Wavell looked around. "If there is no other business, I suggest we adjourn for the day."

Tomahawk II **Marijke,** *Habbaniyah, Iraq*

"So this is the famous *Marijke*?"

The sixteen Tomahawks were lined up in the parking area after the flight in from Kenya. They were only one of the squadrons that had arrived. A Desert Rat Maryland squadron was also trying to make itself comfortable in its new home. One of their pilots was admiring *Marijke* and the line of kill marks painted under her cockpit. Flight Lieutenant Pim Bosede had almost two dozen confirmed kills by the time the fighting had ended. His fame was spreading as one of the first Commonwealth aces. The Tomahawks, their noses painted with the garish shark's mouth, had become as symbolic of the Middle East fighting as the Matilda tank and the Bren Gun carrier.

"She is, and a fine aircraft. A good partner. I'm Bosede; Pim to my friends."

"Sean Mannix, 47 Squadron. That's my Maryland over there. *G-George*. We got pulled out of Egypt a few days ago and ordered here. No idea why."

"Iraq's a nice, quiet area. Guess the powers that be decided we needed a rest."

"Might be, Pim; might be. Why don't you come over and I'll introduce you to my crew?"

Cabinet Office, 10 Downing Street, London, United Kingdom

"According to the note of protest, two Ju-90 reconnaissance aircraft were damaged in the attack." Sir Arnold Robins looked at the copy of the report again. "The damage is really quite minor; amounts to no more than a few bullet holes really. Nobody was hurt, although one of our regular policemen twisted his ankle while searching for the shooters."

"It sounds more like vandalism, or even just youthful high spirits, than an organized attack." Lord Halifax was very reluctant to admit there was anything more to the incident than a few farmers, probably very drunk, taking pot-shots at parked aircraft. He wasn't even certain whether who owned the aircraft would have made much difference.

"The German note says as much, Prime Minister. They make light of the situation and imply that, taken by itself, it is of little account. However, they do suggest it points to a risk that a more organized and effective attack may take place one day and that an ounce of prevention now would be better than a pound of cure later."

"And just what would that ounce of prevention be?" R. A. B. Butler sounded slightly suspicious.

"The note draws our attention to the fact that the police guarding the gate at Tangmere airfield were unarmed. In this case, it would have made no real difference to the situation, but they suggest that the replacement of unarmed British regular police by armed personnel would reassure the authorities in Germany."

"Sounds like a job for the Auxiliaries. When we set them up, defending airfields and factories was explicitly included in their remit."

"My thoughts exactly, Foreign Secretary. The Germans also suggest that improving liaison between the Auxiliaries and the German reconnaissance detachments would be worthwhile. They suggest a corporal's guard of Luftwaffe police be allowed to reside at the bases. Purely to maintain order amongst the German personnel and liaise with the Auxiliaries."

"German troops on British soil. I do not think so." Halifax didn't like the way this was going at all.

"Luftwaffe police, Prime Minister, not troops." Butler was at his oiliest, positively oozing reassurance. "A corporal and eight privates, at most armed with a pistol for the corporal and truncheons for the rest. They would not be allowed off the base and their responsibilities would be restricted to dealing with the German Luftwaffe personnel. I believe, even in Germany, the Luftwaffe police do not even have the power to arrest civilians but must summon the ordinary police to make an arrest. I do not see any great problem here."

"Perhaps not." Halifax read the complaint from the German Embassy again. "I just wish this hadn't happened; that's all. We have no idea who fired those shots?"

"None, Prime Minister. An investigation revealed nothing."

"Pity. Some stern punishment of the offenders might have been more useful than these measures. Very well, Richard, I will approve these measures. Replace the regular police with Auxiliaries and tell the Germans that they may send assign a corporal's guard of Luftwaffe police to each of the bases they use. For deployment on the base. It must be clearly understood they may not set one foot outside the airfield perimeter. See to the arrangements, Sir Arnold."

"Yes, Prime Minister."

Don Muang Airfield, Bangkok, Thailand

Bangkok had proper fighter protection at last. A whole squadron of Tomahawks lined up alongside the runways. They lacked the garish shark's tooth markings sported by the Commonwealth Tomahawks. Instead, they had a leaping tiger painted on to their tails. *The Thai Tigers*. Squadron Leader Suchart rolled the name around in his head. *It had a ring to it.*

The airfield was the staging point for the new aircraft. There were some of the new American dive bombers being readied for transfer to an attack squadron and a number of DB-7 bombers had been flown in from India. Suchart looked around for his friend Pappy, but the American was nowhere to be seen. Left to his own devices, he wandered over to the DB-7s. They were different from any he had seen before. The nose was solid instead of glazed. It had the barrels of eight .50-caliber machine guns sticking out of it. They were also painted a dark blue-gray.

"Looking at your new aircraft Khun Suchart?" The voice from behind him was hearty and encouraging. Suchart turned to see Group Captain Fuen standing behind him.

"These are mine? But, Sir, I am a fighter pilot . . . " Suchart was deeply distressed. The words 'fighter pilots and lesser men' echoed in his mind. *What will Pappy say when he finds out I have been transferred to bombers?*

Group Captain Fuen slapped him on the back. "And these are fighters. Night fighters. You are the only fighter pilot in the Air Force with a kill scored at night. In fact, there are very few men in the world today with that distinction. So you will command our new squadron of night-fighters; the only such squadron in the whole region. They are more than just that though. These are intruders. Your job will not just be to defend our capital at night but also to

406

take the battle to the enemy, hunt him down on his bases and destroy him there. With our bombers in the day and your intruders at night, those who threaten us will get no sleep."

He paused for a second and suddenly the joviality had gone. "Suchart, these aircraft are probably the most important of all the ones that have been delivered to us. Our greatest vulnerability is our wooden cities. If they are set on fire, the results will be a national catastrophe. We could see tens of thousands of our wives and daughters dying in the flames. Our enemies know this well and already they talk of exploiting it. Even the threat of firebombing is something we must take very seriously. So, every defense we can mount against the threat of bombing is vital to us. You understand now? We must learn to fight at night and you are the only one who has done so successfully. Suchart, I do not exaggerate when I say that every person in our capital is relying on you. Don't let them down."

Fuen went off to inspect another group of new aircraft, leaving Suchart to look at the DB-7 with new eyes. He still wasn't entirely convinced it was a fighter. He looked underneath and saw the bomb bay. That increased his doubts on the point a bit further. Then he looked at the battery of machine guns in the nose and remembered his hunt for the Farman bombers over the city. That made him content.

Headquarters, Imperial Japanese Army, Tokyo, Japan

The package arrived on Colonel Masanobu Tsuji's desk. It had been posted from abroad, Singapore, to be precise, and was very carefully wrapped. It slightly mystified him, since he had no idea what was in it. However, he had gone to great lengths to establish a chain of correspondents all over the Far East. All he could think of was that one of them had found something very important indeed. It also meant that the person responsible had been astute enough to work out who he was and discover how to contact him.

The package was a welcome introduction to what was otherwise a frustrating day. With the collapse of his Indochina plan, he was trying to work out how to get at the wealth of resources that lay in South East Asia. It was by no means as easy as he had hoped. Strategic options were closing in fast and the age-old rivalry between the Army and the navy didn't help matters. He sincerely hoped that this package would contain the answers. Something had to. Japan's imperial destiny had been thrown into doubt. He used a knife on his desk to cut the string and brown paper that wrapped the box. Inside that was another cardboard box, also carefully secured. Inside that was a brown paper bag. Tsuji spilled the contents of the bag on to his desk. A dozen bottles. It took a few seconds for the significance of the words "hair removing lotion" to sink in. When it did, his scream of anger could be heard all over the building.

Prisoner of War Camp, Ratchanaburi, Thailand

"You have heard we are to go home?" Major Belloc didn't sound too pleased at the prospect.

"I have, sir." Lieutenant Jordain Roul wasn't that happy with the idea either. The options were to resign from the Army and go back to a France that was very close to being German-occupied, or stay in the Army and go back to a French Indochina that was very close to being Japanese-occupied. Neither really appealed that much. "A lot of the men are saying they would rather stay here."

"And that surprises you?" Belloc sounded almost broken. "We are the Legion; the Fifth *Régiment Etranger d'Infanterie*. We have no home other than the Legion and the men have no place in France until their enlistment is concluded. Worse, we have not just been defeated; we have surrendered. I doubt we have a place in the Legion after this. With no place to go, staying here has its merits."

Roul looked around. The truth was that staying on did look attractive. The prisoner of war camp was clean and well-built. The food wasn't to French taste, but it was fresh and there was plenty of it. There were doctors from the Swiss Red Cross to look after the wounded and they had received everything they asked for. *If this is a sample of what waits for us here, then I can see how the men might find it welcoming.* "I hear the Thais are asking the Germans in the unit if they want to serve as advisors to the new units they are forming."

Belloc laughed. "I heard the same. And that some men were accepting. Although, it seems that those are well-disposed to the present government in Germany will not be welcome here."

"There is General de Gaulle of course. And his Free French movement."

"Yes, there is always General de Gaulle."

Village School, Rattanburi, Thailand

Mongkut Chandrapa na Ayutthya, to his great relief no longer a Sergeant, stopped at the door of the school. The teacher had a big map of the new Thailand pinned to the wall. The areas occupied in the war were marked "The Recovered Provinces." She was teaching the children the names of those provinces and explaining how they had been returned to their rightful owners. She was young herself and very earnest; one of many who had volunteered to leave the cities and come to these country villages to teach the children.

"And so, Our Heroes defeated the French who had taken our land from us and freed all our people. The Japanese didn't like this and they sent a great army to force us back, but Our Heroes met that army and defeated it as well. And so, peace was agreed and Our Heroes are coming home." She looked up and saw Mongkut standing at the door, his army rifle slung over his shoulder. The 11th was receiving a new rifle, the Kar-98k, that was shorter, lighter and more powerful than the old Type 52 he had carried. So the demobilized soldiers had been told they could take their old-model rifles home with them if they wished.

408

"Look children, a great honor has been granted to us. One of Our Heroes has come to visit our school."

"Daddy!" Mongkut heard his daughter squeal with delight. The teacher had arrived after he had left for the Army, so she hadn't known he was Sirisoon's father. She did now. Mongkut didn't care. He was looking at his daughter who had grown so much since he had left. And she was looking at him with her eyes shining.

"Honored Sir, please, could you tell the children about what the war was like?"

For a moment Mongkut smelled the stench of the flamethrowers and roasting flesh. Above all, he remembered the searing hate that had filled him when the beaten Japanese refused to surrender and how he had started to relish their screams as they were burned in their foxholes. *The teacher is young and a girl, she has no idea what she is asking. If she did, she would want me to cut out my tongue before telling them the truth.*

Mongkut entered the schoolroom, making a respectful wai to the portrait of the King on the wall. He sat on the table at the front of the class and told the children about what he had seen of the provinces, how poor the people were and how they needed so much help to recover from the years of occupation. Some of the boys were disappointed. They had wanted to hear about the fighting, but he simply couldn't bring himself to describe it. He showed them where he had been but of the battles themselves he said nothing. In the end, he just said, "the French and Japanese were skilled and fought very hard. But we fought better and we won in the end. Never forget; it is never wrong for us to defend ourselves."And the children had smiled. Only the teacher heard what he added so softly afterwards.

"Even when it has torn out my soul."

The White Horse Public House, Nottingham, United Kingdom

"We know you did it." The man spoke to David Newton very quietly indeed.

"Don't know what you are talking about." The reply was equally quiet.

"Good. But, be aware that there are other people who think like you. And who are ready to do the same when the time comes."

"Drink a good beer, you mean?"

"That's right." Calvert looked at the student with appreciation. He really was an excellent recruit and would go far. Until he got careless and was killed. That was inevitable, of course; it was what happened to all resistance fighters. Eight months from becoming active to becoming dead was the average. "Just don't drink any more beer until we show you the good brands. And how to appreciate them."

"What if I run up a thirst before then? I still owe . . . the bar . . . some debts."

"You'll have to be patient." Calvert looked at the student in front of him with much more sympathy than his expression revealed. "You think you came up short, don't you?"

"I . . . did nothing. Nothing. And she . . . "

"You froze up. Most people do . . . .when having their first beer. I did. It was in Norway. The beer started to flow and I froze up. But, I was in a party and the others kept it running until I was back in the game. You were drinking on your own and everything went to Hell so fast you had no time to recover. Now, you do. Now you can learn to enjoy your beer properly.

"How many people . . . like their beer?"

"That's something you'll never know. You'll know only me. And I won't know the people who drink with you. You won't know their drinking friends either. Think about it."

Newton nodded. "I'll have another beer. You're buying?"

"Of course. If you're drinking."

Epilogue

Imperial General Headquarters-Government Liaison Conference, Tokyo, Japan

The Navy and Army delegations trooped into the conference room. *The Spirit Warriors,* Shingen Takeda thought contemptuously. *They call themselves Samurai and claim to follow Bushido, yet they are nothing but bullying braggarts and brutes who do not understand the meaning of the words honor and bravery. Once, I would have taken the head of any such man who claimed to be a Samurai.*

There was a reason why his uniform was plain and unmarked by decorations or insignia of rank. Officially, it was because that the only thing that anybody needed to know about him was that he was a member of the *Tokubetsu Kōtō Kempeitai.* The Special Higher Military Police Corps. Privately, it was because the thought of wearing a decoration awarded by the Spirit Warriors sickened him. Nevertheless, the unmarked uniform was, in its own way, a decoration. There were 36,000 members of the *Kempeitai*; only 107 belonged to the *Tokubetsi Koto* section. Mostly their identities were unknown other than to the rest of the section. How special they were was something they kept amongst themselves.

The Navy delegation was sitting down. Takeda looked at them. Isoroku Yamamoto, the commander-in-chief of the navy; a gambler, rash and erratic but brilliant. With him was Chuichi Nagumo, commander of the Kido Butai; a stolid, cautious, analytical man. *I wonder which would have been the best way to order these men?* Takeda thought. *Yamamoto, the brilliant, incisive gambler to drive on the cautious, painstaking Nagumo or the careful, analytical Nagumo to restrain the headstrong, impetuous Yamamoto?* Then there was Osami Nagano, Chief of the Navy General Staff; a cipher who was Yamamoto's creature and little else. Tamon Yamaguchi, commander of the aircraft carrier *Hiryu.* The man had a personality cult building around him for reasons that mystified Takeda. *Despite what the Navy thinks, drunken oafishness and mindless aggression do not equal intelligence. The man is a peasant.* Then there was Minoru Genda and Mitsuo Fuchida, the experts on carrier air operations. Finally, there were the commanders of the submarines, the land-based air force, the scouting forces and finally the Navy Minister. Ten men in all.

Accordingly, there were ten men from the Army. In Takeda's eyes, only one of them was of any note. For him, he had respect. General Akihito Nakamura limped in, shaking aside any offer of assistance. Wounded and cut down by Thai rifle fire, then terribly burned by a Thai flamethrower, he had been written off as dead. Six Korean laborers had crossed the river late at night to bring back his body. There had been a thread of life left in it. The General had been nursed back to something approaching health, even though his injuries had left him crippled and cruelly disfigured. It took a real warrior to inspire that kind of loyalty from the lowest members of his command. In such a man, the spirit of the Samurai still lived. Takeda had 'found evidence' that the six Koreans weren't really Koreans at all, but pure-blooded Japanese descendants of the troops that had fought in Korea over three hundred years earlier. As a result, they'd been reinstated as true Japanese citizens. Anybody who wished to argue would have to debate the matter with the *Tokubetsu Kōtō Kempeitai.*

There was one other member of the Army delegation. Colonel Masanobu Tsuji. Takeda had to make a great effort not to chuckle on seeing him. Word of the insults he had received from the Thai 'Ambassador' had spread around the Headquarters, though none dared laugh openly. None save the members of the *Tokubetsu Kōtō Kempeitai.*

Twenty men, plus two from the *Tokubetsu Kōtō Kempeitai* and two from the Palace. The Emperor himself was not present, of course. The recommendations of the Conference would be taken to him for his approval by the 25th man, the chairman of the Conference, Hideki Tōjō. He rapped the gavel and the meeting settled down. "We are here today to decide on whether the Navy strategic plan for a thrust against the Southern Resource Area should be expected or whether, by default, the existing operations should be continued. Admiral Yamamoto?"

"In September of this year, the large aircraft carriers *Shokaku* and *Zuikaku* will be joining *Kido Butai.* At that time, the *Hosho* and *Ryujo* will be withdrawn and assigned to support the Philippines operation. The campaign will open with an attack on the American naval base at Pearl Harbor by all six large carriers of *Kido Butai.* This will eliminate the American Navy as an obstacle to our assault on the southern resources area. They will be incapable of resistance for six months and, in that period, I will run riot.

"Following the attack, the 5th Army Air Force Division and the 11th Naval Air Fleet will attack American bases in the Philippines in support of an invasion by three Army divisions and one independent mixed brigade. These forces will then to attack Manila in a pincer attack. After this, the islands of Manila Bay will be taken. The 28th and 38th Army Divisions will attack the western islands of the Dutch East Indies, The 48th Division will assault Java in the central Dutch East Indies and the Sasebo Combined Naval Landing Force and 1st Yokosuka Special Naval Landing Force will occupy the Celebes.

Other Navy troops will occupy minor American bases such as Guam and Wake Island.

"On land, the 18th, 31st, 33rd and 56th Infantry Division will cross northern Thailand and invade Burma . . ."

Yamamoto's flow was interrupted by a contemptuous snort from General Nakamura. The surge of agreement for the General's reaction from the other army officers went completely over Yamamoto's head. He continued as if it had never happened. "The 5th and 18th Divisions will land in Southern Thailand and invade Malaya, advancing on Singapore. The island has no landward defenses and its fall will be quickly accomplished. The Navy will cover these operations with the surface fleet and aircraft based in Indochina."

Yamamoto's voice droned on, describing the naval groups and logistics side of the operation. Eventually, he summed up. "And so, within six months of commencing operations, the entire southern resource area will be in our hands and we will be able to resist any counterattack." He sat down to ecstatic applause from the Navy. The silence from the Army ranks was deafening. They were mostly interested in continuing the war in China. This southern adventure was a distraction made tolerable only by the need to seize the resources they needed for the China campaign.

Time to inject a little reality into this fantasy. Takeda thought as he turned to Katsuyori, his aide and long-time comrade. "I wonder if General Tojo would find an up-to-date assessment of the forces we will face if this plan is executed of value."

Katsuyori gave the appearance of careful consideration. "I think he would. It is fortunate we have two maps available. I suggest we use one to show the situation in June 1940 and the other today, almost a year later."

The others in the room swallowed their annoyance at the exchange. It was well-known that the *Tokubetsu Kōtō Kempeitai* rarely talked to lesser mortals. They discussed things amongst themselves and others were, sometimes, allowed the privilege of listening. That was all.

"An excellent idea. Very well. A year ago, India had three squadrons of its own, all equipped with biplanes from the 1920s. There were eleven RAF squadrons; six with the same obsolete biplanes, two with Vildebeest torpedo bombers in Singapore and three squadrons of Blenheim bombers, one in India, one in Burma, one in Malaya."

Takeda put three blue circles on the June 1940 map. "Less than fifty modern aircraft and no fighters at all. That has all changed. The RAF and Indian Air Forces have effectively merged and they have been re-equipped. They now have ten squadrons of fighters, all equipped with Mohawk IVs. Two in Ceylon, two in Singapore, one in Malaya, one in Burma and four in northern India. The two torpedo bomber squadrons in Singapore have equipped with DB-7Cs. There are six other DB-7 light bomber squadrons; two in Singapore, the rest in Malaya, Burma and Northern India. They have two maritime reconnaissance squadrons in Ceylon; one with Hudsons, one with Catalinas. Their air force continues to expand as more pilots are trained or arrive from Britain.

"It is the same with their Navy. A year ago, three old cruisers and a half-dozen destroyers. Now, a battleship, two carriers with fighters and torpedo planes, a dozen modern cruisers and two dozen or more destroyers." Takeda finished putting blue circles on the 1941 map and it already was starting to look crowded.

"In the Dutch East Indies, it is the same position. In 1940, nothing but a handful of old biplanes, mostly dating from the 1920s. Now, over a hundred modern monoplane fighters, including Brewster Buffalos, Hawk 75s and Curtiss-Wright Demons. Two more squadrons of DB-7C torpedo bombers and over a hundred Martin medium bombers." More blue circles joined the Indian ones.

"We have the Australians of course; they had nothing in 1940 other than long-obsolete biplanes from the 1920s. Now, nine squadrons of fighters, including five of Tomahawks. Six squadrons of bombers with Beaufort torpedo bombers and Hudsons. Three maritime squadrons with Catalinas and Sunderlands. Two of the Tomahawk squadrons are in Singapore. There is an Australian Army division in Malaya, reinforcing two Indian and a British division."

Takeda finished adding the circles for the Australian forces to the blue swathe that now dominated the southern half of the map. "In total, over the last year, more than a thousand modern aircraft have arrived in the area we wish to claim as our southern resources area. Most of them were ordered by the British and French but were delivered to the Commonwealth countries. The opposition is immensely stronger than it was a year ago. It has been reinforced by the purchasing power of two European nations redirected into the area the Navy plans to attack. I wonder if they have fully considered the implications of this change?"

Katsuyori pushed his lower lip out in an eloquent expression of doubt. "That would require a degree of independent thought and strategic consideration quite beyond them. One wonders also if the Army have actually been consulted about how their troops are to be used. Or, even if they are still available, after the recent debacle."

"The forces assigned to occupy Thailand are ridiculous." General Nakamura's voice was hoarse and strained from the burns he had received. The searing heat of the flamethrower had damaged his throat and lungs. Speaking was a grave hardship for him. In Takeda's eyes, that gave him the privilege of speaking while the *Tokubetsu Kōtō Kempeitai* held the floor. "They have maintained their Army at wartime levels. They have four infantry divisions and a cavalry division along the Mekong and three infantry divisions and a cavalry division in the south. They are forming an armored division as a strategic reserve in Bangkok. They also have re-equipped their air force since

414

the fighting in January. We will need at least nine divisions for the northern operation and the southern operation will need at least five."

"It appears the Navy have not consulted the Army." Takeda looked at Katsuyori and shook his head in disbelief. "Why they have not done so is a grave oversight on their part. I sometimes wonder if they are both serving our Emperor, as their duty demands, or whether they merely cater to their own factional interests. We must contemplate that possibility."

"And that is before we invade Burma and Malaya." Nakamura stopped speaking, his reserve of strength gone, but his words had slashed deep into the heart of the meeting.

"The spirit of the Japanese soldier . . . " Masanobu Tsuji's fanatical voice cut across the crippled general.

"And how many battles against a modern enemy have *you* fought, Colonel?" Nakamura made one last final effort before his strength was exhausted. After a pause he looked disdainfully at the Colonel. "I thought not."

"The Philippines also presents problems." Katsuyori spoke slowly and carefully, apparently completely unaware that the interruption from Tsuji had ever happened. "The Americans have reinforced there as well."

"Indeed they have, yet the Navy appears not to have noticed. The Americans have sent many more bombers, many more fighters. Above all, they have dispersed them all over the Islands. Once, they were concentrated at Davao and Manila. Now, they are on many airbases, some of which we have yet to find.

"McArthur may be an egotistical fool, but the Philippine Army and the American forces grow stronger every day. It is the same in Hawaii. Twice as many troops, three times as many fighters, twice as many bombers and reconnaissance aircraft. Our Embassy there reports that the Americans are flying around-the-clock reconnaissance patrols now and our passenger liners north of the islands report seeing Catalinas and B-17s patrolling the area."

That caused a stir, even in the Navy ranks. The whole basis of the Navy plan was to attack from the north, where there was supposed to be no opposition and patrol aircraft were absent.

Katsuyori shook his head in disbelief. "If the defenses have grown so much in a year, what will they be like in a other six months? Has the Navy even considered how the situation might further change by the end of the year?"

"Who can say? We do know that Australia and India are both starting to build their own fighter aircraft. Not the best in the world, perhaps; but more opposition still. The American production lines continue to accelerate and their new aircraft are much more formidable than the old." Takeda pinned up a picture of a new American fighter, the P-38. For some reason, the sight of the twin-engined fighter sent a chill down Yamamoto's spine. "Their current aircraft may be no match for our A6M and Ki-43 now but in a year's time? Or six months?"

"We have no choice!" Yamaguchi's bellow cut across Takeda's comments.

Katsuyori stared at him coldly, smelling the waves of used sake on his breath from across the room. Once again, his words were directed to Takeda, not Yamaguchi. "Have you ever despaired at the lack of moral character in so many of our officers?"

"We do not despair in the *Tokubetsu Kōtō Kempeitai*. We accept that we must work with what we have, however apparently inadequate it is. Despite its shortcomings. In this case, the shortcomings are so deep-rooted that they have almost become virtues." To Takeda's amusement, Yamaguchi was having great problems working out whether the remarks addressed to Katsuyori were an insult or not. "General Nakamura believes the forces assigned to the occupation of Thailand are inadequate, even before the follow-on operations are considered. He has much experience and from experience comes wisdom. The Army should heed his words."

Count Hisaichi Terauchi shook his head. "There are insufficient troops to allocate any more to that operation. If it cannot be concluded with the troops assigned, then it should not be attempted at all. That prevents the follow-on operations aimed at Burma and Malaya. It means we will not be able to secure Singapore. We can use the troops freed up to reinforce the attacks on the Dutch East Indies, of course. But, without Malaya, Burma and Singapore, the security of the Southern Resource Area is greatly imperilled. But, the Admiral was right. We have no choice."

"This may not be entirely true." The speaker was one of the two civilians in the room. He actually represented the *Inperiaru Zaimushō Sābisu*, the Imperial Treasury Service, the empire's tax collectors. Incorruptible and answering only to the Emperor himself, the *Inperiaru Zaimushō Sābisu* was a body even the *Tokubetsu Kōtō Kempeitai* respected. "There is a choice."

"This should be interesting." Katsuyori's aside to Takeda was, for once, actually intended for his ears alone. "Perhaps we will tax our enemies to death."

Takeda glanced around the room. Once again, the posturing truculence of the Spirit Warriors who dominated the armed forces disgusted him. "Foreigners are the opposition. Our enemies are here in this room and, yes, taxing them to death might well be an option worth considering. It would be less cruel than some of the others we might consider appropriate."

Takeda had spoken for Katsuyori's ears alone, but the man from the *Inperiaru Zaimushō Sābisu* had heard the remark and was nodding thoughtfully. He produced a series of papers from as briefcase and looked owlishly around the room.

"To take the raw materials we need, and secure the access routes to them, is possible, of course. But, would it not be simpler just to buy them?"

He waited politely while the jeers died down. "That was impossible up to now, of course, due to the American blockade and their financial embargoes. But nothing is permanent or unchanging. The world situation now is unprecedented and it may change quite radically without notice. Did this not already happen on June 19th last year? On June 17th, who would have known that within a few weeks, Great Britain would have become a political outcast and the Commonwealth it once led reformed without it? Great changes lead to other changes of comparable magnitude, and we have yet to hear the end of the echoes from June 19th. We failed to anticipate the echoes that have taken place. We must be ready to exploit those that remain.

"One such echo is that the Commonwealth countries have been cast adrift in the harsh world of international trade. They proudly call themselves the Commonwealth of Nations but, the truth is, without Britain, their old trading system is dead. Today, only South Africa is prosperous, for the world needs its gold. India survives just barely and it is doing the best of the other Commonwealth countries. Australia is sliding into deep economic depression and New Zealand does even worse. Outside the Commonwealth, the Netherlands East Indies is also suffering from an economic depression. In each case, the root cause is the same. With their parent countries gone, they have nobody to buy their goods.

"So *we* buy them. We can pay for them with yen, for they will have to accept what we offer. And, when the tides change and the Americans change their position, we can negotiate once again. All we need is patience for that change. In the meantime, we can exploit the economic problems of the resource area to get the materials we need."

Takeda was fascinated to watch the delegates in the room mull the situation over. He could already divide them into two groups. Those who wanted a war because their minds could not conceive of another way of handling their problems, and those who could. Those who could were looking at the two maps, the sparse and empty map of 1940 and that of 1941, with its great swathe of Commonwealth forces occupying the area that had once seemed so ripe for plucking. Tojo was looking at him. Takeda he nodded slightly. *It is time.*

"I call for a vote. Do we accept the Navy plan to seize the Southern Resource Area and thus commit us to the war with the United States it inevitably means?" Tojo looked around the room for the first votes to be declared.

"I vote for it." Yamamoto wasted no time in casting his vote.

"And I." Yamaguchi followed him a split second later.

"And I." Masanobu Tsuji's vote was also a foregone conclusion. His eyes were so focussed on Southeast Asia and his desire for revenge, they ignored everything else.

"And I." Nagano Osami followed his master.

"I vote against." General Nakamura spoke with equal fervor. "This plan is a delusion."

"I vote against." Field Marshal Shunroku Hata, Commander of the *Shina haken gun,* the China Expeditionary Army, was equally firm. The last thing he wanted was resources withdrawn from his thin-stretched army.

"The submarines vote in favor of the plan."

"The naval air force votes in favor of the plan."

"The General Defense Command votes against."

"The Southern Expeditionary Army votes against."

"The Scouting forces vote in favor."

"The Ministry of War votes in favor." That was a shock to Takeda. He had expected Tojo to vote against.

"The Kwantung Army votes against."

"*Kido Butai* votes in favor." *Well, Nagumo has finally climbed off the fence.*

"The General Staff College votes against."

"The Army Air Force votes against."

"Army Operations votes against."

"Army Intelligence votes against."

So that made nine votes in favor of the Navy plan and nine against. There were three votes left, one Army and two Navy. The *Tokubetsu Kōtō Kempeitai* and the two financial experts did not have votes here. Takeda knew that, if the power blocks held good, the Navy plan would be accepted and Japan would be doomed. He didn't know how the Americans would do it but he did know that if the Navy had their way, the war they started would end with Japan being smashed into the dust.

"The Army Minister votes in favor." That was also a shock for Takeda. He was beginning to despair. *Can't these people see what they are doing?*

Fuchida had been staring at the map with its array of Commonwealth air units and working out what the chances of the carrier strike groups were like when they were thrown against the growing forces he could see. He had seen the prospect of formations of carrier aircraft engaging in battle after battle against an apparently neverending stream of opposition. They would win each battle. But, with each victory, the finely-honed sword upon which the Japanese Navy depended would become ever duller and the chips on the blade would weaken it more. Eventually it would break. There was another factor. Battles were by definition unpredictable things and nobody could be sure of their outcome. Those new land-based torpedo bombers could come in at dawn or dusk and drop their deadly loads. Only a few weeks earlier, a tiny handful of British Swordfish torpedo planes from the British carrier *Eagle* had driven back the Italian battlefleet, inflicting grievous losses in the process. That carrier and her Swordfish now operated out of Ceylon. The image of a constant battle of attrition and the ever-present danger of a lucky strike had led him to an ugly conclusion. The planned assault was doomed.

Even if it succeeded, it would have failed for the continuous battles would leave the precious carriers and their fragile air groups ruined beyond quick repair. That meant Japan would be defenseless against the counter-blow that would surely come. There was only one thing he could possibly say.

"The Air Fleet votes against."

"You snivelling coward!" Yamaguchi screamed the insult and struck Fuchida in the face. Blood trickled from the pilot's lip but he stood to attention, ignoring the blow. Takeda knew that pose well; a man who had done his duty as he saw it, regardless of cost to himself. *I am sorry I ever linked you with the Spirit Warriors. Today you showed the true heart of a warrior.*

That made it ten votes to ten. All eyes turned to the one man who had not yet voted. The Head of Navy Operations, Minoru Genda. He was Yamamoto's protégé; a man who had benefitted from having his career steered by Yamamoto from one auspicious posting to the next. Everything he had and everything he was, he owed to the Admiral. Next to him Yamamoto was already smiling with the understanding that, despite Fuchida's defection, the vote was won.

Genda stared at the map and the solid swathe of Commonwealth air power, then at Fuchida, who had realized its implications. Genda's strategic insight, almost unique in this room, warred with his loyalty to his patron. His mind was also filled with images; not of air battles or victories, but with the simple figure of a man playing dice. No matter what the game was, no matter how heavily the dice were loaded, one day that man would lose. Losing was inevitable; the art of war was to ensure that when battles were lost, the consequences of the loss would not be fatal to the cause as a whole.

Here, the man playing dice was staking everything Japan had on each throw and assuming that fortune would not turn its face from him. But, it surely must one day. Then staking everything would mean no prospect of recovery. One other thing kept nagging at his mind. The centerpiece of the plan was to destroy the U.S. Fleet at Pearl Harbor. Yet, attacks on a major naval base were foolhardy. For all the gains it might have offered, the British had backed off attacking the Taranto naval base. Instead, they elected to fight the Italian Navy at sea, in the Strait of Calabria. *Was the entire Navy Plan based on a flawed foundation?*

Genda looked up and saw Takeda staring at him. He remembered, whatever other loyalties he had, his first was to Japan and the Emperor. To them, he owed the best advice he could deliver; not that which suited his own ends. In that respect, he was also almost unique in this room. He made his mind up, taking a deep breath as he did so. "Operations votes against the plan."

Five words, utterly unexpected, caused complete uproar in the conference room. Yamaguchi had to be physically restrained from assaulting Genda. Yamamoto stared at him with a stricken expression; one that revealed his sense of complete betrayal. Tojo's face was expressionless as he banged his gavel. "Operations in China will continue as currently planned, pending further developments. By eleven votes to ten, the proposed plan for an attack on Pearl Harbor and the Southern Resource Area has been rejected."

The End

CPSIA information can be obtained at www.ICGtesting.com
Printed in the USA
LVOW062325251112

308757LV00003B/493/P